Jeff Deaver is the bestselling author of a number of powerful suspense novels. He was a lawyer before quitting work to become a full-time writer. He divides his time between Washington, DC and California. *The Bone Collector* is now a major film starring Denzel Washington and Angelina Jolie.

Praying For Sleep
A Maiden's Grave

Jeffery Deaver

CORONET BOOKS
Hodder & Stoughton

Praying For Sleep first published in Great Britain in 1994
by Hodder & Stoughton
A Maiden's Grave first published in Great Britain in 1995
by Hodder & Stoughton

This paperback omnibus edition published in 2000
by Hodder & Stoughton

A division of Hodder Headline

A Coronet paperback

10 9 8 7 6 5 4 3 2 1

ISBN 0 340 79393 7

Printed and bound in Great Britain by
Mackays of Chatham PLC, Chatham, Kent

Hodder and Stoughton
A division of Hodder Headline
338 Euston Road
London NW1 3BH

And can you, by no drift of conference,
Get from him why he puts on this confusion,
Grating so harshly all his days of quiet
With turbulent and dangerous lunacy?

Hamlet
William Shakespeare

1

Like a cradle, the hearse rocked him gently.

The old vehicle creaked along a country road, the asphalt cracked and root-humped. He believed the journey had so far taken several hours though he wouldn't have been surprised to find that they'd been on the road for days or weeks. At last he heard the squeal of bad brakes and was jostled by an abrupt turn. Then they were on a good road, a state road, and accelerating quickly.

He rubbed his face across a satiny label sewn inside the bag. He couldn't see the label in the darkness but he remembered the words elegantly stitched in black thread on yellow cloth.

Union Rubber Products
Trenton, NJ 08606
MADE IN USA

He caressed this label with his ample cheek and sucked air through the minuscule opening where the zipper hadn't completely seated. The smoothness of the hearse's transit suddenly troubled him. He felt he was falling straight down to hell, or maybe into a well where he'd be wedged immobile, head down, forever. . . .

This thought aroused a piercing fear of confinement and when it grew unbearable he craned his neck and drew back his thick lips. He gripped the inside of the zipper with lengthy teeth, yellow and gray as cat's claws, and with them he struggled to work the mechanism open. One inch, two, then several more. Cold, exhaust-scented air filled the bag. He inhaled greedily. The air diminished the bristle of claustrophobia. The men who took away the dead, he knew, called what he now lay in a "crash bag." But he couldn't recall these men ever taking away anyone dead from a crash. The dead ones died by leaping from the top of the stairwell in E Ward. They died from severed veins in their fat forearms. They died face down in toilets and they died like the man this afternoon—a strip of cloth wound round and round and round his neck.

But he couldn't recall a single crash.

His teeth rose from his lips again and he worked the zipper open further, eight inches, ten. His round shaved head emerged from the jagged opening. With his snarling lips and thick face he had the appearance of a bear—though one that was not only hairless but blue, for much of his head was dyed that color.

Finally able to look about he was disappointed to find that this wasn't a real hearse at all but merely a station wagon and it wasn't even black but tan. The back windows weren't shaded and he could see ghostly forms of trees, signs, power towers and barns as the wagon sped past—his view distorted by the misty darkness of the autumn evening.

In five minutes he began on the zipper again, angry that his arms were pinioned helpless by, he muttered in frustration, "damn good New Jersey rubber." He opened the crash bag another four inches.

He frowned. What was that *noise*?

Music! It came from the front seat, separated from the back by a black fiberboard divider. He generally liked music but certain melodies upset him greatly. The one he now heard, a country-western tune, for some reason set off within him bursts of uneasiness.

I hate this bag! he thought. It's too damn *tight*.

Then it occurred to him that he wasn't alone. That's it—the bag was filled with the souls of crashed and shattered bodies. The jumpers and the drowners and the wrist slitters.

He believed that these souls hated him, that they knew he was an impostor. They wanted to seal him up alive, forever, in this tight rubber bag. And with these thoughts came the evening's first burst of real panic—raw, liquid, cold. He tried to relax by using the breathing exercises he'd been taught but it was too late. Sweat popped out on his skin, tears formed in his eyes. He shoved his head viciously into the opening of the bag. He wrenched his hands up as far as they'd go and beat the thick rubber. He kicked with his bare feet. He slammed the bridge of his nose into the zipper, which snapped out of track and froze.

Michael Hrubek began to scream.

The music stopped, replaced by a mumble of confused voices. The hearse rippled sideways like an airplane in a crosswind.

Hrubek slammed his torso upward then fell back, again and again, trying to force his way out of the small opening, his massive neck muscles knotting into thick cables, his eyes bulging. He screamed and wept and screamed again. A tiny door in the black partition flew open and two wide eyes stared into the back of the vehicle. Surrendering to the fear Hrubek neither saw the attendant nor heard the man's hysterical shout, "Stop! Stop the car. Christ, *stop!*"

The station wagon careened onto the shoulder amid a staccato clatter of pebbles. A cloud of dust surrounded it, and the two attendants, wearing pastel green jumpsuits, leapt out and ran to the back of the hearse. One tore open the door. A small yellow light above Hrubek's face popped on, frightening him further and starting another jag of screaming.

"Shit, he's not dead," said the younger of the attendants.

"*Shit he's not dead?* It's an escape! Get back."

Hrubek screamed again and convulsed forward. His veins rose in deep clusters from his blue skull and neck, and straps of tendon quivered. Flecks of foam and blood filled the corner of his mouth. The belief, and hope, that he was having a stroke occurred simultaneously to each attendant.

"Settle down, you!" shouted the youthful one.

"You're just going to get in more trouble!" his partner said shrilly, and added with no threat or conviction whatsoever, "We've caught you now so just settle down. We're going to take you back."

Hrubek let go a huge scream. As if under the power of this sound alone the zipper gave way and metal teeth fired from the crash bag like shotgun pellets. Sobbing and gasping for air Hrubek leapt forward and rolled over the tailgate, crouching on the ground, naked except for his white boxer shorts. He ignored the attendants, who danced away from him, and rested his head against his own distorted reflection in the pitted chrome bumper of the hearse.

"All right, that's enough of that!" the younger attendant growled. When Hrubek said nothing but merely rubbed his cheek against the bumper and wept, the attendant lifted an oak branch twice the length of a baseball bat and waved it at him with some menace.

"No," the other attendant said to his partner, who nonetheless swung at the massive naked shoulders, as if taking on a fastball. The wood bounced off with hardly a sound and Hrubek seemed not to notice the blow. The attendant refreshed his grip. "Son of a bitch."

His partner's hand snagged the weapon. "No. That's not our job."

Hrubek stood, his chest heaving, and faced the attendants. They stepped back. But the huge man didn't advance. Exhausted, he studied the two men curiously for a moment and sank once more to the ground then scrabbled away, rolling into the grass by the road, oblivious to the cold autumn dew that lacquered his body. A whimper came from his fleshy throat.

The attendants eased toward the hearse. Without closing the back door they leapt inside and the wagon shot away, spraying Hrubek with stones and dirt. Numb, he didn't feel this pummeling and merely lay immobile on his side, gulping down cold air that smelled of dirt and shit and blood and grease. He watched the hearse vanish through a blue cloud of tire smoke, grateful that the men were gone and that they'd taken with them the terrible bag of New Jersey rubber filled with its ghostly occupants.

After a few minutes the panic became a stinging memory then a dark thought and then was nearly forgotten. Hrubek rose to his full six-foot, four-inch height and stood bald and blue as a Druid. He snatched up a handful of grass and wiped his mouth and chin. He studied the geography around him. The road was in the middle of a deep valley; bony ridges of rock rose up on either side of the wide asphalt. Behind him in the west—where the hearse had come from—the hospital was lost in darkness many miles away. Ahead lay the distant lights of houses.

Like an animal released from his captors, he circled in an awkward, cautious lope, uncertain of which direction to take.

Then, like an animal finding a scent, he turned toward the lights in the east and began to run, with an ominous grace and at a great speed.

2

Above them the sky had gone from resonant gunmetal to black.

"What's that? There?" The woman pointed to a cluster of stars above the distant line of alder and oak and occasional white birch that marked the end of their property.

The man sitting beside her stirred, setting his glass on the table. "I'm not sure."

"Cassiopeia, I'll bet." Her eyes lowered from the constellation to gaze into the large state park that was separated from their yard by the inky void of a dim New England lake.

"Could be."

They'd sat on this flagstone patio for an hour, warmed by a bottle of wine and by unusually congenial November air. A single candle in a blue fishnet holder lit their faces, and the scent of leaf decay, ripe and too sweet, floated about them. No neighbors lived within a half mile but they spoke in near whispers.

"Don't you sometimes," she asked slowly, "feel something of Mother around here still?"

He laughed. "You know what I always thought about ghosts? They'd have to be naked, wouldn't they? Clothes don't have souls."

She glanced toward him. His gray hair and tan slacks were the only aspects of him visible in the deepening night (and made him, she reflected, if anything, ghostlike). "I know there're no ghosts. That's not what I mean." She lifted the bottle of California's finest Chardonnay and poured herself more. She misjudged and the neck of the bottle rang loudly on her glass, startling them both.

Her husband's eyes remained on the stars as he asked, "Is something wrong?"

"No, nothing at all."

With long, ruddy and wrinkled hands Lisbonne Atcheson absently combed her short blond hair, shaping the strands but leaving them as unruly as before. She stretched her limber, forty-year-old body luxuriously and looked momentarily at the three-story colonial house rising behind them. After a moment she continued, "What I mean about Mother . . . It's tough to explain." But as a teacher of the Queen's language Lis was bound by the rule that difficulty of expression is no excuse for not expressing, and so she tried once more. "A 'presence.' *That's* what I mean."

On cue, the candle flickered in its cerulean holder.

"I rest my case." She nodded at the flame and they laughed. "What time is it?"

"Almost nine."

Lis slouched down into the lawn chair and pulled her knees up, tucking her long denim skirt around her legs. The tips of brown cowboy boots, tooled with gold vines, protruded from the hem. She gazed again at the stars and reflected that her mother would in fact have been a good candidate for ghosthood. She'd died just eight months ago, sitting in an antique rocking chair as she looked out over the patio where Lis and Owen now sat. The elderly woman had leaned forward suddenly as if recognizing a landmark and said, "Oh, of course," then died in a very peaceful second.

This house too would have been a good site for a haunting. The dark boxy structure contained more square footage than even a fertile eighteenth-century family might comfortably fill. It was sided with weather-stained cedar shakes, brown, scalish, rough. The trim was dark green. Once a Revolutionary War tavern, the house was divided into many small rooms connected by narrow hallways. Beams dotted with powder-post-beetle holes crisscrossed the ceilings, and Lis's father had claimed that several finger-size perforations in the walls and posts were from musket balls fired by rebel militia as they fought the British from room to room.

Hundreds of thousands of dollars had been sunk into the interior design of the house over the past fifty years but for some reason her parents had never properly wired the place; lamps with low-wattage bulbs were all that the circuits could bear. From the patio tonight these lights shone through the small squares of rippled panes like jaundiced eyes.

Lis, still thinking of her mother, said, "It was like the time near the end when she said, 'I just talked to your father and he said he was coming home soon.'" That conversation would have been a tricky one; the old man had been dead for two years at that point. "She *imagined* it, of course. But the feeling was real to her."

And their father? Lis wondered momentarily. No, L'Auberget *père* was probably not present in spirit. He'd dropped dead in a men's room in Heathrow Airport as he tugged angrily at a reluctant paper-towel dispenser.

"Superstition," Owen said.

"Well, in a way he *did* come home to her. She died a couple days later."

"Still."

"I guess I'm talking about what you feel when people are together again, people who knew someone who's gone."

Owen was tired of speaking about the spirits of the dead. He sipped his wine and told his wife he'd scheduled a business trip for Wednesday. He wondered if he could get a suit cleaned in time for his departure. "I'll be staying through Sunday, so if—"

"Wait. Did you hear something?" Lis turned quickly and looked at the dense mesh of lilacs that cut off their view of the back door of the house.

"No, I don't think I . . ." His voice faded and he held up a finger. He nodded. She couldn't see his expression but his posture seemed suddenly tense.

"There," she said. "There it was again."

It seemed like the snap of footsteps approaching the house from the driveway.

"That dog again?" Lis looked at Owen.

"The Busches'? No, he's penned in. I saw him when I went for my run. Deer probably."

Lis sighed. The local herd had feasted on over two hundred dollars in flower bulbs over the course of the summer, and just last week had stripped bare and killed a beautiful Japanese-maple sapling. She rose. "I'll give it a good scare."

"You want me to?"

"No. I want to call again anyway. Maybe I'll make some tea. Anything for you?"

"No."

She picked up the empty wine bottle and walked to the house, a fifty-foot trip along a path that wound through topiary, pungent boxwood and the bare, black lilac bushes. She passed a small reflecting pond in which floated several lily pads. Glancing down, she saw herself reflected, her face illuminated by the yellow lights from the first floor of the house. Lis had occasionally heard herself described as "plain" but had never taken this in a bad way. The word suggested a simplicity and resilience that were, to her, aspects of beauty. Looking into the water tonight she once again prodded her hair into place. Then a sharp gust of wind distorted her image in the water and she continued toward the house.

She heard nothing more of the mysterious noise and she relaxed. Ridgeton was among the safest towns in the state, a beautiful hamlet surrounded by wooded hills and fields that were filled with kelly-green grass, huge boulders, horses bred for running, picturesque sheep and cows. The town had been incorporated even before the thirteen states considered unionizing, and Ridgeton's evolution in the past three hundred years had been more in the ways of earthly convenience than economics or attitude. You could buy pizza by the slice and frozen yogurt, and you could rent Rototillers and videos but when all was said and done this was a walled village where the men were tied to the earth—they built on it, sold it and loaned against it—and the women marshaled children and food.

Ridgeton was a town that tragedy rarely touched and premeditated violence, never.

So tonight when Lis found that the kitchen door, latticed with squares of turquoise bottle glass, was wide open, she was more irritated than uneasy. She paused, the wine bottle in her hand slowly swinging to a stop. A faint trapezoid of amber light spread onto the lawn at Lis's feet.

She stepped around the thicket of lilacs and glanced into the driveway. No cars.

The wind, she concluded.

Stepping inside, she set the bottle on the butcher-block island and made a perfunctory search of the downstairs. No evidence of fat raccoons or curious skunks. She stood still for a moment listening for sounds within the house. Hearing nothing, Lis put the kettle on the stove then crouched to forage through the cabinet that contained the tea and coffee. Just as she placed her hand on the box of rose-hip tea, a shadow fell over her. She stood, gasping, and found herself looking into a pair of cautious hazel eyes.

The woman was about thirty-five. She had a black jacket over her arm and wore a loose-fitting white satin blouse, a short, shimmery skirt, and lace-up boots with short heels. Over her shoulder was a backpack.

Lis swallowed and found her hand quivering. The two women faced each other for a moment, silent. It was Lis who leaned forward quickly and embraced the younger woman. "Portia."

The woman unslung the backpack and dropped it on the island, next to the wine bottle.

"Hello, Lis."

There was a moment of thick silence. Lis said, "I didn't . . . I mean, I thought you were going to call when you got to the station. We'd pretty much decided you weren't coming. I called you and got your machine. Well, it's good to see you." She heard the nervous outpouring of her words and fell silent.

"I got a ride. Figured, why bother them?"

"It wouldn't have been a bother."

"Where were you guys? I looked upstairs."

Lis didn't speak for a moment but merely stared at the young woman's face, her blond hair—exactly Lis's shade—held back by a black headband. Portia frowned and repeated her question.

"Oh, we're out by the lake. It's a strange night, isn't it? Indian summer. In *November*. Have you eaten?"

"No, nothing. I had brunch at three. Lee stayed over last night and we slept late."

"Come on outside. Owen's out there. You'll have some wine."

"No, really. Nothing."

They headed back down the path, thick silence filling the short distance between them. Lis asked about the train ride.

"Late but it got here."

"Who'd you get a ride with?"

"Some guy. I think I went to high school with his son. He kept talking about Bobbie. Like I should know who Bobbie was if he didn't give me his last name."

"Bobbie Kelso. He's your age. His father's tall, bald?"

"I think," Portia said absently, looking out over the black lake.

Lis watched her eyes. "It's been so long since you've been here."

Portia gave a sound that might have been a laugh or a sniffle. They walked the rest of the way to the patio in silence.

"Welcome," Owen called, standing up. He kissed his sister-in-law's cheek. "We'd about given up on you."

"Yeah, well, one thing after another. Didn't get a chance to call. Sorry."

"No problem. We're flexible out here in the country. Have some wine."

"She got a ride with Irv Kelso," Lis said. Then she pointed to a lawn chair. "Sit down. I'll open another bottle. We've got a lot of catching up to do."

But Portia didn't sit. "No thanks. It's still early enough, isn't it? Why don't we get the dirty work over with?"

In the ensuing silence Lis looked from her sister to her husband then back again. "Well . . ."

Portia persisted, "Unless it'd be a hassle."

Owen shook his head. "Not really."

Lis hesitated. "You don't want to sit for a few minutes? We've got all tomorrow."

"Naw, let's just do it." She laughed. "Like the ad says."

Owen turned toward the younger woman. His face was in shadow and Lis couldn't see his expression. "If you want. Everything's in the den."

He led the way and Portia, with a glance at her older sister, followed.

Lis remained on the patio for a moment. She blew the candle out and picked it up. Then she too walked to the house, preceded by sparkling dew lifted off the grass and flung from the tips of her boots, while above her in the night sky Cassiopeia grew indistinct, then dark, then invisible behind a wedge of black cloud.

He walked along the gritty driveway, passing through pools of light beneath the antiquated, hoopy lamps sprouting from the uneven granite wall. From high above, a woman known to him only as Patient 223-81 keened breathlessly, mourning the loss of something only she understood.

He paused at a barred wooden door beside the loading dock. Into a silver plastic box—incongruous in this nearly medieval setting —the middle-aged man inserted a plastic card and flung the door open. Inside, a half dozen men and women, wearing white jackets or blue jumpsuits, glanced at him. Then they looked away uncomfortably.

A white-jacketed young doctor with nervous black hair and large lips stepped quickly to his side, whispering, "It's worse than we thought."

"Worse, Peter?" Dr. Ronald Adler asked vacantly as he stared at the gurney. "I don't know about that. I expect pretty bad."

He brushed his uncombed sandy-gray hair out of his eyes and touched a long finger to a thin, fleshy jowl as he looked down at the body. The corpse was huge and bald and had a time-smeared tattoo on the right biceps. A reddish discoloration encircled the massive neck. His back was as dark with sunken blood as his face was pale.

Adler motioned to the young doctor. "Let's go to my office. Why are all these people here? Shoo them out! My office. Now."

Vanishing through a narrow doorway the two men walked down the dim corridors, the only sounds their footsteps and a faint wail, which might have been either Patient 223-81 or the wind that gushed through the gaps in the building, which had been constructed a century ago. The walls of Adler's office were made from the same red granite used throughout the hospital but he was its director so the walls were paneled. Because this was a state hospital, however, the wormwood was fake and badly warped. The office seemed like that of a bail bondsman or an ambulance-chasing lawyer.

Adler flicked the light on and tossed his overcoat onto a button-studded couch. The summons tonight had found him between the legs of his wife and he'd leapt off the bed and dressed hastily. He noticed now that he'd forgotten his belt, and his slacks hung below his moderate belly. This embarrassed him and he quickly sat at his desk chair. He gazed momentarily at the phone as if perplexed it wasn't ringing.

To the young man, his assistant, Adler said, "Let's have it, doctor. Don't hover. Sit down and tell me."

"Details are pretty sketchy. He's built like Callaghan." Peter Grimes aimed his knobby hair toward the body in the loading dock. "We think he—"

Adler interrupted. "And *he* is . . . ?"

"The one who escaped? Michael Hrubek. Number 458-94."

"Go on." Adler fanned his fingers gingerly and Grimes placed a battered white file folder in front of the director.

"Hrubek, it seems—"

"He was the big fellow? Didn't think he was a troublemaker."

"Never was. Until today." Grimes kept retracting his lips like a fish chewing water and exposing little, even teeth. Adler found this repugnant and lowered his face to the file. The young doctor continued, "He shaved his head to look like Callaghan. Stole a razor to do it. Then he dyed his face blue. Broke a pen and mixed the ink with—" Adler's eyes swung to Grimes with a look of either anger or bewilderment. The young man said quickly, "Then he climbed into the freezer for an hour. Anybody else would've died. Just before the coroner's boys came by to pick up Callaghan, Hrubek hid the corpse and climbed into his body bag. The orderlies looked inside, saw a cold, blue body and—"

A barked laugh escaped from the director's thin lips, on which to his shock he detected the scent of his wife. The smile faded. "Blue? Incredible. Blue?"

Callaghan had died, Grimes explained, by strangulation. "He was blue when they found him this afternoon."

"Then he wasn't *blue* for long, my friend. As soon as they cut the sheet off him, he was *un*-blue. Didn't the fucking orderlies think of that?"

"Well," Peter Grimes said, and could think of nothing to add.

"Did he hurt the meat-wagon boys?" Adler asked. At some point tonight he'd have to total up how many people might sue the state as a result of the escape.

"Nope. They said they chased him but he disappeared."

"They chased him. I'm sure." Adler sighed sardonically, and turned back to the file. He motioned for Grimes to be quiet and began to read about Michael Hrubek.

DSM-III diagnosis: Paranoid schizophrenic . . . Monosymptomatic and delusional . . . Claims to have been committed in seventeen hospitals and escaped from seven of them. Unconfirmed.

Adler glanced up at his assistant. "Escaped from *seven* hospitals?" Before the young man could answer the question, to which there really was no answer, the director was reading once more.

. . . committed indefinitely pursuant to Section 403 of the State Mental Health Law. . . . Hallucinatory (auditory, nonvisual) . . . subject to severe panic attacks, during which Pt. may become psychotically violent. Pt.'s intelligence is average/above average. . . . Difficulty processing only the most abstract thought . . . Believes he is being persecuted and spied upon. Believes he is hated by others and gossiped about . . . Revenge and retribution, often in Biblical or historical contexts, seem to be integral parts of his delusion. . . . Particular animosity toward women . . .

Adler then read the intake resident's report about Hrubek's height, weight, strength, general good health and belligerence. His face remained impassive though his heart revved up a few beats and he thought with dread and clinical admiration, The son of a bitch is a killing animal. Jesus, Lord.

" 'Presently controlled by chlorpromazine hydrochloride, 3200 mgs./daily. P.O. in divided doses.' Is this for *real*, Peter?"

"Yes. I'm afraid so. Three grams of Thorazine."

"Fuck," Adler whispered.

"About which . . ." The assistant rocked against the desk with his thumbs pressed on a stack of books, the digits growing bright red under the pressure.

"Let's have it. All of it."

"He's been cheeking his meds."

Adler felt a bristle of heat course over his face. He whispered, "Tell me."

"There was a movie."

"A movie?"

Grimes clicked together two untrimmed nails. "An adventure film. And the hero pretended to take some drug or something—"

"You mean in the rec room? . . . *What* are you telling me?"

"An adventure film. But he didn't really take them. The pills. He pretended to but he cheeked them and spit 'em out later. Harrison Ford, I think. A lot of patients did that for a few days afterwards. I guess nobody thought Hrubek was that cognitively functional so they didn't watch him that closely. Or maybe it was Nick Nolte."

Adler exhaled slowly. "How long was he off the candy?"

"Four days. Well, make that five."

Flipping through his ordered mind Adler selected the *Psychopharmacology* file cabinet and peeked inside. Psychotic behavior in schizophrenics is controlled by antipsychotic medication. There's no physical addiction to Thorazine, as with narcotics, but going cold turkey off the drug would render Hrubek nauseous, dizzy, sweaty, and intensely nervous, all of which would increase the likelihood of panic attacks.

And panic was what made schizophrenics dangerous.

Off their Thorazine, patients like Hrubek sometimes fly into psychotic rages. Sometimes they murder.

Sometimes voices tell them what a good job they did with the knife or baseball bat and suggest that they go out and do it again.

Hrubek, Adler noted, would also experience severe insomnia. Which meant that the man would be wide awake for two or three days—ample opportunity to spread his mayhem about quite generously.

The moaning grew louder, filling the dim office. Adler's palms rose to his cheeks. Again he smelled his wife. Again he wished he could turn back the clock one hour. Again he wished he'd never heard of Michael Hrubek.

"How'd we find out about the Thorazine?"

"One of the orderlies," Grimes explained, chewing water again. "He found it under Hrubek's mattress."

"Who?"

"Stu Lowe."

"Who else knows? About him cheeking the candy?"

"Him, me, you. The chief nurse. Lowe told her."

"Oh, that's just great. Now listen to me. Tell Lowe . . . tell him it's his job if he ever repeats that. Not a single fucking word. Wait. . . ." A troubling thought occurred to Adler and he asked, "The morgue's in C Ward. How the hell did Hrubek have access to it?"

"I don't know."

"Well, find out."

"This all happened very fast, extremely fast," the flustered assistant blurted. "We don't have half the information we need. I'm getting files, calling people."

"*Don't* call people."

"I'm sorry?"

Adler snapped, "Don't call *anybody* about this without my okay."

"Well, the board . . ."

"Jesus, man, especially the board."

"I haven't yet," said Grimes quickly, wondering what had become of his cockiness.

"Good God!" Adler exploded. "You haven't called the police yet?"

"No, no. Of course not." This was a call he'd been about to make just as Adler arrived at the hospital. Grimes noticed with alarm how violently his own fingers were quivering. He wondered if he'd have a vagus-nerve lapse and faint. Or pee on his boss's floor.

"Let's think about this, shall we?" Adler mused. "He's sure to be wandering around out near . . . *Where* was it?"

"Stinson."

Adler repeated the name softly then touched the file under eight firm fingertips as if preventing it from rising into the inky stratosphere of his Victorian asylum office. His mood lifted slightly. "Who were the orderlies who schlepped the body from the morgue to the hearse?"

"Lowe was one. I think Frank Jessup was the other."

"Send 'em up to me." Forgetting his ill-fitting slacks Adler stood and walked to the grimy window. It hadn't been washed in six months. "You're responsible," Adler said sternly, "for keeping this absolutely quiet. Got it?"

"Yes sir," Grimes said automatically.

"And, goddamn it, find out how he got off E Ward."

"Yessir."

"If anyone . . . Tell the staff. If anyone leaks anything to the press they're fired. No police, no press. Send those boys up here. It's a hard job we've got here, isn't it? Don't you agree? Get me those orderlies. Now."

. . .

"Ronnie, are you feeling better?"

"I'm okay," the young heavyset man snapped. "So what? I mean, what're you going to *do* about it? *Honestly*."

Dr. Richard Kohler felt the cheap bedsprings bouncing beneath Ronnie's weight as the patient scooted away from him, moving all the way to the headboard, as if Kohler were a molester. Ronnie's eyes flicked up and down suspiciously as he examined the man who'd been his father, brother, friend, tutor and physician for the past six months. He carefully studied the doctor's curly fringe of thinning hair, his bony face, narrow shoulders and thirty-one-inch waist. He seemed to be memorizing these features so he might have a good description in mind when he reported Kohler to the police.

"Are you uncomfortable, Ronnie?"

"I can't do it, I can't *do* it, doctor. I get too *scared*." He whined like a wrongly accused child. Then suddenly growing reasonable he said conversationally, "It's the can opener mostly."

"Was it the kitchen? All the work in the kitchen?"

"No no no," he whined. "The *can* opener. It's too *much*. I don't see why you don't *understand* it."

Kohler's body was racked by a yawn. He felt a painful longing for sleep. He'd been awake since 3:00 a.m. and had been here, at the halfway house, since 9:00. Kohler had helped the patients make breakfast and do the dishes. At 10:00 he shuttled four of them to part-time jobs, conferring with employers about his patients and mediating little disputes on their behalf.

The rest of the day he spent with the remaining five patients, who weren't employed or who had today, Sunday, off. The young men and women each had a psychotherapy session with Kohler and then returned to the mundane chores of running a household. They divided up into project groups that did what to healthy people were absurdly simple tasks: peeling potatoes and washing lettuce for dinner, cleaning windows and bathrooms, separating trash for recycling, reading aloud to each other. Some lowered their heads and completed their assignments with furrowed-brow determination. Others chewed their lips or plucked out eyebrows or cried or came close to hyperventilating from the challenge. Eventually the work got done.

Then, catastrophe.

Just before dinner, Ronnie had his attack. A patient standing beside him opened a can of tuna with the electric opener, and Ronnie fled screaming from the kitchen, triggering a chain reaction of hysteria in several other patients. Kohler had finally restored order and they sat down to dinner, Kohler with them. The food was eaten, dishes washed, the house straightened, games played, television programs hashed out (a *Cheers* rerun was the majority selection of the evening and the *M*A*S*H* minority abided grudgingly by the decision). Then meds were taken with juice, or the orange-flavored liquid Thorazine was chugged, and it was bedtime.

Kohler had found Ronnie hiding in the corner of his room.

"What would you like to do about the noise?" Kohler now asked.

"I don't *know*!" The patient's voice was dull as he chewed his tongue—an attempt to moisten a mouth painfully dry from his Proketazine.

Adaptation causes stress—the hardest thing for schizophrenics to cope with—and, Kohler reflected, Ronnie had plenty to adapt to here in the halfway house. He had to make decisions. To consider the likes and dislikes of the other people living with him. He had to plan ahead. The safety of the hospital was gone. Here he was confronted daily with these matters, and a downhearted Kohler could see the young man was losing the battle.

Outside, vaguely visible in the darkness, was a lawn that had been kept perfectly mowed by the patients all summer long and was now hand-stripped of every leaf that made the mistake of falling upon it. Kohler focused on the window and saw his haggard face in the black reflection, his eyes socketlike, his chin too narrow. He thought, for the thousandth time that year, about growing a beard to flesh out his features.

"Tomorrow," Kohler said to his unhappy patient, "we'll do something about it."

"Tomorrow? That's just *great*. I could be *dead* tomorrow, and so could *you*, mister. Don't forget it," snapped the patient—sneering at the man to whom he owed not only such peace of mind as he possessed but probably his life as well.

Even before he'd decided to attend medical school, Richard Kohler had learned not to take personal offense at anything schizophrenic patients said or did. If Ronnie's words troubled him at all, it was only because they offered a measure of the patient's relapse.

This was one of Kohler's clinical errors. The patient, involuntarily committed at Marsden State hospital, had responded well to his treatment there. After many trials to find a suitable medication and dosage Kohler began treating him with psychotherapy. He made excellent progress. When one of the halfway-house patients had improved enough to move into an apartment of her own, Kohler placed Ronnie here. Immediately, though, the stresses accompanying communal living had brought out the worst of Ronnie's illness and he'd regressed, growing sullen and defensive and paranoid.

"I don't trust you," Ronnie barked. "It's pretty fucking clear what's going on here and I don't like it one *bit*. And there's going to be a storm tonight. Electric storm, electric can opener. Get it? I mean, you tell me I can do *this*, I can do *that*. Well, it's bullshit!"

Into his perfect memory Kohler inserted a brief mental notation about Ronnie's use of the verb "can" and the source of his panic attack tonight. It was too late in the evening to do anything with this observation now but he'd review the young man's file tomorrow in his office at Marsden and write up a report then. He stretched and heard a deep bone pop. "Would you like to go back to the hospital, Ronnie?" he asked, though the doctor had already made this decision.

"That's what I'm *getting* at. There isn't that *racket* there."

"No, it's quieter."

"I think I'd like to go back, doctor. I *have* to go back," Ronnie said as if he were losing the argument. "There are reasons too numerous to list."

"We'll do it then. Tuesday. You get some sleep now."

Ronnie, still dressed, curled up on his side. Kohler insisted that he put on his pajamas and climb under the blankets properly, which he did without comment. He ordered Kohler to leave the light on, and did not say good night when the doctor left his room.

Kohler walked through the ground floor of the house, saying good night to the patients who were still awake and chatting with the night orderly who sat in the living room, watching television.

A breeze came through the open window and, enticed by it, Kohler stepped outside. The night was oddly warm for November. It reminded him of a particular fall evening during his last year of medical school at Duke. He recalled walking along the tarmac from the stairs of the United 737. That year the trip between La Guardia and Raleigh-Durham airports had been like a commute for him; he'd logged tens of thousands of miles between the two cities. The night he was thinking of was his return from New York after Thanksgiving vacation. He'd spent most of the holiday itself at Murray Hill Psychiatric Hospital in Manhattan and the Friday after it in his father's office, listening to the old man argue persuasively, then insist belligerently, that his son take up internal medicine—going so far as to condition his continuing financial support of the young man's education on his choice of specialty.

The next day, young Richard Kohler thanked his father for his hospitality, took an evening flight back to college and when school resumed on Monday was in the Bursar's Office at 9:00 a.m., applying for a student loan to allow him to continue his study of psychiatry.

Kohler again yawned painfully, picturing his home—a condominium a half hour from here. This was a rural area, where he could have afforded a very big house and plenty of property. But Kohler's goal had been to forsake land for convenience. No lawn mowing or landscaping or painting for him. He wanted a place to which he might escape, small and contained. Two bedrooms, two baths and a deck. Not that it didn't have elements of opulence— the condo contained one of the few cedar hottubs in this part of the state, several Kostabi and Hockney canvases and what was described as a "designer" kitchen ("But aren't all kitchens," he had slyly asked the real-estate broker, "designed by *somebody*?" and enjoyed her sycophantic laughter). The condo, which was on a hilltop and looked out over miles and miles of patchwork woods and farmland during the day and the sparkling lights of Boyleston at night, was—quite literally—Kohler's island of sanity in a most insane world.

Yet tonight he made his way back into the halfway house and climbed the creaking stairs to a room that measured ten by twelve feet and was outfitted only with a cot, a dresser and a metal mirror bolted to the wall.

He stripped off his suit jacket and loosened his tie then lay on the cot, kicking off his shoes. He looked out the window at a dull spray of stars then, lowering his eyes, saw a ridge of clouds in the west slicing the sky in half. The storm. He'd heard it was supposed to be a bad one. Although he himself liked the rain, he hoped there wouldn't be any thunder, which would terrify many of his patients. But this concern passed immediately from his mind as he closed his eyes. Sleep was all he could think of now. He could taste it. He felt the fatigue ache in his legs. He yawned cold tears into his eyes. And in less than sixty seconds he was asleep.

3

They signed their names a dozen times and became millionaires.

A hundred sheets of paper, filled with scrolly writing, peppered with words like *whereas* and *hereby*, sat on the desk before the two women. Affidavits, receipts, tax returns, releases, powers of attorney. Owen, stern and looking very much the lawyer, circulated each document and said, "Duly executed," every time a signature was scratched upon a sheet. He'd squeeze his notarial seal and sign his own name with a Mont Blanc and then check off another item on his closing sheet. Portia seemed amused at his severity and on the verge of needling him about it. Lis on the other hand—after six years of marriage—had grown used to her husband's playing Rumpole and paid little attention to his gravity.

"I feel," she said, "like a president signing a treaty."

The three of them were in the den, encircling the massive black mahogany desk that Lis's father had bought in Barcelona in the sixties. For this occasion—the closing of his estate—Lis had unearthed a shellacked découpage poster that she herself had made ten years ago. It had been a decoration for the party following the sale of her father's business and his retirement. On the left side of the canvas was pasted a photograph of his company's very first sign, a small hand-painted rectangle from the early fifties, which read, *L'Auberget et Fils Ltd.* Next to it was a glossy photo of the huge billboard that crowned the company when it was sold: *L'Auberget Liquor Importing, Inc.* Around the border was Lis's own diligent, stiff rendering of vines and grapes, done in purple and green marker. The years had turned the shellac coating a deep, sickly yellow.

Although the old man had never discussed the company with his daughters (there was no male heir; the *fils* was strictly for image), Lis—as executrix of the estate—had learned what an astonishing businessman her father had been. She knew from his frequent absences throughout her childhood that he'd been addicted to his job. But she'd never guessed, until their mother died and the money passed to her and Portia, exactly how much that hard work had amassed: nine million, plus this house, the Fifth Avenue co-op and a cottage outside of Lisbon.

Owen gathered up papers and put them into tidy bundles, labeling each with a yellow Post-it tag marked with his boxy writing.

"I'll have copies made for you, Portia."

"Keep them safe," Lis warned.

Portia tightened her mouth at the motherly tone and Lis winced, looking for a way to apologize. But before she could find the words, Owen lifted a bottle of champagne to the desk and opened it. He poured three glasses.

"Here's to . . ." Lis began and noticed the others gazing at her expectantly. She said the first thing into her mind. "Father and Mother."

Glasses chimed together.

"Practically speaking," Owen explained, "that's the end of the estate. Most of the transfers and disbursements've been made. We have one account still open. That's for the outstanding fees—the executrix, law firm and accountant. Oh, and for that other little matter." He looked at Lis. "Did you tell her?"

Lis shook her head.

Portia kept her eyes on Owen. "Tell me what?"

"We just got notice on Friday. You're going to be sued."

"What?"

"A challenge to the bequests."

"No! Who?"

"That problem with your father's will."

"What problem? There a fuck-up someplace?" Portia looked at Owen with amused suspicion.

"Not from me there wasn't. *I* didn't draft it. I'm talking about the problem with his school. Doesn't this ring a bell?"

Portia shook her head and Owen continued, explaining that when Andrew L'Auberget passed away he'd left his entire estate in trust for his wife. When she died the money went to the daughters, with a small bequest going to his alma mater, a private college in Massachusetts.

"Oh, bless me, for I have sinned," Portia whispered sarcastically and crossed herself. Their father had often reminisced—reverently and at great length—about his days at Kensington College.

"The bequest was for a thousand."

"So what? Let 'em have it."

Owen laughed. "Oh, but they don't want *that*. They want the million he was going to leave them originally."

"A *million*?"

"About a year before he died," Lis continued, "the school started admitting women. That was bad enough. But it also adopted a resolution banning gender and sexual-orientation discrimination. You must know all this, Portia." She turned to her husband. "Didn't you send her copies of the correspondence?"

"Please, Lis, a little credit. She's a beneficiary. She *had* to be copied."

"I probably got it. But, you know, if it's got a lawyer's letterhead on it and there's no check inside, who pays any attention?"

Lis started to speak but remained silent. Owen continued, "Your father did a codicil to his will, cutting his bequest to the school to a thousand. In protest."

"The old shit."

"Portia!"

"When he wrote the chancellor telling him about the change, he said he wasn't, I'm pretty much quoting, he wasn't *against* women and deviates. He was simply *for* tradition."

"I repeat, what a shit."

"The school's challenging the codicil."

"What do we do?"

"Basically, all we have to do is keep an amount equal to their original bequest in the estate account until it's settled. You don't have to worry. We'll win. But we still have to go through the formalities."

"Not worry?" Portia blurted. "It's a million dollars."

"Oh, they'll lose," Owen announced. "He *did* execute the codicil during that spell when he was taking Percodan pretty regularly and Lis *was* spending a lot of time at the house. That's what the school's lawyer's going to argue. Lack of capacity and undue influence by one of the other beneficiaries."

"Why do you say they won't win?"

Grim-faced, Lis sipped her champagne. "I don't want to hear this again."

Her husband smiled.

"I'm serious, Owen."

He said to his sister-in-law, "The lawyer for the school? I did a little investigating. Turns out he's been negotiating contracts on behalf of the school with a company his wife's got a major interest in. Big conflict of interest. And á felony, by the way. I'm going to offer him four or five to settle."

Lis said to Portia, "He makes it sound like a legal tactic. To me, it's blackmail."

"Of course it's blackmail," Portia said. "So? But you think this lawyer'll talk the school into settling?"

"He'll be . . . persuasive, I'm sure," Owen said. "Unless he wants an address change to the Bridewell Men's Colony."

"So basically, he's fucked." Portia laughed. She held up her glass. "Good job, attorney."

Owen tapped his glass to hers.

Portia drained her champagne and let Owen pour her more. To her sister she said, "I wouldn't get on this boy's bad side, Lis. He might do to you what he does unto others."

Owen's stony façade slipped and he laughed briefly.

Lis said, "I guess I just feel insulted. I didn't even *know* the school was getting any money in the will. I mean, can you imagine Father even *talking* to me about it? Undue influence? I say let them sue."

"Well, I say let our lawyer handle it." With her working-girl hair rimmed by the black lace headband Portia seemed miraculously transported back to six or seven—the age at which it first was clear that the sisters would be such different people. This process seemed to continue, by inches and miles, Lis sensed, even tonight.

Owen poured more Moët. "Never would've been a problem if your father'd kept his money to himself and his mouth shut. That's the moral: no good deed goes unpunished."

"Your services expensive, Owen?" Portia asked wryly.

"Never. At least not for beautiful women. It's in my retainer agreement."

Lis stepped between these two people, bound to her one by blood and one by law, and put her arms around Owen. "See why he's such a rainmaker?"

"Can't make much rain if he doesn't charge."

"I didn't say I'm free." Owen looked at Portia. "I just said I'm not expensive. You always have to pay for quality."

Lis walked to the stairway. "Portia, come here. I want to show you something."

The sisters left Owen stacking the papers and climbed upstairs. The silence again grew thick and Lis realized that it was her husband's presence that had made conversation possible between the sisters.

"Here we go." She stepped in front of Portia and then pushed open the door to a small bedroom, sweeping on the overhead light. *"Voilà."*

Portia was nodding as she studied the recently decorated room. Lis had spent a month on the place, making dozens of trips to Ralph Lauren and Laura Ashley for fabrics and wallpaper, to antique stores for furniture. She'd managed to find an old canopy bed that was virtually identical to the one that had been Portia's when this was her room years ago.

"What do you think?"

"Taking up interior decorating, are we?"

"That's the *same* curtain material. Amazing that I found it. Maybe a little yellower is all. Remember when we helped Mother sew them? I was, what?, fourteen. You were nine."

"I don't remember. Probably."

Lis looked at the woman's eyes.

"What a job," Portia offered, walking in a slow circle on the oval braided rug. "Incredible. Last time I was here it looked like an old closet. Mother'd just let it go to hell."

Then why don't you like it? Lis wondered silently.

She asked, "Remember Pooh?" and nodded at a mangy Steiff bear, whose glassy eyes stared vacantly at the corner of the room, where a shimmery cobweb had emerged since Lis had last cleaned the place, twenty-four hours ago.

Portia touched the bear's nose then stepped back to the door and crossed her arms.

"What's the matter?" Lis asked.

"It's just that I'm not sure I can stay."

"What do you mean?"

"I wasn't really planning on it."

"You're talking about *tonight*? Portia, really . . . It's too late to go."

"There're trains all night."

Lis's face grew hot. "I thought you'd be here for a couple of days."

"I know we talked about it. I . . . I guess I'd really rather just get the train back. I should've told you."

"You don't even call and say you'll be late. You don't even tell us you've gotten a ride. You just show up, get your money and leave?"

"Lis."

"But you can't just sit on a train for two hours and then turn around and go back. It's crazy." Lis walked to the bed. She reached for the bear then thought better of it. She sat on the chenille spread. "Portia, we haven't spoken in months. We've hardly said a damn word since last summer."

Portia finished her champagne and put the flute on the dresser. A questioning look started to cross her face.

"You *know* what I'm talking about," Lis said.

"Right now's tough for me to be away. Lee and I're going through a hard time."

"When'll be a *good* time?"

Portia waved her hands at the room. "I'm sorry you went to all this work. Maybe next week. A couple weeks. I'll come out earlier. Spend the day."

The silence was suddenly broken by Owen's voice, calling sharply for Lis. Startled, she looked toward the door then back to her lap and found that she'd picked up the bear after all. She stood abruptly, setting the toy back on the pillow.

"Lis," came Owen's urgent voice, "come down here."

"Coming." Then Lis turned to her sister. She said, "Let's talk about it," and before Portia could open her mouth to protest, walked out of the room.

"This smells of being whipped."

"Well, I'd guess."

Before the two men lay a sharp valley that rose fifty feet above them, filled with black rocks and tangles of vine and barkless branches, many dead and rotten. Moisture glittered on undergrowth like a million snake scales, and the dew stained their jumpsuits the same dark blue the uniforms turned when they worked the Piss 'n' Shit Ward.

"Look at that. How d'we even know it's his footprint?"

"Because it's size fourteen and he's barefoot. Who the hell's do you *think* it is? Now shut up."

The moon was fading behind clouds and in the growing darkness each man thought the scene before him was straight out of a horror film.

"Say, meaning to ask—you bumping uglies with Psaltz?"

"Adler's secretary?" Stuart Lowe snickered. "Like that'd be a real smart thing to do. I'm really thinking we should've bitched more. Didn't either of us *have* to come. We ain't cops."

The men were large—both muscular and tall—and sported crew cuts. Lowe, a blond. Frank Jessup was dark. They were easygoing and had neither hatred nor love for the troubled men and women under their care. Their job was a job and they were pleased to be paid decent money in an area that had little money for any work.

They were not, however, pleased about this assignment tonight.

"Was a honest mistake," Lowe muttered. "Who'd've guessed he'd do what he done?"

Jessup leaned against a pine tree and his nostrils flared at the aroma of turpentine. "How 'bout Mona? You fucking *her*?"

"Who?"

"Mona Cabrill. Mona the Moaner. The *nurse*. From D Ward."

"Oh. Right. No. Are you?"

"Not yet," Jessup said. "I myself'd slip her a dose of thiopental and jump her bones the minute she conked out."

Lowe grunted disagreeably. "Let's stay focused here, Frank."

"We'd hear him. Big fellow like that can't walk past without knocking something down. She didn't wear a bra last week. Tuesday. The head nurse sent her home to get one. But it was Tit City for a while."

There was a faint scent of campfire or woodstove smoke in the damp air. Lowe pressed a thick palm into each of his eye sockets while he examined exactly how scared he was. "My point is, they pay cops for this kind of stuff."

"Shhh," Jessup hissed abruptly. Lowe jumped, then—at the bark of laughter—hit his partner very hard on the arm. "You son of a bitch." They sparred for a moment, rougher than they meant to be because they were bleeding off tension. Then they started up the valley once more. The men were spooked, true, but it was more the setting than the escapee; both men knew Michael Hrubek. Lowe had supervised him for most of the four months the patient had been incarcerated at Marsden State hospital. Hrubek could be a real son of a bitch—sarcastic, picky, irritating—but he hadn't seemed particularly violent. Still, Lowe added, "I'm thinking we deep-six it and call the cops."

"We bring him back, we keep our jobs."

"They can't fire us for this. How was we to know?"

"They can't *fire* us?" Jessup snorted. "You're dreaming, boy. You and me're white men under forty. They can fire us 'cause they don't like the way we crap."

Lowe decided they should stop talking. They proceeded in silence thirty yards up the cold, suffocating valley before they noticed the motion. It was indistinct and might have been nothing more than a discarded grocery bag shifting in the breeze. But there was no breeze. Maybe a deer. But deer don't walk through the forest, humming singsong tunes to themselves. The orderlies glanced at each other and took stock of their weaponry—each had a container of Mace and a rubber truncheon. They adjusted their grips on the clubs and continued up the hill.

"He doesn't want to hurt anybody," Lowe announced, then added, "I've worked with him plenty."

"I'm pleased about that," Jessup whispered. "Shut the fuck up."

The moaning reminded Lowe, who was from Utah, of a leg-trapped coyote that wouldn't last the night. "It's getting louder," he said unnecessarily, and Frank Jessup was far too spooked by now to shush him again.

"It's a dog," Lowe suggested.

But it wasn't a dog. The sound came straight from the thick throat of Michael Hrubek, who with an astonishingly loud crash stumbled into the midst of the path twenty feet in front of the orderlies and froze like a fat statue.

Lowe, thinking of the many times he'd bathed and coddled and reasoned with Hrubek, suddenly felt himself the team leader. He stepped forward. "Hello, Michael. How are you?"

The response was mumbled.

Jessup called, "Hey, Mr. Michael! My fave patient! You all right?"

Except for muddy shorts Hrubek was naked. His face was outlandishly alien—with its blue tint, pursing lips and possessed eyes.

"Aren'tcha cold?" Lowe found the voice to say.

"You're Pinkerton agents, you fuckers."

"No, it's me. It's Frank. You remember me, Michael. From the hospital. And you know Stu here. We're the fuckin'-A orderlies from E Ward. You know us, man. Hey . . ." He laughed good-naturedly. "What are you doing without any clothes on?"

"What are you doing *hiding* in yours, fucker?" Hrubek retorted with a sneer.

Suddenly the reality of their mission struck Lowe with a jolt. My God, they weren't in the hospital. They weren't surrounded by fellow

staffers. There was no telephone here, no psychiatric nurses nearby
with two hundred milligrams of phenobarb. He grew weak with fear
and when Hrubek gave a shout and fled up the valley, Jessup not
far behind, Lowe remained where he was.

"Frank, hold up!" Lowe called.

But Jessup didn't wait, and reluctantly Lowe too started after the
huge blue-white monster, who was leaping along the trail. Hrubek's
voice echoed in the damp valley, begging not to be shot or tortured.
Lowe caught up with Jessup and they ran side by side.

The orderlies crashed through the undergrowth, swinging their
truncheons like machetes. Jessup panted, "Jesus, on these rocks!
How can he run on these rocks?" A memory suddenly came to
Lowe—the image of Hrubek standing behind the hospital's main
building, his shoes around his neck, walking barefoot on gravel,
over and over, muttering as if speaking to his feet and encouraging
them to toughen up. That had been just last week.

"Frank," Lowe wheezed, "there's something funny about this. We
oughta—"

And then they were flying.

Sailing through the black air. Trees and rocks tumbling upside
down, over and over. With identical screams they plunged into the
ravine that Hrubek had easily leapt over. The orderlies smacked
against the rocks and branches on their way down and their spinning bodies slammed into the ground with vicious jolts. An icy cold
began to radiate through Lowe's thigh and arm. They lay motionless
in the gray ooze of the mud.

Jessup tasted blood. Lowe examined his bent fingers, attention
to which flagged when he wiped the mud from his forearm and
found that it wasn't mud at all but a wide, foot-long scrape where
skin used to be. "Cocksucker," he wailed. "I'm gonna hurt that
asshole bad, it's the last thing I do. Oh, shit. I'm bleeding to death.
Oh, shit . . ." Lowe rolled into a sitting position and pressed the
scrape, feeling in horror his own hot, torn flesh. Jessup was content

to lie unmoving in the methane-scented mud and breathe a few
cubic centimeters of air, the most his stunned lungs would accept.
He gasped wetly. After a moment he was able to whisper, "I
think—"

Lowe never found out what was on Jessup's mind because at that
moment Hrubek strode into the middle of the ravine. He casually
bent down, pushing Stuart Lowe aside, and plucked the men's tear-
gas canisters from their belts, flinging them deep into the woods.
He turned abruptly back to Lowe, who looked up into Hrubek's
leering face and began to scream.

"Stop that!" Hrubek screamed in return. "Stop that *noise!*"

Lowe did, and using the advantage of Hrubek's own panic scrabbled away. Jessup's eyes closed and he began muttering incoherently.

Lowe lifted the truncheon.

"You're from Pinkerton," Hrubek barked. "*Pink*-er-ton. I'm in
the *pink*, Mr. Fuckin'-A Orderly. Your arm looks pretty *pink* and
tend-er. Nice try, but you shouldn't've come after me—I've got a
death to at-*tend* to."

The rubber stick in Lowe's hand remained poised for a moment
then with a gushing sound landed in the mud at his feet. He took
off, running blindly through the woods, his courage suddenly as
flimsy as the grass and saplings that bent beneath his pounding
feet.

"Oh, don't leave me, Stu," Jessup cried into the mud at his lips.
"I don't want to die alone."

Hrubek watched the disappearing form of Stuart Lowe then knelt
on top of Jessup, pushing his head further into the ground. The
orderly tasted dirt and grass, the flavor of which reminded him of
his childhood. He began to cry.

"You dumb fucker," Hrubek said. Then he raged, "And I can't
wear your *clothes* either." He poked sharply at the stitched label,
Marsden State Mental Health Facility, on Jessup's jumpsuit. "What

good are you?" He began to sing, " '*Good* night, ladies, good night, ladies, I'm going to see you cry. . . .' "

"Will you let me go, please, Michael?"

"You *found* me out, and what I'm doing has to be a surprise. 'Good night, laaaaaaadies, I'm going to see you *die!* ' "

"I won't tell nobody, Michael. Please let me go. Oh, please. I got a wife."

"Oh, is she pret-ty? Do you fuck her *often?* Do you fuck her in unpleasant *ways?* Say, what's her address?"

"Please, Michael . . ."

"Sorry," Hrubek whispered and leaned down.

The orderly's scream was very loud and very brief. To Michael Hrubek's unbounded pleasure, it set in flight an exquisite owl, curiously golden in the ravine's blue light, which soared from a nearby oak tree and passed not five feet from the huge man's astounded face.

". . . repeating, the National Weather Service has issued an emergency storm warning for residents of Marsden, Cooper and Mahican counties. Winds in excess of eighty miles an hour, tornadoes and severe flooding in low-lying areas are expected. The Marsden River is already at flood level and expected to rise at least three more feet, cresting around one or two a.m. We'll bring you bulletins as more information is available. . . ."

Portia found them in the den, leaning over the teak stereo cabinet, both grim.

Classical music resumed and Owen shut the radio off.

Portia asked what the problem was.

"Storm." He turned to look out the window. "The Marsden—it's one of the rivers that feed the lake."

"We were getting estimates on building up the shoreline," Lis said. "But we didn't think there'd be any flooding till the spring."

Lis left the den and walked into the large greenhouse, looking up at the sky, murky but still placid.

Her sister saw her troubled face and glanced at Owen.

"There's no foundation," he explained to her. "The greenhouse. Your parents built it right on the ground. If the yard floods—"

"It'll be the first to go," Lis said. Not to mention, she thought, what the fifty-foot oak tree, hovering overhead, might do to the thin glass panes of the greenhouse roof. She glanced at the brick wall beside her and absently straightened a stone gargoyle, who grinned mischievously as he stuck out his long, curly tongue. "Damn," she whispered.

"Are you sure it'll flood?" Portia asked. She sounded irritated—because, Lis supposed, her escape from the L'Auberget manse tonight was looking complicated.

"If it goes up three feet," Lis said, "it'll flood. It'll come right into the yard. It happened in the sixties, remember? Washed away the old porch. That was right here. Where we're standing."

Portia said she didn't recall.

Lis looked at the windows again, wishing they had time to put plywood on the roof and sides. They'd be lucky to build up the lakefront by two feet and tape half the windows before the storm hit. "So," she said, sighing, "we tape and sandbag."

Owen nodded.

Lis turned to her sister. "Portia, could I ask you to stay?"

The young woman said nothing. She seemed less irritated than daunted by a conspiracy to keep her there.

"We could really use your help."

Owen looked from one sister to the other, frowning. "Weren't you going to stay for a few days?"

"I'm really supposed to get back tonight."

Supposed? Lis wondered. And who had dictated that? The hard-times boyfriend? "I'll take you to the station tomorrow. First thing. You won't miss more than an hour of work."

Portia nodded. "Okay."

"Listen," Lis said sincerely, "I appreciate this."

She hurried outside to the garage, giving a short, silent prayer of thanks for the weather that would keep her sister here at least for the night. Suddenly, however, this benediction struck Lis as a token of bad luck and superstitiously she retracted it. She then went to work assembling shovels and tape and burlap bags.

4

"Three in two years." The tall man in the smart gray uniform rubbed his matching gray mustache and added, "They run away from you all here lickety-split."

Dr. Ronald Adler fiddled with his waistband. With a monumental sigh meant to put himself on the offensive he said, "Aren't there more valuable ways to use this time, Captain? Don? I'll bet there are."

The state trooper chuckled. "How come you didn't report it?"

"We reported Callaghan's, uhm, death," Adler said.

"You know what I'm saying, doctor."

"I thought we could get him back without any fuss."

"How exactly? By one orderly getting his arm exorcised around backwards and the other one crapping in his jumpsuit?"

"He is not essentially a dangerous man," Peter Grimes offered, incidentally reminding both Adler and the state trooper that he was in the room, a fact they had forgotten.

"Any competent staff member would've handled it differently. They were playing cowboy. They fell off the cliff and were injured."

"Fell. Uhm. You boys here tried a cover-up and that don't sit well with me."

"There's nothing to cover up. I don't call you every time Joe Patient wanders off the grounds."

"Don't go scratching me between the ears, Adler."

"We *almost* got him."

"Butcha didn't. Now what's he look like?"

"He's big," Grimes began before his voice froze in fear of careless adjectives.

"How the *hell* big? Come on, gemmuns. Time's awasting."

Adler gave the description then added, "He shaved his head and dyed his face blue. Don't ask, he just did. He has brown eyes, a wide face, dirty teeth, and he's twenty-seven years old."

Captain Don Haversham, a man twice Hrubek's age, jotted notes in even script. "Okay, we got a couple cars headed up to Stinson. I see that doesn't appeal to you, Adler, but it's gotta be done. Now tell me, how dangerous? Will he come jumping outta trees?"

"No, no," the director said, glancing at Grimes, who poked into his mushroom crown of black hair. Adler continued, "Hrubek, he's like—what would you say?—a big lovable dog. This escape, he's playing a game."

"Woof, woof," the captain said. "Seem to recall he was the one involved in that Indian Leap thing. That's not lovable, and that's not a dog."

Then why, Adler inquired, did the captain ask his opinion if the trooper'd already diagnosed Hrubek?

"I want to know if he's *still* dangerous after he's been in the care of you sawbones all these four months. I'd guess he is, though, what with that fellow you got on the slab tonight. Tell me, Hrubek, he taking his pills like a good boy?"

"Yes, he is," Adler said quickly. "But wait a minute. Callaghan was probably a suicide."

"Suicide?"

Grimes again looked toward his boss and tried to match round words and square facts.

"The coroner'll tell us for sure," Adler continued.

"I'm sure he will," Haversham said cheerfully. "Kind of a coincidence though, wouldn't you say? This Callaghan kills himself then your cuddle puppy Hrubek ske-daddles in his body bag?"

"Uhm." Adler pictured locking Haversham into the old hose

room with Billie Lind Prescott, who would, off his Stelazine, masturbate while howling at the top of his lungs for hour after hour after hour.

Grimes said, "The thing is . . ." and, as both men turned to him, stopped speaking.

Adler filled the void, "Young Peter was going to say that in the months Hrubek's been with us he's been a model patient. He sits quietly, doesn't bother anyone."

"He's like a vegetable."

A wet laugh burst from Haversham's throat. He said to Grimes, "Vegetable? Was a dog a minute ago. Must be getting worse. Tell me now, what kind of crazy is he exactly?"

"He's a paranoid schizophrenic."

"Schizo? Split personality? I seen that flick."

"No, not multiple personalities. Schizophrenic. It means he has delusions and can't cope with anxiety and stress."

"He stupid? A retard?"

The professional in Adler bristled at the word but he remained placid. "No. He's got a medium to high IQ. But he's not calculating."

The captain snickered. "He'd have to be kinda sorta calculating, wouldn't you think? To get clean away from a hospital for the criminally insane."

Adler's lips vanished momentarily as he turned them inward in contemplation. The taste of his wife returned and he wondered if he'd get an erection. He didn't, and he said to Haversham, "The escape was the fault of the orderlies. They'll be disciplined."

"Seems to me, they have been. At least the one with the broken arm."

"Listen, Don, can we do this one quietly?"

The captain grinned. "Why, scared of a little publicity, Mr. Three in Two Years?"

Adler paused then spoke in a low voice that barely broke above the ghostly wail that still filled the halls. "Now, listen to me, Captain. You quit jerking my chain. I've got close to a thousand of the most unfortunate people in the Northeast in my care and money to treat about one-quarter of 'em. I can—"

"All right now."

"—I can make some of their lives better and I can protect the general populace from them. I'm doing the fucking best I can with the fucking money I've got. Don't tell me that you haven't had troopers cut back too."

"Well, I have. That's a fact."

"If this escape becomes a big deal some prick of a reporter's going to run with it and then maybe there goes more money or maybe the state'll even look into closing down this place." Adler's arm swept toward the wards filled with his hapless charges—some asleep, some plotting, some howling, some floating through nightmares of madness or perhaps even dreaming dreams of sanity. "If that happens then half those people'll be wandering around outside and they're going to be *your* problem, not mine."

"Simmer down now, doc." Haversham, whose law-enforcement career like most senior officers' was informed more by his skills at self-preservation than detection, said, "Tell me the God's truth. You say a low-security patient wandered away, that's what I'll go with. But you tell me he's *dangerous*, it'll be a whole different ball game. What's it gonna be?"

Adler hiked up his waistband. He wondered if his wife was at home masturbating as ardently as Billie Lind Prescott. "Hrubek's half-comatose," Adler spoke directly into the eyes of Peter Grimes. The young assistant nodded numbly and added, "He's stumbling around in a daze like a gin-drunk fool," and wondered what on earth possessed him to say that.

"Okay," Haversham said with finality. "I'll send it out as a missing-patient notice. You got some fellow wandered off and you're worried about his welfare. That'll make sure it's not scanner-feed.

These boys and girls they call reporters round here won't even notice it, not with a storm gonna take off roofs."

"I appreciate this, Don."

"Now let me ask. You got some bucks to spend?"

"How's that?"

"There's somebody I'm thinking might be a help. But he ain't cheap."

"We're a state hospital," Adler said. "We don't have much money."

"That may be true. But one thing you *do* have is a escaped nutzo who happens to look like Attila the effing Hun. So, what about it? You gonna hear me out?"

"Oh, by all means, Captain. By all means."

A cold and anxious Michael Hrubek stood on broad, naked feet in the center of a large rectangle of ruined grass. His hands gripped the waistband of his muddy and dew-stained shorts, and he stared at the shabby building before him.

The small shop—taxidermy, trapping and hunting supplies— was surrounded by chicken wire suspended from rusted posts with Baggie twist ties. Much of the mesh was squashed to the ground in a way that for some reason depressed Hrubek profoundly.

He had run all the way from the site of the attack on the orderlies to this cluster of lights, ghostly in the fog: a truck stop, which contained this shop, a diner, a gas station and an antique store. Positive he was being pursued by the Secret Service, Hrubek wanted to keep moving. But, as he'd announced aloud to himself, a naked man'd be "too damn obvious. Make no mistake about that."

He'd then noticed a window in this outdoors shop and that had decided the matter.

He now stood in the exact spot where he'd been frozen in place for the past few minutes, gazing into the store at seven tiny animal skulls, boiled and bleached white as clouds.

Oh, look there. Look at that!

Seven was an important number in the cosmology of Michael Hrubek and he now leaned forward, counting them aloud, and enjoying the sound of the numbers in his mouth.

Seven skulls, seven letters, M-I-C-H-A-E-L.

Make no mistake, he thought. This is a special night.

Much of Hrubek's thinking was metaphoric and the image now occurred to him that he was waking up. He liked to sleep. He *loved* to sleep. Hours and hours in bed. His favorite position was on his side with his knees drawn up as far as his massive legs and thick chest and belly would allow. Most of his waking hours too were a type of sleep—a slippery succession of chaotic dreams, a jumble of disconnected faces and scenes that fished past him, products of both his troubled mind and various medications.

Awake!

He bent down and in the dirt at his feet wrote with his stubby finger: *i as I am AWakE tonIght. AWakE!*

He made his way around the store, noting a sign that said the owner was on vacation. He kicked in the side door and entered. Avoiding a tall black bear, mounted in a rearing position, he made a circuit of the shop. He inhaled deeply and smelled musk and boiled game flesh, his hands shaking with exhilaration. He noticed shelves containing clothing and he rummaged through the piles of shirts and coveralls until he found several items that more or less fit. Then socks, and finally an Irish-tweed cap that he liked very much. He placed it on his head.

"Very fashionable," he whispered, looking into a mirror.

Hrubek continued searching until he located a pair of engineer's boots and struggled to pull them on. They were tight but not painful. "John Worker," he muttered, running his hands over his clothes with approval. "John Worker." He poured cleaning fluid onto a rag and scrubbed hard at his face to remove the blue ink from his cheeks and forehead.

He solemnly placed the seven skulls into a green canvas backpack he found in the shop. Then, keeping a suspicious eye on the rearing bear, Hrubek crossed the floor to the sales counter, where he'd noticed a display of cellophane packs of beef jerky. He ripped them open with his teeth, one after another, and chewed down the salty meat, all eight packages.

He was about to leave when he glanced down, beneath the counter, and his face broke into a huge grin.

"A present from Jesus Cry-ist our Weeping Lord."

The pistol was a long-barreled Colt revolver. Hrubek lifted it to his face and smelled it and rubbed the cold blue metal on his cheek, grinning like a boy who'd just pocketed a ten-dollar bill. He put the gun in his backpack and, once more sizing up the bear, slipped from the door.

A wedge of light suddenly filled the grass, accompanied by the clatter of an aluminum door. Hrubek stepped quickly into a large open shed behind the shop and pulled the pistol from the backpack.

A man's voice cut through the night, "You left it out there, you go pick it up. It's rusted, I'll tan your hide, young man."

The man was speaking from a dingy but brightly lit one-story house from whose chimney drifted wood and trash smoke. It was about thirty yards from the shop.

A boy, about eight or nine, walked sullenly past the shed. Without looking inside he disappeared behind the shop. A moment later he started back toward the house, holding a long hammer close to his eyes, inspecting it and scratching hopelessly with his thumbnail at dots of rust.

A noise nearby startled Hrubek. A fat raccoon was in the shed, scuttling over the concrete floor. It hadn't seen him and was nosing obliviously among garbage bags. The boy had heard the scratching of claws on concrete and stopped. Holding the rusted hammer like a club he stepped to the shed door and peered into inky darkness.

Hrubek's heart began to pulsate violently as he wondered what to do if the boy confronted him. What *will* I *tell* him? I know—I will tell him that I am Will-*i-am* Tell. I will shoot him in the head, Hrubek said to himself, and tried to control his panicked breath. The raccoon paused cautiously as it heard the boy's footsteps. Its head turned and, seeing Hrubek, the animal tensed. Baring its fangs it panicked and leapt at the madman's leg. In a short portion of a second Hrubek lunged, seizing the big animal by the neck. Even before the needlelike claws lashed out, Hrubek snapped its spine with a quiet pop.

Nice try, he thought. No such luck.

The animal quivered once and died.

The boy stepped closer to the doorway and listened. When he heard nothing else he walked slowly back into the house. The back-yard spotlight was extinguished.

Hrubek calmed as he absently stroked the fur of the raccoon for a moment then arranged the animal very carefully on its stomach with its rear legs and tail spread out behind, its front paws reaching forward. Salivating with lust Hrubek picked up a screwdriver from a workbench and drove it deep into the back of the animal's skull. Then he extracted the tool and threw the limp corpse into the corner of the garage.

As he was about to leave he looked above his head and saw a row of six animal traps hanging from pegs.

Well, look at this. More presents . . . These'll slow 'em up, make no mistake!

Slipping three of the traps into his backpack, Hrubek stepped outside. He paused in the middle of a dusty patch behind the shop and smelled his hands. Mixed with the gasoline was a musky scent from the raccoon. He held his fingers close to his face and inhaled this smell on the wood-fire-laden air, deep, deep, so deep that his lungs hurt. As if the air overflowed into his groin, he went almost immediately erect. He guided his penis out of his overalls and stroked himself absently, using the slick blood from the screwdriver to lubricate the motion. Eyes closed, he swiveled his head sideways, keeping time with his right arm, feeling the pitch intensify, growing more and more dizzy as he hyperventilated.

He moaned an unearthly sound as he ejaculated, amply and hard, upon the dark earth.

Hrubek wiped his hands on the grass then he adjusted his Irish hat square on his head. Slipping into a stand of bushes he crouched down and made himself comfortable. There was only one more thing he needed right now and he knew in his heart God was about to send it to him.

Owen Atcheson pulled a large pile of burlap bags from a shelf in the greenhouse. They'd made good progress on the shoreline and had already built up one low-lying portion of lawn with several feet of sandbags. His muscles ached and he stretched hard, thinking of a meeting he had scheduled for tomorrow, his trip later in the week.

He glanced outside and saw Lis, beside the lakefront, filling bags with sand.

Moving silently down the aisle he passed plants whose names he neither knew nor cared to know. A timed watering valve clicked open and filled portions of the greenhouse with clouds of mist that obscured plants and the stone bas-reliefs that hung on the brick.

At the far end of the space he stopped. Portia looked up at him with her hazel eyes.

"I thought I saw you in here," he said.

"First aid." She pulled her skirt high, turning away from him and revealing on her thigh a small smear of blood a foot above the back of her knee.

"What happened?"

"Came down for a new roll of tape. I bent over and a fucking thorn got me in the ass. Part of it's still in there, I can feel it."

"Doesn't look too bad."

"Doesn't it? Hurts like hell." She turned around and looked him up and down then gave a short laugh. "You know, you look like a lord of the manor. Very medieval. Sort of like Sir Ralph Lauren."

Her voice seemed laced with mockery but immediately she smiled in a way that seemed to include him in a private joke. Her face contorted as she dug into the tiny wound with a fingernail lacquered red as the blood that dotted her skin.

Four silver rings were on each hand and a complicated spiral earring dangled from one lobe. The other was pierced by four silver hoops. Portia had refused Lis's offer of more practical clothing. She still wore her shimmering gold-and-silver skirt and loose blouse. The greenhouse was chill and it was clear to Owen that she wore no bra beneath the satiny white cloth. He scanned her figure briefly, reflecting that while his wife with her boyish figure might be called striking or handsome, her sister was a purely voluptuous creature. At times it amazed him that they shared the same genes.

"Let me look at it," he said.

Again, she turned her back and lifted her skirt. He clicked on a table lamp and shone it on her pale leg, then knelt to examine the wound.

"Would it really float away?" she asked. "The greenhouse?"

"Probably."

Portia smiled. "What would Lis do without her flowers? Do you have flood insurance?"

"No. The house is below flood level. They wouldn't write the policy."

"I don't imagine the rosebushes'd be covered anyway."

"It depends on the policy. That's a bargained risk."

"Once a lawyer always a lawyer," Portia said. He looked up but again could not tell if she was taunting him. She continued, "That porch Lis mentioned? On this part of the yard? I think she's wrong. I don't think it got washed away. I think Father tore it down to build Mother the greenhouse." Portia nodded toward a display of tall orange-red rosebushes. "Lis acts like it's a holy site. But Mother didn't even particularly want it."

"I thought that Ruth lived for her flowers."

"That's the way Lis tells it. But nope. It was Father who insisted. My own theory is that it was to keep her, let's say, occupied while he was away on business."

"Your mother's name and 'mischief' aren't words I'd ever put together." Owen dabbed away a dot of blood and peered into the wound.

"One never knows. Still waters and all. But then, was Father paranoid, or what?"

"I wouldn't know. I never liked him very much."

"Ooo, that hurts," she whispered as he probed, and lowered her head. "When we were young we had Sunday dinner on that old porch. Two p.m. sharp. Father rang a bell and we had to be there on the button. Roast, potatoes, green beans. We'd eat while he lectured about literature or business or space flights. Politics sometimes. Mostly he liked astronauts."

"It's really in there, the thorn. Just the tip. I can see it."

"Hurts like hell. Can you get it out?"

"I've got some tweezers." He pulled out a Swiss Army knife.

She dug into her pocket and handed him a Bic lighter. "Here." When he looked blank she laughed and said, "Sterilize it. Living in New York you learn to be careful about what you put into your body."

He took the lighter and ran a flame over the end of the tweezers.

"A Swiss Army knife," she said, watching him. "Does it have a corkscrew on it, and everything? Little scissors? A magnifying glass?"

"You know, Portia, sometimes it's hard to tell if you're making fun of somebody."

"It's probably my abrasive big-city attitude. It gets me into trouble sometimes. Don't take it personally." Portia fell silent and turned away, lowering her face to a rosebush. She inhaled deeply.

"I didn't know you smoked." He returned the lighter to her.

"I don't. Not cigarettes. And then, after we'd have our dessert, which was accompanied by . . . ?"

"I have no idea."

"Port."

Owen said he should have guessed.

"Do you like port, Owen?"

"No. I don't like port."

"Ow, Jesus, that hurts."

"Sorry."

He put his large hand on the front of Portia's thigh and held it firmly as he pressed the tiny blade of the tweezers against the base of the thorn. "Keep your hem up, so it doesn't get blood on it." She hiked her skirt slightly higher and he caught a fast view of the lace trim on red panties. He pressed harder with the tweezers.

Her eyes were closed and her teeth seated. "No, I can't stand port either but I *am* an expert on the subject. I paid attention during dear Father's dinnertime speeches. Nineteen seventeen was as good a year as the benchmark year. . . . Which was?" She raised a querying eyebrow. When he didn't respond she exhaled against the pain and said, "Why, 1963, of course. I thought all of you upper-crust gentlemen farmers knew that."

"I don't like to farm any more than I like port."

"Well, garden then." He felt her thigh quivering in his hand. He gripped it tighter. Portia continued, "A really good 1917 port has a bouquet that's reminiscent of tobacco. Sunday nights! After the port—and Father's lecture *about* port or NASA or lit-ra-ture or God knew what—and after our *bolos levados* and jam, we kids had nothing to do." She inhaled deeply, then asked, "Owen, I didn't really have to be here, did I? I could've signed everything in New York, had it notarized and mailed to you, right?"

He paused. "You could have, yes."

"So, what does she really want?"

"You're her sister."

"Does that mean I'm supposed to know why she asked me? Or does it mean she wants my company?"

"She hasn't seen much of you."

Portia laughed breathily. "You got that little sucker yet?"

"It's almost out." Owen glanced at the doorway at which his wife, if inclined to enter the greenhouse at this moment, would catch them at whatever it was that they were doing. He probed again with the tweezers, felt her shiver. She bit her lip and remained silent. Then he lifted out the thorn and stood.

Still holding her translucent skirt, Portia turned. Owen caught another flash of panties then held up the tweezers, the tip bright with her blood. "You'd think it'd be bigger," she said. "Thanks. You're a man of many talents."

"It's not too bad. Just a pinprick. But you should put something on it. Bactine. Peroxide."

"You have anything?"

"In the bathroom upstairs," he answered. "The one next to our bedroom."

She dabbed a Kleenex on the wound and examined the tissue. "Damn roses," Portia muttered, and dropping her hem she started toward the stairs.

5

He encircled her with his arms and pressed his mouth against hers. It was not a gentle kiss. Her fingers found his solid biceps and pulled him closer. Against his bare chest she rubbed her breasts, covered by only the thin cloth of her blouse.

I'm out of control, Owen thought. Out of goddamn control. He closed his eyes and kissed her again.

His tongue slipped between her lips and played with hers. She gripped his lower lip between her teeth and sucked it into her mouth. Then she hesitated and turned away, uneasy.

"No," he commanded. "Kiss me."

"What if she sees us?"

Owen shushed her, observing that her protest was halfhearted. It was as if the risk of being caught was part of her passion. Perhaps most of it.

His hands dropped to her blouse. She shuddered as a button popped off and fell at their feet but she gave no other resistance. The garment separated, and the backs of his hands brushed her exposed breasts.

"Are you—?" she began but he kissed her again and spread his large hand, so that a thumb and little finger each touched a nipple. His other hand curled around the white flesh of her back and pulled her closer.

His hand yanked her skirt high and stuffed the hem of the cloth into her waistband, exposing pale skin. She lifted her hips but he stroked her taut silk panties once and then didn't touch them again.

Instead he took her hand, unzipped his trousers and pulled himself out, closing her fingers around him roughly, silently instructing her to stroke, hard, so hard he was nearly in pain. When she flagged he ordered, "No, harder!"

And she did.

A moment later he stopped her, urgently gripping her shoulders and turning her around so that her back was to him. He rested his palm on the back of her hair and pushed her forward, then tugged the panties down. With both hands on her hips he entered her hard and instantly lost whatever self-restraint remained. He slammed against her. His hands clutched her breasts and he pulled her into him, her breath popping from her mouth in small bursts. He lowered his teeth to the back of her neck and closed them on the nape, biting hard, tasting sweat and perfume. She squirmed and pressed back against him, whimpering.

The sound triggered him. He slipped out and amid fierce spasms left a glistening stream down the inside of her thigh. He let his weight sag onto her back, gasping.

Then he was aware of motion and he realized that she'd been stroking herself all along. His hands slid around to her breasts once more and he pulled on her nipples. A few moments later he could feel her legs tense and, as she called his name in a high-pitched moan, once then again, her body shivered hard. She remained still for a moment then eased forward and rolled onto her back. He rested beside her, on his knees.

Inches apart, not touching.

As if words were wrong, as if words would give away this secret, he said nothing but leaned over and kissed her cheek in a formal, brotherly gesture. She squeezed his hand once.

Then Owen hefted his shovel and disappeared down the culvert, leaving his wife to lie like a trysting college girl beside the dark lake, on a neatly stacked row of sandbags.

.   .   .

Lis Atcheson watched the dull clouds overhead, and glanced uneasily at the house to see if Portia might have witnessed their exhibition.

The water lapped on rocks only feet from her head but seemed, despite the rising level, quite peaceful.

She breathed deeply a number of times and closed her eyes momentarily. What on earth had brought that on? she wondered. Owen was a man with an appetite stronger than hers, that was true, but he had a moodiness too; sex was the first thing to die when he turned sultry or preoccupied. It had been three or four weeks since he'd eased over to her side of the bed.

And the last time they'd found a more adventurous venue? The kitchen, the Cherokee, outdoors? Well, she couldn't remember. Months. Many months.

He'd come up to her ten minutes before, carrying a load of burlap bags from the greenhouse. Her back had been to him and she'd been bending down to muscle a sandbag into place on the levee when she heard the stack of empty bags fall nearby and felt his hands on her hips.

"Owen, *what* are you doing?" She laughed, and felt herself being pulled against him. He was already erect.

"No, we don't have time for this. My God, Portia's doing the upstairs windows! She can look right out!"

Silently he closed his hands over her breasts and kissed her hotly on the back of the neck.

"Owen, no!" She turned around.

"Shhh," was all he said, and his unyielding hands moved up under her skirt.

"Owen, are you nuts? Not now."

"Yes," he said. "Now."

And from behind, too. A position he generally didn't like; he preferred to pin her on her back, helpless, and watch her face as he pulsed on top of her.

What had gotten into him?

Maybe, above the clouds, there's a full moon.

Maybe it's . . .

The water lapped with the rhythm of the blues.

. . . the cowboy boots.

She glanced at the yellow windows of the house—windows from which she was now fully, if dimly, visible. Had Portia seen?

And if she had? Lis wondered. Well, so be it. He's *my* husband, after all.

She closed her eyes and was astonished to find herself drowsy —despite the adrenaline that still coursed in her bloodstream, despite the urgency to finish the sandbagging. Well, here's the miracle of the evening. Oh, my God, forget about floods, forget about orgasms out of doors. . . . I think I'm falling asleep.

Lis Atcheson suffered from insomnia. She might go twenty-four hours without sleep. Sometimes thirty, thirty-six hours, spent wholly alert, completely awake. The malady had been with her for years but had grown severe not long after the Indian Leap incident last May. The nightmares would start fifteen or twenty minutes after she'd slipped under—dreams filled with black caverns, blood, eyes that were dead, eyes that begged for mercy, eyes that were cruelly alive. . . .

Like a whipcrack, she'd be awake.

Eventually her heart would slow, the sweat on her temples and neck would evaporate. And she'd lie in bed, a prisoner of consciousness, growing ill with fatigue and teased by hallucinations. Hour after hour after hour. Gazing at the blue-green digital numerals that flicked ever onward. These numbers took on crazy meanings—1:39 seemed snide, the shape of 2:58 was comforting, 4:45 was a barricade; if she didn't cross it asleep she knew she'd lost the battle for that night.

She could recite all sorts of facts about sleep. Einstein needed ten hours a day, Napoleon only five. The record holder for not sleeping is a Californian who was awake for 453 hours. The average person sleeps between seven and a half and eight hours, a tomcat sixteen. There was a fatal type of insomnia, a type of prion disease that destroyed the thalamus region of the brain. Lis owned exactly twenty-two books on sleep disorders and insomnia; sometimes she recited their titles in lieu of counting sheep.

"It's just a way to avoid the nightmares," Lis's doctor had told her. "You have to tell yourself they're just dreams. Try repeating that. 'They're just dreams; they can't hurt me. They're just dreams; they can't hurt me.' "

She did as instructed but the awkwardness of this tongue-twisting mantra tended to waken her even further.

Yet tonight, Lis Atcheson—lying outside, bare-breasted and skirt to her thigh—felt sleep closing in fast. She grew more and more relaxed as she gazed at the greenhouse, the lights glowing ultramarine blue. She heard Owen slam the shovel onto a sandbag with a ring. She saw Portia's shadow in an upstairs bedroom.

Odd images began to dance in her mind. She recognized this as lucid dreaming. She saw faces melting, people becoming dark shapes, vaporous forms, flowers mutating.

Lis pictured a dark-red, a *blood*-red Victorian John Armstrong rose and that was the last image in her mind before she slipped under.

It was perhaps no more than ten seconds later that a branch snapped, loud as a gunshot. Lis, her ruddy hands folded scrupulously on her chest like the effigy of a long-dead saint, sat up, instantly and irrevocably awake, drawing closed her blouse and pulling down her skirt, as she stared at the dark form of the man who appeared from a row of hemlocks and trod forward.

Easing the '79 Chevy pickup off the back road onto Route 236 he goosed the lazy ticking engine until the truck climbed to seventy.

He heard what he diagnosed as an ornery bearing and chose not to think about it further.

Trenton Heck sat nearly reclining, his left foot on the accelerator and his right straight out, resting on the bench under the saggy flesh of a four-year-old male dog, whose face was full of lamentation. This was the way Heck drove—with his leg stretched out, not necessarily with a hound atop it—and he'd bought a vehicle with an automatic transmission and bench seat solely because of this practice.

Exactly thirty-two years older than the dog, Trenton Heck was sometimes referred to as "that skinny guy from Hammond Creek" though if people saw him with his shirt off, revealing muscles formed from a life of hunting, fishing, and odd jobs in rural towns, they'd decide that he wasn't skinny at all. He was *lean*, he was *sinewy*. Only in the past month had his belly started to roll past his waistband. This was due mostly to inactivity though some of it could be traced to chain-drinking Budweisers and to single suppers of twin TV dinners.

Heck tonight massaged a spot on his faded blue jeans under which was a glossy mess of old bullet wound dead center in his right thigh. Four years old (coming up on the anniversary, he reflected), the wound still pulled his muscles taut as cold rubber bands. Heck passed a slow-moving sedan and eased back into his lane. A big plastic Milk Bone swung from the truck's rearview mirror. It looked real and Heck had bought it to perplex the dog though of course it didn't; Emil was a purebred blood.

Heck drove along the highway at a good clip, whistling a tuneless tune between uneven teeth. A roadside sign flashed past and he lifted his foot off the accelerator and braked quickly, causing the hound to slide forward on the vinyl seat, grimacing. Heck eased into the turnoff and drove a quarter mile down a country lane of bad asphalt. He saw lights in the far distance and a few shy stars but mostly felt an overwhelming sense of solitude. He found the deserted roadside stand—a shack from which a farmer had years ago sold cheese and honey. Heck climbed out of the truck, leaving the engine running and the dog antsy on the seat.

Heck's outfit tonight was what he always wore unless the temperature was crackling cold: a black T-shirt under a workshirt under a blue-jean jacket. Covering the curly brown hair that dipped over his ears was a cap emblazoned with the logo of the New York Mets. The cap had been a present from a woman who could recite all the vital statistics of the Flushing Meadow sluggers going back fifteen years (Jill had a great knuckleball herself) but he didn't care for the team and wore the tattered hat only because it was a present from her.

He looked around uneasily and wandered in a slow circle through the dusty parking area. He glanced at the idling truck and concluded that it was too much of a beacon. He shut off the engine and lights. Enveloped in darkness, he resumed his pacing. Rustling sounded nearby. Heck immediately recognized the sound of raccoon's footfalls. Moments later he identified a residue of musk on a skunk's ass fur as the animal passed silently behind him. These creatures weren't a threat, yet as he paced he kept his hand on the black Bakelite ribbed grip of his old automatic pistol, dangling from an even older cowboy holster, complete with rawhide leg thongs.

Clouds filled the sky. The storm was overdue. Rain if you've gotta, he spoke silently though not heavenward, but keep that wind away for another few hours, Lord. I could use some help here and I could use it bad.

A twig snapped behind him, loud, and he turned fast, coming close to drawing down on a conspicuous birch tree. He knew of few animals in the wild that would snap twigs this way; he recalled only a towering moose lumbering along with her calves, and a seven-foot grizzly bear, gazing at Heck hungrily from the amiable haze of his protected-species status.

Maybe it's a drunk deer, he thought, to cheer himself up.

Heck continued to pace. Then lights filled the parking lot and the car arrived. It parked with a leisurely squeal of brakes. Upright as a boot-camp sergeant, the gray-suited officer walked over the damp ground to where Heck stood.

"Don." Heck offered a limp salute.

"Trent. Glad you were free. Good to see you."

"That storm's on its way," Heck said.

"That Emil of yours could scent through a hurricane, I thought."

That may be, he told Haversham, but he wasn't inclined to get himself lightning-struck. "Now, who's the escapee?"

"That psycho they got at Indian Leap last spring. You remember it?"

"Who don't, round here?"

"Snuck off in somebody's body bag tonight." Haversham explained about the escape.

"Crazy maybe but that shows some smarts."

"He's over near Stinson."

"So he drove a ways, this nutzo?"

"Yup. The coroner's boy, the one who was driving's over there now. So's Charlie Fennel and a couple troopers from J. He's got his bitches with him."

The Troop's dogs weren't true trackers but hunting dogs— Labradors—occasionally drafted for scenting. They had fair noses and being spayed bitches they stayed clear of posts and trees and weren't easily led astray. But they did get distracted. Emil was a track-sure dog; when he was on scent he'd walk right over a rabbit sitting in his path and ignore it, and the only sound you'd hear was the rasp of his anxious breath as he charged along the trail. The girls on the other hand were track-happy and spent much of the time quartering with sloppy enthusiasm and yelping. Still, when you were after a dangerous escapee, it was good practice to go with a pack. He asked Haversham what they could use to scent on.

"Skivvies." The captain handed over a plastic bag. Heck was confident that Haversham knew how to handle scent articles. He'd have made sure that the underwear hadn't been laundered recently and that nobody had touched the cloth with their fingers. The trooper added, "He's running mostly naked, near as we can tell."

Heck thought the captain was joking.

"No sir. He's a big fellow, got lots of padding on him. Adler, that doctor at Marsden, he was telling me these schizos don't feel cold like normal people. It's like they're pretty numb. They don't feel pain either. You can hit 'em and they don't even know they're hit."

"Ooo, that's good to know, Don. Tell me, does he fly too?"

Haversham chuckled then added, "They say he's pretty harmless. He does this a lot. Adler says he's escaped from seven hospitals. They always find him. It's like a game for him. The bag he snuck out in? The fellow's it was, was a suicide."

"Harmless? Didn't they read about Indian Leap?" Heck snickered, and nodded down the road toward Marsden hospital. "Who's crazy in there and who isn't?" Heck was suddenly unable to look at Haversham. "Say, over the phone you mentioned five hundred for my fee. And the reward. Ten *thousand*. That right, Don? Ten?"

"Yessir. The fee's from my assistance fund just like normal. The reward's from the state. From Adler's budget. He's pretty anxious to get this fellow."

"I don't suppose he put it in writing?"

"Adler? Nope. But he's really anxious to see this boy caught. You collar him, you'll get your money, Trent. And you're the only civvy on the case. My boys can't take a penny."

"We'll get him."

The captain looked off into the night and seemed to be debating. Finally he said, "Trenton? I know I told you he wasn't dangerous but keep that close to you." Haversham indicated the pistol on Heck's hip. "I gotta tell you—was probably an accident, from what Adler says, but Hrubek might've attacked a couple orderlies. Cracked one of 'em's arm like a toothpick. Could've died if nobody'd found him."

"Well, is he dangerous, or ain't he?" Heck asked.

"All I'm saying is, keep your eye out. Say, what *is* that piece?"

"That old P-38 of mine." Heck patted his holster, remembering in detail the day he handed his Glock service automatic over to this very man, Heck's eyes frozen on the black gun as he turned it in, grip first, clip out, slide locked open. The badge and the ID card followed. Heck had bought the uniform himself so they let him keep that though he had to sign a form that said he'd never wear it in public, and his face was red with anger and shame as he set his name to paper.

"They still sell ammunition for that old thing?"

"Nine-millimeter parabellum is all it is."

Haversham stuck his head through the passenger window and stroked the hound's head. The dog sat insensible and bored, staring at the motion of the captain's gray hair. "All right, Emil, go do us and your master proud. You hear? You go catch us a crazy man. Good boy, good boy." Haversham turned to Heck. "Isn't he a good old boy?"

And Trenton Heck—who'd midwived bitches and nursed pups with eyedroppers and sucked snake venom out of the shoulders of retrievers and sped to vets at ninety mph to save dogs that could be saved and shot them remorselessly with a merciful bullet when they could not, who didn't speak to dogs except to command them—Trenton Heck just nodded at the captain with a cautious smile. "Better be going. 'Fore that track gets cold."

"How the hell did it happen?" Owen barked. "He's a madman. He *can't* escape! Did they leave the son-of-a-bitch door open?"

"Some mix-up of some kind. They were kind of, you know, sketchy on details." Stanley Weber, duly elected sheriff of the In-corporated Village of Ridgeton, turned out to have been the intruder who'd wakened Lis from her brief sleep. He'd passed by without even noticing her, directed by Portia down to the culvert where Owen was working.

His news was far more disturbing than his unexpected arrival.

"My God, Stan," Lis said, "it's a hospital for the criminally insane. Don't they have bars?"

She was remembering: Eyes set deep in the moonish jolly mad face. Teeth yellow. His howling voice. "*Sic semper tyrannis* . . . Lisbone. . . . Hello, Lis-bone!"

"There's no excuse for it." Owen paced angrily. He was a large man, strong in many ways, and he had a temper that scared even Lis. The sheriff crossed his arms defensively and leaned into the anger. "When did it happen?" Owen continued. "Do they know where he's going?"

"Within the last couple hours. I was on the radio." He pointed to his squad car as if trying to lead Owen's fury off track. "I was speaking to Don Haversham. With the state police?" He added significantly, "He's a good man. He's a captain."

"Oh, a captain. My."

Lis found herself staring at the sheriff's feet; in his heavy, dark boots he appeared less a civil servant than a man of combat on a combat mission. A breath of air stirred, reaching damply into her blouse. She watched a dozen leaves fall straight from the branches of a towering maple as if seeking cover before the storm arrived. Lis shivered and realized the kitchen door was ajar. She closed it.

Footsteps sounded suddenly and Lis glanced at the doorway to the living room.

Portia paused then entered the kitchen, still dressed in her thin, sexy outfit, her abundant breasts provocatively defined by the white silken cloth of her blouse. The sheriff nodded at the young woman, who smiled indifferently. The lawman's eyes dipped twice to her chest. Portia's Discman was stuffed into the pocket of the skirt and a single earplug was stuck in one ear. A tinny chunka-chunka sound came from the dangling plug.

"Hrubek's escaped," Lis told her.

"Oh, no." The second earplug was extracted and she flung the wire around her neck the way a doctor wears a stethoscope. The raspy sound of rock music was louder now, shooting from both tiny plugs.

"Say, could you shut that off?" Lis asked, and Portia absently complied.

Lis, Owen and Portia stood on glazed terra-cotta tile as cold as the concrete stoop outside, all in a line, arms crossed. Their formation struck Lis as silly and she broke ranks to fill a kettle. "Coffee or tea, Stanley?"

"No, thankya. He's just wandering around lost, they say. He got away in Stinson, nearly ten miles east of the hospital."

And fifty miles east of where they now stood, Lis thought. Like having a full gas tank or two twenty-dollar bills in your pocket this was a comfort—maybe insubstantial, maybe useless, but a comfort nonetheless.

"So," Portia said, "he's heading away from here."

"Seems to be."

Lis was remembering: The madman bursting to life, hand and foot shackles jingling, his eyes molesting the trial spectators. And she was the person he undressed most eagerly. "Lis-bone, Lis-bone . . ."

Lis had cried then—in June—hearing his hyena-pitched laugh fill the courtroom and she wanted to cry now. She clamped her teeth together and turned to the stove to make a cup of herbal tea. Owen was still firing angry questions at the sheriff. How many men are out looking for him? Do they have dogs? Did he take any weapons? The sheriff endured this cross-examination gamely then responded, "The fact is they're not doing a whole lot about it. It went out as an information bulletin only. Not an escape-assistance request. I myself'd guess they've pretty much cured him. Shocked him, probably, like they do. With those electrode things. He's out wandering around and they'll pick him up—"

Owen waved his hand and started to speak but Lis interrupted. "If nobody's worried about it, Stan, what are you doing here?"

"Well, I come by to ask if you still got that letter. Thought it might give 'em a clue where he's got himself to."

"Letter?" Owen asked.

Lis, however, knew exactly which letter he was referring to. It'd been her first thought this evening when the sheriff had said the word "Marsden."

"I know where it is," she said, and went to get it.

6

Mrs. Lis-bone Atcheson:

I am in this room I can't breathe I can't hear. I am held here unfAIRly and thEY, yes thEy are stopping me from what I MUST DO. This is very Important. they are holding me and have told lIes About Me to waShingtOn and the enTIRE worlD. they think that I am dANGERous etc but this is their excUSE and EVErybody beliEVEs it. That is beliEVEs "them". they are very Strong & we Must fear them. they arE eVErywhere.

It is a CONSPIRACY. CON + S + PIRACY.

and I know YOU are in it!!!!

Revenge is mine it is not the LORDS because the LORD knows what I have Done and will not let ME rest. He shoots me in the hEAd every nighT!!! I accept my fATE and YOU who are bEAuTiful mUSt too. Come to me for eternal rest forever.

EVErywhere. forEVEr. rEVEnge.

EVE the woman

COME to ME.

i your lover

Michael Hrubek's penmanship featured green, black and blu ink.

And for her name, and his "signature," red.

The sheriff sucked air between shiny white teeth in a loud,

ritating way. "Does any of this make sense to you?" He addressed the question to Owen.

Lis answered, "It's just babble."

Owen glanced at her then added, "We talked about it when it came but we thought it was a kid's prank."

Lis taught sophomore English at Ridgeton High School.

"I'm a tough grader." She laughed wanly. "I've been on my share of sixteen-year-olds' shit lists."

" 'i your lover.' " The sheriff hitched at his gun belt. He stared at the letter for a moment. "Return address?"

Lis flipped through the manilla folder where she'd filed it—in the *Letters, Miscellaneous* slot. Just past, she now noted, *Last Will and Testament—Owen and Lis*. She found the envelope. There was no return address. The postmark was Gloucester.

"That's nowhere near Marsden," she pointed out.

"Let me make a call." The sheriff glanced at Owen, who nodded at the phone.

As she leaned against the counter, sipping the rose-hip tea, Lis remembered a hot Saturday in September, replanting a bush of hybrid tea roses, lemon yellow. Sweat was running along her nose with a tickle. Owen had been working all day and had just returned. About 6:00 p.m., the sun low and wan. He stood in the doorway, his large shoulders slumped, a piece of paper in his hand. Lis glanced up at him and the plant sank through her fingers, a thorn piercing her skin. Because of the sallow, grave expression on her husband's face she hadn't at first noticed the pain. Lis looked down a second later and saw a sphere of blood on her finger. She set the plant on the ground. Owen handed her this very letter and she took it from him slowly, leaving a bloody fingerprint on the envelope— like an old-time wax seal.

Portia now read it. She shrugged, and announced to Lis, "I've got some stuff with me. Stop by the room, you want. It might relax you."

Lis blinked and forced herself to appear blasé. Only her sister, she reflected from an emotional distance, would offer a joint with one-fifth of the town's constabulary standing nearby (his squad car's bumper proclaiming, *Ridgeton Says NO to Drugs*). This was vintage Portia—playful, cunning, perverse. Oh, Portia—the hip, pale, French-braided younger sister with her Discman and her stream of thin-faced boyfriends. She'd been forced to endure an evening in the country, and she was blowing Lis one of the cold kisses her older sister remembered so well.

Lis did not reply. The young woman shrugged and, with a glance at Owen, wandered out of the kitchen.

The sheriff, who hadn't heard Portia's proposition and probably wouldn't have understood it if he had, hung up the receiver. When he spoke, it was to Owen. "Well . . . The long and the short of it is that she doesn't have anything to worry about."

She? Lis repeated to herself. Was this me? Her face burned and she sensed even old-world Owen shift uncomfortably at the sheriff's patronizing attitude.

"They said it didn't mean nothing. Hrubek's a schizo—they don't do well by people face to face. Too nervous to talk or something. So they write these long letters that're just nonsense mostly and when they do make a threat they're like too scared to act on it."

"The postmark?" Lis asked firmly. "Gloucester."

"Oh, about that. I asked. He may still've sent it. He got sent to this hospital there for some tests the first week in September. It's pretty low-security. He might've slipped away and mailed a letter. But, what I was telling you before, he's headed east, *away* from here."

The sheriff and Lis both looked at Owen, who because he was the largest person in the room and the most grave, seemed to be in charge. "What if he isn't?"

"Hell, he's on foot, Owen. The doctor said there's no way he can drive a car. And who's going to give him a ride, a big crazy like that?"

"I'm just asking you," Owen said, "what if he *isn't* going east. What if he changes him mind and comes here?"

"Here?" the sheriff asked and fell silent.

"I want you to put a man on the house."

"I'm sorry, Owen. No can do. We've got—"

"Stan, this is serious."

"—that storm coming up. It's supposed to be a whopper. And Fred Bertholder's in bed with the flu. Sick as a dog. Whole family has it."

"One man. Just until they catch him."

"Look, even the state boys're spread pretty thin. They're on highway detail mostly because of the—"

"Fucking storm," Owen spat out. He rarely swore in front of people he didn't know well; he considered it a sign of weakness. Lis was momentarily shocked at this lapse—not at the cussing itself but the anger that would be behind it.

"We got our priorities. Come on, don't go looking that way, Owen. I'll check in with Haversham every so often. If there's any change I'll be over here like greased lightning."

Owen walked to the window and looked out over the lake. He was either paralyzed with anger or deep in thought.

"Why don't you go to a hotel for the night?" the sheriff suggested with a cheerfulness that Lis found immensely irritating. "Hey, that way you'll get yourselves a good night's rest and not have to worry 'bout nothing."

"Good night's rest," Lis muttered. "Sure."

"Believe me, folks, you got nothing to worry about." He glanced out the window into the sky, perhaps hoping for a searing streak of lightning to justify his deployment of deputies this evening. "I'll stay on top of it, yessir." The sheriff offered a rueful smile as he stepped to the door.

Only Lis said good night.

.   .   .

Owen paced beside the window, gazing out to the lake. He said matter-of-factly, "I think we ought to do that. A hotel, I mean. We'll get a couple rooms at the Marsden Inn."

A quaint little bed-and-breakfast, lousy (Owen's word) with dried flowers, Shaker furniture, country wreaths and dreadfully sincere paintings of live horses, dead birds and glassy-eyed nineteenth-century children.

"Not exactly the best hideout from a crazy man, would you say?"

"It doesn't sound like he could even get halfway to Ridgeton, let alone find a hotel we're staying at. . . . If he was inclined to find us in the first place. Besides, the Inn's only two miles from here. I don't want to have to go far tonight."

"We need to finish the dam and the taping."

Owen didn't speak for a moment. He asked in a distracted voice, "Where do you think he is?"

"I'm not leaving till we get that levee finished. The sandbags, the—"

Owen's eyes flashed. "Why are you arguing?"

Lis blinked. She'd learned to tolerate his temper. She knew it was usually misdirected. Her husband was angry now, yes, but not at her—at the sheriff. Most times she blustered right back at him. But tonight she didn't raise her voice. On the other hand she wasn't going to back down. "I'm not disagreeing. The hotel's fine. But I'm not leaving until we've got at least another foot's worth of sandbags."

His eyes again looked out onto the lake while Lis's dipped to the letter, resting on the butcher block. Lis smoothed it, then folded the paper. It made a crinkling sound and she thought for some reason of dried skin. She shivered and tossed it onto a stack of bills to be filed.

Lis pulled on her jacket. Was he going to argue, or agree? Unable to anticipate his reaction she felt her stomach twisting into a knot. Cautiously she said, "It shouldn't take more than an hour." Still he said nothing. "You think we can get enough bags piled up by then?"

Owen finally turned from the window and asked what she'd just said.

"Sandbags? Can we stack enough in an hour?"

"An hour? I'm sure we can." His serenity surprised her. "Anyway I don't think it's going to be as bad as they say. You know weathermen around here—they're always sounding false alarms."

The driver downshifted to the lowest of his thirteen gears and nudged the huge White tractor-trailer past the restaurant and into the parking area. He locked the brakes and shut off the diesel, then checked a map, spending more time than he thought normal for a smart man like himself to calculate that he'd be in Bangor by four the next afternoon.

A young man, the driver wore his Dolphins cap backwards and Nike Pumps on his feet. In the Blaupunkt was a grunge tape, backed up by a half dozen rap and hip-hop cassettes (a secret never to be shared with any blood relation). He climbed out of the cab, pausing long enough to glance in the side mirror with discouragement at the constellation of acne on his cheek, then dropped to the ground. He was halfway to the diner when the voice barked, "Hey, John Driver!"

The huge man was suddenly next to him, hovering on legs like tree trunks. The driver stopped, astonished, as he looked up into the glistening round face, the spit-flecked grin, the eyes as excited as a kid's at a ball game.

"Howdy," the driver stammered.

The big man suddenly grew awkward and seemed to look for something to say. "That's quite a machine, it is," he offered though he didn't look toward the truck but kept his eyes fixed downward on the driver.

"Uhn, thanks. You excuse me, I'm pretty beat and I'm gonna get some chow."

"Chow, chow. Sure. It's lucky seven. See. One, two, three, four, five, six . . ." His arm was making a circuit of the vehicles in the parking lot. "Seven." The man adjusted the wool tweed cap that was perched on his bowling ball of a head. He seemed bald and the driver wondered if he was a Nazi skinhead. He said, "Lucky," and laughed too loud.

"Uh-oh. That's eight." The fellow was pointing to another truck just pulling into the lot. His mouth twisted up in a smirking grin. "Always some fucker who ruins it."

"That *does* happen. You bet." The driver decided he could outrun this bozo but was as troubled by the thought of looking like a fool in front of fellow truckers as he was of getting stomped. "Well. Yessir. G' night now." He sidled toward the diner.

The big man's eyes flashed with concern. "Wait wait wait! Are you going east, John Driver?"

The young man looked up into the murky eyes. "That's not truly my name," he said cautiously.

"I'm going to Boston. That's the home of our country. I really have to get to *Boston*."

"I'm sorry but I can't give you a lift. I work for—"

"A lift?" the man asked with great curiosity. "A lift?"

"Uhn, I can't give you a *ride*? You know what I'm saying? I work for a company and they'd fire me I was to do that."

"No such luck, huh? No such luck?"

"A rule, I'm saying."

"But what am I going to *do*?"

"They don't like it too much you try for rides in truck stops?" This wasn't a question but he was too frightened to offer the man a declarative sentence. "You might go up the road a spell and thumb?"

"Up the road and thumb."

"Somebody might pick you up."

"Up the road and thumb. I could do that. Can I get to Boston that way?"

"That intersection up there, see the light? That's 118, turn left, that'd be north. It'll get you to the Interstate and that'll put you in Boston in no time."

"Thank you, John Driver. God bless you. Up the road and thumb."

The big man started through the lot in a muscular, awkward lope. The driver said a short prayer of thanks—both for surviving this encounter and, equally important, for ending up with a good story to tell to his fellow truckers, one that needed hardly any embellishment at all.

Peter Grimes returned to the hospital director's office and sat in a desk chair. Adler asked casually, "He did *what*?" as if resuming a conversation recently interrupted.

"I'm sorry?"

Adler slapped a green file folder. "The nurses' duty report. "Hrubek was *authorized* to be in C Ward. He had access to the *grounds*. He just walked right into the morgue. *That's* how he got there. He just *strolled* into the freezer. Oh, Peter, Peter, Peter . . . This is not good." Adler had conceded the dankness of his office and was now wearing a beige cardigan into whose bottom buttonhole he poked his little finger.

"And I found out why," Grimes announced. "He was part of Dick Kohler's program."

"Oh, for God's sake, not the halfway house?"

"No. Restricted to the grounds here. Milieu Suite and the work program. For some reason he had a job at the farm. Milking cows, or something, I suppose." The assistant gazed out the black window toward the part of the grounds where the hospital's nonprofit farm, operated by volunteers and staffed by patients, spread for some ten acres into the rocky hills.

"Why wasn't any of this in the file?" Adler slapped the folder once again, as if disciplining a puppy.

"I think there're some other files we don't have. I don't know what happened to them. Something funny's going on."

"Did the board recommend Hrubek for the program?" Adler, as member of the Marsden Board of Directors, prayed for one particular answer to this question.

"No," Grimes said.

"Ah."

"Maybe Dick Kohler slipped him in somehow."

" 'Slipped him in'?" Adler pounced. "We have to be very buttoned up about this, my friend. Did you mean that: 'slipped him in'? Think now. Think carefully."

"Well, I don't know. Hrubek was always closely supervised. It's not quite clear who okayed it. The paperwork's sketchy."

"So maybe he wasn't," Adler reflected, " 'slipped in' after all? Maybe some other idiot here dropped the ball."

Grimes wondered if he was being insulted.

The hospital director breathed slowly. "Wait a moment. Kohler's not on staff. Does he have an office here?"

Grimes was surprised Adler didn't know. "Yes, he does. It's part of the arrangement with Framington. We supply facilities for the attendings."

"He's *not* an attending," Adler snapped.

"In a manner of speaking, he is." With the trooper absent, Grimes inexplicably felt bolder.

"I want to find out what the hell is going on here and I want to know in the next hour. Who's the E Ward resident on call?"

"I'm not exactly sure. I think—"

"Peter, you've got to get on top of this," Adler snapped. "Find out who it is and tell him to go home. Tell him to take the evening off."

"Yes. Go *home*? Are you sure?"

"And tell him not to talk to anyone. . . . I'm curious about this woman. . . ." Adler looked for a scrap of paper, found it and handed it to Grimes. "Did Hrubek ever mention her? *Anybody* ever mention her?"

Grimes read the name. "Mrs. Owen Atcheson? No. Who's she?"

"She was at Indian Leap. She testified against Hrubek at the trial. She claims she got a threatening letter from him last September when our little boy was playing with blocks at Gloucester. The sheriff says her husband thinks Hrubek's after her."

"Ridgeton," Grimes mused. "Forty miles west of here. Not a problem."

"Oh?" Adler turned his red eyes on the young doctor. "Good. I'm so relieved. Now tell me why you think it's quote not a problem."

Grimes swallowed and said, "Because most schizophrenics couldn't get three miles on their own, let alone forty."

"Ah," Adler said, sounding like a crotchety old Oxford don. "And with what little qualifiers, dear Grimes, did you shore up your substandard assessment?"

Grimes surrendered. He fell silent and fluffed his crinkly hair.

"A, what if he *isn't* on his own, doctor?" Adler barked. "What if there are co-conspirators, witting or un? And B, what if Hrubek isn't *like* most schizophrenics? How 'bout them apples, doctor? Now, get on it. Find out exactly how the son of a bitch got out."

Grimes had not grown so bold that he failed to say, "Yes, sir." And he said it very quickly.

"If this . . . Hold up a minute there. If this—" Adler gestured, unable or unwilling to give a name to the potential tragedy. "If this becomes a problem . . ."

"How's that?"

"Get Lowe on the phone. I need to have another little talk with him. Oh, and where's Kohler?"

"Kohler? He'll be at the halfway house tonight. He sleeps over on Sunday."

"You think he'll be in for rounds tonight?"

"No. He was here at four-thirty this morning. And after evaluations he went right to the halfway house. And he was dead on his feet *then*. I'm sure he's in bed now."

"Good."

"Should I call him?"

"Call him?" Adler stared at Grimes. "Doctor, really. He's the *last* one we want to know about this. Don't say a word to him. Not . . . a . . . word."

"I just thought—"

"No, you didn't just think. You weren't thinking at all. I mean, for God's sake, do you call up the fucking lamb and say, 'Guess what? Tomorrow's Easter'?"

7

The steam rising from the plastic cup of coffee left a foggy ellipse on the inside of the windshield.

Dr. Richard Kohler, slouching in the front seat of his fifteen-year-old BMW, yawned painfully and lifted the cup. He sipped the bitter liquid and replaced the carton on the dash slightly to the right of where it had been. He vacantly watched a new oval paint itself on the glass, overlapping the one that was now fading.

He was parked in the staff lot of Marsden State Mental Health Facility. The chunky car, half hidden under an anemic hemlock, was pointed at a small, one-story building near the hospital's main structure.

The duty nurse on E Ward, a friend and woman he used to date, had called the halfway house twenty minutes ago. She'd told Kohler about Michael's escape and warned him that Adler was stonewalling. Kohler had flushed his face with icy water, filled a thermos with coffee then run groggily to his car and driven here. He'd pulled into the parking lot and chosen this spot for his stakeout.

He now looked up at the gothic façade of the asylum and saw several lights. One of them, he supposed, was burning in the office of good Dr. Adler.

The wittier orderlies called the two doctors Hatfield and McCoy and that pretty accurately described their relationship. Still, Kohler had some sympathy for the hospital director. In his five years as head of Marsden, Adler had been fighting a losing political and budgetary battle. Most of the state mental hospitals had been closed, replaced by small, community-based treatment centers. But there remained a need for places to house the criminally insane as well as indigent and homeless patients.

Marsden was such a place.

Adler worked hard for his chunk of the state purse, and he made sure that the poor souls in his care were treated kindly and had the best of a bad situation. It was a thankless job and one that Kohler himself would have quit medicine before taking on.

But beyond that, Kohler's sympathy for his colleague stopped. Because he also knew that Adler had a $122,000-a-year job, malpractice premiums and state benefits included, and that for his paycheck he worked at most a forty-hour week. Adler didn't keep up with the current literature, didn't attend institutes or continuing-education sessions, and rarely spoke with patients except to dispense the insincere greetings of an incumbent politician.

Mostly though Kohler resented Adler's running Marsden not as a treatment facility but as combination prison and day-care center. Containment, not improvement, was his goal. Adler argued that it wasn't the state's job to fix people—merely to keep them from hurting themselves or others.

Kohler would respond, "Then whose job is it, *doctor*?"

Adler would snap back, "You give me the money, sir, and I'll start curing."

The two doctors had played oil and water since Kohler first came to Marsden, brandishing court-appointment orders and trying unusual forms of therapy on severely psychotic patients. Then, somehow—no one quite knew how—Kohler had set up the Milieu Program at Marsden. In it, noncriminal patients, mostly schizophrenics, learned to work and socialize with others, with an eye toward moving on to the halfway house outside of Stinson and eventually to apartments or homes of their own.

Adler was just smart enough to recognize that he had a plum deal that he'd have trouble duplicating anywhere in this universe and was accordingly not the least interested in having jive New York doctors rocking his delicate boat with these glitzy forms of treatment. Recently he'd tried to have Kohler removed, claiming that the younger doctor hadn't gone through proper state civil-service channels to get the job at Marsden. But the allegation was tenuous since Kohler drew no salary and was considered an outside contractor. Besides, the patients themselves rose in rebellion when they heard the rumor that they might lose their Dr. Richard. Adler was forced to back down. Kohler continued to work his way into the hospital, ingratiating himself with the full-time staff and cultivating friends among the practical power centers—the nurses, secretaries and orderlies. The animosity between Kohler and Adler flourished.

Many of the doctors at Marsden wondered why Kohler—who could have had a lucrative private practice—brought all this trouble on himself. Indeed, they were perplexed why he'd spend so much time at Marsden in the first place, where he received a small fee for treating patients and where the practice itself was so demanding and frustrating that it drove many physicians out of psychiatry—and some out of medicine altogether.

But Richard Kohler was a man who'd always tested himself. An honors art-history graduate student, he'd abruptly given up that career path at the ripe age of twenty-three to fight his way into, then through, Duke Medical School. Those grueling years were followed by residencies at Columbia Presbyterian and New Haven General then private practice in Manhattan. He worked with in-patient borderline and near-functioning psychotics, then sought out the hardest cases: chronic schizophrenic and bipolar depressives. He battled bureaucratic resistance to get visiting-physician status at Marsden, Framington and other state Bedlams, where he put in twelve-, fifteen-hour days.

It was as if Kohler thrived on the very stress that was his schizophrenic patients' worst enemy.

Early in his career the psychiatrist developed several tricks for combatting anxiety. The most effective was a macabre meditation: visualizing that he was slipping a needle into a prominent vein rising from his arm and drawing out a searing white light, which represented the stress. The technique was remarkably successful (though it usually worked best when accompanied by a glass of Burgundy or a joint).

Tonight, sitting in a car smelling of old leather, oil and antifreeze, he tried his old trick, though without the chemical assist. It had no effect. He tried again, actually closing his eyes, and picturing the mystical procedure in vivid detail. Again, nothing. He sighed and gazed again at the parking lot.

Kohler stiffened and slouched further down into the front seat as a white van, on whose side was painted *Intertec Security Inc.*, appeared and zigzagged slowly through the parking lot, casting its spotlights on suspicious shadows.

Kohler clicked on the penlight he used for neuro exams and returned to the papers in front of him. These sheets represented an exceedingly abridged version of Michael Hrubek's personal history. The records about the young man's life were woefully inadequate; since he was an indigent patient, very few details of his hospitalization and treatment history were available. This was another sin that Kohler couldn't lay at the hospital director's feet. Michael was the type of patient whose files were virtually nonexistent and whose past treatment was largely a mystery. He'd lived on the street so often, been expelled from so many hospitals, and used so many aliases with intake personnel that there was no coherent chronicle of his illness. He also suffered from a particular type of mental disease that left him with a jumbled and confused sense of the past; what paranoid schizophrenics reported was a stew of lies, truth, confessions, hopes, dreams and delusions.

Yet, for someone with Kohler's experience, the file he now scanned allowed him to reconstruct in some detail a portion of

Michael's life. This fragment was startlingly illuminating. He was vaguely familiar with the file, having acquired it four months before, when Michael came under his care. Kohler now wished he'd paid more attention to its contents when he first read it. He wished too that he had more time now to review the material it contained. But having skimmed the pages once, he noticed that the white van had left the parking lot. Richard Kohler set the folder on the BMW's floor.

He started the car and drove over the wet asphalt to the one-story building he'd been watching for the past half hour. He circled behind it and located the back door, which was near a battered green dumpster. He braked to a stop, debated for a moment and then—after wisely clipping on his seatbelt—drove the right front bumper of the auto into the door at what seemed to him a leisurely rate of speed. Still, the impact shattered the wood so violently that the door cracked free of both hinges and flew deep into the darkness inside.

He pulled the Chevy onto the shoulder of Route 236. The battered truck listed hard to the left and an Orange Crush empty rolled against the door. The brakes squealed as the truck stopped.

Trenton Heck pushed the door open and stepped out. The soda can fell clattering to the road's rocky shoulder and Heck stooped painfully and pitched the empty under the seat.

"Come," he said to Emil, who, already aimed down the incline of the seat, relaxed some muscle or another and slid forward then out the door. He landed on the ground and stretched then blinked at the flashing lights of a state-police car across the highway.

Next to the lit-up Dodge cruiser sat another black-and-white, and beside that was a tan county-coroner's meat wagon. Four men looked up as Heck crossed the wide strip of black pebbly asphalt. He led Emil away from the cars—he always got the dog out of the truck as soon as possible at a search scene and kept him far from car engines; exhaust dulls dogs' noses.

"Sit," Heck commanded when they were in a patch of grass upwind from the cars. "Down." Emil did as instructed, even though he eagerly noted the presence of some four-legged ladies nearby.

"Hey, Trenton," one of the men called. He was a large man, large all over, not just the belly—food round, not drink round— and his weight pulled hard at the buttons and pockets of his gray uniform. He was holding back two young female Labrador retrievers, who nosed in the dirt.

"Hiya, Charlie."

"Well, if it ain't the Cadillac of trackers." This, from one of the two young troopers standing on the roadside, a man Heck referred to, though not to his face, as "the Boy." He was a narrow-jawed youngster, six years Heck's junior in age though fifteen in appearance. Trenton Heck's idea of dealing with a budget cutback would have been to fire this kid and keep Heck himself on the force at three-quarters salary. But they hadn't asked his opinion and so the Boy, who though younger had hired on two months before Heck, was still a trooper while Trenton Heck had netted eighty-seven dollars last month carting old washing machines and water softeners to the Hammond Creek dump.

"Hey, Emil," the Boy said.

Heck nodded to him and waved to the other trooper, who called back a greeting.

Charlie Fennel and Heck walked toward the tan hearse, beside which stood a young man in a pale-green jumpsuit.

"Not much of a search party," Heck said to Fennel.

The trooper answered that they were lucky to have what they did. "There's a concert letting out at midnight or so down at the Civic Center. You hear about that?"

"Rock 'n' roll," Heck muttered.

"Uhn. Don sent a buncha troopers over there. They had some boy got shot at the last one."

"Don't they have security guards for that sort of thing?"

"Was a guard who shot the kid."

"Doesn't seem like a brilliant use of taxpayers' money, riding herd on a bunch of youngsters paying to deafen themselves."

Then too, Fennel added, the captain had put a good portion of the troops on highway detail. "He figures what with the storm, they'll be picking 'em off the pavement. Say, I hear there's a reward for catching this crazy."

Heck kept his eyes on the grass in front of him and didn't know what to say.

"Listen," Fennel continued in a whisper, "I heard about your situation, Trenton. I hope you get that money. I'm rooting for you."

"Thanks there, Charlie."

Heck had a curious relationship with Charlie Fennel. The same bullet that had left the shiny star-shaped wound in Heck's right thigh had passed first through Fennel's brother's chest as he crouched beside their patrol car, killing the trooper instantly. Heck supposed that some of the man's living blood had ridden the slug into his own body and that because of that he and Charlie Fennel were blood brothers, once removed. At times Trenton Heck thought that he and Fennel ought to be closer. The more time the men spent in each other's company, however, the less they found they had in common. They occasionally talked about a hunting or fishing trip but the plans came to nothing. It was a secret relief to both of them.

Heck and Fennel now paused beside the coroner's meat wagon. Heck lifted his head and inhaled air fragrant with the decomposition so prominent on damp autumn nights like this. He sniffed the air once more and Fennel looked at him curiously.

"No wood smoke," Heck said in response.

"Nope. There don't seem to be."

"So wherever this Hrubek's got himself to, it wasn't toward a house he could smell."

"You learn that from Emil? Heh."

Heck asked the coroner's attendant, "What happened exactly?"

The young man glanced at Fennel, silently asking permission to answer a civilian. Heck had gotten used to the demise of his own authority. When the attendant received a grunt of approval from Fennel, he explained how Hrubek had escaped then added, "We chased him for a ways."

"Chased him, did you?" Heck couldn't resist needling, "Well, it's not hardly your job to catch him. I wouldn't't've blamed you if you'd just hightailed it out of here, to hell with a madman."

"Yeah, well. We didn't. We chased him." The attendant shrugged, young and far above shame.

"All right. Let's get to it." Heck noticed that Fennel had put the tracking harnesses on his dogs some time ago. This had worked them up and confused them. If they weren't immediately going on track, scenting dogs should wear only their regular collars. Heck almost said something to Fennel but didn't. How the trooper ran his dogs was his business; Trenton Heck was no longer a man-tracking instructor.

He took the red nylon harness and quarter-inch nylon track line from his pocket. Emil tensed immediately though he stayed rump-to-ground. Heck hooked him up and wrapped the end of the line around his own left wrist, contrary to the general practice of right-hand grip; drugged up and giddy though this big fellow might be, Heck remembered Haversham's warning and he wanted his shooting hand free. He then took the bag from his other jacket pocket. He opened it, pulling back the plastic from the wad of cotton shorts.

"Jesus," the Boy said, wrinkling his nose. "Dirty Jockeys?"

"Musk is the best," Heck muttered. "Yum . . ." He pushed

the dingy underwear toward the young trooper, who danced away.

"Trenton, stop that! They got crazy-man jism on 'em! Keep 'em away!"

Charlie Fennel laughed hard. Heck subdued his own laughter and then called sternly to Emil, "Okay," which meant for the dog to stand.

They let Emil and the bitches sniff each other, muzzle and ass, as they exchanged their complicated greetings. Then Heck held Hrubek's shorts down toward the ground, taking care not to rub the cloth on the dogs' noses—just letting them get to know a smell that to a human would vanish in an instant, if it was detectable at all.

"Find!" Heck yelled. "Find, Emil!"

The three dogs started shivering and prancing, skittering in circles, noses to the ground. They snorted as they sucked in dust and sour fumes from gasoline or grease and picked out the invisible molecules of one man's odor from a million others.

"Find, find!"

The hound took the lead, straining the line, pulling Heck after him. The other dogs followed. Fennel was a big man but he was being dragged along by two frantic sixty-pound Labradors and he trotted awkwardly beside Heck, who himself struggled to keep up the pace. Soon both men were gasping for breath.

The bitches' noses dropped to the ground sporadically in almost the identical spots on the asphalt of Route 236. They were step-tracking, inhaling at each place Hrubek had put a foot on the ground. Emil tracked differently; he'd scent for a few seconds then raise his head slightly and keep it off the ground for a ways. This was line-tracking, the practice of experienced tracking dogs; continually sniffing on a step-track could exhaust an animal in a couple of hours.

Suddenly Emil veered off the road, south, and started into a field of tall grass and brush, filled with plenty of cover even for a man as large as Hrubek.

"Oh, brother," Heck muttered, surveying the murky heath into which his dog plunged. "Taking the scenic route. Here we go."

Fennel called to the Boy and the other trooper, "Follow along the road. I'll call on the squawker, we need you. And if I call, bring the scattergun."

"He's real big," the coroner's attendant shouted. "I mean, no fooling."

Kohler pulled his BMW out of the Marsden state hospital parking lot and turned onto the long access road that would take him to Route 236. He waved a friendly greeting to a security guard, who was walking quickly toward an alarm bell ringing jarringly in the lot. The guard did not respond.

Although Kohler was a physician and could write prescriptions for any drug that was legally available, Adler had instituted a rule that no controlled substances—narcotics, sedatives, anesthetics— could be dispensed in greater than single-dose quantities without his or Grimes's approval. This edict was issued after a young resident at Marsden was caught supplementing his income by selling Xanax, Miltown and Librium to local high-school students. Kohler had no time to try to bluff his way past the hospital's night pharmacist and found the steel bumper of a German car a much more efficient means than paperwork to requisition what he needed.

As he approached the highway he pulled the car to a stop and examined the fruits of his theft. The hypodermic syringe was unlike most that you'd find in a doctor's office or hospital. It was large, an inch in diameter and five inches long, made of stainless steel around a heavy glass reservoir. The needle mounted to it, protected by a clear plastic guard, was two inches long and unusually thick. Although no one admitted it, least of all the manufacturer, this was actually a livestock syringe. To M.D.s, however, it was marketed as a "heavy-duty model intended for use on patients in agitation-oriented situations."

Sitting beside the instrument were two large bottles of Innovar, a general anesthetic Kohler'd picked because of its effectiveness when injected into muscle tissue—unlike most such drugs, which must be injected into the bloodstream. Familiar primarily with psychiatric drugs, Kohler knew little about Innovar other than the prescribed dosages per kilo of body weight and its contraindications. He knew too that he had enough drug to kill several human beings.

One thing he didn't know for certain but that he figured was probably accurate was that by stealing a Class II controlled substance he'd just committed a felony.

Kohler slipped the bottles and the syringe into the rust-colored backpack he carried in lieu of a briefcase then opened a small white envelope. As a bonus he'd also stolen several chlorphentermine capsules, two of which he now popped into his mouth. The doctor put the car in gear and eased forward, hoping that the diet pills would kick in soon and that when they did they'd have the desired effect. Kohler rarely took medicine of any kind and his system sometimes responded in unexpected ways—it was possible that the amphetaminelike drug would paradoxically make him drowsy. Richard Kohler prayed that this didn't happen. Tonight, he desperately needed his thoughts clear.

Tonight, he needed an edge.

An *agitation-oriented situation* indeed.

As he sped out onto Route 236, looking about him in the dark night, Kohler felt overwhelmed and helpless. He wondered if, despite their antagonisms, he should simply have leveled with Adler and enlisted the man's aid. After all, the hospital director too was trying desperately to conceal Michael's escape and to find him as quietly as possible; for once, the two medicos shared a common goal—though their motives were very different. But Kohler decided this would be a foolish, a *disastrous* thing to do, and might jeopardize Kohler's position at Marsden, perhaps even his career itself. Oh, some of Kohler's concern was perhaps paranoia—a junior version of what Michael Hrubek lived with daily. Yet there was a significant difference between Kohler and his patient: Michael was classified a paranoid because he acted as if enemies sought his darkest secrets while in fact his enemies and secrets were imaginary.

In his own case, Kohler reflected as his car accelerated to eighty, they were quite real.

8

Like a quarter horse cutting cattle from a herd, Emil would wheel and swerve, crossing back and forth through brush or over scrub grass until he picked up the scent once more.

The dog found the spot where Hrubek had tangled with the orderlies then returned to the road. Now, he leapt off the asphalt again and charged back into the brush, the Labradors following his lead.

The searchers trotted through this field for a few minutes, heading generally east, away from the hospital, and parallel to Route 236.

At one point as they were making their way through tall, whispering grass, Heck jerked the lead and growled, "Sit!" Emil stopped abruptly. Heck felt him shivering with excitement as if the track line were an electric wire. "Down!" Reluctantly the dog went horizontal. The bitches wouldn't respond to Charlie Fennel's similar command; they kept tugging at their lines. He pulled them back once or twice and shouted several times for them to sit but they wouldn't. Wishing that Fennel, as well as the dogs, would keep quiet, Heck managed to ignore this bad discipline and strode ahead, playing a long black flashlight over the ground.

"Lookit what I turned up," Heck said. He shone the light on a fresh bare footprint in the earth.

"God double damn," Fennel whispered. "That's size thirteen, if it's an inch."

"Well, we *know* he's big." Heck touched the deep indentation made by the ball of a huge foot. "What I'm saying is, he's sprinting."

"Sure, he's *running*. You're right. That Dr. Adler at the hospital said he'd just be wandering around in a daze."

"He's in some damn big hurry. Moving like there's no tomorrow. Come on, we've got a lot of time to make up for. Find, Emil! Find!"

Fennel started the other dogs on the trail, following the footprints, and they ran ahead. But curiously Emil didn't take the lead. He rose on his muscular legs but stayed put. His nose went into the air and he flared his nostrils, swiveling his head from side to side.

"Come on," Fennel called.

Heck was silent. He watched Emil gazing right to left and back once more. The hound turned due south and lifted his head. Heck called to Fennel, "Hold up. Shut your light out."

"What?"

"Just do it!"

With a soft click the two men and three dogs were enveloped in darkness. It occurred to Heck, as it must have to Fennel, that they were totally vulnerable. The madman might be downwind, ten feet away, with a tire iron or broken bottle.

"Come on, Trenton."

"Let's don't be in too big of a hurry here."

Fifty yards north they could see the slow convoy of the squad car and Heck's pickup. Emil paced, his head wagging back and forth in the air. Heck studied him intently.

"What's he doing?" Fennel whispered. "The track's here. Can't he tell?"

"He knows that. There's something else. Airborne scent maybe. It's not as strong as the track scent but there's something there."

It was possible, Heck considered, that Hrubek, huge and sweating, had given off masses of scent, which would eddy and gather here like smoke, remaining for hours on a humid night like this. Emil was probably scenting on the cloud of these molecules. Still,

Heck was reluctant to pull the hound away. He had faith in the cleverness of animals. He'd seen raccoons dexterously unscrew the lids of jam jars and had once watched a cumbersome grizzly bear (the same one that had eyed him so voraciously) carefully poke not just one but two delicate claw holes in the top of a 7-Up can then drink down the soda without spilling a drop. And Emil, in his master's informed opinion, was ten times smarter than any bear.

Heck waited a moment longer but neither heard nor saw anything.

"Come, Emil." He turned and started away.

But Emil would not come.

Heck squinted into the night. There was a faint glow from the sky but most of the moonlight was now obscured by cloud. Come on, boy, he thought, let's get back to work. Our reward money's jogging east at about five miles an hour.

But Emil dropped his nose and pushed into the grass. He quivered. Heck lifted his pistol in front of him and swung aside a thick whip of green and beige shoots. They continued a few feet farther into the maze of grass. It was there that they found what Emil had been seeking.

The dog was no setter but he was as good as pointing at the quarry—a scrap of paper in a plastic Baggie.

Fennel had come up slowly. He put his back to Heck and scanned the grass nervously, his service automatic sweeping left to right. "Bait?"

This had also occurred to Heck. Felons accustomed to being hunted by dogs sometimes leave a pungent article of clothing or spray of urine in a tactical place on the trail. When the tracker and his hound stop to examine the spot, the fugitive attacks from behind. But Heck studied Emil and said, "Don't think so. He was still around, Emil'd smell more of him."

Still, as he picked up the bag, Heck kept his eyes not on the plastic but on the wall of grass surrounding him, and there were several pounds of pressure on the stiff German trigger of his gun. He handed Fennel the bag and they stepped into a clearing, where they could read without fear of immediate attack.

"From a newspaper," the trooper said. "Tore it out. One side's part of an ad for bras, the other's a, hey, lookie . . . A map. Downtown Boston. Historical sites, you know."

"Boston?"

"Yep. We call the highway patrol? Tell 'em to keep the main roads to Massachusetts covered?"

And Heck, who saw his precious ten thousand dollars vanishing before him, said, "Let's hold off for a bit on that. Maybe he left this here to lead us off."

"Naw, Trenton. If he'd've wanted us to find it, he would've left it in the road, not in man-high grass."

"Maybe," Heck said, very discouraged. "But I still think—"

Crack . . .

A fierce noise like a gunshot sounded next to Heck's ear and he swung around, heart pounding, pistol raised. The volume on Charlie Fennel's walkie-talkie had been full on when he received the transmission. Fennel turned down the squelch and volume knobs and palmed the unit. He spoke softly into it. In the distance, on the road, the red and blue roof lights on the Boy's squad car started spinning.

"Fennel here. Go ahead." He lowered his head as he listened.

What *are* they doing? Heck wondered.

Fennel signed off and put the walkie-talkie back on his belt. He said, "Come on. They've found him."

Heck's heart fell. "They *got* him? Oh, damn."

"Well, not quite. He got himself all the way to a truck stop in Watertown—"

"Watertown? That's seven miles from here."

"—and tried to hitch a ride up to, guess where, Boston. The truck driver told him no so Hrubek took off on foot heading north.

We'll drive over there and pick up the trail. Man, I hope he's winded. I myself don't feel like a half-hour run. Don't go looking so sorrowful, Trenton, you'll be a rich man yet. He's not but a half hour away."

Fennel and the bitches bounded back toward the road.

"Come, Emil," Heck called. The hound hesitated just a moment longer and slowly followed his master, clearly reluctant to forsake the grassy fields, damp and cold though they were, for the slippery plastic bench seat of an old, smelly Chevrolet.

When she heard the deliberate footfalls coming up from the basement stairs, the heavy steps, the dull clink of metal, Lis Atcheson understood immediately, and the mood of the night at once turned icy.

Owen walked into the doorway of the greenhouse and looked at his wife, who was pulling more burlap bags from the stack near the lath house.

"Oh, no!" Lis whispered. She shook her head and then sat on a bench made of hard cherry wood. Owen paused then sat beside her, smoothing her hair over her ear the way he did when he explained things to her—business things, estate things, legal things. But no explanation was necessary tonight. For Owen was no longer in his work clothes. He wore a dark-green shirt and matching baggy pants—the outfit he wore under a bright-orange slicker when he went hunting. On his feet were his expensive waterproof boots.

And in his hands, a deer rifle and a pistol.

"You can't do it, Owen."

He set the guns aside. "I just talked to the sheriff again. They've got four men out after him. Only *four* goddamn men! And he's already in Watertown."

"But that's east of here. He's going *away* from us."

"That doesn't matter, Lis. Look how far he's traveled. That's seven or eight miles from where he escaped. On foot. He's not wandering around in a daze at all. He's up to something."

"I don't want you to do this."

"I'm just going to see exactly what they're doing to catch him." He spoke in an austere, assured voice. It was her father's voice. It was a voice that could hypnotize her.

Still, she said, "Don't lie to me, Owen."

And like Andrew L'Auberget, Owen's eyes contracted, hard as a tick's back. He had a faint smile on his face but she didn't believe it for a second. She might very well have been speaking to one of the marble-eyed trophies Owen had nailed up on his den wall, for all the effect her words had on him. She touched his arm and let her fingers linger on the thick cloth. He pressed his hand over hers.

"Don't go," she said. She pulled him to her. She felt a surge of unfocused ardor. It was more than the memory of their liaison earlier. His strength, his gravity, the hunger in his face—they were all immensely seductive. She kissed him hard, open-mouthed. She wondered if the arousal she felt was truly lust, or was rather an attempt to keep him encircled in her arms all this long night until the danger was past.

Whatever her motives might have been, though, the embrace had no effect. He held her for a moment then stepped to the window. She rose and stood behind him. "Why don't you say it? You're going to hunt him down."

She studied her husband's back and the reflection of a face that should, she supposed, be vastly troubled. Yet he seemed very much at peace with himself. "I'm not going to do anything illegal."

"Oh? What do you call murder?"

"Murder?" he whispered harshly, spinning around, and nodding toward the upstairs of the house. "Don't you ever *think* about what you're saying? What if she heard you?"

"Portia isn't going to turn you in. *That's* not the point. The point is you can't just track somebody down and—"

"You forget what happened at Indian Leap," he snapped. "I sometimes think *I* was more upset by it than you were."

She turned away as if slapped.

"Lis . . ." He calmed quickly, wincing at his own outburst. "I'm sorry. I didn't mean that. . . . Look, he's not a human being. He's an animal. You know what he's capable of. *You* more than anybody."

He continued his argument smoothly: "He escaped this time, he could escape again. He got away long enough to mail that letter to you when he was in Gloucester. Next time he's there maybe he'll wander off. And head this way."

"They'll catch him tonight. They'll put him in jail this time."

"If he's still mentally incompetent he goes right back into the hospital. That's the law. Lis, look at the newscasts, they're emptying the hospitals. You hear about it every day. Maybe next year, the year after, they'll just turn him out on the street. And we'd never know when he might show up here. In the yard. In the *bedroom*."

Then the first tears started and she knew that she'd lost the argument. She had probably known it when she first heard his steps on the basement stairs. Owen was not always right, she reflected, but he was perpetually confident. It seemed wholly natural for him to load up the 4x4 with guns and cruise off into the middle of a stormy night to hunt down a psychopath.

"I want you and Portia to go to the Inn. We've done enough sandbagging."

She was shaking her head.

"I'm insisting."

"No! Owen, the water's already up two feet and it hasn't even started to rain here. The part by the dock? Where the creek flows in? We need another foot or two there."

"I finished that part. I added plenty of bags. It's three feet high. If the crest's higher than that, there's nothing we could do anyway."

She spoke coldly. "Fine. Go if you want. Go play soldier. But I'm staying. I still have to tape the greenhouse."

"Forget the greenhouse. We're insured against wind damage."

"I don't *care* about the money. For heaven's sake, those roses are my life. I'd never forgive myself if anything happened to them." She sat again on the bench. Lis had noticed that she commanded less authority standing beside her husband, with him a foot taller. Seated, though much lower, she paradoxically felt more his equal.

"Nothing's going to happen. A few broken windows."

"You heard the report. Eighty-mile-an-hour winds."

Owen sat beside her and gripped her thigh, pressing hard. His elbow was against her breast. Instead of comfort she felt vulnerability, her defenses breached by his proximity.

"I'm not going to argue this," he said evenly. "I don't want to have to worry about you. I want you to go to the Inn. Once they get him—"

"Once *you* get him, you mean."

"Once they get him I'll call you. You two come back to the house and we'll finish the work together."

"Owen, he's going the other way."

His eyes flashed. "Are you trying to deny it? Lis, he's run seven miles in forty-five minutes. He's up to something. Think about it. Why're you being so damn stubborn? There's a killer out there. A psychotic killer! He knows your name and address."

Lis said nothing. She breathed shallowly.

Owen pressed his face against her hair. He whispered, "Don't you remember him? Don't you remember the trial?"

Lis happened to glance up and see on the wall a stone bust of a leering gargoyle. She heard in her memory Hrubek chanting, "Lisbone, Lis-bone, my Eve of betrayal. My pretty Lis-bone."

A cheerful voice filled the room. "Little late for fishing, isn't it, Owen?" Portia stood in the doorway, eyeing his outfit. "The party breaking up?"

Owen stepped away from his wife but he kept his eyes on her.

"I'll pack a few things," Lis said.

"Going somewhere?" her sister asked.

"The Inn," Owen said.

"So soon? I thought that was later on the program. When the crazy man showed up to boogie. Oops, sorry. Was that in bad taste?"

"He's traveled farther than they thought. I'm going to talk to the sheriff about what they're doing to find him. Lis and you're going to a bed-and-breakfast up the road."

"God, he's not coming this way?" Portia asked.

"No, he's going east." Lis looked at her sister. "It'll just be better to spend the night at the Inn."

"Okay by me." Portia shrugged and went to collect her backpack.

Lis rose. Owen squeezed her leg. What, she wondered, does *that* mean? Thanks? I won? I love you? Hand me my guns, woman?

"I won't be long. A few hours, tops. Come lock the door after me."

They walked into the kitchen and he kissed her for a long moment but she could see that his mind was already in the fields and on the roads where his prey wandered. He pocketed the pistol and slung his deer rifle over his shoulder. He then walked outside.

Lis double-locked the door behind him, watching him climb into the truck. She stepped to the window and looked down at the garage. The black Cherokee backed out and paused for a moment. The interior of the truck was dark and she wondered if he was waving to her. She lifted her own hand.

He pulled into the driveway. Of course Owen was right. He knew more about Hrubek than all of the pros did—the troopers, the sheriffs, the doctors. And, what's more, Lis knew too. She knew Hrubek wasn't harmless, that he wasn't wandering around like a dim animal, that he had something on his mind, damaged though it was. She knew these things not as facts but as messages from her heart.

Her cheek pressed against the window for a moment. She backed away and gazed at the uneven, bubble-flecked glass, realizing something she'd never thought of—that these panes had been made two and a half centuries ago. How, Lis wondered, had the fragile glass survived intact all those turbulent years? When she focused again on the yard, the truck's taillights were gone. Yet she continued for a long time to gaze at the shadowy driveway down which the truck had vanished.

Here I am, she thought in disbelief, a pioneer wife, staring into the wilderness after my husband, who's traveling through the night, on his way to kill the man who would kill me.

The lingering dust raised by the vehicles settled and their taillights vanished behind a hill far to the east. The night was still again. Overhead the clouds that swept in from the west obscured a sallow moon, which sat over a rock outcropping above the deserted highway.

There was as yet no hint of storm. No breeze at all. And for a moment this portion of highway was absolutely silent.

Then Michael Hrubek, pulling his precious Irish cap down over his head, pushed aside the grass and walked directly into the middle of Route 236. He replaced his pistol in the backpack.

GET TO

These words swam into his mind and floated there for a moment, doing slow loop-the-loops. He knew they were vitally important but their meaning kept evading him. They vanished and he was left with a prickling reminder of their absence.

What do they *mean*? he wondered. What was he supposed to *do* with them?

He stood on the asphalt and walked in a circle, searching through his confused mind for the answer. What did *GET TO* mean? Filled with a churning dread, he knew that *they* were jamming his thoughts. They: the soldiers who'd just been pursuing him.

Let's think about this.

GET TO

What could it *possibly* mean?

Hrubek again looked east down the highway, the direction in which the soldiers had disappeared. Conspirators! With their dogs on ropes, sniffing and growling. Fuckers! One man in gray, one man in blue. One Confederate soldier. And one Union, the man with the limp. He was the one Hrubek hated the most.

That man was a con-*spirat*-or, a fucking Union soldier.

GET TO

GETTO

Slowly the hatred began to fade as he thought about how he'd fooled them. He'd been only thirty feet away from the soldiers, holding his cocked gun, crouching down in a bowl of dirt high on a ledge of rock above them. They'd eased into the grass and found the bag he'd carefully placed there. Shivering with fear he'd heard their alien voices, heard the wet snorting of the dogs, the rustle of grass.

Hrubek saw the letters again, GETO. They floated past, then vanished.

Hrubek recalled the colored lights on the police car starting to spin. A moment later the soldiers returned to the cars and the one who hated him most, the lean fucker in blue, the one with the limp, got into the truck with his dog. They sped off east.

Hrubek crouched down and put his cheek against the damp road. Then he stood up.

"Good night, ladies . . ."

It was coming back to him. GETO. He squinted down the highway, westward. He was seeing not the black strip of asphalt but rather the letters, which slowly stopped swirling and began to line up for him. Like good little soldier boys.

GETO 4

Hrubek's mind was filling with thoughts, complicated thoughts, wonderful thoughts. He started walking. "I'm gonna see you cry. . . ."

GETON 4

There!

There it was! He began trotting toward it. The letters were all falling into place.

GETON 47 M

The dogs were gone, the conspirators too. The fucker with the limp, Dr. Richard, the hospital, the orderlies . . . all of his enemies were behind him. He'd fooled them all!

Michael Hrubek searched his soul and found that his fear was under control and that his mission was as lucid as a perfect diamond. He paused and set one of the tiny animal skulls in a nest of grass at the base of the post, muttering a short prayer. He then walked past the green sign that said *RIDGETON 47 MILES*, turned off the road into the cover of brush and began to hurry due west.

9

On her parted lips he rubs the petal of a yellow rose.

His eyes are fixed on hers, two feet away, close enough for him to penetrate the orbit of her perfume, not so close each feels the heat radiating from the other's body in this chill room. She reaches out for him but he motions curtly for her to stop. Her hands acquiesce but then rebelliously reach slowly to her own shoulders and dislodge the satin straps of her nightgown. They fall away and the cream-colored garment drops to her waist. His eyes stray to her breasts but he does not touch her and, as he again commands, she lowers her hands to her sides.

From the green-and-russet tangle of a rosebush, the reigning plant in the darkened greenhouse, he lifts away two more petals. These, pink. He holds them in his large, confident fingers, and lifts them to her eyes, which she closes slowly. She feels the petal skin brush over her lids and continue down her cheek. Again he makes a circuit of her mouth, both petals coursing slowly over her half-open lips.

She wets these lips and tells him playfully that he's destroying one of her prize flowers. But he again shakes his head, insisting on silence. She leans toward him and nearly succeeds in planting a contracted nipple against his forearm but he sways back and their bodies don't touch. A petal caresses her chin then slips from his fingers, spiraling to the slate greenhouse path on which they stand. He snatches another from the shivering bush. Still, her eyes are closed, her hands are at her sides. As he has insisted.

Now, he brushes her earlobes so gently she doesn't at first feel the touch of the flower's skin. He presses the valleys behind her ears and caresses the soft wisps of white-gold hair.

Now, her shoulders, muscled from carrying tubs of earth like that out of which these rosebushes grow.

Now, her throat. Her head tilts back and if she opened her eyes, she'd see a cluster of pale stars awash in the speckled glass. Now, he weakens and kisses her quickly, the petals disappearing from his spreading fingers, which grip her neck and pull her to him. Her breath, matching her desire, rushes inside her, pulling with it his own. She moves her head in a slow circle to increase the pressure of his touch. But he's too fast for her and he dodges away. He stands back again, dropping the crushed petals and tugging more from the thorny stem beside them.

Her eyes still are closed and the anticipation grows unbearable as she awaits the next touch, which occurs on the lower part of her modest breasts, and she seats her teeth as her lips spread in what could be taken for a snarl but is rather evidence of will. The roses move slowly along the arcs of her breasts and she feels too the drag of several of his fingers, a much rougher feel yet equally provocative. . . . Soft and rough. Fingernails, petal flesh. The heat of his touch, the cold of the greenhouse floor on her bare feet.

She feels pressure as slight as a breath. She's astonished that such a large man is capable of such subtle motion. He kisses her again and the sensations from his lips and fingers fire through her.

But he won't hurry. The pressure fades and vanishes and she opens her eyes with a plea for him not to stop. He again closes her eyes and she obeys, listening to a curious ripping sound. Then silence, as her neck and breasts are covered by two huge handsful of petals, which fall away from his hands and trickle to their feet.

He kisses each of her eyes and she takes this as the sign that he wants her to open them. They gaze at each other for a moment and she sees that, no, not all the petals have fallen. One remains. He

*holds it between them, a bright-red oval from a John Armstrong
plant. He opens his mouth and places it on his tongue, like a priest
dispensing host. She desperately works the nightgown over her hips
and reaches for him, enveloping him in her arms, sliding her hands
into the small of his back. He leans forward. Their tongues connect
and as she pulls him down on top of her, they transfer the red petal
back and forth until it disintegrates and they swallow the fragments
as they swallow each other.*

Lis Atcheson remained lost for a moment in this memory then
opened her eyes and gazed out over the flowers in the greenhouse,
listening to the pleasant hiss of spray from the watering system.

"Oh, Owen," she whispered. "Owen . . ."

She set down her packed suitcase and strolled through the damp,
fragrant room, then out the lath-house door to the flagstone patio.
She looked out over the lake.

The black water lapped persistently.

Troubled, she noticed that the level of the lake had risen another
several inches in the last twenty minutes. She glanced to her left,
toward a low-lying portion of the property—the dip in the yard
behind the garage, where Owen had stacked the extra bags. A creek
trickled into the lake there and the marshy shoreline was obscured
with rushes. She couldn't see how well the barrier was holding but
she didn't particularly want to walk down the narrow, slippery path
to find out. Owen was a meticulous—often fanatic—worker and
she guessed that he'd built a solid levee. Her own engineering
efforts, in the center of the yard, looked shoddy. The water was
almost up to the level of the bags she'd dozed upon after she and
Owen had made love; it was only eighteen inches beneath the
top row.

She walked closer to the lake. Above her, no stars. She couldn't
even discern the underside of the clouds; the sky was flat and
smooth, a gray-blue monotone, like the flesh of a shark. Were the

clouds moving or not? Were they a hundred feet in the air, or ten thousand? She couldn't tell.

Vague motion, nearby, startled her. The shell of the large tortoise jerked again as the ungainly creature lumbered toward the lake. Fiercely intent on its goal, the animal scuttled over rocks and roots too high for its reptilian feet, slipping often. Why the urgency? Lis wondered. Was some eerie premonition about the storm prompting the thing to seek the safety of the lake? But what would a tortoise have to fear from the rain? With a loud splash the animal caromed off a willow root and sliced into the water. There, it became a perfect airfoil and cruised eloquently just beneath the surface for a short distance then dove out of sight. Lis watched its wake vanish and the water turn once again to rippling black silk.

She strolled back toward the house, through wide, trellis-covered patches of overturned dirt—her formal garden. She paused before the one rosebush that still retained a number of petals. When she was young, Lis had plotted to dye her hair the copper color of a plant this shade—an Arizona grandiflora—and paid for it with a whipping when her father, in one of his Saturday-morning raids on the girls' room, discovered the Clairol, hidden beneath her mattress.

She clicked a brittle thorn with her nail then lifted away a few dead petals. She rubbed them against her cheek.

The horizon in the west flared brilliantly with a broad gray-green flash. It had vanished by the time her eyes flicked to that portion of the sky.

The petals fell from Lis's hands.

She heard the kitchen door opening then closing. "I'm ready," Portia called. "You have your suitcase?"

Lis walked to the house. Gazing at the yellow windows she said, "Listen, I have to tell you—I've changed my mind."

"You what?"

Lis set her suitcase inside the kitchen door. "I'm going to finish the sandbagging. Taping the greenhouse. It could take an hour or so. I'd really like you to stay too but if you want to leave, I understand. I'll call you a cab."

Emil was sorely tempted by the aroma of grilling burgers and onions but he knew his job and kept his butt planted on the ground.

Trenton Heck himself cast a longing eye toward the truck-stop diner but at the moment the reward money was his main thought and he too ignored the smell of a much-desired cheeseburger. He continued his discussion with the Highway Patrol trooper.

"And he really seemed set on Boston, did he?" Heck asked.

"That's what the driver said. He was babbling about it being the home of our country or something."

Fennel, drawing nearby, said, "He was a history major."

Heck looked up in surprise.

"Yup. That's what I heard."

"He went to *college*?" This made Trenton Heck, with only eleven hours of credits toward an associate degree, feel very bad.

"One year only, before he started to go wacko. But he got himself some A's."

"Well. A's. Damn." Heck pushed aside his personal chagrin and asked the HP trooper if he'd have the truck driver step outside for a minute.

"Uhm, he's gone."

"He's *gone*? Didn't you tell him to wait?"

The trooper shrugged, looking placidly into the civilian's eyes. "It's an escape situation, not an arrest situation. I got his name and address. Figured he didn't need to stay around to be a witness or anything."

Heck muttered to Fennel, "Address isn't going to be real helpful. I mean, what're we supposed to do? Send him a postcard?"

The trooper said, "I asked him a bunch of stuff."

Heck slipped the harness off Emil. The trooper looked even younger than the Boy and would have no seniority over anybody.

The Highway Patrol had a separate budget for salaries and they hardly ever fired anybody. Heck'd had the chance to put in for Highway Patrol when he first joined. But, no, he wanted to fight real crime.

"What was he wearing?"

"Overalls. Boots. Workshirt. Tweed cap."

"No jacket?"

"Didn't seem to be."

"Was he drinking?"

"Well, the driver didn't say. I didn't exactly ask that. Didn't see any need to."

Heck continued, "Was he carrying anything? Bag or weapon. Walking stick?"

The trooper looked uneasily at his notes then at Fennel, who nodded for him to answer the questions. "I don't exactly know."

"Was he threatening?"

"No. Just kind of goofy, the driver said."

Heck grunted in frustration. Then he asked, "Oh, one more thing. Just how big *is* he?"

"The driver said about six five, six six. Three fifty, if he's a pound. WWF wrestler, you know. Legs like a side of beef."

"Side of beef." Heck gazed into the blackness in the east.

Fennel asked him, "Is there enough trail to follow?"

"It's not bad. But I wish it'd rain." Nothing brought out a latent scent better than a gentle mist.

"To hear the weatherman tell it, you're going to get that wish in spades."

Heck hooked up Emil again and refreshed the scent memories of the dogs with Hrubek's shorts. "Find, find!"

Emil took off down the shoulder of the road, Heck paying out the dark-red rope until he felt the twenty-foot knot. Then he followed. Fennel and the retrievers too. But they hadn't gone fifty feet before Emil turned and nosed slowly toward an unlit, dilapidated house squatting in an overgrown yard. A spooky-looking place, with a sagging roof and shingles like old snake scales. In the window was a sign. *Hunting Goods. ETC. Deer dressed and mounted. Pelts bought and sold. Trout too*

"Think he's in there?" The Boy uncomfortably eyed the black windows.

"Hard to say. All that animal work'd confuse even Emil."

Heck and Fennel led the dogs to a cockeyed fencepost and tied them up. The men drew their side arms and simultaneously chambered bullets and put the safeties on. Heck thought, Don't let me get shot again. Oh, please. I got no insurance this time. Though what was behind this prayer wasn't hospital bills of course but the horror of a scalding bullet.

"Trent, you don't have to do this."

"From the sound of this guy, you need everybody you've got."

Conceding, Fennel nodded then motioned the Boy around back. He and Heck walked onto the front porch quietly. Heck looked at Fennel, who shrugged and knocked on the door. There was no answer. Heck leaned forward and looked through a grimy window. He leapt back suddenly. "Jesus! Oh!" His voice clicked into a high register.

Fennel drew down on the window with his Glock. He squinted. Then laughed. Six inches away, through the muddy glass, was the rearing form of a black bear staring out at them, taxidermied into ferocity.

"Goddamn," Heck said reverently. "Son of a bitch, I nearly dampened my pants there."

Fennel pointed to a sign propped in another window. *Closed First Two Weeks of November. Happy huntin'*

"He's telling everybody he's going away? Don't this fellow know about burglaries?"

"He's got himself a watch-bear."

Heck studied the creature with admiration. "That'd be the first thing *I'd* steal."

Then they found the door that Hrubek had kicked in. The men entered cautiously, covering each other. They found the traces of the madman's shopping spree but it was clear he was no longer here. They reholstered their guns and returned outside. Fennel told the Boy to call Haversham and tell him where they were and that Hrubek did in fact seem to be making for Boston.

They were about to continue up the highway when the Boy called, "Hold up a minute, Charlie. There's something here you ought to see."

Heck and Fennel ordered the dogs to sit and then walked around to the back of the building to where the young man was standing, hand on his own pistol. "Look there." He was pointing inside a work shed. There was blood on the ground just inside the doorway.

"Jesus." Out came the Walther again. The safety clicked off.

Heck eased into the shed. The place was chockablock with a thousand odds and ends: hoses, boxes, animal skulls, bones, broken furniture, rusted tools, auto parts.

"Check it out. Over there. We got a 'coon bit the big one."

Fennel shone his light on the limp corpse of a raccoon.

"Think he'd do that? Why?"

"Goddamn," Heck whispered in dismay. He was looking not at the body of the animal, however, but at a narrow beam in the ceiling from which dangled some spring animal traps, toothless but big—the sort that would easily snap the neck of a fox or badger or raccoon.

Or the leg of a dog.

The reason for Heck's dismay wasn't the traps themselves but rather the three empty pegs where, presumably, three other traps had hung until not long ago. Several large bloody bootprints were directly below the pegs.

Heck asked, "Your girls heel?"

"Not when they're on track. Emil?"

"He's slow to, if the scent's fresh. We'll have to tie the lines back and keep 'em next to us. Hell, if he takes to the grass we'll just about have to crawl on our bellies. Hrubek'll be in Boston by the time we get to the county line."

They walked back to the highway and shortened the lines as Heck instructed. He left his pickup at the truck stop with the third deputy, who remained there in case Hrubek wandered back this way. The Boy accompanied Heck and Fennel in his squad car, the headlights dark, just the amber flashers on. The dogs caught a whiff of the scent and started east once more.

"Down the middle of the friggin' road." Fennel laughed nervously. "This boy *is* nuts, that's for damn sure."

But Heck didn't respond. The giddy excitement of earlier in the evening was gone. The night had turned coarse. Their quarry was no longer a big silly fellow, and Trenton Heck felt the same chill he remembered when, four years ago, outside of a neon-lit 7-Eleven, he'd glanced at what he thought was a branch moving in the breeze and saw instead a sphere of muzzle flash and felt a ripping jolt in his leg, as the asphalt leapt up to meet his forehead.

"You think he'd set traps for *dogs*?" Fennel muttered. "Nobody'd do that. Nobody'd hurt a dog."

Heck reached down and held up his hound's right ear, in which was a smooth hole the exact size of a .30-'06 slug. Fennel whistled out his disgust at humankind, and Trenton Heck called, "Find, Emil, find!"

Lis stood in the greenhouse, taping bold X's over the glass that she could remember being glazed into place twenty-five years ago, her mother standing in the construction site, arms crossed, her austere eye on the contractors. Often she frowned because she believed that people wouldn't cheat you if it was obvious that you suspected they were capable of it.

Taping windows as she went, Lis moved slowly around the large room, which was filled with hybrid tea roses in all shades, and grandiflora blushes dotted with the blood-red John Armstrongs, and High Noon yellow climbers twining around an antique trellis. She had large-cluster floribunda Iceberg whites and Fashion corals. A thousand flowers, ten thousand petals.

She preferred the striking shades, the stark colors, especially in the most fragile of flowers.

Recalling the thousands of hours she'd spent here—as a girl, helping her mother, then more recently by herself—she pictured the many times she'd cut back shoots, pruned flowered laterals and snipped away unvigorous stems. Her hands, thorn-pricked and red, would scoop a dormant eye from the budding and peel the bark to make a shield then slide it into the t-cut rootstock, binding the incision with raffia.

Glancing at several recent grafts, she heard a sound behind her and turned to see Portia rummaging through a box on the floor. She was no longer wearing her Manhattan outfit but had finally acknowledged that she was in L. L. Bean country and accepted Lis's offer of jeans, sweater and Topsiders. Lis was overcome with an urge to thank her again for staying. But the girl wasn't interested in gratitude. She seized several rolls of masking tape and disappeared, saying, "Too fucking many windows in this house."

Her footsteps pounded up the stairs, a teenager sprinting to take a phone call.

Lis was suddenly aware of the greenhouse's overhead lights, one bank of which Owen had turned on when he was looking for burlap bags. She now doused them. Lis respected the daily cycle of plants—in the same way that she herself never woke to an alarm if she could avoid it. The rhythm of our bodies, she believed, is linked to our souls' pulse. Plants are no different and in deference to them Lis had installed, in addition to five-hundred-nanometer artificial-sunlight lamps for overcast days, a series of dim blue and green bulbs for nighttime hours. These lights let her flowers sleep—for she believed plants did sleep—while illuminating the greenhouse.

This was what horticulturists call a warm greenhouse. Ruth L'Auberget had scattered archaic heaters around the room but they never worked well. It seemed as if the woman was daunted by technology and had been content to let nature and fate decide whether her roses prospered or died. That wasn't good enough for her daughter. This was after all, Lis reasoned, the computer age, and she had the place outfitted with a microprocessor climate-control system that kept the temperature above sixty-two degrees even on the coldest of nights and operated the automated vents along the roof's peak and roller shades on the south-facing panes (sunlight being as potentially dangerous as frost).

On one side of the thirty-five-by-twenty-foot room were the cuttings, rooted in sand, and the seedlings; on the other were the growing plats for mature bushes, and propagation benches. Soil-warming cables snaked under the cutting area, and hoses, trickle-irrigation pipelines and capillary sand benches provided the water. The connected potting area and lath house were floored in concrete; the greenhouse floor itself was gravel, through which wound a serpentine path of slate—also selected by Lis (to replace the original concrete). The slate was deep green-blue and had been picked by Lis as a reminder of a rose yet to be, the L'Auberget hybrid. This was an ambition of hers—to develop a luminescent teal-colored rose, an All-American Rose Selections designation in her name.

The crossbreeding of this flower had a particular appeal because she'd been told it was impossible; fellow rosarians assured her that the elusive color couldn't be bred. What's more, she was bucking the trend. The current strategy among growers was to cultivate for fragrance and disease resistance. But color and form, now traits in disrepute, were what excited Lis Atcheson. Logically she appreciated the difficulty of the crossbreed. But the irony is that by nature rose lovers have deep romantic streaks and aren't easily discouraged. So, working with a number of yellow varieties and pinks and the Blue Moon hybrid tea, Lis spent hours here grafting and budding as if it were merely a matter of time until she found the evasive color.

From literature, Lis had learned the transcendence of the imagination, which she'd come to believe was God's main prize to us, all things else, even love, being more or less honorable mentions. But from flowers, she learned a better lesson—the persistence of beauty: petals bursting, growing, falling, and curling into dry, colorful flakes.

Roses were more than animate to her; they were virtually human. "Think about it," she'd tell students of hers invited to the greenhouse for informal Saturday-afternoon horticultural lectures. "The history of roses? They migrated west to Europe and America, mostly from the Orient. Their culture? They grow in increasingly sophisticated social clusters. And how about religion? Roses've had as bad a time on *that* subject as we have. They were burned by early Christians because of pagan—excuse the expression—roots. And then what happened? The Pope converted them. Now, ask a Catholic what roses represent—Mary, of course. That's the Mother, by the way, not the prostitute."

Lis's love of flowers began when she was around nine. Skinny and tall, the girl would herd Portia into the huge backyard, where their mother's helper presided. The imported au pair would send the girls on missions to find wildflowers of certain colors, after of course delivering the litany of warnings: the lake, snakes, hornets, bees, abandoned wells, strangers, men with candy, on and on. (The caveats were the product of Andrew L'Auberget; no chubby, carefree Dutch girl could possibly find the world so threatening.)

The speech delivered, paranoia invoked, Jolande would then dole out the assignments. "Leesbonne, a golden flur. Breeng me a gold flur."

Off the children would go.

"Leesbonne, now a red one. A red flur . . . Be careful of that, how you call it, beehive. Poortia, a red one . . ."

The girls would charge off into the woods and return with the blossoms. The daughters would then ask the big girl to trim and wash the bouquet and the trio would deliver the works of art to Ruth L'Auberget, who would nod with approval and thank the girls. She would then tie the blossoms into bright arrangements for the rectory office where she spent her afternoons.

This combination of aesthetics and generosity was irresistible to Lis, and she would sit at the dinner table, too timid to speak, but praying that Mother would report to Father about the flowers—or that talkative Portia would blurt the story to him. Impatient with religion, Andrew L'Auberget only managed to tolerate his wife's involvement in St. John's (it was, the liquor merchant was fast to joke, her only vice). Still, he usually dispensed some backhanded praise. "Ah, very good. Good for you, Lisbonne. And Portia too. You were careful of thorns and wasps?"

His face was stern but Lis believed she heard pleasure in his voice. "Yes, Father."

"And don't run through tall grass. Has our Jolande been careful with you? Broken legs can turn gangrenous very easily. Then off they come. Zip! How about the Reverend Dalcott? He going to snatch you up in a bag and turn you into little Episcopalians?"

"Andrew."

"No, Daddy. He has yellow teeth and his shirt smells funny."

"Portia!"

If he was in a good mood, Father might recite some Robert Burns or John Donne. " *'O my love's like a red, red rose. . . .'* "

Lis harbored a secret belief that the bouquets she'd delivered to her mother had inspired her to build the greenhouse and to start tending roses all year round.

Flowers were what Lis thought about too when her father's mood grew dark and the inevitable willow whip descended on her exposed buttocks. The image of an orange hybrid seemed somehow to anesthetize much of the pain.

Through the mottled windows she now gazed toward the very tree—a black willow—that had sacrificed hundreds of young shoots so that two daughters might grow into proper women. She could see only a vague form, like an image in a dream. It seemed to be just a lighter version of the darkness that filled the yard tonight.

Lis squinted and gazed past the tree. It was then that she saw a curious shape in the water.

What *is* that? she wondered.

Walking outside, she looked again—at a portion of the shoreline a hundred yards from the house. It was a configuration of shapes she'd never noticed. Then she understood—the water had risen so far that it was ganging near the top of the old dam. What she was looking at was a white rowboat that had slipped its moorings and floated to the concrete rim. Half the rocky beach beside the dam was obscured. In thirty years, the water had never been this high. . . . The dam! The thought struck Lis like a slap. She'd forgotten completely about the dam. It was of course the lowest spot on the property. If the lake overflowed, the water would fill the low culvert behind it and flood the yard.

Suddenly from her youth she recalled a sluice gate in the dam, operated by a large wheel. Opening this gate diverted the water to a creek that flowed into the Marsden River a mile or so downstream. She recalled her father's opening the gate once many years ago after a sudden spring thaw. Was it still there? And, if so, did it still work?

Lis walked closer to the house and called, "Portia!"

A second-floor window opened.

"I'm going to the dam."

The young woman nodded and looked up at the sky. "I just heard a bulletin. They're calling it the storm of the decade."

Lis nearly joked that she'd picked a fine night for a visit but thought better of it. Portia eased the window shut and continued her methodical taping. Lis walked cautiously into the culvert that led to the dam and, plunging into darkness, picked her way along the rocky creek bed.

The two Labs suddenly jerked into a frenzy. The trackers simultaneously drew their guns, Heck thumb-cocking his. The men exhaled long as the animal—a raccoon fat on village garbage—jogged away from them, the concentric rings of its tail vanishing into underbrush. The indignant animal reminded Heck of Jill's father, who was a small-town mayor.

Heck, lowering the prominent hammer of his old German pistol, downed Emil and waited while Charlie Fennel futilely scolded the Labs and then refreshed their memory with Hrubek's shorts. As he waited Heck gazed around him at the seemingly endless fields. They'd come five miles from the shack where Hrubek had stolen the traps, and the dogs were still scenting on the asphalt. Heck had never pursued an escapee who stuck so persistently to the road. What seemed like blood-sure stupidity now looked pretty smart: by doing just the opposite of what everybody expected, Hrubek was making damn good time. Heck had a vague thought, which lasted merely a second or two, that somehow, they were making a very bad mistake about this fellow. This impression was punctuated by a shiver that dropped from his neck to his tailbone.

Charlie Fennel's dogs were soon back on the trail and the men hurried along the deserted strip of highway under a sky black as a hole. To stem his own uneasiness Heck leaned over and said, "Know what's coming up this week?"

Fennel grunted.

"St. Hubert's Day. And we're going to be celebrating it."

Fennel hawked and spit in a long arc then said, "Who's we?"

"Emil and me. St. Hubert's Day. He's the patron saint of hunters. St. Hubert hounds—that's what he bred—"

"Who?"

"St. *Hubert*. This is what I'm telling you. He was a monk or something. He bred the dogs that eventually became bloodhounds." Heck nodded at Emil. "That boy goes farther back than I do. Part of St. Hubert's Day is a blessing of the hounds. Aren't you Irish, Charlie? How come you don't know this stuff?"

"Family's from Londonderry."

"You've got those Labs there. We ought to get a priest to bless our dogs. What do you think about that, Charlie? How 'bout over at St. Mary's. Think that priest'd do that for us?" Fennel didn't answer and Heck continued, "You know bloodhounds go back to Mesopotamia?"

"Where the hell's that?"

"Iraq."

"Now *that*," Fennel said, "was a stupid little war."

"I think we should've kept going, tromp, tromp, tromp, all the way to Baghdad."

"I'll second that." Then Fennel laughed.

Heck, grinning, asked, "What's so funny?"

"You're a crazy man after a crazy man, Trenton."

"Say what you will, I think I'm going to find me a priest and get Emil blessed after this is over."

"If he catches the guy."

"No, I think I'll just do it anyway."

The road down which they now pursued Hrubek was a dark country highway, which threaded through a string of small towns and unincorporated portions of the county. If Hrubek had Boston in mind he was taking the long route. But, Heck concluded, it was also the smarter way to travel. Along these roads there'd be hardly any local police, and the houses and traffic would be sparse.

They followed the dogs, still short-lined because of the traps, only three miles east before Hrubek broke away and turned north, onto a small dirt lane. A hundred feet away they found a filthy roadside diner, which looked bleaker yet because of the sloppily taped X's on the windows.

Thinking that Hrubek might be inside, Fennel sent the Boy around back and he and Heck snuck up to the windows of the streamlined, aluminum-sided restaurant. Cautiously they lifted their heads and found themselves gazing straight into the eyes of the cook, waitress and two diners, who, forewarned by the baying Labradors, were staring out the windows.

Heck and Fennel, feeling somewhat foolish, stepped through the door, holstering their guns.

"A posse," the waitress exclaimed, drops of viscous gravy falling from the tilting plate she held.

But, no, nobody here had seen Hrubek, even though to judge by Emil's scenting he'd passed within feet of the window. Without an explanation, or a farewell, the men and the dogs vanished as quickly as they'd come. Emil picked up the scent once more and led them northeast along the dirt road.

Not two hundred yards from the diner they found the spot where Hrubek had taken to the fields. "Hold up," Heck whispered. They stood beside a small grass-filled path—an access road for mowing tractors. The drive darkened as it passed through a dense stand of trees.

Fennel and Heck tied back the track lines until they were shorter than pet-store leads. They found, however, that they didn't need the animals any longer; not more than fifty yards into the woods they heard Hrubek.

Fennel gripped Heck's arm and they stopped short. The Boy

dropped to a crouch. They heard a mad moaning rising from the trees.

Heck was so excited to have found Hrubek that he forgot he was a civilian. He began communicating to Fennel and the Boy with the hand signals law enforcers use when they silently close in on their quarry. Up went his finger to his lips and he pointed toward the source of the sound then motioned Fennel and the Boy forward. Heck bent low to Emil and whispered, "Sit," then, "Down." The dog eased to the ground, obedient but irritated that the game was over for him. Heck loose-tied him to a branch.

"I'll take over from here, you want," Fennel whispered in a casual way but with enough timber to remind Heck who was in charge. Heck was of course willing to yield the role of commander, which was never his in the first place, but no way was he going to miss the hogtying party; he didn't want any argument about the reward money. He nodded toward Fennel and unholstered his Walther.

The Boy, who with his fiery eyes and a big automatic in his fingers didn't look so boyish anymore, circled around to the side, north of the trees, as Fennel had indicated. Heck and Fennel went up the middle of the road. They moved very slowly; they couldn't use their flashlights and the grove was darkly shadowed by the hemlocks, whose branches were dense and lay upon one another like ragged petticoats.

The moaning grew louder. To a man, it chilled their hearts.

When Heck saw the truck—a long semi, parked cockeyed in the shadows—he felt a burst of queasiness, thinking that the moaning was not Hrubek at all but the driver, whom the madman had attacked and gutted. Perhaps he was listening to a sucking chest wound. He and Fennel glanced at each other, exchanging this identical thought in silence, and continued their cautious approach.

Then Heck saw him, an indistinct shape not far away.

Michael Hrubek, so thick around the middle he seemed deformed.

Moaning like a moon-crazed dog.

He lay on the ground, trying to get up. Perhaps he'd fallen and hurt himself, or had been hit by the massive truck.

Maybe he'd heard the Labs and was feigning injury, waiting for his pursuers to get close.

Opposite Heck and Fennel, on the other side of the clearing, the Boy appeared in a crouch. Fennel held up three fingers. The young trooper responded by mimicking it. Then Fennel clicked the safety off his gun and lifted his hand above his head. One finger. Two fingers . . . Three . . . The men jumped into the clearing, three dark pistols pointed forward, three long flashlights pumping their dazzling halogen light onto the massive body of their quarry.

10

"Freeze!"

"All right, don't you move!"

For the love of Mary, Trenton Heck thought, his legs weakening in shock, what's happening here?

The madman, lying on the ground in front of the three lawmen, was shrieking like a bluejay. He suddenly split clean in two, half of him leaping into the air, white as death.

What is going on here? Heck trained the flashlight on the part of the madman that remained on the ground—the part that was now grasping about for something to pull over her ample breasts.

"Shit, son of a bitch!" the man's upper half shouted in an edgy tenor. "What the hell you think you're doing?"

The Boy started laughing first then Fennel joined in and, if Heck hadn't been so upset at losing his reward money, he'd have laughed too. The sight of the skinny man, searching desperately for his shorts, the long condom whipping back and forth as it dangled from his quickly shrunk member . . . Well, it *was* the funniest thing Heck had seen for a month of Sundays.

"Don't hurt me," the woman wailed.

"Son of a bitch," the skinny man growled once more. Heck's humor returned and he whistled the "Dueling Banjos" tune from *Deliverance.*

In a Kentucky-mountain voice Charlie Fennel said, "Naw, I want *him.* He's a purty one."

"Sooo-eee," Heck called. "Here, piggy, piggy, piggy!"

The woman wailed again.

"Oh, shit . . ." The young man fumbled with his pants.

"Calm down now." Fennel shone the light on his badge. "We're state troopers."

"That wasn't funny, I don't care who y'all are. *She* wanted to do it. She picked me up at that diner up the road. It was *her* idea."

The woman had calmed in proportion to the amount of clothing she'd pulled on. "*My* idea? I'll thank you not to make me sound cheap."

"I didn't want—"

"That's your all's business," Fennel said, "but it's *our* business you've had a hitchhiker on the back of your rig for the past ten miles. An escapee."

Heck too understood that this is what had happened and he was angry at himself for not thinking of it sooner. Hrubek had clung to the back bumper guard or loading platform of the truck. That was why the scent had been so weak, and why it had never wavered from the road.

"Jesus, that fellow at the truck stop in Watertown? The big guy? Oh, my everloving Lord!"

"You're *that* truck driver?" Heck asked. "He asked you about going to Boston?"

"Shitabrick, maybe he's still on the rig!"

But the Boy had already circled around and checked out the truck's roof and undercarriage. "He's not here, nope. And the back's padlocked. He must've took off into the fields when the truck stopped."

"Oh, Jesus," the driver whispered reverently, "he's a killer, ain't he? Oh, Jesus, Jesus . . ."

The woman had started crying again. "This is the last time, I swear. Never again."

Fennel asked how long the driver had been there.

"Fifteen minutes, I'd guess."

"You love bunnies hear anything?"

"Nothing, not a single thing," the driver said, eager to please.

"I didn't hear anything either," the woman replied, sniffling, "and I don't like your, you know, attitude."

"Uhn," Fennel responded, then said to the young man, who was buttoning up his shirt, "Now I suggest you get back in that rig and take this lady home and get on your way."

"Take her home? Forget about it."

"You prick," she snapped. "You damn well better."

"I think you ought to do that, son," Heck said.

"Okay. If she don't live too far from here. I've got a load of auto parts I got to get to Bangor by—"

"You prick."

Fennel had checked the bushes around the semi. "No sign of him," he called.

"Well, with the sound these two were making," Heck said, chuckling, "I'd run too. Well, let's get on with it. He can't be more than a half mile from here. We should—"

The Boy said, "Uh, Trenton, I think there's a problem."

Heck looked up to see the young trooper pointing at a small sign that in their silent approach they'd passed but not noticed. Its back was to Heck and Fennel. They strode to it, turned and read.

Welcome to Massachusetts

Heck looked at the scripty green letters and wondered why anybody'd waste a nicely painted sign here on this dim country road, home of madmen, horny truck drivers and loose waitresses. He sighed and looked at Fennel.

"Sorry, Trenton."

"Come on, Charlie."

"We got no jurisdiction here."

"Why, he isn't but a half mile away! He could be two hundred yards from us right now. Hell, he could be watching us from one of those trees over there."

"The law's the law, Trenton. We need to get the Mass troopers in."

"I say let's just go get him."

"We can't cross the state line."

"Hot pursuit," Heck said.

"Won't work. He ain't a felon. Adler said that Hrubek didn't kill that fellow was in the body bag. It was a suicide."

"Come on, Charlie."

"If he ain't so crazy—and it looks like maybe he ain't—and we nab him in Massachusetts, he might sue us for assault or kidnapping. And he could damn well win."

"Not if we get our stories straight."

"Lie, you're saying."

Heck didn't speak for a moment. "All we do is we find him and bring him back. That'd be that."

"Trenton, did you ever falsify a case report?"

"No."

"You ever perjure yourself on the stand?"

"You know I never did."

"Well, you're not wearing a badge now and I know you feel different about those of us who are. But the fact is, we just can't stroll over state lines."

Rising through Heck's prominent anger now was a sudden understanding—that the interest Charlie Fennel and the young trooper had in the search was this: to do their job. Oh, they'd give the pursuit of Michael Hrubek 110 percent and they'd bust their balls and put in all sorts of god-awful overtime and even risk their life. But for that one purpose only: *to do their job.*

Leaving the jurisdiction wasn't their job.

"I'm sorry, Trenton."

"Didn't any of us notify the Mass troopers before," Heck said.

"It'll take 'em a half hour to get the first cars here. Maybe more. If he hops another ride he'll be long, long gone by then."

"Then that's what'll happen," Fennel said. "That's the way it is. . . . I know what the money means to you."

Heck stood with his hands on his narrow hips, looking at the sign for a few moments. Then he nodded slowly. "Let's don't have words over it. You gotta do what you think's right, Charlie."

"I'm pretty sorry about this, Trenton."

"Okay. No hard feelings." He walked back to Emil. "If you two'll excuse us."

"No, Trenton," Fennel said in a firm monotone.

Heck ignored Fennel and continued walking to where Emil was loose-tied to a forsythia whip.

"Trenton . . ."

"*What?*" Heck's voice bristled as he turned.

"I can't let you go by yourself either."

"Don't ride me, Charlie. Just don't do it."

"By yourself? You're a civilian. *You* couldn't argue hot pursuit even if he *was* a felon. You cross that line, it's kidnapping for sure. You could get yourself into a real fix."

"And what if he kills somebody else? You're happy just to let him go."

"There are rules for how this works and I'm going to stick to 'em. And I'm going to see that you do too."

"You're saying you'd stop me?" Heck spat out. "Use that gun? Use that fancy *de*-partmental Glock of yours?"

Fennel was clearly stung by this but he received no apology from Heck, whose fists were balled at his side, as if spoiling for a school-yard fight.

"Don't be stupid, Trenton," Fennel said kindly. "Think about it. That Dr. Adler's a peckerhead to start with. You think he's going to pay you a penny of reward, you snag his boy out of state? You know he'll cheat you if he can. And what if some pansy civil-liberties lawyer gets a hold of you for kidnapping some poor retard. Bang, your ass is hung out to dry."

It wouldn't have hurt so bad, Heck knew, if they hadn't been so close—if he'd gotten a notice that Hrubek was, say, in Florida or Toronto. But they were so *damn* close. . . . Trenton Heck glanced at Fennel then gazed across the empty fields, which seemed white, as if dusted with snow or lime. He saw in the vague, indiscernible distance the shape of a man's back, crouching low as he ran. But as Heck's eyes squinted the back became a shrub and he understood that he was seeing only what his imagination had created.

Without a word to the two men Heck untied his hound and slipped off the harness, replacing it with the jangling ID collar. He said, "Come," and returned to the squad car to wait for the others, Emil trotting along beside.

They didn't notice him for a full minute so he spent that time looking around the shabby office—the cheap desk, the vibrating fluorescent light, the carpet of shocking green, the books with torn jackets or no jackets at all, stacks of recycled manilla folders, the shoddy walls.

Owen Atcheson was himself a homeowner and handy with tools. He recognized that the paneling came from a cheap store and was mounted by cheaper labor. The carpet was stained and the windows were streaked with grease though Owen also observed that the glass in the frames holding the doctor's diplomas was shiny as diamond.

"Excuse me."

The men turned. The one in uniform—this would be Haversham, the captain, the *good man*—pivoted on the heels of his short boots. The other one—whose office this was, a sandy-haired man of about fifty—seemed to have had only two hours of a much-needed sleep. Still, he had keen eyes, which now tersely examined his visitor.

Owen introduced himself then asked, "You're Dr. Adler?"

"I am," said the hospital director, neither polite nor contrary. "What can I do for you?"

The trooper, whose eyes suggested that he remembered the name, surveyed Owen's clothing.

"I live in Ridgeton. It's west of here about—"

"Yes. Ridgeton. I know where it is."

"I'm here about Michael Hrubek."

Adler's eyes flashed with brief alarm. "How'd you find out that he's wandered away?"

"Wandered away?" Owen asked wryly.

"Who exactly are you?"

The trooper spoke up. "It's your wife . . . ?"

"That's right."

Adler nodded. "The woman at the trial? That sheriff called about her a while ago. Some letter Hrubek sent." The doctor squinted, wondering, it seemed, where Owen might fit in the zodiac of the evening.

"You haven't caught him yet?"

"Not quite. You really don't have anything to worry about."

"No? That was a pretty frightening letter your patient sent my wife."

"Well, as I think we explained"—his gaze incorporated Haversham—"to your sheriff, Hrubek is a paranoid schizophrenic. What they write is usually meaningless. There's nothing for you to wor—"

"*Usually* meaningless? Then not *always*. I see. Don't you think there's something to it if he threatened my wife at the trial, then wrote this letter a few months back and here he goes and escapes?"

Adler said, "It's not really your concern, Mr. Atcheson. And we're really quite busy—"

"My wife's safety is my concern." Owen glanced at the doctor's left hand. "It's a man's job to look after his wife. Don't you look after yours?" He noticed with some pleasure that Adler had in this short time grown to dislike him. "Tell me why there are only four men in the search party."

The hospital director's front teeth danced together briefly with several short taps. "The men after him're experienced dog-trackers. More efficient than a dozen troopers just wandering around in the dark."

"He's in Watertown?"

"He was. He seems to be going north. He *is* going north, I should say."

From outside, the sound of hammering boomed. Owen recalled that entering the hospital grounds he'd seen workmen carrying sheets of plywood toward large plate-glass windows in what seemed to be a cafeteria.

"Have they actually spotted him?" Owen asked curtly, and watched the doctor's dislike become active hatred. But Owen was a lawyer; he was used to this.

"I don't think so," Adler said. "But they're very close."

Owen believed posture was a man's most important attribute. He could have hair or no hair, be shaven or stubbled, tall or short, but if he stood up straight he was respected. Now, at attention, he stared down this doctor, who may have believed that Hrubek was harmless but on the other hand *was* here late on Sunday, looking like death itself, with an officer of the state police at his side.

He asked, "He escaped in Stinson?"

Dr. Adler glanced at the far ceiling. He nodded impatiently toward Haversham, who strode to the desk and with a capped Bic pen touched a location on the map. "Here's why your wife's got nothing to worry about. We're tracking him here." He touched a spot near the intersection of Routes 236 and 118. "He escaped . . ." The doctor's eyes bored into Haversham at this choice of word. The captain paused then continued. "He wandered off here, just over the Stinson line."

"And how did he get to Stinson?"

Adler plucked a sentence from inventory and responded quickly, "There was a mix-up. He took another patient's place in a transport van."

Haversham took a moment to detach his gaze from the hospital director's serene face and continued, "Then he eluded two orderlies *here*. In Watertown, *here*, he asked a driver for a ride to Boston. Oh, and he dropped a map of Boston while he was running. He's on Route 118 now."

"Boston? What kind of lead does he have?"

"Just a half hour. And our people are gaining fast. We should have him within twenty minutes."

"Now, if you'll excuse us," Adler said, "we've got some work to do."

Owen had the pleasure of staring the troubled man down once more and said to the state trooper, "I hope you'll do my wife and me the courtesy of keeping the Ridgeton sheriff informed about what's happening here."

"I'll do that, sure."

Nodding to the trooper and ignoring Adler, Owen left the office. He was walking down the dank, murky corridor when the captain stepped into the hall and caught up with him.

" 'Scuse me, sir? A question?"

The trooper was a big man though Owen was bigger and Haversham stepped back a pace so that he wasn't looking up into Owen's eyes at so steep an angle. "You out doing some camping when you heard about this?"

"I'm sorry?"

"The reason I ask is, you're dressed like you've been camping. Or hunting."

"I just threw on some clothes and drove over here."

"All the way from Ridgeton?"

"It's straight down the highway. I'll confess. I didn't obey the posted."

"You might've called." When he received no response the captain continued, "You armed, by any chance?"

Owen asked if Haversham wanted to see his pistol permit.

"That won't be necessary, no. What line of work you in?"

"I'm an attorney."

"Lawyer, huh?" This seemed to please Haversham. "What sort?"

"Corporate mostly."

"The doctor back there, he's got a pretty low opinion of this Hrubek. And I suspect you and your wife do too. Now this fellow may be criminally insane but in the eyes of the law he isn't no dog. He's a human being and if somebody was to shoot him down they'd be guilty of murder just the same as they'd shot a minister. But I don't need to tell you that, being a lawyer and all."

"Let me ask you something, Captain. Have you ever seen Michael Hrubek up close? You ever faced him?"

"I sympathize with you, sir. But I'm telling you, we find him dead somewhere, I personally'll be coming to talk to you. Even if you get off with manslaughter, that'll be the end of your legal practice."

Owen looked back into the calm eyes of the captain, who finally said, "Those are just some things to consider."

"Duly noted, Captain. Good night to you now."

From the corner of his eye Michael Hrubek—running through tall grass—noticed headlights on a service road that paralleled his path along the highway. The car was keeping pace with his speed and he believed it was following him. The vehicle stopped suddenly, made a sharp turn and headed in his direction. "Conspirators!" he crowed. Amid the panic that enveloped him like a cloud of hornets he tripped and fell forward onto the shoulder. Cinders, pebbles and bits of glass embedded themselves in his palms and blood appeared. He screamed briefly, picked himself up and ran forty feet into the forest, crashing through a line of low brush then dropping onto the ground. A few moments later the green cube of a car drove past slowly and stopped.

A door slammed and a man climbed out. The conspirator walked in a slow circle near the perimeter of the forest. Hrubek curled up on his side. He closed his eyes and prayed that he might fall asleep so that he'd grow invisible.

"Michael!" the man called tentatively, as if undecided whether to shout or whisper. "Are you there?"

Something familiar about the voice.

"Michael, it's me."

Dr. Richard! the stunned patient realized. Dr. Richard Kohler from Marsden!

Or was it? Careful here. Something funny's going on.

"Michael, I want to talk to you. Can you hear me?"

Hrubek opened his eyes and gazed out from between two ferns. It *looked* like Dr. Richard. How did those fuckers *do* it? Hrubek nervously scooted under a bush. His eyes flicked up and down suspiciously as he examined the man, studying the doctor's thin frame, dark-blue suit, black penny loafers and Argyle socks. His backpack the color of old blood. Sure, this looked just like Dr. Richard. Identical! Hrubek gave the conspirator credit for disguising himself so cleverly.

Smart fucker, make no mistake.

"They told me you'd run off. Michael, is that you? I thought I saw you."

The footsteps grew closer, crushing leaves beneath the dainty feet. Hrubek pulled his own backpack to his side. It was heavy and clinked with the sound of metal and chains. He froze at the noise then rummaged inside quietly. At the bottom he found the pistol.

"Michael, I know you're scared. I want to help you."

He aimed the pistol at the shadowy form that approached. He'd shoot the impostor in the head. No, that'd be too merciful. I'll aim for the belly, he thought, and let him die like a battlefield soldier, slowly, with a gut wound from a .54 Minié ball.

. . . for I love the bonnie blue boy who gave his life for me. . . .

The footsteps came closer. The beam from a tiny flashlight swept the ground, lit a patch of grass two feet from his foot, then moved on. Hrubek held the gun close to his face. He smelled oil and metal. As he gazed back into the clearing, a dreadful thought came into his mind: What if this *wasn't* an impostor. Maybe this really *was* Dr. Richard. Maybe *he* was a conspirator too! Maybe he'd been a traitor all along. From the first fucking day they'd met. Four months of betrayal!

"I've been looking all over for you. I want to give you some medicine. It'll make you feel better."

How do you feel better when you're dead? Hrubek responded silently. How does poison make you feel *bet-ter*? If I were a *bettor*, I'd say you were a bad *bet*, you fucker.

The conspirator was ten feet away. Hrubek's right hand began to shake as it gripped the gun, which was pointed directly at the belly of Dr. Richard the betrayer (or John Conspirator the impostor).

"I'm your last chance. There are people who want to hurt you. . . ."

Well, I *knew* that all along. You're telling me something *new*? How'd you like to be in the *news*? CNN can do a story about your blown-up guts. He pulled the hammer back. The click was very soft but inexplicably it released in Hrubek a flood of fear. He began to quiver. The gun slipped from his hand and he remained paralyzed for a long moment. Finally his vision grew blacker than the black forest around him and his mind froze, seated like a hot drill bit in oak.

When he opened his eyes again and was aware of his surroundings, some minutes had passed. The air felt colder, more oppressive, heavy with moisture. The conspirator was gone, his car too. Hrubek found the gun and lowered the hammer carefully, then stowed the weapon in his bag. As he rose to his feet, dazed and discomfited, and started jogging through the night once more, Hrubek wondered whether the entire incident had been just a dream. But he concluded that even if it hadn't been real the apparition was certainly a message from God: to remind him that tonight he could trust no one, not even those who were—or who *pretended* to be—his closest friends on earth.

11

She called it the Berlin Wall.

A six-foot-high stockade fence of gray cedar, surrounding most of the four acres of the L'Auberget estate. Lis now walked along a stretch of this fence on her way to the dam. To enclose the property had cost Andrew L'Auberget eighteen thousand dollars (and they'd been *1968* dollars, no less). But despite the price he was adamant about the barricade. Lis jokingly named it after the German barrier (the reference shared only with Portia and friends, never with her father) though the man's concern hadn't been the Red Peril. Terrorist kidnappings were his main fear.

He'd become convinced that he, as a successful businessman with several European partnerships, was targeted. "God*damn* Basques," he railed. "Goddamn them! And they know all about me." The SDS, the Black Panthers! "I'm in *Who's Who in American Business*. There for the whole world to see! Where I live! My children's names! They could read *your* name, Lisbonne. Remember what I told you about answering the door? Tell me what you'd do if you saw a Negro walking around outside the gate. Tell me!"

The fence, even Lis the naïve child supposed, was easily breachable and less a deterrent to the bad guys than an inconvenience to the family, who had to walk three-quarters of a mile around it if they wanted to go for walks in the woods across Cedar Swamp Road. But like the builders of its namesake, L'Auberget's purpose seemed only partially to keep the enemy out; he also wanted to restrain his own citizenry. "I will not have the children wandering off. They're *girls*, for God's sake!" Lis had often heard this declaration, or variations on it.

As she walked along tonight Lis reflected with some irony that while its German counterpart was now dust, Andrew L'Auberget's cedar folly was still as strong as ever. She noticed too that if the water did overflow the dam, the fence would make a perfect sluice, preventing any flood from spilling off the property into the woods and directing it straight to the house.

She now approached the beach—a small crescent of dark sand. Just beyond was the dam, an old stone-and-cement slab twenty feet high, built around the turn of the century. It was against this wide lip of cement that the white rowboat she'd seen from the house thudded resonantly. Behind the dam was the narrow spillway fed by the overflow; usually dry, tonight it gushed like a Colorado rapid, the water disappearing into the creek that ran beneath the road. The dam was part of the L'Auberget property though it was under the technical control of the state Corps of Engineers, which had been granted an easement to maintain it. Why weren't they here tonight? she wondered.

Lis continued a few feet toward the dam, then stopped, uneasy, reluctant to go further, watching the white jet of water shoot into the creek.

Her hesitation had nothing to do with the safety of the dam or the ragged spume. The only thought on her mind at the moment was the picnic.

Many, many years before: a rare event—a L'Auberget family outing.

That June day had been a mixture of sun and shade, hot and cold. The family strolled from the house to this beach, and hadn't gotten more than ten yards before Father started carping at Portia. "Calm down, quiet down!" The girl was five, even then cheerfully defiant and boisterous. Lis was horrified that because of the girl's rowdiness Father would call off the picnic and she bluntly shushed her little sister. Portia tried to kick Lis in retaliation and, with a dark glance from her husband, Mother finally swept up the squirming girl and carried her.

Lis, then eleven, and her father hefted picnic baskets packed by him so efficiently that she nearly tore muscles under the weight. Still, the girl didn't complain; she'd endured eight months of her father's absence while he was in Europe on yet another business trip and nothing on earth would stop her from walking at his side. She was thrilled speechless when he complimented her on her strength.

"How about here?" Father asked, then answered himself. "Yes, I think so."

It seemed to Lis that he'd developed a minuscule accent in his recent travels. Portuguese, she supposed. She observed his dark slacks and white dress shirt buttoned at the neck, without tie, and short boots. This was hardly American fashion in the nineteen sixties but he'd have nothing to do with Brooks Brothers or Carnaby Street and remained faithful to the look favored by his Iberian business associates. It wasn't until after he died that Lis and her mother would laugh that Andrew's style could best be described as postimmigrant.

That afternoon he'd watched his wife arranging the meal and gave her strident instructions. The food was cut geometrically, cooked perfectly, sealed in containers airtight as the NASA capsules that so fascinated him. Mother set out expensive stainless-steel utensils and ceramic plates the shade of milky plums.

A Warre's port appeared and they each had a glass, Father asking Mother her opinion of it. He said she had an uneducated palate and for that reason was worth more than a dozen French sommeliers. Lis had never heard her mother utter a single negative syllable about any of the wines in her husband's inventory.

On the day of Lis's birth, Andrew L'Auberget was in Portugal, where he happened to drop a bottle of Taylor, Fladgate 1879 because he was so startled by the sharp ringing of his partner's telephone—on the other end of which happened to be his mother-in-law with the news that he was now a father. The story goes that he laughed about the catastrophe and insisted—there, on the phone—that they name Lis after the city in which she'd destroyed seven hundred dollars' worth of port. Two things about this incident had always seemed significant to Lis. The first was the generosity with which he treated the loss.

And second: why wasn't he with his wife at such a time?

That day at the beach, sitting beside the dam, he'd lifted a silver spoon and, against Mother's protests, poured a scant teaspoon down Lis's throat.

"There, Lisbonne, what do you think? That's a 1953. Not renowned, no, but good. What do you think?"

"Andrew, she's eleven! She's too young."

"I like it, Father," Lis said, repulsed by the wine. By way of compliment she added that it tasted like Vick's.

"Cough syrup?" he roared. "Are you mad?"

"She's too *young*." Mother sent Lis out of harm's way and the girls went off to play until lunch was ready.

While Portia sat in a cove of grass and picked flowers, Lis noticed a motion from the state park nearby and stepped closer to explore. A boy of about eighteen stood with a girl several years younger. She was backed against a tree and he was clutching the bark on either side of her shoulders. He would ease forward and kiss her then back away quickly as she wrinkled her nose in mock disgust. He reached suddenly for her chest. Lis was alarmed, thinking that a wasp or bee had landed on her and he was trying to pick it off. She felt an urge to call out to him to leave it alone. They sting when they're scared, she nearly shouted, astonished that a high-school boy wouldn't know this plain fact of nature.

It wasn't of course a bee he was after but the button of her shirt. He undid it and slipped his fingers inside. The girl crinkled her face again and slapped his knuckles. He withdrew his fingers reluctantly, laughed then kissed her again. The hand crawled back inside and this time she didn't stop him. Their tongues met outside their mouths and they kissed hard.

An eerie radiation of warmth consumed Lis. She couldn't tell from which portion of her body it arose. Maybe her knees. Drawing some vague conclusions about the spectacle of the two lovers, Lis cautiously lifted her own hand to her blouse, beneath which was her swimsuit. She undid buttons, mimicking the young man, and eased her fingers under her suit as if his hand directed hers. She probed, with no discernible results at first. Then as she fumbled the heat seemed to rise from her legs and center somewhere in her belly.

"Lisbonne!" her father called harshly.

Gasping, she jumped.

"Lisbonne, what are you doing? I *told* you not to wander far!" He was nearby though apparently he hadn't seen her crime—if a crime it was. Her heart quivering madly, she began to cry and dropped to her knees. "Looking for Indian bones," she called in a shaking voice.

"How horrible," her mother shouted. "Stop that this minute! Come wash your hands."

"You should respect the remains of the dead, young lady! When you're dead and laid out, how'd you like someone to molest *your* grave?"

The girls returned to the picnic blanket, washed and sat down to the meal, while Father talked about the paste that astronauts would have to eat on extended space flights. He tried, without success, to explain to Portia what zero gravity meant. Lis was unable to get down more than a few bites of anything. When they finished she hurried back to the cleft in the bushes on the pretense of looking for a dropped comb. The couple was no longer there.

Then came the part of the day that Lis had been dreading. Father took her down to the dark water. He removed his shirt and slacks, beneath which he wore his burgundy trunks. He had a dense body—not strong but with fat distributed evenly, in approximation of muscles.

Her shirt came off, then her culottes, revealing the plain red swimsuit. A thin woman now, Lis was a thinner girl then, but she pulled in her stomach vehemently—not in shame at a belly but hoping, futilely, that it might inflate her chest.

They strode into the cold lake. A championship swimmer in college, Andrew L'Auberget was, he'd told his daughter on a number of occasions, troubled by her fear of the water. He never missed an opportunity to get her into a pool or river or ocean. "It's dangerous, yes. It's far too easy to drown. That's why you must learn to swim, and swim like a fish."

Nervously she flexed her knees, feeling the gracious bed of mud beneath her arched toes. Father made a stern show of these lessons. When he noticed that she was resisting putting her head under water he ordered her to take a breath and pushed her face beneath the waves. Panic finally sent her scrambling upright. As she sputtered and shivered he laughed and told her, "See, that wasn't so bad. Again, for ten seconds. I can do it for two minutes. Two whole minutes without a breath!"

"No, I don't want to!"

"You take that tone, you'll go under for twenty seconds."

She practiced her strokes, beating the water with splayed fingers, which he forced closed into paddles. He supported her and held her buoyant while she swam in place.

"Calm down, girl! Water won't kill you. Calm *down*!"

She rested on his palm, trying to coordinate her legs and arms. Just as she struck a rhythm that approximated a breaststroke, a wave rolled in and lifted her from his hand. For a moment she was actually swimming on her own. Then the crest passed and lowered her once more. But when she drifted back down, she'd moved forward a foot or so and she came to rest with her groin on his fingers. For a tense moment neither father nor daughter moved and—compelled by an urge she understood no better today than then—Lis pressed her legs together, capturing his hand in that spot.

And then she smiled.

Lisbonne L'Auberget looked at her father and gave him a slight smile—not one of seduction or power or pride. Least of all physical pleasure. No, just a smile that sprang spontaneously to her cold, blue lips.

And it was for this transgression, Lis later speculated, rather than the fluke contact of bodies, that she was so ruthlessly punished. The next thing she recalled was being dragged from the water, her arm almost popping from its socket, and being flung to the hard ground, where she lay on her belly, as her father's hand—the same hand that had moments before cradled the most enigmatic part of her body—now rose and fell viciously upon another.

"Don't you ever!" he roared, unwilling to give a name to the offense. "Don't you ever! Don't you ever!" The raw words kept time with the loud slap of his palm upon her wet buttocks. She felt little sting from the powerful blows—her skin was numb from the cold—but the greater pain was in her soul anyway. She cried of course and she cried hardest when she saw her mother start toward her then hesitate. The woman refused to look then turned away, leading her sister from the shore. Portia looked back once with an expression of cold curiosity. They disappeared toward the house.

Nearly thirty years ago. Lis remembered those few minutes perfectly. This very spot. Except for the level of the water and the height of the trees, the place was unchanged. Even the darkness of night was somehow reminiscent of that June. For though the picnic had been at lunchtime, she had no memory of sunlight; she recalled the whole beach being shrouded, as murky as the water in which her father had dunked her.

Tonight, Lis finally managed to push the memory aside and

walked forward slowly over the gray sand of the beach to the dam. The lake was already pouring over a low portion of it—a cracked corner on the side nearest the house. Some of this spillage made its way into the runoff and the creek beyond but much of it was gathering in the culvert that led to the house. She leapt over this flood and walked to the wheel, set into the middle of the dam.

It was a piece of iron two feet in diameter, its spokes in graceful curves like wisteria vines, the foundry name prominently forged in some gothic typeface. The wheel operated a gate, two by three feet, now closed, over which flowed the water that gushed into the spillway. Opening it all the way would presumably lower the lake by several feet.

Lis took the wheel in both hands and tried to twist it. Rose breeders develop good muscles—from twenty-five-pound bags of loam and manure if not the plants themselves—and Lis strained hard. But the whole mechanism was frozen solid with rust.

She found a rock and pounded on the shaft dully, chipping paint and sending a few sparks flying like miniature meteorites. She tried the wheel again without success then drew back and hammered the mechanism once more, hard. But the rock dipped into the spume of water and was ripped from her hand. It bent back her fingers as it catapulted deep into the culvert. She cried out in pain.

"Lis, you all right?"

She turned and saw Portia climbing cautiously over the slippery limestone rocks. The young woman walked up to the gate.

"The old dam. Still here."

"Yup," Lis said, pressing her stinging fingers. She laughed. "But then where would a dam go? Give me some muscle here, would you?"

They tried the wheel together but it didn't move a millimeter. For five minutes the sisters hammered at the worn gears and the wheel's shaft but were unable to budge the mechanism.

"Been years since anybody opened it, looks like." Portia studied the gate and shook her head. She then gazed at the lake. It stretched away, a huge plain of opaque water at their feet.

"You remember this place?" Lis asked.

"Sure."

"That's where we were going to launch the boat." Lis nodded at the beach.

"Right. Oh, is this it? The same boat?" Portia touched the gunwale of the rowboat.

"That? Of course not. It was that old mahogany sailboat. Father sold it years ago."

"What were we going to do? Run away? Sail someplace? Nantucket?"

"No, England, remember? That's when we'd read books out loud. After lights out. I'd read you some Dickens story. And we were going to live in Mayfair."

"No, it was Sherlock Holmes. I didn't mind them. But Dickens you did solo. That was more than I could take."

"You're right. Baker Street. Mrs. Hudson. I think it was the idea of a housekeeper bringing us tea in the afternoon that we liked best."

"And doing the dishes afterwards. Can you sail to Boston from here?"

"*I* can't sail to the other side of the lake from here."

Portia peered into the water. "I'd forgotten all about the beach. I think one of my dolls drowned here. Barbie. Probably worth a hundred bucks nowadays. And we'd steal Oreos, then sneak down here and eat them. We'd come here all the time." She tried unsuccessfully to skip a stone. "Until the picnic."

"Until the picnic," Lis echoed softly, dipping a hand into the dark water. "This is the first time I've been back."

Portia was astonished. "Since *then*?"

"Yep."

"That was when? Twenty years ago?"

"Try thirty."

Portia shook her head as the number sunk in. The rowboat gave a hard thud and bounced into the dam. She watched it for a moment then said, "It'll go over if we don't do something." Portia eased the boat to the beach and tied it to a sapling. She stepped back, wiping the bits of rotten rope from her hands, and exhaled a fast laugh.

"What?"

"I was thinking. I don't know if I ever asked what happened."

"Happened?" Lis asked.

"That day? The picnic? I'd seen him mad but I'd never seen him *that* mad."

Was it true? Had they never talked about it? Lis's eyes were fixed on the jagged tops of three pines, rising out of the forest; the protruding trees were all different heights and for some reason put her in mind of Calvary. "I don't know," Lis answered. "I sassed him, probably. I don't remember."

"I wish I'd been older. I'd've turned him in."

Lis didn't speak for a moment. "See that?" She pointed to a rock the size of a grapefruit sticking up out of the sand and mud. The water was now an inch away from it. "After he finished spanking me, I crawled over to it. Tried to pick it up. I was going to hit him and push him into the lake."

"You? The girl who never fought back?"

"I remember being on my hands and knees, wondering what it'd be like to be in jail—whether they had separate jails for boys and girls. I didn't want to be in jail with a boy."

"Why didn't you do it?"

After a moment Lis replied, "I couldn't get it out. That's why." Then abruptly she said, "We better get some sandbags here. It looks like we've got about a half hour till it overflows."

Trenton Heck stared into the night sky through the sliding door of his trailer. In front of him, on a red vinyl placemat, sat a plate of tuna salad and rice; at Emil's feet was a bowl filled with Alpo and spinach. Neither had eaten very much.

"Oh, Lord."

The plate got pushed across the table and Heck swiped up a quart bottle of Budweiser, gulping three stiff swallows. He realized that he'd lost his taste for beer as well as his appetite and set the bottle back on the table.

Aside from a glaring light above the table the trailer was dark. He walked over the yellow-and-brown shag carpet to his green easy chair, a Sears "Best," and clicked on the pole lamp. It gave an immediate comfort to the long space. The trailer was large, a three-bedroom model. It was sided in sunlight-yellow aluminum, the windows flanked by black vinyl shingles.

Although Heck had lived here for four and a half years and had accumulated almost everything that a married then divorced man would by rights accumulate in that time, the rooms were not cluttered. Trailer makers are savvy about closets and storage areas; most of Heck's earthly possessions were stowed. Apart from the furniture and lamps the only visible accessories were photographs (family, dogs), trophies (silver-plated men holding pistols in outstretched hands, gold-plated dogs), a half dozen needlepoints that his mother had produced during the period of her chemotherapy (easy sentiments—"Love is where the home is"), cassettes for the stereo (Willie, Waylon, Dwight, Randy, Garth, Bonnie, k.d.,) and a couple of small-bore targets (center-riddled with tight groupings).

Because he was feeling sorry for himself he read the foreclosure notice again. Heck opened the blue-backed paper and laughed bitterly as he thought, Damn, that bank moves fast. The auction was a week from Saturday. Heck had to vacate the Friday before. That part was as unpleasant to read as the next paragraph—the one explaining that the bank was entitled to sue him for the difference between what they made by selling his property in the foreclosure and the amount he still owed.

"Damn!" His palm crashed down. Emil jumped. "God*damn* them! They're taking everything!"

How, he thought bitterly, can I owe *more* than what I bought with the money they lent me? Yet he knew some things about the law and supposed that suing him for this sum was well within their rights as long as they gave him notice.

Trenton Heck knew how fast and bad you could ruin a man's life as long as you gave him notice first.

He figured he could live without the trailer. The worse tragedy—what hurt him like a broken bone—was losing the land. The trailer had always been intended as a temporary residence at best. Heck had bought these acres—half pine forest and half low grass—with some money an aunt had left him. The first time he'd seen the property he knew he had to own it. The thick, fragrant woods giving way to yellow-green hills gently sloped like a young girl's back. A wide stream slicing off the corner of the property, no good for fishing but wonderful just for sitting beside as you listened to the water gush over smooth rocks.

And so he'd bought it. He hadn't asked the advice of his sensible father, or his temperamental fiancée, Jill. He went to the bank, horrified at the thought of depleting a savings account larger than any he'd ever possessed in his life, and put the money down. He walked away from the office of a surly lawyer the owner of four and seven-eighths acres of land that featured no driveway, well or septic tank.

Or a dwelling either.

Unable to afford a house, Heck bought a trailer. He'd allowed Jill a part in *that* decision, and the young waitress—born never to be cheated—had slugged walls and measured closets and interrogated salesmen about BTUs and insulation before insisting that they buy the big one, the fancy one, the *Danger—Wide Load* trailer ("You owe me it, Trenton"). The dealer's men eased the long vehicle onto the pinnacle of the prettiest hill on the property, right next to the spot where he planned to build his dream split-level.

These hopes of construction he believed could be achieved as easily as he'd built his hundred-yard driveway: easing his pickup back and forth between the trailer and the road fifty times. But the savings he'd planned to replenish never materialized, and therefore neither did the house. Finally it came to the point where he could no longer afford the trailer either. When the first overdue notices arrived, Heck recalled to his dismay that the bank had loaned for the trailer on condition it take back a mortgage on the land as well—all his beautiful acreage.

The same land that as of a week from Saturday was going to be somebody else's.

Heck folded the papers and stuffed them behind a statement from the veterinarian. He walked to the plate-glass picture window, which faced west, the direction the storm would be coming from in just a few hours. In the truck, on the drive back home, he'd heard several announcements about the storm. One of them reported that a twister had cut a swath through a trailer park in a town seventy miles west of here. There'd been no deaths but several injuries and a great deal of damage.

Hearing this newscast, just as he happened to click on the old radio, seemed to Heck a bad omen. Would his trailer survive intact? he wondered, then whispered, "And what the hell does it matter?" He picked up a roll of masking tape and peeled off a long strip. He lay down one long diagonal of an X. He started to do the cross strip, then paused and flung the tape across the room.

Walking into the bedroom he sat on the spongy double bed. He imagined himself explaining this whole matter to Jill—the foreclosure, the lawsuit—although he often grew distracted because when he pictured this conversation he pictured it very explicitly and couldn't help but notice that his ex was wearing a hot-pink peek-aboo nightgown.

Heck continued to speak to her for a few minutes then became embarrassed at the unilateral dialogue. He lay back on the bed, gazing at the roiling clouds, and began another silent conversation—this time not with Jill but with Heck's own father, who at this moment was many miles away, presumably asleep, in a big colonial house that he'd owned for twenty years, no mortgage, free and clear. Trenton Heck was saying to him, It's just for a little while, Dad. Maybe a month or so. It'll help me get my life together. My old room'll be fine. Just fine.

Oh, those words sounded flat. They sounded like the excuses offered by the red-handed burglars and joyriders Heck used to nab. And in response his father glanced down the long nose that Heck was grateful he hadn't inherited and said, "For as long as you like, son, sure," though he was really saying: "I knew all along you couldn't handle it. I knew it when you married that blonde, not a woman like your mother, I *knew*. . . ." The old man didn't tell his son the story about the time he was laid off from the ironworks in '59 then got himself together and started his own dealership and made himself a comfortable living though it was tough. . . . He didn't have to, because the story'd *been* told—a dozen times, a hundred—and was sitting right there, perched in front of their similar but very different faces.

Times aren't what they were, Heck thought as he nodded his flushed thanks. Though he was also thinking, I'm just not like you, Dad, and that's the long and the short of it.

He took a swig of beer he didn't really want and wished that Jill were back. He imagined the two of them packing boxes together, looking forward to a joint move.

A truck horn sounded in the distance, an eerie carrying wail, and he thought of the lonely whippoorwill in the old Hank Williams song.

Oh, come on, he thought, rain like a son of a bitch. Heck loved the sound of the rain on metal roof of the trailer. Nothing sent him off to sleep better. If I ain't going to get my reward money, at least give me a good night's sleep.

Trenton Heck closed his eyes, and, as he began to doze, he heard the truck's plaintive horn wail once more in the distance.

12

Owen Atcheson knew the harrowing logic of cornered animals and he understood the cold strategy of instinct that flowed like blood through the body of both hunter and prey.

He would stand motionless for hours, in icy marshes, so still that a drake or goose would pulse carelessly thirty feet above his head and die instantly in the shattering explosion from Owen's long ten-gauge. He'd move silently—almost invisibly—inches at a time, along rock faces to ease downwind of a deer and without using a telescopic sight place a .30 slug through the relaxed shoulder and strong heart of the buck.

When he was a boy he'd doggedly follow fox paths and set dull metal traps exactly where the lithe blond animals would pass. He'd smell their musk, he'd see the hint of their passage in the grass and weeds. He'd collect their broken bodies and if one chewed through the stake line he'd track it for miles—not just to recover the trap but to kill the suffering animal, which he did almost ceremoniously; pain, in Owen Atcheson's philosophy, was weakness, but death was strength.

He'd killed men too. Picked them off calmly, efficiently, with his black M-16, the empty bullet casings cartwheeling through the air and ringing as they landed. (For him, the jangle of spent shells had been the most distinctive sound of the war, much more evocative than the oddly quiet cracks of the gunfire itself.) They charged at him like children playing soldier, these men and women, working the long bolts of their ancient guns and he'd picked them off, *ring, ring, ring.*

But Michael Hrubek wasn't an animal driven by instinct. He wasn't a soldier propelled by battle frenzy and love—or fear—of country.

Yet what was he?

Owen Atcheson simply didn't know.

Driving slowly along Route 236 near Stinson, he looked about for a roadside store or gas station that might have a phone. He wanted to call Lis. But this was a deserted part of the county. He could see no lights except those from distant houses clinging to a hilltop miles away. He continued down the road several hundred yards to a place where the shoulder widened. Here he parked the Cherokee and reached into the back. He slipped the bolt out of his deer rifle, pocketing the well-oiled piece of metal. From the glove compartment he took a long black flashlight, a halogen with six D cells in the tube, the lens masked by a piece of shirt cardboard to limit the refraction of the light. Locking the doors he once again checked to see that his pistol was loaded then walked in a zigzag pattern along the shoulder until he found four hyphens of skid marks—where a car had stopped abruptly then sped off just as fast.

Playing the light over the ground he found where Hrubek had jumped from the hearse: the bent grass, the overturned stones, the muddy bare footprints. Owen continued in a slow circle. Why, he wondered, had Hrubek rolled in the grass? Why had he ripped up several handsful of it? To staunch a wound? Was he trying to force himself to vomit? Was it part of a disguise? Camouflage?

What was in his mind?

Six feet from the shoulder was a muddle of prints, many of them Hrubek's, most of them the trackers' bootprints and the dogs' paw-prints. Three animals, he noticed. Here Hrubek had paced for a time then started running east through the grass and brush just beyond the shoulder. Owen followed the trail for a hundred yards then noted that Hrubek had turned off the road, plowing south, aiming for a ridge of hill paralleling the highway fifty feet away.

Owen continued along this track until it simply vanished altogether. Dropping to his knees he scanned the area, wondering if the man was smart enough to deer-walk, an evasion technique used by professional poachers: stepping straight down on the ground, avoiding the most telltale signs of passage (not prints but overturned pebbles, leaves and twigs). But he could find no bent blades of grass—the only evidence most deer-walkers leave behind. He concluded Hrubek had simply backtracked, aborting his southward journey and returning to the path beside the road.

Fifty yards east he found where Hrubek had once again done the same—turned south, walked a short way then backtracked. So, yes, he was moving east but at the same time was drawn to something south of the road. Owen followed this second detour some distance from the highway. He stood in the midst of a field of tall grass and once more saw that the trackers had paused here.

Shutting off the flashlight, he took his pistol from his pocket and waded into the pool of cold darkness that rolled off the rocky hills in front of him and gathered at his feet like snow. He paused here and, against all reason, closed his eyes.

Owen Atcheson tried to rid himself of the hardened, savvy, forty-eight-year-old WASP lawyer inside him. He struggled to become Michael Hrubek, a man consumed by madness. He stood this way, swaying in the darkness, for several minutes.

Nothing.

He could get no sense whatsoever of Hrubek's mind. He opened his eyes, fingering his pistol.

He was about to return to the Cherokee and drive on to the truck stop in Watertown when a thought came to him. What if he was allowing Hrubek too *much* madness? Was it possible that, even if his world was demented, the rules that governed that world were as logical as everyone else's? Adler was fast to talk about mix-ups and doped-up patients ambling off. But step back, Owen told himself. Why, look at what Michael Hrubek's done—he's devised a plan to escape from a hospital for the criminally insane, he's executed it and he's managed to evade professional pursuers. Owen decided it was time to give Hrubek a little more credit.

Returning to the spot where Hrubek's trail ended he placed his feet squarely in the huge muddy indentations left by the madman's feet. With eyes open this time, he found himself looking directly at the crest of the rocky hill. He gazed at it for a moment then walked to the base of the rock. He dabbed his fingers in mud and smeared it on his cheekbones and forehead. From his back pocket he took a navy-blue stocking cap and pulled it over his head. He started to climb.

In five minutes he found what he sought. The nest on the top of the rocks contained broken twigs and grass and the marks of boots. Their indentations were deep—made by someone who'd weigh close to three hundred pounds. And they were fresh. He also found button marks from where the man had lain prone and looked at the highway below, maybe waiting for the trackers and their dogs to leave. Pressed into the mud was a huge handprint above the word *rEVEnge*. Hrubek had been here no more than an hour before. He'd gone east, yes, but only for clothes, perhaps, or to lead his pursuers astray. Then he'd backtracked west along a different route to this outcropping, which he'd spotted on his way east.

The son of a bitch! Owen descended slowly, forcing himself to be careful, despite his exhilaration. He couldn't afford a broken bone now. At the bottom of the rocks he played his flashlight over the ground. He found a small patch of mud nearby and observed bootprints walking away from the rocks—the same prints he'd seen on the top of the cliff. Although they weren't widely spaced, they were toe-heavy, an indication that Hrubek was jogging or walking fast. They led to the road then back south into the fields, where they turned due west.

Following these clear imprints Owen walked for a short way through the grass. He decided that he would make certain that Hrubek was indeed going west then would return to his truck and cruise slowly along the highway, looking for his quarry from the road. Just another ten yards, he decided, and climbed through a notch in a low stone fence, leading to a large field beyond.

It was there that he tripped over the hidden wire and fell, face forward, toward the steel trap.

The big Ottawa Manufacturing coyote trap had been laid brilliantly—in a section of the path with no handholds for arresting falls, just beyond the stone wall so that a searcher couldn't get his other foot to the ground in time to stop his tumble. In an instant Owen dropped the flashlight and covered his face with his left arm, lifting his pistol and firing four .357 magnum rounds at the round trigger plate in a desperate effort to snap it closed before he struck it. The blue-steel device danced under the impact of the powerful slugs. Stones, twigs and hot bits of shattered bullets flew into the air as Owen twisted sideways to let his broad shoulder take the impact of the fall.

When he landed, his head bounced off the closed jaws of the trap and he lay, stunned, feeling the blood on his forehead and fighting down the horrific image of the blue metal straps snapping shut on his face. An instant later he rolled away, assuming that Hrubek had used the trap as Owen himself would have—as a diversion—meant to hold him immobile and in agony while Hrubek attacked from behind. Owen glanced about, huddling beside the fence. When there was no immediate assault he ejected the spent and unfired cartridges then reloaded. He pocketed the two good rounds and scanned the area once more.

Nothing. No sound but a faint wind in the lofty treetops. Owen stood slowly. So the trap had been meant merely to injure a scenting dog. In fury Owen picked up the bullet-dented trap and flung it deep into the field. He found the spent shells and buried them then, by touch, surveyed the damage to his face and shoulder. It was minor.

His anger vanished quickly and Owen Atcheson began to laugh. Not from relief at escaping serious injury. No, it was a laugh of pure pleasure. The trap said to him that Michael Hrubek was a worthy adversary after all—ruthless as well as clever. Owen was never as alive as when he had a strong enemy that he was about to engage—an enemy that might test him.

Hurrying to the Cherokee he started the engine and drove slowly west, staring at the fields to his left. He was so intent on catching sight of his prey that he grazed a road sign with the truck's windshield. Startled by the loud noise he braked quickly and glanced at the sign.

It told him that he was exactly forty-seven miles from home.

Michael Hrubek, crouched down in a stand of grass, caressed his John Worker overalls and wondered about the car at which he stared.

Surely it was a trap. Snipers were probably sighting on it with long-barreled muskets. Snipers in those trees just ahead, waiting for him to sneak up to the sports car. He breathed shallowly and reminded himself not to give away his position.

After he'd passed the *GET TO* sign he'd hurried west through the fields of grass and pumpkin vines, paralleling the dim strip of Route 236. He'd made good time and had stopped only once—to place one of the animal traps beside a stone fence. He'd set a few leaves on top of the metal and hurried on.

Now, Hrubek raised himself up and looked again at the car. He saw no one around it. But still he remained hidden, in the foxhole of grass, waiting, aiming the blade sight of his gun at the trees

ahead and looking for any sign of motion. As he smelled the grass
a dark memory loomed. He tried his best to ignore it but the image
refused to disappear.

Oh, what's that on your head, Mama? What're you wearing there?
Mama . . .

Take off that hat, Mama, I don't like it one bit.

Fifteen years ago Michael Hrubek had been a boy both very
muscular and very fat, with waddling feet and a long trunk of a
neck. One day, playing in the tall grass field behind an old willow
tree, he heard: "Michael! Miiii-chael!" His mother walked onto the
back porch of the family's trim suburban home in Westbury, Pennsylvania. "Michael, please come here." She wore a broad-brimmed
red hat, beneath which her beautiful hair danced like yellow fire
in the wind. Even from the distance he could see the dots of her
red nails like raw cigarette burns. Her eyes were dark, obscured
by the brim of the hat and by the amazing little masks that she
dabbed on her eyes from the tubes of mask carrier on her makeup
table. She did this, he suspected, to hide from him.

"Honey . . . Come here, I need you." Slowly he stood and walked
to her. "I just got home. I didn't have time to stop. I want you to
go by the grocery store. I need some things."

"Oh, no," the boy said tragically.

She knew he didn't want to, his mother said. But Mr. and Mrs.
Klevan or the Abernathys or the Potters would be here at any minute and she needed milk and coffee. Or something. She *needed* it.

"No, I can't."

Yes, yes, he could. He was her little soldier. He was brave,
wasn't he?

He whined, "I don't know about this. There are reasons why I
can't do it."

"And mind the change. People short-change you."

"They won't let me cross the street," Michael retorted. "I don't
know where it is!"

"Don't worry, honey, I'll give you the instructions," she said soothingly. "I'll write it down."

"I can't."

"Do it for me. Please. Do it quickly."

"I don't know!"

"You're twelve years old. You can do it." Her composure was steadfast.

"No, no, no . . ."

"All you have to do"—her mouth curved into a smile—"is go by the store and get what I need. My brave little soldier boy can do that, can't he?"

But the Klevans or the Milfords or the Pilchers arrived the next minute and his mother didn't get a chance to write down the directions for him. She sent him on his way. Michael, frightened to the point of nausea, a five-dollar bill clutched in a death grip, started out on a journey to the nearby store.

An hour passed and his mother, stewing with mounting concern and anger, received a phone call from the market. Michael had wandered into the store ten minutes before and had caused an incident.

"Your son," the beleaguered manager said, "wants the store."

"He wants the *store*?" she asked, bewildered.

"He said you told him to buy the store. I'm near to calling the police. He touched one of our checkers. Her, you know, chest. She's in a state."

"Oh, for the love of Christ."

She sped to the market.

Michael, shaking with panic, stood in the checkout line. Confronted with the apparent impossibility of doing what he'd been told to do—*Go buy the store*—his conscious thought dissolved and he'd belligerently grabbed the checker's fat arm and thrust the cash into her blouse pocket as she stood, hands at her side, sobbing.

"Take it!" he screamed at her, over and over. "Take the money!"

His mother collected him and when they returned home, she led him straight into the bathroom.

"I'm scared."

"Are you, darling? My little soldier boy's scared? Of what, I wonder."

"Where was I? I don't remember nothing."

" 'Anything.' 'I don't remember anything.' Now get out of those filthy clothes." They were stained with sawdust and dirt; Michael had belly-flopped to the floor, seeking cover, when his mother, eyes blazing beneath her stylish hat, charged through the pneumatic door of the supermarket. "Then I want you to come out and tell my guests you're sorry for what you did. After that you'll go to bed for the day."

"Go to bed?"

"Bed," she snapped.

Okay, he said. Okay, sure.

Was he being punished or comforted? He didn't know. Michael pondered this for a few minutes then sat on the toilet, faced with a new dilemma. His mother had dumped his clothes down the laundry chute. Did she want him to apologize naked? He gazed about the room for something he might wear.

Five minutes later Michael opened the door and stepped out into the living room, wearing his mother's nightgown. "Hello," he said, trooping up to the guests. "I tried to buy the fucking store. I'm sorry." Mr. Abernathy or Monroe stopped speaking in mid-sentence. His wife raised a protective hand to her mouth to stop herself from blurting something regrettable.

But his own mother . . . Why, she was smiling! Michael was astonished. Though her masked eyes were cold she was smiling at him. "Well, here's our pretty little soldier boy," she whispered. "Doesn't Michael look fashionable?"

"I found it behind the door."

"Did you now?" she asked, shaking her head.

Michael smiled. *Fashionable*. He felt pleased with himself and repeated his apology, laughing harshly. "I tried to buy the fucking store!"

The guests, holding the cups that contained tea not coffee and lemon not milk, avoided each other's eyes. Michael's mother rose. "I've changed my mind, Michael. You look so nice why don't you go out and play?"

"Outside?" His smile faded.

"Come along. I want you outside."

"I'd feel funny going outside wearing—"

"No, Michael. Outside."

"But they might see me." He began to cry. "Somebody might see me."

"Now!" she screeched. "Get the fuck outside."

Then she escorted him by the hand, thrusting him out the front door. Two of the neighborhood girls stared at him as he stood on the doorstep in the pale-blue nightgown. They smiled at first but when he began to stare back, muttering to himself, they grew uncomfortable and went inside. Michael turned back to his own front door. He heard the lock click. He looked obliquely through the dirty glass window and saw his mother's face, turning away. Michael walked to the willow tree in the backyard and for the rest of the afternoon huddled by himself in a nest of grass similar to the one in which he sat tonight. Looking for snipers and staring at the car.

As he listened to the rustle of this grass, feeling it caress his skin as it had so long ago, Michael Hrubek remembered much of that day. He didn't, however, remember it with perfect clarity for the very reason that made it so significant in his life—it was his first break with reality, his first psychotic episode. The images of those few hours were altered by his mind and by the intervening years, and were buried beneath other memories, many of which were just as haunting and sorrowful. Tonight, moved by the smell and feel of the grass, he might have delved deeper into that event—

as Dr. Richard had been encouraging him to do—but he'd grown so agitated by now that he could wait no longer. Snipers or no, he had to act. He rose and made his way to the road.

The sports car had apparently broken down earlier in the evening. The hood was up and the windows and doors were locked. A red triangular marker sat in the road near the rear fender. Hrubek wondered if its purpose was to help snipers sight on their target. He sailed it into the brush like a Frisbee.

"MG," he whispered, reading the emblem on the hood. He concluded this meant "My God." Paying no attention to the inside of the car he walked directly to the trunk. A gift! Look at this. A gift from My God! The rack was locked but he simply grabbed the mountain bicycle in both hands and pulled it free. Bits of metal and plastic from the mountings cascaded around him. He set the bicycle on the ground and caressed the tubes and leather and gears and cables. He felt a chill from the metal and enjoyed this sensation very much. He lowered his head to the handlebar and rubbed his cheek on the chrome.

He took a marker from his pocket and wrote on his forearm: *Oh, strANGE aRe the works of GOD. Thank YOU GOD for thIs beautIFul gIFt*. Next to these words he drew a picture of a serpent and one of an apple and wrote the name *EVE*. He licked the name and stepped back, studying his new means of transportation with an uneasy but grateful gaze.

Richard Kohler found himself in an alien world.

He was wearing a wool-blend suit, a silk tie, red-and-green Argyles and a single penny loafer—what other proof did he need, he reflected, that he was no outdoorsman?

Bending forward as far as he dared he pulled his other shoe out of a pool of soupy, methane-laced mud and wiped it on the grass beside him. He stepped back into the wet loafer and continued his journey westward.

Curiously this forest invoked in him a claustrophobia that he'd never felt anywhere else—even in his dark tiny office, where he would often spend fifteen straight hours. His pulse was high, his limbs itched from this fear of confinement and he was having trouble breathing. He also heard noises where no noises should be and his sense of direction was terrible. He was on the verge of admitting to himself that, yes, he was lost. His points of reference—trees, signposts, bushes—were vague and shifty. More often than not, as he walked toward them, they simply vanished; sometimes they turned into grotesque creatures or faces in the process.

Over his shoulder was his ruddy backpack, containing the syringe and drugs, and on his arm was a black London Fog raincoat. He was too hot to wear it and he wondered why on earth he'd brought the coat with him. The radio updates about the impending storm suggested that a helmet and armor would be better protection than gabardine.

Kohler had parked his BMW up the road, a half mile from here, and had made his way through a field into this forest, making slow progress. His leather soles slipped off the damp rocks and he'd fallen twice onto the hard ground. The second time he'd landed on his wrist, nearly spraining it. The vicious thorns of a wild rosebush hooked his pant leg and it took five painful minutes to free himself.

Kohler recognized, though, that he'd been lucky. The nurse who'd alerted him to the escape reported that the young man had run from the hearse in Stinson and had apparently gotten as far as Watertown.

As Kohler had sped in that direction down Route 236, he was certain that he'd sighted Michael in a clearing. The doctor raced to the turnoff, climbed from the car and searched the area. He'd called his patient's name, pleaded with him to show himself, but received no response. Then the doctor had driven off once more. But he hadn't gone far. He pulled off onto a side road and waited. Ten minutes later he believed that he'd seen the same figure hurrying on once more.

Kohler had found no sign of Michael since. Hoping he might stumble across him by chance, the psychiatrist had taken to the wilderness again, heading in the direction in which Michael seemed to be headed—west.

Where are you, Michael?

And why are you out here tonight?

Oh, I've tried so hard to look into your mind. But it's as dark as it ever was. It's as dark as the sky.

He tripped again, on a strand of wire this time, and tore his slacks on a sharp rock, gouging his thigh. He wondered if there was a danger of tetanus. This thought discouraged him—not the risk of disease but the reminder of how much basic medicine he'd forgotten. He wondered if his knowledge of the human brain compensated for the long-forgotten facts of physiology and organic chemistry he once had learned and recited so easily. Then these thoughts faded, for he found the sports car.

There was nothing remarkable about the vehicle itself. He didn't for a minute think that Michael had lifted the hood and tried to hotwire it. His patient would be far too frightened at the thought of driving a car to steal one. No, Kohler was intrigued by something else—a small object resting on the ground behind the rear bumper.

The tiny white skull ironically was the exact shade of the car itself. He stepped closer and picked it up, looking carefully at the delicate bones. A tiny fracture ran through the cheek. Trigeminal, he thought spontaneously, recalling the name of the fifth pair of cranial nerves.

Then the skull teetered on the tips of his fingers for an instant and tumbled with a soft crack onto the trunk of the car, rolling into the dust of the shoulder. Kohler remained completely still as the muzzle of the pistol slid along his skin from his temple to his ear, while a fiercely strong hand reached out and fastened itself to his shoulder.

13

Trenton Heck pointed the Walther up at the turbulent clouds and eased the ribbed hammer down. He put the safety on and slipped the gun back into his holster.

He handed the wallet back to the skinny man, whose hospital identification card and driver's license seemed on the up and up. The poor fellow wasn't quite as pale as when Heck had tapped the muzzle to his head a few minutes before.

But he wasn't any less angry.

Richard Kohler dropped to his knees and unzipped the backpack Heck had tossed onto the grass before frisking him.

"Sorry, sir," Heck said. "Couldn't tell whether you were him or not. Too dark to get a good look, with you crouched down and all."

"You come up on Michael Hrubek that way and he'll panic," Kohler snapped. "I guarantee it." He rummaged inside the pack. Whatever was so precious inside—just a couple of bottles, it looked like—didn't seem to be damaged. Heck wondered if he'd caught himself a tippler.

"And I'll tell you something else." The doctor turned, examining Heck. "Even if you'd shot him, he'd've turned around and broken your neck before he died." Kohler snapped his fingers.

Heck gave a brief laugh. "With a head wound? I don't know about that."

"There's apparently a lot you don't know about him." The doctor rezipped the pack.

Heck supposed he couldn't blame the man for being pissed off but he didn't feel too bad about the ambush. Kohler, it turned out, had been padding down the same path Hrubek must've taken earlier in the evening. In the dark, how was Heck to know the difference? True, the doctor was undoubtedly a lot punier. But then so are all suspects after they turn out not to be suspects.

"What's your interest here exactly, sir?" Heck asked.

Kohler eyed his civvy clothes. "You a cop, or what?"

"Sort of a special deputy." Though this was untrue and he had no more police powers than an average citizen. Still he sensed he needed some authority with this wiry fellow, who looked like he was in the mood to make trouble. Heck repeated his question.

"I'm Michael's doctor."

"Quite a house call you're making tonight." Heck looked over the doctor's suit and penny loafers. "You've did some fine tracking to get yourself all the way here, considering you haven't got dogs."

"I spotted him up the road, headed in this direction. But he got away."

"So he's nearby?"

"I saw him a half hour ago. He can't've gotten that far."

Heck nodded at Emil, whose head was up. "Well, for some reason the scent's vanished. That's got me worried and Emil antsy. We're going to quarter around here, see if we can pick it up."

The tone was meant to discourage company, as was the pace that Heck set. But Kohler kept up with man and dog as they zigzagged across the road and along the fields surrounding it, their feet crunching loudly on leaves and gravel. Heck felt the stiffening of his leg muscles, a warning to go slow. The temperature was still unseasonable but it had dropped in the last half hour and the air was wet with the approaching storm; when he was tired and hadn't slept his leg was prone to seize into agonizing cramps.

"Now that I think about it," Heck said, "you were probably better off tracking him without dogs. He fooled our search party damn good. Led us all in the opposite direction he ended up taking."

Kohler once again—for the fourth time, by Heck's count—glanced at the Walther automatic. The doctor asked, "Led you off? What do you mean?"

Heck explained about the false clue—dropping the clipping that contained the map of Boston.

The doctor was frowning. "I saw Michael in the hospital library yesterday. Tearing clippings out of old newspapers. He'd been reading all morning. He was very absorbed in something."

"That a fact?" Heck muttered, discouraged once again at Hrubek's brainy talents. He continued, "Then he pulled a trick I've only heard about. He pissed on a truck."

"He what?"

"Yep. Took a leak on a tire. Left his scent on it. The truck took off for Maine and the dogs followed it 'stead of going after his footsteps. Not many people'd know about that, let alone psychos."

"That's not exactly," Kohler said coolly, "a word we use."

"My apologies to him," Heck responded with a sour laugh. "Funny thing: I was just falling asleep—you know how this happens sometimes?—and I heard a truck horn. It just come to me—what he'd done. Emil's good but following airborne scent of a man hanging on to a tractor-trailer? Naw, that didn't seem right. For that many miles? I drove back to the truck stop and sure enough picked up his backtrack. That's a trick of the pros. Just like he hid that clipping in the grass. See, I wouldn't've believed it, it'd been lying out in the open. He's clever. He's fooled dogs before, I'll bet."

"No. Impossible. He's never escaped from anything in his life. Not a calculated escape."

Heck looked at Kohler to see if he could spot the lie. But the doctor seemed sincere, and Heck added, "That's not what I heard."

"From who?"

"From my old boss at the state police. Don Haversham. He's the one called me about the search. He said something 'bout seven hospitals your boy'd hightailed it outta."

Kohler was laughing. "Sure. But ask Michael which ones. He'll tell you they were prison hospitals. And when he escaped he was on horseback, dodging musket balls. See what I mean?"

Heck wasn't quite sure that he did. "Musket balls. Heh. We've gotta head through this brush here."

They plunged down a steep dirt path into a valley below. Kohler was soon winded by the arduous trek. When they reached flat ground, he caught his breath and said, "Of course you don't know for certain that he *isn't* headed for Boston."

"How's that?"

"Well, if he was smart enough," the doctor pointed out, "to fool you into thinking he was going east, maybe now he's fooling you into thinking he's going *west*. Double bluff."

Well. This was something Heck hadn't thought about. Sure, why couldn't Hrubek just do the same thing all over again and turn east? Maybe he *did* have Boston in mind. But he thought for a minute and then told Kohler the truth: "That might be but I can't search the whole of the Northeast. All I can do is follow my dog's nose."

Though he was painfully aware that this particular nose presently had no notion of where his prey was.

"Just something to think about," the doctor said.

They followed the path through a valley beside an old quarry. Heck remembered in his youth, a solitary boy, he'd taken an interest in geology. He'd spent many hours pounding with a hammer in a quarry similar to this one, snitching honest quartz, mica and granite rocks for his collection. Tonight, he found himself staring at the tall cliffs, scarred and chopped—the way bone was gouged by a doctor's metal tools. He thought of the X-rays of his shattered leg, showing where the bullet cracked his femur. Why, he'd wondered at the time, as he wondered now, had the goddamn doctor shown him that artwork?

The hound turned abruptly several times, paused then turned again.

"Has he got the track?" Kohler asked, whispering.

"Nope," Heck replied in a conversational voice. "We'll know when he does."

They walked behind Emil as he snaked along the base of the tall yellow-white cliffs around pools of brackish water.

They emerged from the rocky valley and climbed slowly. They found themselves once again back at the disabled MG. Heck was grimacing. "Hell, back to square one."

"Why're you out here by yourself?" Kohler asked, breathing heavily.

"Just am."

"There's a reward for him."

Heck looped the track line for a moment. Finally he said, "How'd you know that?"

"I didn't. But it explains why you're out here by yourself."

"And how 'bout you, doc? If you spotted him, how come you didn't call out the Marines?"

"He panics easily. I can get him back without anybody getting hurt. He knows me. He trusts me."

Emil suddenly stiffened and turned to the forest, tensing. In an instant Heck drew and cocked his pistol. The underbrush shook.

"No!" Kohler shouted, glancing at the gun. He started forward into the bush.

But Heck gripped him by the arm and whispered, "I'd be quiet there, sir. Let's don't give our position away."

There was silence for a moment. Then the muscular doe bounded in a gray-brown arc over a low hedge and vanished.

Heck put the gun away. "You oughta be a little more careful. You're kinda trusting, you know what I mean?" He looked south along the road, where the gray asphalt disappeared into the hills.

Emil'd shown no interest in that direction but Heck thought they ought to try it nonetheless. He started to hold the plastic bag containing Hrubek's shorts down to the dog once more. But Kohler stopped his arm.

"How much?" the doctor asked.

"How's that, sir?" Heck stood.

"How much is the reward?"

Emil was aware that a scent article was dangling over his head and he shivered. Heck closed the bag up again to keep the dog from growing too skittish. He said to the doctor, "That's sort of between me and the people paying it, sir."

"Is that Adler?"

Heck nodded slowly.

"Well," Kohler continued, "he's a colleague. We work together."

"If he's a buddy then how come you don't know 'bout it? The reward?"

Kohler asked, "How much, Mr. Heck?"

"Ten thousand."

"I'll give you twelve."

For a moment Heck watched Emil rock back and forth eager to run. He said to Kohler, "You're joshing."

"Oh, no. I'm quite serious."

Heck snorted a laugh but his face grew hot as he realized that he was looking at a man who could actually write a check for twelve thousand dollars. And probably have some left over afterwards. "Why?"

"Thirteen."

"I'm not bargaining with you. What do you want me to *do* for that kind of money?"

"Go home. Forget about Michael Hrubek."

Heck looked slowly around him. He noticed in the west, far away, a diffuse flash of lightning. It seemed to stretch for a hundred miles. He gazed at the huge expanse of countryside, the muddy horizon against the black sky. He found the view disturbing, for the very reason that this unexpected money was so appealing. How could he possibly find one man in that vast emptiness? Heck laughed to himself. Why did God always drop temptations in front of you when you wanted them the most?

"What's in this for you?" Heck asked again, to stall.

"I just don't want him hurt."

"I'm not going to hurt him. Not necessarily."

"You were about to use that gun."

"Well, if I *had* to I would. But I'm not going to shoot anybody in the back. That's not my way. Wasn't when I was a trooper. Isn't now."

"Michael isn't dangerous. He's not like a bank robber."

"Doesn't matter if he's dangerous like a crazed moose protecting her calves or dangerous like a Mafia hit man. I'm looking out for me and my dog and if that means shooting the man's coming at me with a rock or tire iron so be it."

Kohler gave a little smile that made Heck feel he'd somehow lost a point.

"Look, he's set out traps for dogs. I don't give much quarter to a man like that."

"He did *what*?" The smile vanished from Kohler's face.

"Traps. Spring animal traps."

"No. Michael wouldn't do that."

"Well, you may say that but—"

"Have you seen any?"

"I know he took some. Haven't found any yet."

The doctor didn't speak for a moment. Finally he said, "I think you're being used, Mr. Heck."

"What do you mean by that?" He was ready to take offense but the psychiatrist's voice was suddenly soothing, the voice of someone on his side, trying to help.

"Adler knows that a dog'll make a schizophrenic snap. Chasing someone like Michael is the worst thing in the world for him. A patient like that, cornered? He'll panic. He'll panic *bad*. You'll *have* to shoot him. Adler wants this whole thing wrapped up as smooth as possible. Fourteen thousand."

Lord. Heck squeezed his eyes shut and opened them just in time to see another flash of lightning. At his feet Emil rocked on his paws and had just about had it with this human-conversation stuff.

Take the money and go back home. Call up the bank, feed them a big check. Fourteen'd buy him another nine, ten months. Maybe in that time HQ'd find money to reinstate all the troopers let go in the last three years. Maybe one of the thirty-six security companies that had Heck's résumé would find an opening.

Maybe Jill'd come home with her knuckleball and tip money and her lacy nightgowns.

Fourteen thousand dollars.

Heck sighed. "Well, sir, I understand you're concerned about your patient and all, and I respect that. But there're other people to think about too. I wasn't a trooper for nothing. Emil and me have a chance to capture this fellow. And I'd say it's probably a better shot than you have—even with your talk about double bluffs and all. No offense."

"But he isn't dangerous. That's what nobody understands. You *chasing* him, that's what makes him dangerous."

Heck laughed. "Well, you psychiatrists have your own way of talking, I don't doubt. But those two fellows he almost killed tonight might disagree with you some."

"Killed?" Kohler's eyes flickered, and the doctor seemed as badly shaken as when Heck had pressed the black barrel of the gun against his skin. "What're you talking about?"

"Those orderlies."

"What orderlies?"

"He had the run-in with those two fellows near Stinson. I thought you knew about it. Just after he escaped."

"You know their names?"

"No, sure don't. They were from the hospital. Marsden. That's all I know."

Stepping away from Heck, Kohler wandered to the car. He picked up the small skull. He rubbed it compulsively in his hands.

"So," Heck continued, "I think I gotta turn down your offer."

Kohler stared at the night sky for a moment then turned to Heck. "Just do me a favor. If you find him, don't threaten him. Don't chase him. And whatever you do, for God's sake, don't sic that dog on him."

"I'm not looking at this," Heck said coolly, "like a fox hunt."

Kohler handed him a card. "That's my service. You get close to him, call that number. They'll page me. I'd really appreciate it."

"If I can, I will," Heck said. "That's the best I can say."

Kohler nodded and looked around, orienting himself. "That's 236 down there?"

"Yessir," Trenton Heck said, then leaned against the fender of the car and—with a slight laugh—watched the peculiar sight of this narrow man in a suit and tie, muddy as a ditchdigger, sporting a fine-looking overcoat and a backpack as he strolled down this deserted country road late on a stormy night.

Dr. Ronald Adler's eyes coursed up and down the Marsden County map. "Made it all the way to the state border. Who'd've thought?" He added with neither elation nor interest, "The Massachusetts Highway Patrol should have him within an hour or so. I want a worst-case plan."

"Are you talking about the reward?" Peter Grimes asked.

"Reward?" the director snapped.

"Uhm. What do you mean by worst-case?"

Adler seemed to know exactly but didn't speak for a moment, perhaps out of some vestigial superstition that medical training had not wholly obliterated. "If he kills a trooper when they find him. Or kills anybody else for that matter. *That's* what I mean."

"Okay, that's possible, I suppose," Grimes offered. "Unlikely."

Adler turned his attention back to the E Ward supervisor's reports. "Is all this accurate?"

"Absolutely. I'm sure."

"Hrubek was in the *Milieu Suite*? Kohler was doing *individual* psychoanalysis with him? This delusion therapy he's always boring people with?"

And publishing about in the best professional journals, Grimes reflected. He said, "So it appears."

"NIMH guidelines. We *all* know them. The criteria for individual psychotherapy in schizophrenic patients are that they be young, intelligent, have a past history of achievement. And are more acute than chronic . . . Oh, and that they have some success in a sexual relationship. That's hardly Michael Hrubek."

The assistant came a half breath away from saying, Not unless you call rape a successful relationship. He wondered if Adler would have fired him or laughed.

"A history like his"—Adler riffled pages—"and *still* Kohler puts him in therapy. One way you could view it is that Kohler was *more* than negligent in this whole matter. Let's just take that tack for a minute, shall we? Is that door open? My door there. Close it, why don't you?"

Grimes did, while Adler flipped through one doctor's assessment of Hrubek, in which was recorded the patient's plans to remove this therapist's internal organs with a single bare hand—a process that Hrubek described articulately and, all things considered, with an impressive knowledge of human anatomy.

When Grimes dropped again into his chair, Adler had snapped closed the file and was gazing at the ceiling. His hand dipped into his crotch, where he adjusted something. He said, "You realize what Herr Dr. Kohler has done?"

"He—"

"Do you know the case of Burton Scott Webley? Burton Scott Webley the Third. Or Fourth. I don't recall. Do you know about him? Do they teach you such arcane things in . . . Where did you go to school?"

"Columbia, sir. I'm not familiar with the case, no."

"Co-lum-bi-a," Adler stretched the four syllables out with elastic disdain. "Webley the Third or Fourth. He was a patient in New York. I don't know. Creedmoor perhaps. Or Pilgrim State. Don't let's quibble. No, wait. It was private. Top doctors, like our friend, *Sigmund* Kohler. *Cum laude* sort of doctors. Co-lum-bi-a sort of doctors."

"Got it."

"You see, Kohler has this idea that our mental hospitals are chockablock with van Goghs. Poets and artists. Misunderstood geniuses, vision and madness locked together—the beast with two backs." When he noticed Grimes staring at him blankly, Adler continued, "Webley was a paranoid schizophrenic. Delusional. Monosymptomatic. Twenty-eight years of age. Sound familiar, Grimes? Delusions centered around his family. They were trying to get him, blah, blah, blah. Felt his father and aunt were having an incestuous relationship. Including bouts of televised sodomy. On network TV, if I'm not mistaken. He had a bad episode and threatened the aunt with a pitchfork. Well, he's involuntarily committed. Insulin-shock therapy is all in vogue and his doctors put him into a hundred seventy comas."

"Jesus."

"Then the ECS department third-rails him for six months after his blood sugar becomes an embarrassment. With that much amperage, well, he came out of it rather tattered, as you'd suspect."

"This was when?"

"Hardly matters. A little while after they unplugged him, he sees the senior psychiatrist, who does a new diagnostic. Webley is neat and clean and coherent. And very sharp. Astonishing indeed, considering the SmithKline cocktails he's on. He's polite, he's responsive, he's eager to undergo therapy. The doctor schedules the full battery of tests. Webley takes, and passes, all twenty-five of them. A miracle cure. He'll be written up in the *APA Journal*."

"I can guess what's coming."

"Oh, can you, Grimes?" Adler fixed him with an amused gaze. "Can you *guess* that after he was released, he took a taxi to his aunt's house then raped and dismembered her, looking for the hidden microphone that'd recorded the evidence used to commit him? Can you *guess* that her fifteen-year-old daughter walked into the house as his little search was in progress and that he did the same to her? Any inkling that the only thing that saved the eight-year-old son was that Webley fell asleep amid the girl's viscera? You look sufficiently pale, Grimes.

"But I have to tell you the end of the story. The *shocking* part: it was all *calculated*. Webley had an IQ of 146. After he took himself off his brain candy, he snuck into the library and memorized the correct answers to each of those twenty-five tests and, I submit, honed his delivery pretty fucking well."

"You think Hrubek did the same thing to Kohler? What this Webley did?"

"Yes! Of *course* that's what I mean! Kohler bought a bill of goods. Lock, stock and barrel. Callaghan's death, any *other* deaths tonight—they're ultimately Kohler's fault. *His* fault, Peter."

"Sure. Of course."

"Tell me, what do you think of him? Of Kohler?"

"Pompous little shit."

Adler was pleased to have someone second this sentiment though it reminded him how much he detested Grimes for being such a toady. "I think there's more to it. Why is he being so blind? Kohler's not stupid. Whatever else, he's not stupid. Why?"

"I don't really—"

"Peter, I'd like you to do something for me."

"Look, sir—"

"Some detective work." When the otherwise thin Adler dropped his head to look over the top of his glasses he developed an alarming double chin.

Because it was very late in the evening and he was tired of treading lightly through hospital politics, Peter Grimes chose not to be coy. "I don't think I'd like to do that."

" 'Like to do that'?" Adler snapped. "Don't give me any of your bluster. I want to see fear in your face, young man. You're not union. If I wanted your fucking balls, I'd have them in an instant and a hell of a lot easier than I could castrate those orderlies. Don't you forget that. Now are you listening? Some detective work. Write it down if you can't remember it. Are you ready?" he inquired sarcastically, forgetting for the moment that he was speaking not to an incompetent secretary but to a doctor of medicine.

As man and dog returned to the sports car, Heck grew convinced that Hrubek had hitched a ride or snuck into the back of a repair vehicle that had answered the distress call.

Hiding in trucks for real this time, is he? Heck wondered. He leaned against the car and shivered slightly as a breeze came up.

Oh, man, here I give up almost a year's salary, sounding all grandiose and righteous and look what happens? I lose the trail completely. What would you've done, Jill? Tell me you'd've told him to stuff it too.

But no, Heck knew. Jill would've skedaddled home and tucked Kohler's check in her jewelry box. By now she'd be fast asleep.

In her pink nightgown.

Oh, baby . . .

Then, suddenly, Emil's nose shot into the air and the dog stiffened. He turned north, toward Route 236, and began to trot forward. Heck followed, feeling the line go taut and Emil pick up the pace.

What's going on here?

The breeze blew over them again and Emil began to run.

Glancing down at the asphalt, Heck closed his eyes in disgust. "Goddamn! What was I thinking of? Bicycle!"

Heck commanded Emil to stop then examined the asphalt and found a tread mark leading unsteadily from the car toward the highway. The tread was very wide; the rider could easily weigh three hundred pounds.

The surest clue though was Emil, whose nose was in the air. When a dog raises his nose and switches from trailing ground scent to trailing airborne, it's a good sign that the quarry's on a bike or motorcycle. They'd probably been upwind of the scent until the breeze a moment ago blew a bit of it back in their direction. Emil's ears twitched and he doled his weight from the left paw to the right and back again, ready to run.

Heck was too. Airborne scent is the hardest to track and even a moderate wind will disrupt it. A storm of the sort that was expected would surely obliterate it altogether.

Strapping the thong over his pistol, he wrapped Emil's red lead around his left hand.

"Find, Emil. Find!"

The hound broke from the starting gate and surged down the road. They were on the trail once again.

What's different?

Standing on the edge of the lake not far from the patio, Lis was momentarily disoriented. This place seemed both familiar and foreign. Then she understood why. The lake had risen so high that the shape of the shoreline had changed. What had been a voluptuous outcropping of lawn and reeds was now concave, and a cluster of small rock islands roughly in the shape of the constellation Orion had vanished—completely covered with water.

She turned back to her labors.

The two women hadn't returned to the dam but chose to build the new levee closer to the house, filling and piling sandbags where the culvert met the lawn. Even if the lake were to overflow the dam a line of bags here would, if it held, stop the water from reaching the house. Besides, she decided, they hardly had the time or strength to cart several tons of sand a hundred yards through a rocky culvert slowly filling with water.

Portia filled the bags and Lis dragged or carried them to their impromptu line of defense. As they worked, Lis glanced occasionally at her sister. The rings and crystal necklace were gone and her delicate hands and short, perfect nails—fiery red—were covered by canvas gloves. In place of the black lace headband was a Boston Red Sox cap.

Portia lunged energetically with the shovel, absorbed in the task, scooping huge wads of sand and pitching them into bags. Lis, with years of gardening and landscaping behind her, had always assumed herself the stronger of the two. But she saw now that they were, in strength at least, on par. Thanks, she supposed, to the hours Portia spent on health-club treadmills and racquetball courts. Occasionally the young woman would stop, pull off a glove to see what sort of honorable callus she might be developing, then return to the job. Once, as she gazed out into the forest, Portia twined a strand of hair around her finger and slipped an end into her mouth. Lis had seen her do this earlier in the evening—a nervous habit that she'd perhaps developed recently.

But then, Lis thought, how would I know if she'd picked it up recently or not? She reflected how little she knew of her sister's life. The girl had for all practical purposes left home at eighteen and rarely returned for any length of time. When she had, it was usually for a single night—a Saturday or Sunday dinner—with her current flame in tow. She even spent the majority of holidays elsewhere—usually with boyfriends, sometimes workmates. A Christmas for two in a far-off inn, however romantic, didn't appeal much to Lis. During summer breaks from college Portia would travel with girlfriends, or work at internships in the city. When she'd dropped out of school her junior year, the girl had abandoned her Bronxville apartment and moved to Manhattan. Lis was then working at Ridgeton High School and living in a small rental house in Redding. She'd been hoping that after her sister left Sarah Lawrence, the young woman might come back to the area. But no, Portia smilingly deflected the suggestion, as if it were pure craziness. She added that she *had* to move to New York. It was time for her to "do the city."

Lis remembered wondering what exactly this meant, and why her sister seemed to treat it as an inevitable rite of passage.

What, Lis wondered, was life like when you "did" the city? Did Portia's daytime hours pass quickly or slow? Did she flirt with her boss? Did she gossip? What did she eat for dinner? Where did she buy her laundry soap? Did she snort cocaine at ad-agency parties? Did she have a favorite movie theater? What did she laugh at, *Monty Python* or *Roseanne*? Which newspaper did she read in the morning? Did she sleep only with men?

Lis tried to recall any time in recent years when she and Portia had spoken frequently. During the prelude to their mother's death, she supposed.

Yet even then "frequently" was hardly the word to use.

Seventy-four-year-old Ruth L'Auberget had learned the hopeless diagnosis a year ago August and had immediately taken up the role of Patient—one that, it was no surprise to Lis, her mother seemed born to play. Her monied, Boston *sous*-Society upbringing had taught her to be stoic, her generation to be fatalistic, her husband to expect the worst. The role was, in fact, simply a variation on one that the statuesque, still-eyed woman had been acting for years. A formidable disease had simply replaced a formidable husband (Andrew having by then made his unglamorous exit in the British Air loo).

Until she got sick, the widow L'Auberget had been foundering. A woman in search of a burden. Now, once again, she was in her element.

Buying clothes for a shrinking figure, she chose not the shades she'd always worn—colors that made good backgrounds, beige and taupe and sand—but picked instead the hues of the flowers she grew, reds and yellows and emerald. She wore loud-patterned turbans, not scarves or wigs, and once—to Lis's astonishment—burst into the Chemo Ward announcing to the young nurses, "Hello, dahlings, it's Auntie Mame!"

Only near the very end did she grow sullen and timid—mostly at the thought, it seemed, of an ungainly and therefore embarrassing death. It was during this time that, on morphine, she'd described recent conversations with her husband in such detail that Lis's skin would sting from the goosebumps. Mother only imagined it, Lis recalled thinking—as she'd protested to Owen tonight on the patio.

She'd just imagined it. Of course.

The chills, however, never failed to appear.

Lis had thought that perhaps their mother's illness might bring the sisters closer together. It didn't. Portia spent only slightly more time in Ridgeton during the months of Mrs. L'Auberget's decline than she had before.

Lis was furious at this neglect, and once—when she and her mother had driven into the city for an appointment at Sloan-Kettering—she resolved to confront her sister. Yet Portia preempted her. She'd fixed up one of the bedrooms in the co-op as a homey sickroom and insisted that Lis and Ruth stay with her for several days. She broke dates, took a leave of absence from work and even bought a cookbook of cancer-fighting recipes. Lis still had a vivid, comic memory of the young woman, feet apart, hair in anxious streamers, standing dead center in the tiny kitchen as she slung flour into bowls and vegetables into pans, searching desperately for lost utensils.

So the confrontation was avoided. Yet when Ruth returned home, Portia resumed her distance and in the end the burden of the dying fell on Lis. By now, much had intervened between the sisters, and she'd forgiven Portia for this lapse. Lis was even grateful that only she had been present in the last minutes; it was a time she would rather not have shared. Lis would always remember the curiously muscular touch of her mother's hand on Lis's palm as she finally slipped away. A triplet of squeezes, like a letter in Morse code.

Now Lis suddenly found herself gasping for breath and realized that, in the grip of memory, she'd been working with growing fervor, the pace increasingly desperate. She paused and leaned against the pile of bags, already three-high.

She closed her eyes for a moment and was startled by her sister's voice.

"So." Portia plunged the shovel into the pile of sand with a loud *chunk*. "I guess it's time to ask. Why did you really ask me out?"

14

At her sister's feet Lis counted seven bags, filled, waiting to be piled up on the levee. Portia filled two more and continued, "I didn't have to be here for the estate, right? I could've handled it all in the city. That's what Owen said."

"You haven't been out for a long time. I don't get into the city very much."

"If you mean we don't *see* each other very much, well, that's sure true. But there's something else on your mind, isn't there? Other than sisters socializing."

Lis didn't speak and watched another bag vigorously fill with wet sand.

"What is this," Portia continued, "kiss and make up?"

Lis refused to let herself be stung by the mocking tone. Gripping a bag by the corners she carried it to the culvert and slung it fiercely on top. "Why don't we take five?"

Portia finished filling another bag then planted the shovel and pulled off the gloves, examining a red spot on her index finger. She sat down, beside her sister, on the low wall of bags.

After a moment Lis continued, "I'm thinking of leaving teaching."

Her sister didn't seem surprised. "I never could quite see you as a teacher."

And what exactly *did* she see me as? Lis wondered. She assumed Portia had opinions about her career—and about the rest of her life, for that matter—but couldn't imagine what they might be.

"Teaching's been good to me. I've enjoyed it enough. But I think it's time for a change."

"Well, you're a rich woman now. Live off the fat of the land."

"Well, I'm not going to just quit."

"Why not? Stay home and garden. Watch Oprah and Regis. There're worse lives."

"You know Langdell Nursery?"

"Nope." The young woman squinted, shaking her head. "Oh, wait, that place off 236?"

"We used to go there all the time. With Mother. They'd let us water flowers in the hothouse."

"Vaguely. That's where they had those big bins of onions?"

Lis laughed softly. "Flower bulbs."

"Right. It's still there?"

"It's for sale. The nursery and a landscaping company the family owns."

"Jesus, look." Portia was gazing across the lake into the state park. The water had pushed an old boathouse off its pilings. The ghostly white structure of rotting clapboard dipped slowly into the water.

"The state was going to tear it down." Lis nodded toward the boathouse. "The taxpayers just saved a few dollars, looks like. The nursery, I was saying? . . ." She rubbed her hands together a few times and felt her palms go cold as the nervous sweat evaporated. "I think I'm going to buy the place."

Portia nodded. Again a bit of yellow hair wound between her fingers and the tips of the strands slipped into her mouth. In the muted light, her face seemed particularly pale and her lips black. Had she refreshed her lipstick before coming out here to stack sandbags?

"I need a partner," Lis said slowly. "And I was thinking I'd like it to be you."

Portia laughed. She was a pretty woman and could instantly, as if by turning on a switch, become entirely sensual or charming or cute. Yet she often laughed with a deep breathiness that, Lis felt, instantly killed her appeal. This usually occurred when, as now, she was critical in an obscure way, leaving it to others to deduce their slipups.

Heat bristled at Lis's temples as the blush washed over her face. "I don't know business. Finances, marketing, things like that. You do."

"I'm a media buyer, Lis. I'm not Donald Trump."

"You know more than I do. You're always talking about getting out of advertising. You were thinking about opening a boutique last year."

"Everybody in advertising talks about quitting and opening a boutique. Or a catering company. You and me in business?"

"It's a good deal. Langdell died last year and his wife doesn't want to keep running the place. They're asking three million for everything. The land alone's worth two. Mortgage rates are great now. And Angie said she'd be willing to finance some of it herself, as long as she gets a million and a half at the closing."

"You're serious, aren't you?"

"I need a change, Portia. I love gardens and—"

"No, I think it makes sense for you. I meant, you're serious about *us*. Working together."

"Of course I am. You handle the business and finance, and I handle the product—there, doesn't that sound professional? The 'product'?"

Portia had been staring at the pile of bags she'd filled. She picked one up, carried it to the wall, dropped it into place. "Heavy bastards, aren't they?" she gasped. "Maybe I oughta shovel less."

"I've got a lot of ideas. We'd expand the formal gardens and open a specialty hothouse for roses. We could even have lectures.

Maybe do videos. How to crossbreed. How to start your first garden. You know people in film production. If we work hard, it could really fly."

Portia didn't speak for a minute. "Fact is, I was going to quit anyway after the first of the year. Just stay long enough to get my bonus."

"Really? That's when I was thinking of buying the place. February. Or March."

The young woman added quickly, "No, I mean I was going to take the year off. A couple years maybe. I wasn't going to work at all."

"Oh." Lis straightened one of the sandbags, which teetered between the two women. "And do what?"

"Travel. Club Med it for a while. I wanted to learn how to windsurf. Demon of the sea."

"Just . . . not do anything?"

"I hear that tone, Mother."

Lis fought down the wave of anger. "No, I'm just surprised."

"Maybe I'll do Europe again. I was poor when I did the backpacking routine. And, God, those trips with Mother and Father? The pits. Señor L'Auberget, fascist tour guide. 'Come on, girls, what the hell're you up to? The Louvre closes in two hours. Portia, don't you dare look back at those boys. . . .' Ha, and you—you were probably the only kid in the history of the world who went to bed without dinner because she bitched about leaving . . . what was that?"

"The sculpture gardens at the Rodin museum," Lis said in a soft voice, laughing wanly at the memory. "A culture victim at seventeen."

After a moment Portia said, "I don't think so, Lis. It wouldn't work."

"For a year. Try it. You could sell out your share if it isn't for you."

"I could also lose the money, couldn't I?"

"Yes, I suppose you could. But I won't let it go under."

"What does Owen think?"

Ah, well, there was that.

"He had some reservations, you could say."

You could also say that it nearly broke up their marriage. Lis began thinking about opening a nursery just before their mother died and it was clear that the sisters would be inheriting a large sum of cash. Owen had wanted to put the money into conservative stocks and invest in his law firm, hiring several attorneys and expanding into new offices. That would be the best return on the investment, he'd told her.

But she was adamant. It was *her* money, and a nursery would be perfect for her. If not the Langdells', then another one somewhere nearby. Always the practical counselor, he rattled off a list of concerns.

"You're crazy, Lis. A nursery? It's seasonal. It's weather-dependent. With landscaping, there're major liability issues. You'll have INS problems with the workers. . . . You want to garden, we'll build another one here. We'll get an architect, we can—"

"I want to *work*, Owen. For heaven's sake, I don't tell you to stay home and read law books for fun."

"You can make a living at law," he'd snapped.

The more he argued, the more insistent she grew.

"Jesus, Lis. At best, you'll probably clear a few thousand a year. You'd make more if you put it in the bank and earned passbook interest."

She flung a *Money* magazine down on the table. "There's an article on profitable businesses. Funeral homes are number one. I don't *want* a funeral home."

"Quit being so damn pigheaded! At least in the bank the money's insured. You're willing to risk it all?"

"Mrs. Langdell showed me the books. They've been profitable for fifteen years."

He grew ominously quiet. "So you've talked to her about it already. Before you came to me?"

After a moment she confessed that she had.

"Don't you think you might've asked first?"

"I didn't commit myself."

"You haven't even got your hands on the money yet and you're pretty fucking eager to throw it away."

"It's my *family's* money, Owen."

Most scripts of domestic confrontation would call for a little parrying at this point. Your money? *Your* money? I supported you when the teachers went on strike. . . . When you lost your big bank client two years ago, it was my salary—a teacher's salary!—that got us through. . . . I'm doing all the estate legal work for free. . . . All those months when we couldn't pay the light bill because you joined the country club . . .

But Owen had done then what Owen did best. He closed his mouth and walked away. He grabbed his old .22 pump rifle and walked out into the woods to plink cans and hunt squirrels and rabbits.

For several hours Lis was left alone with the distant pops of gunshots and the memory of the coldness in his eyes when he'd walked out the door.

And for several hours she wondered if she'd lost her husband.

Yet when he returned he was calm. The last he said about the nursery was, "I'd counsel against it but if you want to go ahead anyway, I'll represent you."

She'd thanked him but it was several days before his moodiness vanished.

Tonight, Lis started to tell her sister some of Owen's concerns but Portia wasn't interested. She simply shook her head. "I don't think so."

After a moment Lis asked, "Why?"

"I'm not ready to leave the city yet."

"You wouldn't have to. I'd do the day-to-day things. We'd get together a couple times a month. You could come out here. Or I could go into the city."

"I really need some time off."

"Think about it, at least. Please?" Lis exclaimed breathlessly to her sister's face, pale and obscure in the darkness.

"No, Lis. I'm sorry."

Angry and hurt, Lis picked up a large sandbag and tossed it onto the edge of the levee. She misjudged the distance though and it tumbled into the lake. "Shit!" she cried, trying to retrieve the bag. But it had slipped deep beneath the surface.

Portia spun some strands of hair once more. Lis stood. Several waves splashed loudly at their feet before Lis asked, "What's the real reason?"

"Lis."

"What if I said I didn't want to buy a nursery. What if I was all hot for a boutique on Madison Avenue?"

Portia's mouth tightened but Lis persisted, "What if I said, Let's start a business where you and I travel around Europe and try out restaurants or rate châteaux? What if I said, Let's start a wind-surfing school?"

"Lis. Please."

"Goddamn it! Is it because of Indian Leap? Tell me?"

Portia spun to face her. "Oh, Jesus, Lis." She said nothing more.

The surface of the lake grew light suddenly, as a huge flash, bile green, filled the western horizon. It vanished behind a slab of thick clouds.

Lis finally said, "We've never talked about it. For six months, we haven't said a *word*. It just sits there between us."

"We better finish up here." Portia seized her shovel. "That was some mean son-of-a-bitch lightning. And it wasn't that far away."

"Please," Lis whispered.

A groan filled the night, and they turned to see the boathouse slide completely off the pilings and into the water. Portia said nothing more and started shoveling once again.

Listening to the *chunk* of the sandbags filling, Lis remained near the shore, gazing out over the lake.

As the boathouse sank, a vague white form appeared in the trees behind it. For a moment, Lis was sure that it was an elderly woman limping slowly toward the lake. Lis blinked and stepped closer to shore. The woman's gait suggested she was ill and in pain.

Then, like the boathouse, the apparition eased off the shore and into the water, where it sank beneath the still, onyx surface. A piece of canvas tied to a cleat on the frame, or a six-mil plastic tarp, Lis supposed. Not a woman at all. Not a ghost.

She'd just imagined it. Of course.

The night Abraham Lincoln died, after spending many hours with a horrid wound in the thick mass of sweat-damp hair, the moon that blossomed out of the clouds in the Eastern part of the United State was blood red.

This freak occurrence, Michael Hrubek had read, was verified by several different sources, one of whom was a farmer in Illinois. Standing in a freshly planted cornfield, 1865, April 15, this man looked up into the radiant evening sky, saw the crimson moon and took off his straw hat out of respect because he knew that a thousand miles away a great life was gone.

There was no moon visible tonight. The sky was overcast and turbulent as Hrubek bicycled unsteadily west along Route 236. It was a painstaking journey. He was now accustomed to the mountain bike and was riding as confidently as a Tour de France racer. Still, whenever a crown of light shone over the road before him or behind, he stopped and vaulted to the ground. He'd lie under cover of brush or tree until the vehicle passed then would leap onto his bike once again, his hammish legs pedaling fast in low gear; he didn't know how to upshift.

A flash of light startled him. He looked across a field and saw a police car patrolling slowly, shining a spotlight on a darkened farmhouse. The light clicked out and the car continued east, away from Hrubek. His anxiety notched up a few degrees as he pedaled on, and he found himself thinking of his first run-in with the police.

Michael Hrubek had been twenty years old and the arrest was for rape.

The young man had been attending a private college in upstate New York, an area pretty enough at the height of a vibrant summer but for most of the year as bleak as the depressed economy in the small city and fields surrounding the campus.

During his first semester Michael had been reclusive and fidgety but he'd done well in his studies, especially in his two courses in American history. Between Thanksgiving and Christmas, however, he grew increasingly anxious. His concentration was poor and he seemed unable to make even the simplest decisions—which class assignment to do first, when to go to lunch, whether it was better to brush his teeth before he urinated or after. He spent hour after hour staring out the window of his room.

He was then nearly as large as he was now, with long curly hair, Neanderthal eyebrows grown together and a round face that paradoxically seemed kind as long as he didn't smile or laugh. When he did, his expression—in fact usually one of bewilderment—appeared to be pure malice. He had no friends.

Michael was therefore surprised, one gray March Sunday, to hear a knock on his door. He hadn't showered for several weeks and had been wearing the same jeans and shirt for nearly a month. No one could remember, he least of all, when he had last cleaned the room. His roommate had long ago escaped to a girlfriend's apartment, a desertion that delighted Michael, who was certain that the student had been taking pictures of him while he slept. On this

Sunday he'd spent two hours hunched over his desk, repeatedly reading T. S. Eliot's "The Love Song of J. Alfred Prufrock." He found this task was like trying to read a block of wood.

"Yo, Mike."

"Who is it?"

The visitors were two students—juniors who lived in the dorm. Michael stood in the open door, gazing at them suspiciously. They smiled their clean-cut smiles and asked how he was doing. Michael stared at them and said nothing.

"Mikey, you're working too hard. Come on. We got a party in the rec room."

"Have something to eat, come on."

"I have to *study*!" he whined.

"Naw, naw, come on. . . . Let's party. You're working too totally hard, man. Have something to eat."

Well, Michael *did* like to eat. He ate three big meals a day and snacked constantly. He also tended to acquiesce to people's requests; if he didn't—if he refused to do what they wanted—his gut erupted with fiery bursts of worry. What would they *think* about him? What would they *say*?

"Maybe."

"Hey, excellent. Party down!"

So Michael reluctantly followed the two young men down the hall toward the dorm's common room, where a loud party was in progress. As they passed a darkened bedroom the juniors paused to let Michael precede them. They suddenly swiveled and pushed him into the room, slamming the door shut and tying it closed.

Michael howled in panic, tugging furiously at the knob. He stumbled, looking unsuccessfully for a light. He stormed to the window, ripped down the shade and was about to break the glass and jump forty feet to the grass lawn when he noticed the room's other occupant. He'd seen her at one or two parties. She was an overweight freshman with a round face and curly hair cut very short. She had thick ankles and wore a dozen bracelets around her pudgy wrists. The girl was passed-out drunk, lying on the bed, skirt up to her waist. She wore no panties. Her hand held a glass that contained the dregs of orange juice and vodka. She had apparently regained consciousness long enough to vomit then passed out again.

Michael leaned close and studied her. Instantly, the sight of her genitals (his first glimpse of female private anatomy) and the smell of liquor and puke sent him into paroxysms of fear. He screamed at the insensible girl, "What are you *doing* to me?" Then he flung himself into the door again and again, the huge noise resounding throughout the dormitory. In the hallway outside, laughter pealed. Michael fell back onto the bed, hyperventilating. Claustrophobia clutched him and sweat flowed from every pore. A moment later his mind mercifully shut down and his vision went black. The next thing he remembered was the cruel grip of two security guards, brutally pulling him to his feet. The now-conscious girl, tugging down her skirt, was screaming. Michael's pants were undone and his limp penis hung out, cut and bloodied by the zipper of his trousers.

Michael recalled nothing of what had happened. The girl claimed she had just gone to bed, having caught the flu. She'd opened her eyes and found Michael spreading her legs and penetrating her violently, despite her desperate protests. Police were called, parents notified. Michael spent the night in jail, under the cautious eye of two very uncomfortable deputies, unprepared for a prisoner who glared at them and threatened to make them "dead fuckers" if they didn't bring him a history book from his room.

The evidence was in conflict. Although there were traces of three different condom lubricants found in and around the girl's vagina, Michael wasn't wearing a condom when the guards captured him nor were any located in the room. The defense lawyer's tack was that the girl herself had lifted Michael's penis from his jeans and alleged rape, rather than admit that she'd taken on a succession of students after drinking herself semiconscious—a theory that, while politically incorrect, might very well have appealed to the jury.

On the other hand there were several purported witnesses to the crime, including the girl herself. Then too Michael had threatened or glared at half the campus at one time or another—particularly women.

But the most damning evidence of all: Michael Hrubek himself —a big, scary boy, more than twice the girl's size, who'd been caught, the prosecutor was only too pleased to point out, with his pants down. Nailing shut his own coffin, Michael grew incoherent after the incident and began to mutter violent epithets. Taking the stand in court would have been a disaster. The lawyer pled him down to one count of sexual assault and he was given probation on condition that he withdraw from school and voluntarily commit himself to a state hospital near his home, where he'd undergo a treatment program for violent sex offenders.

After six months he was discharged from the hospital and returned to his parents' home.

Once he was back in Westbury, reason and madness rapidly began to merge. One day, the autumn after the rape, Michael announced to his mother that he wanted to return to college. He added, "I'm only going to take history. They better let me do that. Oh, and I want to become a priest. I'm not going to study anything else. No math, no English, no al-ge-*bra*! Just fucking forget about it! I'm only going to study *history*."

His bleary-eyed mother, lolling in her unmade bed, her blond hair stiff as straw, laughed in astonishment at his demands. "Go back to college? Are you serious? Look what you did! Do you know what you did to that girl?"

No, Michael *didn't* know what he'd done. He had no idea. All he remembered was some girl lying about him and because of that he'd been forced to abandon his precious history classes. "She's a fucker! She lied! *Why* can't I go back? Aren't I *fashionable* enough to go to school? Well, aren't I? Priests are very fashionable. Someday I'll write a *his*-tory about them. They often fuck little boys, you know."

"Go to your room!" his mother tearfully shouted, and he—a man in his twenties, a man twice her size—scurried off like a whipped dog.

Often he'd whine, "Please? I want to go back to *school!*" He promised to study hard and become one fucker of a priest to make her happy. He said he'd wear a crown of thorns on his bloody head and make people rise from their graves.

"Jesus wore thorns because He *rose* from the dead," he explained one day to her. "That's why roses have thorns."

"I'm going out, Michael," she would cry.

"Are you *go*-ing to run away from me? Where are you *go*-ing? To al-ge-*bra* class? Are you going to wear a bra while a priest fucks you?"

His mother left the house. She no longer called him her little soldier boy. She no longer had nails as red as burning cigarette embers, and the masks of her eyes often ran in streaks down the matte skin of her cheeks.

Oh, Mama, what are you wearing? Take that hat off your head. Take off that crown. All those bloody thorns! I don't like that, not one bit. Please! I'm sorry for what I said about you and the soldiers. Please, please, *please*, take that off!

It was an extremely agitated Michael Hrubek who, upon this damp night in November, bicycled doggedly down Route 236 at twenty miles an hour, lost in these hard memories—which was why he didn't hear the police car, dark and silent, until it was within ten feet of the bike's rear wheel. The lights and siren burst to life.

"Oh God oh God oh God!" Hrubek screamed. Panic exploded throughout his body.

A voice came over the loudspeaker, jarring as a firecracker. "You there! Stop that bicycle and get off." A spotlight was trained on the back of Hrubek's head.

John Cops! he thought. Agents! FBI! Hrubek coasted to a stop and the deputies stepped from their squad car.

"Just climb off that, young man."

Hrubek swung awkwardly off the bike. The men cautiously approached. One whispered, "He's a mountain. He's huge."

"All right there. Could we see some identification?"

Fucking fucker conspirators, Hrubek thought. Politely he asked, "Are you federal agents?"

"Agents?" One of them chuckled. "No, we're just police officers. From Gunderson."

"Step over here, sir. You have a driver's license?"

Hrubek sat down, his back to the officers, and bowed his head.

The policemen looked at one another, wondering how they might deal with this. Hrubek upped the ante by crying out, "I'm soooo upset! He took everything. He hit me on the head with a rock. *Look* at my hand." He held up his scraped palm. "I've been *look*-ing for help."

They continued forward but stopped a safe distance away. "Somebody attacked you, you say? Are you hurt? If you could just let us see some ID."

"Is it him?" one asked.

"We just want to see some identification, sir. A driver's license. Anything."

"He took my wallet. He took everything."

"You've been robbed?"

"There were several of them. Took my wallet and my watch. That watch," Hrubek reported solemnly, "was a present from my mother. If you'd *watched* the roads better, you might've prevented a serious crime."

"I'm sorry if you've had some misfortune, sir. Could you give us your name and address. . . ."

"John W. Booth is my name."

"Didn't think it was that," one cop said to the other, as if speaking in front of an infant.

"Don't recall. The notice said he's harmless."

"May be, but he's big."

One cop walked closer to Hrubek, who rocked and moaned in mournful tears. "We'd appreciate you standing up, Johnnie, just coming over to the car. People at the hospital're worried about you. We want to take you back there." In a singsong voice he added, "Wouldn't you like to go home? Get some pie and milk maybe? Some nice apple pie?" He stood behind Hrubek, training his flashlight on the man's empty hands then shining it again on the back of the glossy and somewhat blue head.

"Thank you, sir. You know, I would like to be getting back, now that you mention it. I miss the place." Hrubek turned and grinned amiably as he reached up very slowly to shake the officer's hand. The policeman too smiled—in curiosity at the young man's sincere gesture—and gripped Hrubek's meaty fist, realizing too late that the madman was intending to break his wrist. The bone snapped and, shrieking, the officer dropped to his knees, the flashlight falling onto the ground beside him. His partner reached for his gun but Hrubek had already trained the stolen Colt on him.

"Nice try," he announced with damp lips that pulled into a wry smile. "Drop that, drop that!"

The cop did. "Oh, Jesus."

Hrubek took the injured cop's gun from his holster and tossed it away. The man huddled on the ground, cradling his wrist.

"Look, fellow," his partner pled, "you're going to get in nothing but trouble over this."

Hrubek chewed on a fingernail then he looked down at the cops.

"You can't stop me. I can *do* it. I'm *going* to do it, and I'm going to do it quickly!" These words rose like a mad battle cry. He shook a fist above his head.

"Please, young man, put that gun down." The injured policeman's voice broke and his eyes and nose dripped pitifully. "Nothing serious's happened. Nobody's been really hurt yet."

Hrubek turned a triumphant eye on him. He spat out, "Oh, nice *try*, John Cop. But that's where you're wrong. *Everybody*'s been hurt. Everybody, everybody, everybody! And it's not over yet."

Owen Atcheson parked his truck along Route 236 next to a large, freshly turned field about seven miles west of the high rock overlook where he'd located Hrubek's nest. As anticipated, he'd found deep indentations of footsteps, indicating Hrubek was moving parallel to the road. From the depth and spacing of the toe prints it was clear he was moving fast, running.

Owen stopped at a closed gas station and used the pay phone to call the Marsden Inn. The clerk told him that Mrs. Atcheson and her sister had called and said they'd be delayed some. They hadn't checked in yet.

"Delayed? Did they say why?"

"No, sir, they didn't. Is there any message?"

Owen debated. He thought of trying to encode a message for her: Tell her the visitor's heading west but she's not to call anyone about it. . . . But there was too much risk that the clerk would be suspicious or get the message wrong.

Owen said, "No, I'll try them at home."

But there was no answer at the house. Just missed them, he thought. He'd call them at the Inn later.

The night was very dark now, the cloud cover complete, the air growing colder, compressing around him. He used his flashlight sparingly, only when he thought he saw a clue and even then lowering the light almost to the ground before clicking it on, to limit the radiation of the light. He then moved on—but slowly, very slowly. Every soldier knows—as between the hunter and the hunted, the prey has the vastly greater advantage.

Owen fell several times, catching his boot on a fence wire or forsythia tendril. He went down hard, always rolling and absorbing the impact with his shoulder and sides, never risking breaking a finger or wrist. He saw no more traps. Only at one point did Owen despair. The trail vanished completely. This happened in a vast grassy field, twenty acres square and bordered on all sides with dense woods. Owen was two hundred yards from Route 236. He stood in the center of this field and looked around him. The field extended through a break in the long line of rocky hills and offered an easy route south toward train tracks and more populated parts of the county. Freight trains came through here regularly and it was conceivable that Hrubek had leapt onto one. Or maybe he'd simply continued through the notch in the hills south toward Boyleston, a town that had both Amtrak and Greyhound stations.

Losing hope, Owen moved aimlessly through the grass, pausing to listen for footsteps, and hearing only owls or distant truck horns or the eerie white noise of an expansive autumn night. After ten minutes of meandering he noticed a glint coming from a line of trees west of him. He headed instinctively toward it. At the grove of maples he went into a crouch and moved slowly through a cluster of saplings until he came to a break in the foliage. With his gun he pushed aside a bough of dew-soaked hemlock, inhaling in surprise as drops of water fell with chill pinpricks on his neck and face.

Walking in slow circles around the old MG, Owen studied the ground. He kicked aside a white animal skull. He recognized it instantly as a ferret's. There were dozens of footprints and tire prints covering the asphalt and the shoulder. Some seemed to be Hrubek's but they were largely obliterated by people who had been here after him. He saw dog prints too and wondered momentarily if the trackers had learned that Hrubek was going west. But there was evidence of only one animal, not the three that he'd seen pursuing Hrubek from the site of his escape.

He circled the car again, weaving over the shoulder and through the bushes nearby. No sign of Hrubek's prints in any direction. Hands on hips, he glanced at the car once more. This time he noticed the bike rack but then he immediately dismissed the idea that Hrubek had stolen a cycle. What kind of escapee, he reasoned, would make a getaway on a bike, riding down open highways?

But wait. . . . Michael Hrubek was a man whose madness had its own logic. A bicycle? Why not? Owen examined the road around the car and found faint tread marks, rather wide ones—either balloon tires or those of a bike ridden by a heavy cyclist. He glanced back at the car. The carrier rack seemed broken as if the bike had been removed by sheer force.

Owen continued to follow the tread marks. At the intersection of this country lane and Route 236 he found where the rider had paused, perhaps debating which way to go.

He was not surprised to find, beside the tread, the clear imprint of Hrubek's boot.

Nor was he surprised to find that the rider had decided to turn west.

15

The house was little more than a shotgun cabin at the end of a dirt-and-rock road winding through this scruffy forest. The BMW squealed to a stop in a rectangle of mud amid discarded auto parts, sheet metal, termite-chewed firewood and oil drums torch-cut as if someone had intended to make a business of manufacturing barbecues but gave up after running out of acetylene, or desire.

Richard Kohler climbed out of the car and walked to the cabin. Rubbing his deep-set red eyes with a scrawny knuckle, he knocked on the screen door. No answer, though he heard the tinny, cluttered sound of a TV from inside. He rapped again, louder.

When the door opened he smelled liquor before he smelled wood smoke, and there was a lot of wood smoke to smell.

"Hello, Stuart."

After a long pause the man responded, "Didn't expect to see you. Guess I might've. Raining yet? It's supposed to be a son-of-a-bitch storm."

"You mind if I come in for a few minutes?"

"My girlfriend, she's out tonight." Stuart Lowe didn't move from the doorway.

"It won't take long."

"Well."

Kohler stepped past the orderly and into the small living room.

The couch was draped with two blankets and had the appearance of a sickbed. It was an odd piece of furniture—bamboo frame, cushions printed with orange and brown and yellow blotches. It reminded Kohler poignantly of Tahiti, where he'd gone on his honeymoon. And where he'd gone after his divorce, which had occurred thirty-three months later. Those two weeks represented his only vacations in the last seven years.

Kohler chose a high-backed chair to sit in. The orderly, no longer in his regulation blue jumpsuit, was now wearing jeans and a T-shirt and white socks without shoes. His arms were covered with bandages, his left eye was blackened, and his forehead and cheeks were flecked with small puncture wounds brown-stained from Betadine. He now sat back on the couch and glanced at the blankets as if he were surprised to find the bedclothes sitting out.

On the TV Jackie Gleason was screaming in a shrill and thoroughly unpleasant way at Audrey Meadows. Lowe muted the program. "They snag him yet?" Lowe asked, glancing at the phone, by which he presumably would already have learned if they'd snagged him.

Kohler told him no.

Lowe nodded and laughed vacantly at Jackie Gleason shaking his fist.

"I want to ask you a few things about what happened," Kohler asked conversationally.

"Not much to tell."

"Still."

"How'd you hear about it? Adler wanted it kept quiet."

"I've got my spies," Kohler said, and did not smile. "What happened?"

"Uh-hum. Well, we seen him and we run after him. But it was pretty dark. It was *damn* dark. He must've knowed the lay of the land pretty good and he jumped over this ravine but we fell into it."

Lowe closed his mouth and once more examined the screen, on which an automobile commercial now played. "Look at all that writing on there. Giving all that financing crap. Who can read that in three seconds? That's stupid, they do that."

The room wasn't shabby so much as dim. The prints on the walls weren't bad seascapes but they were dusky. The carpet was gray, as were the blankets that Lowe was pretending he hadn't been wrapped in five minutes before.

"How you feeling?"

"Nothing broke. Sore, but not like Frank. He took the worst of it."

"What'd Adler say to you?"

Lowe found some serviceable words and submitted them. Nothing much. Wanted to know how Lowe was feeling. Where Hrubek seemed to be going. "Truth be told, he wasn't real happy we dropped the ball in the first place and he got loose."

Across the bottom of the TV screen ran a banner announcing that a tornado had touched down in Morristown, killing two people. The National Weather Service, the streaming type reported, had extended the tornado and flash-flood warnings until 3:00 a.m. Both men stared at these words intently and both men forget them almost as soon as the bulletin ended.

"When you found him tonight, did Michael say anything?"

"Can't hardly recall. I think something about us wearing clothes and him not. Maybe something else. I don't know. I was never so scared in my life."

Kohler said, "Frank Jessup was telling me about Michael's meds."

"*Frank* knows about that? I didn't think he did. Wait, maybe I mentioned it to him."

The doctor nodded at the screen. "Art Carney's my favorite."

"He's a funny one, sure is. I like Alice. She knows what she's about."

"Frank wasn't sure how long Michael'd been cheeking them. He said two days."

"Two?" Lowe shook his head. "Where'd he hear that? Try five."

"I think they want to keep it quiet."

Lowe began to relax. "That's what Adler told me. It's not *my* business. I mean, with . . ." The comfort vanished instantly and Kohler noticed Lowe's hand seeking the satin strip on the blanket beside him. "And I just spilled the beans, didn't I? Oh, fuck," he spat out, bitterly discouraged at how easily his mind had been picked.

"I had to know, Stu. I'm his doctor. It's my job to know."

"And it's my job, period. And I'm gonna lose it. Shit. Why'd you trick me?"

Kohler wasn't giving any thought to Lowe's employment. He felt his skin crackling with shock at this confirmation of his hunch. In his last session before the escape, yesterday, Michael Hrubek had looked Kohler in the eye and had *lied* about the Thorazine. He'd said he was taking all his meds and the dosage was working well. Three thousand milligrams! And the patient had given it up purposefully and lied about doing so after he'd been off the pills for five days. And he'd lied very well. Unlike psychopaths, schizophrenic patients are rarely duplicitous in such calculating ways.

"You've got to come clean, Stu. Hrubek's a time bomb. I don't think Adler understands that. Or if he does he doesn't much care." Kohler added soothingly, "You know Michael better than most of the *doctors* at Marsden. You've got to help me."

"I got to keep my job is what I've got to do. I'm making twenty-one thousand a year and spending twenty-two. Adler'll have my nuts for what I told you already."

"Ron Adler isn't God."

"I'm not saying anything else."

"Okay, Stuart, you gonna help me, or do I have to make some phone calls?"

"Fuck." A can of beer flew from the big hand into the gray wall and with a spray of foam fell gushing onto the dingy shag carpet. It was suddenly vitally important for Stuart Lowe to tend the embers of his fire. He leapt up and pitched three fresh logs onto the heap of the dying flames. A gorgeous cascade of orange sparks bounced to the hearth. Lowe returned to the couch and said nothing for a moment. Kohler believed this meant that he accepted the terms of the agreement, which was of course no agreement at all. The signal of surrender was the soft pop as the TV was shut off.

"Did he stockpile all the Thorazine or flush it? You have any idea?"

"We found it. He stockpiled it."

"How much?"

Lowe said resignedly, "Five full days. Thirty-two hundred a day. This'll be the sixth."

"When you saw him tonight, was there any indication of what he had in mind?"

"He was just standing there in the buff, looking at us like he was surprised. But he wasn't surprised at all."

"What do you mean?"

"Nothing," Lowe spat out. "I don't mean a fucking thing."

"Tell me what he said. Exactly."

"Didn't *Frank* tell you? You already talked to him." He looked at Kohler bitterly to see if he had been as big a fool as he thought. The doctor had no choice but to oblige. "Frank's still recovering from surgery. He won't be conscious till morning."

"Jesus Christ."

"*What* did Michael say? Come on, Stu."

"Something about a death. He had a death to go to. I don't know. Maybe he meant a funeral or graveyard. I was pretty shook, you know. I was trying to fight him off Frank."

Kohler didn't respond and the orderly continued, "With those rubber things they give us."

"The truncheons?"

"I tried. I was trying to get him upside the head but he don't feel no pain. You know that."

"That's one thing about Michael," Kohler agreed, observing what a sorrowful liar Lowe was and feeling pity for this man, who'd obviously abandoned his partner to die a terrible death.

"That's all I heard. Then Michael grabbed away the club and come after me. . . ."

"Now tell me what Adler really said to you."

Lowe exhaled air through puffed-out cheeks. He finally said, "I wasn't supposed to say nothing about the meds. To nobody. And he wanted to know if Michael'd said anything about that lady in Ridgeton. He sent her a note or something."

"What lady?"

"Some broad at his trial, I don't know. Adler asked me if Michael'd ever mentioned her."

"Did he?"

"Not to me he didn't."

"What about this note?"

"I don't know nothing about it. Adler said to keep quiet about that too."

"When did he send it to her?"

"How the fuck should I know?"

"What's this woman's name?"

"You're going to ruin me, aren't you? I didn't get your patient back and you're going to fuck me over. Why don't you just admit it?"

"What's her *name*, Stu?"

"Liz something. Wait. Liz Atcheson, I think."

"Is there anything else you can tell me?"

"No," Lowe blurted so quickly all Kohler could do was fill the ensuing silence with his serene, unyielding gaze. The orderly finally said miserably, "Well, the wire."

"Wire?"

"I told Adler and Grimes and they made me swear I wouldn't say anything. Oh, Jesus . . . What a time I've had."

Kohler didn't move. His red, stinging eyes gazed at Lowe, who said *sotto voce*, as if Ronald Adler were making this a threesome, "We didn't fall."

"Tell me, Stu. *Tell* me."

"We could've jumped over that ravine easy. But Michael strung a trip wire for us. He knew we were coming. Strung a piece of fishline or bell wire and led us over it."

Kohler was dumbfounded. "What are you saying?"

"What am I saying?" Lowe blurted furiously. "Aren't you listening? Aren't you *listening*? I'm saying your patient may be off his brain candy and may be a schizo but he was fucking clever enough to lead us into a *trap*. And he damn near killed both of us." The orderly sealed his testimony by clicking the television back on and slouched into the couch, refusing to say anything more.

Passing over the Gunderson town line Trenton Heck braked deftly with his left foot as he skidded around a deer that stepped into the road and stopped to see what a collision with a one-ton pickup might do to her.

He eased back into the right lane and continued caroming down Route 236. He was driving like a teenager and he knew it, even taking the extreme measure of strapping a very unhappy Emil into the passenger seat with the blue canvas seatbelt, which the hound immediately began to chew through. Behind the truck swirled a wake of dust and bleached autumn leaves.

"Stop," Heck barked over the roar of the engine, knowing that "Don't chew," let alone "Leave that seatbelt be," would register in Emil's mind as mere human grunts, worth ignoring. The familiar command was pointless, however, and Heck let the matter go. "Good fellow," Heck said in a rare moment of sentiment, and reached over to scratch the big head, which slipped away in irritation.

"Damn," he muttered, "I'm doing it again." He realized that the hound's evasive maneuver reminded him of the way Jill had dodged away from his embrace the day after she'd served him with papers.

Got to stop thinking about that girl, he now ordered.

But of course he didn't.

"Mental cruelty and abandonment," Heck had read after the process server left. He hadn't even comprehended at first what these documents were. Abandonment? He thought they meant Jill herself was being sued for leaving the scene of an accident. She was a terrible driver. Then like a firecracker going off inside him he understood. Heck had been little good for anything for the month after that. It seemed that all he did was work with Emil and spend hours debating the separation with Jill—or rather with Jill's picture, since by then she'd moved out. Sitting on the bed where they'd romped so friskily he tried to recall her arguments. It seemed that he hadn't upheld his end of a vague bargain that had been made the morning following one particularly romantic, playful night. Their seventh date. At sunrise he'd found her plowing through his kitchen cabinets, looking for the Bisquick mix, and he'd interrupted the frenzied search to blurt a proposal. Jill had squealed and in her eagerness to hug him dropped a bag of flour. It detonated with a large white mushroom cloud. With happiness in her eyes and a little-girl pout on her lips, she cried, talking at curious length about the home that had been denied her all her life.

The marriage had been a stormy union, Heck was the first to admit. When you were on Jill's side, heaven's gate opened up and she rained her good nature on you and if you were her man there were plenty of other rewards. But if you didn't share her opinion or—good luck—if you opposed her, then the flesh over her cheekbones tightened and her tongue somehow contracted and she commenced to take you down.

Trenton Heck in fact had not been all that certain about getting married. Unreasonably, he was disappointed at having a fiancée with one syllable in her name. And when Jill grew angry—he couldn't always predict when this would happen—she became a tiny fireball. Her eyebrows knit and her voice grew husky, like the tone he believed hookers took when confronting obnoxious clients. She would mope aggressively if he said they couldn't afford a pair of high-heeled green shoes dusted with sequins, or a microwave with a revolving carousel.

"You're icky to me, Trenton. And I don't like it one bit."

"Jill, honey, baby . . ."

But the fact remained that she was a woman who'd leap into his arms at unexpected times, even at the mall, and kiss his ear wetly. She would smile with her entire face when he came home and talk nonstop about some silliness in a way that made the whole evening seem to him like good crystal and silver. And he could never forget the way she'd wake suddenly in the middle of the night, roll over on top of him, and drive her head into his collarbone, humping with so much energy that he fought hard not to move for fear it would be over too fast.

Slowly though the pouts began to outnumber the smiles and humps. The money, which was like a lubricant between their spirits, grew sparse when he was denied a raise and the mortgage on the trailer was adjusted upward. Heck began to like Jill's waitress friends and their husbands less and less; there was much drinking in that group and more silliness than seemed normal for people in their thirties. These were clues and he supposed he'd been aware of them all along. But when he finally understood that she really *meant* mental cruelty and abandonment—*his* mental cruelty and *his* abandonment—it knocked the wind clean out of him.

Exactly twenty-two months ago, at nine-forty-eight one Saturday night, Jill let slam the aluminum door of their trailer for the last time and went to live by herself in Dillon. The ultimate insult was that she moved into a mobile-home park. "Why didn't you just stay with *me*?" he blurted. "I thought you left because you wanted a house."

"Oh, Trent," she moaned hopelessly, "you don't understand nothing, do you? Not . . . a . . . thing."

"Well, you're in a trailer park, for God's sake!"

"Trent!"

"What'd I say?"

So Jill left to live in a mobile home somehow better than the one that Trenton Heck could offer her and once there, he supposed, entertain men friends. Billy Mosler, Heck's truck-driving buddy from next door, seemed relieved at the breakup. "Trenton, she wasn't for you. I'm not going to say anything bad about Jill because that's not my way—"

Watch it, you prick, Heck thought, eyeing his friend belligerently.

"—but she was too dippy for you. Bad choice in a woman. Don't look at me that way. You can do better."

"But I *loved* her," Heck said, his anger sadly tamed by a memory of Jill making him a lunch of egg salad one autumn afternoon. "Oh, damn, I'm whining, aren't I? Damn."

"You didn't *love* her," Billy Mosler said sagely. "You were *in love* with her. Or, *in lust* with her, more like. See the difference?"

Watch it, prick. Heck recovered enough to begin glaring once more.

The worst of the sting wore off after a few months though still he mourned. He drove past her restaurant a hundred times and would call her often to talk to her about the few things they could still talk about, which was not much. Many times he got her answering machine. What the hell does a waitress need an answering machine for, he brooded, except to take men's phone calls? He grew despairing when the machine picked up on the second ring, which meant that someone had called before him. Heck saw his ex-wife all over the county. At Kmart, at picnics, driving in cars he didn't recognize, in Jo-Jo's steakhouse, in liquor-store parking lots as she hiked her skirt up to adjust her slip, rolled at the waist to compensate for her being four foot eleven.

There weren't this many Jills in the universe but Trenton Heck saw them just the same.

Tonight, his ex-wife fading very reluctantly from his mind, Heck turned off the highway. Emil stirred with relief as the truck braked to a fast stop and the evil seatbelt came off. His master then hooked up the harness and track line and together they bounded off down the road.

Emil easily picked up Hrubek's scent and trotted down the highway, mimicking more or less the bicycle's passage. Because they were on the asphalt with good visibility, Heck saw no need to keep the hound short-lined; Hrubek wouldn't be setting traps on the surface of the road. They made good time, coursing past abandoned shacks and farms and lowlands and pumpkin fields. Still, after passing two intersections—and verifying that the madman was continuing west on Route 236—Heck ordered Emil back to the truck. Because of the bicycle, which Hrubek could pedal at fifteen or twenty miles an hour, Heck continued to drop-track—driving for several miles then stopping just long enough to let Emil make sure they were still on scent. For a diligent dog like Emil to follow a bicyclist was certainly possible—especially on a damp night like this—but doing so would exhaust him quickly. Then too Heck, with his damaged leg, was hardly up for a twenty-mile run after a man on wheels.

As he drove, scanning the road before him for a bicycle reflector or Hrubek's back, Trenton Heck thought about the meeting with Richard Kohler. He recalled the doctor's slight scowl when Heck had rejected his offer. This reinforced Heck's fear that maybe he'd blown it bad, that he'd chosen exactly the opposite from what a smart person would've picked. He often had trouble choosing the sensible thing, the thing everybody else just *knew* was best. The thing that *both* Jill and his father would appraise and say, "Damn good choice, boy."

He supposed in some ways it *was* crazy to turn down that money. But when he actually pictured taking the check, folding it up, going home—no, no, he just couldn't have done it. Maybe God hadn't made him like Emil, doling out to him a singular, remarkable knack. But Trenton Heck felt in his heart that if he had any purpose at all, it was to spend his hours tracking behind his dog through wilderness just like this. Even if he never found Hrubek tonight, even if he never caught a *glimpse* of him, being here *had* to be better than sitting in front of the tube with a quart of beer in his hand and Emil fidgeting on the back deck.

What troubled Heck more than turning down Kohler's offer was altogether different, maybe something more dangerous. If it was really his goal to catch Hrubek before he hurt someone, then why didn't he just call Don Haversham and tell him that Hrubek had changed direction? Heck was in Gunderson now and would be coming up on Cloverton soon. Both towns had police departments and, despite the storm, probably a few men to spare for a roadblock. Calling Haversham, he thought, was the prudent thing to do, the proper procedure. It promised the least risk to everyone.

But of course if the local police or troopers caught Hrubek, Adler would surely balk at paying Heck the ten thousand.

So, steeped in guilt and uneasiness, Heck pressed the stiff accelerator with his left foot and continued after his prey, speeding west in secret and under cover of the night—just like, he laughed grimly, Michael Hrubek himself.

He was twenty-two miles from Ridgeton when the idea of an automobile slipped into his mind and rooted there.

A car'd be so much *nicer* than a bicycle, so much more *fashionable.* Hrubek had mastered pedaling and now found the bike a frustrating way to travel. It flicked sideways when it hit rocks and there were long stretches of inclines that required him to ride so slowly that he could have walked faster. His teeth ached from the air he sucked into his lungs with the effort of low-gear pedaling. When he hit a bump the heavy animal traps bounced and jabbed him in the kidney. But more than anger at the bike, Hrubek simply felt the *desire* for a car. He believed he had the confidence to drive. He'd fooled the orderlies and whipped the cops and tricked all the fucker conspirators who were after him.

And now he wanted a car.

He recalled the time he'd pumped a tank of gas for Dr. Anne when she'd driven Hrubek and several other patients to a bookstore in a mall near Trevor Hill Psychiatric Hospital. Knowing—and compulsively reciting—the statistics on auto fatalities on American highways, he was terrified at the thought of the drive but reluctantly agreed to go along. The psychiatrist asked him to sit in the front seat. When they stopped at the gas station, she asked, "Michael, will you help me fill up the tank?"

"Noooo."

"Please?"

"Not on your life. It's not safe and it's not fashionable."

"Let's do it together."

"Who knows what comes out of those pumps?"

"Come on, Michael. Get out of the car."

"Nice try."

But he *did* it—opening the tank door, unscrewing the lid, turning on the pump, squeezing the nozzle handle. Dr. Anne thanked Hrubek for his help and, glowing with pride, he climbed back into the front seat, snapping his belt on without her telling him to do so. On their next outing she let him drive the gray Mercedes through the hospital parking lot, arousing the envy of the patients and the amusement—and awe—of several doctors and nurses.

Yep, he now decided, the bike's got to go.

He coasted to the bottom of a long hill, where he stopped at a darkened gas station, its windows spattered with mud and grease. What had caught his interest was an old lime-green Datsun parked beside the air pump. Hrubek climbed off the bicycle. The car's door was unlocked. He sat in the driver's seat, smelling oil and mold. He practiced driving. He was very tense at first then relaxed and gradually remembered what he knew about cars. He moved the steering wheel. He put the gearshift lever in D. He practiced pushing the accelerator and the brake.

He looked down at the wheel pedestal and saw a key in the ignition. He turned it. Silence. He climbed out. He supposed the car might need a battery or maybe gasoline. He opened the hood and found that what the car needed, however, was an engine. Some fucker had stolen it, he observed, and slammed the hood closed.

Can't trust anybody.

Hrubek walked to the front of the store and looked in. A soda machine, a snack machine, a wire tray holding boxes of doughnuts and pastries. Twinkies. He liked Twinkies. He muttered a line he had once heard on TV: "A wholesome snack." Repeating this phrase over and over he walked to the back of the station. "Be smart," he whispered. "Use the back door." He hoped there was an engine lying around inside. Could he install it himself in the green car? he wondered. You probably just plugged them into the engine compartment. (Hrubek knew all about plugs; because the electrical appliances in his parents' house contained listening devices or cameras, Michael had settled into the daily routine of unplugging them every morning. The VCR in the Hrubek household was perpetually flashing 12:00).

He strode to the back door of the gas station and knocked out the glass in the window then undid the deadbolt. He walked inside and perused the place. He found no ready-to-mount auto engines, which was an immense disappointment though this setback was largely mitigated by the doughnuts on the rack by the door. He immediately ate an entire package and put another in his backpack.

Taste That Beats the Others Cold promised the torn and faded poster taped to the ancient Pepsi machine in the front of the store. He easily ripped open its door and pulled out two bottles of soda. He had forgotten all about glass containers—in mental hospitals you get soda in plastic cups or not at all. He popped the cap off with his teeth and, sitting down, he began to drink.

In five minutes the parking lot outside turned silver, then white. This attracted Hrubek's attention and he rose, walking to the greasy glass to determine the source of the light. A glistening metallic-blue 4x4 truck pulled into the driveway. The door opened and the driver climbed out. She was a pretty woman with frothy blond hair. To a phone pole beside the air pump she taped a poster advertising a church auction to be held tomorrow night.

"Will they auction their *memorabilia*?" Hrubek whispered. "Will they sell their memory-*labia*? Will the priest stick his finger in your *pussy*?" He glanced inside the truck. The woman's passenger was a teenage girl, her daughter, it seemed. He continued, speaking now in a conversational tone, addressing the girl. "Oh, you're very beautiful. Do you like al-ge-*bra*? Are you wearing one over your tits? Did you know that ninety-nine percent of schizophrenics have big cocks? The *cock* crowed when Jesus got betrayed—just like Eve. Say, is the priest going to stick his *snake* in you? You may know that as a serpent."

The driver returned to the truck. Oh, she looks beautiful, Hrubek thought, and couldn't decide whom he liked best, mother or daughter. The 4x4 turned back onto the highway and a moment later pulled into a driveway or side road a hundred yards west on Route 236. It vanished. He stood for a long moment at the window, then blew hot breath onto the cold glass in front of him, leaving a large white circle of condensation, in the center of which he drew a very good likeness of an apple, complete with leaves and stem and pierced by what appeared to be a worm hole.

Their Maginot Line, four feet high, was starkly illuminated by another sudden flash of distant lightning.

The women, both exhausted, stepped back from their handiwork as they waited for thunder that never sounded.

Portia said, "We oughta break a bottle of champagne over it." She leaned heavily on the shovel.

"Might not hold."

"Fucking well better." The water in the culvert leading to the dam was already six inches high.

"Let's finish taping the greenhouse and get out of here."

They stowed the tools and Lis pulled a battered tarp over the depleted pile of sand. She still felt hurt by Portia's rebuff earlier but, as they strolled back to the house like two oil-workers at day's end, Lis nonetheless had a sudden urge to put her arm around her sister's shoulders. Yet she hesitated. She could picture the contact but not the effect and that was enough to stop the gesture. Lis recalled bussing cheeks with relatives on holidays, she recalled handshakes, she recalled palms on buttocks.

That was the extent of physical contact in the L'Auberget family.

Lis heard a clatter not far away. The wind had pushed over a set of aluminum beach chairs beside the garage. She told her sister she was going to put them away and started down the hill. Portia headed up to the house.

Pausing in the driveway, Lis felt a sharp gust of wind—an outrider of the storm. Ripples swept across the surface of the lake and a corner of the tarp covering the sand snapped like a gunshot. Then calm returned, as if the breeze were a shiver passing through a body.

In the silence that followed she heard the car.

The tires crunched on the glistening white stone chips that she and Owen had spread in the driveway last summer during a heat spell. She'd feared then for their hearts under the scalding sun and insisted that they finish the job after dusk. Lis Atcheson knew that the visitor tonight was driving over fragments of premium marble from a quarry somewhere in New England. But for some reason the thought came to her that the sound was of wheels on crushed bone and once there the horrid image would not leave.

The car moved urgently through the stand of pines through which the serpentine driveway ran. It pulled into the parking area, paused then headed toward her. Blinded by the beams, she couldn't identify the vehicle, which stopped a dozen yards away.

Lis stood with arms crossed, her feet separated, frozen like a schoolgirl playing statue. For a long moment neither she nor the driver moved. She faced the car, whose engine was still running, lights on. Finally, before uneasiness became fear, she cleared her throat and walked forward into piercing shafts of white light.

16

"They haven't caught him yet?"

Lis motioned with her hand toward the back door and Richard Kohler preceded her into the kitchen.

"No, I'm afraid not." He stepped to the counter and set a small backpack on the butcher block. He seemed quite possessive about it. His thin face was alarmingly pale.

"Lis, there's a car—"

Portia walked into the doorway and paused, glancing at Kohler. Lis introduced them.

"*Portia?*" Kohler repeated. "Don't hear that name much nowadays."

She shrugged and neither sister said a word about the burdens of being the daughter of a man utterly devoted to the business of fortified wine.

"I'm going to tape the west windows. In the parlor. That's where it'll hit worst."

"You're right. We forgot to do those. Thanks."

When she left, Lis turned to the doctor. "I don't have much time. As soon as we're finished here, we're going to a hotel for the evening." She added pointedly, "Because of Hrubek."

It was the moment when he'd tell her there was nothing to worry about, the moment when he'd laugh and say that his patient was harmless as a puppy. He didn't.

What he said was, "That's probably not a bad idea."

On the other hand he didn't seem particularly alarmed or suggest that they get the hell out of the house immediately and flee for safety.

"Do they know where he is?"

"Not exactly, no."

"But he *is* going away from here? East?"

"I saw one of the men tracking him not too long ago. He's still east of the hospital but it looks like he may have gone east and then turned around."

"He's coming west?"

"I'd say he's more likely wandering in circles. He isn't as disabled as some people are making him out to be, but I don't think he'd be able to get this far."

"What exactly can I do for you, doctor? I'd like to be out of here in twenty minutes or so."

"I'm worried about Michael. I'd like to find him before the police do. Not many people know how to handle a patient like him. He could hurt himself or somebody else if they try to arrest him like any other prisoner."

"Well, what can *I* do?"

"I understand he sent you a letter not long ago."

"In September."

"It had to do with the . . . incident last May?"

"It doesn't seem to have to do with anything. It's mostly gibberish."

Kohler lifted his eyes but not his head and stared directly at her. "Mrs. Atcheson, I need to know about Indian Leap. Will you help me?"

Six large water spots were evident on the counter beside the sink. Lis lifted a sponge and rubbed them away.

"You see, I'm Michael's attending psychiatrist. But I frankly don't have a clue about what's going on in his mind tonight. What happened last May was very . . . significant in his life."

"Significant?" she repeated, appalled at the word.

"I don't mean to downplay the tragedy."

"Well, what exactly can I tell you?"

"I've read some newspaper stories. I have a few files. But Marsden hospital's practically broke. We have very sketchy records. I don't even have a transcript of his trial."

This struck her as the epitome of bureaucratic nonsense, and she said so.

"Transcripts cost two dollars a page," he explained. "Michael's would have cost six thousand dollars. The state can't afford it."

"It seems to be just common sense to spend money like that."

He gestured in concession.

"I really don't think there's time." She nodded outside. "My sister and I have hotel reservations. And the storm . . ."

"It won't take long." He curled two fingers of his right hand around two fingers of his left, and Lis pictured the gangly teenage Richard Kohler asking a pretty girl to dance.

"The fact is, I'd rather not talk about it."

"Yes, of course . . ." Kohler hesitated and seemed to be examining her. "But you have to understand my perspective. It's important that I find him quickly. If he wanders up to someone's house . . . If he gets scared and panics. People could get hurt. Inadvertently."

Lis stood silent, looking down at the ruddy tile floor.

"*That's* what I'm concerned about, you see. Getting him back before there's an . . . accident. And, I have to tell you, there *is* a chance he's on his way here. Very slight, but it is a possibility. If you help me I might be able to prevent that."

After a long moment Lis said, "Cream and sugar?"

Kohler blinked.

"You've glanced at the coffee maker three times in the last minute."

He laughed. "I've been trying my best to stay awake."

"I'll give you twenty minutes, doctor. Not a minute more."

"Thank you very much," he said sincerely.

She stepped to the cupboard.

"Hope it's no trouble." His eyes were hungrily fixed to the can of Maxwell House.

"Can I ask a question?"

"Please."

"Could you fall asleep now?" Lis asked.

"I beg your pardon?"

"If you were home now would you be able to fall asleep?"

"At home? Yes. In my car, yes. On your front lawn. On your kitchen floor. Anytime, anyplace."

She wagged her head at this miracle and watched the pot fill with black liquid. Impulsively she decided to have a cup too. "I won't be asleep before eleven tomorrow night, whatever happens tonight."

"Insomnia?" he asked.

A condition on which she was an expert, she explained. Warm milk, hot baths, cold showers, hypnosis, self-hypnosis, valerian roots, biofeedback, medication. "You name it, I've tried it."

"In my practice I work with patients' dreams a lot. But I've never done much with sleep disorders."

She doctored her coffee with milk. Kohler took his black. "Let's go in here," she said.

With their thin mugs of steaming coffee in hand they walked into the greenhouse, at the far end of which was an alcove. As they sat in the deep wrought-iron chairs, the doctor looked about the room and offered a compliment, which because it had to do only with square footage and neatness meant he knew nothing of, and cared little for, flowers. He sat with his legs together, body forward, making his thin form that much thinner. He took loud sips, and she knew he was a man accustomed to dining quickly and alone. Then he set the cup down and took a pad and gold pen from his jacket pocket.

Lis asked, "Then you have no idea where he's going tonight?"

"No. He may not either, not consciously. That's the thing about Michael—you can't take him literally. To understand him you have to look behind what he says. That note he sent you, for instance; were certain letters capitalized?"

"Yes. That was one of the eeriest things about it."

"Michael does that. He sees relationships between things that to us don't exist. Could I see it?"

She found it in the kitchen and returned to the greenhouse. Kohler was standing, holding a small ceramic picture frame.

"Your father?"

"I'm told there's a resemblance."

"Some, yes. Eyes and chin. He was, I'd guess . . . a professor?"

"More of a closet scholar." The picture had been taken two days after he'd returned from Jerez, and Andrew L'Auberget was shown here climbing into the front seat of the Cadillac for the drive back to the airport. Young Lis had clicked the shutter as she stood shaded by her mother's protruding belly, inside of which her sister floated oblivious to the tearful farewell. "He was a businessman but he really wanted to teach. He talked about it many times. He would've made a brilliant scholar."

"Are you a professor?"

"Teacher. Sophomore English. And you?" she asked. "I understand medicine runs in the genes."

"Oh, it does. My father was a doctor." Kohler laughed. "Of course he wanted me to be an art historian. That was his dream. Then he grudgingly consented to medical school. On condition that I study surgery."

"But that wasn't for you?"

"Nope. All I wanted was to be a psychiatrist. Fought him tooth and nail. He said if you become a shrink, it'll chew you up, make you miserable, make you crazy and kill you."

"So," Lis said, "he was a psychiatrist."

"That he was."

"Did it kill him?"

"Nope. He retired to Florida."

"About which, I won't comment," she said. He smiled. Lis added, "Why?"

"How's that?"

"Why psychiatry?"

"I wanted to work with schizophrenics."

"I'd think you'd make more money putting rich people on the couch. Why'd you specialize in that?"

He smiled again. "Actually, it was my mother's illness. Say, is that the letter there?"

He took it in his short, feminine fingers and read it quickly. She could detect no reaction. "Look at this: '. . . *they are holding me and have told lIes About Me to waShingtOn and the enTIRE worlD*.' See what he's really saying?"

"No, I'm afraid I don't."

"Look at the capitalized letters. 'I AM SO TIRED.' "

The encoded message sent a chill through her.

"There are a lot of layers of meaning in Michael's world. 'Revenge' contains the name 'Eve.' " He scanned the paper carefully. " 'Revenge,' 'eve,' 'betrayal.' "

He shook his head then set the letter aside and turned his hard eyes on her. She suddenly grew ill at ease. And when he said, "Tell me about Indian Leap," a full minute passed before she began to speak.

Heading northeast from Ridgeton, Route 116 winds slowly through the best and the worst parts of the state: picturesque dairy and horse farms, then small but splendid patches of hardwood forests, then finally a cluster of tired mid-size towns studded with abandoned factories that the banks and receivers can't give away. Just past one of these failed cities, Pickford, is a five-hundred-acre sprawl of rock bluffs and pine forest.

Indian Leap State Park is bisected by a lazy S-shaped canyon, which extends for half a mile from the parking lot off 116 to Rocky Point Beach, a deceptive name for what's nothing more than a bleak rock revetment on a gray, man-made lake about one mile by two in size. Rising from the forest not far from the beach is what the State Park Service, still overly generous, calls a "peak," though it's really just a flat-topped summit six hundred feet high.

These rocks have their ghosts. In 1758 a small band of Mohegans, trapped on the side of this mountain, jumped to their deaths rather than be captured by rival Pequots. The women flung their screaming children before them then leapt to the rocks below with their men. Lis could still recall in perfect detail the bad, earnest illustration in her fifth-grade textbook of a squaw, looking more like Veronica Lake than a princess of the Mohican Confederacy, reaching for her tearful child as they were about to sail into the air. The first time she'd come here, a skinny wan girl, Lis walked these trails close to tears, thinking of the sorrow—whole families flying through the air. Even now, thirty years later, sitting across from Kohler, she felt the chill horror the story had evoked in her childhood.

Six months ago, on May 1, the Atchesons and the Gillespies— a couple they knew from the country club—planned a picnic at Indian Leap. Accompanying them were Portia and a former student of Lis's, Claire Sutherland.

The morning of the outing—it was a Sunday—had begun awkwardly. Just as Lis and Owen were about to leave, he got a call from his firm and learned that he had to go into the office for several hours. Lis was used to his zealot's schedule but was irritated that he acquiesced today. He'd worked almost every Sunday since early spring. The couple fought about it—genteelly at first, then more angrily. Owen prevailed, though he promised he'd meet them at the park no later than one-thirty or two.

"I didn't realize until later how lucky it was that he won that argument," she told Kohler softly. "If he hadn't gone into work . . . It's funny how fate works."

She continued with her story. Portia, Claire and Lis rode with Dorothy and Robert Gillespie in their Land Cruiser. It was a pleasant two-hour drive to the park. But as soon as they arrived, Lis began to feel uneasy, as if they were being watched. Walking to the lodge house to use the phone she believed she saw, in a distant cluster of bushes, someone looking at her. Because she had the impression that there was something of recognition in the face, which she took to be a man's, she believed for an instant that it was Owen, who'd changed his mind and decided not to work after all. But the face vanished into the bushes and when she called her husband's office, he answered the phone.

"You haven't left yet?" she asked, disappointed. It was then noon; he wouldn't be there before two.

"Fifteen minutes, I'll be on my way," he announced. "Are you there yet?"

"We just got here. I'm at the gift store."

"Oh"—Owen laughed—"get me one of those little pine outhouses. I'll give it to Charlie for making me come in today."

She was irritated but agreed to, and they hung up. Lis went into the store to buy the souvenir. When she stepped outside a moment later and rejoined the others at the entrance to the park, she glanced over her shoulder. She believed she saw the man staring again, studying the five of them. She was so startled she dropped the wooden outhouse. When she picked it up and looked back again, whoever it might have been was gone.

Kohler asked her about the others on the picnic.

"Robert and Dorothy? We met them at the club about a year ago."

The foursome had coincidentally picked adjacent poolside tables. They became friends by default, being about the only childless couples over thirty in the place. This mutual freedom broke the ice and they gradually got to know each other.

Owen and Lis were initially no match socially for their friends. Not yet inheritors of the L'Auberget fortune, the Atchesons lived in a small split-level in Hanbury, a grim industrial town ten miles west of Ridgeton. In fact the country-club membership itself, which Owen had insisted on so that he might court potential clients, was far too expensive for them, and many nights they'd eaten sandwiches or soup for dinner because they had virtually no cash in the bank. Robert, on the other hand, made buckets of money selling hotel communications systems. Owen, a lawyer in a small firm with small clients, masked his chagrin under careful smiles but Lis could see bitter jealousy when the Gillespies pulled up in front of the Atchesons' tacky house in Robert's new forest-green Jag or Dorothy's Merc.

There was the matter of temperament too: Robert had lived in Pacific Heights and on Michigan Avenue, and spent several years in Europe. ("No, no, I kid you not! It was Tourette sur Loup. Ever hear of it? A medieval city in the mountains northwest of Nice, and what do we find in the town square? A cross-dressing festival. Really! Tell 'em, Dot!")

He seemed ten years younger than his forty-one and you couldn't help but feel the tug of his boyish enthusiasm. With Robert, all the world was a sales prospect and you willingly let yourself be hawked. Owen had more substance but he was quiet and had his temper too. He didn't like taking second place to a handsome, wealthy charmer who resembled JFK in both appearance and charisma.

But then last March, when Ruth died, the Atchesons became

wealthy. This had little effect on Lis, who'd grown up with money, but it transformed Owen.

For her part Lis too had felt some reservations about the four-some. Her discomfort, though, lay mostly with Dorothy.

Dorothy, with the voice of a high-school cheerleader. With the perfect figure—and the clothes to showcase it. With a round, Middle Eastern face, and dark eyes always flawlessly made up.

Lis could honestly say though that she felt more pique than jealousy. It was mostly Dorothy's fawning that irritated her. The way she'd stop whatever she was doing to run errands for her husband, or errands she *thought* he'd want done. Robert seemed embarrassed by this excessive obeisance, which always seemed put-on, calculated, and Lis silently played the woman's game of spouse sniping, concluding that what Robert really needed in a mate was a partner, not this little geisha, even one decked out with world-class boobs.

Yet when it was clear that they'd never be close friends, the reservations Lis felt about the woman faded. She grew more tolerant and even asked for Dorothy's advice on makeup and clothes (about which she *was* a generous wellspring of data). They never became sisterly but Dorothy was someone to whom Lis could confide sins down to, say, the fourth level of hell.

It had been Dorothy, Lis recalled, who'd heard that the weather the next Sunday was supposed to be particularly beautiful and had suggested the picnic.

"And who was Claire?"

Eighteen years old, the girl had been in Lis's English class her sophomore year. She was intensely shy, with a pale, heart-shaped face. "She was somebody," Lis explained, "you hoped wouldn't become too beautiful because it seemed there was no way she could handle the attention."

But beautiful she was. Seeing her on the first day of class, several years ago, Lis was struck immediately by the girl's ethereal face, still eyes and long, delicate fingers. Teachers peg students instantly, and Lis had felt an immediate fondness for Claire. She'd made an effort to stay in touch as the girl made her way through her junior then senior years. Lis rarely singled out any youngsters from school; only on one or two other occasions had she maintained relationships with students, or former students, outside of class. She generally kept her distance, aware of the power she had over these young people. When she wore light-colored blouses she noticed boys' eyes lose control and dart across her chest while their cheeks grew red and their penises, she supposed, irrepressibly hard. The shy or unattractive girls worshipped her; those in the inner clique were disdaining and jealous—for no reason other than that Lis was a woman, and they were not quite. She handled all of these feelings with consummate dignity and care, and usually kept home and classroom absolutely separate.

But she made an exception for Claire. The girl's mother was a drunk and the woman's boyfriend had served time for sexual abuse of a stepchild in a prior marriage. When Lis learned Claire's history, she began letting the girl into her life in small ways—occasionally asking her to help in her greenhouse or to attend Sunday-afternoon brunches. Lis knew this attraction to the girl had an enigmatic, almost a dangerous, side—the time, for instance, that Claire had stayed after class to discuss a book report. Lis noticed a tangle in the girl's shimmery blond strands and with her own brush began working it out. Suddenly, she realized: teacher-student contact, with the door closed! Lis virtually leapt from her chair, away from the startled girl, and vowed to be more circumspect.

Still, over the past two years, they'd seen each other often, and when Claire mentioned wistfully on the Friday before the picnic that her mother would be away all Sunday, Lis didn't hesitate to invite her along.

That May 1 the picnickers set up camp on Rocky Point Beach. Portia left immediately for a run—an improvised 10K through the winding canyons. She runs marathons, Lis told Kohler.

"So do I," the doctor said.

Lis laughed, astonished, as ever, that people actually engaged in this sport for fun.

"We sat on the beach for a while, Dorothy, Robert, Claire and I. Watching the boats. You know, just chatting and drinking soda and beer."

They had been there for about a half hour when Dorothy and Robert began to argue.

Dorothy had left Lis's book in the truck. "*Hamlet*," she explained. She'd been preparing for final exams and had carted along a well-read and annotated volume. "I had my hands full with picnic things and Dorothy said she'd get the book. But it had slipped her mind." Lis had told her not to worry; she wasn't in the mood to work anyway. But Robert leapt up and said he'd get it. Then Dorothy made some sour comment about his doing anything for anybody in a skirt. It was supposed to be a joke, Lis supposed, but it fell flat—since she'd managed to insult both Lis and Robert at the same time.

"Robert asked her what she meant by that. Dorothy waved her hand and said, 'Just go get the fucking book, why don't you?' Something like that. Then she told him he ought to jog all the way to the parking lot. 'Work off some of that fat. Look, he's getting tits.'"

Lis was embarrassed for Claire's sake. Robert jogged off angrily and Dorothy sullenly returned to her magazine.

Lis had pulled off her shorts and unbuttoned her workshirt, beneath which she wore a bikini. She lay back on a warm rock and closed her eyes, trying not to go to sleep (daytime naps are taboo for insomniacs). Claire, with whom Robert had struck up an immediate friendship en route to the beach, had seemed the most anxious of anyone for him to return. After he'd been gone a half hour, she stood and said she was going to look for him. Lis had watched the girl as she strolled toward the towering, weathered rocks. Repulsive and fascinating, the cliffs seemed hard as polished bone. They reminded her of the yellow skull sitting on the lab table in the school's biology classroom.

Lis noticed Claire standing in the mouth of the canyon about a quarter mile from the beach. Then she vanished.

"And I thought suddenly," Lis told Kohler, "where is everyone? What's going on? I felt very concerned. I picked up my purse and started toward the place where I'd seen Claire disappear." Then she saw a flash of color ahead of her. She believed it was yellow, the color of Claire's shorts, and leaving Dorothy behind she hurried into the canyon. Lis was perhaps a hundred yards into the ravine when she found the blood.

"Blood?"

It was right outside a cave. The entrance had been chained off at one time but the post holding the chain had been pulled out of the ground and flung aside. No way, she thought, was she going inside. But she knelt down and looked into the passageway. The air was chill and it smelled of wet stone and clay and mold.

Then she felt a shadow over her. A huge man appeared just feet away, standing behind her.

"Michael?" Kohler asked.

Lis nodded.

Hrubek started howling like an animal. Holding a bloody rock, he looked right at her and screamed, "*Sic semper tyrannis!*"

Richard Kohler held up a thin hand, indicating for her to wait. He made his first notation of the evening.

"You didn't think of going to find a park ranger?" Kohler asked.

Lis suddenly grew angry. Why had he asked her this? It was the sort of question the lawyers had asked, and the police. Did I think of looking for a ranger? Well, for God's sake, wouldn't we *always* do it differently if we could? Wouldn't we recast our whole *lives*? That's why time doesn't reverse, of course—to keep us sane.

"I thought about it, yes. But I don't know, I just panicked. I ran into the cave."

Inside, it wasn't completely dark. Thirty, forty feet above her, shafts of pale light streamed inside.

The walls rose straight up to an arched roof full of stalactites. Lis, breathless and frightened, leaned against a wall to steady herself. A high-pitched moaning of some sort filled the air. It was like wind over a reed, like someone imitating an oboe. Terrible! She looked at the trail at her feet and saw more blood.

Then Hrubek slipped through the cave opening. Lis turned and raced down the path. No idea where she was going, not really thinking, she simply ran. Once out of the main chamber she fled down a long corridor, about eight feet high. Hrubek was somewhere behind her. As she ran she noticed the tunnel was growing smaller. By now it had shrunk to six feet, and the sides were closing in. Once she slammed into a rock, cutting her forehead and leaving a scar that still remained. By then the chamber had narrowed down to five feet and she was running crouched over. Then, four feet. Soon she was crawling.

Ahead of her the tunnel grew even smaller though on the other side of a very narrow opening it seemed to widen and grow brighter. But escaping that way would mean crawling through a tunnel that was no more than twelve or so inches high. With Hrubek right behind her.

"The thought of being, well, exposed to him like that. I mean, wearing just my swimsuit . . . I couldn't do it. I turned to my left and crawled through a larger entrance."

It was black, completely black, but she felt cool air circulating and assumed it was a large space. She climbed inside, feeling her way along the smooth floor. Looking back she could see the entrance—it was slightly lighter than the surrounding walls. Slowly it darkened then grew less dark again, and she heard a hissing sound. He was in this small cave with her. She lay flat on the ground and bit a finger to keep silent while she sobbed.

"You have no idea what noise is until you've been in a place like that. I was sure my heartbeat or the sound of blood in my ears would give me away. I think I could hear my own tears falling on the floor of the cave."

All the while Hrubek was shuffling around her. He passed her, no more than five feet away. Then he paused and sniffed the air and muttered, "There's a woman in here. I can smell her pussy."

Lis ran. She couldn't bear it any longer. "I scrambled to the opening and turned back down the narrow corridor, the way I'd come. That is, I thought I did. But somehow I took a wrong turn."

In one sense it was lucky. The light was better here and the roof of the cave high. She saw discarded cigarettes and beer cans—which led her to believe she was heading toward an exit. She kept moving toward the light.

"Then I felt a breeze stirring and way up ahead I heard running water. I ran toward it as fast as I could. Then I turned the corner. That's where I found the body." She gazed through the misty windows into the yard, now filled with a blustery wind. "I didn't recognize it at first. There was too much blood."

17

Robert Gillespie lay on the cave floor.

"He was twisted like a rag doll and had a huge gash in his head. But he wasn't dead."

She'd taken Robert's hand and leaned close, urging him to keep breathing. She'd get help, she said. But then she heard footsteps. Ten feet away Hrubek stood staring at them. He was smiling cynically, muttering.

"He was talking," Lis told Kohler, "about conspirators."

Stumbling backwards Lis landed on her purse. Inside, she felt a knife. She'd packed it for the picnic, she explained, wrapping it in a paper towel and placing it in her bag so no one would reach blindly into the picnic basket and cut themselves. She pulled it out now and ripped the towel away from the blade—it was very sharp, a Chicago Cutlery, nine inches long. She pointed it at Hrubek and told him to keep back. But he just kept walking at her, saying, "*Sic semper tyrannis!*" again and again. Her nerve broke. She dropped the knife and ran.

"That was the knife that he used?" Kohler asked. "I remember reading that the victim was stabbed as well as beaten. Sexually mutilated too."

After a moment Lis answered, "Robert was badly hurt but he probably could've survived. According to the evidence at the trial they think he would've recovered from the rock blows. He died from the stabbing." She paused. "And the mutilation? Yes, Hrubek stabbed Robert in the groin. A number of times."

. . .

Only fifty feet away Lis found the exit and scrabbled through it. She collapsed on the ground and caught her breath. Then she headed into the canyon. But after running only a dozen yards she pulled up with a fierce cramp in her side. Hrubek was twenty or thirty feet behind her. He was saying, "Come here. You're a very beautiful woman but what's that on your hair? I don't like your hair that way. What's that on your *head*?" She'd gotten some of Robert's blood on her hair. This upset Hrubek. He was very angry. She supposed that he was worried it was evidence. "What did you do to yourself?" he called. "That's not *fashionable*. You shouldn't've done that!"

He stepped toward her and she dropped to her knees, rolling under a jutting overhang about a foot and a half high. It went back into the rock maybe six feet and there she wedged herself, shivering in the cold and fighting the panic from confinement. As she stared at the path, his feet appeared. He wore shoes. Huge ones. Wingtips. This astonished her. For some reason she expected him to be barefoot, with long yellow toenails. She wondered if he'd killed a man for the shoes. Then he bent down and lay on his belly.

" 'Nice try,' he kept saying. 'Come on out here. You're Eve, aren't you? Beautiful lady. Ought to shave that fucking hair off.' "

She wedged herself as far back as she could, her face pressing into the rock. When he groped for her, she screamed and the piercing sound of her own voice stunned her ears. He screamed too, crying at her to shut up. He grunted and tried again to grab her. With a huge effort he jammed his arm forward. The tip of his middle finger eased against her thigh. Those were the only parts of their bodies close enough to touch. Lis felt the feathery trail of his callused skin move toward her knee. The sensation was like a burn and it remained, searing, even when Hrubek stood and vanished.

Lis lay, whimpering and fighting the grip of claustrophobia. Where was he? she wondered. Did she dare leave? It'd been a half hour since she'd disappeared from the beach. She knew Owen wouldn't have arrived yet but Portia and Dorothy might've come looking for her. Claire too would be somewhere nearby.

Outside she noticed rain beginning to spatter on the stone path.

"I started to push myself out. Then I heard two things. One was Hrubek's voice. He was very close and talking to himself. The other sound was thunder."

It shook the ground. She was worried that the rock above her might shift and trap her where she lay. But this fear was soon replaced by a more immediate one—that she would drown. Huge gushes of water suddenly flowed down the arroyo and the cave began to fill.

She eased closer to the opening. If Hrubek had reached in again, he could have grabbed her easily. Her head was sideways—the only way it would fit into the narrow space—and she was twisting her mouth upward, desperately gasping for air. Soon, filthy water was surging around her face, flowing over her lips. She spat it out and started choking. More thunder, more torrents of water, tumbling over the stone. She pushed toward the opening but couldn't make headway. Fighting the rush of water she finally got far enough through the current to fling her hand outside the cave. Blindly, she gripped a rock and pulled herself toward it.

"Then the rock moved. It wasn't a rock at all but a shoe. I pulled back quickly but a huge hand grabbed me by the wrist and tugged me out." Lis looked away from Kohler. "My swimsuit snagged on a rock and tore open."

She was half-naked. But she had no choice—she couldn't stay in the cave any longer. She remembered thinking she wished that she had the courage to choose to die by drowning rather than be raped and murdered by the madman. As she was drawn out of the cave, her mind was filled with images of Hrubek's huge hands prodding her breasts and reaching between her legs. She began to cry.

Then a man's voice said, "It's all right, ma'am, it's all right. What's the matter?"

She collapsed into the arms of the park ranger.

Leaning against the rock in the torrential rain she told him about Robert and Hrubek. He began asking questions but Lis couldn't concentrate. All she could hear was a horrid keening that filled the air. It seemed to come from earth itself, resonating from the rocks, stretching out thinner and thinner, impossibly thin, an unsustainable note that nonetheless refused to stop. " 'What *is* that?' I asked. 'Make it stop. Oh, for God's sake.' "

And soon it did, Lis explained to the psychiatrist.

For, as Lis found out just moments later from another ranger, an underground stream, swollen with rain, had overflowed into the cave where Lis had found Robert's body—the cave where Claire had been all along. The sound had been the girl's wail for help that had been stifled by the rising waters in which she'd drowned.

Stopping the truck abruptly and extinguishing the lights, Owen Atcheson gazed about him, surveying this dismal stretch of deserted road.

He slipped the pistol out of his pocket and stepped into the clearing, playing his flashlight on the dusty shoulder. Hrubek's bike had been laid or had fallen on its side and there were footprints around it. Several of these he recognized as the madman's boots but the others weren't familiar to him. It was clear that at one point Hrubek had sat on the ground—the sides of his heels made deep cut marks and his hams wide indentations in the dirt of the highway's shoulder.

He couldn't make any sense of what'd happened here. He noticed the bicycle treads led on again, continuing west down Route 236, yet still he studied the turnoff carefully, trying to get a clearer idea of how Hrubek's mind worked. He saw a grassy access road nearby:

a path disappearing into the forest. A number of tire treads led toward it, some fresh.

Beyond this was a long road descending through trees, bushes, tall grass, vines, mist. Where the path flattened out again and vanished into the murky shadows of the forest was a car, sitting cockeyed in the brush. Owen shone his flashlight toward it but the distance was too great for illumination; all he saw was a vague image of the vehicle. He deduced it was an abandoned hulk because it appeared to be two-tone; Detroit had stopped making those a long time ago. He didn't bother to explore the vehicle further but returned to the road and drove slowly west, checking every hundred yards or so for the weaving bike tread.

And pondering again the biggest problem of the evening.

His was no moral dilemma. Oh, Owen Atcheson had absolutely no ethical difficulty with walking right up to Hrubek and putting a bullet into his forehead. No, it was simply practical, one that Haversham had reminded him of in Adler's office: how could he kill Michael Hrubek without ending up disbarred and in jail himself.

If Hrubek had been a convicted felon, Owen would have an easier time of it. Fleeing felons could legally be shot in the back (Owen now squinted as he recited from cold memory the rules in the state Penal Code). But Hrubek was *not* a felon. Although the jury found that he had in fact killed Robert Gillespie, the verdict that was entered was not guilty by reason of insanity.

This meant that there were only two justifiable ways to kill Hrubek. First, to be attacked by him in a place from which Owen couldn't reasonably escape: an enclosed room, a blocked tunnel, a bridge. Second, to catch Hrubek in the Atcheson house, where Owen could legally shoot him without provocation and have nothing but an inconvenient trip to police HQ to show for it. And possibly not even that.

One of these scenarios would have to be engineered. But he was still too far from his prey to figure out exactly how. No, there was nothing to do now but continue on, driving slowly through the misty night, amid this troubled uncertainty—not of purpose, but of means. He gave in to the mood of combat, thinking purely of the mechanics of the kill: Which shot would be the most effective? Which gun should he use? How far would a man of Hrubek's size be able to run with a mortal wound? (Like a cape buffalo or bear, a frighteningly long way, he guessed.) Was Hrubek himself stalking his pursuers? Was he even now laying another steel-jawed trap? Or something more deadly? From his military days, Owen knew the huge variety of booby traps that can be created out of gasoline, naphtha, fertilizer, nails, tools, lumber, wire.

He was considering these matters when he passed an old roadside gas station and general store, closed and dark. He slowed and studied the road carefully. The station had apparently attracted Hrubek too; the bike treads turned into the driveway. Owen pulled the truck past the lot and stopped very slowly to keep the damp brakes from squealing. He took his pistol from his pocket and, verifying that he still had the rifle bolt with him, climbed out of the truck.

He noticed in the front of the building, near one of the pumps, a box of doughnuts, half-empty. It seemed a little too prominent— as if it'd been left here to lure pursuers into a trap—and when Owen walked to the back of the building he walked very quietly. Yes, the window was broken and the deadbolt unlatched. He inhaled slowly, to steady himself, then pushed the door open—fast, to keep the hinges from squealing—and stepped inside and moved immediately out of the doorway.

Standing still, he let his eyes grow accustomed to the gloom. His mouth was open wide—a soldier's trick to mute a loud inhalation should he be startled. When he heard nothing for five full minutes, he walked in a crouch among the shelves filled with auto parts and greasy cartons.

Foot by foot, Owen covered the back room of the store and found no evidence of Hrubek. Through the open doorway and smeared glass beyond he saw the highway. A car drove past and the light flooded around him, creating a thousand shadows that flipped from left to right, coalescing then spreading out again into darkness. The headlights had dimmed his night vision and he waited five minutes until he could see well enough to continue.

Owen found another empty doughnut carton. Powdered sugar and cinnamon were scattered on the floor. He made his way toward the narrow doorway that opened onto the front room. He stopped suddenly, listening to a rumbling. It grew louder. Lights flickered outside, outlining the old-time gas pumps. A burping explosion from a truck's exhaust stack filled the air as the driver revved the engine to upshift coming off the long incline of the highway. The truck thundered past.

Owen partially closed his eyes to protect them from the light.

That was when he felt, more than saw, the movement. He opened his eyes in alarm and gazed at the dark shape swinging into the doorway. Before it reached him he leapt backwards. But he misjudged and tripped over a metal table, falling backwards and dropping his gun. His head struck the steel edge on the way down and he lay on the concrete floor, stunned, while the shadowy form of his assailant filled the doorway, not more than three feet from him.

Beckoning, the glossy truck sat like a blue jewel in the driveway.

"That'll take me to Ridgeton in no time at all. Make no mistake, no time at all."

O beautiful truck, I could sit upon your seat while the priest's beautiful daughter sits upon his cock. . . .

From the old gas station Hrubek had cycled to the long gravel driveway down which had vanished the 4x4 that contained the woman and her daughter. He couldn't see any lights and guessed that their house must be a half mile or more from the highway.

He'd slowly trudged through the field beside the driveway, pausing to take the last trap from his canvas bag and place it under some strands of tall grass. He continued on, carrying the bicycle with him, thinking, What a truck that is! Why would I go *by* a *bi*-cycle store to *buy* a fucking *bi*-cycle when I can drive a truck?

He had paused, taken the rear wheel in both hands and eased his shoulders back. Like a discus thrower he spun around twice and sent the bike flying through the air; it fell into a clump of plants thirty feet away. He was disappointed it didn't explode on impact, though he had no idea why it should. He continued up the driveway, thinking less about the truck than the woman's beautiful hair. That's what intrigued him the most. He supposed she had breasts, he supposed she had a pussy, he supposed she had masks on her eyes. But what captivated him so was her hair. It reminded him of his own hair before he cut it all off. When had he done that? Tonight? No, last year. And why? He couldn't remember. Microphones probably.

Hrubek had walked a half mile until he came to the place where he now stood—the driveway beside the house. "Now be smart," he told himself gravely. By this he meant: there'd be a husband. A woman with such soft hair and a delicate face wouldn't live alone. She'd be married to a big man with cold eyes—a conspirator, like the limping fucker with the dog.

He crouched and walked closer, hiding in a stand of juniper, the dew soaking through his overalls. He looked at the three-story colonial. The lights were golden, the trim garden was filled with Indian cornstalks and fat pumpkins on runners, the house itself was solid, symmetrical, plumb-even, a picture-book place, its red front door decorated with a dried-flower wreath.

He turned away and studied the shiny truck in the driveway. Next to it was a sporty yellow motorcycle. He vaguely remembered that he'd ridden a cycle several times at college and recalled being thrilled, as well as terrified, by the sensation. The cycle looked very nice, bright and springy. But the truck had captivated him first and it continued to possess his heart.

Hrubek walked up to the house and, standing in the side yard, he peered through a window. He tasted bitter paint where his lips pressed against the sill. Through a thick screen and thicker glass he could see the kitchen. There she was! The woman with the beautiful hair. Yes, she *was* beautiful. Much prettier than she'd seemed at the gas station. Tight blue jeans, a white silky blouse . . . And hair cascading to her shoulders—no hats for her, just tangles of soft, blond hair. The daughter was heavier and wore a thick sweatshirt with the sleeves drooping over her hands. A third woman in the room was dark and her face was tight and sultry. Hrubek didn't like her at all. The women vanished from sight for a moment. The kitchen door opened. The mother and daughter were carrying boxes out of the house. "Last load," the woman said. "Be back soon."

In a high edgy voice the girl said, "Mom, I'm tired."

"It's the church auction. And you volunteered to help."

"Mom," she repeated hopelessly.

Hrubek thought, Don't whine, you little fucker.

He heard a ringing. He squinted into the darkness of the driveway. Oh, no! The keys to the truck! *His* truck! They were taking it away. He stood and tensed to leap into the driveway. As he watched them load the boxes into the back of the truck, he rocked back and forth, willing himself to act.

"See you later, Mattie."

"Bye," the dark woman called and returned to the kitchen. Through the window Hrubek saw her pick up the phone. The pretty woman and her daughter the whiny little shit climbed into the truck. Hrubek couldn't move; if he stepped out of hiding, the woman on the phone would call for help. The engine started. Overcome by a burst of anxiety, Hrubek nearly leapt forward but he restrained himself and closed his eyes, squinting furiously until his head screamed with pain and he regained control. He hunkered down beneath a holly bush, whose leaves were sharp as knives.

The truck rolled past him, crunching gravel. When it was past he stepped away from the house and watched it disappear, and neither the mother nor daughter heard Hrubek's anguished hiss of rage.

With a resounding thud he kicked the motorcycle's fender. He gazed at the cycle for a moment then continued to the back door of the house. Quietly he opened the screen and looked through the small window high in the back door. The dark-complected woman, still on the phone, was gesturing broadly and shaking her head as she talked. This made Hrubek think she'd be a screamer. On the stove was a tea kettle just starting to steam over a high flame. As he silently twisted the knob back and forth, checking that the door was not locked, Hrubek thought, She's having tea, that means she isn't about to leave and won't be expected anywhere soon.

Hrubek congratulated himself on this smart thinking and he continued to act smart—he didn't open the door and step into the kitchen until the woman had hung up and walked across the kitchen to the stove, far away from the phone.

Owen Atcheson, his ear numb from striking the table leg as he fell, scrabbled away from the door, and unable to find his gun grabbed a soda bottle lying nearby. He cracked it hard against the floor and held the shard like a knife. He crouched and made himself ready for attack.

The assailant didn't move.

Owen waited a moment longer. Finally he stood. Owen grabbed his pistol from the floor. When he heard no breathing and saw no other motion, he flicked on the light switch.

Taste T

Beats t

Others C

In fury Owen kicked shut the door of the old Pepsi machine. "Jesus," he spat out. The lock had been broken—by Hrubek undoubtedly—and the door, dislodged by the semi as it rumbled past, had swung open into the doorway. His anger was so great he nearly put a bullet through the navel of the bikini-clad girl on the old, faded poster taped to the door. He jammed the gun into his pocket and trotted outside to his truck.

Only a few hundred feet west he found the tread again, turning into a private road or driveway of a residence. He couldn't see a house from the road and, observing the length of the drive and the size of the property, guessed that the family was wealthy. Horse ranchers maybe. He looked back at the ground and noted that Hrubek had left the drive and was traveling through the brush. Making his way silently on the patches of dirt, Owen followed the madman's clear path. A flash in the distant west caught his eye. Lightning.

Attempting to circle in front of Hrubek, he made his way west from the driveway into the field of tall, flesh-colored grass and moved south. From here he was able to see, a quarter mile away, a stately house. Although it was late, there were many lights on, giving a homey glow to the place.

But that impression vanished when Owen noticed a single unsettling token—the kitchen door was wide open, sending a shaft of bone-white light onto the gravel driveway, as if someone had fled quickly from the house.

Or maybe, Owen reflected, had *entered* quickly. And was still inside.

18

One who loves flowers and literature can't doubt the existence of God. The lesson He's got for us, though, probably isn't so hot. We see miracles daily, that's true. On the other hand God's got the universe to mind and doesn't have much time for passengers on colliding trains, kids dragged to death behind buses, and dear friends murdered by a madman in a state park.

"That," Lis explained to Richard Kohler, "was the thought I just couldn't get out of my mind. For months after the murder I repeated it to practically everyone I met. I'm sure they thought I was totally mad."

Kohler nodded her bit of theology politely aside and frowned sympathetically. "You lost two friends at the same time. How terrible. I didn't know about the girl's death."

Lis was silent for a long moment. Finally she said, "No, it wasn't featured in the news about the trial. Her death was considered accidental."

"May I ask . . . ?"

Lis glanced at him inquiringly.

"Did you hear anyone call for help?"

"How do you mean?"

"Claire, I'm thinking of. Before you saw Michael and ran into the cave, did you hear her scream?"

When Lis didn't respond, Kohler added, "It just seems that with Michael chasing her down the path . . . I mean, he *was* chasing her, wasn't he?"

Lis couldn't guess the purpose of his questions. After a moment she said, "I didn't hear anything. There weren't any screams."

"Why would she go into the cave in the first place?"

"I don't know."

"It's curious, isn't it? You'd think with Michael after her, she'd continue running down the canyon. A cave is the last place I'd want to be with Michael chasing me."

She was testy. "I can't speak for her. Obviously."

"I'm just wondering. Later, did you think about it? A young girl, being chased by a huge man like Michael. I would've thought she'd scream at some point."

"Maybe she did. Maybe I didn't hear her. I don't really—"

"It was close to where you were looking for her though, wasn't it?" Kohler persisted. "From the way you described it, I—"

"It was *close* to where I was, yes, but . . ." She felt cross-examined and forced herself to be calm. "I don't know. Maybe I blocked it out. Maybe she did scream, and I don't remember it. That's possible, isn't it?"

"Oh, sure. Post-trauma stress. Very possible."

"Well, then."

Kohler said something, perhaps by way of apology, but Lis didn't hear. She was thinking: Claire. My poor Claire. And pictured the girl's pale eyes, the hair that tumbled over her shoulders like water, the white mouth that needed lipstick the girl was too bashful to apply.

She had grieved for Robert, yes, but it was the girl's death that hurt her the deepest. She hadn't known that she could be so attached to a youngster. Lis had always felt a certain uneasiness around children, even her students. She rarely put it that way and tended to think of her and Owen's childlessness as circumstance. But the truth was, she just hadn't wanted a son or daughter. She couldn't picture the Atcheson family on a picnic, austere Owen cradling an infant Andy, herself dropping a line of formula onto her wrist to test the temperature. Baby showers. Strollers. PTA meetings. Embarrassing conversations about the facts of life . . . .

But about Claire Lis felt differently. Claire she'd sought out. Lis viewed the girl through a rare crack in the wall of distant time and saw in the student's eyes and halting manners the effigy of another thin, shy girl from years before. A child whose father was both intimate and hating, and whose mother dared to be truly present only when her man was not. Lis could not refuse the covert pleas for help—like the times the girl stayed after class to ask intelligent if calculated questions about Jacobean drama, or happened—too coincidentally—to find herself walking beside her teacher on the deserted riverside behind the school.

Lis was again picturing Claire's face when she realized that the psychiatrist was asking her a question. He wanted to know about the trial.

"The trial?" she repeated softly. "Well, I got to the courthouse early . . ."

"Just you?"

"I refused to let Owen come with me. It's hard to explain but I wanted to keep what happened at Indian Leap as separate as possible from my home. Owen spent the day with Dorothy. After all, *she* was the widow. She needed comforting more than I."

Inside the courtroom, when Lis first saw Hrubek—it'd been five and a half weeks since the murder—he looked smaller than she recalled. He was pale, sickly. He squinted at her and his mouth twisted into an eerie smile. As she walked down the aisle Lis tried to keep her eyes on the prosecutor, a young woman with a mass of flyaway hair. She'd been prepping Lis all week for the court appearance. Lis sat behind her but in full view of Hrubek. His hands were manacled in front of him and he lifted them as far as he could then simply stared at her, his lips moving compulsively.

"God, it was eerie."

"That's just dyskinesia," Kohler explained. "It's a condition caused by antipsychotic drugs."

"Whatever, it was scary as hell. When he spoke he almost gave me a heart attack. He jumped up and said, 'Conspiracy!' And 'Revenge,' or something. I don't remember exactly."

Apparently these outbursts had happened before because everyone, including the judge, ignored him. As she walked past he grew very calm and asked her in a conversational tone if she knew where he was on the night of April 14 at 10:30 p.m.

"April *14*?"

"That's right."

"And the murder was May 1, wasn't it?"

"Yes."

"Did April 14 mean anything to you?"

She shook her head. A small notation went into Kohler's book. "Please go on."

"Hrubek said, 'I was murdering somebody. . . .' I'm not quoting exactly. Something like, 'I was murdering somebody. The moon rose blood red and ever since that day I have been the victim of a conspiracy—' "

"Lincoln's assassination!" Kohler looked at her with raised eyebrows.

"I'm sorry?"

"Didn't it happen in mid-April?"

"I think it *was* around then, yes."

Another notation.

With disdain Lis observed the brief smile that crossed Kohler's lips then she continued, "He was saying, 'I've been implanted with tracking and listening devices. I've been tortured.' Sometimes he was incoherent, sometimes he sounded like a doctor or lawyer."

Lis was the main prosecution witness. She swore her oath then settled in a huge wooden chair. On its seat was a crocheted cushion and she wondered if it had been made by the wife of the grizzled, slouching judge. "The prosecutor asked me to tell the court what happened that day. And I did."

Her testimony seemed to take an eternity. She later learned she was in the spotlight for all of eight minutes.

She was dreading cross-examination by the defense attorney. But she wasn't called. Hrubek's lawyer said simply, "No questions," and she spent the next several hours in the gallery.

"All I could do was stare at the plastic bags that contained the rock stained with Robert's blood, and the kitchen knife. I sat in the back of the courtroom with Tad. . . ." Kohler lifted an inquiring eyebrow. "He's a former student of mine. He does work for me around the yard and greenhouse. I told everybody I knew not to attend the trial. But Tad ignored me. He was there all day long, cheerful and smiling. We sat together."

Before she testified, the young man found her in the corridor outside and handed her a paper bag. Inside was a yellow rose. He'd trimmed the thorns and cut the stem back, wrapped it in wet paper towels. Lis had cried and kissed him on the cheek.

"Was it a long trial?" Kohler asked.

Not really, she explained. The defense lawyer didn't dispute the fact that Hrubek had killed Robert. He relied on the insanity defense—Hrubek lacked the mental state to understand that his acts were criminal. Under the M'Naghten rule, Lis relayed to Kohler what she'd learned during the jury instruction, the death becomes an act of God. The lawyer didn't even put Hrubek on the stand. He offered medical reports and depositions, which were read out loud by a clerk. This all had to do with Hrubek's inability to appreciate the consequences of his actions.

All that time the madman had sat at the defense table, hunched over, twining his dirty hair between blunt fingers, laughing and muttering, filling sheet after sheet of foolscap with tiny frantic

characters and lines. She hadn't paid any attention to these doo-
dlings then but understood later that he hadn't been as crazy as it
appeared—this was undoubtedly how he'd recorded her name and
address.

A verdict of not guilty by reason of diminished capacity was
entered. Under Section 403 of the Mental Health Law, Hrubek
would be classified as dangerously insane and would be incarcerated indefinitely in a state hospital, to be re-evaluated annually.

"I left the courthouse. Then—"

"And what about the incident," Kohler asked, palms meeting as
if he were clapping in slow motion, "with the chair?"

"Chair?"

"He jumped up on a chair or table."

Ah, yes. That.

The courtroom began to empty. Suddenly a huge voice rose over
the murmuring of the spectators and press. Michael Hrubek was
shouting. He threw a bailiff to the ground and climbed onto his
chair. The manacles clanked and he lifted his arms over his head.
He began screaming. His eyes met Lis's for a moment and she
froze. Guards subdued Hrubek, and a bailiff hustled her out of the
courtroom.

"What did he say?"

"Say?"

"When he was on the chair. Did he shout anything?"

"I think he was just howling. Like an animal."

"The article said he shouted, 'You're the Eve of betrayal.' "

"Could be."

"You don't remember?"

"No. I don't."

Kohler was shaking his head. "Michael had therapy sessions with
me. Three times a week. During one he said, 'Betrayal, betrayal.
Oh, she's *courting* disaster. She sat in that *court*, and now she's

courting disaster. All that betrayal. Eve's the one.' When I asked him what he meant, he became agitated. As if he'd let an important secret slip. He wouldn't talk about it. He's mentioned betrayal several times since then. You have any thoughts on what it might mean?"

"No. I don't. I'm sorry."

"And afterwards?"

"After the trial?" Lis sipped the strong coffee. "Well, I took a trip to hell."

After the publicity faded and Hrubek was committed in Marsden, Lis resumed the life she'd led before the tragedy. At first her routine seemed largely unchanged—teaching summer school, spending Sundays at the country club with Owen, visiting friends, tending the garden. She was perhaps the last person to notice that her life was unraveling.

Occasionally she'd skip a shower. She'd forget the names of guests attending her own cocktail parties. She might happen to glance down as she walked through the corridors of the school and find that she was wearing mismatched shoes. She'd teach Dryden instead of the scheduled Pope and berate students for failing to read material she'd never assigned. Sometimes in lectures and in conversations she found herself gazing at embarrassed, perplexed faces and could only wonder what on earth she'd just uttered.

"It was as if I was sleepwalking."

She withdrew into her greenhouse and mourned.

Owen, patient initially, grew tired of Lis's torpor and absentmindedness and they began to fight. He spent more time on business trips. She stayed home more and more frequently, venturing outside only for her classes. Her sleep problems grew worse: it was not unusual for her to remain awake for twenty-four hours straight.

Adding to Lis's difficulty was Dorothy, who stepped as brusquely

into widowhood as she slipped into the front seat of her Mercedes
SL. She was gaunt and pale and didn't smile for two months. Yet
she functioned, and functioned quite well. Owen several times held
her out as an example of someone who took tragedy in stride. "Well,
I'm not *like* her, Owen. I never have been. I'm sorry."

When Dorothy sold her house and moved to the Jersey shore in
July, it was not she but Lis who cried during their farewell lunch.

Lis's life became school and her greenhouse, where she would
snip plants and wander like a lost child over the slate path, her
face occasionally damp as the leaves of a plantain lily.

But gradually she improved. She took Prozac for a time, which
made her jaw quiver and fingers tremble and infused her dreams
with spectacular effects. It also aggravated the insomnia. She
switched to Pamelor, which was gentler.

And then, one day, she simply stopped taking the pills and hung
up her housecoat.

"I can't tell you what happened. Or when exactly. But I suddenly
just knew it was time to get on with my life. And I did."

"I'd had some clues that Michael's delusion involves American history," Kohler told her. "Particularly the Civil War . . . '*Sic semper
tyrannis*'—that's what Booth shouted after he shot Lincoln."

" 'Thus ever to tyrants.' " Lis the schoolteacher added, "It's also
the state motto of Virginia."

"And the April 14 reference. The assassination."

"What does Lincoln have to do with anything?"

Kohler shook his head. "Michael's been very reluctant to talk to
me about his delusions. Only hints, cryptic phrases. He didn't
trust me."

"Even you, his doctor?"

"*Especially* me, his doctor. That's the nature of his illness. He's
paranoid. He's always accusing me of trying to get information out
of him for the FBI or Secret Service. He has a core delusion but I

can't get to the bottom of it. I suppose it centers on the Civil War, Lincoln's death, conspirators. Or some event he associates with the assassination. I don't know."

"Why's his delusion so important?"

"Because it's central to his illness. It explains to him why every day is so unbearably hard. A schizophrenic's life," Kohler lectured, "is a search for meaning."

And whose isn't? Lis wondered.

"It's a very controversial matter right now," the doctor said, adding that he himself was considered a bit of a renegade. She thought he was a little too smug with this characterization of himself. "Schizophrenia is a physical illness. Just like cancer or appendicitis. You have to treat it with drugs. No one disputes that. But I differ from most of my colleagues in thinking that you can also treat schizophrenic patients very effectively with psychotherapy."

"I can't really imagine Hrubek lying on a couch talking about his childhood."

"Neither could Freud. He said schizophrenic patients shouldn't be treated with psychoanalysis. Most psychiatrists agree. The current treatment is to get them on brain candy—that's how the cynics among us refer to their medication—and force them to accept reality, teach them to order in restaurants and do their own laundry then turn them loose. And it's true—extended analysis, with the patient on the couch, that's wrong for people like Michael. But certain types of psycho*therapy* work very well. Seriously ill patients can learn to function at a very high level.

"Most psychiatrists think that schizophrenic patients ramble incoherently, that their delusions are meaningless. I think that almost everything they say is meaning*ful*. The more we try to translate their words into *our* way of thinking, yes, the more pointless those words are. But if we try to grasp their *metaphoric* meaning, then doors open up. Take a Napoleon, okay? That's the popular image of a schizophrenic. I won't try to convince a patient that he isn't

Napoleon. And I wouldn't just pat him on the head and say, "*Bonjour*," when I pass him in the hall. I'd try to find out *why* he thinks he's the emperor of France. Nine times out of ten there's a reason. And once I know that, I can start to unlock doors. I've had remarkable results with patients—and some of them are a lot sicker than Michael." He added bitterly, "I was *just* getting inside him, I was almost there . . . When this happened."

"You make him sound innocent."

"He *is* innocent. That's the perfect word for him."

She thought angrily, Oh, isn't the good doctor used to people buying his bill of goods? The malleable patients who nod their damaged heads and shuffle off to obey. The sorrowful families pecking through his pompous words for comfort like birds for seed. Young, terrified interns and nurses. "How on earth," she asked, "can you *romanticize* him? He's just a set of muscles free to do whatever he wants. He's a machine run amok."

"Not at all. Michael's tormented by the inability to achieve what he thinks he can become. That conflict shows itself as what we call madness. To him, his delusions are merciful explanations for why he can't be like the rest of the world."

"You seem to be saying his disease isn't anybody's fault." She waved her arm at the clouds speeding past. "Well, neither are tornadoes but we'd stop them if we could. We should *stop* Hrubek. Somebody should . . . lock him up and throw away the key." She'd come a split second away from saying, track him down and shoot him. "He's just a psychopath!"

"No, he isn't. That's a very different diagnosis from schizophrenia. Psychopaths adapt well to society. They seem normal—they have jobs and families—but they're completely detached from morality and emotion. *They're* evil. A psychopath would kill you because you took his parking place or wouldn't give him ten dollars. And he wouldn't think twice about it. Michael would only kill for the same reasons you would—self-defense, for instance."

"Please, doctor. Michael's harmless? Is *that* what you're telling me?"

"No, of course not. But . . ." Kohler's voice faded. "I'm sorry. I've upset you."

After a moment Lis said, "No. We see things differently, that's all." But she said it quite coolly.

"It's late. I've used up my twenty minutes." He rose and walked toward the kitchen. When they approached the back door, he asked, "One thing I'm still curious about. Why would he associate you with betrayal? 'The Eve of betrayal.' 'Revenge.' 'Forever.' Why?"

"Well, I suppose because I testified against him." She lifted her palms at the simplicity of this deduction.

"You think that's it?"

"I suppose. I really don't know."

Kohler nodded and fell silent. A moment later his mind made another of its odd leaps, punctuated by a stab at his pale scalp with a nervous finger. "There's a car lot outside of town, isn't there?"

She thought she'd misheard him. "A car lot? What did you say?"

"Cars. A dealership."

"Well, yes. But . . ."

"I'm thinking of the big one. All lit up. A Ford dealership."

"Klepperman's Ford, that's right."

"Where is it exactly?"

"Half mile outside of town. On Route 236. Just over the hills east of town. Why?"

"Just curious."

She waited for an explanation but none came and it was clear that the interview, or interrogation, or whatever it had been, was over. Kohler cleared his throat and thanked her. She was grateful he was leaving; the visit had angered her. But she was confused too. What had he learned that was so helpful?

And what had he not told her?

Outside, walking to his car, they both looked up at the thick clouds. The wind was fierce now and whipped her hair in an irritating way, flinging it into her face.

"Doctor?" Lis stopped him, touching his bony upper arm. "Tell me, what are the odds that he's on his way here?"

Kohler continued to gaze at the clouds. "The odds? The *odds* are that they'll find him soon, and even if not, that he'd never make it this far alone. But if you want my opinion I think you should go to that hotel you mentioned."

He glanced at her for a moment then it was clear that his thoughts were elsewhere, maybe wandering with his terrified, mad patient through brush and forests, lost on highways, sitting in a deserted cabin somewhere. As she watched him walk to his car, she pushed aside her anger for a moment and saw Kohler for the ambitious young physician that he was, and tough and devoted. And undoubtedly damn smart too. But she sensed something else about him and was unable for a few moments to fathom exactly what that might be. His car had disappeared down the long driveway before she understood. Dr. Richard Kohler, Lis decided, was a very worried man.

The ambulance and the police car arrived simultaneously, their urgent lights painting the underside of the trees with peculiar metallic illumination. The brakes squealed and the yard was filled with uniformed men and women, equipment, stretchers, electric boxes dotted with lights and buttons. The medics trotted toward the large colonial house. The police too, holstering their long flashlights as they ran.

Owen Atcheson sat on the back steps beside the kitchen door, which was still open. His head was in his hands as he watched the medics run toward the doorway. One said to him, "You called 911? Reported a woman was attacked?"

He nodded.

"Where is she?"

"In the kitchen," Owen said, exhaustion and discouragement thick in his voice. "But you can take your time."

"How's that?"

"I said there's no rush. The only place she's going tonight is the morgue."

19

"Who is it? Not Mary Haddon? Jesus, not their *daughter*?"

"No, that's not her."

"That's not Mary?"

"*Look* at her, for God's sake! It's not Mary."

But nobody wanted to look. They'd look at the wall calendar, the Post-it notes, the shattered teacup, the scraps of paper clinging to the avocado-colored refrigerator door under fruit-shaped magnets. They'd look everywhere but at the terrible creature tied with bell wire to the maple captain's chair. The senior medic walked carefully into the room, minding the huge slick of blood on the tile floor. He bent down and studied the intricately tied knots. Her head, loosened by the deep cut to her throat, lolled backwards, and her blouse was pulled open. The awkward letters cut into her skin were stark against her blue-white chest.

"Fucking mess," one of the young cops said.

"Hey, let's don't have any of that talk here," a plainclothes detective said. "Check out the house. All the bedrooms."

"I think Joe and Mary're over at the church. The charity auction's tomorrow and he's chairman. I heard they're working late. Oh, I hope their daughter's with them. Man, I hope that."

"Well, call 'em up or get a car over there. Let's get on with this."

One cop entered and looked at the corpse. "Lord, that's Mattie! Mattie Selwyn. She's the Haddons' housekeeper. I know her brother."

The nervous banter continued. "Oh, this is a bad thing. What's that in her lap, that little white thing? . . . Jesus, some kind of skull or something. A badger?"

"Why tonight?" a deputy lamented. "Storm'll be here any time. Already had a twister in Morristown. Couple people died. You hear? Man—"

Owen stood in the doorway and looked again at the carnage. He shook his head.

"You the one who called us, sir?" the detective asked, running his hand through his salt-and-pepper hair.

Owen nodded and wiped sweat from his face. After calling 911 he'd glanced into a window and seen on his face the mud smeared on his cheekbones and forehead to mask the glossiness of his skin. He had washed his face before the police arrived. Still, his hand-kerchief now came away from his forehead dirty and he supposed he looked a mess. He explained about Hrubek's escape, the bicycle, following him here. The detective said, "Yessir, we had a notice about that runaway. But we thought he was heading east."

"I *told* them he wasn't," Owen said heatedly. "I *told* them he'd turn west. They wouldn't listen. Nobody took this thing seriously from the start. And now look. . . ."

"We also heard he was harmless," the detective said bitterly, staring at the body. Then he glanced at Owen. "What's your role in this exactly?"

He told them that he'd come out to see what the state police were doing to capture the escapee, who appeared to have a grudge against his wife. As he spoke he realized that the story *was* out-landish and he was neither surprised nor offended when the officer asked, "Could I see some ID, please?"

Owen handed over his driver's license and his attorney's regis-tration card.

"You don't mind if we confirm this?"

"Not at all."

The detective picked up the phone and called his office. A moment later he nodded and hung up. He walked back to Owen and returned the ID. "Are you armed, sir?"

"Yes."

"I assume you have a firearm permit, Mr. Atcheson?"

"I do, yes. And four years of combat experience." He said this because the detective was about his age and had a serenity in the face of butchery like this that comes from only one thing—surviving firefights. The detective squinted a bit of reluctant camaraderie into his face.

One cop stuck his head into the foyer and, his wide eyes on the dead woman, said to the detective, "Found something, Bob. We got motorcycle tracks. They look fresh."

The detective asked Owen, "Yours?"

"No."

The cop continued, "Only, the helmet's still on the ground. It seemed—"

The policeman who'd identified the housekeeper called from the living room, "That helmet? Was hers, Mattie's. She drove a Honda. Yellow one, I think."

The detective called, "Where do the tracks head?"

"They go behind the garage, down a path then out over to 106. They turn south."

Owen asked, "To 106? That's the road to Boyleston."

"Sure is. He was to head down 106 on a motorcycle, he'd be there in forty, fifty minutes."

"Boyleston's the closest Amtrak station, isn't it?"

The detective nodded. "That's right. Notice we got said he was making for Massachusetts. They were thinking he'd gone on foot but, sure, he could take the train. Maybe he doubled back. Like a feint, you know."

"That makes sense to me."

The detective barked an order to a uniformed sergeant, telling him to notify the Boyleston police about the murder and to send two of their own cars south on 106. Immediately. As the cops turned back to the body and busied themselves with fingerprints and crime-scene photos, Owen stepped outside and strolled around the property, looking for tracks. He studied the estate's rolling pastures, a horse stable and several small barns that had been converted into garages.

"You see anything?" the detective called to him.

"Nope."

"Say, Mr. Atcheson, we'll need a statement from you. And I'm sure Attorney Franks, our prosecutor, will be wanting to talk to you."

"In the morning, I'd be happy to."

"I—"

"In the morning," Owen said evenly.

The officer kept eye contact for a moment then chased to his wallet for a business card, which he handed to Owen. "You'll call me then? Nine a.m. sharp?"

Owen said he would.

The detective, tours of duty aside, looked Owen up and down. "I understand what you're going through, sir. I myself might be inclined to head off after him this minute, I was in your position. But my advice is for you to stay out of this whole thing."

Owen merely nodded and gazed south toward the ruddy haze of lights that would be Boyleston. He stepped aside as the medics brought the woman's body out of the door. He stared at it, seeing not so much the dark-green bag as, in his mind's eye, the bloody black strokes of the letters that had been cut into her chest.

The words they spelled were *forEVEr rEVEnge*

He lost the scent on the outskirts of Cloverton.

Emil was once again quartering, zigzagging across the asphalt, his master in tow, looking for a trail he simply couldn't find. Even

Trenton Heck, who supported his dogs 110 percent, was having an uneasy time of it.

The big obedience problem with tracking was that you never knew exactly what was in the dog's mind. Maybe just as you lowered the scent article to his nose, the hound got a whiff of deer and with the shout of "Find!" he'd bounded off in pursuit of a big buck who'd trotted nearby hours ago. The hound would be doing exactly what he believed he'd been ordered to do, and woe to the handler who failed to slip him a Bac'n Treat just the same as if he'd treed the escaping convict. Yet Heck replayed the evening and didn't see how Emil could be mistaken. Come on, boy, he thought fervently. I got faith in you. Let's do it.

Emil started toward a water-filled ditch but Heck ordered him back. It occurred to him that a man who'd lay traps would also poison water though Heck was more worried about natural contamination. It was his rule to let dogs drink only water from home. (When his fellow troopers would snicker at this and mutter, "Evian," or "Perrier," he'd tell them, "Fine, boys, just go to Mexico yourselves sometime and drink from the tap. See how you enjoy it. For your hound, anyplace that ain't home could be Mexico.") Tonight he took a jar from the truck and gave Emil a long drink. The hound lapped greedily. They started on the trail again.

Far distant in the west, lightning flashed in mute bands at the horizon, and a misty rain had started falling. This, Heck supposed, was what had ruined the scent. Earlier he'd been welcoming the rain but that was when Hrubek was on foot. The madman was now on a bicycle and they were following a very different type of trail. Dogs detect three different scents—body scent in the air, body scent pressed into the ground, and track scent, which is a combination of crushed vegetation and smells released by whatever the prey might step on. Rain intensifies and freshens the latter two. But add a hard rain to airborne scent on asphalt—which is chock-full of chemicals that foul dogs' noses—and you've got the worst possible combination to track over.

"Come on, why don't you get off that damn bike?" Heck muttered. "Can't you hoof it? Like a normal escapee?"

Emil slowed and looked around him. A bad sign. *I got you for your nose, boy, not your eyes. Hell, I can see better'n you.*

The hound slowly strolled off the road and into a field. His leg on fire, Heck led the dog along a grid search pattern, loping in huge squares over the ground, moving slowly under the guidance of the flashlight for fear of the steel traps. Emil paused for long moments, sniffing the ground then lifting his nose. Then he ambled off and repeated the process. As Heck watched the hound his sense of futility grew.

Then Heck felt a tug on the track line and he looked down with hope in his heart. But immediately the line went slack, as Emil gave up on the false lead and returned to nosing about in the ground, breathing in all the aromas of the countryside and searching in vain for a scent that, for all Heck knew, might have vanished forever.

Michael Hrubek's father was a grayish, somber man who had, over the years, grown dazed by the disintegration of his family. Rather than avoiding home, however, as another man might have done, he dutifully returned every evening from the clothing store in which he was the formal-wear manager.

And he returned quickly—as if afraid that in his absence some new pestilence might be threatening to destroy whatever normalcy remained in his house.

Once home though he spent the tedious hours before bed largely ignoring the chaos around him. For diversion he took to reading psychology books for lay people and excerpts from *The Book of Common Prayer* and—when neither proved to be much of a palliative—watching television, specifically travel and talk shows.

Michael was then in his mid-twenties and had largely given up his hopes of returning to college. He spent most of his time at home with his parents. Hrubek senior, attempting to keep his son happy and, more to the point, out of everyone's hair, would bring Michael comic books, games, Revell models of Civil War weaponry. His son invariably received these gifts with suspicion. He'd cart them to the upstairs bathroom, subject them to a *pro forma* dunking to short out sensors and microphones then stow the dripping boxes in his closet.

"Michael, look: Candyland. How 'bout a game later, son? After supper?"

"Candyland? Candyland? Do you know *anybody* who plays Candyland? Have you ever met a single person in the fucking *world* who plays Candyland? I'm going upstairs and taking a bath."

For his part, Michael avoided his father as he avoided everyone else. His rare forays outside the house were motivated by pathetic missions. He once spent a month looking for a rabbi who would convert him to Judaism and he devoted three fervent weeks to hounding an anxious Armed Forces recruitment officer, who couldn't shake the young man even after explaining a dozen times that there was no longer a Union Army. He took a commuter train to Philadelphia, where he stalked an attractive black newscaster and once cornered her on the street, demanding to know if she was a slave and if she enjoyed pornographic films. She got a restraining order that the police seemed eager to enforce with whatever vigor was necessary but Michael soon forgot about her.

On Saturday mornings his father would make a big pancake breakfast and the family would eat amid such ranting from Michael that his parents eventually tuned out the noise. Michael's mother, most likely still in her nightgown, would pick at her food until she could face the plate no longer. She would rise slowly, put on lipstick, because that's what proper ladies did after meals, and after spending several frantic minutes looking for the *TV Guide* or the remote control, she would return to bed and click on the set. His father did the dishes then took Michael to a doctor whose small office was above an ice-cream parlor on Main Street. All that Michael remembered about this man was that with almost every sentence he said, "Michael."

"Michael, what I'd like to do today is for you to tell me what some of your earliest memories are. Can you do that, Michael? An example would be: Christmas with your family. Christmas morning, Michael, the very first time—"

"I don't know, fucker. I can't remember, fucker. I don't know anything about Christmas, fucker, so why do you keep asking me?"

Michael said "fucker" even more often than the doctor said "Michael."

He stopped seeing this psychiatrist after his father's insurance company refused to reimburse the family for any more visits. He spent more and more time in his room, sometimes reading history, sometimes wearing his mother's clothing, sometimes screaming out the windows at people who walked past. The Hrubeks' pale-blue home became a renowned house of terror among the children of Westbury, Pennsylvania.

This was his life for the years following his expulsion from college—living at home, going on his mad sorties, dunking toys, eating junk food, reading history, watching television.

It was around his twenty-fifth birthday, in April, that Michael withdrew into his room and stopped talking to anyone. One month later he tried to burn down the house to stop the voices that came from his mother's bedroom. The following Saturday Hrubek senior dressed his son in an ill-fitting suit and took him, along with three books, a change of underwear and a toothbrush, to a state mental hospital in New York. He lied about state residency, and had the boy admitted to the facility under an involuntary-commitment order intended to last for seventy-two hours.

His father hugged Michael and told him the hospital would stabilize his condition and make him well enough to live at home. "I'll have to think about that," a frowning Michael responded, not knowing that those would be the last words ever spoken between father and son.

Upon his return to Westbury, the depleted man sold the house at a loss and moved to the Midwest, where his family had come from years before.

After six weeks the hospital's Third-Party Payments Section gave up trying to track down his father, and Michael became a guest of the state.

This hospital was bleak—an institutional desert, where the long hours were broken only by Pill Time and Meal Time and Shock Time. At this point in his illness, however, Michael was more evasive than aggressive and didn't need electroconvulsive-shock treatment. His pills calmed him down and he spent the days sitting placidly in his room until his butt grew sore then he'd stand and stare out the windows barred by wire lattice that dangled with tiny streamers of greasy dust.

Once a week he would talk to a doctor.

"You have to take your meds. . . . Are you taking them? Good. You see, we're aiming to get you to the point where you're aware, I'm speaking of a conscious awareness, that your concerns are a function of your illness not of the reality around you. . . ."

Michael would grunt disagreeably and remind himself to keep a suspicious eye on the fellow.

After six weeks in the hospital Michael Hrubek was diagnosed as mildly schizophrenic, nonviolent, possibly paranoid, and was among eighty-seven similar patients released when the hospital closed one of its wings due to budget cutbacks.

Because Third-Party Payments had never informed Discharge that the location of Michael's father was unknown, the release notice was sent to a fictitious address in Valhalla, New York. On the day Michael was discharged an orderly parked him on a bench in the waiting room and told him to wait for a family member to pick him up. Four hours later Michael told the duty nurse that he was going to say goodbye to one of the groundskeepers. Instead, he wandered unchallenged through the front gate—thus beginning a lengthy and harrowing journey that would lead him to cities throughout the Eastern Seaboard, to hospitals of varying degrees of renown and infamy, to idyllic Trevor Hill Psychiatric and his beloved and betraying Dr. Anne, to the snakepit of Cooperstown, to the deaths at Indian Leap, to Marsden State Mental Health Facility, to Dr. Richard . . . and finally—after so many miles and so very many lifetimes—to the astonishing place in which Michael found himself tonight: the driver's seat of a black, thirty-year-old Cadillac Coupe de Ville, speeding not toward Boyleston at all, but straight down Route 236 west to Ridgeton, which was now less than twenty miles away. As he drove, musical words flew from his lips:

"Cadillac, hard tack . . . Hard tack, horseback . . . Soldier boys, gray and blue . . ."

His hands left a residue of sweat on the white steering wheel and he kept repeating to himself which pedal was the accelerator and which was the brake. He'd sometimes find himself easing over the center line and in panic forget which lane he was supposed to be in. Then, remembering, he'd forget how to steer back into the proper lane and would drive English-style for some distance before gradually returning to the right.

On and on he drove, a steady forty miles an hour in a fifty-five zone. He swallowed and moaned often and muttered to himself, and he wanted nothing so much as to fall onto the smooth plain of the upholstered seat, cover his head and fall fast asleep. But he didn't. No, Michael remained as upright as a soldier on guard duty, looking straight into the darkness where the guns of his enemy waited.

His eyes left the asphalt only once, to glance at the sign that said, RIDGETON 17 MILES, then returned to the highway. With pleasure he inhaled the sweet smell of the heater that blasted air into his face. The memories he'd had this November evening, Michael thought with a burst of rare perception, had traveled as far as he had. And he thought now about an afternoon long ago, sitting in the library of one of his hospitals, singing a song that he himself had written. He recalled that he'd sung it over and over until the librarian asked him to stop and then he sang it in his head, silently mouthing the words.

Now, ensconced in his luxurious black car, he once again sang it and he sang it loud.

> *"Hard tack, horseback, the Capital's asleep.*
> *The soldier boys are crying. Somewhere a woman weeps.*
> *Hard tack, the moon's back, and bloody in the sky.*
> *I'm going to the graveyard, where the body lies. . . ."*

Michael points the black nose of the car down a long hill and feels the gradual, smooth acceleration of the engine. Unexpectedly though, despite the glory of newfound speed, despite his immense pride at mastering this machine that a year ago would have paralyzed him with terror, Michael Hrubek begins to cry.

He gulps hot air into his lungs, fueling the sobbing, and feels the moisture on his wide cheeks. His throat stings.

Why am I crying? Michael wonders, barely conscious that he *is* crying.

He really has no idea. But somewhere deep in his mind is the answer that he cries for man's genius in making this exquisite automobile. He cries for all the miles he's traveled tonight. And for the vague memory of a woman wearing a very unfashionable hat on her otherwise perfect head.

For the past dead and for those soon to be.

And he cries for what is surely sitting above the thickening storm clouds over his car right now—a moon blood red.

I'm going to the graveyard, where the body lies. . . .

20

Lis was taping the top row of windows in the greenhouse when the storm finally hit.

Her face was inches from the glass as she was reaching out to lay a strip on a hard-to-reach pane. Suddenly a slash of rain cracked against the window. She twisted away, dropping the tape, thinking for an instant that someone had flung a handful of gravel at the panes. She nearly tumbled backwards off the ladder.

She climbed down and retrieved the masking tape, surveying the sky. Worried that a window might shatter into her face if she continued to tape, Lis again considered leaving—now. But the north windows, those facing the storm, were still to be done.

Ten minutes, she decided. She'd allow herself that.

Climbing up once again she thought about Kohler's advising her to leave. Yet she felt no extreme urgency. He hadn't seemed particularly concerned on her behalf. Besides, she reasoned, the Ridgeton sheriff would certainly have called if he'd learned that Hrubek was headed for town.

As she laid the X's on the squares of glass, her eyes fell on the lake and the forest. Beyond them, barely visible in the rain, was a huge expanse of countryside—a muddy horizon of fields and woods and rocks disappearing into the black windy sky. The sweep of terrain seemed so limitless, so perfectly able to contain the infection of Michael Hrubek, that it was foolish to think that he might even get close to Ridgeton. The vastness of the landscape would protect her husband too; how could either man possibly find the other?

And where was Owen at this moment?

In her heart she believed he'd be back soon. Perhaps even before she and Portia left for the Inn. Returning empty-handed, angry and frustrated—because he'd missed his chance to play soldier.

And because he had lost an opportunity to do penance.

Oh, Lis had understood that from the start. She knew that his errand tonight had a tacit purpose. It was part of a complicated debt he seemed to feel he owed his wife.

And perhaps he did, she reflected. For Owen had spent much of last year in the company of another woman.

He'd met her at a legal continuing-education conference. She was a trust-and-estates lawyer, thirty-seven years old, divorced with two children. He offered these facts as proof of the virtue of his infidelity; no young, gum-snapping bimbo for *him*.

Yale-educated.

Cum laude.

"Do you think I give a *fuck* about her credentials?" Lis had shouted.

When she'd first seen a MasterCard receipt for a hotel in Atlantic City, dated the weekend he was supposed to be in Ohio on business, she was devastated. Never before a victim of adultery, Lis hadn't realized that illicit sex is only a part of the infidelity game. There's illicit affection too, and she wasn't sure which hurt the worst.

Why, bedding the bitch in Trump's Palace, her highly educated thighs squeezing Owen's, flicking tongues, shared spit, exposed nipples and cock and cleft . . . Those were bad enough. But Lis was almost more stung by the thought of their joined palms, romantic walks on the turbulent Jersey beach, the two of them sitting on a bench and Owen sharing his most private thoughts.

Stern Owen! Her *quiet* Owen.

Owen from whose mouth *she* had to pry words.

Much of this was speculation of course (he'd learned his lesson and volunteered nothing more after blurting out the woman's CV).

But the thought alone of an intimacy deeper than sex was horrifying to Lis and her fury at their furtive conversations and entwined fingers grew beyond all reasonable proportion. For weeks after his confession she was racked by a sensation that she might at any moment erupt in madness—anytime, anywhere.

By the time she confronted him, the affair was over, he said. He'd taken his wife's head in his long hands, stroking her hair, jiggling the earrings he'd given her (during the height of his infidelity, Lis had noted with ire, and that night pitched the jewelry out). The woman had asked him to leave Lis, Owen said, and marry her. He refused, they fought and the affair ended bitterly.

After the initial, cataclysmic weeks following this confession, after the long nights of silence, after those funereal Sunday mornings, after an intolerable Thanksgiving, they began to discuss the matter as couples do—tactically, then obliquely, then reasonably. Lis now had only vague memories of the conversations. You're too demanding. You're too strict. You're too quiet. You're too reclusive. You're not interested in what I do. You have to loosen up sexually. You come on like a rapist. You never complained. . . . Yes but you scare me sometimes I can't tell what you're thinking yes but you're so stubborn yes but . . .

The second-person pronoun occurs never so often as in the aftermath of infidelity.

Finally they decided to consider divorce and went their separate ways for a time. During this period Lis finally admitted to herself that the affair was no surprise. Not really. Owen's having an attorney for a lover, well, *that* was a shock, yes. He didn't fare well with strong women. To hear him tell it, his best relationship prior to Lis had been with a young Vietnamese woman in Saigon during the war. He was tactfully reluctant to go into many details but he described her glowingly as sensitive and demure. It took Lis some translating, and prying, to figure out that this meant she was subservient and complacent and she spoke very little English.

That's a relationship? she wondered, unnerved to find that this was the sort of woman her husband had sought out. Still, there seemed to be something more to the liaison. Something dark. Owen wouldn't go into the details and Lis was left to speculate. Maybe he had accidentally wounded her and stayed with her out of loyalty, slipping her stolen rations and medicines and nursing her to health. Maybe her father was a Viet Cong whom Owen had killed. Plagued with guilt, he'd offered some reparation and fallen in love.

This all seemed far too romantic, operatic even, for Owen Atcheson, and she ultimately attributed the affair to youthful lust, and his fond memories of it to the revisionist ego of a middle-aged man. But there was no denying that a servile young thing had a certain appeal to him. The greatest friction between them—and his worst flares of temper—arose when she opposed him. She could rattle off a hundred examples—buying the nursery, urging him to be more of a sexual partner, suggesting they see a therapist when the marriage hit rough spots, traveling less.

And yet, ironically, his domineering side did have a certain appeal to Lis. As troubling as this was, she couldn't deny it. She still recalled seeing him for the first time. She was in her mid-thirties, an age at which most Ridgeton women were sensible mothers several times over. Lis had attended a town-council meeting, where Owen was representing a building developer seeking a P&Z variance. Stern and unyielding, Owen Atcheson stood at the podium and comfortably withstood the assault of wrathful citizens. Lis stayed long after her own minor ministerial proceeding and watched him play the king's knight. She was captivated by his cold articulation and, watching him grip the podium with his large hands, actually found herself aroused.

She engineered a chance meeting in the parking lot afterwards, suggesting they exchange phone numbers. "Who knows? Maybe I'll need a good lawyer someday."

One week later he asked her to dinner and she accepted at once.

On the first date he showed up scrubbed and trimmed, wearing a blue blazer and khaki slacks, carrying a dozen roses. Owen ordered for her, picked up the check discreetly, held open every door she walked through and capped the evening with a chaste kiss after escorting her to the door.

He did everything by the book and she felt absolutely nothing for him.

He didn't call her afterwards and—despite a brief sting to the ego—she decided she was relieved not to hear from him. She went out with several other men casually, thinking no more about the austere Owen Atcheson. Then one Saturday, six months later, they ran into each other in a store on Main Street. He claimed he'd been meaning to call but had been traveling extensively. Why, Lis had wondered, did men think this made you feel better, explaining how much they'd *wanted* to call but had not?

As she and Owen stood awkwardly at the counter of Ace Hardware, he glanced down at the white plastic tubing she was buying. It was for her garden, she explained. Did she need any help installing it? When she hesitated he looked into her eyes and said he didn't have many talents but there were a few things he was very good at. Plumbing was one.

"All right," she said.

They returned to the small bungalow she was renting. With Owen supervising, together they hooked up the irrigation system in half an hour. When the work was finished, he walked to the spigot, beckoning her to follow. He took her hand and placed it on the knob then enfolded her fingers with his. "Shall we?" he asked, and turned the faucet on full as he lifted her chin with his free hand and kissed her hard on the mouth.

They spent the rest of the afternoon in Lis's brass bed, not even bothering to climb beneath the blue gingham covers, their dirty work-clothes strewn about them on the stairs and floor.

They were married eight months later.

Throughout their six years together Lis had frequent doubts about their future yet she'd never thought that infidelity would end the marriage; more likely, she believed, one of them would just pack and leave—maybe after, in a fit of temper, he finally delivered one of the slaps he'd come close to inflicting on her in the past. Or after she'd insisted, no, no compromises, that he choose between her and another weekend at the office.

So his affair was a sobering event. She was, at first, fully ready to divorce him and start life on her own. Initially this had a great appeal to her. But Lis Atcheson was not at heart an angry woman and as the weeks went by she found she needed to remind herself to be indignant about the affair. This equilibrium made the idea of living alone again less attractive. Besides, he was excruciatingly contrite, which gave her a curious power over him—the only upper hand she'd ever attained in the marriage.

A practical matter too: Ruth L'Auberget, who'd been ill with cancer throughout this time, finally passed away, and the daughters were heirs to a complicated estate. Lis, with no interest in financial matters, found herself relying more and more on Owen. Business and money were, after all, aspects of his profession and as he became involved in managing the estate the couple grew close once again.

Their life became easier. Lis bought the 4x4. As agreed among the sisters and Ruth L'Auberget, Lis and Owen moved into the Ridgeton house with its dream greenhouse and Portia received the co-op. Owen bought suits from Brooks Brothers and fancy shotguns. He went deep-sea fishing in Florida and hunting in Canada. And he continued to take business trips, often overnight. But Lis believed his pledge of fidelity. Besides, she reasoned, Owen clearly liked being wealthy, and the money, stock and house were all in Lis's name.

So when, tonight—after they'd learned of Hrubek's escape—Owen had stood before her, armed with his black guns, Lis had looked past his grim mouth and the consuming hunt lust in his eyes and had seen a husband trying the only way he could to fix a love altered by his own carelessness.

Well, bless you, Owen, for your errand tonight, Lis thought, tapping the last of the windows. Your efforts are appreciated. But hurry home now, won't you?

The wind was rising. It drove a whip of rain across the roof and north side of the greenhouse with such a clatter than Lis gasped.

It was time to leave.

"Portia! Let's go."

"I've got a couple more to do," she called from upstairs.

"Leave 'em."

The woman appeared a minute later. Lis studied her for a moment and was surprised to see that in these country clothes, so atypical of Portia, the sisters looked very much alike.

"What?" Portia asked, noting Lis's gaze.

"Nothing. You ready?" Lis handed her a yellow rain slicker and pulled her own on.

Portia slung her backpack over one shoulder. Lifting her small Crouch & Fitzgerald suitcase Lis nodded toward the door. They walked outside into the rain that now was falling steadily. A sudden gust ripped the baseball cap from Portia's head. She shouted in surprise and ran to retrieve the hat while her sister double-locked the back door, and they stepped along the soggy path to the edge of the parking area.

Lis turned to look back at the house. With the windows barred by X's of tape, and the old, warping shingles, the colonial had a battle-weary air, as if it squatted in the middle of a no-man's-land. Her eyes were on the greenhouse when she heard her sister ask, "What *is* that?"

Lis spun around. "My God."

Spreading out before them was a field of mud and water, nearly a foot deep, covering much of the driveway and filling the garage.

They waded through the chill, slimy water and gazed at the lake. It wasn't their levee that had given way; it was the sandbags by the dock—the ones that Owen had assured Lis he'd stacked high and solid. The rising lake had pushed them over and the water was backing into the creek behind the garage. Amid eddies and whirlpools, the stream was filling the yard.

"What do we do?" Portia shouted. Her voice was harsh and unsettling; despite the quick-moving current, the flood was virtually silent.

There wasn't much they *could* do, Lis decided. The water was flowing in through a twenty-foot gap—too large for the two of them to dam. Besides, the garage was in a low-lying area of the property. If the level of the lake didn't rise much more, the house and most of the driveway would be safe.

She said, "We leave is what we do."

"Fine with me."

They waded into the garage and climbed into the Acura. Lis slipped the key into the ignition. She paused superstitiously—concerned that the flood had shorted out the battery or ruined the starter. She looked at Portia then turned the key. The engine kicked to life and purred smoothly. Backing out carefully, Lis eased the car through the flood up the incline of the driveway.

They were nearly out of the dark pool surrounding the garage when the car shuddered and the front wheels, the drive wheels, dug through the gravel and into the slick mud below, where they spun uselessly, as if they rested in ruts of ice.

This, Lis recalled, had been her second concern.

He eased his BMW around the curve on Route 236 and sped out of Ridgeton through the cutting rain.

Richard Kohler now descended through the hills and swept to the right, heading due east once again. There it was. Perfect. Just perfect! He laughed out loud, thinking that the scene was far more impressive than he'd remembered. He pulled into the back of the lot, parked and shut the engine off. He unzipped his backpack, extracting Michael Hrubek's file—the one he'd started to read earlier that evening.

This battered folio had been penned by sixty-five-year-old Dr. Anne Weinfeldt Muller, a staff psychiatrist at Trevor Hill Psychiatric Hospital.

Trevor Hill was a renowned private facility in the southern part of the state. Michael had been Anne Muller's patient for merely five months but her insights into his plight, and his improvement under her care, were inspiring. It was, Kohler reflected, a true tragedy that no one would ever know how effective Muller's treatment of Michael Hrubek might have been.

Like Kohler, Anne Muller divided her time among various hospitals and happened to have come across Michael at a small state facility where she worked with severe schizophrenics. Impressed by his intelligence and struck by his unusual delusions, she campaigned to pry open the doors of expensive Trevor Hill and have Michael admitted as a *pro bono* patient. The hospital administrators—preferring patients that were more "mainstream" than Michael (that is, able to pay their bills)—had resisted her efforts at first but had finally acquiesced, largely because of her own prestige and talent and pigheaded manner.

His first day had been spent in a restraint camisole. Then he'd calmed and the feared garment had come off. Kohler glanced again at Muller's notes, jotted in the first week of the young man's commitment:

Pt. is hostile & suspicious. Afraid of being struck. ("You hit me on the head, you're one dead fucker, make no mistake.") No apparent visual hallucinations, some auditory . . . Motor activity is extreme restraint at times necessary. . . . Affect flat or inappropriate (Pt. began sobbing when noticed book of Ameri-

*can history; later Pt. laughed when asked about maternal
grandmother and said she was "one dead fucker") . . . Cognitive functioning good but flights of ideas indicate purely random thinking at times. . . .*

Although the many state hospitals in which Michael had been
committed undoubtedly blended together into a grim stew of memories, Trevor Hill might very well have stood out pleasantly in his
mind. In state facilities, patients wore filthy clothing and sat in drab
rooms with blunt crayons or Play-Doh for entertainment. Many of
the men and women had the indentations of lobotomies on the
crowns of their heads and were regularly third-railed by electroconvulsive-shock technicians or sent into insulin comas. But Trevor
Hill was different. There were far more orderlies and doctors per
patient than in the state hospitals, the library was full of books,
wards were sunny and windows unbarred, the grounds landscaped
with trim paths and gardens, and rec rooms stocked with learning
toys and games. ECS was used occasionally but medication was the
major tool of treatment.

Yet, as with all schizophrenic patients, getting the right drug and
dosage for Michael was a major task. One young resident at Trevor
Hill had naïvely asked him what medicines he'd taken in the past
and the patient answered like a diligent medical student. "Oh, lithium. Generally, chlorpromazine and its derivatives are contraindi-
cated for me. I'm a schizophrenic—make no mistake about that—
but a big component of my disease is manic-depression. You may
know that as bipolar depression. So, lithium has generally been my
drug of choice."

The impressed resident prescribed lithium and under the drug's
effect Michael went berserk. He threw the ward's television through
a window, leapt out after it and got halfway through the main gate
before being tackled by three burly orderlies.

After this incident Dr. Muller took over treatment personally. She put Michael on a loading dose of Haldol—a dosage larger than he would ultimately need but intended to stabilize him fast. He improved immediately. Then began the fine tuning, balancing the drugs' effectiveness against the side effects of weight gain, dry mouth, the uncontrollable moving of the lips that antipsychotic drugs cause, the nausea. His regimen included, at various times, Thorazine, Stelazine, Mellaril, Moban, Haldol, and Prolixin. Thirty milligrams of this, one hundred of that, up it to two hundred, no, better mix it. Eighteen hundred of Thorazine, no, go higher, switch to Haldol, ninety milligrams of it, well, that's the same as forty-five hundred of Thorazine, too high, how's his dyskinesia? Okay, back to Stelazine . . .

Muller finally settled on what Kohler himself found worked best with Michael: high levels of Thorazine. Michael's treatment consisted of this workhorse drug and his therapy with Dr. Anne. She met with him every Tuesday and Friday. And what was distinctive about his sessions with this psychiatrist was that unlike so many of his doctors in the past she *listened* to what he had to say.

"You've said a couple of times now, Michael, that you're worried about what's 'ahead.' Do you mean your immediate future?"

"I never said that," he snapped.

"Did you mean something ahead of you in the hallway? Was someone upsetting you?"

"I never said a word like that. Someone's making up things about me. The government's usually to blame, the fuckers. I don't want to talk about it."

"Do you mean 'a head,' like someone's head, a skull?"

He blinked and muttered, "I can't go into it."

"If it's not the head maybe you mean someone's face? Whose?"

"I can't fucking go into it! You're going to have to use truth serum on me if you want that information. I'll bet you have already. You may know that as scopolamine." He fell silent, a smirk upon his face.

The therapy was no more sophisticated than this. Like Kohler, Anne Muller never tried to dissuade Michael of his delusions. She dug into them, trying to learn what was inside her patient. He resisted with the resilience of a captured spy.

But after four months Michael's paranoid and contrary nature suddenly vanished. Muller herself grew suspicious—she'd come to recognize that Michael had a calculating streak in him. He grew increasingly cheerful and giddy. Then she learned from the orderlies that he'd taken to stealing clothes from the laundry room. She assumed that his apparently improved temperament was a ruse to shift suspicion about the theft.

Yet before Muller could confront him, Michael began to deliver the loot to her. First, two mismatched socks. He handed them to her with the bashful smile of a boy with a crush. She returned the articles to their owners and told Michael not to steal anymore. He grew very grave and told her he was "unable at this time to make a commitment of that magnitude."

Important principles were involved, he continued. "Very important."

Apparently so, for the next week, she received five T-shirts and more socks. "I'm giving these clothes to you," he announced in a whisper, then walked away abruptly as if late for a train. The gift-giving went on for several weeks. Muller was far less concerned about the thefts themselves than understanding what Michael's behavior meant.

Then, when she was lying in bed at three in the morning, the epiphany occurred. She sat up, stunned.

In the course of a long, disjointed therapy session that day, Michael had lowered his voice and, eyes averted, whispered, "The reason is, I want to get my *clothes* to you. Don't tell anyone. It's very risky. You have no idea *how* risky."

Clothes to you. *Close* to you. I want to get close to you. Muller bolted from her bed and drove immediately to her office, where she

dictated a lengthy report that began with a subdued introduction
tantamount to a psychiatrist's shout of joy:

*Major breakthrough yesterday. Pt. expressed desire for emo-
tional connection with Dr., accompanied by animated affect.*

As the treatment continued, Michael's paranoia diminished further. The thefts stopped. He grew more sociable and cheerful and
he required less medication than before. He enjoyed his group-
therapy sessions and looked forward to outings that had previously
terrified him. He started doing chores around the hospital, helping
out the library and gardening staffs. Michael, Muller reported, had
even driven her car several times.

Kohler now looked up from the report and gazed across the gritty
parking lot. Lightning flashed in the west. Then he read the final
entry in the file, written in a hand other than Anne Muller's. He
found he could picture the scene upon which these notes were
based only too well:

*Michael lies on his bed, looking through a history book, when a
doctor comes into his room. He sits on the bed and smiles at the
patient, inquiring about the book. Michael immediately stiffens. Little
sparks of his paranoia begin to burn.*

"Who're you, what do you want?"

"I'm Dr. Klein. . . . Michael, I'm afraid I have to tell you that
Dr. Muller is sick."

"Sick? Dr. Anne is sick?"

"I'm afraid she's not going to be meeting with you."

Michael doesn't know what to say. "Tomorrow?" *he manages to
blurt, wondering what this man has done with his doctor and friend.*
"Will I see her tomorrow?"

"No, she's not coming back to the hospital."

"She left me?"

"Actually, Michael, she didn't leave you. She left all of us. She passed away last night. Do you know what it means, 'passed away'?"

"It means some fucker shot her in the head," he answers in an ominous whisper. "Was it you?"

"She had a heart attack." .

Michael blinks a number of times, trying to comprehend this. Finally a bitter smile snaps onto the patient's face. "She left me." He begins nodding, as if relieved to hear long-anticipated bad news.

"Your new doctor is Stanley Williams," the man continues soothingly. "He's an excellent psychiatrist. He trained at Harvard and he worked at NIMH. That's the National Institutes for Mental Health. How's that for credentials, Michael? Very sharp fellow, you'll be pleased to know. He's going to—"

The doctor manages to dodge the chair, which splinters against the wall with the sound of a gunshot. He leaps into the corridor. The heavy oak door restrains Michael for about ten seconds then he finishes kicking his way into the hall and storms through the hospital to find his Dr. Anne. He breaks the arm of an orderly who tries to subdue him and they finally net him like an animal, a nineteenth-century technique that had been used at Trevor Hill only once since it opened.

One week later, his advocate and therapist dead, Michael Hrubek and his sole material possessions—toothbrush, clothes and several books of American history—were shipped to a state mental hospital.

His life was once again about to become an endless stream of Pill Time and Meal Time and Shock Time. And it would have too, except that after sitting in the hospital's intake waiting room for two hours, temporarily forgotten about, he grew agitated and strolled out the front door. He waved goodbye to a number of patients and orderlies he'd never met and continued through the gate, never to return.

Dr. Richard Kohler noted that the date of that disappearance had been exactly fourteen months ago; the next official record about Michael Hrubek was an arrest report written by the unsteady hand of a trooper at Indian Leap State Park on the afternoon of May 1.

The psychiatrist set aside Anne Muller's file and picked up the small notebook filled with the jottings he had made at Lis Atcheson's house. But before he read he stared for a moment outside at the drops of thick rain that rattled on the windshield, and he wondered just how much longer he'd have to wait.

21

"Where'd you find this?"

Under the bed, up a tree, in between Mona the Moaner's legs . . .

Peter Grimes didn't respond and to his great relief the hospital director seemed to forget the question.

"My God. He's been talking to DMH for *three months*? Three fucking months! And look at all of this. Look!" Adler seemed almost more astonished at the volume of paperwork that Richard Kohler had generated than by the contents of those papers.

Grimes noticed that his boss was touching the sheets rather gingerly, as if afraid of getting his fingerprints on them. This was perhaps Grimes's imagination but it made the young doctor extremely uncomfortable—largely because it seemed like an excellent idea, one he wished had occurred to him earlier, before he'd left the evidence of his identity imprinted all over the documents.

Adler looked up, his thoughts hovering, and to keep him from asking again where the papers had come from, Grimes read from the sheet that happened to be face up in front of the two men. " 'Dear Dr. Kohler: Further to your proposal dated September 30 of this year, we are pleased to inform you that the Finance Division of the State Department of Mental Health has provisionally agreed to fund a program for inpatient treatment of severely psychotic individuals according to the guidelines you have set forth in the aforementioned proposal. . . .' "

"God*damn* him," Adler interjected with such vehemence that Grimes was afraid to stop reading.

286 \ Jeffery Deaver

" 'A preliminary budget of 1.7 million dollars covering the first year's financial needs for your program has been provisionally approved. As agreed, funding will come from existing allocations to the state mental-health hospital system, in order to bypass the necessity of a public referendum,' "

But stop he did when Adler muttered "bypass" as if it were an obscenity and snatched away the sheet to read the final paragraph himself. " 'This is to confirm that your proposal is conditioned upon approval by the Board of Physicians of the State Department of Mental Health, following your final presentation of the six case studies and verbatims upon which your proposal was based (Allenton, Grosz, Hrubek, McMillan, Green, Yvenesky). A representative of the Board will contact you directly regarding times for oral presentations of those case studies. . . .' "

Adler slammed the paper to the desk and Grimes decided that, while his fingerprint paranoia was perhaps misplaced, the hospital director should be somewhat more careful. If Kohler noticed damaged pages he might complain of a suspected theft—to which, Grimes was painfully aware, there'd been a witness. A half hour before, the assistant had summoned an irritable Slavic janitor to open the door of Kohler's office. Not a seasoned burglar, Grimes had neglected to send him away and had failed to notice that the squat man planted himself on the threshold to watch with amusement the young doctor's heist from start to finish.

"Our *money*. He's getting our money, on top of everything else! And, look at this. Look at it, Grimes. He's using *our* patients to fuck us! He's selling us out—our patients, our money—for *his* program."

Adler grabbed the phone and made a call.

As he gazed out the window, Grimes considered Kohler's scheme and he was both shocked and impressed. Kohler had used Michael Hrubek as a shining example of how his combination of drugs, delusion therapy and milieu resocialization treatment could produce dramatic improvements in chronic, dangerous schizophrenic patients. The Department of Mental Health had agreed to give Kohler a great deal of money and let him create a little fiefdom—carved out of Marsden hospital itself, at Adler's expense no less. But of course if Hrubek wasn't captured quietly, if he injured or killed someone, the DMH Board of Physicians would abort Kohler's plan as unworkable and dangerous.

Still, it was an admirable scheme, Grimes thought, and he regretted playing a part in the downfall of a talented man, one who probably would've been a better choice to hitch his star to—if of course Kohler's career had survived this evening. Which it surely would not.

The rain spattered the greasy windows. A huge wail of wind ended in a crash of plate glass from somewhere in the courtyard below. Several other patients had joined Patient 223-81 and a chorus of frightened wailing filled the halls. Grimes looked absently out the window and tried to avoid thinking about the effect on patients if a tornado touched down nearby.

Adler slammed down the phone and looked at him. "He's not at the halfway house. Some son of a bitch tipped him off."

"Who, Kohler?"

"He got a call a couple hours ago. He's *out* there. He's after Hrubek right now."

"By himself?"

"He *has* to go by himself. He has to get Hrubek to come back like a quiet little lamb. Then he'll claim he simply walked up to him and asked him to come home. And the son of a bitch will. *After* Kohler hits him with a taser or a tranquilizer gun . . . Shit! The break-in."

"I'm sorry?" the assistant asked cautiously.

"Security said somebody broke into the pharmacy tonight."

"Right. Well, they said it was a car accident, looked like. We won't know till morning if anything's missing."

"Oh, something's missing, you can bet on it. That son of a bitch lifted a tranquilizer gun. He's going to . . ." Adler spat out, "Jesus, he's going to make Hrubek look like the fucking little puppy *I've* said he is all along. Jesus Lord."

Grimes impersonated a fish again, chewing water urgently, and wondered aloud what they might do next.

"I want to be ready to pre-empt the press. If this . . ." He tried out several words for size before saying, "If this situation becomes critical—"

"If it's a worst case."

"Yes, if it's worst-case, we'll have to go public immediately. I want a release. Write it up—"

"A press release?"

"What *else* would I mean? Can you draft one up? Subject, verb. Subject, verb. That too much for you? And let's go over it, you and me. Say that, unbeknownst to staff, no, say unbeknownst to *administrators* and *officials*, a private physician with privileges here gave Hrubek access to all wards, which allowed him to escape. Say 'with privileges'; don't say 'attending.' Let's confuse the morons. Then say that this was in defiance—"

"Defiance?"

"—of clear instructions that any transfer of Section 403 patients must be approved by the office of the director before they go into any milieu, group, or off-ward therapy."

Instructions, yes, well, his assistant stammered. But there *were* no instructions to that effect, were there? Oh, it made sense, yes. There probably *should* be, yes. But at the moment there were none.

"The memo," Adler said impatiently. "Don't you remember? The 1978 memo?"

Grimes glanced out the window. Adler was referring to a directive that required notice to the director's office before criminally insane patients could be moved into medium- or low-security wings, even temporarily—if, for instance, the showers on E Ward weren't working. While this *was* a rule, yes, it was observed only by the most (Grimes allowed himself the diagnosis) anal-retentive of the doctors at Marsden.

"This seems a little . . ." Now words evaded Assistant Grimes.

"And put a copy in here. What's the matter?"

"I just . . . The issue isn't really access, is it?"

"Well, what *is* the issue?" Adler said this with a sneer in his voice and Grimes had an urge to call him a schoolmarm, which certainly would have cost him his job faster than jokes about rape.

"Kohler doing delusion therapy. *That's* what set Hrubek off. *That's* what we can hang him with."

This was, Adler reflected, a good point. Hrubek's roaming the halls near the morgue was essentially the *orderlies'* fault. They missed his medicine stockpile and they were careless with Callaghan's body. But Kohler's sin, as Grimes accurately pointed out, was far more serious. He had somehow awakened Hrubek's *desire* to escape. The means *were* largely irrelevant. Those fantasies ought to have been tucked away inside Hrubek, tucked away very deeply—or, better yet, behaviorially conditioned out of him. Say what you might, electrodes and food could turns rats into quite model animals. Why, witness young Grimes. . . .

Still, the hospital director assessed, Kohler's errors would be tough to sell to the public—simple people who would want simple answers in the event that Hrubek knifed a trooper to death or raped a girl. He thanked Grimes for his insight and then added, "Let's just lay the access issue at our friend's feet, shall we? By the time it's all sorted out, he'll be everybody's whipping boy, and no one'll really care exactly what he did."

And his assistant, pleased to have been patted on the head, nodded instantly.

"Don't be too specific. We have to massage the facts. Say, because of his involvement in Kohler's program Hrubek was free to get into the freezer, the morgue and the loading dock. None of the other Section 403 criminally insane have that access. That's true, isn't it?"

It was, Grimes confirmed.

"*But for* his involvement in the program he never would've escaped. *Sine qua non.*"

"You want me to say that?"

"Well, not '*sine qua non*,' obviously. You know what I'm saying? You get the picture? And don't use Kohler's name. Not at first. Make it sound like we're concerned about, you know . . ."

"His reputation?"

"Good. Yes, his reputation."

The only mechanic answering the phone tonight was in Roenville, about fifteen miles west on Route 236. The man chuckled and answered that sure he had a truck but it'd be four or five hours before he could get somebody over to Ridgeton.

"Already got three roads out in this part of the county alone. And my men're getting a wreck off Putnam Valley Highway. Injuries. Mess of 'em. Hell of a night. Just one hell of a night. So, you wanna go on the list?"

Lis said, "That's okay," and hung up. She then called the Ridgeton Sheriff's Department.

"Why, hello, Mrs. Atcheson," the dispatcher answered respectfully. The woman's daughter was in Lis's class; parents tended to address her as formally as their children did. "How you weatherin' the storm tonight? So to speak. Ha. It's something, isn't it?"

"We're getting by. Say, Peg, is Stan around?"

"Nup, not a soul here. Everybody's out. Even Fred Bertholder, and he's got the flu like nobody oughta have. And they didn't cancel that rock concert like they oughta've. Can you believe that? A lotta youngsters got stranded. What a mess."

"Have you heard anything from Marsden hospital, about Hrubek?"

"Who'd that be?"

"That man who escaped tonight."

"Oh, him. You know, Stan called the state police about that just 'fore he went out. He's in Massachusetts."

"Hrubek? In Massachusetts?"

"Yes'm."

"You're sure?"

"They tracked him to the state line then our boys had to call off the search. Handed it over to the Mass troopers. They're top-notch at finding people even though they don't have any sense of humor. That's what Stan says."

"Have they . . . ? Have they found him?"

"I don't know. The storm'll hit there in an hour, hour and a half, so I don't suppose a drugged-up psycho's a real high priority but that's me speaking not them. They might not take to madmen from out of state. Being so serious and all. You know, Mrs. Atcheson, been meaning to speak to you about that C-minus Amy got."

"Could we talk about it next week, Peg?"

"Absolutely. It's just that Irv coached her like a demon, and he reads all the time. Knows his literature, and I don't mean just schlock either. He read *Last of the Mohicans* even before it was a movie."

"Next week?"

"Absolutely. Good night to you, Mrs. Atcheson."

She hung up and wandered out to Portia, who stood sipping a Coke on a small screened-in porch off the kitchen. They didn't use the place much for entertaining. The sun never reached it, and the view of the yard and lake was all but cut off by a tall growth of juniper.

"This is pretty," her sister commented, running her hand along an elaborate railing of mahogany, carved in the shapes of flowers, vines and leaves. The wind blew an aerated mist of icy rain toward the house and the women stepped back suddenly.

"That's right, you haven't seen it."

Lis had noticed the balustrade at an upstate demolition site and knew at once that she had to have it. In one of her brashest moments she'd laid quick, cold dollars into the ponderous hands of the wrecking-crew captain. It was probably an illicit deal, for he turned his back as she dragged off the delicate sculpture, which she then spent another two thousand dollars incorporating into the railing here.

Friends wondered why such a beautiful piece of woodwork accented a dark, out-of-the-way porch like this. But the carving had one frequent admirer: Lis herself spent many nights here, bedded down in a chaise longue she'd commandeered for the times when the insomnia was particularly bad. The porch was open on three sides. If there was wind the breezes flowed over her as she lay beneath the blankets and if there was rain the sound was hypnotic. Even when Owen was away on business, she'd often come down here. She supposed it was risky, being alone and so exposed to the night. Yet the game of finding sleep is a crucible of trade-offs and an insomniac can't afford the luxury of separating slumber and vulnerability.

"I heard," Portia said. "No tow truck?"

"Nope."

"Can we walk?"

"Two miles? In this rain and wind?" Lis laughed. "Rather not."

"What about Hrubek?"

"Supposedly in Massachusetts."

"So why don't we just sit it out? Get a fire going and tell ghost stories?"

If only they'd left twenty minutes sooner . . . Angrily Lis remembered Kohler. If he hadn't stopped by, they'd be at the Inn by now. She felt a chill thinking that it was as if Michael Hrubek had sent an agent to detain her.

Portia asked, "Well? We're staying?"

Overhead the wind sliced through the treetops with a hissing sound—the noise electric trains make—of motion not propulsion. The rain pounded the soaked earth.

"No," Lis said finally, "we're leaving. Let's get some shovels and dig out the car."

Animals are far easier than humans to pursue for long distances, for three reasons: They eat whenever they're hungry. They don't control elimination of wastes. They have limited options for locomotion.

The world at large, Trenton Heck reflected, may have considered Michael Hrubek an animal but so far his journey west had all the trappings of a trip by a damn clever human being.

Heck was in despair. The driving rain had virtually erased all the airborne scent and he could find no other evidence of Hrubek's trail. Emil had quartered again and again over the highway and surrounding fields for an hour and had found nothing.

But now, just outside of Cloverton, Heck found that the madman had lapsed momentarily. His animal's impulse to eat had overcome his need for evasion.

At first Heck didn't think anything of the Hostess doughnut box lying in the driveway of the old gas station. Then he noticed it wasn't empty. This said to him that it couldn't have been there more than a half hour. No self-respecting raccoon, he concluded, would let pastry sit uneaten for longer than that.

As Heck and Emil walked up to the box, the dog immediately tensed. Heck knew this had nothing to do with a canine fondness for sugar and grease, and he scanned the ground carefully. There! Hrubek's bootprints, just visible on the concrete apron near the pumps. All right! His heart thudded at this good luck. Just west of the station Heck found a tread mark in the dirt beside the highway. For some reason Hrubek was now keeping to the shoulder and in the rain it was easy to follow the tread ·by sight. Heck and Emil returned to the truck and drove west. He saw that the track continued only for another hundred yards or so then cut suddenly across the highway, aiming directly for a long driveway or private road.

Heck stopped the truck and got Emil harnessed up, once again short-lined because of Heck's fear of the traps. He picked up the scent immediately and together man and dog crashed through brush, the hound in heaven—his coat glistening with misty rain, his lungs filling with great gulps of cool air, his familiar master beside him, his simple dog's mind and solid body doing what God had created them for.

As they ran, Heck remembered another dog who loved fields, Sally Dodgeson's St. Anne—Emil's predecessor.

Sal was a smarter dog than Emil and with a faster gait and lither step. Those last two qualities, however, had been her downfall; she developed the curse of large working dogs, hip dysplasia. Heck retired her early and spent the bulk of his—and Jill's—sparse savings on operations. The surgery was not successful and it was a terrible thing to watch Sal, a young invalid, staring at the fields she'd loved to run through. Often she made pathetic attempts to escape and Heck would have to go retrieve the struggling animal, carrying her in his arms, his heart as broken as hers. The condition and the pain that accompanied it grew worse.

On the last visit to the vet Heck himself took the syringe from the doctor and injected the lethal dosage. Oh, it was a hard thing to do, and he wept, but Trenton Heck would let no stranger put down a dog of his.

When he returned home, Jill asked, too improvidently for his taste, "Would you cry for me that way?"

Heck was stung but he told her the truth and said of course he would. But the timing of his response was somehow off and Jill got huffy. She went out that night with her girlfriends, a batch of fun-loving waitresses, and he mourned alone, which was his preference anyway. The next morning at seven, Jill having returned just three hours before, Heck arose by himself and went to the breeder to talk about bloodhound pups.

Heck had used a classic dog-handler's trick to pick Emil out of a litter of five mournful-looking, irresistibly adorable bloodhound puppies. The breeder set up a piece of quarter-inch plywood next to the pen where the young pups were playing. In the middle of the board was a tiny hole. Heck crept up to the wood sheet and, unseen by the litter, watched through the hole as they rolled and nipped and tried out their long legs. In a few minutes one of the puppies lifted his head with a spark of curiosity in his eyes—a glint clearly visible despite the folds of skin that nearly obscured them. He tilted his head back and looked around then stumbled toward the hole behind which was Trenton Heck's right eye. The dog sniffed the alien scent for two minutes before becoming bored and returning to romp with his sorrowful-faced brothers and sisters.

The next day Heck did the same thing and again the ungainly puppy, tripping over his huge ears and paws, was drawn to investigate—while his siblings slept or played, oblivious to the intruder. When, the next week, the dog passed the scent test three for three, Trenton Heck stood, scooped up the dog and, one-handed, wrote a very large check to the breeder.

When Emil was twelve months old, the training started. Heck used only inductive training—dispensing rewards, never punishing. During the first six months of this work Heck's slacks stank of the meaty dog treats. Then he weaned the dog off food and onto praise as a reward tool. The training was a thousand times harder on Heck than on Emil, who had only to learn what commands to obey and to grasp how those words related to using his nose to do what it wanted to anyway.

Heck on the other hand had to make sure the training remained fun. Smart dogs like Emil get bored easily and Heck was forced to devise ways to keep the scenting interesting but feasible. Knowing when to stop for the day, figuring out when Emil was frustrated or horny or in a bad mood—those were his tasks. He had to pick scent articles that were challenging but not impossible (a scrap of leather was too easy; Bic pens and Jill's trashy romance novels too hard).

Heck, who at the time had a full-time trooper job and a wife who ate up much of his time, would rise at 4:00 a.m. to train his hound—a hardship for him but not for Emil, who woke immediately and joyously, knowing he was on his way to the fields. Oh, Trenton Heck worked. He knew the old tracking adage: "If you're not handling the dog right, it's your fault. If the dog's not tracking right, it's your fault."

But Emil did track right. He had a remarkable nose—one of the few, in his vet's estimation, that were two or three million times more sensitive than a human nose. He learned fast and the hound so exploited his nature that Heck, whose marriage was rocky and whose job was going nowhere, occasionally felt bad watching this astonishing dog and lamented that he himself had no consuming skill or drive to match Emil's.

After six months of training, Emil could follow a mile-and-a-half trail in record time, shaming the German shepherds that were the troop's unofficial trackers. By age two Emil had his American Kennel Club TD classification and a month later Heck took him up to Ontario, where he was awarded his Tracking Dog Excellent certification by pursuing a stranger over a thousand-yard trail that was five hours old, never hesitating on the turns or the cross-tracks meant to confuse the hound. After the TDE rating Emil more or less joined Haversham's troop, to which Heck was assigned, though the state technically had no budget for dogs. The troop did, however, spring for membership (dog and man) in the National Police Bloodhound Association, which two years ago gave Emil the famed Cleopatra Award for finding a lost boy who'd fallen into the Marsden River and been swept downstream in a heavy current, after which he'd wandered deep into a state park. The trail, through water, marsh, cornfields and forest, was 158 hours old—a record for the state.

Heck had taken to reading a lot about bloodhounds and believed that Emil was the descendant (spiritual, there being no true lineage) of the greatest of all tracking bloodhounds, Nick Carter, who was run by Captain Volney Mullikin down in Kentucky at the turn of the century, a dog credited with more than 650 finds resulting in criminal convictions.

Emil himself had put a fair number of people behind bars. Much tracking work involves trailing suspects from crime scenes or linking weapons or loot to defendants. Emil, because of his AKC papers and his solid history of tracking, was a permitted "witness," though he appeared on the stand through his spokesman, one Trenton Heck. Most of the dog's assignments, however, involved locating escapees like Michael Hrubek.

Tonight in fact it was the anticipated triumph in tracking down the psycho and earning Heck his reward that preoccupied him as they pushed through the brush. He should have had his mind on what he was doing though for he didn't see the spring trap until Emil stepped right onto it.

"No!" he cried, jerking back hard on the line, pulling the hound off balance. "Oh, no! What'd I do?" But Emil had already fallen sideways onto the large Ottawa Manufacturing trap. He yelped in pain.

"Oh, Jesus, Emil . . ." Heck dropped to his knees over the animal, thinking about splints and the emergency vet clinics, frighteningly aware that he had no bandages or tourniquets to staunch the flow of blood from a severed vein or artery. As he reached for his dog, however, his trooper instincts took over and realized that the trap might be a diversion.

He's waiting for me, it's a trick!

Heck flicked rain from his eyes, lifting the Walther, and spun about, wondering from which direction the madman would come charging at him. He paused momentarily, debated and when he heard nothing turned back to Emil. He'd have to risk an attack; he wasn't going to leave the dog unattended. Holstering the gun he reached for Emil, Heck's hands shaking and his heart only now beginning to pulse quickly in the aftermath of the fright. But the dog suddenly shook himself snootily and stood upright, unharmed.

What had happened? Heck gazed at the animal, who, as far as he could tell, had landed square on the burnished trigger plate of the trap.

Then he understood—the jaws had been sprung *before* Emil stepped on the trigger.

"Oh, Lord." He gripped the dog around his neck and hugged him hard. "Lord." The dog eased back and shook his head, embarrassment now piled on top of his indignation.

Heck crouched down and examined the trap. It was identical to those at the shop on Route 118. Hrubek obviously had set it. But how had it been sprung? There were two possibilities, Heck supposed. First, that a small animal, its head lower than the steel jaws, had bounded onto the trigger and set it off. The second possibility was that someone had come by, seen the trap and popped it with a stick or rock. This, Heck decided, was the likely explanation— because next to the trap he saw several bootprints in the mud. One set was Hrubek's. But someone else had been here as well. He looked closely at the prints and his heart plummeted.

"Oh, damn!" he whispered bitterly.

He recognized the sole. He'd seen these prints—of expensive L. L. Bean outdoorsman's boots—earlier in the evening, not far from the overhang where he and Emil had picked up Hrubek's westward trail, miles back.

So I've got some competition here.

Who is it? he wondered. A plainclothes trooper or cop maybe. Or more likely—and more troubling—a bounty hunter like Heck himself, seeking the reward money. Heck thought of Adler. Had he sent an orderly to find the patient? Was the hospital director playing a game of ends against the middle?

With the stake being Heck's reward money?

He rose and, clutching his gun, examined the two men's tracks carefully. Hrubek had continued south along the private road. The other tracker was coming *from* that direction and heading back toward Route 236. He'd done so after Hrubek—some of his prints covered the madman's—and he'd been running, as if he'd learned where Hrubek was headed and was in pursuit. Heck followed the L. L. Bean prints to the highway and found where the man had stopped and studied a tread mark, left recently by a heavy car. The tracker had then sprinted to the shoulder of Route 236, where he'd climbed into a vehicle and hurried west, spinning his wheels furiously. From the tread marks it was clear that the man was driving a truck with four-wheel drive.

The scene told him that Michael Hrubek had got himself a vehicle and was probably just minutes ahead of this other pursuer.

Heck looked around the turbulent night sky and saw a distant flash of silent lightning. He wiped the rain from his face. He debated for a long moment and finally concluded he had no choice. Even Emil couldn't track prey inside a moving car. Heck would speed west down the highway, relying on luck to reveal some sign of the prey's whereabouts.

"I'll leave the belt off, Emil," Heck said, leading the dog into the pickup. "But you sit tight. We're gonna waste some fuel here."

The hound sank down on Heck's outstretched leg, and as the truck sped onto the highway with a gassy roar, closed his droopy eyelids and dozed off.

22

Seven miles outside of Cloverton, along Route 236, Owen spotted the car parked by the roadside near a stand of evergreens.

Oh, you smart son of a bitch!

He drove past the old Cadillac then abruptly slowed and turned off the road, parking the truck in a cluster of juniper and hemlock.

He'd gambled, and he'd won.

About time, he thought. I'm due for a little luck.

Walking over the grounds at the murder site in Cloverton, Owen had noticed that two of the small barns near the house contained antique autos. He'd slipped inside and looked under the blue Wolf car covers to find an old '50 Pontiac Chief, a Hudson, a purple Studebaker. In one building, a stall was empty, and the car cover was dropped in a heap on the floor—the only disorder in the entire barn. His inclination was to dismiss the possibility of Hrubek's stealing such an obvious getaway car. But, remembering the bicycle, Owen yielded to his instincts and, after a brief search of the ground, he found recent tread marks of a heavy auto leading from the barn, down the driveway and then west on Route 236. Without a word to the Cloverton police he'd left the house and sped not to Boyleston but after the old car.

Now he climbed from the truck and walked back toward the Cadillac, the sound of his passage obscured by the steady rain and sharp slashes of wind. He paused and squinted into the night. Sixty, seventy feet away a large form stood with his back to Owen, urinating on a bush. The man's bald head was tilted back as he looked up into the sky, staring at the rain. He seemed to be singing or chanting softly.

Owen crouched down, slipping his pistol from his belt. He considered what to do next. When it had seemed that Hrubek was heading for the house in Ridgeton, Owen had planned simply to follow him there and then slip into the house ahead of him. If the madman broke in, Owen would simply shoot him. Maybe he'd slip a knife or crowbar into the man's hand—to make a tidier scene for the prosecutor. But now Hrubek had a car and it occurred to Owen that maybe Ridgeton wasn't his destination after all. Maybe he really would turn south and make for Boyleston. Or simply keep going on 236 and drive to New York, or even further west.

Besides, here was his quarry, defenseless, unsuspecting, alone —an opportunity Owen might not have again, wherever Hrubek was ultimately headed.

He made his decision: better to take the man now.

But what about the Cadillac? He could leave his truck here, dump the body in the trunk of the old car then drive it to Ridgeton himself. Once there he'd lug the body inside the house and—

But, no, of course not. The blood. The .357 hollow points would cause a lot of damage. Some forensic technician was sure to examine the Cadillac's trunk.

After a moment of debate Owen concluded that he'd simply leave the car here. Hrubek was crazy. He'd become scared of driving and had abandoned it, continuing on foot to Ridgeton. It occurred to him too that he probably shouldn't kill Hrubek here—the coroner might be able to determine that he'd died an hour or so before Owen claimed he had.

He decided that he'd just immobilize Hrubek now—shoot him in the upper arm and in the leg. Owen would lug him into the back of the Cherokee and drive on to Ridgeton.

And there the patient would be found, in the Atchesons' kitchen. Owen would be sitting in the living room, staring numbly out the window, staggered by the tragedy of it all—having fired two shots to try to stop him and finally a third, a lethal, bullet, when the big man would not heed Owen's orders to halt.

The blood in the Cherokee? Well, that was a risk. But he'd park it behind the garage. There'd be no reason for any investigators to see it, let alone have a forensic team go through the truck.

He analyzed the plan in detail, deciding that, yes, it was chancy but the risks were acceptable.

Cocking the pistol he made his way closer to the looming shape of Hrubek, who'd now finished his business and was staring up at the turbulent sky, listening to the sharp hiss of the wind in the tips of the pine trees and letting the rain fall into his face.

Owen got no further than five steps toward his prey before he heard the distinctive double snap of a pump shotgun and saw the policeman aim the muzzle at his chest.

"On the ground, freeze!" the young man's trembling voice called.

"What are you doing?" Owen cried.

"Freeze! Drop your gun! Drop that gun!"

Then Hrubek was running, a thick dark mass fleeing toward the Cadillac.

"I'm not going to tell you again!" the cop's voice was high with panic.

"You fucking idiot," Owen yelled, his temper flaring. He stepped toward the cop.

The trooper lifted the shotgun higher. Owen froze and dropped the Smith & Wesson. "Okay, okay!"

The sound of the Cadillac firing to life filled the clearing. As the car sped past them, the trooper glanced in shock at the sound. Owen easily shoved the shotgun muzzle to the side and drove his right fist into the side of the trooper's face. The young man dropped like deadweight and Owen was on him in a minute, slugging the trooper again and again, anger exploding within him. Gasping, he finally managed to control himself and looked down at the bloody face of the unconscious cop.

"Fuck," he spat bitterly.

The sudden crack sounded some yards behind him. It seemed like a gunshot and Owen dropped into a crouch, snatching up his pistol. He heard nothing else other than the wind and the drumming of the rain. The distant horizon lit up for a moment with huge sheets of lightning.

He turned back to the cop and handcuffed the man's wrists behind his back. He then stripped off the regulation patent-leather belt and bound the officer's feet. He stared in disgust for a moment, wondering if the trooper had gotten a good look at him. Probably not, he concluded. It was too dark; he himself hadn't seen the cop's face at all. He'd most likely figure that Hrubek himself had attacked him.

Owen ran back to his truck. He closed his eyes and slammed his fist on the hood. "No!" he shouted at the wet, breezy sky. "No!"

The left front tire was flat.

He bent down and noted that the bullet that had torn through the rubber was from a medium-caliber pistol. A .38 or 9mm probably. As he hurried to get the jack and spare, he realized that in all his plans for this evening this was something that he'd never considered—that Hrubek might be inclined to defend himself.

With a gun.

They stood side by side, holding long-handled shovels, and dug like oyster fishermen beneath the brown water for their crop of gravel. Their arms were in agony from filling and lugging the sandbags earlier in the evening and they could now lift only small scoops of the marble chips, which they then poured around the sunken tires of the car for traction.

Their hair now dark, their faces glossy with the rain, they lifted mound after mound of gravel and listened with some comfort to the murmuring of the car's engine. From the radio drifted classical music, interrupted by occasional news broadcasts, which seemed to have no relation to reality. One FM announcer—sedated by the sound of his own voice—came on the air and reported that the storm front should hit the area in an hour or two.

"Jesus Christ," Portia shouted over the pouring rain, "doesn't he have a window?"

Apart from this, they worked silently.

This is mad, Lis thought, as the wind slung a gallon of rain into her face. Nuts.

Yet for some reason it felt oddly natural to be standing in calf-high water beside her sister, wielding these heavy oak-handled tools. There used to be a large garden on this part of the property—before Father decided to build the garage and had the earth plowed under. For several seasons the L'Auberget girls grew vegetables here. Lis supposed that they might have stood in these very spots, raking up weeds or whacking the firm black dirt with hoes. She remembered stapling seed packets to tongue depressors and sticking them into the earth where they'd planted the seeds the envelopes contained.

"That'll show the plants what to look like, so they'll know how to grow," Lis had explained to Portia, who, being four, bought this logic momentarily. They'd laughed about it afterwards and for some years vegetable pinups had been a private joke between them.

Lis wondered now if Portia too recalled the garden. Maybe, if she did, she would take the memory as proof that going into business with her sister might not be as improbable as it seemed.

"Let's try it," she called through the rain, nodding toward the car.

Portia climbed in and, with Lis pushing, eased her foot delicately to the gas. The car budged an inch or two. But it sank down into the mud almost immediately. Portia shook her head and got out. "I could feel it. We're close. Just a little more."

The rain pours as they resume shoveling.

Lis glances toward her sister and sees her starkly outlined against a flare of lightning in the west. She finds herself thinking not about gravel or mud or Japanese cars but about this young woman. About how Portia moved to a tough town, how she learned to talk tough and to gaze back at you sultry and defiant, wearing her costumes, her miniskirts and tulle and nose rings, how she glories in the role of the urbane femme lover.

And yet . . . Lis has her doubts. . . .

Tonight, for instance, Portia didn't really seem at ease until she discarded the frou-frou clothes, ditched the weird jewelry and pulled on baggy jeans and a high-necked sweater.

And the boyfriends? . . . Stu, Randy, Lee, a hundred others. For all her talk of independence, Portia often seems no more than a reflection of the man she is, or isn't, with—precisely the type of obsolete, noxious relationship that she enthusiastically denounces. The fact is she never really *likes* these excessively handsome, bedroom-eyed boys very much. When they leave her—as they invariably do—she mourns briefly then heads out to catch herself a fresh one.

And so Lisbonne Atcheson is left to wonder, as she has frequently, who her sister really is. Is she truly the stranger she seems?

Lis just doesn't know. But she's decided to find out. If not through the nursery business, then in some other way. For a thought occurred to her recently—not long after Indian Leap, in fact. A thought she just can't shake: that the only way the dark heritage of the L'Aubergets can be redeemed—*if* it can be redeemed at all— is through the two surviving members of the family.

These two, together.

She can't say exactly why she wants this reconciliation. But none-

theless Lis feels, inexplicably, that this is something she must try.
As a student told her last week, after she caught him cheating,
"Hey, you play the odds."

They sling more gravel, as the rain falls heavily in thick dashes
through the car's white headlight beams. Then the stuffy announcer
fades in to tell his listeners that coming up next will be Handel's
Water Music. He's apparently oblivious to the joke, and moves on
to other news, while the sisters look at each other for an instant,
and laugh, then return to their task.

The Cadillac raced down the highway amid the sticky rush of thick
tires on wet asphalt and the hum of the grand engine's eight calm
cylinders.

Michael Hrubek was still anxious from the run-in with the conspirators twenty minutes before. The fuckers! He'd escaped, yes,
but his hands quivered violently and his heart pounded. His mind
kept slipping off track, and he'd forget where he was and what he
was doing. The echo of the gun's loud crack, the memory of the
feel as it jumped in his hand, were prominent in his thoughts.

"*Cadillac*," he sang frantically, "*hard tack, sic semper ty-
ran-ak . . . Dr. Anne, won't you come back?*"

After the death of Dr. Anne Muller, Michael began to wander.
He occasionally spent time in state hospitals but lived mostly on
the street, surviving on cheese sandwiches from social workers and
scrounging through dumpsters outside restaurants. He was ravaged
by anxiety and paranoia though the latter condition had a positive
consequence: fearing drugs, all of which he believed to be poison-
ous, he remained uninfected by AIDS, hepatitis and other serious
illnesses.

After several months in the Northeast he meandered south to
Washington, D.C., intending to apologize for his past crimes to
Andrew Johnson, Ulysses S. Grant or the current President, whom-

ever he met first. He managed to get to the White House gate and knocked on the door of the guard's station.

"It's vital that I talk to you about this assassination business, John Guard. It's *vital!*"

Picked up, bang, by the Secret Service.

"That was stupid," he told himself glumly as he waited in an interrogation room somewhere in the Treasury Department. "Shouldn't've done that."

But he wasn't tortured as he'd expected. He was simply asked a series of what he called mind-messing questions and released after two hours. He knew that during the session the agents had somehow planted a tracking device in his body and he threw himself in the reflecting pool of the Washington Monument to short out the battery. He felt better after this dip and moved into Arlington National Cemetery, where he lived for a month.

Finally he grew bored with the capital and wandered back north, looking for his father. After a month of sporadic searching Michael believed he found his family's house in an old neighborhood of Philadelphia. He walked through the unlocked front door to see if anyone was home. Someone was, though it turned out to be not his father but the wife of a police detective.

Picked up, bang, for that one too.

Released the next day he hiked all the way to Gettysburg and lay in the middle of the battlefield, howling in shame for his role in ending the life of the greatest President the United States had ever known.

Picked up, bang.

Phillie, Newark, Princeton, New York, White Plains, Bridgeport, Hartford.

That was Michael's life: hospitals and the street. He slept in boxes, he bathed in rivers when he bathed, and he wandered purposefully. Every day was an intense experience. He saw truths with a piercing clarity. There were truths everywhere! Raw and painful truths. In red cars zipping down the street, in the motion of a tugboat easing into a slip, in the part of a teenage boy's hair, in a symmetrical display of watches in a jewelry-store window. He considered each of these revelations, always wondering if it might ease the burden of his anxiety and fear.

Did it *say* something to him? Did it offer solace?

Michael met people in his wanderings and they sometimes took to him. If he was clean and was wearing clothing recently given to him by a priest or social worker, someone might sit beside him on a park bench as he read a book. With a Penguin Classic in your hand, you were easily forgiven rumpled clothes and a short stubble of beard. Like any businessman out on a fine Sunday afternoon, Michael would cross his legs, revealing sockless ankles in brown loafers. He'd smile and nod and, avoiding the subjects of murder, rape and the Secret Service, talk only about what he saw in front of him: sparrows bathing in spring dust, trees, children playing flag football. He had conversations with men who might have been chief executives of huge corporations.

This nomadic life finally came to an unpleasant end in January of this year when he was arrested and charged with breaking into a store in a small, affluent town fifty miles south of Ridgeton. He'd shattered the window and torn apart a female mannequin. He was examined by a court-appointed psychiatrist, who believed there were sexual overtones to the vandalism and declared him violently psychotic. Giving his name as Michael W. Booth he was involuntarily committed and sent to Cooperstown State Mental Hospital.

There, even before an intake diagnostic interview, Michael was shuttled into the Hard Ward.

Still in a restraint camisole he was deposited in a cold, dark room, where he remained for three hours before the door opened and a man entered. A man bigger even than Michael himself.

"Who're you?" Michael challenged. "Are you John Wilkes Orderly? Do you work for the government? I've been to Washington, D.C., the capital of this great country. Who the *hell* do you—"

"Shut the fuck up." John Orderly slammed him into the wall and then shoved him to the floor. "Don't scream, don't shout, don't talk back. Just shut the fuck up and relax."

Michael had shut the fuck up but he hadn't relaxed. *Nobody* relaxed at Cooperstown. This was a place where patients simply gave up, surrendering to their madness. Michael spent much time sitting by himself, looking out windows, jiggling his legs with nervous energy, repeatedly muttering a single song—"Old Folks at Home." The staff psychologist who spent about seven minutes a week with Michael never pursued this compulsion but if he had he'd have found that the old Stephen Foster song contained the line "Oh, darkie, how my heart is yearning," which to Michael referred not to a slave but to darkness, specifically night. Night brought the hope of sleep, and sleep was the only time when he was at peace in this terrible place.

Cooperstown—where nurses would put two women patients in a room together with a single, oiled Coke bottle and watch from the door.

Cooperstown—where John Orderly would bend Michael over the tin washbasin and press into him again and again, the pain crying up through his ass into his jaw and face, the cold metal of the orderly's keys bouncing on the patient's thigh and matching the rhythm of his thrusts.

Cooperstown—where Michael slipped far, far from reality and came to believe with certainty that he was living in the time of the Civil War. In his month on the Hard Ward Michael had access to only one book. It was about reincarnation and after reading it a dozen times, he understood how he could in fact be John Wilkes Booth. He carried Booth's soul around with him! The spirit had flown from the old wounded body and circled for a hundred years. It alighted upon the head of Michael's mother just as the baby struggled out of her, leaving the red marks on her stomach that she had told him were his fault but not to worry about.

Yes, within him was the soul of Mr. John Wilkes Booth, a fair actor but a damn good killer.

One day in March of this year, John Orderly took Michael by the arm and pushed him into Suzie's room. He slammed the door shut and aimed the video camera through the window.

They were alone, Michael and this twenty-four-year-old patient, on whose pretty face was only one blemish—a tiny indentation of scar in the middle of her forehead. Suzie looked at Michael carefully with her sunken eyes. She was someone whose only earthly power was in knowing what was expected of her. She observed that Michael was a man and immediately hiked her skirt over bulging thighs. Down went her panties and she rolled onto her hands and knees.

And Michael, knowing that John Orderly was just outside the door, also knew what to do—exactly the same. Pants down, on his hands and knees. Here they remained, butts bare to the world, while John Orderly fled down the hallway when a doctor unexpectedly happened by. The psychiatrist glanced inside the room and opened the door. He inquired what the patients were doing.

Michael answered, "Waiting for John Orderly. I'm ready for him and so is she. Make no mistake. Like all men of medicine, John Orderly's got a very big cock."

"Oh, my God."

The investigation resulted in the dismissal of five orderlies, two nurses and two doctors from Cooperstown. Michael, however, never learned John Orderly's fate because as one of the most victimized patients he was immediately transferred out of the Hard Ward into the voluntary-commitment section of the hospital. "Due to stabilization of his condition," the report said. "Prognosis for improvement: fair to good." In fact Michael was far sicker than when he'd been admitted but the administrators wanted to isolate him from the questioning reporters and state mental-health examiners who descended on the hospital to investigate what one newspaper dubbed "Psycho Ward Atrocities."

Reforms were instituted, the reporters went elsewhere for their stories, and Cooperstown fell from the public eye—just as Michael himself was largely forgotten within the halls of the hospital.

A month after the scandal he was still a resident of the Cooperstown Soft Ward. One weekend he found himself unusually agitated. On Saturday evening the anxiety increased to massive proportions and he began to feel the walls of his room closing in on him. Breathing grew difficult. He suspected the Secret Service was behind this; agents frequently bombarded him with beams that electrified his nerves.

Michael didn't know that his anxiety was due not to the federal government but to something much simpler: his medication instructions had been misplaced and he'd received no Haldol for four days.

Finally in desperation he decided to find the one person in his recent memory who might help him. He had, he recalled, accused Dr. Anne of being a conspirator and had even announced on hundreds of occasions that he was happy she was dead. He decided that the only way to find relief was to retract his cruel pronouncements and apologize to her. He spent the night plotting his escape from Cooperstown, a plan that involved diversionary fires and costumes and disguises. The elaborate scheme proved unnecessary, however, because on Sunday morning he simply dressed in jeans and a T-shirt and walked out the front gate of the hospital, right past a guard unaware that he was a Hard Ward patient in the Soft Ward wing.

Michael had no idea exactly where Dr. Anne might be. But he knew Trevor Hill was in the southern part of the state and that was the direction in which he started to jog that spring morning. Soon he became lost in a tangle of country roads and the more lost he became, the greater was his anxiety. Panic crawled over his skin like hives. At times he took to sprinting, as if fear were an animal snapping at his heels. Other times he hid in bushes until he felt unseen pursuers pass him by. Once, he summoned up his courage and climbed onto the back of a flatbed truck, on which he rode for an hour, hiding under the canvas tarps, until the driver stopped at a roadside diner. Noticing that there were four trucks parked in the lot and fearing this very unlucky number, Michael leapt off and escaped down a nearby country lane.

Around noon he found himself in the middle of a large parking lot. He paused, caught his breath and walked through the lot toward a row of trees, nauseous with anxiety. He ran through the lot and disappeared into the bushes just beyond the large wooden sign. He glanced at the words that were carved into it as if by a huge wood-burning iron.

Welcome to Indian Leap State Park

Michael Hrubek thought of that day now, six months later, as he steered his black Cadillac over the crest of a hill on Route 236. He saw before him a long smooth straightaway sailing into a distance filled with flashes of lightning and the soft glow of lights that perhaps were those of Ridgeton. He cringed as rain clattered on the roof and windshield.

"Betrayal," he muttered. Then he repeated the word, bellowing. He was scalded with anxiety. "Eve of betrayal! Fuckers!"

In an instant his pulse rate leapt to 175 and sweat sprung from his pores. His teeth clattered like galloping hooves on concrete. His mind snapped shut. He forgot *GET TO*, he forgot Lis-bone, he forgot Eve, the conspirators and Dr. Anne and Dr. Richard. . . . He forgot everything but the icy clutch of fear.

His hands quavered on the steering wheel. He gazed at the Cadillac's hood with shock—as if he'd suddenly awakened and found himself riding a rampaging bull.

I'll fight this, he thought. God, please help me fight this! He lowered his head and chewed on his inner cheek. He tasted blood. *I will* fight it!

And for a very brief moment he did.

For a very brief moment he gripped the ivory wheel firmly and forced the car back into the right lane of the highway.

For this brief moment Michael Hrubek was not a maladroit lunatic, a host holding an ancient killer's soul. He was not driven by unbearable guilt. Abraham Lincoln was merely a great, sad figure from history whose face graced copper pennies, and Michael himself was just a big, strong, young man filled with much promise, driving a gaudy old car down a country road, scared to death, yes, but more or less in charge of himself.

And then this delusion vanished.

He could fight it no longer. He lost all conception of the controls and it was the pedal on the right upon which he stamped his huge foot in an effort to stop the skid. He covered his eyes, howled a plea for help and kept his foot to the floorboard as the car disappeared into a low stand of juniper and began turning over and over and over.

23

You've got this thing to do ahead of you. . . .

Owen Atcheson remembered his platoon lieutenant looking steel-eyed and crazed from hits of local funnydust but sounding calm as a college professor. "You've got this thing ahead of you, and you've got to go out and meet it. . . ."

Owen and three others Marines more often than not rolled their eyes at this pep talk. But, inspired by it nonetheless, they then clipped on their gear and blackened their faces and disappeared into the jungle to cut the throats of thin soldiers or murder politicians with silenced pistols or rig gelignite and C4 satchel charges.

Owen thought of those times now—as he stood on the ridge of a hill, looking at the antique Cadillac that sat upright, its roof half-staved in and windows spidered with fractures, one parking lamp the only light that had survived the crash. He opened the cylinder of his gun. He'd owned revolvers all his life and, fastidious about safety, had always kept the chamber under the hammer empty. He now loaded a sixth shell into the gun and swung the cylinder closed. He started toward the car. The incline was steep and Owen needed one hand to steady himself as he climbed down to a low hedge.

He felt a stunning exhilaration and told himself that he shouldn't be enjoying this so much. The thrill diminished when he recalled that Hrubek was armed and saw that there was no way to approach the car under cover. It had crashed through a line of juniper and tumbled for thirty feet into the center of a grassy clearing.

The rain wasn't heavy and the wind was subdued; his approach
would be noisy. And Hrubek—assuming his injuries hadn't prevented him from doing so—had also had plenty of time to establish
a defensive position. Owen considered tactics for a moment then
decided not to bother with a cautious approach. He clutched the
gun hard, inhaled long then ran at top speed, ready to aim and
shoot from a tumbling position. As he sped across the grass, a
primitive howl bubbled in his throat and he suppressed the urge to
let this grow into the Marines' battle cry.

He charged the car straight on and slid into the grass like a
runner stealing home, ending up behind the rear bumper. The
muddy leaves scattered by his run settled around him and he looked
about frantically. The rear windshield was less obscured than the
others but he still was unable to tell if Hrubek was inside. He
crouched, using the trunk as cover, and looked behind the car.

Nothing.

He moved toward the rear door. . . .

Underneath!

Owen dropped to his stomach with a grunt and aimed the gun
under the car. A shattered pipe hung like an arm and startled him
but Hrubek wasn't hiding there. He stood and breathed deeply
several times then switched his gun to his left hand and yanked
the car's right rear door open.

Empty. The Cadillac held no evidence of Michael Hrubek other
than a smell of animallike musk and sweat and fragments of shattered animal skulls—like the one Hrubek had left on the woman's
lap in the house in Cloverton. The keys were in the ignition.

Owen stood and looked around him. The spongy leaves had left
no footprints and there was no sign of blood or other trail. Owen
stepped behind the Cadillac and turned his back to it as he scanned
the vast forest, damp and gray and dark. His heart fell. He knew
how hard it was to track on wet leaves and through dark woods.
And after an accident this bad Hrubek might be disoriented

316 \ **Jeffery Deaver**

or stunned and could wander pointlessly in any direction. He
might—

The trunk!

Owen cocked the gun and spun on his heels, aiming at the broad
dented plain of metal—a perfect hiding place. The trunk was secured by a keyhole button but—since the Caddie was an older
car—it did not automatically lock. Owen approached. He touched
the cold chrome latch, pushed it in. The mechanism snapped open.
He pulled the lid up and leapt back.

The spacious trunk had ample room for someone as large as
Michael Hrubek. But it did not in fact contain him.

Owen turned toward the forest and in a crouch ran to the closest
opening in the tall fence of brush and trees. In an instant he was
swallowed up by the cold darkness around him. He shone his
shielded flashlight on the ground in a slow U pattern. After ten
minutes he found two of Hrubek's bootprints. They led deeper into
the forest. He smelled pine in the damp air. The psycho might have
headed out of the deciduous trees and Owen would find a clear
trail in pine needles. He had proceeded only thirty feet when he
heard a thud and a snap nearby—a careless footstep, it seemed.

He aimed his pistol toward the sound.

Owen gauged his footsteps perfectly and placed them on foliage-
free ground, making no noise as he moved. He crouched, pistol in
front of him, and stepped onto the bed of fragrant needles.

The man was sitting on a fallen tree trunk and massaging his
outstretched leg, as if taking a break on a Sunday-afternoon hike.

"Looks like we just missed him," the lanky man in a New York
Mets cap said to Owen, looking up without a trace of surprise in
his face. "So you're the other bounty hunter. Guess we got a few
things to talk about."

The woman was thirty-six years old and had lived in this prim little
bungalow all her life, the past six of those years, after her mother's

death, alone. She hadn't seen her father since the day the old man got his other daughter pregnant, was arrested for it and taken away. One week after the trial the sister too moved away.

The woman's life consisted of filling cartons with electronic circuit boards that did something she had no desire to understand, of lunch with one or two fellow workers, sewing, and—for entertainment—church and the newspaper on the day of rest, and television on the other six.

The house was an island of caution and simplicity in a grassy clearing carved out of what had been one of the oldest forests in the Northeast. The half acre of grass was almost a perfect circle and was marred only by a rusted hull of a pickup that would never go anywhere under its own power and a doorless refrigerator her father had been meaning to cart to the dump one Saturday morning ten years ago when he chose instead to pay a visit to his daughter's bedroom.

Blonde, thin and fragile, the woman had a plain face and a good figure though on the rare occasions when she and a few girlfriends went to the rocky beach at Indian Leap or the riverside at Klamath Falls, she would wear a high-necked swimsuit that she'd bought mail-order so she wouldn't have to try it on in a store. She dated some—mostly men she met at church—though she rarely enjoyed the outings and had recently started to think of herself, with some comfort, as a spinster.

Tonight she'd just finished preparing a bedtime snack of Jell-O with mandarin oranges and a cup of hot milk, when she heard the noise in the yard. She walked to the window and saw nothing other than blowing leaves and rain then returned to the maple dining table.

She sat down, said grace and put her napkin in her lap then lifted a spoonful of Jell-O as she opened *TV Guide*.

The knocking on the front door seemed to shake the whole house. The spoon fell to the table and the gelatin cube wobbled off her lap then escaped onto the floor. She stood abruptly and shouted, "Yes, who is it?"

"I'm hurt. I had an accident. Can you help me?"

It was a man's voice.

She hesitated, walked to the front door, hesitated again then opened it as far as the chain allowed. The big fellow was bent over, clutching his arm. He seemed like a working man.

"Who are you?"

"I was driving by and my car, she rolled over and over. Oh, I'm hurt. Please let me in."

No way on God's green earth, thank you very much. "I'll call an ambulance, you wait right there."

The woman closed the door and deadbolted it then went to the table that held the rotary-dial phone. She picked it up. She banged the button down several times and when the silence continued said, "Oh, dear."

It was then that she realized the sound she'd heard a few moments before was coming from the place where the phone line ran into the house. This thought stayed with her only a moment though because Michael Hrubek had grown tired of waiting outside and kicked open the door. Huge and wet, he walked into the living room and said, "Nice try. But your phone, it doesn't work. I could've told you that."

Standing beneath a cluster of thick pine trees, which offered some shelter from the streaming rain, Owen asked how Trenton Heck happened to find the Cadillac.

"I followed his track to Cloverton. That's where I picked up your prints and tire tread. I saw you headed west. Then I saw the Jeep parked up there and figured it might belong to you. My dog picked up Hrubek's scent right away beside the Caddie."

"Did the detective have any more news?"

"How's that?"

"I don't recall his name." Owen patted his pockets for the card he had been given. "The detective in Cloverton. At the house where he killed that woman?"

"*What?*" Heck blurted.

"You didn't know? Didn't you stop at the house?"

"I didn't see a house. I hightailed it west as soon as I saw your prints."

To a troubled Trenton Heck, Owen explained about the killing, the terrible butchery in Cloverton. He then told him about the antique cars stowed in a barn. "I figured he'd try to lead us off track with that motorcycle. He drove it south a few hundred yards and dumped it in a marsh somewhere to fool everybody, I'd guess. Then he took the Cadillac and came here. That man is too damn smart."

Heck asked, "What's your interest in all this?"

Owen stooped down and retied his boots, which were muddy and scuffed but looked as expensive as Heck had guessed they'd be. The tall man stood and said, "Was my friend he killed at Indian Leap. And my wife saw him do it."

Heck nodded, thinking that this put a whole new spin on the evening. "Tell you what, let me get my dog. He stays and keeps quiet when he's told but mostly it addles him." He walked off into the woods, glancing at the signposts of bushes and trees for direction.

"You're quiet when you move," Owen said, impressed. "You hunt?"

"A bit." Heck chuckled.

They found Emil sitting nervously, shifting weight from paw to paw. He calmed as soon as he saw his master.

Owen asked, "Purebred blood?"

"Edouard Montague of Longstreet the Third. He's as pure as they come."

"Quite a name."

"That's what he came with but it wouldn't do of course, not

around here. So I call him Emil and he answers to it. If he ever mates a pure bitch I'll have to put his full name on the papers but till then it's our secret."

Walking back to the clearing beside Heck, Owen asked, "How'd you follow the scent if he was on a bicycle?"

"That's nothing for Emil. Hell, he's gone through a foot of snow in a blizzard. So you think maybe he's after your wife?"

"I don't really know. But it's too dangerous to leave in the hands of cops who don't know what they're doing."

This rankled Heck and he said, "You got your state troopers on the case, you know."

"Well, a lot of mistakes've been made, I should tell you." Owen glanced at Heck's pistol. "You mentioned a bounty. You're a professional tracker?"

"I hire out my dog, yep."

"How much's the reward?"

Hot-faced, eyes fixed on the dark forest, Heck said, "Ten thousand dollars." He spoke emphatically, as if making clear to Owen that even if he was just a hired hand he wasn't coming cheap.

"Well then," Owen said, "let's go catch this psycho and make you some money. What do you say?"

"Yessir."

Heck roused Emil with Hrubek's scent and off they went through the woods. The track was easy to follow now, with abundant ground scent in the moist forest. The dog's excitement and the uncanny atmosphere of the woods at night urged them forward in a kind of dazed ecstasy, and they could do nothing but give in to this lust. They crashed through the brush. Hrubek could've heard them coming from a hundred yards away but there was nothing to be done about it. They couldn't have both stealth and speed, and they chose the latter.

. . .

Michael watched her carefully, irritated that she was crying so much. It made him very anxious. The blonde woman didn't speak. All the points of her face—her nose and chin and cheekbones— were red from the silent tears. She quivered and shredded a paper napkin between her fingers while Michael paced. "I had to take down your telephone. Stop that crying. The line's sure to be tapped anyway."

"What," she sobbed, "are you going to do to me?"

He walked through the living room, his huge muddy feet pounding on the boards. "This is a nice place. Stop crying! I like your eyes. You don't have masks on them. Where did you get it? The *house*, I'm speaking of."

She glanced at the small cap on his head. "What are you—?" He repeated his question sharply and she stammered, "My mama died and she left it to me. I've got a sister. It's half hers." As if he intended to steal it, she added, "We own it free and clear."

Michael lifted the Irish cap by the brim, courteously tipping it to her. He rubbed his hand over his smooth head. In the bright light a residue of the blue ink was still visible. He saw her staring at the cap as he replaced it. He smiled. "Fashionable, isn't it?"

"I'm sorry?"

He frowned. "My hat. *Fashionable*. Isn't it?"

"Yes," she exclaimed. "Very. Extremely."

"My car rolled over and over and over. She was a good car while she lasted." He walked closer and examined her body. He thought it was strange that although she was a woman she didn't frighten him. Maybe because she was so frail. He could lift her with one hand and could snap her neck as easily as he had the raccoon's earlier in the evening. What's that smell? Oh, it's woman. The smell of woman. This brought back an indistinct and troubling memory. He felt darkness around him, claustrophobia, fear. Rocks and water. Bad people. What was it? His anxiety notched up a few degrees.

He also found he had a fierce erection. He sat down so that she wouldn't notice.

The wind slammed against the windows and the sound of the rain grew louder. The clatter of muskets, he thought. Lead balls cracking apart a thousand heads . . . He covered his ears at this unnerving sound. After a moment he realized that she was staring at him.

"People are after me," he said.

"You're a *convict*?" she whispered. "You escaped from the prison over in Hamlin?"

"Nice try. Don't expect to get anything out of me. You know too much as it is."

She shivered as he leaned forward and stroked her fine hair. "That's nice," he muttered. "And you're not wearing a fucking hat. Good . . . Good."

"Don't hurt me please. I'll give you money. Anything . . ."

"Give me a penny."

"I have some savings. About three thousand but it's in the bank. You could meet me there at nine tomorrow. You're welcome to—"

Michael roared, "A *penny*!"

She dug frantically into her purse. He looked over her shoulder. "You don't have a microphone in there? A panic button or anything?"

She looked mystified then whispered, "No. I'm getting you the penny like you asked."

Guilty, Michael said, "Well, you can't be too careful."

He held out his massive hands and she dropped the coin into his palm. He held it up behind her head. "What seven-letter word is on the penny?"

"I don't know."

"Guess," he said petulantly.

She wrung her hands together. "*E Pluribus Unum*. In God We Trust. Legal Tender. No. United States. Oh, God, I can't think!" Then, *sotto voce*, she began murmuring the Lord's Prayer.

"It's right behind seven-letter Abraham Lincoln." Without looking at the coin he said, "The word is right *behind* him, seven letters, like the barrel of a gun pointed at his head."

He poked her scalp with a blunt finger. She closed her eyes and whispered, "I don't know."

Michael said, " 'Liberty.' " He dropped the penny on the floor. "I'm pretty hungry. What's to eat?"

She stopped crying. "You're hungry?" She gazed at the kitchen. "I have some roast beef, some vegetarian chili. . . . You're welcome to it."

He walked to the table and sat down, easing into the chair. He delicately opened a paper napkin. It covered only a part of his huge lap.

She asked, "Can I stand up?"

"How can you get me dinner if you don't stand up?"

She hurtled into the kitchen and busied herself preparing a plate while Michael sang, " 'For I love the bonnie blue gal who gave her heart to me.' " He played with the pepper mill. " 'Her arms, her arms, are where I want to be! . . .' "

She returned, setting a tray in front of him. Michael roared, " 'For I love the bonnie blue gal who gave—' " He stopped abruptly, picked up the fork and cut a piece off the beef. This, together with a portion of Jell-O, he put on the pink saucer and placed it in front of her.

She glanced at the food then looked inquiringly at him.

"I want *you* to eat that!" he said.

"I've already . . . Oh, you think it's poison."

"I don't *think* it's poison," he sneered. "I don't *think* there's a posse outside that window. I don't *think* you're a Pinkerton agent. But you can't be too *careful*. Now come on. Quit being a shit."

She ate. Then she smiled and went blank-faced again. He studied her for a moment and set his fork down. "Do you have some milk?"

"Milk? I have low-fat is all. Is that all right?"

"Some *milk*!" he blared, and she jumped to get it. When she returned he'd already started to eat. He drank the glass down, taking with it a mouthful of food. "I used to work in a dairy."

"Well, yes." She nodded politely. "That must be a nice place to work."

"It was very nice. Dr. Richard got me the job."

"Who is he?"

"He was my father."

"Your father was a doctor?"

"Well," he scoffed, "I don't mean a father like *that*."

"No," she agreed quickly, seeing the darkness fall over his face. He stopped eating. She told him she liked his tweed cap. He touched it and smiled. "I like it too. I have hair but I cut it off."

"Why did you do that?"

"I can't tell you."

"No, don't tell me anything you don't want to."

"If I don't *want* to, I won't. You don't have to give me permission."

"I wasn't giving you permission. I didn't mean to sound like I was. You can do whatever you want."

"Don't I know it." Michael cleaned his plate.

"Would you like some more?"

"Milk. I'd like more milk." When she was in the kitchen he added, "Please."

As he took the tall glass from her he intoned in an FM disc jockey's voice, "A wholesome snack."

She barked a laugh and he smiled. As he poured the milk down she asked, "What are you doing?"

"I'm drinking milk," he answered with exasperation.

"No. I mean, what are you doing out tonight? There's supposed to be a storm like we haven't seen in a donkey's age."

"What's a donkey's age?" He squinted.

She stared at him with a vacant face. "Uhm, now that you ask, I don't exactly know. It means for a long time."

"Is it like an *expression*? Is it like a *cliché*?"

"I guess so."

He stared down, his eyes as empty and filmy as the glass in his hand. "Did you know that 'anger' is five-sixths of 'danger'?"

"No, I didn't. But it surely is. How about that?"

"So there."

She broke the very dense silence by asking, "What did you do in the dairy?"

Michael's erection had not gone away. His penis hurt and this was beginning to anger him. He reached into his pocket and squeezed himself then stood and walked to the window. He said, "What's the biggest town near here that has a train station?"

"Well, Boyleston, I suppose. It's south about forty, fifty miles."

"How would I get there?"

"Go west to 315. It'll take you right there. That becomes Hubert Street and it goes right past the train station. Amtrak."

"In no time at all?"

"No time at all," she agreed. "Why are you going there?"

"I told you," he snapped. "I can't say!"

Her hands went into her lap.

Michael began rummaging through his backpack. "I'm sorry, I'm very sorry," he said to her. But he uttered these words, then repeated them, with such deep longing that it was clear he was apologizing not for being curt but rather for something else—something he was *about* to do, something far graver than bad manners. He sat down beside her, his thigh pressing hard against hers, and as she cried, he set a small white animal skull in her lap and, very gently, began stroking her hair.

Under clouds so fast and turbulent they seemed like special effects from a science-fiction movie, Portia L'Auberget inhaled the scents of decaying leaves and the musky lake. Several feet away her sister lifted the shovel and dropped a huge pile of gravel around the front wheels of the stranded car.

The young woman flexed her hands. They stung and she supposed the skin was starting to blister from the wet gloves. Her muscles were on fire. Her head ached from the pounding rain.

And she was troubled by something else, a vague thought— something other than the storm. At first she wondered if it might be the escape. Yet she'd never really believed that someone like Michael Hrubek could make it all the way to Ridgeton from the mental hospital, certainly not on a night like this.

No, some nebulous memory kept rising up disturbingly then vanishing. It seemed that it had something to do with this portion of the yard. She was picturing . . . what was it? Plants? Had there been a garden here of some sort? Ah, yes. It *was* here. The old vegetable garden.

Then she remembered Tom Wheeler.

How old had they been? Twelve or thirteen probably, both of them. One fall afternoon—maybe November, like tonight—the skinny red-haired boy had shown up in the yard. Portia strolled outside and they sat on the back steps. She managed simultaneously to both ignore and converse with him, teasing mercilessly. Finally he suggested that they go to the state park. "Why?" she asked. "I dunno," he responded. "Hang out, you know. Got the new Jefferson Airplane." He nodded lethargically at an eight-track-tape player at his feet. She told him no, she didn't want to, but a moment later she disappeared into the house and returned with a blanket.

He started for the state park.

"Uh-uh," Portia announced. "This way."

And led him to the vegetable garden. Here she spread the blanket in partial view of the house and lay down, kicking off her Keds and stretching sumptuously. But somebody might see, he protested.

Somebody could be watching right now! She placed his hand on her breast and he stopped worrying about voyeurs. Portia lay on her back, surrounded by slug-chewed pumpkins and short blond cornstalks. Tommy beside her, covering her hot mouth with his; she had to breathe for long stretches through her nose. She now recalled smelling this same scent of wet, late fall. Drowsy flies strafed them. Finally, confusing him by not protesting, she allowed his pale, freckled hand to pass the elastic barrier. He glanced at the windows of the house then jabbed with a shaking finger, leaving inside her a glow of pain and on her bare hip a large wet spot that matched the one spreading across the front of his dungarees.

They lay awkwardly, side by side, for a few minutes then he suddenly whispered, "I think there's somebody there."

Though he'd said that only to escape and he rose quickly and vanished down the driveway. Hearing the resonant guitar licks fade, Portia grew dizzy as she watched the thick clouds pass overhead and wondered about the mysteries of bodies. She spent a long time unsuccessfully trying to convince herself to feel bad that he'd fled.

Portia now realized, with a twist in her belly, that it was not this memory of speedy Tommy Wheeler at all that was so troubling. It was Indian Leap.

She had almost not accompanied her sister and brother-in-law on the picnic. She had no interest in the out-of-doors, no interest in state parks—especially the park to which she'd been dragged by teachers on tedious field trips and in which she later spent hours gazing at treetops, as she lay beneath boyfriends, or friends of boyfriends, or sometimes strangers.

No, it was essentially a decision by default. She was fed up with the quiet anxiety of solo life in Manhattan: The dinners of turkey sandwiches and cole slaw. The companionship of rented movies. The tired come-ons in bars and at parties, delivered as if the men actually thought she hadn't heard it all a thousand times before.

Socializing with lean, ponytailed girlfriends who'd discard you in
an instant if doing so moved them an inch closer to a Better Job
or an Available Man.

So, on that May 1, she'd reluctantly packed bagels and lox and
cream cheese and magazines and bikini and sunscreen. She endured the surly rent-a-car clerk, she endured the traffic, she endured the tense company of the poor, shy Claire. She suffered
through all the stress of a day in the country. Yet there was one
aspect of the trip that didn't require enduring. Robert Gillespie,
Portia thought at first, was hardly a catch. As she sat in the back
of his 4x4 with Lis and Claire, en route to Indian Leap, she re-
viewed his ledger and came up mostly with debits: only marginally
cute, fifteen pounds overweight, too smooth, too pompous, too talkative, a wife who was a complete cipher.

There was, Portia realized, no logical basis for finding him irresistible. But irresistible he was. While Lis had dozed in the back
of the truck and while dull Dorothy liberally applied her oh-puh-
leaze red nail polish, Robert deluged Portia with questions. Where
did she live, did she like the city, did she know this or that restaurant, did she like her job? It was all a come-on. Of course it
was. But still . . . And his liquid eyes danced with excitement as
they talked. Portia recalled thinking helplessly, Oh, it's true: seduce
my mind and my body will follow.

By the time they arrived at the park, Portia L'Auberget was his
for the asking.

As they walked along the path from the parking lot to the car,
he glanced at her running shoes and discreetly asked—in a way
that was both intimate and lighthearted—if they might take a run
together.

She responded, "Maybe."

He took this to mean yes. "Let me leave before you," he whispered. "Then I'll meet you near the old cave. Give me ten minutes.
Then follow me."

"Maybe."

When they got to the beach she appraised her power over him and decided not to abdicate a single bit of it. She did a few fast stretches then jogged away first, blatantly ignoring him. She ran a half mile to the secluded gully he'd mentioned. Past the cave was a stand of pine trees, beneath which was an inviting nest of soft needles, some green, some ruddy. Portia sat on a nearby rock, wondering if he'd join her. Maybe he'd retaliate for her defiance by remaining with his wife and Lis. She'd certainly have more respect for him if he did. Yet Portia L'Auberget had no particular desire, or need, to respect men, especially men like Robert Gillespie, and decided he fucking well better show; she'd make his day miserable if he didn't. She examined the small clearing, which was gloomy and shadowed by the steep walls of pale rock rising on either side of the trees. Overhead the sky had turned heavily overcast. Much less romantic, she reflected, than a Club Med beach in Curaçao or Nassau. On the other hand there were no condoms littering the ground here.

She scooted from the rock to the needle bed, separated from sight of the clearing by a tall line of bushes and young hemlocks. A half hour passed, then forty minutes, and finally Robert came jogging toward her. He caught his breath and earned many points by not saying a word to Portia about disregarding his instructions. He was studying his chest, pouting.

She laughed. "What?"

"My wife says I'm getting tits."

Portia pulled off her T-shirt and sports bra. "Let's compare."

They rolled back under the pine trees. Robert kissed her firmly, stroking her bare nipples with the backs of his hands. He closed his fingers around hers and placed them on her breasts. She began fondling herself while his tongue slid down to her navel then continued to her thighs and knees. He remained there, teasing, until Portia finally seized his head in both hands and directed it firmly between her legs. Her thighs rose as her head pressed back hard into the pine bed, needles fixing themselves in her sweat-damp hair. Staring through half-closed lids at the speeding clouds she gasped for breath. He rolled on top of her, and their mouths met hard, brutally. He had just entwined her legs around his waist and was thrusting into her savagely when a branch snapped near their heads.

Claire walked out of a stand of trees and stopped, frozen, six feet from them. Her hand rose to her mouth in shock.

"Oh, my God," Portia shouted.

"Claire, honey . . ." Robert began, as he rolled to his knees.

Claire, speechless, stared at his groin. Portia remembered thinking, My God, she's eighteen. This can't be her first hard-on.

It took a moment for Robert to recover some wits and he looked frantically for his shirt or shorts. As the girl's eyes remained fixed on him, Portia watched the young blonde. This curious à trois voyeurism aroused her all the more. Robert grabbed his shirt and wrapped the knit garment about his waist, abashed and grinning. Portia didn't move. Then Claire choked a sob and turned, running past the cave and back up the path.

"Oh, shit," Robert muttered.

"Don't worry."

"*What?*"

"Oh, don't take it so seriously. Every teenager gets a shock at some point. I'll talk to her."

"She's just a kid."

"Forget her," Portia said offhandedly, then whispered, "Come on over here."

"She's going—"

"She's not going to say anything. Hmm, what's that? You're still interested. I can tell."

"Jesus, what if she tells Lis?"

"Come on," she urged breathlessly. "Don't stop now. Fuck me!"

"I think we ought to get back."

Portia dropped to her knees and pulled his shirt away, taking him deep into her mouth.

"No," Robert whispered.

He was standing, head back, eyes closed, shuddering uncontrollably and gasping when Lis stepped into the clearing.

Claire must have run into her almost immediately and Lis had either learned, or deduced, what had happened. She stood above the half-naked couple and stared down at them. "Portia!" she raged. "How could you?" Her expression of horror matched Robert's perfectly.

The young woman stood and wiped her face with her bra. She turned to face her sister and with detachment watched Lis's throat grow remarkably red as the tendons rose and her jaw quivered. Robert pulled up his running shorts, looking around again for his shirt. He seemed incapable of speaking. Portia refused to act like a caught schoolgirl. "How could you?" Lis gripped her arm but Portia stepped away abruptly. Meeting her sister's furious gaze she dressed slowly then, saying nothing, left Lis and Robert in the clearing.

Portia walked back to the beach, where Dorothy was starting to pack up; the temperature had dropped and it was clearly going to rain. She looked at Portia and seemed to sense something was wrong but said nothing. The wind picked up and the two women hurried to gather up the picnic baskets and blankets, carting them to the truck. They made one more trip back to the beach, looking for their companions. Then the downpour began.

Moments later sirens filled the park and police and medics arrived. It was in a rain-drenched intersection of two canyons that Portia met her sister, red-eyed and muddy and disheveled, looking like a madwoman, being led by two tall rangers out of a flooded arroyo.

Portia had stepped toward her. "Lis! What—?"

The slap was oddly quiet but so powerful it brought Portia down

332 \ *Jeffery Deaver*

on one knee. She cried out in pain and shock. Neither woman moved, and Lis's hand remained frozen in the air as they stared at each other for a long moment. A shocked ranger helped Portia to her feet and explained about the deaths.

"Oh, no!" Portia cried.

"Oh, no!" Lis mimicked with bitter scorn then stepped forward, pushed the ranger aside and put her mouth close to her sister's ear. In a rasping whisper she said, "*You* killed that girl, you fucking whore."

Portia faced her sister. Her eyes grew as cold as the wet rocks around them. "Goodbye, Lis."

And goodbye it had been. Apart from a few brief, stilted phone conversations, those words had been virtually the last communication between the sisters until tonight.

Indian Leap. It was the first thing in Portia's mind when Lis had invited her here this evening—just as it had reared in her thoughts when the subject of the nursery was raised, and, for that matter, every time Portia had thought of moving back to Ridgeton, which —though she'd never confess it to Lis—she'd considered frequently in the past few years.

Indian Leap . . .

Oh, Lis, Portia thought, don't you see? *That's* what dooms the L'Auberget sisters, and always will. Not the tragedy, not the deaths, not the bitter words or the months of silence afterwards, but the past that led us to that pine bed, the past that's certain to keep leading us to places just as terrible again and again and again.

The past, with all its spirits of the dead.

Portia now looked at her sister, ten feet away, as Lis put aside the shovel and waded toward the front seat of the car.

The sisters' eyes met.

Lis frowned, troubled by Portia's expression. "What is it?" she asked.

But just then a low whistle squealed from the car's grille. The engine choked, and kicked hard several times as the fan blade slapped water. Then with a shudder it died, leaving the night filled only with the sounds of the wind, the rain and the lilting music of a clever baroque composer.

24

"Well, I didn't go for help because it's over a half mile to the neighbors and if you've listened to the radio you *know* what kind of storm it's supposed to be. I mean, doesn't it make *sense*?"

The words fired from the pale mouth of the petite blonde. She'd stopped crying but was pouring down brandy from a dusty bottle in a medicinal way. "And anyway," she said to Trenton Heck, "he told me not to and if you ever saw him you'd *do* what he told you. Oh, my Lord. All I kept thinking was, Lucky me, lucky me, I had communion today."

Owen Atcheson returned from the side yard to the house's tiny living room, where Heck and the fragile woman stood.

"Lucky me," she whispered and tossed down a belt of liquor. She started to cry again.

"He just pulled one wire out," Owen reported. He lifted the receiver. "I got it working."

"He's got my car. It's a beige Subaru station wagon. An '89. Apologized about ten times. 'I'm sorry I'm sorry I'm sorry. . . .' Phew." Her tears stopped. "That's what I mean when I call him strange. Well, you can imagine. Asked me for the keys and of course I gave them. Then off he went, squatting behind the wheel. Missed the drive completely but found the road. Guess I'll write that vehicle off."

Owen grimaced. "If we'd gone that way he would've come right to us."

Heck looked again at the tiny skull, resting on the paper towel in which she'd handed it to him, unwilling to touch the bone itself.

"Well," the woman continued, "you can find him on 315."

"How's that?"

"He's going to Boyleston. Route 315."

"He said that?"

"He asked me about the nearest town with a train station. I told him Boyleston. He asked me how to get there. And then asked me for fifty dollars for a train ticket. I gave it to him. And a little more."

Heck stared at the phone for a minute. Can't keep it a secret anymore, he thought. Not with Hrubek killing one woman and terrorizing another. He sighed and sucked air through bent teeth. Very conspicuous in Heck's mind now was the thought that if he'd called Haversham like he'd thought of doing—after figuring out that Hrubek was heading west—they might've caught him before he got to that house in Cloverton. All law enforcers, Heck too, had inventories of times when their mistakes and failings had gotten other people hurt—times that occasionally returned hard and kept them from sleeping, and sometimes did worse than that. Though he was removed from the sorrow at the moment, he supposed that that woman's death would be the most prominent in his personal store of those events, and he could only guess how bad it would later come back to him.

Now though he wanted only one thing—to see this fellow caught—and he snatched up the receiver. He placed a call to the local sheriff and reported Hrubek's theft of the Subaru and where he seemed to be going. He turned to the woman. "Sheriff says he'll send somebody out to the house to take you to a friend's or relative's, ma'am. If you want."

"Tell him yes, please."

Heck relayed this information to the sheriff. When he hung up, Owen took the phone and called the Marsden Inn and was surprised to find that Lis and Portia still hadn't checked in. Frowning, he called the house. Lis picked up on the third ring.

"Lis, what are you doing there?"

"Owen? Where are you?"

"I'm in Fredericks. I tried to call you before. I thought you'd left. What're you doing there? You were supposed to be at the Inn an hour ago."

A momentary hollowness on the line. He heard her calling, "It's Owen." What was going on? Through the line he heard a roll of thunder. Lis came back on and explained that she and Portia had stayed to build up the sandbags. "The dam was overflowing. We could've lost the house."

"Are you all right?"

"We're fine. But the car's stuck in the driveway. The rain's terrible. We can't get out. There're no tow trucks. What are you doing in Fredericks?"

"I've been following Hrubek west."

"West! He *did* turn around."

"Lis, I have to tell you . . . He killed someone."

"No!"

"A woman in Cloverton."

"He's coming here?"

"No, it doesn't look like it. He's going to Boyleston. To get a train out of state, I'd guess."

"What should we do?"

He paused. "I'm not going after him, Lis. I'm coming home."

He heard her exhale a sigh. "Thank you, honey."

"Stay in the house. Lock the doors. I'm only fifteen minutes away. . . . Lis?"

"Yes?"

He paused. "I'll be there soon."

Heck and Owen said goodbye to the woman and hurried out into the rain, buffeted by the terrible wind. They followed the driveway to the dim road that led back to the highway.

Owen glanced at Heck, who was trudging along morosely.

"You're thinking about your reward?"

"I have to say I am. They'll probably get him in Boyleston for sure. But I *had* to call and tell them. I'm not going to risk anybody else getting hurt."

Owen thought for a moment. "You're still due that money, I'd say."

"Well, the hospital's gonna have a different opinion on that, I'll guarantee you."

"Tell you what, Heck, you burn on down that highway to Boyleston, and if you get him first, fine. If not, we'll sue the hospital for your money and I'll handle the case myself."

"You a lawyer?"

Owen nodded. "Won't charge you a penny."

"You'd do that for me?"

"Surely would."

Heck was embarrassed at Owen's generosity and after a moment he shook the lawyer's hand warmly. They continued in silence to the clearing where the ruined Cadillac sat.

"Okay, Emil and I'll head south here. It's a beige Subaru we're looking for, right? Let's hope he doesn't drive Japanese any better'n he drives Detroit. Okay, let's do it." On impulse he added, "Say, after this's over with, let's stay in touch, you and me. What do you say? Do some fishing?"

"Hey, that's a fine idea by me, Heck. Happy hunting to you."

Heck and Emil limped, and trotted, back to the battered Chevy pickup fifty yards down the road. They climbed in. Heck started up the rattling engine, then sped through the fierce rain toward Route 315, his left foot on the accelerator and an eye on his modest prize.

The sign revolved slowly in the turbulent night sky.

Dr. Richard Kohler looked toward the flashes of light in the west and laughed out loud at the metaphor that occurred to him.

Wasn't this how Mary Shelley's doctor had animated his creature? Lightning?

The psychiatrist now recalled very clearly the first meeting with the patient who would play the monster to Kohler's Frankenstein. Four months ago, two weeks after the Indian Leap trial and Michael's incarceration in Marsden, Kohler—overcome with morbid and professional fascination—had walked slowly into Marsden's grim, high-security E Ward and looked down at the huge, hunched form of Michael Hrubek, glaring up from beneath his dark eyebrows.

"How are you, Michael?" Kohler asked.

"They're lis-ten-ing. Sometimes you have to keep your mind a complete blank. Have you ever done that? Do you know how *hard* it is? That's the basis of Transcendental Meditation. You may know that as TM. Make your mind a complete blank, doctor. Try it."

"I don't think I can."

"If I hit you with that chair your mind'd be a *complete* blank. But the downside is that you'd be a dead fucker."

Michael had then closed his mouth and said nothing more for several days.

Marsden was a state hospital, like Cooperstown, and offered only a few dismal activity rooms. But Kohler had finagled a special suite for patients in his program. It was not luxurious. The rooms were drafty and cold and the walls were painted an unsettling milky green. But at least those in the Milieu Suite—so named because Kohler's goal was to ease the patients here gradually back into normal society—were separated from the hospital's sicker patients and this special status alone gave them a sense of dignity. They also had learning toys and books and art supplies—even the dangerous and officially forbidden pencils. Art and expression were encouraged and the walls were graced by the graffiti of paintings, drawings and poems created by the patients.

In August Richard Kohler commenced a campaign to get Michael into the Milieu Suite. He chose the young man because he was smart, because he seemed to wish to improve, and because he had killed. To resocialize (one did not *cure*) a patient like Michael Hrubek would be the ultimate validation of Kohler's delusion-therapy techniques. But more than precious DMH funding, more than professional prestige, Kohler saw a chance to help a man who suffered and who suffered terribly. Michael wasn't like the many schizophrenic patients who were oblivious to their conditions. No, Michael was the most tragic of victims; he was just well enough to imagine what a normal life might be like and was tormented daily by the gap between who he was and who he so desperately wanted to be. Exactly the sort of patient Kohler wished most to work with.

Not that Michael leapt at the chance to join the psychiatrist's program.

"No fucking way, you fucker!"

Paranoid and suspicious, Michael refused to have anything to do with the Suite, or Kohler, or anyone else at Marsden for that matter. He sat in the corner of his room, muttering to himself and suspiciously eyeing doctors and patients alike. But Kohler persisted. He simply wouldn't leave the young man alone. Their first month together—and they saw each other daily—they argued bitterly. Michael would rant and scream, convinced Kohler was a conspirator like the others. The doctor would parry with questions about Michael's fantasies, trying to break him down.

Finally, tuckered out by Kohler's aggressiveness and by massive dosages of medicine, Michael reluctantly agreed to join his program. He was gradually introduced to other patients, first one on one, then in larger groups. To get the young patient to talk about his past and his delusions, Kohler would bribe him with history books, filching them from the library at Framington hospital because the collection at Marsden was almost nonexistent. In their individual sessions Kohler kept pushing the young man, turning up the emotional heat and forcing him to spend time with other patients, probing into his delusions and dreams.

"Michael, who's Eve?"

"Oh, yeah, right. Like I'm going to tell *you*. Forget about it."

"What did you mean by 'I want to stay ahead of the blue uniforms'?"

"Time for bed. Lights out. Nighty-night, doctor."

So it went.

One cold, wet day six weeks ago, Michael was in Marsden's secluded exercise area, walking laps under the surly eyes of the guards. He gazed through the chain-link fence at the bleak, muddy New England farm on the hospital grounds. Like most schizophrenics Michael suffered from blunted affect—hampered display of emotion. But that day he was suddenly swept up by the bleak and sorrowful scenery and started to cry. "I was feeling sorry for the poor damp cows," Michael later told Kohler. "Their eyes were broken. God should do something for them. They'll have a hard time."

"Their eyes were broken, Michael? What do you mean?"

"The poor cows. They'll never be the same. Good for them, bad for them. It's so obvious. Their eyes are *broken*. Don't you understand?"

The flash came to Kohler like an ECS jolt. "You mean," he whispered, struggling to control his excitement, "you're saying the *ice* is broken."

With this backhanded message—like the one about getting close to Dr. Anne Muller—Michael was trying to express his inmost feelings. In this case, that something about his life had changed fundamentally. He shrugged and began to cry in front of his therapist—not in fear but out of sorrow. "I feel so *bad* for them." Gradually he calmed. "It seems like a difficult life to be a farmer. But maybe it's one that'd suit me."

"Would you be interested," Kohler asked, his heart racing, "in working on that farm?"

"The farm?"

"The work program. Here at the hospital."

"*Are you mad?*" Michael shouted. "I'd get kicked in the head and killed. Don't be a stupid fucker!"

It took two weeks of constant pressure to talk Michael into the job—far longer, in fact, than it took Kohler to gin up the paperwork to arrange the transfer. Michael was technically an untouchable at Marsden because he was a Section 403 commitment. But there is no easier mark than state bureaucracy. Because Kohler's voluminous documentation referred to "Patient 458-94," rather than "Michael Hrubek," and because the supervisors of vastly overcrowded E Ward were delighted to get rid of another patient, Hrubek was easily stamped, approved, vetted and blessed. He was assigned simple tasks on the farm, which produced dairy products for the hospital and sold what little surplus there was at local markets. At first he was suspicious of his supervisors. Yet he never once had a panic attack. He showed up for work on time and was usually the last to leave. Eventually he settled into the job—shoveling manure, lugging sledgehammers, fence stretchers and staples from fencepost to fencepost, carting milk pails. The only times you'd suspect he wasn't your average farm boy was when he'd use white fence paint on Herefords to even up markings he found unpleasant or scary.

Still, as soon as he was told not to paint the cows, he shamefacedly complied.

Michael Hrubek, who'd never in his life earned a penny of his own money, was suddenly making $3.80 an hour. He was having dinner in the hospital cafeteria with friends and washing dishes afterwards, he was writing a long poem about the Battle of Bull Run, and he was an integral part of Kohler's delusion-therapy program, not to mention the cover boy of his proposal to the State Department of Mental Health.

And now, Kohler reflected sorrowfully, he was a dangerous escapee.

Oh, where are you, Michael, with your broken eyes?

One thing he was convinced of: Michael was en route to Ridgeton. The visit with Lis Atcheson had been doubly helpful. Partly for what it revealed about Michael's delusion. But also for what it revealed about *her*. She'd lied to him, that was clear. He'd tried to deduce exactly where her story about Indian Leap deviated from the truth. But she seemed to be a woman used to living with secrets, with feelings unexpressed, passions hidden, and so he hadn't been able to spot the lie. Yet Kohler felt that whatever she wasn't telling him was significant—very likely significant enough to prod Michael out of the haze of his deluded but secure life and urge him to make this terrifying journey through the night.

Oh, yes, he was on his way to Ridgeton.

And here waiting for him, huddled in the driving rain, was Richard Kohler, a man willing to bribe bounty hunters with thousands of dollars he could scarcely afford, to troop through hostile wilderness, to track down and meet his edgy and dangerous patient all by himself and spirit him back to the hospital—for Michael's sake and the sake of the thousands of other patients Kohler hoped to treat during his lifetime.

The doctor now gazed over the spacious parking lot and drew his black overcoat about him in a futile effort to ward off the heavy rain and gusts of wind. He opened his backpack and lifted out the sturdy metal syringe then filled the reservoir with a large dosage of anesthetic. He flicked the bubbles to the top and fired a small spurt into the air to expel them. Then he leaned back, his face pelted with rain, and he looked up once more at the perpetual motion of the sign above his head.

25

"Look at this!"

A mile down the road Michael rounded a curve and barked a sudden laugh. He calmly recalled which pedal was the brake and he pressed it gently, slowing to ten miles an hour.

"Look!" He leaned forward, his head almost to the windshield, and gazed into the sky, filled with rain that reflected red, white and blue lights in a million spatters.

"Oh, God, what could this *mean*?" His skin hummed with emotion and upon his face a vast grin was spreading. Michael pulled onto the shoulder and stopped the Subaru. He stepped out into the rain and, as if in a trance, began walking through the parking lot, his John Worker boots scraping on the asphalt. He paused at the base of the shrine and stood with his hands clasped before him, reverently, staring up into the sky. He dug into his backpack and observed that he had two skulls left. He selected the one in worse condition—it was cracked in several places—and set it at the base of the sign.

The voice came from nearby. "Hello, Michael."

The young man wasn't startled in the least. "Hello, Dr. Richard."

The thin man sat on the hood of a white car, one of fifty, all in a row. Doesn't he look small, doesn't he look wet? Michael thought, reminded once again of the raccoon he'd killed earlier in the evening. Such little things, both of them.

Dr. Richard scooted off the Taurus. Michael glanced at him but his eyes were drawn irresistibly to the radiant sign revolving above their heads.

Michael ignored the middle portion of the sign, noting only that the word *MERCURY* was bloody red. What he stared at were the two words in blue, Union-soldier blue: On the top, *FORD*. On the bottom, *LINCOLN*.

"That's where you killed him, isn't it, Michael? The theater?"

This is surely a miracle. Oh, God in your infinite brilliance . . .

"Ford . . . Lincoln . . . Ford's Theater . . . Yessir, I sure did. Make no mistake. I snuck into the presidential box at ten-thirty on April 14, the year of our Lord eighteen hundred and sixty-five. It was Good Friday. I came up behind him and put a bullet into his head. The President didn't die right away but lingered until the next day. He linnnnn-gered."

"You yelled, '*Sic semper tyrannis.*' "

"They've been after me ever since." Michael looked at his doctor. No, he was no impostor. It was truly Dr. Richard. You look tired, doctor, Michael thought. I'm awake and you're asleep. What do you make of that? He gazed up at the sign again.

"I want to help you."

Michael chuckled.

"I'd like you to come back with me to the hospital."

"That's nuts, Dr. Richard. I just *left* there. Why would I want to go back?"

"Because you'll be safe. There are people looking for you, people who want to hurt you."

Michael snapped, "*I've* been telling you that for months."

"That's true, you have." The doctor laughed.

Michael took the pistol from his pocket. Dr. Richard's eyes flicked down momentarily but returned immediately to his patient's. "Michael, I've done a lot for you. I got you the job on the farm. You like that job, don't you? You like to work with the cows, I know you do."

The pistol was warm. It was comfortable in his hand. It was, he thought, quite *fashionable*. "I've been wondering if—wouldn't this be strange—if this was the same gun I'd used."

"To shoot Lincoln?"

"The very same gun. That would have a special *meaning*. That would make a lot of *sense*. Do you like the *scent* of blood, Dr. Richard? When do you think a soul makes the a-*scent* to heaven? Do you think souls linnnnger on earth a while?"

Why is he stepping closer to me? Michael wondered. When he's this close, it's easier to read my mind.

"I wouldn't know."

Michael held the pistol close to his face, smelling the metal. "But how do you explain that it was just there for me? This gun. It was just *there* in the store. The store with the heads."

A shudder ran through Michael Hrubek.

"What heads?"

"All the little heads. White and smooth. Beautiful little white heads."

"Those skulls?" Dr. Richard nodded toward the sign pole.

Michael blinked but said nothing.

"So you shot Lincoln, did you, Michael?"

"Sure did. I was willing and *abe*-le."

"Why didn't you ever tell me about it? In any of our sessions?"

Michael's stomach twisted with unbridled anxiety. "It was . . ."

"Why?"

Fear prickled at his neck. Between rapid breaths, Michael answered, "It was too terrible. I did a terrible thing. *Terrible!* He was such a great man. And look what I did! It was . . . It hurts! Don't fucking ask me any more."

"What," Dr. Richard asked gently, "was so terrible about it? What was too terrible to tell me?"

"Many things. Too numerous to go into."

"Tell me about one."

"No."

"Just pick one thing and tell me, Michael."

"No."

"Please. Now. Quick."

"No!" What's this fucker up to?

"Yes, Michael. Tell me." For an instant the thin doctor's eyes grew fierce and commanding. He ordered, "Now! Tell me!"

"The moon," Michael blurted. "It . . ."

"What about the moon?"

"It rose bloody red. The moon is a sheet of blood. Eve is wrapped in the sheet."

"Who's Eve, Michael?"

"Nice try, fucker. Don't expect me to say anything more." Michael swallowed and looked around nervously.

"Where did the blood come from?"

"The moon. Ha, just kidding."

"Where, Michael? Where did the blood come from? Where?!"

In a whisper: "From . . . their head."

"*Whose* head, Michael?" Dr. Richard said, then shouted, "Tell me! Whose head?"

Michael began to speak then he smiled grimly and snarled, "Don't try to trick me, fucker. *His* head. His, his, his head. Abraham Lincoln's head. The sixteenth President of the United States' head. The rail-splitter from Illinois's head. *That's* who I meant. I put a fucker of a bullet in his head."

"Is that what you mean when you'd say 'ahead,' Michael? You were talking about somebody who got hurt in the head? Who? Who *else* got hurt, besides Lincoln?"

Michael blinked, and sizzled in panic. "Seward, you're thinking of! Secretary of State. But he got *stabbed*! If you're going to trick me, get your facts straight. He didn't enjoy the evening much either, by the way."

"But someone else got *shot*, didn't they?"

"No!"

"Think, Michael. Think back. You can tell me."

"No!" He pressed his hands over his ears. "No, no, no!"

"Where did all that blood come from? Blood everywhere!" Dr. Richard whispered. He leaned forward. "So much blood. Enough blood to cover the moon. Sheets and sheets of it."

Enough blood to cover the sheet . . .

Michael cried, "There was so *much* of it."

"Who else, Michael? Who else got shot? Please tell me."

"I *tell* you, you *tele*graph the CIA and the Secret Service!"

"It'll be our secret, Michael. I won't tell another living soul."

"Will you tell a *dead* soul?" he roared, throwing his head back and raving into the pouring rain. "*They're* the ones we have to worry about! All the *dead* souls! *That's* where the danger is!"

"Who, Michael? Tell me."

"I . . ."

Oh, what's that on your head? What's that you're wearing?

Daddy'll be home soon. Daddy'll make her take it off.

Her beautiful head, all ruined. No, no!

"Michael, talk to me! Why are you crying?" Dr. Richard gripped his arm. "What are you thinking?"

He's thinking: I came into the house. I'd been in the backyard doing many important things. I came into the house and there she was, and there were no masks on her eyes and her fingernails weren't burning. There she was in the bedroom, wearing the same nightgown she'd worn for days and days and days. Very *fashionable*. The *very* thing to wear to go by the store to buy the store. The *very* thing to wear when you're holding a gun, this *very* gun. John Wilkes Booth had given it to her.

"Michael! What's the matter? Look at me! What are you thinking?"

He's thinking: Booth must have been her lover and he gave her this gun—to protect her from dead Union *soldi*ers. But she *sold* me out. She betrayed me!

"Did you say betrayal? I can't hear you. You're muttering. What are you saying, Michael?"

She held the gun in her hand. She was lying in bed in her nightgown. She sat up when I came into the doorway and she said . . . She said . . . She said, "Oh, you."

Michael heard her words tonight, as he'd heard them a million times before—spoken not in surprise or contempt or supplication but out of infinite disappointment.

He's thinking: And then she kissed her gold hair with the lips of the gun, and blood flew high as the moon and covered her head like a red glistening hat. It covered the sheets.

Oh, you . . . Oh, you . . .

Michael had stood in the doorway of her bedroom as he watched the blond hair grow dark under the crimson hat. Then he leaned down and touched her quivering hand awkwardly, the first physical contact between mother and son in years. Her unfocused eyes grew dark as eclipses, her forked fingers shuddered once and relaxed and then slowly lost whatever warmth they'd once held, though Michael let go long, long before her flesh grew cold.

"The beautiful head . . ."

"*Whose*, Michael?"

Then the memories vanished, as if a switch had been shut off. The tears stopped and Michael found himself gazing down at Dr. Richard, who was now only a foot or so from him.

"Who?" said the doctor desperately.

"Nice try," Michael said, cheerfully sarcastic. "But I don't think so."

Dr. Richard closed his eyes for a moment. His lips tightened then he sighed. "Okay, Michael. Okay." He fell silent for a moment then said, "How 'bout we drive back to the hospital together? I've got the BMW. We talked about going for a ride sometime. You said you'd like that. You said a BMW was one fucker of a car."

"Fucker of a *Nazi* car," Michael corrected.

"Let's go, come on."

"Oh, but I can't, Dr. Richard. I'm going to pay a little visit to Lis-bone. Oh, that was bad, what happened there. I've got some evening up to do."

"Why, Michael? Why?"

"She's the Eve of betrayal," he answered as if it were self-evident.

Dr. Richard's face slowly relaxed. He looked away for a long moment. Then his face brightened—every bit of his face except his eyes, Michael noticed. "Hey, you've got a car too. I'm impressed, Michael."

"It's not like a Cadillac," he sneered.

"Look over there," the doctor said casually. "At that row of cars. All those *Lincolns*. Row after row of *Lincolns*."

"That's interesting, Dr. Richard," Michael said agreeably, studying not the cars but his doctor's face. "But what's more interesting is why you've been hiding your hand behind you all night, you fucker!"

"God, no!" The doctor's left cross thudded harmlessly into the huge chest, as Michael ripped the syringe from the narrow fingers.

"What've we got *here*? This is shiny, oh, this is pretty. You've got a present for me? Oh, I know all about you! You came out all by yourself to stick me in the back and turn me over to the conspirators. So nobody'd know about me, nobody'd know about Dr. Richard's little secret who ran away. Don't tell the world until you're ready. Right? Stick me in the back then stick me in a crash bag, you fucker?"

"No! Don't do this!"

Michael leaned forward. "*Oh, you . . .*" he whispered, and moved the long needle with its razor-sharp beveled edge even with the doctor's eyes. It moved closer and closer, passing inches from his face as the man's thin muscles struggled uselessly against Michael's overwhelming strength.

"Please, no!"

The needle turned directly toward the doctor and started toward his chest.

"No!"

Then, with a skill that came from years of careful observation, Michael eased the needle deep into the doctor's skin and injected the drug.

From Dr. Richard's lips came a mournful wail, which seemed not to be a cry of pain but appeared to come rather from a deeper sort of anguish—the sound perhaps of a man realizing that the last image in his thoughts as he died would be the look of betrayal upon the face of someone that he had, in a way, loved.

"How far away was he?" Portia asked.

"Fredericks. It's only eight or nine miles from here. But the roads're bound to be terrible."

They had changed clothes and shared the hair dryer. Lis stood in the kitchen window and saw, through the rain, a dot of light reflecting on the lake, a mile away. The house of their closest neighbor—a couple Owen and Lis knew casually. They were young, married only six months. The woman was very much a hausfrau and on several occasions had talked to Lis breathlessly and with queasy candor about wifedom. She asked many questions and watched with squinting eyes, her elbows on a vinyl placemat, as Lis awkwardly dished out advice about relationships. For heaven's sake, Lis thought, how would *I* know if you should have sex with your husband even if you've got the flu? As if there were rules about such things.

"You're all packed?" Portia asked.

"Packed? Nightgown, toothbrush, underwear. It'll be about a six-hour stay. God, what I want is a hot bath. They might even catch him before Owen gets here. Hey, I need a drink. Brandy?"

"Tastes like soap."

"Acquired taste, granted. Grand Marnier?"

"More my style." '

Lis poured two glasses and wandered into the doorway of the greenhouse.

"We make a good dam. It's still holding."

A huge burst of wind shook the windows. It howled through the open vents, loud enough to obscure conversation. The leafless trees whipped back and forth and whitecaps broke on the surface of the lake. Lis said that she'd never seen the water this turbulent. A huge streak of lightning split the sky to the west and the floor seemed to drop beneath their feet when the thunder rolled over the house.

"Let's retreat. To the living room?"

Lis was happy to agree.

They sat in silence for a moment. Lis avoided her sister's eyes and glanced instead at a cluster of photographs on the end table. Pictures from their childhoods: Portia, sassy and sexy. Lis, studious and vigilant and, well, plain. Tall, stern Andrew, complete with anachronistic mustache and ubiquitous white shirt. And gracious Mother with her uplifted matriarchal jaw, her eyes commanding everyone except her husband, in whose presence she was timid.

"Portia," Lis said slowly, eyes now on the frames, not the photographs, "I'd like to talk to you about something."

Her sister looked toward her. "The nursery business?"

"No," Lis finally answered. "It's about Indian Leap. What happened there. Between us, I mean. Not the murder. You don't want to talk about it, I know. But will you just listen to what I have to say?"

Portia was silent. She licked the sweet liquor from the rim of her glass and waited.

Lis sighed. "I never wanted to see you again after that day."

"You must've figured that was how I felt too. Since we *haven't* seen each other."

"I've felt so guilty."

"I don't want an apology."

"Hitting you, saying the things I said . . . I was out of control. I've never been that way before. Never in my life. I was everything I always prayed I'd never be."

"You had a good teacher." Portia tapped the photo of their father. "Got your right hook from him, it felt like."

Lis didn't smile; she felt ill with shame and anger. She looked now for signs of forgiveness, softening. But Portia merely sat hugging her glass and staring—almost bored, it seemed—into the greenhouse. The eerie moaning of the wind continued.

Absently, Lis said, "I went to the Dairy Queen the other day. Remember it?"

"They're still around? I haven't been inside one for years."

"No, remember. There *is* no inside."

"That's right. Sure."

Lis pictured them as young girls, with their Dutch bodyguard Jolande, buying the soft vanilla cones at a little screen window and sitting on a sticky picnic bench beside the parking lot. During the day bees hovered, and at night moths and beetles died fast, brilliant deaths as they flew into the mesmerizing purple glow of the bug zapper.

"We'd get the cherry coatings," the younger sister squinted as she recalled.

"And the ice cream was always melting and running down the cone. It was always a race—trying to lick it off before it got to our hands."

"Sure, I remember."

They fell silent, as the whine from the wind grew more piercing. Lis walked to the greenhouse and closed the vent tightly. The sound waned but didn't cease completely. When she returned she said,

"I never mentioned it to you, Portia, but I had an affair last spring, and there are some things I have to tell you about it."

He cruises at seventy miles an hour, the tach on the dash edging red on the uphill grades, the engine a tortured whine. Owen Atcheson passes the Sav-Mor, now closed, the plate glass taped with huge X's, as if instead of a fall storm a hurricane is anticipated. Then he speeds past a housing development, and beyond that, the Ford dealership, the blue and red sign turning like a lighthouse beacon slowly in the sky.

Then Route 236 begins to curve through the hills that border Ridgeton—the hills that are also part of the same geologic glitch that, two hours away, rises high above the stone valley of Indian Leap, where Robert Gillespie had died broken and bloody.

Owen slows to take these turns then speeds again to fifty, hurrying through the red light at the intersection of 116. The road now rises along the crest of a long hill and he catches a glimpse of water thirty feet below him, off to the right. From the dark creek rise the spindly black legs of the old Boston, Hartford & New York railroad trestle. He slows for the road's only hairpin turn and lifts his foot off the brake to accelerate onto the long straightaway that will take him into downtown Ridgeton.

The beige Subaru seems to drift leisurely from the cleft of bushes where it was hidden, pointed nose out. Owen sees, however, that the car's rear wheels spin furiously, shooting mud and water behind them, and the import is actually moving at a good clip. In the instant before the huge hollow bang, he thinks he might escape, so close do the vehicles approach without striking. Then the car hits the Cherokee solidly amidships with a terrible jolt that twists Owen's neck badly. Pain explodes in his face with a burst of yellow light.

The Subaru stops short of the cliff's edge as the truck eases over the side. It teeters for what seems an eternity, giving Owen Atcheson plenty of time to see the face of Michael Hrubek, a mere six feet away. He's grinning madly, pounding on the wheel, and shouting as he tries frantically, it seems, to make himself heard. Owen stares back but never does figure out what the message might be because just then the truck lurches forward and starts its plunge toward the creek far below.

26

Portia laughed shortly and asked with astonishment, "You? An affair?"

The older sister's eyes were fixed on the sheets of gray rain that cascaded down the windows.

"Me. Wouldn't've guessed, would you?"

There, Lis thought. I've done it. The first time I've confessed. To anyone. There's lightning nearby but so far it hasn't struck me dead.

"You never said anything." Portia was clearly amused. "I had no clue."

"I was afraid, I guess. That Owen would find out. You know him. That temper of his."

"Why would I tell Owen?"

"I didn't think you would. It just seemed to me that the more people who knew, the more the chance word would get out." She paused. "Well, there's something else too. . . . I was ashamed. I was afraid of what you'd think."

"Me? Why on earth?"

"An affair isn't anything to be proud of."

"Were you just fucking? Or were you in love?"

Lis was offended, yet Portia's question seemed motivated merely by curiosity. "No, no, no. It wasn't just physical. We *were* in love. I really don't know why I didn't tell you before. I should have. There've been too many secrets between us." She glanced at her sister. "Owen had an affair too."

The young woman nodded knowingly. Lis was horrified that Portia had somehow learned this already. But, no, it turned out that she'd simply pegged Owen as a man with a wandering eye.

This offended Lis too. "Well, it was only one time," she said defensively.

"Frankly, Lis, I'm surprised you waited as long as you did to find somebody."

"How can you say that?" Lis retorted. "I'm not the sort . . ." Her voice faded.

"Not like *me*?" her sister asked wryly.

"I mean that I wasn't *looking* for anyone. We were trying to work it out, Owen and me. He'd given up the woman he was seeing and we were making a conscious effort—"

"Conscious effort."

Lis listened for mockery and believed she heard none. She continued doggedly, "—an *effort* to keep our marriage together. The affair . . . just happened."

She'd begun the liaison at an awkward time, right in the middle of the terrible sequence of last winter: Owen's affair, the slow death of her mother, her increased discontent with teaching, taking over the estate. . . . The worst *possible* time, she thought, then reflected: As if there's a convenient moment for cataclysm.

Lis's affair, unlike the tidy Hollywood version that she imagined Owen's to have been, had tormented her mercilessly. It would've been far easier, she told herself, if she'd been able to separate the dick from the soul. But she couldn't and so of course she fell in love—as her paramour did with her. At first, Lis admitted, she was partly drawn to her lover out of retaliation. It was petty, yes, but there it was—she wanted to get even with Owen. Besides, she found, she simply couldn't control herself. The affair was all-consuming.

Portia asked, "It's over now?"

"Yes, it's over."

"Well, what's the big deal?"

"Oh," Lis said bitterly, "but it is a *big deal*. I haven't told you everything."

Lis opened her mouth to speak and for an unbearable moment she was about to confess everything. She truly believed that she was going to blurt out every scathing fact.

And she probably would have if the car hadn't arrived just then.

Portia turned from her sister and looked out the kitchen window toward the driveway.

"Owen!" Lis stared out the window, both overjoyed at his arrival and bitterly disappointed that the conversation with her sister was being interrupted.

They walked into the kitchen and peered through the sheets of rain.

"No, I don't think it's him," her sister said slowly. They watched the headlights make their snaking way along the driveway. Lis counted the flares as the beams hit the orange reflectors along the route. Portia was right. Although she couldn't make out the vehicle clearly through the bushes and trees, it was light-colored; Owen's Cherokee truck was black as a gun barrel.

Lis flung open the kitchen door and looked out through the dazzling rain.

It was a police car. A young deputy climbed out. He glanced at the Acura sitting in the middle of the flood and ran into the kitchen, flicking rainwater from his face in an effeminate way. He was round with the tautness of recent fat and had the face of a man on an unexpected assignment.

"Lis." He pulled his hat off. "I'm sorry to have to tell you this. We just found Owen's truck at the bottom of a ravine."

"Oh, God!" Lis's hands flew to her eyes and she pressed hard, as if they stung with smoke.

"He'd been run into—by that fellow Hrubek, looks like. The psycho. Knocked him off the road. Seemed to be a ambush."

"No! Hrubek's going to Boyleston. You're wrong!"

"Well, he ain't going to Boyleston in the car he was driving. Front end's mashed in."

Lis turned instinctively toward where her purse lay on the counter. "How badly hurt is he? I have to go to him."

"We don't know. Can't find him. Or Hrubek either."

"Where did it happen?" Portia asked.

"By the old railroad trestle. Near downtown."

"Downtown *where*?" Lis snapped.

His fat mouth fell silent. Perhaps he suspected her of hysteria. He said, "Well, downtown Ridgeton."

No more than three miles from where they stood.

The wreck wasn't too bad, the deputy explained. "We think Hrubek took off and Owen's after him."

"Or, Owen's running, with Hrubek after *him*."

"We thought of that too. The sheriff and Tom Scalon are out looking for them. All the phones in this part of town're out. Stan had me drive over to tell you. He's thinking you oughta leave. Till they find him. But your car's outta commission, looks like."

Lis didn't respond. Portia told him that they couldn't get a tow truck.

"Believe you'll need more'n a tow for that particular vehicle." He nodded toward the sunken Acura. "Anyway, I'll take you. Just get your stuff together."

"Owen . . ." Lis looked around her, scanning the woods in vain.

"I'm thinking," the deputy said, "we oughta get a move on."

"I'm not going *anywhere* until we find my husband."

Perhaps she sounded ferocious, for the deputy added cautiously, "I understand how you feel. . . . But I don't exactly know there's a lot you can do here but fret. And I'll—"

"I'm not going anywhere," she said slowly. "You understand?"

He looked at Portia, who gave no response. Finally he said, "Have it your way, Lis. That's your business. But Stanley said to make sure you're okay. I better call him and tell him you don't want to leave." He waited a moment more, as if this might intimidate her into leaving. When she turned away he walked out into the rain once more and climbed into the front seat of the cruiser to make the radio call.

"Lis," Portia protested. "There's nothing we can do."

"Go sit in the car with him if you want. Or have him take you to the Inn. I'm sorry, but I'm not leaving."

Portia glanced outside, at a tree bending under a furious gust of wind. "No, I'll stay."

"Go lock the windows. I'll check the doors."

Before he'd left, Owen had deadbolted the front door. Lis now fixed the security chain, thinking momentarily how tiny the brass links seemed compared with the manacles that had gripped Hrubek's hands at trial. She then locked and chained the door off the kitchen utility room. She wondered if Owen had remembered the lath-house door—the only way one could enter or leave the greenhouse from the outside. She walked toward it but paused halfway. She noticed a large rose plant—a Chrysler Imperial hybrid cultivated into a tree. Last year, one week after Owen confessed his affair, he had bought her this plant. It was the only one he'd ever purchased without her guidance. On the day of rest after owning up to Ms. Trollop, Esq., he appeared with the massive scarlet rosebush in the back of his truck. At the time Lis nearly pitched it out. Then she decided not to. The plant owed its reprieve to a passage from a class assignment in *Hamlet*, which her students were then studying.

Cut off even in the blossoms of my sin . . . No reckoning made, but sent to my account, with all my imperfections on my head.

The coincidence was too great to dismiss—this combination of literature, horticulture and real-life drama. So what could Lis do but resist the urge to destroy it? She rooted the damn thing and wondered if the plant would survive. It of course proved to be one of her hardier specimens.

Lis stepped forward and cradled the flower. It was a paradox of her love for plants that her gardener's hands had toughened so much that she could no longer feel the delicacy of petals. She brushed the backs of her hands over the blossoms, then started once again toward the door. She'd taken only a few steps when she saw vague motion from outside.

Walking cautiously to a window, thick with condensation and the sheets of rain, she wiped the glass with her sleeve and saw to her shock the indistinct form of a tall man standing near the house. Hands on his hips, he was trying to find the front door, it appeared. He wasn't the young deputy. Maybe, she thought, another officer had accompanied him, though this fellow didn't seem to be in uniform.

He noticed the side door that led into the utility room and walked to it, oblivious to the downpour. He knocked politely, like a man picking up a date. Lis walked cautiously to the door, and looked out through the curtain. Although she didn't recognize him he had such a pleasant, innocent face, and looked so completely wet, that she let him in.

"Evening, ma'am. You must be Mrs. Atcheson." He wiped his lanky hand on his pants, leaving it just as wet as before, and offered it to her. "Sorry to trouble you. My name's—"

But he didn't have the chance to complete the introduction just then because a large bloodhound pushed his way uninvited into the greenhouse and started to shake himself enthusiastically, showering them both with a million drops of rain.

Owen Atcheson, lying half in and half out of the chill creek, slowly came to. He sat up, praying that he wouldn't faint again.

After the Cherokee had stopped tumbling, Owen hadn't waited for Hrubek to come leaping down the hill after him. He'd examined his left shoulder and felt the indentation where the bone ought to be. He'd made certain his pistol and ammunition were in his pocket and flung the bolt of the deer rifle far into the dark creek, exhaling at the astonishing pain caused by this slight effort.

Then he'd struggled to his feet and run clumsily through the stream, putting distance between himself and the truck.

Two hundred yards into the forest that surrounded downtown Ridgeton he'd stopped and rolled onto his back, lying against a flat rock softened by an old growth of moss. He'd slipped a length of oak branch into his mouth and chewed down hard, gripping his left biceps with his right hand. With excruciating concentration he had forced himself to relax and slowly, slowly manipulated the bone, eyes closed, breathing staccato bursts and sending his teeth deep into the wood. Suddenly, with a pop, the shoulder had reseated itself in the cuff. He cried out softly as the amazing pain made him vomit and then he fainted and slid into the creek.

Now, his eyes open, he crawled to the shore and lay on his side.

He allowed himself no more than five minutes of recuperation before standing up. He removed his belt and tightly bound his left arm to his side. The temporary sling increased the pain but would safeguard against a catastrophic jolt of agony that might make him faint again. He lifted his head and breathed deeply. The rain was falling steadily now and the wind whipped into his face. He threw his head back and inhaled the wet air. After a few moments he began to struggle through the woods, slowly making his way north, around downtown Ridgeton. He didn't want Hrubek to find him of course but neither did he wish to be spotted by anyone else—least of all a meddling sheriff or deputy. After a torturous mile he came to the intersection of North Street and Cedar Swamp Road. He found a pay phone and lifted the receiver. He was not surprised to hear only silence.

Driving north on Cedar Swamp was the only way to reach their address. It was possible to approach the house from the opposite direction but only after driving around two hundred acres of state park and into a different township then back south once again. Hrubek had rammed him so hard the Subaru was surely useless; the psycho would now be on foot too. If the Atcheson property was his destination, he'd have to come this way.

Despite the delay to reset his shoulder Owen doubted that Hrubek had preceded him here. Unfamiliar with the area the man would first need to find a map. Then he'd have to orient himself and find the correct streets, many of which were not clearly marked.

Owen struggled into the intersection cautiously—a soldier on advance patrol, sighting out ambush and fire zones, high ground, backfields, perimeters. He saw a drainage ditch and a corrugated metal pipe, four feet wide. A good hidey-hole, he thought, falling easily into combat-speak. He pictured Hrubek loping cautiously down the middle of the road then Owen himself stepping out, silently, coming up behind with the pistol at his side.

The rain was cool and fragrant with the scents of a deep autumn. Owen inhaled this liquid air deeply then slipped down into the icy water that filled the ditch, guarding his damaged arm. But he was no longer faint and was able to ignore the worst of the pain. As he moved in his military crouch, he recited to himself the profile of kill areas: chest head abdomen groin, chest head abdomen groin. . . . He repeated this gruesome mantra again and again as around him the rain grew fiercer.

Lis Atcheson escorted the man into the kitchen and handed him a towel. She decided that in the baseball cap, with the curly hair dipping toward his shoulders, he looked very much like the backhoe operator who'd dug the trench for their new septic tank last year. He stood with one hip cocked in a stiff way that made her wonder if he had fallen and injured it. He looked mussed enough, she thought, to have taken a tumble recently.

"I'm from over in Hammond Creek? East of here?" Trenton Heck spoke as if no one had ever heard of Hammond Creek—a town with which she wasn't in fact familiar.

Lis introduced Portia, who glanced at Heck in a dismissing way. With a juvenile grin Heck waited for an explanation of the exotic name. "Like the car," he laughed. The young woman offered nothing but her hand, and that unsmilingly.

The young officer was in the squad car, trying to get an update on Hrubek's whereabouts.

"Mr. Heck—" Lis began.

"Trenton. Or Trent," he said good-naturedly, laughing. "Mr. Heck, ha."

"Would you like something?"

He declined a beer but guzzled a can of Coke in less than thirty seconds then leaned against the kitchen island, looking out the windows in an analytical, self-assured way that made Lis wonder if he was an undercover policeman. But, no, he explained, he was more of a consultant. When he told her how Hrubek had led the trackers astray then doubled back, Lis shook her head knowingly. "He's no fool at all."

"Nup."

"I thought he was supposed to be crazy," said Portia, who was rubbing the dog's head with an enthusiasm the hound did not share.

"Well, he is that. But he's a clever son of a gun is what he is too."

Lis asked how he happened to come here.

"I met your husband over in Fredericks. We found this woman. Hrubek told her he was headed for Boyleston. So I went that way and your husband was going to keep on coming this way. The deputy tells me they think Hrubek drove him off the road."

"We don't know where he is. We don't know where *either* of them are. Why'd you change your mind and come this way?"

It was something he just felt, Heck explained. He was halfway to Boyleston when he decided that Hrubek was leading them off track again. "He'd been too, you know, methodical about moving west and trying to throw us off or stop us. He even set out traps for Emil here."

"No!"

"Surely did. I was thinking, he's been clever up till now and there's no reason for him to stop being clever."

"But why didn't you just call the police?"

He was suddenly awkward; she thought he was blushing. Eyes fixed on the window, he gave the women his account, which contained not a single period or comma, all about a reward and his being laid off and having been a state trooper for nearly but not quite ten years and a recession and a trailer that was about to be foreclosed on.

Heck then asked about Owen.

"There're men out looking for him. The sheriff and another deputy."

"I'm sure he'll be okay," Heck said. "He seems to know what he's about. Was in the service, I'll bet."

"Two tours of duty," Lis said distractedly, gazing outside.

Heck, paying no attention to the sisters, dropped to his knees and began drying the dog with paper towels in a wholly absorbed, methodical way, even blotting the inside of his collar and wiping the gaps between his stubby claws. He went through the same ritual as he dried his pistol. Watching this, Lis understood immediately that Trenton Heck was both simpler and sharper than she, and she resolved to take him more seriously than she'd been inclined to.

The deputy returned and squeegeed the water from his cheeks with thick fingers.

"Stanley tells me he notified the troopers about Owen's truck. They're passing that info along to some fellow in the state police named Haversham—"

"He's in charge of the search, sure. My old boss," Trenton Heck said. He seemed not to like this news. Because, Lis supposed, he was not keen on losing or sharing his reward. He added, "He'll probably send a Tactical Services squad—"

"What's that?" the deputy asked.

"Don't you know? Like SWAT."

"No fooling?" The deputy was impressed.

Heck continued, "They'll be here in forty minutes, I'd guess. Maybe a little longer."

"Why don't they send them by helicopter?"

"*Helicopter?*" Heck snorted.

Lis looked past the others for a moment as a sheet of lightning canopied the sky. She felt the thunder in her chest. The deputy was asking her something but she didn't hear a word of it and when she left the room she was running. Portia stepped after her and, alarmed, called, "Lis, are you all right? What is it?"

But Lis was by then taking the stairs two at a time.

In the bedroom she found the Colt Woodsman, a thin .22 automatic pistol that Owen kept beside the bed. He'd insisted that she learn to use it and had made her fire the pistol a dozen times into a paper target tacked to a pile of rotten wood behind the garage. She'd done so, dutiful and nervous, her hand jerking unartfully with every shot. She hadn't touched it since then, perhaps three or four years ago.

She hefted the gun now and noted that, unlike rose petals, the checkered grip and metal of this long pistol left strong sensations upon her callused hands.

The pistol disappeared into her pocket. She walked slowly to the window. The immense blackness outside it—lacking any reference point—hypnotized her and drew her forward. Like a sleepwalker she approached the glass, three feet, two, compelled to find something visible on the other side of the blue-green panes—a branch, an owl, a cloud, the verdigris Pegasus weather vane atop the garage, *anything* that would make the darkness less infinite and permanent. Lightning lit the flooded driveway. She recalled waving goodbye to her husband. She realized with a shock that that gesture might have been the last communication between them ever, and, worse, perhaps one that he had not even seen.

She gazed into the night. Where are you, Owen? Where? Lis knew he was near. For she'd by now realized that, injured or not, he was making his way back to the house, trying to get Hrubek onto their property and complete his mission—to kill him and make it look like self-defense. They could be a mile from the house, or fifty yards away. It was only a matter of time.

Another bolt of lightning streaked from the sky and hit nearby. Lis gasped, stepping back, as the thunder rattled the badly glazed eighteenth-century panes. The storm now came forward like a wave, a wall of indifferent water a thousand feet high. It sped frantically across the lake, whose surface was oddly illuminated as if the globules of rain emitted radiation when they collided with the dark water.

A huge growl of thunder enveloped the house, finishing with a sharp whipcrack. Lis hurried downstairs. She pulled her rain slicker from a hook and said, "I'm going outside. I'm going to find my husband."

27

On April 15, 1865, Doctor Samuel A. Mudd splinted John Wilkes Booth's leg and put him to bed in one of the cots that served as a small infirmary in his home office.

Dr. Mudd had an idea who his patient was and what he'd done the night before but the doctor chose not to ride to town and report Booth to the authorities because his wife was afraid to be left alone with the eerie, feverish man and begged him not to go. Mudd got arrested as part of the conspiracy to assassinate Lincoln and came one vote from being hanged. He was finally released from prison but he died a ruined man.

Michael Hrubek, now reflecting on Mudd's ordeal, thought: He had a woman to thank for that. Just goes to show.

He also thought a doctor might not be a bad idea right at the moment. His wrist burned wildly; it had slammed into the steering wheel when he drove his car into the conspirator's truck. It didn't hurt much but the forearm was glossy, swollen nearly double. From fingers to elbow it was a log of flesh.

As he walked through the rain, however, he grew too excited to worry about his injuries.

For Michael Hrubek was in Oz.

The town of Ridgeton was magical to him. It was the end of his quest. It was the Promised Land and he looked at every strip of pale November grass and every rain-spattered parking meter and mailbox with respect. The storm had darkened most of downtown and the only lights were battery-driven exit and emergency signs.

The red rectangles of light added to the mythic quality of the place.

Standing in a booth, he flipped through a soggy phone book and found what he sought. He recited a prayer of gratitude then turned to the map in the front of the book and located Cedar Swamp Road.

Stepping back into the rain Michael hurried north. He passed darkened businesses—a liquor store, a toy store, a pizza restaurant, a Christian Science reading room. Wait. A *scientific* Jesus Our Lord bless us? Jesus Cry-ist was a physic-ist. Cry-ist was a chem-ist. He laughed at this thought then moved on, catching ghostly images of himself in the plate-glass windows. Some of them were protected by wrinkled sheets of amber plastic. Some were painted black and were undoubtedly used for surveillance. (Michael knew all about one-way mirrors, which could be purchased for $49.95 from Redding Science Supply Company, plus shipping, no COD orders please.)

" 'Good night, ladies,' " he sang as he splashed through a torrent of water in the gutters. " 'Good night, ladies . . .' "

The street ended at a three-way intersection. Michael stopped cold and his heart suddenly began to crawl with panic.

Oh, God, which way? Right or left? Cedar Swamp is one way but it is *not* the other. Which? Left or right?

"Which *way*?" he bellowed.

Michael understood that if he turned one direction he would get to 43 Cedar Swamp Road and if he turned the other he would not. He looked at the signpost and blinked. And in the very small portion of a second it took to close and open his eyelids, his rational mind seized like an overheated engine. It simply stopped.

Explosions of fear surged through him, so intense that they were visible: black and yellow and orange sparks popped through the streets, caroming off the windows and wet sidewalks. He began a fearful keening and his jaw shook. He sank to his knees, pummeled by voices—the voices of old Abe, of the dying soldiers, of the conspirators. . . .

"Dr. Anne," he moaned, "why did you *leave* me? Dr. Anne! I'm so afraid. I don't know what to do! What should I do?"

Michael hugs the signpost as if it's his only source of blood and oxygen and he cries in panic, searching his pockets for the pistol. He must kill himself. He has no choice. The panic is too great. Unbearable terror cascades over him. One bullet in the head, like old Abe, and it'll all be over. He no longer cares about his quest, about betrayal, about Eve, about Lis-bone and revenge. He must end this terrible fear. The gun is here, he can feel its weight, but his hand is shaking too badly to reach into his pocket.

Finally he rips the wool and slips his hand inside the rent cloth, feeling the harsh grip of the pistol.

"I . . . can't . . . STAND . . . IT! OH, PLEASE!"

He cocks the gun.

The brilliant light swept across his closed eyes, filing his vision with bloody illumination. A voice was speaking, saying words he couldn't hear. He relaxed his grip on the gun. His head jerked upright and Michael realized that someone was talking to him, not Dr. Anne or the deceased President of the United States or conspirators or good Dr. Mudd.

The voice was that of a scrawny man in his late fifties, sticking his face out of a car window not three feet from where Michael huddled. He apparently hadn't seen the gun, which Michael now slipped back into his pocket.

"Say, you all right, young man?"

"I . . ."

"You hurt yourself?"

"My car," he mumbled. "My car . . ."

The gray and skinny man was driving a battered old Jeep with a scabby canvas top and vinyl sheets for windows. "You had an accident? And you couldn't find a phone that worked. Sure, sure. They're mostly all out. 'Cause the storm. How bad you hurt?"

Michael breathed deeply several times. The panic diminished.

"Not bad but my car's in a state. She wasn't that good. Not like the old Cadillac."

"No. Well. Come on, I'll ride you over to the hospital. You should get looked at."

"No, no, I'm fine. But I'm turned around. You know where Cedar Swamp is? Cedar Swamp Road, I mean."

"Sure I do. You live there?"

"People I'm suppose to see. I'm late. And they'll be worried."

"Well, I'll drive you over."

"You'd do that for me?"

"I think I ought to be taking you to the emergency room what with that wrist of yours."

"No, just get me to my friends. There's a doctor there. Dr. Mudd, you know him?"

"Don't believe I do, no."

"He's a good doctor."

"Well, that's good. Because that wrist is pretty surely broken."

"Give me a ride"—Michael stood up slowly—"and I'll be your friend till your dying day."

The men hesitated for an uncomfortable moment, then said, "Uh-huh . . . Well, hop in. Only mind the door. You're a tall one."

"Owen's trying to make it back here to the house," Lis explained. "I'm sure of it. And I think Hrubek's chasing him."

"Why wouldn't he just go to the station house?" the deputy asked.

"He's worried about us being here, I'm sure," Lis said. She said nothing about the real reason that Owen wouldn't go to the police.

"I don't know," the deputy said. "I mean, Stan told me—"

"Look, there's nothing to talk about," Lis said. "I'm going out there."

The deputy objected uneasily, "Well, Lis . . ."

Portia again echoed his thoughts. "Lis, there's nothing *you* can do."

Heck took off his pitiful baseball cap and scratched his head. When he replaced the hat, he left a forelock of curly hair dipping toward his right eye. He was studying her. "You testified at his trial?"

Lis looked back at him. "I was the chief prosecution witness."

He was nodding slowly. Finally he said, "I arrested me a fair number of men and testified at their trials. None of them ever came after me."

Lis looked into Heck's eyes, which immediately fled to an old Shaker chair. She said, "You were lucky, then, weren't you?"

"That I was. But it's pretty, you know, rare for an escapee to come after somebody. Usually they just hightail it out of the state."

He seemed to want a response but she gave none other than, "Well, Michael Hrubek probably isn't your typical escapee."

"No argument from me there." Heck didn't continue his line of thought.

Lifting the bright rain slicker from the hook by the door Lis said to her sister, "You stay here. If Owen gets back before I do, honk the horn."

Portia nodded.

"Uhn, ma'am?"

Lis glanced at Heck.

"That might make you a bit, you know, obvious, don't you think?"

"How's that?"

"The, uhn, yellow."

"Oh, I didn't think about that."

Heck lifted away the sou'wester and hung it up. Lis reached for her dark bomber jacket but Heck held up a hand. "Tell you what. I'm thinking let's don't any of us go tripping over our own tails here. I know how you feel and everything, him being your husband

374 \ Jeffery Deaver

and all. But I'm speaking as somebody's done this sort of thing before. I get paid to track people. Let me go out there by myself. No, let me finish. I'll go out and look for your husband and if he's anywhere nearby I'll stand a chance of finding him. Probably a sight better than you. And not only, if you're wandering around out there too, it'll just distract me." His voice was taut, anticipating Lis's protest.

She guessed his essential motive was the reward. Yet what he said was true. And even if Lis happened to find her husband, she wondered how persuasive she would be in urging him to give up the hunt for Hrubek and return home. He hadn't listened to her before; why would he now?

"Okay, Trenton," Lis said.

"What I think we should do is I'll go out in the woods, toward the front gate. He could climb the fence, of course, but I'll risk that. He won't be swimming the lake, not in this wind. That's for sure."

Heck then glanced at the deputy. "I'd say you stay closer to the house. Like a second line of defense. Somewhere near here."

The deputy's interest was rekindled. He'd done his duty and what more could he say to an ornery woman of the house? Now he had allies and might see some action and glory after all. "I'll back the car into the bushes over there," he said excitedly. "How'd that be? I can see the whole of the yard and he won't catch a glimpse of me."

Heck told him that was good idea then said to Lis, "I know your husband's a hunter. Now, you might not feel too comfortable with side arms but you think maybe you could turn one up for yourself?"

Lis took perverse glee in lifting the pistol from her pocket. She held it, muzzle down, finger outside the trigger guard—just as Owen had solemnly instructed her. Portia was appalled. The deputy guffawed. But Trenton Heck merely nodded with satisfaction as if one more item had been crossed off a checklist. "I'll leave Emil with you here. Storm's too fierce even for him. Keep him by you. He's not an attack dog but he's big and he'll make a bushel of noise if someone was to come by uninvited."

"I don't have anything darker that'll fit," Lis said, nodding at the sou'westers.

"That's okay. I'm pretty impervious to water. But I'll take a Baggie for my gun. It's an old German Walther and rusts easy."

He slipped the pistol into a bag and tied the end closed, returning the gun to his cowboy holster. He gazed outside and stretched his leg out for a moment, wincing. She supposed that whatever was wrong with his thigh wouldn't be helped by the rain. The pain seemed quite severe.

The deputy went outside to the car though not before he'd unsnapped the thong of his automatic and circled his fingers around the grip several times like a bad actor in a bad western. Lis heard the car start. He backed into the bushes halfway between the garage and the house. He could turn on his spotlights and illuminate the entire backyard from where he was parked.

Trenton turned to her and spoke in a low voice. "You know how to use that weapon, I'll bet, but I don't suppose you ever *did* use it, not in a situation like this." He didn't wait for confirmation but continued, "What I'd like you to do is shut all the lights out in the house. Sit yourselves away from the windows. I'll keep my eye on the property as best I can. Flick the lights if you need me and I'll come running."

Then without a word to either woman, or his dog, he vanished into the sheets of rain. Lis closed the door behind him.

"Jesus, Lis," Portia whispered but there were so many things she might be shocked by that her sister had no idea to what she was referring.

Thoughts of his wife are long gone from Dr. Ronald Adler's mind. The way she tastes, the arc of her thigh, her skin's texture, the smell of her hair—memories that so occupied him earlier in the evening are wholly absent now.

For Captain Haversham called him not long ago with the news.

"Cloverton," the trooper growled. "Hrubek just killed a woman. The lid's off it now, doc."

"Oh, my God." Adler closed his eyes and his heart seemed to fibrillate as he was lanced with the mad thought that Hrubek had committed this crime solely for the purpose of betraying him. He held the phone in quivering hands and heard the trooper explain with ill-concealed fury how Hrubek had murdered a woman and carved her up, then stolen a motorcycle to escape to Boyleston.

"A *motorcycle*. Carved her up?"

"Cut words on her boobs. And two cops in Gunderson are missing. They were cruising down Route 236 and called in with a report on him. Last we heard. We're sure he's killed 'em and dumped the bodies somewhere. Low-security? Harmless? Jesus *Christ*, man. What were you *thinking* of? I'll be in your office in a half hour." The phone went dead.

Adler is now on his way back to his office from the hospital's cafeteria, where he had taken Haversham's dismaying call and where he had then sat, numb, for the next thirty minutes. But the doctor isn't making very good progress.

Alone in the dark hallway he pauses and spends a moment considering the chain reaction of miraculous physiology that's now causing his neck hair to stir, his eyes to water, and his genitals to contract alarmingly. And although he's thinking about the vagus nerve and adrenaline release and synaptic uptake, what's most salient in his mind is how fucking scared he is.

The corridor is 130 feet long. Twenty doors open off it and all but the last one—his—are closed and dark. Every other bulb in the overhead fixtures has been removed as an economy measure and of those remaining most are burnt out. Three corridors also lead off this one. They too are dark as graves.

Adler looks down the dark hallway and wonders, Why aren't I walking?

He's left the elevator alcove and he knows that Haversham is waiting impatiently in his office. Yet here the doctor stands frozen with fear. His arms are weak, his legs too. He squints away an unfunny apparition—a huge pale form that has stuck its head out of a corridor nearby and darted back into hiding.

The patient's ghostly wailing is displaced by the howl of the wind. It reverberates in Adler's chest, and he thinks, All right. Enough. Please.

Adler walks five paces. Again he stops—on the pretext of flipping through a file he carries.

It is at this moment that he is struck by the sudden awareness that Michael Hrubek has returned to kill him.

That there's no logic to this mission doesn't lessen Adler's growing panic one bit. He gasps as the elevator, summoned from below, grinds downward. He hears a patient somewhere utter a guttural moan of infinite, inexpressible sorrow. As this sound strokes his neck, he places one foot before the other and doggedly starts walking.

No, no—Michael Hrubek has no need to kill him. Michael Hrubek doesn't even *know* him personally. Michael Hrubek couldn't have made the journey back to the hospital in this short time, even if he *did* feel like eviscerating the director.

Dr. Ronald Adler the veteran of the state mental-health-hospital system, Dr. Ronald Adler the fair-to-middlin' graduate of a provincial medical school—these Dr. Ronald Adlers believe that he's probably safe.

Yet the man whose head was entwined between his wife's fragrant legs earlier in the night, the man who mediates board-meeting conflicts far better than he cures madness, the man who now pads down this murky, stone hallway—*these* Ronald Adlers are paralyzed by the sound of his own gritty footsteps.

Please, don't let me die.

His office now seems miles away, and he gazes at the white trapezoid of light falling onto the concrete from his open doorway. He continues on, passing one of the arterial corridors, and exhales a fast astonished laugh at his inability to turn and look down it. If he does he will see a Technicolor film clip of Michael Hrubek reaching into Adler's mouth. The hospital director cannot purge from his thoughts the passages of Hrubek's transcripts he read earlier in the evening. He recalls in particular detail the patient's lively discussion of locating and rupturing a spleen.

Enough. Please!

Adler passes by the corridor safely but a new worry intrudes— that he'll lose control of his bladder. He's insanely furious at his wife—for gripping his cock earlier in the evening and unwittingly putting in mind the now-consuming fear of incontinence. He must urinate. He absolutely *must*. But the men's room is a lengthy way down the corridor he now approaches. The restrooms are dark this time of night. He considers pissing against the wall.

I don't want to die.

He hears footsteps. No, yes? Whose are they?

The ghosts of one woman and two troopers.

What's that *sound*?

Hah, they're his own feet. Or perhaps not. He pictures the urinal. He turns toward it and begins to walk through the dim hall, and as he does a thought comes to mind: that Michael Hrubek's escape tugs at everything he's ever done wrong as a doctor. The escape is the crib sheets that accompanied him into organic-chemistry exams, it's the charts he misplaced, the misprescribed medications, the aneurysms he forgot to inquire about before dispensing large dosages of Nardil. The madman's escape is like lifting a twenty-pound line and watching rise from a murky pond some diseased fish snagged by your hook, bloated and near death—a prize you regret ever seeking, a token you wish would forever go away.

.   .   .

"Listen to me, you son of a bitch," Haversham growled, after he hung up the telephone. His audience—the hospital director and a glazed-eyed Peter Grimes—stared at him numbly. A grating rain fell heavily on the windows of Adler's office. The wind screamed.

"We just got ourselves another notice," Haversham continued. "This one's from Ridgeton. Seems there's a report somebody crashed into a truck and drove it off the road. Both drivers disappeared into the woods. The truck got hit was registered to Owen Atcheson."

"Owen—?"

"The husband of that woman testified against Hrubek. The fellow who was here before."

So now, maybe four dead.

"They know for a fact it was Hrubek who did it?"

"They *think*. They don't *know*. That's what we need you for."

"Oh, Jesus," Adler muttered. He touched his eyes and pushed until he heard soft pops of pressure beneath the lids. "Four dead," he whispered.

"It's up to you, doc. We need to know where to put our resources."

What was he talking about? Resources?

"No cuddly-pup psychocrap. I want a straight answer. We've had two reports—Boyleston and Amtrak, or Ridgeton and that woman testified against him. Where's he headed?"

Adler gazed at him blankly.

"I think they want to know where to send their men, sir," Grimes explained delicately.

"That's the problem, yeah. Two reports. They don't jibe. Nobody knows jack shit for certain."

Adler looked from his assistant to the tall cowboy of a trooper and thought: Sleep deprivation, that's my problem. "Well, the Ridgeton sheriff has men he can send, doesn't he?"

"Sure he does. Only they got but four in the whole of the department. They sent somebody out to the house so the woman's safe. But I need to know where to deploy. We gotta *catch* this boy! I got four Tactical Services troopers ready to go. The rest of the men won't be available for close to an hour. Where should I send the van? It's your call."

"*Me?* I don't know the facts," Adler blurted. "I need *facts*. I mean, are they sure Hrubek hit Atcheson? Where did he get a car? Was he actually *sighted* on the motorcycle? We can't decide anything until we know that. And—"

"You've got all the facts there are," Haversham muttered, gazing steel-eyed at the doctor. "This boy's been in your care here for four months. Whatever you know about him is all you got to go on."

"Ask Dick Kohler. *He's* Hrubek's doctor."

"We would. But we don't know where he is and he ain't answering his pager."

Adler looked up as if to ask, Why me? He leaned forward and pressed his palms together. He chewed compulsively on a red index finger.

Boyleston . . .

The doctor's finger left his mouth and traced along the same map on which earlier in the evening he had plotted Michael Hrubek's capture and Richard Kohler's downfall.

Ridgeton . . .

Suddenly his face began to bristle, and nothing in this mad universe was as important to Dr. Ronald Adler as capturing his errant patient. Capturing him alive if possible but if not then putting him on a slab with his meaty toe tagged for burial in potter's field, lying cold and blue and still.

Oh, let this night be over, he prayed. Let me slip back home and lie against the hot breasts of my wife, let me find sleep under the thick comforters, let this night end with no more deaths.

Adler ripped open Hrubek's file and leafed frantically through the sheets. They spun out and scattered on his desk. He began to read.

Hrubek, Adler considered, displays classic paranoid-schizophrenic symptoms—thought content illogical, flights of ideas, loose association, pressure of speech and increased motor activities typical of manic episodes, blunted and inappropriate affect. . . .

"No, no, no!" Adler spat out in a whisper, garnering troubled glances from the two men nearby. What, he raged to himself, do these words *mean*? What is Hrubek *doing*? What is *driving* him?

Who *is* Michael Hrubek?

Adler spun his desk chair and gazed out the rain spattered window.

Item: Hrubek suffers from auditory hallucinations and his speech is a typical schizophrenic's word salad. He might have told that truck driver, "Boston," meaning to say, "Boyleston."

Item: Revenge, the purported reason for going to Ridgeton, is a common element of paranoid-schizophrenic delusions.

Item: A schizophrenic would shun the circuitous path of getting to Boyleston via Cloverton.

Item: Amtrak runs through Boyleston. Train travel has a far lower stress factor than air travel, and accordingly would be preferred by a psychotic.

Item: Despite being off Thorazine, he *is* driving a vehicle. Thus Hrubek has, through will or miracle, tamed his anxiety and might make the more arduous and complicated journey south to Boyleston rather than the logistically simpler trip to Ridgeton.

Item: With all his tricks tonight, his false clues and cleverness, Hrubek was displaying astonishing cognitive functionality. He could easily be setting up a feint to Ridgeton, intending all along to go to Boyleston.

Item: But on the other hand he might be *so* high-functioning that he was double-feinting—appearing to head for Ridgeton when that town was in fact his destination.

Item: He's capable of unmotivated murder.

Item: Some of his delusions have to do with United States history, politics and government agencies. And several times in his therapy sessions he mentioned Washington, D.C.—a place he could get to via Amtrak.

Item: He has a hatred of women, and he has a rape conviction. He threatened the Atcheson woman several months ago.

Item: He has a fear of confrontation.

Item: He cheeked his medicine, in anticipation of this evening, indicating a long-thought-out plot.

Item . . . *Item* . . . *Item* . . .

A thousand facts cascaded though the doctor's sumptuous mind. Dosages of Haldol and Stelazine, intake-interview observations, milieu-therapy encounters, verbatims of his delusional ramblings, psychopharmacologists' and social workers' reports . . . Adler spun back to confront the files, spearing some sheets of paper beneath his narrow fingers and clutching others randomly. He looked at a page of transcript but he saw instead Michael Hrubek's face—eyes that revealed no ebullience or lethargy, no affection or contempt, no trust or doubt.

Adler sat very still for a moment. Suddenly, he looked up at the lined, exhausted face of the state trooper and spoke what he devoutly believed to be the truth. "Hrubek's making for the train station. He's going to Washington, D.C. Send your troopers to Boyleston. Now!"

The two sisters went about their tasks, combing the house, shutting out lights. They walked in silence, jumping at the noise when there was thunder and at the shadows when there was not. Finally, the house was lit only by ambient light from outside and a few blue up-lamps in the greenhouse, which Lis had left on for the comfort of the faint illumination; she reckoned they'd be invisible from the outside. Shadows fluttered on the walls and floors. Together, they returned to the kitchen and sat side by side on a bench, facing an army of pine and birch trees through the rain-swept backyard.

Five minutes of quiet passed, the rain battering the greenhouse, the wind screaming through the holes and cracks in the old house. Finally Lis was no longer able to keep from speaking. "Portia, there's something I started to tell you tonight."

"Earlier?"

"The affair," Lis whispered discreetly, as if Owen were in the next room.

"I don't know if this is the time—"

Lis touched her sister's knee. "This thing's been between us too long. I can't stand it anymore."

"*What*'s between us? Lis, this isn't really the time to have a talk. For heaven's sake."

"I *have* to talk to you."

"Later."

"No, now!" Lis said heatedly. "Now! If I don't do it now, I may never."

"And why's it so important?"

"Because you have to understand why I said those terrible things to you. And I have to know something from you too. Look at me. Look!"

"Okay, you told me you were seeing somebody. So what? What does Indian Leap have to do with it?"

"Oh, Portia . . ."

Lis must have unknowingly inhaled a huge lungful of air; her chest stung suddenly and she lowered her forehead to her drawn-up knees to ease the pain. In the turbulent silence that flowed between them Lis felt the pain drift away and she lifted her head again to face her sister. As she was about to speak, a faint, not unpleasant roll of thunder filled the room and as it did Portia's eyes narrowed with understanding. She said, "Oh, no."

"Yes," Lis said. "Yes. My lover was Robert Gillespie."

28

"So how long you known the Atchesons?"

The Jeep driver had a narrow face and gray wattles running down his throat. He downshifted the old vehicle and nursed it up a hill north of downtown Ridgeton, exhaust popping and the gears in agony. The big man next to him was studying the shifting with more interest than the driver thought natural.

"Years and years I've known them," he said. "Many years."

"I know Owen," the driver said. "Talked to him a few times. We run into each other at Ace Hardware some. A decent sort. For a lawyer."

"A hundred years, I'd guess."

"Pardon me?"

"Lis-bone especially."

"I didn't think she pronounced it that way. But you know 'em better'n me, I'd guess." The Jeep bounded over a rough spot of road. "You're lucky I come by. Nobody's out on the streets tonight because of the storm. Those weathermen with their toupees and funny names, they said it's going to be a pisser of a storm but naw it's just a little rain is all it is."

The big man didn't respond.

The Jeep hissed past the intersection of Cedar Swamp and North Street and for a moment the driver thought that he saw someone turn quickly, startled by their passage, and drop over the side of a small hill near the drainage ditch. Simultaneously the sky filled with a huge sphere of lightning and shadows danced every which way. A branch fell nearby. The driver put the apparition down to a freak arrangement of lights and fog and rain. He sped up and followed the winding, uneven course of Cedar Swamp. "Shameful on the part of the county. When're they going to get around and do it up right? Put some new asphalt along here? This road's mostly mud and twigs."

"Mud and twigs," the big man fired back. "Mud and twigs."

I believe I may've made a mistake here. "What happened to your car?"

"Mud and twigs maybe, something *you* seem to know a lot about."

When his rider added nothing more, the driver said, "Ahn."

"She slipped out from under me on a slick road. She went and twisted. Rolled over and over."

"What about the police?"

"They're busy elsewhere. Two of them. Two young men. I was particularly sorry about them. Poor Gunderson boys. But I had no choice."

Never again, the driver thought. Never ever again, rain or no rain, cracked wrist bone or no.

The big man stared intently at the trees then with great concentration unlocked and relocked his door seven times. He asked, "You ever been in the army?"

What's the best answer to give? The driver said, "Did a tour, yessir. Was stationed in—"

"Army intelligence?"

"Nope. I was a GI."

The big man frowned. "What's *that*?"

"Government Issue. A dogface. Combat infantryman."

"A GI."

"Yessir."

"GI, GI. *Gee, I* wonder if you know where Abraham Lincoln was shot."

"Uhm."

"In the head. Or during a play. They're *both* right answers."

"I knew that, sure." Oh, brother, what've I done to myself here? "Quite a storm after all. I stand corrected. Glad I got four-wheel drive."

"Four-wheel drive," the man said. "Yes. What *is* that exactly? What *is* four-wheel drive?"

"You don't know that?" The driver blurted a laugh. "Everybody knows what four-wheel drive is." The big man turned to him with a malevolent glare and the driver rubbed the back of his hand across a stubbled cheek, adding, "That was most probably a joke."

"Nice try," the man snapped, leaning across the gearshift, placing his round face very close to the driver's. "But if somebody was *away* in a different *country* for a long time, isn't it possible that they might not know what four-wheel drive is?"

"Put that way, it's more'n possible."

"What if somebody from *1865*, for instance, just showed up now? Are you saying it's not *possible* that they might not know what four-wheel drive is?"

"More'n possible," he repeated miserably. "You know, I'm thinking we should really stop by that hospital. Get your arm looked at."

The big man wiped his face with his stubby peasant fingers, yellow as his teeth, and then took from his pocket a blue-black pistol. He lifted it to his face and smelled it then licked the barrel.

"Ah," the driver whispered and began to pray.

"Take me to the Atchesons' place," the man bellowed. "Take me there now and use all of those damn four-wheeled drivers of yours!"

Several miles up the road the driver pulled the Jeep to a stop, bladder loose and hands quivering. I'll never forgive myself for doing this to the Atchesons, he thought, but this's the way it's gotta be. "That there's the driveway."

"Nice try but I don't see the sign."

"There it is. There! Underneath that rose on the mailbox. See the name? Are you going to kill me?"

"You get out of this car and I want to make it so it won't work anymore."

"The Jeep?"

"Yes. I want to make it so it won't work."

"Okay, I can do that. Let's both get out. Only I'm asking you not to hurt me."

"You ever have a mind to go to Washington?"

"D.C. you're speaking of?"

"Of course D.C.! Who gives a *shit* about Seattle?"

"No, no! Never have. I swear."

"Good. Show me how to dismember this truck."

"You take off the distributor cap and pitch it away. This thing'll never start."

"Do that."

The driver opened the blunt hood of the car and ripped the cap off. It sailed into the woods. He looked completely forlorn. The rain matted his hair and ran into the deep grooves of his face. The big man turned to him. "Now, you think I'm stupid. You're trying reverse psychology. You say you don't *want* to go to Washington hoping I'll say go there? Is that right?"

The man choked. "That's about right, sir."

"Well, I want you to run. You run all the way to Washington, D.C., and tell them that revenge is here."

"Are you going to shoot me in the back?"

"You tell them that."

"Are you going to—"

"RUN!"

He ran, never looking back, believing that he'd die before he got ten feet. Then before he got twenty. Then fifty. Running through the streams of rain, waiting for death. He never turned and so he never saw the big man, holding the pistol high in front of him like a nineteenth-century Pinkerton detective, stalk slowly down the driveway of gravel and mud.

Lis stared at the young woman's face. Even in the dark she could clearly see silver dots of reflection in her eyes. Yet Lis would have turned on all the lights in the kitchen, risked attracting a hundred Michael Hrubeks, to witness her sister's expression at this moment, to see if her words were lies or the truth.

"Tell me honestly, Portia. Did you know about us, Robert and me? Before you . . . made love with him."

Either way I lose, she thought. Either her lover had betrayed her. Or her lover *and* her sister. Still, she had to know the answer.

"Oh, Lis, of course not. I wouldn't do that to you. Didn't you know that?"

"No! How *could* I know. You're my sister but . . . No, I *didn't* know." Lis wiped tears, looking down. "I thought he might have told you, and you, well, you just decided to go ahead anyway."

"No, of course he didn't."

Lis's heart hadn't beat this hard since she'd been in the cave at Indian Leap, fleeing from her mad pursuer. "I didn't know. All these months, I just didn't know."

"Believe me, Lis. Think about it. Why would Robert say anything? He wanted to get laid. He wasn't going to spoil it by confessing that he was my sister's lover."

"When I saw the two of you there together . . ." She closed her eyes and massaged her temple. "And tonight, when you were flirting with Owen . . ."

"Lis."

"Weren't you?"

Portia's lips pressed together tightly. Finally she said, "I flirt, sure. It doesn't mean I want somebody. If Robert'd told me about

you two, I'd've said no. Men look at me. It's a power I have. Sometimes I think it's *all* I have."

"Oh, Portia. It was Robert of course I was so angry with. Not
you. I wanted to hit *him*. I wanted to kill . . ." Her voice faded. "I
felt so betrayed. Claire died because of him. After she saw you two,
she was so upset she ran off and got lost in the cave."

"Half the guys I go out with are Roberts. You can spot 'em a
mile away. Lis, he was all wrong for you."

"No! It's not what you think. It wasn't just a fling. We were
equals, Robert and me. Dorothy was dragging him down. They hated
each other. They fought all the time. And Owen? He doesn't love
me the same way. Not at all. I could feel it. After being with Robert,
all I felt was the absence of Owen's love. The night before the
picnic, that Saturday night . . . Owen was working late in Hartford.
And Robert came over."

"Lis—"

"Let me finish. Owen called and said he wouldn't be home before
two or three. Robert and I made love in the greenhouse. We were
there for hours. He'd pull the petals off flowers and he'd touch me
with them—" Lis closed her eyes and lowered her head once more
to her knees. "And then he proposed."

"Proposed?" From Portia's lips popped her breathy laugh. "He
asked you to *marry* him?"

"He and Dorothy had been unhappy for a long time. She'd been
cheating on him for several years. He wanted to marry me."

"And you said no, right?"

"And," Lis whispered, "I said no."

Portia shook her head. "So he was pissed at you. And when I
turned my big hazel eyes on him in the truck, he jumped at the
bait. Oh, brother, did I put my foot in it, or what?"

"I didn't want to *end* it with him. I just couldn't leave Owen. I
wasn't ready to. He'd given up that woman for me. I thought I
should try to make it work."

"Mistake, Lis. Mis-take. Why didn't you go for it? My God, it may've been your only chance to dump the last of the family."

Lis shook her head, confused. "You?"

"No, no! Owen. You should've done it years ago."

"What do you mean, last of the family?"

Portia laughed. "Doesn't Owen remind you just a little of Father?"

"Oh, don't be crazy. There's no comparison. Why, look what he's doing tonight." She waved at the window. "He's out there for me."

"Owen's a despot, Lis. Just like Father."

"No! He's a good man. He's solid. He *does* love me. In his way."

"Well, Father put a roof over our heads. You call that love?" Portia had grown angry. "You call it love when somebody says, 'You didn't clean up very well this week' or 'How dare you wear that low-cut blouse'? Then lifts up your skirt and leaves those darling little welts on you? The willow tree's still in the backyard, I see. If I'd moved here, that's the first thing that would've gone. I'd've chopped that son of a bitch to the ground in ten seconds flat.

"Tell me, Lis, how did *you* explain the marks in gym class? You probably changed into your uniform with your back to the locker. *I* told everybody I had an older lover who tied me up and jerked off while he whipped me. Oh, don't look so horrified. You talk about love. . . . *Love?* For Christ's sake, if we grew up in such normal circumstances, how come you hide away in this Neverland and why'm I the easiest fuck on East Seventy-second Street?"

Lis buried her head in her arms, the tears streamed.

Her sister said, "Lis, I'm sorry." She laughed. "Look what being back here does. It makes me crazy. I've had more of a dose of family than I can deal with. I knew I shouldn't have come on the picnic. I shouldn't've come tonight."

Lis touched her sister's knee, observing that Portia was once more wearing her gaudy silver rings, and the flecked crystal, like a huge grain of salt, again hung from her neck. A moment passed and Portia lowered her hand onto her sister's toughened, ruddy fingers but offered no pressure and soon withdrew it.

Then Lis too took back her hand and looked out the window, staring at the rain snaking down the glass. Finally she stood up. "There's something I have to do. I'll be back in a minute."

"Do?"

"I'll be right back."

"You're going outside?" Portia sounded frightened, mystified.

"The padlock on the basement door. I have to see about it."

"No, Lis. Don't. I'm sure Owen checked it."

"I don't think so."

Portia shook her head and watched Lis take the gun from her pocket and awkwardly pull the slide to put a bullet in the chamber. "Lis . . ."

"What?"

"Nothing. I . . . Nothing."

Carefully pointing the muzzle toward the floor, Lis dons the bomber jacket. She pauses at the back door, looking back. The old house is dark, this house three stories high and filled with flowers and books and the spirits of many dead. She thinks how odd it is that we're awed by our mortality only during the small moments—when we think of painted fingernails, or a passage of music, or the proximity of sleeping bodies—never at mean, ruthless times like these. She flicks off the safety catch of the gun and feels no fear whatsoever as she steps into the rain-drenched yard.

Owen Atcheson, every inch of his skin wet, in agony, ducked against the muddy embankment of the drainage ditch and cringed like a child as a shaft of lightning engulfed the sky above him. The thunder shook his teeth and sent spasms of pain through his left arm.

After all this, he thought, please don't let me get electrocuted.

He looked along Cedar Swamp Road, down which the Jeep had

vanished five minutes before, sending rooster tails of dirty rain into the air behind it. He'd recognized it as Will McCaffrey's. He supposed the old coot had worked overtime at the mill and was finally heading home.

Owen sank back into the dirty, foaming water. This unpleasantness didn't bother him. On hunting trips, he'd endured leeches, mosquitoes and temperatures of 110 degrees and 30 below. Tonight, he carried only his pistol and twenty rounds of ammunition; on other occasions he'd borne not only his weapons but an eighty-pound pack and, more than once, the body of a fallen comrade as well.

These hardships he could cope with. Far more troubling was the question—where the hell was his prey?

Owen surveyed the terrain for the dozenth time. Yes, he supposed, it'd be possible for Hrubek to avoid the road completely and reach the house through the forest. But that would require a compass and hours of time, and would force him to swim the lake or skirt the shore, which was thickly overgrown and virtually impassable. Besides, Hrubek had shown a strong preference for roads—as if his impeded mind believed that people could be connected only via asphalt or concrete.

Roads, Owen reflected. Cars . . .

The Jeep . . .

McCaffrey, he recalled, didn't live north of town. His bungalow was on the west side. He'd have no need or occasion to take Cedar Swamp, certainly not to reach his house. The only reason someone who didn't live near here would come this way was to take the shortcut to the mall in Chilton. And there sure weren't any stores open there this time of night.

Owen looked up the dark, rain-swept road for a moment then struggled from the water and began the agonizing run to his wife and his home.

29

Trenton Heck slowly climbed the face of the huge rock shelf that cut the Atcheson property in two.

The surface was slick with rain but slipperiness was not the greatest impediment to his twenty-foot climb; rather, Heck's disobedient leg made for very slow progress. He was as exhausted as he was drenched by the time he reached the summit and collapsed on the rocky plain. He caught his breath while he massaged his thigh and scanned the driveway and forest below him. He saw nothing but the mesmerizing flutter of leaves as the rain poured down. After resting for a moment he rose slowly and in a crouch eased along the crest of this hill, parallel to the vague white strip of driveway in the shallow valley below. He made his way slowly from the house toward Cedar Swamp Road—keen to spot Hrubek, yes, but even more eager to find Owen, a man with whom Heck felt considerable kinship. And a man maybe weaponless, maybe injured.

As he moved cautiously toward the road, he found himself thinking about Lis Atcheson. He kept returning to the question that had occurred to him on the hectic drive here after he'd abandoned his journey to Boyleston. Limping into cover behind a tall oak tree for a futile inspection of the rain-drenched panorama beneath him, he wondered again: why exactly was Michael Hrubek after her?

Of course the fellow was maybe completely mad, Heck allowed. Lord knew, enough people seemed to think so. But if Heck understood right, Hrubek'd need one hell of a motive to go through with a trip like this—a journey that clearly terrified him. It'd be like Heck himself standing up and with full intent walking right toward someone threatening to shoot him in the leg again.

Why would a man bring that kind of heartache on himself?

Lis testifying against him? Naw, there had to be more to it. It was true, as he'd told her, that convicts rarely make matters worse for themselves by hurting witnesses.

The only time . . .

Well, usually the only time they carried out threats was when the witness had lied. But why would she've done that?

These musings were interrupted by something Heck saw in the distance: a large cube of faint blue light. It was in the direction of the house. He made his way closer and squinted through the rain. The lights of the greenhouse. She must have forgotten to turn them off. The radiance was, he thought, an unfortunate beacon but there was nothing to be done about it now.

Lightning flared through the forest and Heck was jarred by the encompassing blast of thunder. The lightning troubled him—not from fear of a hit but because he couldn't afford to be light-blinded. Also, a nearby strike would make him, if even for a fraction of a second, as sharp a target as if he'd been flare-lit.

Thunder sounded again.

Or *was* it thunder? The sound was more of a crack than a boom. And now that he thought about it, the noise seemed to have come from the driveway of the Atcheson place. Alarmed, he looked toward the house again for Lis's summoning signal but no lights flashed.

Through the plastic bag he thumbed the old Walther nervously and stalked toward Cedar Swamp Road, surveying the dense forest around him—with its mulchy, cluttered carpet of downed foliage. In this tangle he saw a dozen shadows that clearly resembled the man he sought. Then he forgot about the thunder that resembled a gunshot and grew depressed. The task of finding either Owen or Hrubek suddenly seemed hopeless.

"Oh, man," Heck muttered. Here he'd turned down Kohler's bribe, he'd helped get a woman killed, and he could just *hear* Adler saying, Oh, no, sorry Mr. Heck, it really was Tactical Services that caught Hrubek.

But here's a hundred bucks for your trouble.

"Damn."

Five minutes later he was engaged in a conversation with Jill about his troubles when he saw out of the corner of his eye a flash of light coming from the direction of the house. He stepped forward quickly, thinking at first that it was a summons from Lis. But then he stopped and, squinting through the rain, noted how remarkable it was that light would reflect so vibrantly off a bald, blue-tinted head.

Michael Hrubek was not fifty feet away.

The madman was oblivious to Heck and hiding in a stand of bushes overlooking the garage.

Lord, he's a monster, Heck thought, his face burning at the first sight of his quarry. He trained the Walther, still in the Baggie, on the man's back. He flicked up the thumb safety and, walking as silently as he could, closed the distance between them. When he was thirty feet away Heck took a deep breath and called, "Hrubek!"

The big man jumped and barked out a frightened, pathetic cry. He looked back through the streaming rain toward Heck, his eyes scanning the darkness.

"I want you to lie down on the ground. Do it. I got a gun here."

Okay, Heck thought, he's going to run. You going to shoot him or not? Decide now. Otherwise you chase him.

Hrubek's eyes darted and his tongue appeared, circling his open lips. He seemed like a confused bear, rearing in fright.

Heck decided. Shoot. Park one in his leg.

Hrubek ran.

Heck fired twice. The bullets kicked up leaves behind the fleeing figure, who was covering ground like a wide receiver, dodging trees and crashing over saplings, falling, scrabbling through leaves then leaping to his feet again. He howled in fear. Heck pursued in a fast lope. Though Hrubek carried nearly twice Heck's weight, he set a furious pace and kept his distance for a long ways. But slowly Heck began to gain.

Then suddenly he cried out at a searing eruption of agony. A cramp seized his game leg from calf to hip. Heck dropped to his side, his leg out straight, twitching, muscles hard as oak. He contorted desperately, trying to find a position that would ease the pain. Slowly it subsided on its own, leaving him exhausted and breathless. When he sat up and looked around him Hrubek was gone.

Heck rolled upright and stood, gasping. He scooped up his gun and hurried along the low ridge near where Hrubek had disappeared. Orienting himself, he located the house, a hundred yards away. Through the rain he saw a thousand trees and ten thousand shadows, any one of which might be hiding his prey.

As he started toward the house, hurrying as fast as he dared on the trembling leg, Heck heard the gunshot not more than ten feet behind him. At the same time he felt, with more shock than pain, the tug of the bullet as it tore through his back. "Oh," he gasped. He staggered a few steps, wondering why no one had ever suggested that Hrubek might have a gun. He dropped his pistol and looked down at the pucker of his workshirt where the hot bit of metal had exited.

"Oh, no. Damn."

Dimly, in his mind's eye, Trenton Heck saw his ex-wife Jill in her freshly pressed waitress uniform. Then, as in his actual life, she vanished from him quickly, as if she had far more important matters to attend to, and he dropped to his knees, falling forward and beginning an endless tumble down the hill of slick leaves.

"Lis!" Portia called, as her sister returned to the kitchen and hung up the bomber jacket, shaking the water out of her hair.

Glancing at Portia she locked the door then turned and stared into the backyard, which was just a blur in the heavy rain.

"That noise," Portia blurted.

"What noise?"

"Didn't you *hear* it?" The younger sister paced, and wrung her hands compulsively. "It seemed . . . I mean, it wasn't thunder. I thought there were gunshots. I was worried—where *were* you?"

"I had trouble getting through the mud to the basement door. It was locked after all. Waste of time."

Portia said, "Maybe we should tell the deputy." Lightning struck nearby and she jumped at the thunder. "Shit. I *hate* this."

It was fifty or sixty feet to the police car. Lis stood at the door and waved but received no response from the deputy. Portia said, "He can't see you. Let's go tell him. With the rain he might not've heard anything. All right, don't look at me that way. I'm *scared*. What do you expect? I'm so fucking scared."

Lis hesitated then nodded. She put on the jacket again and a black rain hat that was Owen's—more for camouflage than to protect her drenched hair. Portia pulled on the baseball cap and a navy-blue windbreaker—useless against the rain but less conspicuous than the slicker. Then Lis flung open the door. Portia stepped outside and Lis followed, clutching the gun in her pocket. They were immediately overwhelmed by the storm. They leaned into the torrent of rain and wind and struggled toward the car. Halfway there Lis's hat vanished toward the turbulent lake.

It was from this direction—the lake—that the figure suddenly appeared. He grabbed Lis around the shoulders and they fell together into the saturated mud of one of her rose gardens. The fall emptied her lungs and she bent double, gasping for breath, unable to call for help. His full weight was on her, pinning her to the ground. She yanked at the pistol but the rear lip of the receiver caught in the cloth of her pocket.

Portia turned and saw the assailant. She screamed and made a dash for the police car, as Lis kicked him away. She succeeded only in sliding through a muddy trench and catching herself, in an ungainly sitting position, on the thorny stalk of a blossomless Prospero rose shrub. She was held immobile as the man, his head lowered like an animal's, crawled through the muck after her, muttering eerie sounds. Lis ripped the pocket flap open and pulled the Colt from it. She placed the black muzzle against his head just as Trenton Heck looked up and said, "Help me."

"Oh, my God."

"I'm . . . Can you help me?"

"Portia!" she shouted, pocketing the automatic once again. "It's Trenton. He's hurt. Get the deputy. Tell him."

The young woman stood at the door of the patrol car.

"It's *Trenton*," Lis shouted over the wind and rain. "Tell the deputy!"

But Portia didn't move. She stepped back from the car and began to scream. Lis ripped her jacket from the rosebush and crawled away from Heck. Lis approached her sister cautiously, frowning. Smoke poured from the front seat of the cruiser. Portia pressed her hands over her face then fell to her knees, gagging. A moment later she vomited violently.

When the deputy had been shot—point-blank in the face—the cigarette he held fell into his lap and started his uniform smoldering.

"Oh, no," Portia was crying, "no, no . . ."

Lis pushed her sister aside then scooped up mud and patted out the embers. She too gagged at the smell of burnt cloth, hair and skin.

"The radio!" Portia screamed. She stood, wiping her mouth, and shouted the word twice more before Lis understood. But only a curly black wire protruded from the dash; the handset had been torn off. Lis bent to the deputy once more though there was nothing to be done. He was pasty and cold. Lis stepped away and glanced at the Acura. The water was up to the windows now and had filled the car, covering the cellular phone inside.

Together, the women stumbled through the mud to where Trenton Heck lay on his side. They managed to get him to his feet and struggled toward the back door. The rain pelted their faces and stung; it lay on them heavily like a dozen wet blankets. Halfway to the house a huge gust of wind slapped them from behind and Portia slipped into a trench of mud, pulling unconscious Heck after her. It took long, agonizing minutes to get him out of the soggy yard and to the kitchen. Portia collapsed in the open doorway.

"No, don't stop here. Get him inside."

"I have to rest," Portia gasped.

"Come on, *you're* the runner. You got the stamina genes in the family."

"Jesus."

The women dragged him into the living room and laid him on the couch.

Emil joined them but apparently the hound had no sixth sense of disaster. He sniffed once at his master's boot and went back to the corner he'd commandeered, where he flopped down and closed his eyes. Portia locked the door and turned on a small lamp in the living room. Lis pulled Heck's workshirt open.

"Oh, my God—a bullethole." Portia's voice was high with shock. "Get something! I don't know. A towel."

Lis walked into the kitchen. As she pulled a handful of paper towels off the roll she heard a noise outside—faint at first then growing until it rivaled the howl of the wind. Her heart froze, for the sound reminded her of Claire's final keening, emanating up through the ground from the caves of Indian Leap. Dazed by this terrible memory and her present fear Lis stumbled to the door and stared out. She saw nothing but rain and wind-bent foliage, and it was a moment before she realized that the sound was Michael Hrubek's unearthly cry, calling from nowhere and from everywhere, "Lis-bone, Lis-bone, Lis-bone . . ."

30

Trenton Heck lapsed into and out of consciousness. Lis tried to find his pulse and couldn't, though when she rested her head on his chest his heart seemed to beat stridently.

"Can you hear me?" she shouted.

Like a sleepwalker he muttered unearthly sounds. He hardly responded to what must have been excruciating pain when Lis pressed the towels firmly against the ragged black-bordered hole in his stomach.

Portia sat in the corner of the living room, her arms folded around her knees, her head down. Lis stood and walked past her. Standing in the dark kitchen she looked out over the yard, and saw no sign of Hrubek, who had ceased calling to her. Still, the macabre sound of his voice, chanting her name, resonated in her mind. She felt tainted, abused. Oh, please, she thought, despairing. Just leave me alone. Please.

For a long moment Lis stood at the window. Then she turned to her sister. "Portia."

The woman looked at her and began shaking her head. "No."

"Put this on." Lis handed her the bomber jacket.

"Oh, Lis, no."

"You're going for help."

"I can't."

"Yes, you can."

"I'm not going out there."

"You know where the sheriff's department is. It's on—"

"The car's stuck."

"You're going to take the deputy's."

Portia gasped. "No. *He's* in it."

"Yes, you are."

"I'm not going. No. Don't ask."

"A left out the drive. A mile and a half down Cedar Swamp you come to North Street. Another left, then drive about six miles. The sheriff's on the right side of the road. Cedar Swamp'll be washed out, parts of it. You'll have to go slow till you get to town."

"No!" Portia's face was awash with tears.

With fingers white from the rain and red from a man's blood Lis seized her sister's shoulders. "I'm going to put you in the car and you're going to drive to the sheriff's."

Portia's eyes flicked to the crimson stains on the sweater. Her voice cracked as she said, "You're getting his—"

"Portia."

"—*blood* on me! No!"

Lis pulled the blue-black gun from her pocket and held it in front of her sister's astonished face. "Don't say another word. You're going to climb into that car and get the fuck out of here! Now let's go!"

She grabbed Portia by the collar and thrust her out into the rain.

With their arms around each other's shoulders, they stumbled toward the car. The ground was so marshy that it took them five minutes to get to the cruiser. The muddy water that surrounded the garage now was approaching the bend in the driveway, four feet deep. Soon the deputy's car too would be submerged.

Once, they lost their balance and fell into the muck. Lis's knee stuck in the ooze and Portia actually had to pull her out with both hands. Foot by foot they made their way through the grimy sluice of water toward the car.

Twenty feet to go.

"I can't look," Portia whispered.

Lis left her at the edge of the driveway and struggled to the squad car by herself. The rain was still heavy but there seemed to be a faint illumination from somewhere in the sky—though it was too early for dawn. Perhaps, Lis thought, her eyes had simply gotten used to the darkness. All her senses seemed honed, like an animal's. She was attuned to the falling temperature, the smells of rain, smoke and compost, the slickness of the mud and pages of wet leaves beneath her. She was poised to attack anyone who might slip into the field of this blood radar.

Reaching for the door handle she looked back at her sister. What is that? she wondered, looking over Portia's shoulder. A dozen yards away a large cloud seemed to form, slowly growing blacker than the surrounding haze of rain. It floated forward unsteadily in their direction.

And finally stepped clearly into view. Michael Hrubek waded toward them, one arm outstretched, the other dangling, apparently injured. In the damaged hand hung a pistol, dwarfed by his fingers.

He was staring directly at Portia.

"Lis-bone . . . Lis-bone . . ."

The young woman spun around and screamed, falling backwards into the mud.

Lis froze. Oh, my God! He thinks she's me!

Hrubek reached toward her. "Eve . . ."

Lifting the dark Colt Woodsman with both her hands Lis pulled the trigger, once, twice, more perhaps. She yanked the sharp tongue of metal so hard she nearly broke her finger. The bullets zipped into the night, missing Hrubek by inches.

He howled and, covering his ears, fled into the brush. Lis ran to her sister and pulled her to the car.

Portia was limp with fear, her head lolling. Lis thrust the gun at her. She took it and stared at the black barrel while Lis reached into the police car, grabbing the beefy deputy by the shoulders. With a huge effort Lis pulled him out of the car and dropped him irreverently into the mud then reached inside and started the engine. She snatched the Colt away from Portia, who started to back away. Lis closed her tough hands on her sister's arms and shoved her into the front seat. Easing into the pool of blood, Portia cringed as if the liquid seared her thighs. She was sobbing, quaking. Lis slammed the door. "Go."

"I . . . Get his legs . . . Get his legs out!" Portia wailed, gesturing down at the deputy, whose knees were directly in front of the rear tires.

"Go!" Lis shouted and reached through the window, pulling on the headlights and dropping the gearshift into drive. As the car jerked forward, the side mirror knocked into Lis. She slipped on a layer of wet pulverized leaves and fell to the swampy ground. Slowly the police car drove over the deputy and into the driveway. Portia gunned the engine. With a panicked spray of mud and marble chips the car sped forward. It vanished, sashaying down the long driveway, sending up plumes of dark water in its wake.

Lis clambered to her feet, blinded for a moment—the rear tires of the squad car had sprayed her with mud. She leaned back, letting the downpour clean her face, flushing her eyes. When she could see once more, she noticed that Michael Hrubek was wading toward her again, cautiously, churning through the water, already halfway across the yard.

Lis slapped her side. The gun was gone. When she'd fallen, it had slipped out of her torn pocket. She dropped to her knees and patted the sticky ooze around her but couldn't find the pistol. "Where?" she cried. "Where?" Hrubek was just thirty feet away, advancing slowly through the waist-high flood surrounding the garage. Finally she could wait no longer and fled into the house, slamming the door behind her.

She double-locked it and from a wooden block took a long carving knife. She turned to face the door.

But he was gone.

Stepping cautiously to the window she surveyed the backyard carefully. She couldn't see him anywhere. She stepped away from the glass, fearing that he might suddenly pop into view.

Where? *Where?*

His absence was almost as frightening as watching him stalk toward her.

Hurrying from the kitchen into the living room, she knelt and checked on Trenton Heck. He was still unconscious but his breathing was steady. Lis stood and gazed around the room, her eyes looking at but not really seeing her family's pictures, the porcelain-bird collection, the Quixote memorabilia her father had brought back from Iberia, the chintz furniture, the overwrought paintings.

A crash outside. Breaking glass. Hrubek was circling the house. A shadow fell across a living-room window then vanished. A moment later his silhouette darkened another curtain and moved on. An unbearable minute of silence. Suddenly a huge kick shook the front door. She gasped. Another kick slammed into the wood. A panel broke with a resounding crack. He kicked it again but the wood held. She saw Hrubek's bulk move past the narrow doorside window.

Her head swiveled slowly, following his circuit of the house. She heard him rip open the toolshed door then slam it shut.

Silence.

A fist rapped on a bottle-glass window in the far guest room. The pane broke but she heard nothing else and guessed the windows were too high and the lattice too solid for Hrubek to climb through.

Silence again.

Then he howled and pounded on a wall, ripping cedar shakes from the side of the house.

As she scanned the rooms, her eyes fell on the basement door. My God, she thought suddenly. Owen's guns. His collection was downstairs. She'd get one of his shotguns.

Yet as she took a step toward the basement she heard a crash from outside. Then more—powerful blows that seemed to shake the foundation of the house. Wood splintered. And with a huge bellow Hrubek kicked his way through the outside basement entrance. The padlock on the door had stopped him for all of thirty seconds. His feet scraped on the concrete floor. A moment later the stairs began to creak, the stairs leading up to the hallway in which she stood.

Oh, Christ . . .

The door to the basement was deadbolted but the fixture was thin brass, more cosmetic than substantial. She looked for something with which to wedge the door closed. Just as the knob started to turn, she lifted a heavy oak dining-room chair and shoved it into hallway, wedging the door shut.

The knob turned sharply. She leapt back, wondering if he could still shatter the door, just kick his way in. But he didn't. After a minute of playing with the knob—almost timidly—he started back down the stairs. The blanket of silence returned, broken by an eerie laughter and the sound of his feet scraping on the basement floor. He muttered words she couldn't hear. After five minutes, even these stopped. Was he still there? Would he set the house afire? What was he doing?

She heard no other sound from downstairs. Or from outside either, other than the steady patter of rain. Michael Hrubek had vanished again. Holding the knife in one hand and leading Heck's hound with the other, Lis Atcheson walked into the greenhouse and sat in a dark corner to wait.

The rain clattered like marbles on the greenhouse roof. Portia'd been gone twenty minutes. It was only eight miles or so to the

Sheriff's Department but the road might now be completely impassable. It could take her an hour or more to get through. Yet as the time passed and she heard nothing more of Hrubek, she began to relax. She even let herself wonder if maybe, just maybe, he'd fled. She felt a glow of euphoria and reflected that perhaps this was all that comfort ever was: believing that we're safe despite the clear and unobvious dangers from which we're protected by nothing more than single-strength glass.

She found herself wondering about Owen. She refused to think the worst. No, no. He was fine. With so much flooding he'd probably ducked into a garage or house to wait out the worst of the storm. She looked up at the black sky above her head and uttered a short prayer for dawn—exactly the opposite of what she usually prayed for, lying in bed, trying so desperately to sleep.

A prayer for light, for morning, for rampaging red and blue and white lights atop approaching cars.

She smelled a rose, whose scent now wafted past her face. Only twenty minutes more. Or nineteen. Or fifteen. Help will be here by then. Surely Michael Hrubek was lost in the forest. Surely he'd fallen and broken his leg.

Lis scratched the dog's ears. "It's all right, your master'll be all right," she said to him as he tilted his head. Lis put her arm around the drooping shoulders. The poor thing. He was as nervous as she —his ears were quivering and his neck was a knot of muscle. Lis eased back and looked at him, the folds of skin and bored-looking eyes. His nose was in the air and his nostrils began twitching. She smiled. "You like roses too, boy? Do you?"

He stood. His shoulder muscles tensed.

An unearthly growl rumbled from deep in his throat.

"Oh, my Lord," Lis cried. "No!"

He sniffed the air hard, his legs eager, his head lifting and falling. He began to walk quickly back and forth over the floor. Lis leapt to her feet and grabbed the knife, looking around her at the misted glass of the greenhouse. She couldn't see through it. Where was he?

Where?

"Stop it," she shouted to the dog, who continued to pace, sniffing the air, growing more and more frantic. Her palms were suddenly slick with cold sweat and she wiped them and gripped the handle of the knife once again.

"Stop it! He's *gone*! He's not here anymore. Stop howling!" She was turning in circles, looking for an enemy only the dog could detect. The growling became a bay, a banshee's wail, ricocheting off every inch of window.

"Oh, please!" she begged. "Stop!"

And he did.

Silently the hound spun around and ran straight to the lath-house door—the one Lis recalled she'd been on her way to check when Heck had arrived.

The door that she'd forgotten completely about.

The door that now burst open and struck the hound in his ribs, knocking him down, stunned. Michael Hrubek stepped into the greenhouse. He stood, dripping and huge and muddy, in the center of the concrete floor. His head swiveled, taking in the gargoyles, the flowers, the mists—all the details—as if he were on a garden-club tour. In his hand was the muddy pistol. Seeing Lis, he called her name in an astonished whisper and his mouth hardened into a smile—a smile that arose from neither irony nor triumph nor even mad humor, but was instead reminiscent of an expression one might find upon the faces of the dead.

31

Standing before her, he was so much larger than she remembered.

At the trial he'd seemed small, a dense bole of evil. Here, now, he filled the large greenhouse, expanding to touch every wall, the gravel floor, the peaked roof. He wiped rain from his eyes. "Lisbone. Do you remember me?"

"Please . . ." she whispered. The narcotic of fear flooded through her and stilled her voice.

"I've traveled very far, Lis-bone. I fooled them all. I fooled them pretty good. Make no mistake."

She stepped back several feet.

"You told them I killed that man. R-O-B-E-R-T. Six letters in his name. You lied. . . ."

"Don't hurt me. Please."

A fierce growling came from the hound, who was standing tall and tense behind Michael. The flesh of the dog's mouth was drawn back from his ardent yellow teeth. Michael looked down and reached for him as if the dog were a stuffed toy. The hound dodged the hand and sank its teeth into Michael's swollen left forearm. Lis thought he'd scream in agony but the huge man seemed not to feel the bite at all. He lifted the dog by its teeth and dragged him to a large storage closet. He pulled the slavering jaw from his arm and threw the animal inside, slamming the door.

Oblivious to the gleaming razor-sharp knife in her hand Michael turned to Lis. Why bother? He can't feel pain, he's huge, he has a gun. . . . Still, she held the knife firmly in her hand and it was pointed directly at his heart.

"Lis-bone. You were in court. You were part of that betrayal."

"I *had* to be in court. I had no choice. They *make* you be a witness. You understand that, don't you? I didn't mean you any harm."

"Harm?" He sounded exasperated. "Harm? There's harm all *around* you! How could you *miss* it? The fuckers are everywhere!"

Trying to stall him she said sympathetically, "You must be tired."

Ignoring this he said, "I have to tell you something. Before we get down to it."

Down to it.

A chill ran from her neck to her thighs.

"Now *listen* carefully. I can't speak loudly because this room is sure to be bugged. You may know that as sur*veil*lance, where they watch you from behind *veils* or masks or TV screens. Are you *listening*? Good."

He began a lecture, frantic yet passionless. "Justice cures betrayal," he said. "I killed someone. I admit it. It wasn't a fashionable thing to do and I know now it wasn't smart." He squinted, as if trying to recall his text. "True, it was not what *you* think of as killing. But that doesn't excuse me. It doesn't excuse anybody. *Anybody!*" He frowned and glanced at words written in red ink on his hand. They had bled, like old tattoos.

The monologue continued, his subject betrayal and revenge, and he paced the greenhouse floor, occasionally turning his back on Lis. At one point she almost leapt forward and plunged the blade into his back. But he turned quickly, as if suspicious of her, and continued to speak.

With its faint blue-green lights the room seemed far removed from this time and place. It reminded her of a scene from a book she'd read years ago, perhaps the first novel of her childhood. *Twenty Thousand Leagues Under the Sea.* It seemed, in her own numb dementia, that they stood not in a rural greenhouse but in a Victorian submarine and that she was an innocent harpooner, watching the mad captain rant while the dark ocean passed over and around them.

Michael talked about cows and Christian Scientists and women who hid behind unfashionable hats. He mourned the loss of a beloved black car. Several times he mentioned a Dr. Anne and, scowling, a Dr. Richard. Was that, she wondered, Kohler?

Then he wheeled toward her. "I wrote you a letter. And you never answered it."

"But you didn't put a return address on it. And you didn't sign it. How would I know who it was from?"

"Nice try," he snapped. "But you *knew* I sent it."

His eyes were so piercing she said at once, "I knew, yes. I'm sorry."

"*They* kept you from writing, didn't they?"

"Well—"

"The spirits. The con-*spirat*-ors."

She nodded and he rambled on. He seemed to think her given name had seven letters in it. This pleased him enormously and she was terrified that he'd find some correspondence or a bill that would reveal the extra letter and he'd kill her for this deceit.

"And now it's time," he said solemnly, and Lis shivered again.

He pulled his backpack off and set it beside him. Then he undid his overalls, pulling them down over his massive thighs. The fly of his boxer shorts parted and, stunned, she saw a dark stubby penis, semi-erect.

Oh, God . . .

Lis gripped the knife, waiting for him to put down the pistol and pull his engorged prick free. She'd leap the instant he did.

But Michael never let go of the gun. His left hand, the damaged one, was deep within his stained and filthy underwear, as if exciting himself further. But after a moment, when he removed his fingers, she saw he was holding a small plastic bag. The opening had been tied shut with a piece of string and he squinted like an absorbed child as he carefully untied it with his good hand. He paused to pull his overalls up once more and with some frustration reclipped the straps.

He pulled from the bag a piece of newspaper. It was damp and tattered. He held it out like a tray and on it he reverently placed a tiny perfect animal skull, which he'd taken from his backpack. When she didn't touch either of these, he smiled knowingly at her caution and laid them on the table beside her. He opened and smoothed the newspaper clipping then pushed it halfway to her, stepping back like a retriever that had just deposited a shot quail at a hunter's foot.

His hands were at his side, the gun muzzle down. Lis planned her assault. She would slip closer and aim for his eyes. What a horrible thought! But she had to act. Now was the time. She tightened her grip and glanced at the clipping. It was a local newspaper's account of the murder trial, the margins filled with the minute scrawl of his handwriting. Bits of words, pictures, stars, arrows—a good freehand drawing of what seemed to be the presidential seal. A silhouette of Abraham Lincoln. American flags. These all surrounded a photograph Lis recognized: her own grainy black-and-white image, taken as she walked down the courthouse steps toward the car after the verdict.

She and Michael were now six feet apart. She casually stepped closer, lifting the clipping, tilting her head toward it as she pretended to read. Her eyes were on the gun in his hand. She smelled his foul odor, she heard his labored breathing.

"There's so *much* betrayal," he whispered.

She gripped the knife. His eyes! Aim for the eyes. Do it. Do it! Left eye, then right. Then roll beneath a table. Do it! Don't hesitate. She eased her weight forward, ready to leap.

"So much betrayal," he said, and flecks of his spittle pelted her face. She didn't back away. He looked down at the gun and transferred it to his good hand. Lis's grip tightened on the knife. She was incapable of praying but many thoughts filled her mind: Of her father. And mother. Oh, and please, Owen, I hope you're alive. Our love was perhaps damaged but at least, at times, it *was* love. And Portia I love you too—even if we'll never become what I hoped we might.

"All right," Michael Hrubek said. He turned the gun over in his palm and offered it to her, grip first. "All right," he repeated gently. She was too afraid to take her eyes from the pistol for more than an instant but in that brief glance at his face she saw the abundant tears that streamed down his cheeks. "Do it now," he said with a choked voice, "do it quickly."

Lis did not move.

"Here," he insisted, and thrust the gun into her hand. She dropped the clipping. It spun to the floor like a leaf. Michael knelt at her feet and lowered his head in a primitive signal of supplication. He pointed to the back of his head and said, "Here. Do it here."

It's a trick! she thought madly. It *must* be.

"Do it quickly."

She set the knife on the table and held the gun loosely. "Michael . . ." His first name was cold in her mouth. It was like tasting sand. "Michael, what do you want?"

"I'll pay for the betrayal with my life. Do it now, do it quickly."

She whispered, "You didn't come here to kill me?"

"Why, I'd no more kill you than hurt that dog in there." He laughed, nodding toward the supply closet.

Lis spoke without thinking. "But you set traps for dogs!"

He twisted his mouth up wryly. "I put the traps down to slow up the conspirators, sure. That was just a smart thing to do. But they weren't *set*. They were sprung already. I'd never hurt a dog. Dogs are God's creatures and live in pure innocence."

She was shocked. Why, his whole journey this evening meant nothing. A man who'd kill people and revere dogs. Michael had traveled all these miles to play out some macabre, pointless fantasy.

"You see," he offered, "what people say about Eve isn't true. She was a *victim*. Just like me. A victim of the devil, in her case. Government conspirators, in mine. How can you *blame* someone who's been *betrayed*? You can't! It wouldn't be *fair*! Eve was persecuted, and so am I. Aren't we alike, you and me? Isn't it just *amazing*, Lis-bone?" He laughed.

"Michael," she said, her voice quivering, "will you do something for me?"

He looked up, his face as sad as the hound's.

"I'm going to ask you to come upstairs with me."

"No, no, no . . . We can't *wait*. You have to do it. You have to! That's what I've come for." He was weeping. "It was so terrible and hard. I've come so far. . . . Please, it's time for me to go to sleep." He nodded at the gun. "I'm so tired."

"A favor for me. Just for a little while."

"No, no . . . They're all *around* us. You don't understand how dangerous it is. I'm so *tired* of being awake."

"For me?" she begged.

"I don't think I can."

"You'll be safe there. I'll make sure you're safe."

Their eyes met and remained locked for a long moment. Whatever Michael saw in hers, Lis never guessed. "Poor Eve," he said slowly. Then he nodded. "If I go there, for you"—he looked at the gun—"then you'll do it and do it quickly?"

"Yes, if you still want me to."

"I'll go upstairs for you, Lis-bone."

"Follow me, Michael. It's this way."

She didn't want to turn her back on him, yet she felt that some fragile fiber of trust—spun from madness perhaps but real to him —existed between them. She wouldn't risk breaking it. She led the way, making no quick gestures and saying nothing. Climbing the narrow stairs she directed him to one of the spare bedrooms. Because Owen kept confidential legal files here, a strong Medeco lock secured the door. She opened the door and he walked inside. Lis clicked on the light and told Michael to sit in a rocking chair. It had been Mrs. L'Auberget's and was in fact the chair she'd died in, leaning forward expectantly and squeezing Lis's hand three times. He went to the chair and sat. She told him kindly, "I'm going to lock the door, Michael. I'll be back soon. Why don't you close your eyes and rest?"

He didn't answer but examined the chair with approval and began to rock. Then he lowered his lids as she'd suggested and lay his head against the teal-green afghan that covered the chair back. The rocking ceased. Lis closed the door silently and locked it and walked back to the greenhouse. She stood in the exact center of the room for a long time before the swarm of emotions surrounded her.

Another line from Shakespeare slipped into her thoughts. *"No beast so fierce but knows pity."*

"Oh, my God!" Lis whispered. "My God . . ."

She dropped to her knees and began to sob.

Ten minutes later Lis was wiping Trenton Heck's sweaty forehead. He seemed to be hallucinating and she had no idea if bathing his face helped at all. She squeezed a sponge over his skin and wiped away the effluence in a delicate and superstitious way. She was standing up to get more water when she heard a sound at the door. She walked into the kitchen, wondering why she hadn't heard the sheriff's cars arrive or seen their lights. But it wasn't the police. Lis cried out and ran to the door to let Owen inside. Gaunt and muddy, he stumbled into the kitchen, his arm bound to his side with his belt.

"You're hurt!" she cried.

They embraced briefly then he turned, gasping, and gazed outside, surveying the yard like a soldier. Pulling his pistol from his pocket he said, "I'm all right. It's just my shoulder. But, Christ, Lis—the deputy! Outside. He's dead!"

"I know. I know. . . . It was horrible! Michael shot him."

Leaning against the doorjamb he gazed into the night. "I had to run all the way from North Street. He snuck past me."

"He's upstairs."

"We've got to get away from the windows. . . . What?"

"He's upstairs," she repeated, stroking her husband's muddy cheek.

Owen stared at his wife. "Hrubek?"

She held up Michael's filthy gun and handed it to him. Owen shifted his gaze from Lis's haggard face to the pistol.

"This is *his*? . . . What's going on?" He laughed shortly, then his smile faded as she told him the story.

"He wasn't going to kill you? But why did he *come* here?"

As she fell against Owen's chest once more, mindful of his shoulder, she said, "His brain's gone completely. He wanted to sacrifice himself for me, I think. I don't really know. I don't think he does either."

"Where's Portia?"

"She's gone for help. She should've been here by now so I guess the car got stuck."

"The roads are mostly out in the north part of town. She'll probably have to walk."

Lis told him about Trenton Heck.

"That's his truck outside, sure. Last I heard he was going to Boyleston."

"Bad luck for him he didn't," she said. "I don't know if he's going to make it. Could you look at him?"

Owen did, examining the unconscious man with expert hands. He knew a lot about wounds from his military service. "He's in

shock. He needs plasma or blood. There's nothing I can do for him."
He looked around. "Where is he? Hrubek?"

"I locked him in the small bedroom upstairs, the storeroom."

"And he just *walked* up there?"

"Like a puppy . . . Oh!" Her hand flew to her mouth. Lis went
to the closet and set free Trenton Heck's dog. He was not pleased
at the confinement but strode out unhurt.

She hugged Owen again then walked into the greenhouse, picking up the newspaper clipping. She read, *The BETRAYER hIdeS
as the crusher of heADs. i AM to be sacrificed to save POOR EVE*

She exhaled in repulsion at the madman's macabre words.
"Owen, you should see this." Lis glanced up and saw her husband
studying Michael's pistol. He flipped the cylinder open and was
counting how many bullets were inside. Then he did something
whose purpose she couldn't understand. He pulled on his leather
shooting gloves and wiped the gun with the soft cloth.

"Owen, what are you doing? . . . Honey?"

He didn't respond but continued this task methodically.

It was then that Lis realized he still intended to kill Michael
Hrubek.

"No, you can't! Oh, no . . ."

Owen didn't look up from the gun. He spun the cylinder slowly
so that, she supposed, a bullet was aligned under the hammer. With
a loud click the gun snapped shut.

Lis pled, "He wasn't going to hurt me. He came here to *protect*
me. His mind's gone, Owen. It's *gone*. You can't kill him!"

Owen stood very still for a moment, lost in thought.

"Don't do it! I won't let you. Owen? . . . Oh, God!"

A ragged white flash of light enveloped his hand and all the
panes of the greenhouse rattled at once. Lis threw her palm toward
her face in a mad effort to deflect the bullet, which narrowly missed
her cheekbone and snipped a lock of her tangled hair as it streaked
no more than an inch from her left ear.

32

She fell to the floor, toppling a small yellow rose shrub, and lay on the teal slate, her ear ringing, smelling her own burnt hair.

"Are you mad?" she shouted. "Owen, it's me! It's *me*!"

As he lifted the gun once more, there was a blur of motion, a brown streak. The dog's teeth struck Owen's injured arm just as they had Michael's. But her husband, not numb to the pain, cried out. The pistol flew from his hand and clattered behind him.

Then he was frantically kicking the dog, hammering on its solid shoulder with his good fist. The hound yelped in pain and fled out the lath-house door, which Owen slammed shut.

Lis leapt for the pistol but Owen intercepted her, grabbing her wrist and throwing her to the rocky floor. She rolled, opening patches of skin on her elbow and cheek. She lay for a moment, gasping, too shocked to cry or say a word. As she climbed to her feet, her husband walked slowly toward the pistol.

My *husband*, she thought.

My own husband! The man I've lain with the majority of nights for the past six years, the man by whom I would've borne children had circumstances been different, the man with whom I've shared so many secrets . . .

Many secrets, yes.

But not all.

As she ran into the living room, then down the basement stairs, she caught a glimpse of him standing, gun in hand, looking toward her—his quarry—with a piercing, assured stare.

His gaze was cold and for her money the madness in Michael Hrubek's eyes was twice as human as this predatory gaze.

Poor Eve.

No light. None. The cracks in the wall are large enough to admit air. They're large enough to bleed brown rain, which here falls not from the sky but from the saturated earth and stone of the house's foundation. If the time were two hours later, perhaps the uneven wall would admit the diffuse light of dawn. But now there's nothing but darkness.

The scuffling sounds outside the door.

He's coming. Lis lowers her head to her drawn-up knees. The wound on her cheek stings. Her torn elbows too. She makes herself impossibly small, condensing her body, and in doing so exposing wounds she didn't know she had. Her thigh, the ball of her ankle.

A huge kick against the wooden door.

She sobs silently at the jolt, which is like a blow to her chest. It seems to send her flying into the stone wall behind her and her mind reels from the crash. In the hallway outside Owen says nothing. Was the blow one of frustration or was it an attempt to reach her? The door is locked, true, but perhaps he doesn't know it can be locked from the inside. Perhaps he believes the room is empty, perhaps he'll leave. He'll flee in his black Jeep, he'll escape through the night to Canada or Mexico. . . .

But, no, he doesn't—though he seems satisfied that she's not inside this tiny storeroom and moves on elsewhere in the rambling basement to check other rooms and the root cellar. His footsteps fade.

For ten minutes she has huddled here, furious with herself for choosing to hide rather than flee from the house. Halfway to the outside basement door—the one Michael had kicked open—she'd paused, thinking, No, he'll be waiting in the yard. He can outrun me. He'll shoot me in the back. . . . Lis then turned and ran to this old room in the depths of the basement, easing the door shut behind her, locking it with a key only she knows about. A key she hasn't touched for twenty-five years.

Why, Owen? *Why* are you doing this? It's as if he's somehow caught a virus from Michael and is raging in a fever of madness.

Another crash, on the wall opposite, as he kicks in another door. She hears his feet again.

The room's dimensions are no more than six by four and the ceiling is only chest-high. It reminds her of the cavern at Indian Leap, the black one, where Michael had whispered that he could smell her. Lis thinks too of the times as a girl when she huddled in this same space, then filled with coal, while Andrew L'Auberget was in the backyard stripping a willow branch. Then she'd hear *his* footsteps too as he came for his daughter. Lis read *Anne Frank: Diary of a Young Girl* a dozen times when she was young and although she understands the futility of concealment she always hid.

But Father found her.

Father hurt her doubly when she'd tried to escape from him.

Still, she made this castle keep as defensible as she might— stockpiling crackers and water and a knife and flinging all but one of the green brass keys to the ancient lock into the lake, hiding the remaining one on a nail inside, above the door.

But the mice got the crackers, the water evaporated, a cousin's child found the knife and took it home with him.

And the key proved irrelevant for when Father said open the door she opened it.

Metal sounds on concrete and rings as it falls. Owen grunts as he retrieves the crowbar. Lis cries silently, and lowers her head. She finds in her hand the clipping—Michael's macabre gift, spookier to her than the skull. As the blows begin, she clutches the newsprint desperately. She hears a grunt of effort, silence for the length of time it takes the metal to traverse the passageway outside then a resounding crash. The oak begins to shatter. Yet her room, so far, is inviolable. It's the old boiler room next door that Owen is assaulting. Of course . . . That room has a head-high window. He'd be thinking that she would logically pick the room that offers an exit. But no—smart Lis, Lis the teacher, Lis the scholar after her father's own heart, has cleverly chosen the room without an escape route.

Another crash, and another. A dozen more. The wood shrieks as nails are extracted. A huge crack. His footsteps recede. He's looked inside and seen that she isn't there and that the window is still covered with dusty plywood.

She hears nothing. Lis realizes that she can see again. A tiny shaft of light bleeds into the room around her through a crack in the thin wall shared with the boiler room. Her eyes grow accustomed to the illumination and she peers out, seeing nothing. She cannot hear her husband and she is left alone in this cell with the spirit of her father, a dozen pounds of ancient anthracite, and the clipping, which she now understand holds the explanation as to why she is about to die.

The BETRAYER hIdeS as the crusher of heADs. i AM to be sacrificed to save POOR EVE

The paper is smeared and disintegrating. But she's able to read most of Michael's handwriting.

. . . heADs. i AM . . .

AD . . . AM

ADAM

These sentences, circled, are connected by lines resembling blood veins to the photo accompanying the article. The person they point to, however, is not Lis. They extend to the left of the photograph and converge upon the man who holds open the car door for her.

The BETRAYER hIdeS as the crusher of heADs. i AM to be sac-rificed . . .

Michael's inked lines encircle Owen.

The BETRAYER IS ADAM.

Is this the purpose of Michael's journey tonight? Has he come here as an angel of warning, not of revenge? She opens the clipping fully. It is stamped, *Library Marsden State Mental Health Facility.*

Think now. . . .

Michael saw the article in the hospital, perhaps long after the trial. Perhaps in September—just before he sent his note to her. She tried to recall his words. . . . Eve of betrayal. Perhaps his message was not that she was the *betrayer* but rather the *betrayed.*

Perhaps . . .

Yes, yes! Michael's role at Indian Leap was that of witness, not murderer.

"Lis," Owen says calmly. "I know you're down here somewhere. It's useless, you know."

She folds the clipping and sets it on the floor. Perhaps the police will find it in the investigation that will follow. Perhaps the owner of this house fifty years from now will notice the clipping and wonder about its meaning and the people depicted in the photo before tossing it out or giving it to his daughter for a scrapbook. More likely, Owen will comb the house and tidily dispose of it, like every other clue.

He is, after all, meticulous in his work.

No more prayers for dawn. The storm rages and the sky outside is as dark as the hole in which she hides. There are no whipsawing lines of colored lights filling the night. Owen's grisly task will take only seconds: a bullet into her with Michael's gun then one for the madman with his own. . . . Owen would be found sobbing on the floor, clutching Lis's body, raging at the same police who'd ignored him when he begged for protection of his wife.

She hears his footsteps on the gritty corridor outside.

And then, the same as with her father, Lisbonne rises to her feet and, dutifully and with a minimum of fuss, unlocks the door then pulls it gratingly aside.

"Here I am," she says, just as she used to.

Ten feet away Owen holds the crowbar. He's somewhat surprised to see her appear from this direction and he seems, if anything, disappointed that he was careless enough to let his enemy get behind him. She says to him softly, "Whatever you want, Owen. But not here. In the greenhouse." And before he can speak, she has turned her back to him and started up the stairs.

33

He whispers, "You thought I'd never find out."

Lis backs into a rosebush and senses a thorn easing into her thigh. She feels little pain, she hardly hears the rain pummeling the glass roof above them.

"How pathetic of you, Lis. How pathetic. Sneaking into hotels. Strolling on the beach . . ." He shook his head. "Don't look so shocked. Of course I knew. Almost from the beginning."

Her throat clogs with fear and her eyes dip momentarily shut. "And that's why you're doing this? Because *I* had an affair? My God, you—"

"Whore!" He lunges forward and strikes her in the face. She falls to the ground. "My wife. *My* wife!"

"But *you* were seeing someone!"

"That gives you license to cheat? That's not the law in any jurisdiction that I know of."

Lightning flashes though it's now in the east. The heart of the storm has passed over them.

"I fell in love with him," she cries. "I didn't plan on it. Why, you and I spent months talking about divorce."

"Oh, of course," he says in a snide voice, "that excuses you."

"Robert loved me. You didn't."

"Robert was interested in anything in a skirt."

"No!"

"He fucked half of the women in Ridgeton. A few of the men too probably—"

"That's a lie! I loved him. I won't have you . . ."

But through these protests another thought rises into her mind. She considers months and dates. She considers their reconciliation after Owen's affair—just around the time Mrs. L'Auberget was diagnosed as terminally ill. She considers his resistance to buying the nursery. Her tears slow and she looks at him coldly. "It's something else, isn't it? It's not just that I was seeing Robert."

The estate. Of course. Her millions.

"You and Robert talked about getting married," Owen says, "you talked about divorcing me, cutting me out of everything."

"You talk like it's money *you* earned. It was my father's. And I've always been more than generous. I . . . Wait. How did you know Robert and I talked about getting married?"

"We knew."

Stunned by a blow sharper than his palm a moment before, Lis understands. *We* knew. "Dorothy?"

Owen wasn't seeing a lawyer at all. *Dorothy* was his lover. Was and still is. Obedient Dorothy. They planned Lis's death all along. For Owen's insane pride and for the money. Charming, careless Robert had perhaps left some evidence of the affair around the Gillespie household, or perhaps had simply not stopped talking when he should have.

"Who do you think called the day of the picnic to get me into work? That wasn't my secretary. Oh, Lis, you were so blind."

"You were at the park after all. I *thought* I saw you."

"I stopped at the office and had my calls forwarded from there to the phone in the Acura. I was at the park fifteen minutes before you. I followed you to the beach."

And he waited.

Dorothy forgot Lis's copy of *Hamlet* intentionally, thinking that she'd go back to the truck alone for it. Owen would be waiting for her.

But it was Robert, not Lis, who went after the book, hoping to meet Portia. Robert must have wandered past Owen, who attacked him at the mouth of the cave. Bleeding badly, Robert had run inside and Owen had pursued him. Claire must have heard Robert's calls for help and followed.

And it would have been Owen who found the knife Lis had dropped near Robert's body.

"The mutilation! Why, you bastard!"

"Let the punishment fit the crime."

"Michael never hurt Robert?"

"Hurt him? The son of a bitch tried to save him! He was crying, he was saying, 'I'll get that blood off your head, don't worry, don't worry.' Some crap like that."

"And you've been waiting for something like this. . . ." She laughs, looking around her at the night. "You didn't go out there to kill him at all. You went to *bring* him here! You were going to let him . . . let him finish the job tonight!"

"At first I thought that was why he escaped—to come after you. Then I tracked him to Cloverton. He—"

"That woman . . . Oh, Owen . . ."

"No, he didn't hurt her. He just tied her up so she couldn't reach the phone. I found her in the kitchen. He'd been muttering to her that he was on his way to Ridgeton to save someone named Lisbonne from her Adam."

"*You* did it?" she whispers. "You killed her?"

"I didn't *plan* it. It wasn't *supposed* to be this way! I made it look as if he'd done it. I dumped her motorcycle in a river. The cops thought he was going to Boyleston but I knew he was headed this way."

Of course he did. He knew all along that Michael had a motive for coming to Ridgeton—to find the woman who'd lied about him in court.

"And you shot Trenton. And the deputy outside!"

He grows eerily calm now. "It got out of hand. It started simple and it got out of hand."

"Owen, please, listen to me. Listen." She hears in her voice the same desperate but soothing tone with which she'd addressed Michael a half hour before. "If you want the money, for God's sake, you can have it."

But looking at his face, she knows that the money isn't the point at all. She thinks of her conversation with Richard Kohler. Michael might be mad, yes, but at least his demented world is incorruptibly just.

It's her *husband* who's the psychopath; he's the one immune to mercy.

Lis realizes now that he must have begun planning her death from the very beginning of the evening—when he first heard about Michael's escape. Making a scene about the sheriff's putting men here, insisting she go to the Inn—they were just efforts to make him look innocent. Why, after he murdered Michael, he'd have rung up Lis at the Inn and told her to return. All's safe, my love. Come home. But he'd be waiting for her. For her and . . .

"Oh, God," she whispers.

Portia too.

She realizes that he must have intended to kill her as well.

"No!" Her wail fills the greenhouse. "No!"

And she does the very thing she'd left her basement hideout for, the very thing she prayed for strength to do but never believed herself capable of until this instant—she turns, picks up the kitchen knife from the table behind her and swings the blade at him with all her strength.

She's aimed for his neck but instead hits his cheek. His head bounces back from the impact of the metal. The gun flies from his hand. He blinks in shock.

Blood appears instantly, sheets of blood covering his head like a crimson veil.

For an instant they stand motionless, staring at one another, their thoughts as frozen as their bodies. Neither breathes.

Then with the howl of a combat soldier Owen leaps for her. She falls to the ground, dropping the knife, holding her hands over her face to ward off his maniacal pummeling. She takes a stunning strike on her jaw. Her vision crinkles momentarily to black. She drives her fist into his left shoulder. His cries are like an animal's as he leans away, clutching the tormented joint.

But he recovers quickly and renews the assault, his fury over-powering her. She's no match for his strength or weight, even with the wound on his face and a damaged arm. Soon she's on her back, her shoulders and neck lacerated by bits of gravel. His hand is on her throat, squeezing hard. The lights of the greenhouse, blue and green, dim lights all, grow dimmer as her lungs beg for oxygen they can't have. Her hands flail toward his hugely bloody face. They strike only air then fall to the ground. A dust of blackness fills her eyes. She says something to him, words he cannot possibly hear, words she herself does not understand.

In her last moment of consciousness a small shadow forms at some distant focal point—part of her brain dying, she thinks. This shadow grows from a tiny mass to an encompassing darkness that hangs in the air, a wad of black storm cloud. Then the glass roof directly above the struggling couple disintegrates into a million shards, and bits of wood and glass envelop the hurtling shadow like bubbles of air following a high diver into water.

The massive body lands sideways, unbalanced, half on Owen, half on a tall Imperial rose tree, whose thorns dig deep parallel scratches like musical-staff lines along Michael's cheek and arm. He sobs in panic from the twenty-foot leap—a terror that for anyone would be overwhelming and for him must be beyond compre-hension.

A long boomerang of glass slits Lis's neck. She rolls sideways away from the struggling men and huddles, covering the wound with a shaking hand.

Through the gaping hole in the glass roof a light mist falls and a few swirling leaves descend. Bulbs shatter under the cold moisture from the sky and the room is suddenly immersed in blue darkness. Then a sound fills the air, a sound that Lis believes at first is the rejuvenated storm. But, no, she realizes that it's the howling of a human voice inflected with madness—though whether it's Michael's or Owen's or perhaps even her own, Lis Atcheson will never know.

Here, in this storm-tossed yard, the vigilant and serious sheriff's deputies dispersed doggedly, combing the house and grounds.

Here the medics, directed first to pale Trenton Heck, took his vital signs and determined that he hadn't lost a critical quantity of blood. Here the same medics stitched and dressed Lis's own sliced neck, a dramatic but unserious wound, whose scar would be with her, she guessed, for the rest of her days.

And here Portia was flying into her sister's arms. Embracing her hard, Lis smelled shampoo and sweat and felt one of the young woman's silver hoop earrings tap against her lips. They hugged for a full minute and when Lis stepped away it was the younger of the two sisters who was crying.

A mud-spattered state-police car arrived, its rooftop speaker already turned to the receiving channel and stuttering with broadcasts, all of which were related to the cleanup efforts following the storm. A tall, gray-haired man stepped out of the car. Lis thought he resembled a cowboy.

"Mrs. Atcheson?" he called.

She caught his eye and he started for her but then paused halfway through the muddy yard to gaze with undisguised surprise, then concern, at Trenton Heck, lying on a gurney. He was barely conscious. The two men said a few words to each other before the medics carted the lanky tracker off to an ambulance.

Don Haversham approached her and asked if she felt like answering a few questions.

"I suppose."

As they were talking, a doctor emerged from one of the ambulances and put a butterfly bandage on the cut on Lis's arm then retreated, saying only, "Hardly a scratch. Wash it."

"No stitches?"

"Nup. That bump on your head, that'll go away in a day or two. Don't worry."

Unaware that she had a bump on her head she said she wasn't worried. She turned back to Haversham and spoke with him for the better part of half an hour.

"Oh, listen," she asked, after she'd finished her account, "could you get in touch with a Dr. Kohler at Marsden hospital?"

"Kohler?" Haversham squinted. "He's disappeared. We were trying to find him."

"Hey, would that be a *Richard* Kohler?" The Ridgeton sheriff had overheard them.

"That's him," Lis said.

"Well," the sheriff responded, "fella of that name was found drunk a hour ago. At Klepperman's Ford."

"Drunk?"

"Sleeping off a bad one on the hood of a Mark IV Lincoln Continental. To top it off, had a raincoat laid over him like a blanket and this skull, looked like a badger or skunk or something, sitting on his chest. No, I'm not fooling. If that ain't peculiar I don't know what is."

"Drunk?" Lis repeated.

"He'll be okay. He was pretty groggy so we got him in a holding cell at the station. Lucky for him he was *on* the car and not driving it, or he could kiss that license *good*-bye."

This hardly seemed like Kohler. But nothing would have surprised her tonight.

She led Haversham and another deputy into the house and coaxed Michael outside. Together they walked him to an ambulance.

"Looks like that's a broken arm *and* ankle," the astonished medic said. "And I'd throw in a couple cracked ribs too. But he don't seem to feel a thing."

The deputies stared at the patient with fear and awe, as if he were the mythical progeny of Jack the Ripper and Lizzie Borden. Michael, upon Lis's solemn promise that it was not poison, consented to a shot of sedative and allowed his own wounds to be cleaned though only after Lis asked the medic to dab antiseptic on her wrist to prove it was not acid. Michael sat in the back of the ambulance, hands together, staring down at the floor, and said not a word of farewell to anyone. He seemed to be humming as the doors closed.

Then Owen, battered but conscious, was taken away.

As was the horrible rag-doll body of the poor young deputy, his blood, all of it, lost in his squad car and in a bed of muddy zinnias.

The ambulances left, then the squad cars, and Lis stood next to Portia in the kitchen, the two sisters finally alone. She looked at the younger woman for a moment, examining the bewilderment on her face. Perhaps it was shock, Lis pondered, though more likely a virulent strain of curiosity, for Portia suddenly began asking questions. Although Lis was looking directly at her, she didn't hear a single one of them.

Nor did she ask Portia to repeat herself. Instead, smiling ambiguously, she squeezed her sister's arm and walked outside, alone, into the blue monotone of dawn, heading away from the house toward the lake. The bloodhound caught up with her and trotted alongside. When she stopped at the far edge of the patio, near the wall of sandbags the sisters had raised, the dog flopped onto the muddy ground. Lis herself sat on the levee and gazed at the gun-metal water of the lake.

The cold front was now upon Ridgeton and the trees creaked with incipient ice. A million jettisoned leaves covered the ground like the scales of a giant animal. They'd glisten later in the sun, brilliant and rare, if there was a sun. Lis gazed at broken branches and shattered windows and shingles of wood and of asphalt yanked from the house. The heavens had rampaged, true. But apart from a waterlogged car the damage was mostly superficial. This was the case with storms around here; they didn't cause much harm beyond dousing lights, stripping trees, flooding lawns and making the good citizens feel temporarily humble. The greenhouse, for instance, had seen several howling tempests and had never been damaged until tonight—and even then it'd taken a huge madman to inflict the harm.

Lis sat for ten minutes, shivering, her breath floating from her lips like faint wraiths. Then she rose to her feet. The hound too stood and looked at her in anticipation, which, she supposed, meant he'd like something to eat. She scratched his head and walked to the house over the damp grass, and he followed.

Epilogue

The blossoms of the floribunda are complicated.

This is a twentieth-century rose plant, and the one that Lis Atcheson now trimmed, a shockingly white Iceberg, was a hearty specimen that spilled in profusion into the entryway of her greenhouse. Visitors often admired the blossoms and if she was to enter it in competition she was confident that it would be a blue-ribbon rose.

Today, as she cut back the shoots, she wore a dress that was patterned in dark-green paisley, the shade of a lizard at midnight. The dress was appropriately somber but it wasn't black; she was on her way to a sentencing hearing, not a funeral.

Although the results would make her a widow of sorts, Lis was not in mourning.

Against his lawyer's recommendation Owen rejected a plea bargain—even after Dorothy turned state's witness in exchange for a manslaughter charge. Owen insisted that he could beat the rap by pleading insanity. An expert witness, a psychiatrist, took the stand and in a long-winded monologue characterized Owen as a pure sociopath. This diagnosis, however, apparently didn't have the same allure to juries that Michael's illness did. After a lengthy trial Owen was convicted of first-degree murder on the first ballot.

Last week Lis signed the contract to purchase Langdell's Nursery and that same day she gave notice to the high school; at the end of the spring semester her twelve-year bout as an English teacher would officially end.

Surprising her older sister, Portia had asked for the nursery's P&L statements and balance sheet, which she'd then shown to her current boyfriend—Eric or Edward, Lis couldn't recall. An investment banker, he'd seemed impressed with the company and recommended that Portia buy into the deal while she still could. The young woman had spent several days considering the proposition then waffled in a big way and declared that she wanted more time to think about it. She'd promised Lis an answer when she returned from the Caribbean, where she planned to spend February and March.

Portia had spent the night and would be accompanying Lis to the hearing today. Following Owen's arrest, the young woman had stayed for three weeks in the Ridgeton house, helping Lis clean and repair. But a week after the indictments were handed up, Lis decided that she wanted to be on her own again and insisted that her sister return to New York. At the train station Portia suddenly turned to her. "Listen, why don't you move into the co-op with me?" Lis was touched by the offer although it was clear that the majority of Portia's heart voted against it.

But the city was hardly for Lis and she declined.

Cranking closed the upper vanes of the greenhouse today, shutting out the winter air, Lis had this thought: We face death in many ways and most are hardly as dramatic as finding the ghosts of our dead ancestors in greenhouses or learning that it's your husband who's traveled miles to slice your thin throat as you lie drowsing in bed. Reflecting on these subtler confrontations with mortality, Lis thought of her sister and she understood that Portia wasn't being perverse or cruel all those long years of separation. Nothing so premeditated as that. There was a simpler point to her escape from the family: she did what she had to.

Too many willow switches, too many lectures, too many still-as-death Sunday dinners.

And who knew? Maybe old man L'Auberget changed his tune

after Lis's fateful swimming lesson, and climbed into the sack with Portia when she was twelve or thirteen. She, after all, was the pretty one.

There was a time when this thought would have been madness and seething heresy. But madness had since come to roost in Lis's own backyard and if the night of the storm—the delicate euphemism the sisters had settled upon—taught her anything it was that there are only real two heresies: lies and our willing acceptance of them.

Trenton Heck would also be at the hearing today. He had an interest in this case beyond justice. Before being removed as director of Marsden hospital by the Department of Mental Health, Dr. Ronald Adler had reneged on the reward Heck felt he was due. Adler's successor could find no moral, let alone legal, reason to pay over the money, which Adler apparently had no authority to pledge in the first place. And so with a certain reluctant desperation Heck sued Owen for shooting him in the back.

The insurance company wouldn't pay off for such malfeasance and Heck was horrified to find that suing Owen ultimately meant suing Lis. He immediately offered to withdraw the case but Lis told him that he more than anyone deserved to profit from this tragedy and over her exasperated lawyer's objections wrote him a check for far more than he asked.

There was, Lis understood, no reasonable connection between the two of them, Trenton Heck and herself, yet in some ways she felt they were stations along the same route. Still, when he asked her out to dinner last week, she declined. It was true that he needed something in his life other than a mobile home and a dog. But she doubted that it was for her to provide whatever that might be.

One person who wouldn't be at the hearing was Michael Hrubek.

On Thanksgiving, at the patient's shy request, Lis had paid him a visit at the Framington State Mental Health Facility, where he was once again under the care of Richard Kohler. Michael at first had been peeved that Lis, as an agent of God, refused to take his life in exchange for that of a nineteenth-century President. But he had apparently come to accept that saving her was part of a complicated spiritual bargain that only he understood and had acquiesced to remaining on this good earth for the time being.

Michael himself had an upcoming trial—for the murder of a fellow prisoner during his escape from Marsden. The evidence clearly suggested that the man's death was a suicide and the case was going forward only because Michael's escape made fools of the hospital and the police. Michael, his attorney assured Lis, would emerge from the trial not only innocent but with a better public image than that of the prosecutor, who, at least one editorial pointed out, ought to have better things to worry about than the death of Bobby Ray Callaghan, an institutionalized killer.

There were other charges too. Auto theft, breaking and entering, assault and the intentional confinement of two extremely unhappy Gunderson police officers in their squad-car trunk, one of them with an extremely painful broken wrist. Michael was admittedly the perpetrator. But he probably would serve no time in prison, the lawyer reported. All he need do was tell the judge the truth—that he was simply evading Pinkerton agents pursuing him for Abraham Lincoln's assassination—and, bang, he'd be out of the lockup and back into his hospital room in no time.

Michael Hrubek was a good example of using history to your own advantage.

Lis now pulled on her coat and called to her sister that it was time to leave. They were taking two cars; after the hearing she was planning to spend an hour or two at Framington.

She'd been back to the hospital several times since Thanksgiving. She was still somewhat wary about seeing him. But she'd found that when sitting across from Michael, sometimes in the company of Richard Kohler, sometimes not, she got an indefinable pleasure from his company. When she entered the room, he took her hand with a delicacy and awe that sometimes moved her nearly to tears. She would like to understand the immensely complex matrix of his emotions. She'd like to understand why he undertook his quest to save her, of all people, and why—even though it was rooted in madness—that journey touched her so.

But those were questions beyond Lis Atcheson, and she was content simply to sit with him in a lounge overlooking the snowy fields and drink coffee and soda from plastic cups while they talked about dairy cows or the state of American politics or insomnia—a problem, it seemed, they both suffered from.

With dancing eyes, Michael would listen carefully to what she had to say then lean forward, sometimes touching her arm for emphasis, and offer his thoughts—some of them illuminating, some preposterous, but always delivered as if he were speaking God's own truths.

And who's to say, Lis sometimes thought, that he isn't?

A Maiden's Grave

ACKNOWLEDGMENTS

I'd like to give special thanks to Pamela Dorman at Viking, an editor with the persistence and patience (not to mention just plain guts) to keep authors striving for the same level of excellence she achieves in her craft. My deepest appreciation too to Deborah Schneider, dear friend and the best agent in the world. And to the entire Viking/NAL crew, especially Barbara Grossman, Elaine Koster, Michaela Hamilton, Joe Pittman, Cathy Hemming, Matthew Bradley (who's earned the title Combat Publicist a hundred times over), and Susan Hans O'Connor. No mention of gratitude would be complete without acknowledging the fine folks at Curtis Brown in London, especially Diana Mackay and Vivienne Schuster, and at my top-notch British publisher, Hodder Headline, notably my editor, Carolyn Mays, and Sue Fletcher and Peter Lavery. Thanks to Cathy Gleason at Gelfman-Schneider, and thanks and a "hey" to my grandmother Ethel Rider and my sister and fellow author, Julie Reece Deaver, and to Tracey, Kerry, David, Taylor, Lisa (Ms. X-Man), Casey, Chris, and Bryan Big and Bryan Little.

Arkansas River

Webber & Stoltz
slaughterhouse

windmill

Chevy →

school bus →

100 yards

press–pool table

command van

to Crow Ridge

field
hospital

to press tent and rear staging

N

THE CROW RIDGE BARRICADE
– July 17 –

I

THE KILLING ROOM

8:30 A.M.

"Eight gray birds, sitting in dark.
 "Cold wind blows, it isn't kind."

The small yellow school bus crested an abrupt rise on the highway and for a moment all she could see was a huge quilt of pale wheat, a thousand miles wide, waving, waving under the gray sky. Then they dipped down once again and the horizon was gone.

"Sitting on wire, they lift their wings
 "and sail off into billowy clouds."

When she paused she looked at the girls, who nodded approvingly. She realized that she'd been staring at the thick pelt of wheat and ignoring her audience.

"Are you nervous?" Shannon asked.

"Don't ask her that," Beverly warned. "Bad luck."

No, Melanie explained, she wasn't nervous. She looked out again at the fields that streamed past.

Three of the girls were drowsing but the other five were wide awake and waiting for her to continue. Melanie began again but was interrupted before she'd recited the first line of the poem.

"Wait—what kind of birds are they?" Kielle frowned.

"Don't interrupt." From seventeen-year-old Susan. "People who interrupt are Philistines."

"Am not!" Kielle shot back. "What is that?"

"Crass dummy," Susan explained.

"What's 'crass'?" Kielle demanded.

"Let her finish!"

Melanie continued:

"Eight little birds high in sky,

"They fly all night till they find sun."

"Time out." Susan laughed. "It was *five* birds yesterday."

"Now *you're* interrupting," lean tomboy Shannon pointed out. "You Philadelphian."

"Philistine," Susan corrected.

Chubby Jocylyn nodded emphatically as if she also had caught the slip but was too timid to point it out. Jocylyn was too timid to do very much at all.

"But there are eight of you so I changed it."

"Can you do that?" wondered Beverly. At fourteen, she was the second-oldest student.

"It's *my* poem," Melanie responded. "I can make it as many birds as I want."

"How many people will be there? At recital?"

"One hundred thousand." Melanie looked quite sincere.

"No! Really?" offered enthusiastic eight-year-old Shannon, as a much older eight-year-old Kielle rolled her eyes.

Melanie's gaze was again drawn to the bleak scenery of south-central Kansas. The only color was the occasional blue Harvestore prefab silo. It was July but the weather was cold and heavily overcast; rain threatened. They passed huge combines and buses filled with migrant workers, their Porta-Pottis wheeling along behind. They saw landowners and sharecroppers, piloting their huge Deeres, Masseys, and IHs. Melanie imagined them glancing nervously at the sky; this was harvest time for the winter wheat, and a storm now could ruin eight months of arduous work.

Melanie turned away from the window and self-consciously examined her fingernails, which she trimmed and filed religiously every night. They were coated with faint polish and looked like perfect flakes of pearl. She lifted her hands and recited several poems again, signing the words elegantly. Now all the girls were awake, four looking out the windows, three watching Melanie's fingers, and round Jocylyn Weiderman watching her teacher's every move.

These fields go on forever, Melanie thought. Susan's gaze followed Melanie's. "They're blackbirds," the teenager signed. "Crows."

Yes, they were. Not five or eight, but a thousand, a flock of them. The birds watched the ground, the yellow bus, and the overcast sky, gray and purple.

Melanie looked at her watch. They weren't even to the highway yet. It would be three hours before they got to Topeka.

The bus descended into another canyon of wheat.

She sensed the trouble before a single clue registered in her conscious thoughts. Later she would conclude that it was no psychic message or premonition; it was Mrs. Harstrawn's big, ruddy fingers flexing anxiously on the steering wheel.

Hands, in motion.

Then the older woman's eyes narrowed slightly. Her shoulders shifted. Her head tilted a millimeter. The small things a body does that reveal what the mind is thinking.

"Are girls asleep?" The question was blunt and the fingers returned immediately to the wheel. Melanie scooted forward and signed that they weren't.

Now the twins, Anna and Suzie, delicate as feathers, were sitting up, leaning forward, breathing on the older teacher's broad shoulders, looking ahead. Mrs. Harstrawn waved them back. "Don't look. Sit back and look out opposite window. Do it. Now! The left window."

Then Melanie saw the car. And the blood. There was a lot of it. She shepherded the girls back to their seats.

"Don't look," Melanie instructed. Her heart pounded fiercely, her arms suddenly weighed a thousand pounds. "And put seatbelts on." She had trouble making the words.

Jocylyn, Beverly, and ten-year-old Emily did as instructed immediately. Shannon grimaced and peeked, Kielle blatantly ignored Melanie. Susan got to look, she pointed out. Why couldn't *she?*

Of the twins, it was Anna who'd gone still, hands in her lap and her face paler than usual, in sharp contrast to her sister's nut-brown tan. Melanie stroked the girl's hair. She pointed out the window on the left side of the bus. "Look at wheat," she instructed.

"Totally interesting," Shannon replied sarcastically.

"Those poor people." Twelve-year-old Jocylyn wiped copious tears from her fat cheeks.

The burgundy Cadillac had run hard into a metal irrigation gate. Steam rose from its front end. The driver was an elderly man. He lay sprawled half out of the car, his head on the asphalt. Melanie could now see a second car as well, a gray Chevy. The collision had happened at an intersection. It looked like the Cadillac had had the right of way and had slammed into the gray car, which must have run a stop sign. The Chevy had skidded off the road into the tall wheat. There was no one inside; its hood was twisted and steam plumed from the radiator.

Mrs. Harstrawn brought the bus to a stop, reached for the worn chrome handle of the door.

No! thought Melanie. Keep going! Go to a grocery store, a 7-Eleven, a house. They hadn't passed anything for miles but surely there was something up ahead. Don't stop. Keep going. She'd been thinking those words but her hands must have been moving because Susan responded, "No, we have to. He is hurt."

But the blood, Melanie thought. They shouldn't get his blood on them. There was AIDS, there were other diseases.

These people needed help but they needed *official* help.

Eight gray birds, sitting in dark . . .

Susan, eight years younger than Melanie, was the first one out of the school bus, running toward the injured man, her long, black hair dancing around her in the gusting wind.

Then Mrs. Harstrawn.

Melanie hung back, staring. The driver lay like a sawdust doll, one leg bent at a terrible angle. Head floppy, hands fat and pale.

She had never before seen a dead body.

But he isn't dead, of course. No, no, just a cut. It's nothing. He's just fainted.

One by one the little girls turned to gaze at the accident; Kielle and Shannon first, naturally—the Dynamic Duo, the Power Rangers, the X-Men. Then fragile Emily, whose hands were glued together in prayer. (Her parents insisted that she pray every night for her hearing to return. She had told this to Melanie but no one else.) Beverly clutched her chest, an instinctive gesture. She wasn't having an attack just yet.

Melanie climbed out and walked toward the Cadillac. Halfway there she slowed. In contrast to the gray sky, the gray wheat, and the pale highway, the blood was so very red; it was on everything—the man's bald head, his chest, the car door, the yellow leather seat.

The roller coaster of fear sent her heart plummeting toward the ground.

Mrs. Harstrawn was the mother of two teenage boys, a humorless woman, smart, dependable, solid as vulcanized rubber. She reached under her colorful sweater, untucked her blouse and tore off a strip, making an impromptu bandage, which she wrapped around a deep gash in the man's torn head. She bent down and whispered into his ear, pressed on his chest and breathed into his mouth.

And then she listened.

I can't hear, Melanie thought, so I can't help. There's nothing I can do. I'll go back to the bus. Keep an eye on the girls. The roller coaster of her fear leveled out. Good, good.

Susan crouched too, stanching a wound on his neck. Frowning, the student looked up at Mrs. Harstrawn. With bloody fingers she signed, "Why bleeding so much? Look at neck."

Mrs. Harstrawn examined it. She too frowned, shaking her head.

"There's hole in his neck," the teacher signed in astonishment. "Like a bullet hole."

Melanie gasped at this message. The flimsy car of the roller coaster dropped again, leaving Melanie's stomach somewhere else—way, way above her. She stopped walking altogether.

Then she saw the purse.

Ten feet away.

Thankful for any distraction to keep her eyes off the injured man, she walked over to the bag and examined it. The chain pattern on the cloth was some designer's. Melanie Charrol—a farm girl who made six-

teen thousand, five hundred dollars a year as an apprentice teacher of
the deaf—had never in her twenty-five years touched a designer acces-
sory. Because the purse was small it seemed precious. Like a radiant
jewel. It was the sort of purse that a woman would sling over her shoulder when she walked into an office high above downtown Kansas City
or even Manhattan or Los Angeles. The sort of purse she'd drop onto a
desk and from which she'd pull a silver pen to write a few words that
would set assistants and secretaries in motion.

But as Melanie stared at the purse a tiny thought formed in her
mind, growing, growing until it blossomed: Where was the woman who
owned it?

That was when the shadow fell on her.

He wasn't a tall man, or fat, but he seemed very solid: muscled the
way horses have muscle, close to the skin, rippled and defined.
Melanie gasped, staring at his smooth young face. He wore a glossy
crewcut and clothes gray as the clouds speeding by overhead. The grin
was broad and showed white teeth and she didn't believe the smile for
a second.

Melanie's first impression was that he resembled a fox. No, she concluded, a weasel or a stoat. There was a pistol in the waistband of his
baggy slacks. She gasped and lifted her hands. Not to her face but to
her chest. "Please, don't hurt me," she signed without thinking. He
glanced at her moving hands and laughed.

From the corner of her eye she saw Susan and Mrs. Harstrawn stand
uneasily. A second man was striding up to them; he was huge. Fat and
tall. Also dressed in overwashed gray. Shaggy hair. He was missing a
tooth and his grin was hungry. A bear, she thought automatically.

"Go," Melanie signed to Susan. "Let's go. Now." Eyes on the yellow
skin of the bus, she started walking toward the seven unhappy young
faces staggered in the windows.

Stoat grabbed her by the collar. She batted at his hand, but cautiously, afraid to hit him, afraid of his anger.

He shouted something she didn't understand and shook her. The grin
became what the grin really was—a cold glare. His face went dark.
Melanie sagged in terror and dropped her hand.

"What's . . . this?" Bear said. "I'm thinking we . . . about that."

Melanie was postlingually deaf. She began losing her hearing at age eight, after her language skills were honed. She was a better lipreader than most of the girls. But lipreading is a very iffy skill, far more complicated than merely watching lips. The process involves interpreting movements of the mouth, tongue, teeth, eyes, and other parts of the body. It is truly effective only if you know the person whose words you are trying to decipher. Bear existed in a different universe from Melanie's life of Old English decor, Celestial Seasonings tea and small-town, midwestern schools. And she had no idea what he was saying.

The big man laughed and spit in a white stream. His eyes coursed over her body—her breasts beneath the high-necked burgundy blouse, her long charcoal-gray skirt, black tights. She awkwardly crossed her arms. Bear turned his attention back to Mrs. Harstrawn and Susan.

Stoat was leaning forward, speaking—probably shouting, as people often did with the Deaf (which was all right because they spoke more slowly and their lip motion was more pronounced when they shouted). He was asking who was in the bus. Melanie didn't move. She couldn't. Her sweaty fingers gripped her biceps.

Bear looked down at the injured man's battered face and tapped his booted foot lethargically against the head, watching it loll back and forth. Melanie gasped; the casualness of the kick, its gratuitousness, was horrifying. She started to cry. Bear pushed Susan and Mrs. Harstrawn ahead of him toward the bus.

Melanie glanced at Susan and shot her hands into the air. "No, don't!"

But Susan was already moving.

Her perfect figure and runner's body.

Her one hundred and twelve muscular pounds.

Her strong hands.

As the girl's palm swung toward Bear's face he jerked his head back in surprise and caught her hand inches from his eyes. The surprise became amusement and he bent her arm downward until she dropped to her knees then he shoved her to the ground, filthying her black jeans and white blouse with dust and mud. Bear turned to Stoat and called out something.

"Susan, don't!" Melanie signed.

The teenager was on her feet again. But Bear was prepared this time and turned to meet her. When he grabbed her his hand found her breasts and lingered there for a moment. Suddenly, he grew tired of the game. He hit her solidly in the stomach and she dropped to her knees, clutching herself and struggling for breath.

"No!" Melanie signed to her. "Don't fight."

Stoat called to Bear, "Where . . . he?"

Bear motioned toward a wall of wheat. He had a curious expression on his face—as if he didn't approve of something but was afraid to be too critical. "Don't . . . time . . . this bullshit," he muttered. Melanie followed his eyes and looked into the shafts of wheat. She couldn't see clearly but from the shadows and dim outlines it appeared to be a man, bending down. He was small and wiry. It seemed that his arm was raised, like in one of those Nazi salutes. It remained poised there for a long moment. Beneath him, she thought, was the form of a person, dressed in dark green.

The woman who owned the purse, Melanie understood in a terrible flash.

No, please, no . . .

The man's arm descended leisurely. Through the undulating wheat she saw the dull glint of metal in his hand.

Stoat's head bent slightly; he'd heard a sudden noise. He winced. Bear's face broke into a smile. Mrs. Harstrawn's hands rose to her ears, covering them. Horrified. Mrs. Harstrawn could hear perfectly.

Melanie stared into the wheat, crying. She saw: The shadowy figure crouching lower, over the woman. The elegant movement of the tall wheat, swaying in the intemperate July wind. The motion of the man's arm rising and falling slowly, once, twice. His face studying the body lying in front of him.

Mrs. Harstrawn fixed Stoat with a stoic gaze. ". . . us go and . . . won't bother you. We won't . . ."

Melanie was comforted to see the woman's defiance, her anger. The sturdy set of her jaw.

Stoat and Bear ignored her. They herded Susan, Mrs. Harstrawn, and Melanie toward the bus.

Inside, the younger girls huddled in the back. Bear pushed Mrs.

Harstrawn and Susan inside and gestured toward his belt, where his gun bulged. Melanie was the last person inside before Stoat, who shoved her into the back. She tripped and fell on top of the sobbing twins. She hugged them hard then gathered Emily and Shannon into her arms.

The Outside . . . Caught in the terrible Outside.

Melanie glanced at Stoat and saw him say, "Deaf as . . . all of them." Bear squeezed his fat torso into the driver's seat and started the bus. He looked in the rearview mirror and frowned then spun around.

In the distance, at the end of the ribbon of asphalt, was a dot of flashing lights. Bear pressed the pad on the steering wheel and Melanie felt the vibrations of the horn in her chest.

Bear said, "Man, what the fuck's . . . think we . . ." Then he turned his head and the words were lost.

Stoat shouted toward the wheat. He nodded when, apparently, the man answered. A moment later the gray Chevy sped out of the field. Badly damaged but still drivable, it rolled onto the shoulder, paused. Melanie tried to glance into the front seat for a glimpse of the man behind the wheat but there was too much glare. It appeared there was no driver at all.

Then the car accelerated fast, fishtailing onto the asphalt. The bus followed, easing forward into the faint clouds of blue tire smoke. Bear slapped the steering wheel, turned for a moment and barked some words to Melanie—angry words, vicious words. But she had no idea what they might be.

The brilliant flashing lights grew closer, red and blue and white. Like the Fourth of July fireworks over the park in Hebron two weeks ago, when she'd watched the streamers of color crisscross the sky, felt the explosions of the white-hot bangs against her skin.

She looked back at the police car and knew what would happen. There'd be a hundred squad cars all converging up ahead. They'd pull the bus over and these men would get out. They'd put their hands up and be led off. The students and teachers would go down to a station-house somewhere and make statements. She'd miss the Theater of the

Deaf performance in Topeka this time—even if they still had time to make it—but there was no way she'd get up on stage and recite poetry after all of this.

And the other reason for her trip?

Maybe it was a sign that she shouldn't go, shouldn't have made those plans. It was an omen.

All she wanted to do now was go home. Back to her rented house, where she could lock the door and have a cup of tea. Okay, a hit of blackberry brandy. Fax her brother in the hospital in St. Louis, tell him and her parents the story. Melanie fell into a nervous habit, twining her blond hair around her bent middle finger, the other digits extended. This hand shape was the symbol for "shine."

Then there was a sudden jolt. Bear had turned off the asphalt and was following the gray car down a dirt road. Stoat was frowning. He asked Bear something Melanie didn't see. The big man didn't answer but just spit out the window. Another turn and another, into hillier country. Getting close to the river.

They passed under an electric wire covered with a hundred birds. Big ones. Crows.

She looked at the car ahead of them. She still couldn't see him clearly—the driver, the man from the wheat field. At first Melanie thought he had long hair, then a moment later he seemed bald or crew-cut, then appeared to be wearing a hat.

With a skidding turn the gray car spun to the right and bounded down a narrow weed-filled driveway. Melanie guessed that he'd seen the dozens of police cars up ahead—the cars racing toward them to save them. She squinted and looked. No, nothing ahead of them. The bus turned and followed the Chevy. Bear was muttering, Stoat was looking back at the police car.

Then Melanie turned and saw where they were headed.

No! she thought.

Oh, please no.

For she knew her hope about the men surrendering to the trooper who was fast approaching was just a fantasy. She understood where they were going.

The worst place in the world.

The gray car suddenly broke into a large, weed-filled field. At the end of the field, on the river, squatted a red-brick industrial building, long abandoned. Dark and solid as a medieval fort. The acreage in front of the plant still held a few of the fences and posts from the animal pens that had subdivided the area long ago but mostly the field had been reclaimed by the Kansas prairie of mid-high grass, sedge, bluestem, and buffalo grass.

The Chevy raced right for the front of the building, the bus following. Both skidded to a stop just to the left of the door.

Melanie peered at the ruddy brick.

When she was eighteen, and a student herself at the Laurent Clerc School, a boy had brought her here, supposedly for a picnic but of course to do what boys of eighteen will do—and what Melanie too wanted, she believed at the time. But once they'd snuck inside, carting a blanket with them, she'd looked at the gloomy rooms and panicked. She'd fled and had never seen the perplexed boy, or the building, again.

But she remembered it. An abandoned slaughterhouse, a place of death. A place that was hard and sharp and dangerous.

And dark. How Melanie hated the dark. (Twenty-five years old and she had five night-lights in a six-room house.)

Stoat flung open the bus door, dragged Susan and Mrs. Harstrawn out after him.

The police car—a single trooper inside—paused at the entrance to the field. He leapt out, pistol in his hand, but he stopped short when Bear grabbed Shannon and put a gun to her head. The eight-year-old surprised him by spinning around, kicking his knee hard. He flinched in pain then shook her until she stopped squirming. Bear looked across the field at the trooper, who made a show of putting his gun back into his holster and returning to his car.

Bear and Stoat pushed the girls toward the slaughterhouse door. Bear slammed a rock into the chain that bound the door closed and snapped the rusted links. Stoat grabbed several large bags from the trunk of the gray car, where the driver continued to sit, staring up at the building. The glare still prevented Melanie from seeing clearly but he seemed relaxed, gazing with curiosity at the turrets and black windows.

Bear yanked open the front door and he and Stoat pushed the girls inside. The place stank of cave more than building. Dirt and shit and mold and some sweet-sickly decay, rancid animal fat. The interior was a maze of walkways and pens and ramps and rusted machinery. Pits surrounded by railings and parts of old machines. There were rows and rows of rusted meat hooks overhead. And it was just as dark as Melanie remembered.

Bear herded the students and their teachers into a semicircular, tiled room, windowless and damp. The walls and cement floors were stained dark brown. A worn wooden ramp led to the left side of the room. An overhead conveyor holding meat hooks led away from the right side. In the center was a drain for the blood.

This was the room where the animals had been killed.

Cold wind blows, it isn't kind.

Kielle grabbed Melanie's arm and pressed against her. Mrs. Harstrawn and Susan embraced the other girls, Susan gazing with raw hatred at whichever of the men happened to catch her eye. Jocylyn sobbed, the twins too. Beverly struggled for breath.

Eight gray birds with nowhere to go.

They huddled in a cluster on the cold, damp floor. A rat scurried away, his fur dull, like a piece of old meat. Then the door opened again. Melanie shielded her eyes against the glare.

He stood in the cold light of the doorway.

Short and thin.

Neither bald nor long-haired but with shaggy, dirty-blond strands framing a gaunt face. Unlike the others he wore only a T-shirt, on which was stenciled the name L. Handy. But to her he wasn't a Handy at all—and definitely not a Larry or a Lou. She thought immediately of the actor in the Kansas State Theater of the Deaf who had played Brutus in a recent production of *Julius Caesar*.

He pushed inside and carefully placed two heavy canvas bags on the floor. The door swung shut and once the ashen light vanished she could see his pale eyes and thin mouth.

Melanie saw Bear say, "Why . . . here, man? No fucking way out."

Then, as if she could hear perfectly, Brutus's words sounded clearly in her mind, the phantom voice that deaf people hear sometimes—a human voice yet with no real human sound. "It don't matter," he said slowly. "Nope. Don't matter at all."

Melanie was the one he looked at when he said this and it was to her that he offered a faint smile before he pointed to several rusty iron bars and ordered the other two men to wedge the doors tightly shut.

9:10 A.M.

He'd never forgotten an anniversary in twenty-three years.

Here's a husband for you.

Arthur Potter folded back the paper surrounding the roses—effervescent flowers, orange and yellow—mostly open, the petals perfect, floppy, billowing. He smelled them. Marian's favorite. Vibrant colors. Never white or red.

The stoplight changed. He set the bouquet carefully on the seat beside him and accelerated through the intersection. His hand strayed to his belly, which pressed hard against his waistband. He screwed up his face. His belt was a barometer; it was hooked through the second-to-the-last hole in the worn leather. Diet on Monday, he told himself cheerfully. He'd be back in D.C. then, his cousin's fine cooking long digested, and could concentrate on counting grams of fat once more.

It was Linden's fault. Let's see . . . last night she'd made corned beef, buttered potatoes, buttered cabbage, soda bread (butter optional, and he'd opted), lima beans, grilled tomatoes, chocolate cake with vanilla ice cream. Linden was Marian's cousin, in the lineage of the McGillis forebear Sean, whose two sons, Eamon and Hardy, came over in steerage, married within the same year and whose wives gave birth to daughters, ten and eleven months, respectively, after the vows.

Arthur Potter, an only child orphaned at thirteen, son of only children, had enthusiastically adopted his wife's family and had spent years plotting the genealogy of the McGillises. Through elaborate correspondence (handwritten on fine stationery; he did not own a word processor) Potter kept up religiously, almost superstitiously, with the meanderings of the clan.

Congress Expressway west. Then south. Hands at ten to two, hunched forward, glasses perched on his pale fleshy nose, Potter cruised through working-class Chicago, the tenements and flats and two-family row houses lit by the midwestern summer light, pale in the overcast.

The quality of light in different cities, he thought. Arthur Potter had been around the world many times and had a huge stockpile of ideas for travel articles he would never write. Genealogy notes and memos for his job, from which he was soon to retire, would probably be the only Potter literary legacy.

Turn here, turn there. He drove automatically and somewhat carelessly. He was by nature impatient but had long ago overcome that vice, if a vice it was, and he never strayed above the posted limit.

Turning the rented Ford onto Austin Avenue, he glanced in his rearview mirror and noticed the car.

The men were in a blue-gray sedan, as nondescript as could be. Two clean-shaven, clean-living, clean-conscienced young men, and they were tailing him.

They had Federal Agent printed on their foreheads.

Potter's heart thudded. "Damn," he muttered in his low baritone. Furious, he tugged at a jowl and then wrapped the green paper tighter around the flowers as if anticipating a high-speed chase. When he found the street he sought, however, and made the turn, he was doing seven cautious miles per hour. His wife's bouquet rolled against his ample thigh.

No, he didn't speed. His strategy was to decide that he was mistaken, that the car contained two businessmen on their way to sell computers or printing services and that it would turn off on its own route soon.

And leave me in peace.

But the car didn't do any such thing. The men maintained an innocuous distance, traveling at the identical, irritatingly slow speed of Potter's Ford.

He pulled into the familiar driveway and continued a lengthy distance, then rolled to a stop. Potter climbed out of his car quickly, cradling the flowers to his chest and waddling up the walk—defiantly, he hoped, daring the agents to stop him here.

How had they found him?

He'd been so clever. Parking the car three blocks from Linden's apartment. Asking her not to answer the phone and to leave her machine off. The fifty-one-year-old woman, who'd be a Gypsy if she could have rearranged her genes (so different from Marian, despite their common blood), excitedly accepted his instructions. She was used to the inexplicable ways of her cousin-in-law. She believed his manner was somewhat dangerous, if not sinister, and he could hardly dissuade her of that, for so it was.

The agents parked their car behind Potter's and climbed out. He heard their footsteps on the gravel behind him.

They didn't hurry; they could find him anywhere, and they knew it. He could never get away.

I'm yours, you self-confident sons of bitches.

"Mr. Potter."

No, no, go away! Not today. Today is special. It's my wedding anniversary. Twenty-three years. When you're as old as I am you'll understand.

Leave. Me. Alone.

"Mr. Potter?"

The young men were interchangeable. He ignored one and thus he ignored both.

He walked over the lawn toward his wife. *Marian*, he thought, *I'm sorry for this. I've brought trouble with me. I am sorry.*

"Leave me alone," he whispered. And suddenly, as if they'd heard, both men stopped, these two somber men, in dark suits, with pale complexions. Potter knelt and laid the flowers on the grave. He began to peel back the green paper but he could still see the young men in the corner of his eye and he paused, squeezing his eyes closed and pressing his hands to his face.

He wasn't praying. Arthur Potter never prayed. He used to. Occasionally. Although his livelihood entitled him to some secret, personal superstitions he'd stopped praying thirteen years ago, the day Marian the living became Marian the dead, passing away in front of his joined fingertips as he happened to be in the middle of an elaborate negotiation with the God he had, all his life, more or less believed existed. The address he'd been sending his offers to turned out to be empty as a rusted can. He was neither surprised nor disillusioned. Still, he gave up praying.

Now, eyes closed, he lifted those same fingertips and gave a backhanded wave, warding off the indistinguishable men.

And federal agents, yes, but God-fearing agents perhaps (many of them were), they kept their distance.

No prayers, but he spoke some words to his bride, lying in the same place where she had lain for these long years. His lips moved. He received responses only because he knew her mind as well as his own. But the presence of the men in the matching suits kept intruding. Finally he rose slowly and looked at the marble flower etched into the granite above her tombstone. He'd ordered a rose but the flower looked like a chrysanthemum. Perhaps the stonecarver had been Japanese.

There was no point in delaying any longer.

"Mr. Potter?"

He sighed and turned away from the grave.

"I'm Special Agent McGovern. This is Special Agent Crowley."

"Yes."

"Sorry to trouble you, sir. Mind if we have a word?"

McGovern added, "Maybe we could step to the car."

"What do you want?"

"The car? Please." No one says "please" quite the way an FBI agent does.

Potter walked with them—he was flanked—to their vehicle. He realized only when he was standing beside it that the wind was steady and ridiculously cold for July. He glanced at the grave and saw the green paper of the flowers roll in the steady breeze.

"All right." He stopped abruptly, deciding to walk no further.

"We're sorry to interrupt your vacation, sir. We tried to call the number where you're staying. There was no answer."

"Did you send somebody over there?" Potter was worried that Linden would be upset if agents came calling.

"Yessir, but when we found you we radioed them."

Potter nodded. He looked at his watch. They were going to have shepherd's pie tonight. Green salad. He was supposed to pick up something to drink. Samuel Smith Nut Brown Ale for him, oatmeal stout for them. Then, after dinner, cards with the Holbergs next door. Hearts or spades.

"How bad is it?" Potter asked.

"A situation in Kansas," McGovern said.

"It's bad, sir. He's asked you to put together a threat management team. There's a DomTran jet waiting for you at Glenview. Particulars are in here."

Potter took the sealed envelope from the young man, looking down, seeing to his surprise a dot of blood on his own thumb—from, he supposed, a latent thorn somewhere on the stem of a rose with petals like a woman's floppy-brimmed summer hat.

He opened the envelope and read through the fax. It bore the speedy signature of the director of the Federal Bureau of Investigation.

"How long since he went barricade?"

"First report was around eight forty-five."

"Any communication from him?"

"None yet."

"Contained?"

"Completely. Kansas state troopers and a half-dozen agents from our Wichita office. They're not getting out."

Potter buttoned then unbuttoned his sports coat. He realized that the agents were looking at him with too much reverence and it set his teeth on edge. "I'll want Henry LeBow as my intelligence officer and Tobe Geller for communications. Spelled with an *e* but you pronounce it Toby."

"Yessir. If they're unavailable—"

"Only them. Find them. Wherever they are. I want them at the barricade in a half-hour. And see if Angie Scapello is available. She'd be at headquarters or Quantico. Behavioral Science. Jet her out too."

"Yessir."

"What's the status of HRT?"

The Bureau's Hostage Rescue Team, consisting of forty-eight agents, was the largest tactical barricade force in the country.

Crowley let McGovern deliver the unfortunate news.

"That's a problem, sir. One team's deployed to Miami. A DEA raid. Twenty-two agents there. And the second's in Seattle. A bank robbery that went barricade last night. Nineteen there. We can scramble a third team but we'll have to pull some agents off the other two. It'll be a while before they're assembled on site."

"Call Quantico, put it together. I'll call Frank from the plane. Where is he?"

"The Seattle incident," the agent told him. "If you want us to meet you at the apartment so you can pack a bag, sir . . ."

"No, I'll go right to Glenview. Do you have a siren and light?"

"Yessir. But your cousin's apartment's only fifteen minutes from here—"

"Say, if one of you could take the paper off those flowers, there on that grave, I'd appreciate it. Maybe arrange them a little, make sure the wind doesn't blow them away."

"Yessir, I'll do that," Crowley said quickly. So there *was* a difference between them; McGovern, Potter realized, was not a flower arranger.

"Thank you so much."

Potter started down the path again, following McGovern. The one thing he'd have to stop for was chewing gum. Those military jets climbed so fast his ears filled up like pressure cookers if he didn't chew a whole pack of Wrigley's as soon as the wheels left the asphalt. How he hated to fly.

Oh, I'm tired, he thought. So damn tired.

"I'll be back, Marian," he whispered, not looking toward the grave. "I'll be back."

II

THE RULES OF ENGAGEMENT

10:35 A.M.

As always, an element of circus.

Arthur Potter stood beside the FBI resident agency's best car, a Ford Taurus, and surveyed the scene. Police cars drawn into a circle like pioneers' wagons, press minivans, the reporters holding their chunky cameras like rocket launchers. There were fire trucks everywhere (Waco was on everyone's mind).

Three more government-issue sedans arrived in caravan, bringing the total FBI count to eleven. Half the men were in navy-blue tactical outfits, the rest in their pseudo Brooks Brothers.

The military jet bearing Potter, reserved for civilian government transport, had touched down in Wichita twenty minutes before and he'd transferred to a helicopter for the eighty-mile flight northwest to the tiny town of Crow Ridge.

Kansas was just as flat as he'd expected, though the chopper's route took them along a wide river surrounded by trees, and much of the ground here was hilly. This, the pilot told him, was where the mid-high-grass and short-grass prairies met. To the west had been buffalo country. He pointed toward a dot that was Larned, where a hundred years ago a herd of four million had been sighted. The pilot reported this fact with unmistakable pride.

They'd sped over huge farms, one- and two-thousand-acre spreads. July seemed early for harvest but hundreds of red and green-and-yellow combines were shaving the countryside of the wheat crop.

Now, standing in the chill wind beneath a dense overcast sky, Potter was struck by the relentless bleakness of this place, which he would have traded in an instant to be back amid the Windy City tenements he'd left not long before. A hundred yards away was a red brick industrial building, like a castle, probably a hundred years old. In front of it sat a small school bus and a battered gray car.

"What's the building?" Potter asked Henderson, special agent in charge of the FBI's Wichita resident agency.

"An old slaughterhouse," the SAC responded. "They'd drive herds from western Kansas and Texas up here, slaughter 'em, then barge the carcasses down to Wichita."

The wind slapped them hard, a one-two punch. Potter wasn't expecting it and stepped back to keep his balance.

"They've lent us that, the state boys." The large, handsome man was nodding at a van that resembled a UPS delivery truck, painted olive drab. It was on a rise overlooking the plant. "For a command post." They walked toward it.

"Too much of a target," Potter objected. Even an amateur sportsman could easily make the hundred-yard rifle shot.

"No," Henderson explained. "It's armored. Windows're an inch thick."

"That a fact?"

With another fast look at the grim slaughterhouse he pulled open the door of the command post and stepped inside. The darkened van was spacious. Lit with the glow from faint yellow overhead lights, video monitors, and LED indicators. Potter shook the hand of a young state trooper, who'd stood to attention before the agent was all the way inside.

"Your name?"

"Derek Elb, sir. Sergeant." The red-haired trooper, in a perfectly pressed uniform, explained that he was a mobile command post technician. He knew SAC Henderson and had volunteered to remain here and help if he could. Potter looked helplessly over the elaborate panels and screens and banks of switches and thanked him earnestly. In the center of the van was a large desk, surrounded by four chairs. Potter sat in one while Derek, like a salesman, enthusiastically pointed out the surveillance and communications features. "We also have a small arms locker."

"Let's hope we won't be needing it," said Arthur Potter, who in thirty years as a federal agent had never fired his pistol in the line of duty.

"You can receive satellite transmissions?"

"Yessir, we have a dish. Any analog, digitized or microwaved signal."

Potter wrote a series of numbers on a card and handed it to Derek. "Call that number, ask for Jim Kwo. Tell him you're calling for me and give him that code right there."

"There?"

"That one. Tell him we want a SatSurv scan fed into—" he waved his hand at the bank of monitors—"one of those. He'll coordinate the tech stuff with you. All that loses me, frankly. Give him the longitude and latitude of the slaughterhouse."

"Yessir," Derek said, jotting notes excitedly. In seventh heaven, techie that he was. "What is that, exactly? SatSurv?"

"The CIA's satellite surveillance system. It'll give us a visual and infrared scan of the grounds."

"Hey, I heard about that. *Popular Science*, I think." Derek turned away to make the call.

Potter bent down and trained his Leica field glasses through the thick windows. He studied the slaughterhouse. A skull of a building. Stark against the sun-bleached grass, like dried blood on yellow bone. That was the assessment of Arthur Potter English lit major. Then, in an instant, he was Arthur Potter the Federal Bureau of Investigation's senior hostage negotiator and assistant director of the Bureau's Special Operations and Research Unit, whose quick eyes noted relevant details: thick brick wall, small windows, the location of the power lines, the absence of telephone lines, the cleared land around the building, and stands of trees, clusters of grass, and hills that might provide cover for snipers—both friend and foe.

The rear of the slaughterhouse backed right onto the river.

The river, Potter mused. Can we use it somehow?

Can *they?*

The roof was studded with parapets, a medieval castle. There was a

tall, thin smokestack and a bulky elevator hut that would make a helicopter landing difficult, at least in this choppy wind. Still, a copter
could hover and a dozen tactical officers could rappel onto the building
with little difficulty. He could make out no skylights.

The long-defunct Webber & Stoltz Processing Company, Inc., he decided, resembled nothing so much as a crematorium.

"Pete, you have a bullhorn?"

"Sure." Henderson stepped outside and, crouching, jogged to his car
to get it.

"Say, you wouldn't have a bathroom here, would you?" Potter asked
Derek.

" 'Deed we do, sir," said Derek, immensely proud of Kansas technology. The trooper pointed to a small door. Potter stepped inside and
put on an armor vest beneath his dress shirt, which he then replaced.
He knotted his tie carefully and pulled on his navy-blue sports coat
once again. He noted that there was very little slack on the draw strap
of the Second Chance vest but in his present state of mind his weight
had virtually ceased to trouble him.

Stepping outside into the cool afternoon, he took the black megaphone from Henderson and, crouching, hurried through a winding path
between hills and squad cars, telling the troopers, eager and young
most of them, to holster their pistols and stay under cover. When he
was about sixty yards from the slaughterhouse he lay on a hilltop and
peered at it through the Leica glasses. There was no motion from inside. No lights in the windows. Nothing. He noted that the glass was
missing from the front-facing windows but he didn't know if the men
inside had knocked it out for better aim or if local schoolboys had been
practicing with rocks and .22s.

He turned on the bullhorn and, reminding himself not to shout and
thus distort the message, said, "This is Arthur Potter. I'm with the Federal Bureau of Investigation. I'd like to talk to you men in there. I'm
having a cellular telephone brought up. I'll be getting it to you in about
ten or fifteen minutes. We are not planning an assault. You're in no
danger. I repeat: We are not planning an assault."

He expected no response and received none. In a crouch he hurried back to the van and asked Henderson, "Who's in charge locally? I want to talk to them."

"Him, there."

Crouching beside a tree was a tall, sandy-haired man in a pale blue suit. His posture was perfect.

"Who is he?" Potter asked, polishing his glasses on his lapel.

"Charles Budd. State police captain. He's got investigative and tactical experience. No negotiating. Spit-shined record."

"How long on the force?" To Potter, Budd looked young and callow. You expected to see him ambling over the linoleum in the Sears appliance department to shyly pitch an extended warranty.

"Eight years. Flew upstream fast to get the ribbons."

Potter called, "Captain?"

The man turned his blue eyes to Potter and walked behind the van. They shook firm hands and made introductions.

"Hey, Peter," Budd said.

"Charlie."

To Potter he said, "So you're the big gun from Washington, that right? Pleasure to meet you, sir. Real honor."

Potter smiled.

"Okay, sir, near as I can tell, here's the situation." He pointed to the slaughterhouse. "There's been movement in those two windows there. A glint, maybe a gun barrel. Or a scope. I'm not sure. Then they—"

"We'll get to that, Captain Budd."

"Oh, hey, call me Charlie, why don't you?"

"Okay, Charlie. How many people you have here?"

"Thirty-seven troopers, five local deputies. Plus Pete's boys. Yours, I mean."

Potter recorded this in a small black notebook.

"Any of your men or women have hostage experience?"

"The troopers? A few of them probably've been involved in your typical bank robbery or convenience store situations. The local cops, I'm sure they never have. Most of the work round here's DWI and farm workers playing mumbledypeg on each other Saturday night."

"What's the chain of command?"

"I'm supervisor. I've got four commanders—three lieutenants and one sergeant waiting for rank—overseeing those thirty-seven, pretty evenly split. Two squads of ten, one nine, one eight. You're writing all this down, huh?"

Potter smiled again. "Where are they deployed?"

Like the civil war general Budd would one day resemble he pointed out the clusters of troopers in the field.

"Weapons? Yours, I mean."

"We issue Glocks here, sir, as sidearms. We've got about fifteen riot guns between us. Twelve-gauge, eighteen-inch barrels. I've got six men and a woman with M-16s, in those trees there and over there. Scopes on all of 'em."

"Night scopes?"

He chuckled. "Not round here."

"Who's in charge of the local men?"

"That'd be the sheriff of Crow Ridge. Dean Stillwell. He's over yonder."

He pointed to a lanky, mop-haired man, whose head was down as he talked to one of his deputies.

Another car pulled up and braked to a quick stop. Potter was greatly pleased to see who was behind the wheel.

Short Henry LeBow climbed from the car and immediately pulled on a rumpled tweed businessman's hat; his bald crown had offered a glistening target more than once during the two hundred hostage negotiations he and Potter had worked together. LeBow trudged forward, a pudgy, shy man, and the one hostage-incident intelligence officer Potter would rather work with than anyone else in the world.

LeBow listed under the weight of two huge shoulder bags.

The men shook hands warmly and Potter introduced him to Henderson and Budd.

"Look what we have here, Henry. An Airstream trailer to call our very own."

"My. And a river to catch fish in. What is that?"

"The river? The Arkansas," Budd said, with the emphasis on the second syllable.

"Takes me back to my youth," LeBow offered.

At Potter's request Henderson returned to his car to radio the FBI resident agency in Wichita and find out when Tobe Geller and Angie Scapello would arrive. Potter, LeBow, and Budd climbed into the van. LeBow shook Derek's hand then opened his satchels, extracting two laptop computers. He turned them on, plugged them into a wall socket, and then connected a small laser printer.

"Dedicated line?" LeBow asked Derek.

"Right there."

LeBow plugged in and no sooner had he gotten all his equipment on line than the printer started to groan.

"Goodies already?" Potter asked.

LeBow read the incoming fax, saying, "Prison department profiles, probation reports, yellow sheets and indictments. Very preliminary, Arthur. Very *raw*." Potter handed him the material delivered by the agents in Chicago and the voluminous notes he'd begun jotting on the plane. In terse words they described the escape of Lou Handy and two other inmates from a federal prison in southern Kansas, their murder of a couple in a wheat field several miles from the slaughterhouse and the taking of the hostages. The intelligence officer looked over the hard copies and then began typing the data into one of his computers.

The door opened and Peter Henderson entered. He announced that Tobe Geller would be here momentarily and Angie Scapello would be arriving within the hour. Tobe had been flown in via Air Force F-16 from Boston, where he'd been teaching a course in computer-programming profiling as a way to establish the identity of criminal hackers. He should arrive any minute. Angie was taking a Marine DomTran jet from Quantico.

"Angie?" LeBow said. "I'm pleased about that. Very pleased."

Agent Scapello resembled Geena Davis and had huge, brown eyes that no amount of failing to wear makeup could make less seductive. Still, LeBow's excitement had nothing to do with her appearance and everything to do with her specialty—hostage psychology.

En route to the barricade Angie would stop at the Laurent Clerc School and gather as much information about the hostages as she could. If Potter knew her at all he guessed she was already on the horn to the school, writing up profiles of the girls.

LeBow taped a large sheet of blank paper on the wall above the desk and hung a black marker by a string from it. The sheet was divided in half. The left was headed "Promises," the right, "Deceptions." On it LeBow would record everything Potter offered to Handy and every lie he told the man. This was standard procedure in hostage negotiations. The use of the crib sheet could be explained best by Mark Twain, who'd said that a man needs a good memory to be an effective liar.

Surprised, Budd asked, "You really going to lie to him?"

LeBow smiled.

"But what exactly is a lie, Charlie?" Potter asked. "The truth's a pretty slippery thing. Are any words ever one hundred percent honest?" He tore pages from his notebook and handed them to LeBow, who took the small sheets, along with the faxes that were spewing from the printer, and began typing on the keyboard of the computer that was labeled "Profiles," the word written long ago on a piece of now dirty masking tape. The label on the second computer read "Chronology." The latter screen contained only two entries:

0840 hours. Hostages taken.

1050 hours. Threat Management Team—Potter, LeBow—in place.

The backlit liquid-crystal screens poured eerie blue light onto the man's round face; he looked like an Arthur Rackham rendering of the man in the moon. Charlie Budd gazed at the man's fingers, flying invisibly over the keys. "Lookit that. He's worn off half the letters."

LeBow grumbled to Potter, "Saw the building. Lousy situation. Too well shielded for SatSurv and not enough windows for infrared or mikes. The wind's a problem too."

As in most barricades the bulk of information here would have to come from traditional sources—released or escaped hostages and the troopers who took food and drinks to the HTs and stole a glance inside.

LeBow tapped computer buttons and created a small window on the chronology computer. Two digital stopwatches appeared. One was headed "Elapsed"; the other, "Deadline."

LeBow set the elapsed time clock to two hours, ten minutes and pushed a button. It began moving. He glanced at Potter with a raised eyebrow.

"I know, Henry." If you don't contact the hostage taker soon after the taking they get nervous and begin to wonder if you're planning an assault. The negotiator added, "We'll give Tobe a few minutes then have the briefing." He looked out over the fields behind them, the tall pale blanket of grass waving in the chill breeze. A half-mile away the combines moved in gentle, symmetrical patterns, cropping the wheat fields like a new recruit's scalp.

Potter examined a map of the area. "All these roads sealed off?"

"Yessir," Budd said. "And they're the only way in."

"Set up a rear staging area there, Charlie." He pointed to the bend in the road a mile south of the slaughterhouse. "I want a press tent set up near there. Out of sight of the barricade. Do you have a press officer?"

"Nup," Budd said. "I usually give statements 'bout incidents around here if somebody's got to. Suppose I'll have to here."

"No. I want you with me. Delegate it. Find a low-ranking officer."

Henderson interrupted. "This is a federal operation, Arthur. I think I should make any statements."

"No, I want somebody state and without much rank. That way we'll keep the press in the tent, waiting. They'll be expecting somebody with the answers to show up. And they'll be less likely to go poking around where they shouldn't."

"Well, I don't exactly know who'd be good at it," Budd said uncertainly, looking out the window, as if a trooper resembling Dan Rather might just wander past.

"They won't have to be good," Potter muttered. "All they have to do is say that I'll make a statement later. Period. Nothing else. Pick somebody who's not afraid to say 'No comment.' "

"They won't like that. The press boys and gals. I mean, there's a fender-bender over on Route 14 and reporters here're all over the scene. Something like this, I'll bet they'll be coming in from Kansas City even."

SAC Henderson, who'd served a stint in the District, laughed.

"Charlie—" Potter controlled his own smile—"CNN and ABC networks are already here. So's the *New York Times*, the *Washington Post*, and the *L.A. Times*. Sky TV from Europe, the BBC, and Reuters. The rest of the big boys're on their way. We're sitting in the middle of the week's media big bang."

"No kidding. Brokaw, too, you think? Man, I'd like to meet him."

"And set up a press-free perimeter one mile around the slaughter-house, both sides of the river."

"What?"

"Put five or six officers in four-by-fours and start cruising. You find any reporter in that zone—anybody with a camera—you arrest them and confiscate the camera."

"Arrest a reporter? We can't do that. Can we? I mean, look at 'em all out there now. Look at 'em."

"Really, Arthur," Henderson began, "we don't want to do that, do we? Remember Waco."

Potter smiled blandly at the SAC. He was thinking of a hundred other matters, sorting, calculating. "And no press choppers. Pete, could you get a couple Hueys down here from McConnell in Wichita? Set up a no-fly zone for a three-mile radius."

"Are you serious, Arthur?"

LeBow said, "Time's awasting. Inside for two hours, seventeen."

Potter said to Budd, "Oh, and we need a block of rooms at the near-est hotel. What'd that be?"

"Days Inn. It's up the road four miles. In Crow Ridge. Downtown, as much as they've got a downtown. How many?"

"Ten."

"Okay. What's the rooms for?"

"The parents of the hostages. Get a priest and a doctor over there too."

"Maybe they should be closer. If we need them to talk to their kids, or—"

"No, they shouldn't be. And station four or five troopers there. The families are not to be disturbed by reporters. I want anybody harassing them—"

"Arrested," Budd muttered. "Oh, brother."

"What's the matter, Trooper?" LeBow asked brightly.

"Well, sir, the Kansas state song is 'Home on the Range.' "

"Is that a fact?" Henderson asked. "And?"

"I know reporters, and you're gonna be hearing some pretty discour-aging words 'fore this thing's over."

Potter laughed. Then he pointed to the fields. "Look there, Charlie—those troopers're all exposed. I *told* them to stay down. They're not paying attention. Keep them down behind the cars. Tell them Handy's killed officers before. What's his relationship with weapons, Henry?"

LeBow typed and read the screen. He said, "All indictments have involved at least one firearms count. He's shot four individuals, killed two of them. Fort Dix, M-16 training, he consistently shot low nineties on the range. No record of sidearm scores."

"There you have it," Potter told Budd. "Tell them to keep their heads *down*."

A light flashed toward them. Potter blinked and saw, in the distance, a combine had just turned on its lights. It was early of course but the overcast was oppressive. He gazed at the line of trees to the right and left of the slaughterhouse.

"One other thing, Charlie—I want you to leave the snipers in position but give them orders not to shoot unless the HTs make a break."

"HTs—that's the hostage takers, right?"

"Even if they have a clear shot. Those troopers you were telling me about, with the rifles, are they SWAT?"

"No," he said, "just damn fine shots. Even the girl. She started practicing on squirrels when she was—"

"And I want them and everybody else to unchamber their weapons. Everybody."

"What?"

"Loaded but not chambered."

"Oh, I don't know 'bout that, sir."

Potter turned to him with an inquiring look.

"I just mean," Budd said quickly, "not the snipers too?"

"You can pull the bolt of an M-16 and shoot in under one second."

"Not and steady a scope you can't. An HT could get off three shots in a second." The initials sat awkwardly in his mouth, as if he were trying raw oysters for the first time.

He's so eager and talented and correct, Potter mused.

What a day this is going to be.

"The takers aren't going to come out and shoot a hostage in front of us before we can react. If it comes to that, the whole thing'll turn into a firefight anyway."

"But—"

"Unchambered," Potter said firmly. "Appreciate it, Charlie."

Budd nodded reluctantly and reiterated his assignment: "Okay, I'm gonna send somebody down to give a statement to the press—or not to give a statement to the press, I should say. I'll round up reporters and push 'em back a mile or so, I'll get us a block of rooms, and tell everybody to keep their heads down. And deliver your message about not loading and locking."

"Good."

"Brother." Budd ducked out of the van. Potter watched him crouching and running down to a cluster of troopers. They listened, laughed, and then started herding the reporters out of the area.

In five minutes the captain returned to the command van. "That's done. Those reporters're about as unhappy as I thought they'd be. I told 'em a Feebie'd ordered it. You don't mind me calling you that, I hope." There was an edge to his voice.

"You can call me whatever you like, Charlie. Now, I want a field hospital set up here."

"Medevac?"

"No, not evacuation. Trauma-team medics and triage specialists. Just out of clear range of the slaughterhouse. No more than sixty seconds away. Prepped for everything from third-degree burns to gunshot wounds to pepper spray. Full operating suites."

"Yessir. But, you know, there's a big hospital not but fifteen miles from here."

"That may be, but I don't want the HTs to even hear the sound of a medevac chopper. Same reason I want the press copters and our Hueys out of earshot."

"Why?"

"Because I don't want to remind them of something they might not think of themselves. And even if they do ask for a chopper I want the option to tell them that it's too windy to fly one in."

"Will do."

"Then come back here with your commanders. Sheriff Stillwell too. I'm going to hold a briefing."

Just then the door opened and a tanned, handsome young man with black curly hair bounded inside.

Before he greeted anyone he looked at the control panels and muttered, "Excellent."

"Tobe, welcome."

Tobe Geller said to Potter, "Boston girls are beautiful and they all have pointy tits, Arthur. This better be important."

Potter shook his hand, noting that the dot of earring hole was particular prominent today. He recalled that Tobe had explained the earring to his superiors in the Bureau by saying he'd done undercover work as a cop. He never had; he simply liked earrings and had quite a collection of them. The MIT graduate and adjunct professor of computer science at American University and Georgetown shook everyone's hand. He then looked down at LeBow's laptops, sneered, and muttered something about their being antiquated. Then he dropped into the chair of the communications control panel. He and Derek introduced themselves and were immediately submerged in a world of shielded analog signals, subnets, packet driver NDIS shims, digital tripartite scrambling, and oscillation detection systems in multiple landline chains.

"Just about to brief, Tobe," Potter told him and sent Budd to run his errands. To LeBow he said, "Let me see what you've got so far."

LeBow turned the profile computer to Potter.

The intelligence officer said. "We don't have much time."

But Potter continued to read, lost in the glowing type of the blue screen.

11:02 A.M.

The jackrabbit—not a rabbit at all but a hare—is nature's least likely fighter.

This is an animal made for defense—with a camouflaging coat (gray and buff in the warm months, white in the winter), ears that rotate like antennae to home in on threatening sounds, and eyes that afford a three-hundred-and-sixty-degree view of the terrain. It has a herbivore's chiseling teeth and its claws are intended for tugging at leafy plants and—in males—gripping the shoulders of its mate when creating future generations of jackrabbits.

But when it's cornered, when there's no chance for flight, it will attack its adversary with a shocking ferocity. Hunters have found the bodies of blinded or gutted foxes and wildcats that had the bad judgment to trap a jackrabbit in a cave and attack it with the overconfidence of sassy predators.

Confinement is our worst fear, Arthur Potter continues during his lectures on barricades, and hostage takers are the most deadly and determined of adversaries.

Today, in the command van at the Crow Ridge barricade, he dispensed with his *Wild Kingdom* introduction and told his audience simply, "Above all, you have to appreciate how dangerous those men in there are."

Potter looked over the group: Henderson, LeBow, and Tobe were the federal officers. On the state side there was Budd and his second-in-command, Philip Molto, a short, taciturn officer in the state police, who seemed no older than a high-school student. He was one of the tactical unit commanders. The others—two men and a woman—were solemn, with humorless eyes. They wore full combat gear and were eager for a fight.

Dean Stillwell, the sheriff of Crow Ridge, looked pure hayseed. His lengthy arms stretched from suit coat sleeves far too short and his mop of hair could have been styled from the early Beatles.

When they had assembled, Charlie Budd had introduced Potter. "I'd like you to meet Arthur Potter of the Federal Bureau of Investigation. He's a famous hostage negotiator and we're pretty lucky to have him with us today."

"Thank you, Captain," Potter had jumped in, worried that Budd was going to begin a round of applause.

"Just one more thing," the young captain had continued. He glanced at Potter. "I forgot to say this before. I've been in touch with the attorney general. And he's mobilizing the state Hostage Rescue Unit. So it's our job—"

Keeping an equable face, Potter had stepped forward. "Actually, Charlie, if you don't mind . . ." He'd nodded toward the assembled officers. Budd had fallen silent and grinned. "There'll be no state HRT involvement here. A federal rescue team is being assembled now and should be here later this afternoon or early this evening."

"Oh," Budd began. "But I think the attorney general—"

Potter glanced at him with a firm smile. "I've already spoken to him and the governor on the plane here."

Budd nodded, still grinning, and the negotiator proceeded with the briefing.

Early that morning, he explained, three men had murdered a guard and escaped from Callana maximum-security federal penitentiary outside Winfield, Kansas, near the Oklahoma border. Louis Jeremiah Handy,

Shepard Wilcox, and Ray "Sonny" Bonner. As they drove north their car was struck by a Cadillac. Handy and the escapees murdered the couple inside and got as far as the slaughterhouse before a state trooper caught up with them.

"Handy, thirty-five, was serving a life sentence for robbery, arson, and murder. Seven months ago he, Wilcox, Handy's girlfriend, and another perp robbed the Farmers & Merchants S&L in Wichita. Handy locked two tellers in the cash cage and set the place on fire. It burned to the ground, killing them both. During the getaway the fourth robber was killed, Handy's girlfriend escaped, and Handy and Wilcox were arrested. Visual aids, Henry?"

With an optical scanner LeBow had digitized mug shots of the three HTs and assembled them onto a single sheet of paper, showing front, side, and three-quarter views, highlighting distinguishing scars and characteristics. These were now spewing out of his laser printer. He distributed stacks to the people assembled in the van.

"Keep one of those and pass them out to the officers under you," Potter said. "I want everybody in the field to get one and memorize those pictures. If it comes down to a surrender things may get confusing and we've got too many plainclothesmen here to risk misidentification of the HTs. I want everybody to know exactly what the bad guys look like.

"That's Handy on top. The second one is Shep Wilcox. He's the closest thing Handy has to a friend. They've worked together on three or four jobs. The last fellow, the fat one with the beard, is Bonner. Handy apparently's known him for some time but they've never worked together. Bonner's got armed robbery on his sheet but he was in Callana for interstate flight. He's a suspected serial rapist though they only got him for his last assault. Stabbed the victim repeatedly—while he was in flagrante. She lived. She was seventeen years old and had to change her eleventh plastic surgery appointment to testify against him. Henry, what can you tell us about the hostages?"

LeBow said, "Very sketchy so far. Inside we have a total of ten hostages. Eight students, two teachers from the Laurent Clerc School for the Deaf in Hebron, Kansas, about fifteen miles west of here. They were on their way to a Theater of the Deaf performance in Topeka.

They're all female. The students range in age from seven to seventeen. I'll be receiving more data soon. We do know that they're all deaf except the older teacher, who can speak and hear normally."

Potter had arranged for a sign language interpreter but even so he knew the problems they could anticipate; he'd negotiated in foreign countries many times and negotiated with many foreigners in the United States. He knew the danger—and the frustration—of having to translate information precisely and quickly when lives hung in the balance.

He said, "Now, we've established a threat management team, consisting of myself; Henry LeBow, my intelligence officer and record keeper; Tobe Geller, my communications officer, and Captain Budd, who'll serve as a state liaison and my right-hand man. I'm the incident commander. There'll also be a containment officer, who I haven't picked yet.

"The TMT has two jobs. The primary one is to effect the surrender of the HTs and the release of the hostages. The secondary job is to assist in a tactical resolution if an assault is called for. This includes gathering intelligence for the hostage rescue team, distracting the HTs, manipulating them however we can to keep casualties to an acceptable level."

In barricade incidents everybody wants to be the hero and talk the bad guys out with their hands up. But even the most peace-loving negotiator has to keep in mind that sometimes the only solution is to go in shooting. When he taught the FBI's course in hostage negotiation one of the first things Potter told the class was, "Every hostage situation is essentially a homicide in progress."

He saw the looks in the eyes of the men and women in the van, and recalled that "cold fish" was among the kinder terms that had been used to describe him.

"Any information you learn about the takers, the hostages, the premises, anything, is to be delivered immediately to Agent LeBow. Before me if necessary. I mean *any* information. If you find out one of the HTs has a runny nose, don't assume it isn't important." Potter glanced at two hip young troopers rolling their eyes at one another. Looking directly at them, the agent said, "It might mean, for instance, that we could slip knockout drops in cold medicine. Or it might indicate a cocaine addiction we could use to our advantage."

The young men were above contrition but they reined in their sarcasm.

"Now I need that containment officer. Lieutenant Budd here thought that perhaps some of you have had hostage experience." He looked out over the group of cocky young law enforcers. "Who has?"

The woman state trooper spoke up quickly. "Yessir, I have. I took the NLEA hostage rescue course. And I've had negotiating skills training."

"Have you negotiated a release?"

"No. But I backed up the negotiator in a convenience store robbery a few months ago."

"That's right," Budd said. "Sally led the tactical team. Did a fine job too."

She continued, "We got a sniper inside the store, up in the acoustic tile. He had all of the perps acquired in his sights. They surrendered before we had to drop any of them."

"I've had some experience too," a trooper of about thirty-five offered, his hand on the butt of his service automatic. "And I was part of the team that rescued the teller in the Midwest S&L robbery last year in Topeka. We iced the perps, nailed 'em cold, not an injury to a single hostage."

One other trooper had trained in the army and had been part of two successful hostage rescue assault teams. "Saved them without a single shot being fired."

Peter Henderson had been listening with some dismay. He piped up. "Maybe I better take that job, Art. I've had the standard course and the refresher." He grinned. "And I read your book. Couple times. Should've been a best-seller. Like Tom Clancy." His face went somber and he added softly, "I think I really ought to. Being federal and all."

Dean Stillwell lifted his head then glanced at the troopers, decked out in flak jackets and dark gray ammunition belts. The movement of his moplike hair gave Potter the chance to avoid answering Henderson and he asked Stillwell, "You going to say something, Sheriff?"

"Naw, I wasn't really."

"Go ahead," Potter encouraged.

"Well, I never took any courses, or never shot any—what do you call them?—hostage takers. HTs, heh. But I guess we have had us a coupla situations down here in Crow Ridge."

Two of the troopers smiled.

"Tell me," Potter said.

"Well, there was that thing a couple months ago, with Abe Whitman and his wife. Emma. Out on Patchin Lane? Just past Badger Hollow Road?"

The smiles became soft laughter.

Stillwell laughed good-naturedly. "I guess that does sound funny. Not like the terrorists you all are used to."

Budd glanced at the troopers and they went straight-lipped again.

"What happened?" Potter asked.

Stillwell, looking down, said, "What it was, Abe's a farmer, pig farmer born and bred, and none better."

Now Peter Henderson, SAC though he was, struggled to stifle his own smile. Budd was silent. Potter gestured for Stillwell to continue and, as always, Henry LeBow listened, listened, listened.

"He took a bad hit when the pork belly market went to heck and gone last spring."

"Pork belly?" the woman trooper asked incredulously.

"Just tumbled." Stillwell missed, or ignored, the mockery. "So what happens but the bank calls his loans and he kind of cracks up. Always been a little bit of a nut case but this time he goes off the deep end and holes up in his barn with a shotgun and the knife he used for dressing the pigs he kept for his own table."

"Cooked up that pork belly, did he?" a trooper asked.

"Oh, not just bacon," Stillwell explained earnestly, "That's the thing about pigs. You know that expression, don't you? 'You can use everything but the squeal.' "

Two troopers lost it at this point. The negotiator smiled encouragingly.

"Anyway, I get a call that something's going on out at his farm and go out there and find Emma in front of the barn. His wife of ten years. He'd slit her from groin to breastbone with that knife and cut her hands off. Abe had his two sons in there, saying he was going to do the same to them. That'd be Brian, age eight, and Stuart, age four. Sweet youngsters, both of 'em."

The troopers' smiles were gone.

"Was about to cut off little Stu's fingers one by one just as I got there."

"Jesus," the woman trooper whispered.

"What'd you do, Sheriff?"

The lanky shoulders shrugged. "Nothing fancy. In fact, I didn't really know *what* to do. I just talked him up. I got close but not too close 'cause I've been hunting with Abe and he's a heck of a shot. Hunkered down behind a slop trough. And we just talked. Saw him inside of the barn there, not but fifty feet in front of me. Just sitting there, holding the knife and his boy."

"How long did you talk for?"

"A spell."

"How long a spell?"

"Must've been close to eighteen, twenty hours. We both got hoarse from shouting, so I had one of my boys go out and get a couple of those cellular phones." He laughed. "I had to read the instructions to figure out mine. See, I didn't want to drive the cruiser up and use the radio or a bullhorn. I figured the less he saw of cops, the better."

"You stayed with it the whole time?"

"Sure. In for a penny, in for a pound, is what I say. Well, twice I stepped away for, you know, natural functions. And once to fetch a cup of coffee. Always kept my head down."

"What happened?"

Another shrug. "He came out. Gave himself up."

Potter asked, "The boys?"

"They were okay. Aside from seeing their mother that way, course. But there wasn't much we could do about that."

"Let me ask you one question, Sheriff. Did you ever think of exchanging yourself for the boys?"

Stillwell looked perplexed. "Nope. Never did."

"Why not?"

"Seemed to me that'd draw his attention to the youngsters. I wanted him to forget about them and concentrate just on him and me."

"And you never tried to shoot him? Didn't you have a clear target?"

"Sure I did. Dozens of times. But, I don't know, I just felt that was the last thing I wanted to have happen—anybody to get hurt. Him, or me, or the boys."

"Correct answers, Sheriff. You're my containment officer. Is that all right with you?"

"Well, yessir, whatever I can do to help, I'd be proud to."

Potter glanced at the displeased state commanders. "You and your officers will report to the sheriff here."

"Say, hold up here, sir," Budd began, but didn't quite know where to take it from there. "The sheriff's a fine man. We're friends and everything. *We've* gone hunting too. But . . . well, it's like a technical thing. See, he's local, municipal, you know. These're mostly state troopers. You can't put them under his command. That'd need, I don't know, authorization or something."

"Well, I'm authorizing it. You can consider Sheriff Stillwell federal now," Potter said reasonably. "He's been deputized."

LeBow looked quizzically at Potter, who shrugged. There was no procedure that either of them knew about for field-deputizing federal agents.

Peter Henderson's face, alone among the crowd at the briefing, was still smiling. Potter said to him, "You too, Pete. I want any agents not involved in intelligence gathering, forensics, or liaising with HRT under Sheriff Stillwell's direction."

Henderson nodded slowly, then said, "Could I talk to you for a minute, Art?"

"We don't have much time."

"Just take a minute."

Potter knew what was coming and understood that it was important for it not to happen in front of the other commanders. He said, "Let's step outside, what do you say?"

In the shadow of the van Henderson said in a harsh whisper, "I'm sorry, Arthur. I know your reputation but I'm not putting my people under some hick."

"Well, Pete, my reputation's irrelevant. What counts is my authority."

Again Henderson nodded reasonably, this man in a white shirt immaculately starched and a gray suit that would gain him entrance into any restaurant within a mile of Capitol Hill.

"Arthur, I ought to be more involved in this thing. I mean, I *know* Handy. I—"

"How do you know him?" Potter interrupted. This was news to him.

"I had agents on the scene at apprehension. At the S&L. I interviewed him after the collar. I helped the U.S. Attorney make the case. It was our forensics that put him away."

Since Handy'd been caught in the act and there were direct eyewitnesses, forensics would be a mere technicality. On the DomTran flight Potter had read the interview conducted by, apparently, Henderson. The prisoner had said virtually nothing except "Fuck you."

"Anything you can tell us about him would be appreciated," Potter said. "But you don't have the sort of experience we need for containment."

"And Stillwell does?"

"He has a containment officer's temperament. And judgment. He's not a cowboy."

Or, thought Potter, a bureaucrat, which was just as bad, if not worse.

Finally Henderson looked down at the muddy ground. He growled, "No fucking way, Potter. I've been stuck in this hellhole plenty long enough. Not a damn thing happens down here except copping applesauce and Dictaphones from the Air Force base. And Indians pissing into fucking Minuteman silos. I want a piece of this."

"You don't have any barricade experience, Pete. I read your sheet on the way here."

"I have more law enforcement experience than that Gomer Pyle you've picked. For chrissake, I've got a law degree from Georgetown."

"I'm putting you in charge of the rear staging area. Coordinating medical, press liaison, the facilities for the hostages' families, and supplies for the containment troopers and hostage rescue when they get here."

There was a pause as Henderson gazed at his fellow agent—only a few years older—with shocked amusement then, suddenly, pure contempt, which was sealed with an abrupt nod and a chill grin. "Fuck you, Potter. I know the other part of your reputation. Grandstanding."

"It's an important job, rear staging," Potter continued, as if Henderson hadn't spoken. "It's where you'll be the most valuable."

"Fucking holier than thou . . . You've gotta have the limelight, don't you? Afraid somebody a little showier, with a little more class might play better on camera?"

"I think you know that's not my motive."

"Know? What do I know? Except that you breeze into town with the Admiral's blessing, send us off to get your fucking coffee. After the shootout—where, who knows, a dozen troopers and a hostage or two're killed—you give your press conference, take credit for the good stuff, blame us for the fuckups. And then you're gone. Who's left to deal with the shit you leave behind? Me, that's who."

"If there's nothing else—"

Henderson buttoned his suit jacket. "Oh, there'll be something else. Don't you worry." He stalked off, ignoring Potter's matter-of-fact suggestion not to present too much of a target to snipers in the slaughter-house.

11:31 A.M.

Arthur Potter stepped back into the van, the eyes of the assembled troopers following him cautiously. He wondered if they'd overheard the exchange between him and Henderson.

"Now," the agent continued, "the rules of engagement."

Potter dug a fax from his jacket pocket.

On the jet from Glenview, Potter had spoken via conference call with the Bureau's director, its assistant director of criminal investigations, and Frank D'Angelo, commander of the Bureau's HRT, and had written the rules of engagement for the Crow Ridge barricade. This had taken much of the flight and the result was a single-spaced two-page document that covered every eventuality and gave Potter specific orders about handling the situation. It had been written with much circumspection. Alcohol, Tobacco and Firearms and the FBI had taken serious flak for the handling of the Koresh standoff in Waco and the Bureau itself had been vilified for the Randall Weaver barricade in '92, in which the rules of engagement had been written so broadly that sharpshooters believed that they had orders to shoot any armed adults if they had clear shots. Weaver's wife was mistakenly killed by an FBI sniper.

Potter was looking mostly at Stillwell when he said, "Your job is to contain the HTs. Containment is a tactical function but it's purely passive. There'll be no rescue attempts whatsoever."

"Yessir."

"You'll keep the takers inside whatever perimeter I decide is active. It might be the building itself, it might be a line a hundred yards around the building. Whatever it is, they are not to cross that boundary alive. If any one of them does, whether or not they have a hostage with them, your troops're green-lighted. You know what that means?"

"They're cleared to shoot."

"That's correct. And you shoot to kill. No attempts to wound. No threats. No warning shots. Lethal fire or no fire at all."

"Yessir."

"There are to be no shots through open windows or doorways, even if you see a hostage threatened, without express authorization from someone on the threat management team."

Potter noticed that Budd's face grew dark when he heard this.

"Understood," Stillwell said. The commanders nodded reluctantly.

"If you're fired upon, you'll take defensive positions and wait until you have the okay to return fire. If at any time you or another officer are actually threatened with deadly force, you may use deadly force to protect yourself or that person. But only if you're convinced that there is a true present danger."

"A present danger," a trooper muttered sarcastically.

They're hoping for a turkey shoot, Potter thought. He glanced at the clock on LeBow's computer. "We're going to establish contact in about five minutes. I'm going to warn the takers about the perimeter and I'll let you know, Sheriff, that they've been so notified. From that moment on you're instructed to contain them as I've outlined."

"Yessir," the sheriff answered calmly, and brushed his mop of hair, mussing it further.

"For the time being, the kill zone will be any area outside the building itself. After they send somebody out to get the phone nobody comes outside unless it's under a flag of truce."

Stillwell nodded.

Potter continued. "Henry here will be feeding you data that's tactically relevant. Types of weapons, location of hostage takers and hostages, possible exits, and so on. There's to be no contact directly between you and the HTs. And don't listen in on my conversations with Handy."

"Right. Why not?"

"Because I'm going to be establishing rapport with him and trying to be reasonable. You can't afford to have any sympathy for him. You have to be able to green-light him instantly."

"Fine by me."

"Now, I don't want any accidents," Potter said. "Lieutenant Budd has already told all the troopers to unchamber weapons. That correct? Snipers included?"

Budd nodded. His mouth tightened. Potter wondered just how angry the captain was. Thinking: He'll be angrier yet before this is over.

"My men," one of the troopers said stiffly, "don't have itchy trigger fingers."

"Not now they don't. But they will. In ten hours you'll be drawing down on your own shadow. Now, Dean, you might see reflections from inside. You'll be thinking rifle scopes. But they'll probably just be mirrors, like periscopes. Takers who've done time learned that trick inside prison. So tell your people not to panic if they see a flash."

"Yessir," Stillwell said slowly, the way he seemed to say everything.

Potter said, "Now a few final words. Generally, criminal hostage takers are the easiest to deal with. They're not like terrorists. Their purpose isn't to kill anyone. It's to escape. Given enough time they're going to realize that the hostages are more of a liability than anything and dead hostages mean nothing but trouble. But the psychology of what's going on now is that they're not thinking rationally. They're pumped up on adrenaline. They're scared and confused.

"We have to defuse the situation. Make Handy believe that he'll survive the incident through rational action. Time works in our favor. We don't establish any deadlines. We want to stretch this out longer than any of us can stand. And then longer. And then longer still.

"When HRT gets here we'll prepare for a tactical resolution but that'll still be our last resort. As long as Handy is still talking to us there won't be any rescue attempt. We'll call it the pork belly approach to hostage rescue." Potter smiled toward Stillwell, then continued,

"Delay is the name of the game. It wears down the HTs, makes them bored, brings them and the hostages closer together."

"Stockholm syndrome," one of the commanders said.

"Exactly."

"What's that?" another one asked.

Potter nodded to LeBow, who said, "It's the psychoanalytic process of transference as applied to a hostage taking. The term comes from a bank robbery in Stockholm about twenty years ago. The robber forced four employees into the bank vault. They were later joined by a former prison-mate of the taker. They all stayed together for over five days and when they finally gave up, several of the hostages were madly in love with their captors. They'd come to feel that it was the police who were the bad guys. The robber and his cellmate had formed strong feelings of affection for the hostages too and wouldn't think of hurting them."

"Time to get to work," Potter announced. "Sheriff, you'll proceed with containment. I'll make initial contact with the takers."

Bashful Dean Stillwell motioned to the commanders. "If you all'd come outside, maybe we'll move some of those troopers of yours around a bit. If that's all right with you. What do you say?"

"Pork belly" was the only response, but it was said very softly. Potter believed he was the only one who heard.

The water poured like a shower, a silver stream falling through gaps in the ceiling high above them, probably from rank pools of old rainwater on the roof.

It dripped onto rusting meat hooks and chains and rubber conveyor belts and disintegrating machinery, just outside the killing room, where Melanie Charrol sat, looking over the girls. The seven-year-old twins, Anna and Suzie, huddled against her. Beverly Klemper brushed her short blond hair from her face—round with baby fat still, though she was fourteen—and struggled to breathe. The others were clustered together at the far side of the killing room. Ten-year-old Emily Stoddard rubbed frantically at a rust stain on her white tights, tears running down her face.

Melanie glanced at Mrs. Harstrawn and Susan Phillips, crouching together, speaking in abrupt sign. The teenage girl's pale face, framed by her stark hair, was still filled with anger. Her dark eyes were the eyes of a resistance fighter, Melanie thought suddenly. Their conversation had to do with the students.

"I'm worried they'll panic," Susan said to the older teacher. "Have to keep them together. If somebody runs, those assholes will hurt them."

With the audacity of an eight-year-old, Kielle Stone signed, "We *have* to run! There're more of us than them. We can get away!"

Susan and Mrs. Harstrawn ignored her, and the little girl's gray eyes flashed with anger.

All the while Melanie agonized: I don't know what to do. I don't *know*.

The men weren't paying much attention to the girls at the moment. Melanie rose and walked to the doorway. She watched them pull clothes out of canvas bags. Brutus stripped off his T-shirt and with a glance at her walked under the stream of water, letting it cascade over him as he gazed up at the murky ceiling, eyes closed. She saw his sinewy muscles, his hairless body, marred by a dozen pink scars. The other two men looked at him uncertainly and continued to change clothes. When they pulled off their workshirts she could read the names stenciled on their T-shirts. Stoat's said *S. Wilcox*. Bear's, *R. Bonner*. But still, seeing Bear's fat, hairy body and Stoat's lean one, his slippery eyes, she thought of them only by the animal names that had instinctively occurred to her.

And, seeing the look of amused malice on his face as he stood under the cascading water, arms outstretched like Christ's, she understood that Brutus was a far better name for him than *L. Handy*.

He now stepped from the stream of water, dried off with his old shirt, and pulled on a new one, dark green flannel. He picked the pistol up from the oil drum and gazed at his captives, that curious smile on his face. He joined the other men. They looked cautiously out one of the front windows.

This can't be happening, Melanie said to herself. It's impossible. People were expecting her. Her parents. Danny, going into surgery tomorrow. She'd been in her brother's recovery rooms after every one of his half-dozen operations in the past year. She felt the absurd urge to tell these men that they *had* to let them go; she couldn't disappoint her brother.

Then there was her performance in Topeka.

And of course her plans afterwards.

Go say something to him. Now. Plead with him to release the little girls. The twins, at least. Or Kielle and Shannon. Emily.

Beverly, racked with asthma.

Go. Do it.

Melanie started forward then looked back. The others in the killing room—all nine of them—were staring at her.

Susan held her eyes for a moment then gestured for her to return. She did.

"Don't worry," Susan signed to the girls, then pulled the tiny, chestnut-haired twins to her. Smiling. "They're going to leave soon, let us out. We'll be in Topeka late, that's all. What do you want to do after Melanie's recital? Everybody tell me. Come on!"

Is she crazy? Melanie thought. We're not going to . . . Then realized that Susan was saying this to put them at ease. The girl was right. The truth didn't matter. Keeping the younger girls comforted did. Making sure there was no excuse for the men to get close to them; the memory of Bear gripping Susan's breasts, holding Shannon tight to his fat body came starkly to mind.

But no one wanted to play the game. Until Melanie signed, "Go out for dinner?"

"Arcade!" Shannon signed suddenly. "Mortal Kombat!"

Kielle sat up. "I want to go to real restaurant. I want steak medium rare and potatoes and pie—"

"Whole pie?" Susan asked, mock astonishment on her face.

Choking back tears, Melanie couldn't think of anything to say. Feebly she signed, "Yes. Whole pies for everyone!"

The girls glanced at her but their eyes returned immediately to Susan.

"Might get bellyaches." Mrs. Harstrawn gave an exaggerated frown.

"No," Kielle responded. "Whole pie would be *crass*." She gave an indignant glance to Susan. "Only Philistines eat whole pies. We'll order one piece each. And I'm going to have coffee."

"They don't let us drink coffee," Jocylyn stopped rubbing her tearful eyes long enough to sign.

"*I'm* having coffee. Black coffee," Shannon the knee-kicker signed.

"With cream," Kielle continued. "When my mother makes coffee she puts it in glass cup and pours cream in. It swirls like cloud. I'm going to have coffee in real restaurant."

"Coffee ice cream maybe." Beverly struggled to suck air into her lungs.

"With sprinkles," Suzie offered.

"With sprinkles *and* Reese's Pieces," echoed Anna, her junior by thirty-some seconds. "Like at Friendly's!"

And, once again, Melanie could think of nothing to say.

"Not *that* kind of restaurant. I mean *fancy* restaurant." Kielle didn't understand why nobody else was excited at the prospect.

A huge smile on Susan's face. "We're all decided. Fancy restaurant. Steak, pie, and coffee for everybody. No Philistines allowed!"

Suddenly twelve-year-old Jocylyn broke into hysterical tears and leapt to her feet. Mrs. Harstrawn was up in an instant, cradling the rotund girl, pulling her close. Slowly she calmed down. Melanie lifted her hands to say something comforting and witty. Finally she signed, "Whipped cream on everyone's pie."

Susan turned to Melanie. "You still ready to go on stage?"

The young teacher stared back at her student for a moment then smiled, nodding.

Mrs. Harstrawn, eyes flitting nervously to the main room of the slaughterhouse, where the men stood talking, their heads down, signed, "Maybe Melanie can recite her poems again."

Melanie nodded and her mind went blank. She had a repertoire of two dozen poems she'd been planning on performing. Now she could remember nothing but the first stanza of her "Birds on a Wire." Melanie lifted her hands, signed:

"Eight gray birds, sitting in dark.
"Cold wind blows, it isn't kind.
"Sitting on wire, they lift their wings
"and sail off into billowy clouds."

"Pretty, isn't it?" Susan asked, looking directly at Jocylyn. The girl wiped her face on the sleeve of her bulky blouse and nodded.

"*I* wrote some poems," Kielle signed emphatically. "Fifty of them.

No, more. They're about Wonder Woman and Spider-Man. And X-Men too. Jean Grey and Cyclops. Shannon's read them!"

Shannon nodded. On the girl's left forearm was a faux tattoo of another X-Man, Gambit, which she'd drawn with Pentel marker.

"Why don't you tell us one?" Susan asked her.

Kielle thought for a minute then confessed that her poems still needed some work.

"Why are birds gray in your poem?" Beverly asked Melanie. Her signing was abrupt, as if she had to finish every conversation before one of her wrenching asthma attacks.

"Because we all have a little gray in us," Melanie answered, amazed that the girls were actually rallying, distracted from the horror unfolding around them.

"If it's about us I'd rather be pretty bird," Suzie said, and her twin nodded.

"You could have made us red," suggested Emily, who was dressed in a Laura Ashley floral. She was more feminine than all the rest of the students combined.

Then Susan—who knew facts that even Melanie did not; Susan, who was going to attend Gallaudet College next year with straight A's—explained to the other girls' fascination that only male cardinals were red. The females were brownish gray.

"So, they're cardinals?" Kielle asked.

When Melanie didn't respond the little girl tapped her shoulder and repeated the question.

"Yes," Melanie answered. "Sure. It's about cardinals. You're all flock of pretty cardinals."

"Not archbishops?" Mrs. Harstrawn signed, and rolled her eyes. Susan laughed. Jocylyn nodded but seemed stymied that someone had once again beaten her to a punch line.

Tomboy Shannon, devourer of Christopher Pike books, asked why Melanie didn't make the birds hawks, with long silver beaks and claws that dripped blood.

"It is about us then?" Kielle asked. "The poem?"

"Maybe."

"But there are nine, including you," Susan pointed out to her teacher with the logic of a teenager. "And ten with Mrs. Harstrawn."

"So there are," Melanie responded. "I can change it." Then thought to herself: Do something. Whipped cream on pie? Bullshit. Take charge!

Do something!

Go talk to Brutus.

Melanie rose suddenly, walked to the doorway. Looked out. Then back at Susan, who signed, "What are you doing?"

Melanie's eyes returned to the men. Thinking: Oh, don't rely on me, girls. That's a mistake. I'm not the one to do it. Mrs. Harstrawn's older. Susan's stronger. When she says something, people—hearing or deaf— always listen.

I can't. . . .

Yes, you can.

Melanie took a step into the main room, feeling the spatter of water that dripped from the ceiling. She dodged a swinging meat hook, walked closer to the men. Just the twins. And Beverly. Who wouldn't let seven-year-old girls go? Who wouldn't have compassion for a teenager racked by asthma?

Bear looked up and saw her, grinned. Crew-cut Stoat was slipping batteries into a portable TV and paid no attention. Brutus, who had wandered away from the other two, was gazing out the window.

Melanie paused, looked back into the killing room. Susan was frowning. Again she signed, "What are you doing?" Melanie sensed criticism in her expression; she felt like a high-school student herself.

Just ask him. Write the words out. *Please let little ones go.*

Her hands were shaking, her heart was a huge, raw lump. She felt the vibrations as Bear called something. Slowly Brutus turned.

He looked at her, tossed his wet hair.

Melanie froze, feeling his eyes on her. She pantomimed writing something. He walked up to her. She was frozen. He took her hand, looked at her nails, a small silver ring on her right index finger. Released it. Looked into her face and laughed. Then he walked back to the other two men, leaving her alone, his back to her, as if she posed no threat whatsoever, as if she were younger than the youngest of her students, as if she were not there at all.

She felt more devastated than if he'd slapped her.

Too frightened to approach him again, too ashamed to return to the killing room, Melanie remained where she was, gazing out the window at the row of police cars, the crouching forms of the policemen, and the scruffy grass bending in the wind.

Potter gazed at the slaughterhouse through the bulletproof window in the truck.

They'd have to talk soon. Already Lou Handy was looming too large in his mind. There were two dangers inherent in negotiating. First, making the hostage taker bigger than life before you begin and therefore starting out on the defensive—what Potter was beginning to feel now. (The other—his own Stockholming—would come later. He'd deal with it then. And he knew he would have to.)

"Throw phone ready?"

"Just about." Tobe was programming numbers into a scanner on the console. "Should I put an omni in it?"

Throw phones were lightweight, rugged cellular phones containing a duplicate transmitting circuit that sent to the command post any conversations on the phone and a readout of the numbers called. Usually the HTs spoke only to the negotiators but sometimes they called accomplices or friends. These conversations sometimes helped the threat management team in bargaining or getting a tactical advantage.

Occasionally a tiny omnidirectional microphone was hidden in the phone. It'd pick up conversations even when the phone wasn't being used by the HTs. It was every negotiator's dream to know exactly what was said inside a barricade. But if the microphone was found, it might mean reprisals and would certainly damage the negotiator's credibility—his only real asset at this stage of the situation.

"Henry?" Potter asked. "Your opinion. Could he find it?"

Henry LeBow tapped computer keys and called up Handy's rapidly growing file. He scrolled through it. "Never went to college, got A's in science and math in high school. Wait, here we go. . . . Studied electronics in the service for a while. He didn't last long in the army. He knifed his sergeant. That's neither here nor there. . . . No, I'd say don't put the mike in. He could spot it. He excelled in engineering."

Potter sighed. "Leave it out, Tobe."

"Hurts."

"Does."

The phone buzzed and Potter took the call. Special Agent Angie Scapello had arrived in Wichita and was being choppered directly to the Laurent Clerc School in Hebron. She and the Hebron PD officer who'd be acting as interpreter would be arriving in a half-hour.

He relayed this information to LeBow, who typed it in. The intelligence officer added, "I'll have CAD schematics of the interior in ten minutes." LeBow had sent a field agent to dig up architectural or engineering drawings of the slaughterhouse. These would be transmitted to the command post and printed out through computer-assisted drafting software.

Potter said to Budd, "Charlie, I'm thinking we've got to consolidate them. The hostages. The takers're going to want power in there but I don't want to do that. I want to get them a single electric lantern. Battery powered. Weak. So they'll all have to be in the same room."

"Why?"

LeBow spoke. "Keep the takers and the hostages together. Let Handy talk to them, get to know them."

"I don't know, sir," the captain said. "Those girls're deaf. That's gonna be a spooky place. If they're in a room that's lit with just one lantern, they'll . . . well, the way my daughter'd say, they'll freak."

"We can't be worried much about their feelings," Potter said absently, watching LeBow transcribe notes into his electronic tablet of stone.

"I don't really agree with you there, sir," Budd said.

Silence.

Tobe was assembling the cellular phone, while he simultaneously gazed at six TV stations on a single monitor, the screen split miraculously by Derek Elb. All the local news was about the incident. CBS was doing a special report, as was CNN. Sprayed-haired beauties, men and women, held microphones like ice cream cones and spoke into them fervently. Potter noticed that Tobe'd taken to the control panel of the command van as if he'd designed it himself, and then reflected that perhaps he had. He and red-haired Derek had become fast friends.

"Think about it, though," Budd persisted. "That's a scary place at high noon. At night? Brother, it'll be awful."

"Whatever happens," Potter replied, "these next twenty-four hours aren't going to be very pleasant for those girls. They'll just have to live with it. We need to bunch them up. A single lantern'll do that."

Budd grimaced in frustration. "There's a practical matter too. I'm thinking if it's too dark they might panic. Try to run. And get hurt."

Potter looked at the brick walls of the old processing plant, as dark as dried blood.

"You don't *want* them to get shot, do you?" Budd asked in exasperation, drawing LeBow's glance, though not Potter's.

"But if we turn the power on," the agent said, "they'll have the whole slaughterhouse to hide themselves in. Handy could put them in ten different rooms." Potter pressed his cupped hands together absently as if making a snowball. "We *have* to keep them together."

Budd said, "What we could do is get a generator truck here. Feed in a line. Four or five auto repair lights—you know, those caged lights on hooks. Just enough current to light up the main room. And that way if you ordered an assault we could shut down the juice any time we wanted. Which you couldn't do with a battery unit. And, look, at some point we're gonna have to communicate with those girls. Remember, they're deaf. If it's dark, how're we gonna do that?"

That was a good point, one that Potter hadn't considered. In an assault someone would have to issue sign language evacuation instructions to the girls.

Potter nodded. "Okay."

"I'll get on it."

"Delegate it, Charlie."

"I aim to."

Tobe pushed buttons. A hiss of static filled the van. "Shit," he muttered. He added to LeBow, "Got two men with Big Ears closer than they ought to be," referring to small parabolic microphones that under good conditions could pick up a whisper at a hundred yards. Today they were useless.

"Damn wind," LeBow muttered.

"Throw phone's ready," Tobe announced, pushing a small olive-drab backpack toward Potter. "Both downlink circuits're ready to receive."

"We'll—"

A phone buzzed. Potter grabbed it.

"Potter here."

"Agent Potter? We haven't met." A pleasant baritone boomed out of the speaker. "I'm Roland Marks, the assistant attorney general of the state."

"Yes?" Potter asked coolly.

"I'd like to share some thoughts with you, sir."

Potter's impatience surged. There's no time for this, he thought to himself.

"I'm very busy right now."

"Some thoughts about state involvement. Just my two cents' worth."

Potter had Charlie Budd, he had his containment troops, he had his command van. He needed nothing else from the state of Kansas.

"This isn't a good time, I'm afraid."

"Is it true that they've kidnaped eight young girls?"

Potter sighed. "And two teachers. From the deaf school in Hebron. Yes, that's right. We're just about to establish contact and we're on a very tight schedule. I don't—"

"How many takers are there?"

"I'm afraid I don't have time to discuss the situation with you. The governor's been briefed and you can call our special agent in charge, Peter Henderson. I assume you know him."

"I know Pete. Sure." The hesitant voice suggested he had little confidence in the man. "This could be a real tragedy, sir."

"Well, Mr. Marks, my job is to make sure it doesn't turn out that way. I hope you'll let me get on with it."

"I was thinking, maybe a counselor or priest could help out. In Topeka we've got ourselves this state employee assistance department. Some top-notch—"

"I'm hanging up now," Potter said rather cheerfully. "Pete Henderson can keep you informed of our progress."

"Wait a minute—"

Click.

"Henry, pull some files. Roland Marks's. Assistant AG. Find out if he can make trouble. See if he's filed to run in any elections, got his eye on any appointments."

"Just sounds like some do-good, knee-jerk, bleeding-heart liberal to me," scowled Henry LeBow, who'd voted Democratic all his life, Eugene McCarthy included.

"All right," Potter said, forgetting immediately about the attorney general's call, "let's get a volunteer with a good arm. Oh, one more thing." Potter buttoned his navy jacket and lifted a finger to Budd. He motioned to the door. "Step out here, would you please, Charlie?"

Outside they stood in the faint shadow of the van. "Captain," Potter said, "you better tell me what's eating you. That I stepped on your toes back there?"

"Nope," came the chilly response. "You're federal. I'm state. It's in the Constitution. Preeminence, they call it."

"Listen," Potter said firmly; "we don't have time for delicacies. Get it off your chest now. Or live with it, whatever it is."

"What're we doing? Taking off our insignias and going at it?" Budd laughed without much humor.

Potter said nothing but lifted an eyebrow.

"All right, how's this? What's eating me is I know you're supposed to be good at this and I've never done a negotiation before. I hear you barking orders right and left like you know exactly what you're doing but don't you think there's one thing you neglected to mention?"

"What?"

"You didn't say hardly three words about those girls in there."

"What about them?"

"I just thought you should've reminded everybody that our number-one priority is getting those girls out alive."

"Oh," Potter said, his mind elsewhere as he scanned the battlefield. "But that's not our number-one priority at all, Charlie. The rules of engagement are real clear. I'm here to get the takers to surrender and, if they don't, to help Hostage Rescue engage and neutralize them. I'll do everything in my power to save the people inside. That's why it's me, not HRT, running the show. But those men in there aren't leaving Crow Ridge except in body bags or handcuffs. And if that means those hostages have to die, then they're going to die. Now if you could find me that volunteer—a fellow with a good arm to pitch the phone. And hand me that bullhorn too, if you'd be so kind."

NOON

As he walked through a shallow gully that eventually ran into the south side of the slaughterhouse, Arthur Potter said to Henry LeBow, "We'll want engineer reports on any modifications to the building. EPA too. I want to know if there're any tunnels."

The intelligence officer nodded. "It's being done. And I'm checking on easements too."

"Tunnels?" Budd asked.

Potter told him about the terrorist barricade at the Vanderbilt mansion in Newport, Rhode Island, three years before. The Hostage Rescue Team had completely surprised the HTs by sneaking through a steam tunnel into the basement of the building. The tycoon had ordered the furnace installed away from the house so the noise and smoke wouldn't disturb his guests, never knowing that his sense of social decorum would save the lives of fifteen Israeli tourists a hundred years later.

The agent noticed that Dean Stillwell had reorganized troopers and agents in good defensive positions around the building. Halfway to the slaughterhouse Potter paused suddenly and looked toward the glint of water in the distance.

To Budd, Potter said, "I want all river traffic stopped."

"Well, um, that's the Arkansas River."

"So you told us."

"I mean, it's a big river."

"I can see."

"Well, why? You thinking they'll have accomplices floating in on rafts?"

"No." In the ensuing silence Potter challenged Budd to figure it out. He wanted the man to start *thinking*.

"You're not afraid they'd try and swim out to a barge? They'd drown for sure. It's a mean current here."

"Ah, but they might want to try. I want to make sure they don't even think of it. Just like keeping the choppers away."

Budd said, "Okay. I'll do it. Only who should I call? The coast guard? I don't think there's any such thing as a coast guard on rivers here." His frustration was evident. "I mean, who should I call?"

"I don't know, Charlie. You'll have to find out."

On his cellular phone Budd placed a call to his office and ordered them to find out who had jurisdiction over river traffic. He ended the conversation by saying, "I don't know. You'll have to find out."

SAC Peter Henderson was at the rear staging area, setting up the medical unit and coordinating with other troopers and agents coming into the area, particularly the BATF agents and U.S. marshals, on site because there'd been firearm violations and an escape from a federal prison. The SAC's bitter parting words still echoed in Potter's mind. *Oh, there'll be something else. Don't you worry.*

He said to LeBow, "Henry, while you're looking up our friend Roland Marks, check out Henderson too."

"*Our* Henderson?"

"Yep. I don't want it to interfere with working the incident but I need to know if he's got an agenda."

"Sure."

"Arthur," Budd said, "I was thinking, maybe we should get this fellow's mother here. Handy's, I mean. Or his father or brother or somebody."

It was LeBow who shook his head.

"What? I ask something stupid?" Budd asked.

The intelligence officer said, "Just watching too many movies, Captain. A priest or family member's the last person you want here."

"Why's that?"

Potter explained, "Nine times out of ten their family's part of the reason they're in trouble in the first place. And I've never known a priest to do anything more than rile up a taker." He was pleased to notice that Budd took this not as a chastisement but as information; he seemed to store it somewhere in his enthusiastic brain.

"Sir." Sheriff Dean Stillwell's voice floated to them on the breeze. He trooped up and mussed his moppish hair with his fingers. "Got one of my boys gonna make the run with that phone. Come over here, Stevie."

"Officer," Potter said, nodding, "what's your name?"

"Stephen Oates. I go by Stevie mostly." The officer was lanky and tall and would look right at home in white pinstripes, working on a chaw of tobacco out on the pitcher's mound.

"All right, Stevie. Put on that body armor and helmet. I'm going to tell them you're coming. You crawl up to that rise there. See it? By that old livestock pen. I want you to stay down and pitch the knapsack as far as you can toward the front door."

Tobe handed him the small olive-drab satchel.

"What if I hit those rocks there, sir?"

"It's a special phone and the bag's padded," Potter said. "Besides, if you hit those rocks, you should get out of law enforcement and try out for the Royals. All right," he announced, "let's get this show on the road."

Potter gripped the bullhorn and crawled to the top of the rise where he'd hailed Handy last time, sixty yards from the black windows of the slaughterhouse. He dropped onto his belly, caught his breath. Lifted the bullhorn to his lips. "This is Agent Potter again. We're sending a telephone in to you. One of our men is going to throw it as close to you as he can. This is not a trick. It's simply a cellular phone. Will you let our man approach?"

Nothing.

"You men inside, can you hear me? We want to talk to you. Will you let our man approach?"

After an interminable pause a piece of yellow cloth waved in one window. It was probably a positive response; a "no" would presumably have been a bullet.

"When you come out to get the phone we will not shoot at you. You have my word on that."

Again the yellow scrap.

Potter nodded to Oates. "Go on."

The trooper started toward the grassy rise, staying low. Still, Potter noted, a rifleman inside could easily hit him. The helmet was Kevlar but the transparent face mask was not.

Of the eighty people now surrounding the slaughterhouse, not a soul spoke. There was the hiss of the wind, a far-off truck horn. Occasionally the sound of the chugging engines of the big John Deere and Massey-Ferguson combines swam through the thick wheat. It was pleasant and it was unsettling. Oates scrabbled toward the rise. He made it and lay prone, looking up quickly, then down again. Until recently, throw phones were bulky and hard-wired to the negotiator's phone. Even the strongest officer could pitch them only thirty feet or so and often the cords got tangled. Cellular technology had revamped hostage negotiation.

Oates rolled from one clump of tall bluestem to another like a seasoned stuntman. He paused in a bunch of buffalo grass and goldenrod. Then kept going.

Okay, thought Potter. Throw it.

But the trooper didn't throw it.

Oates looked once more at the slaughterhouse then crawled over the knoll, past rotting posts and rails of livestock pens, and continued on, a good twenty yards. Even a bad marksman would have his pick of body parts from that range.

"What's he doing?" Potter whispered, irritated.

"I don't know, sir," Stillwell said. "I was real clear about what to do. I know he's pretty worried about those girls and wants to do everything right."

"Getting himself shot isn't doing anything right."

Oates continued toward the slaughterhouse.

Don't be a hero, Stevie, Potter thought. Though his concern was more than the man's getting killed or wounded. Unlike special forces and intelligence officers, cops aren't trained in anti-interrogation techniques. In the hands of somebody like Lou Handy, armed with only a knife or a safety pin, Oates'd spill everything he knew in two minutes, telling the location of every officer on the field, the fact that HRT wasn't expected for some hours, what types of guns the troopers had, anything else Handy might be curious to know.

Throw the damn phone!

Oates made it to a second rise and quickly looked up at the slaughterhouse door again then ducked. When there was no fire he squinted, drew back, and launched the phone in a low arc. It passed well over the rocks he'd been worried about and rolled to a stop only thirty feet from the arched brick doorway of the Webber & Stoltz plant.

"Excellent," Budd muttered, clapping Stillwell on the back. The sheriff smiled with cautious pride.

"Maybe it's a good omen," LeBow suggested.

Oates refused to present his back to the darkened windows of the slaughterhouse and eased backward into the grass until he was lost to sight.

"Now let's see who's the brave one," Potter mumbled.

"What do you mean?" Budd asked.

"I want to know who's the gutsiest and most impulsive of the three in there."

"Maybe they're drawing straws."

"No. My guess is that two of them wouldn't go out there for any money and the third can't wait. I want to see who that third one is. That's why I didn't ask for Handy specifically."

"I bet it's him, though," Budd said.

But it wasn't. The door opened and Shepard Wilcox walked out.

Potter studied him through the binoculars.

Taking a casual stroll. Looking around the field. Wilcox sauntered toward the phone. A pistol butt protruded from the middle of his belt. "Looks like a Glock," Potter said of the gun.

LeBow wrote down the information in a small notebook, the data to be transcribed when he returned to the command post. He then whispered, "Thinks he's the Marlboro man."

"Looks pretty confident," Budd said. "But I suppose he's got all the cards."

"He's got *none* of the cards," the negotiator said softly. "But either one'll give you all the confidence in the world."

Wilcox snagged the strap of the phone's backpack and gazed again at the line of police cars. He was grinning.

Budd laughed. "It's like—"

The crack of the gunshot echoed through the field and with a soft *phump* the bullet slapped into the ground ten feet from Wilcox. In an instant he had the pistol in his hand and was firing toward the trees where the shot had come from.

"No!" cried Potter, who leapt up and raced into the field. Through the bullhorn he turned to the cops behind the squad cars, all of whom had drawn their pistols or lifted shotguns and chambered rounds. "Hold your fire!" He waved his hands madly. Wilcox fired twice at Potter. The first shot vanished into the cloudy sky. The second split a rock a yard from Potter's feet.

Stillwell was shouting into his throat mike, "No return fire! All unit commanders, no return fire!"

But there was return fire.

Dirt kicked up around Wilcox as he flung himself to the ground and with carefully placed shots shattered three police car windshields before reloading. Even under these frantic conditions Wilcox was a fine marksman. From a window of the slaughterhouse came the repeated explosions of a semiautomatic shotgun; pellets hissed through the air.

Potter remained standing, in plain view, waving his hands. "Stop your firing!"

Then, suddenly, complete silence fell over the field. The wind vanished for a moment and stillness descended. The hollow cry of a bird filled the gray afternoon; the sound was heartbreaking. The sweet smell of gunpowder and fulminate of mercury, from primers, was thick.

Gripping the phone, Wilcox backed toward the slaughterhouse.

To Stillwell, Potter called, "Find out who fired. Whoever fired the first shot—I want to see him in the van. The ones who fired afterwards—I want them off the field and I want everybody to know why they're being dismissed."

"Yessir." The sheriff nodded and hurried off.

Potter, still standing, turned the binoculars onto the slaughterhouse, hoping to catch a glimpse of the inside when Wilcox entered. He was scanning the ground floor when he observed a young woman looking through the window to the right of the slaughterhouse door. She was blond and seemed to be in her mid-twenties. Looking right at him. She was distracted for a moment, glanced into the bowels of the slaughterhouse then back to the field, terror in her eyes. Her mouth moved in a curious way—very broadly. She was saying something to him. He watched her lips. He couldn't figure out the message.

Potter turned aside and handed LeBow the binoculars. "Henry, fast. Who's that? You have any idea?"

LeBow had been inputting the identities of those hostages they had information about. But by the time he looked, the woman was gone. Potter described her.

"The oldest student's seventeen. It was probably one of the two teachers. I'd guess the younger one. Melanie Charrol. She's twenty-five. No other information on her yet."

Wilcox backed into the slaughterhouse. Potter saw nothing inside except blackness. The door slammed shut. Potter scanned the windows again, hoping to catch another glimpse of the young woman. But he saw nothing. He was silently duplicating the motion of her mouth. Lips pursed together, lower teeth touching the upper lips; lips pursed again, though differently, like in a kiss.

"We should make the call." LeBow touched Potter's elbow.

Potter nodded and the men hurried back to the van in silence, Budd behind them, glaring at one of the troopers who'd returned fire at Wilcox. Stillwell was reading the man the riot act.

Lips, teeth, lips. What were you trying to say? he wondered.

"Henry," Potter said. "Mark down: 'First contact with a hostage.' "

"Contact?"

"With Melanie Charrol."

"What was the communication?"

"I don't know yet. I just saw her lips move."

"Well—"

"Write it down. 'Message unknown.' "

"Okay."

"And add, 'Subject was removed from view before the threat management team leader could respond.' "

"Will do," replied meticulous Henry LeBow.

Inside the van Derek asked what happened but Potter ignored him. He snatched the phone from Tobe Geller and set it on the desk in front of him, cradled it between his hands.

He looked out through the thick window over the field, where the flurry of activity after the shooting had stopped completely. The front was now quiet; the errant officers—three of them—had been led off by Dean Stillwell, and on the field the remaining troopers and agents stood with dense anticipation and fear and joy at the prospect of battle—a joy possible because there're thirty of you for each of them, because you're standing behind a half-ton Detroit picket line and wearing an Owens-Corning body vest, a heavy gun at your side, and because your spouse awaits you in a cozy bungalow with a beer and hot casserole.

Arthur Potter looked out over this cool and windy afternoon, an afternoon with the taste of Halloween in the air despite the midsummer month.

It was about to begin.

He turned away from the window, pushed a rapid-dial button on the phone. Tobe flipped a switch and began the recording. He hit another button and the sound of the ringing crackled through a speaker above their heads.

The phone rang five times, ten, twenty.

Potter felt LeBow's head turn toward him.

Tobe crossed his fingers.

Then: *Click.*

"We've got an uplink," Tobe whispered.

"Yeah?" The voice rang through the speaker.

Potter took a deep breath.

"Lou Handy?"

"Yeah."

"This is Arthur Potter. I'm with the FBI. I'd like to talk to you."

"Lou, that shot, it was a mistake."

"Was it now?"

Potter listened carefully to the voice, laced with a slight accent, mountain, West Virginian. He heard self-confidence, derision, weariness. All three combined to scare him considerably.

"We had a man in a tree. He slipped. His weapon discharged accidentally. He'll be disciplined."

"You gonna shoot him?"

"It was purely an accident."

"Accidents're funny things." Handy chuckled. "I was in Leavenworth a few years back and this asshole worked in the laundry room choked to death on a half-dozen socks. Had to've been a accident. He wouldn't go chewing on socks on purpose. Who'd do that?"

Cool as ice, Potter thought.

"Maybe this was that kinda accident."

"This was a run-of-the-mill, U.S.-certified accident, Lou."

"Don't much care what it was. I'm shooting one of 'em. Eenie meenie miney . . ."

"Listen to me, Lou. . . ."

No answer.

"Can I call you Lou?"

"You got us surrounded, don'tcha? You got assholes in the trees with guns even if they can't sit on branches without falling. Guess you can call me what you fucking well like."

"Listen to me, Lou. This's a real tense situation here."

"Not for me it ain't. I ain't tense at all. Here's a pretty little blond one. No tits to speak of. Think I'll pick her."

He's playing with us. Eighty percent he's bluffing.

"Lou, Wilcox was in clear view. Our man was only eighty yards away, M-16 with a scope. Those troopers can drop a man at a thousand yards if they have to."

"But it's awful windy out there. Maybe your boy didn't compensate."

"If we'd've wanted your man dead he'd be dead."

"That don't matter. I keep telling you. Accident or not," he snarled, "gotta teach you people some manners."

The bluff factor dropped to sixty percent.

Stay calm, Potter warned himself. Out of the corner of his eye he watched young Derek Elb wipe his palms on his pants and stuff a piece of gum into his mouth. Budd paced irritatingly, looking out the window.

"Let's just put it down to a mishap, Lou, and get on with what we have to talk about."

"Talk about?" He sounded surprised. "Whatta we gotta talk about?"

"Oh, lots," Potter said cheerfully. "First of all, is everybody doing okay in there? You have any injuries? Anybody hurt?"

His instinct was to ask specifically about the girls but negotiators try never to talk about the hostages if possible. You have to make the HT think that the captives have no bargaining value.

"Shep's a little bent outta shape, as you'd imagine, but otherwise everybody's right as rain. Course, ask again in five minutes. One of 'em ain't gonna be feeling so good."

Potter wondered: What did she say to me? He pictured Melanie's face again. Lips, teeth, lips . . .

"You need any first-aid supplies?"

"Yeah."

"What?"

"A medevac chopper."

"That's kind of a tall order, Lou. I was thinking more bandages or morphine, something like that. Antiseptic."

"Morphine? That wouldn't be to make us all dopey, would it? You'd like that, bet."

"Oh, we wouldn't give you enough to dope you up, Lou. You need anything at all?"

"Yeah, I need to shoot somebody's what I need. Little blondie here. Put a bullet 'tween the tits she don't have."

"That wouldn't do anybody any good now, would it?"

Potter was thinking: He likes to talk. He's unstable but he likes to talk. That's always the first hurdle, sometimes insurmountable. The quiet ones are the most dangerous. The agent cocked his head and prepared to listen carefully. He had to get into Handy's mind. Fall into his speech patterns, guess what the man is going to say, how he's going to say it. Potter would play this game all night until, by the time things were resolved one way or another, part of him would *be* Louis Jeremiah Handy.

"What's your name again?" Handy asked.

"Arthur Potter."

"You go by Art?"

"Arthur, actually."

"Ain't you got the info on me?"

"Some. Not much."

Potter thought spontaneously: *I killed a guard escaping.*

"I killed me a guard when we were escaping. Didn't you know that?"

"Yes, I did."

Potter thought: *So the girl without any tits don't mean shit to me.*

"So killing this girl, little blondie here, it don't mean nothing to me."

Potter pushed a mute button—a special device on the phone, which cut off his voice without a click on the other end. "Who's he talking about?" he asked LeBow. "Which hostage? Blond, twelve or under?"

"I don't know yet," the intelligence officer responded. "We can't get a clear look inside and don't have enough information."

Into the phone he said, "Why d'you want to hurt anybody, Lou?"

He'll change the subject, Potter guessed.

But Handy said, "Why not?"

Theoretically Potter knew he should be talking about frivolous things, stretching out the conversation, winning the man over, making him laugh. Food, sports, the weather, conditions inside the slaughter-house, soft drinks. You never talked to the HTs about the incident it-self at first. But he was assessing the risk that Handy was about to kill the girl and the bluff ratio was down to thirty percent; he couldn't af-ford to chat about hamburgers and the White Sox.

"Lou, I don't think you want to kill anybody."

"How d'you figure?"

Potter managed a chuckle. "Well, if you start killing hostages I'll have to conclude that you're planning to kill them all anyway. That's when I send in our hostage rescue team to take you all out."

Handy was laughing softly. "*If* them boys was there."

Potter and LeBow frowned at each other. "Oh, they're here," Potter said. He nodded at the "Deceptions" side of the bulletin board and LeBow jotted, *Handy told that HRT is in place.*

"You're asking me to hold off killing her?"

"I'm asking you not to kill anyone."

"I don't know. Should I, shouldn't I? You know how that happens sometimes, you just don't know what you want? Pizza or a Big Mac? Just can't fucking decide."

Potter's heart stuttered for a moment, for it seemed to him that Handy was being honest: that he really couldn't decide what to do, and that if he spared the girl it wouldn't be Potter's reasoned talk that saved her but whim, pure and simple, on Handy's part.

"I'll tell you what, Lou. I'm apologizing to you for the gunshot. I'll give you my word it won't happen again. In exchange for that, will you agree not to shoot that girl?"

He's smart, calculating, always thinking, the agent concluded. There wasn't a thing psychotic about Handy that Potter could identify. He wrote on a sheet of paper *IQ?* and pushed it toward LeBow.

Don't have it.

Handy's humming came through the phone. It was a song that Potter had heard a long time ago. He couldn't place it. Then through the speaker the man's amplified voice said; "Maybe I'll wait."

Potter sighed. LeBow gave him a thumbs-up and Budd smiled.

"I appreciate that, Lou. I really do. How's your food situation?"

Are you for real? Potter speculated.

"What're you, first you play cop, then you play nurse, now you're a fucking caterer?" .

"I just want to keep everybody real calm and comfortable. Get you some sandwiches and sodas if you want. What do you say?"

"We're not hungry."

"Could be a long night."

Either: silence or *Won't be that long at all.*

"Don't think it's gonna be that long. Listen here, Art, you can chat me up 'bout food and medicine and any other crap you can think of. But the fact is we've got some things we're gonna want and we better have 'em without no hassles or I start killing. One by one."

"Okay, Lou. Tell me what they are."

"We'll do some talking here between us. And get back to you."

"Who's 'us,' Lou?"

"Aw, shit, you know, Art. There's me and Shep and my two brothers."

LeBow tapped Potter's arm. He was pointing to the screen. It read:

Handy is one of three brothers. Bench warrant out on Robert, 27. LKA, Seattle; failed to appear for grand larceny trial, fled jurisdiction. Eldest brother, Rudy, 40, was killed five years ago. Shot six times in the back of head by unknown assailant. Handy was suspected; never charged.

Potter thought of the delicate lines on his genealogy charts. What would Handy's look like; from whom did his blood descend? "Your brothers, Lou?" he said. "Is that right? They're inside with you?"

A pause.

"And Shep's four cousins."

"That's a lot of folk you got there. Anybody else?"

"Doc Holliday and Bonnie 'n' Clyde and Ted Bundy and a shitload of the gang from Mortal Kombat, and Luke Skywalker. And Jeffrey Dahmer's hungry ghost."

"Maybe we better surrender to *you*, Lou."

Handy laughed again. Potter was pleased at the sliver of rapport. Pleased too that he managed to say the magic word "surrender," plant it in Handy's thoughts.

"My nephew collects superhero comics," the agent said. "He'd love an autograph. Spider-Man wouldn't be in there too, would he?"

"Might just be."

The fax machine whirred and a number of sheets scrolled out. LeBow snatched them up and flipped through them rapidly, paused at one and then scribbled on the top, *HOSTAGES*. He pointed to a girl's name, followed by a block of handwritten text. It was preliminary data from Angie Scapello.

Hostage negotiation is the process of testing limits. Potter read the fax and noticed something. He said casually, "Say, Lou, like to ask you a question. One of those girls in there's got some serious health problems. Would you let her go?"

It was surprising how often direct requests of this sort worked. Ask a question and go silent.

"Really?" Handy sounded concerned. "Sick, huh? What's the trouble?"

"Asthma." Maybe the joking and the cartoon-character chat was having an effect on Handy.

"Which one is she?"

"Fourteen, short blond hair."

Potter listened to the background noise—just hollowness—as Handy, he assumed, looked over the hostages.

"If she doesn't get her medicine she could die," Potter said. "You release her, you do that for me, and when we get down to the serious negotiating I'll remember it. Tell you what, release her and we'll get you some electricity in there. Some lights."

"You'll turn the power on?" Handy asked so suddenly it startled Potter.

"We checked into that. The place is too old. It's not wired for modern current." Potter pointed to the "Deceptions" board and LeBow wrote. "But we'll run a line in and get you some lights."

"Do that and then we'll talk."

The balance of power was shifting subtly to Handy. Time to be tough. "All right. Fair enough. Now listen, Lou, I have to warn you. Don't try to get out of the building. There'll be snipers sighting on you. You're perfectly safe inside."

He'll be angry, Potter anticipated. A mini tantrum. Obscenities and expletives.

"Oh, I'm perfectly safe anywhere," Handy whispered into the phone. "Bullets pass right through me. I have strong medicine. When do I get some lights?"

"Ten minutes, fifteen. Give us Beverly, Lou. If you do—"

Click.

"Damn," Potter muttered.

"Little eager there, Arthur," LeBow said. Potter nodded. He'd made the classic mistake of negotiating against himself. Always wait for the other side to ask you for something. Understandably he'd pushed when he heard Handy's hesitation and upped the stakes himself. But he'd scared off the seller. Still, at some point he'd have to go through this exercise. Hostage takers can be pushed a certain distance, and bribed a certain amount further. Half the battle was finding out how far and when to do which.

Potter called Stillwell and told him he'd warned the takers about leaving the slaughterhouse. "You're green-lighted to contain them, as discussed."

"Yessir," Stillwell said.

Potter asked Budd, "What's the ETA on that power truck?"

"Should be just ten minutes." He was looking out the window morosely.

"What's the matter, Charlie?"

"Oh, nothing. I was just thinking that was good what you did there. Talking him out of shooting her."

Potter sensed there was something else on Budd's mind. But he said only, "Oh, Handy was the one who decided not to shoot. I had nothing to do with it. The problem is, I don't know why yet."

Potter waited five minutes, then pushed speed dial.

The phone rang a million times. "Could you please turn that down a little, Tobe?" Potter nodded at the speaker above his head.

"Sure. . . . Okay, uplink."

"Yeah?" Handy barked.

"Lou, you'll have a power line in about ten minutes."

Silence.

"What about the girl, Beverly?"

"Can't have her," he said abruptly, as if surprised that Potter hadn't figured this out yet.

Silence for a moment.

"Thought you said if you got power—"

"I'd think about it. I did, and you can't have her."

Never get drawn into petty bickering. "Well, have you done any thinking about what you fellows want?"

"I'll get back to you on that, Art."

"I was hoping—"

Click.

"Downlink terminated," Tobe announced.

Stillwell brought the trooper in, a short, swarthy young man. He leaned the offending weapon by the door, its black bolt locked back, and walked up to Potter.

"I'm sorry, sir, I was on this branch and there was this gust of wind. I—"

"You were told to unchamber your weapon," Potter snapped.

The trooper stirred and his eyes darted around the room.

"Here now," Stillwell said, looking faintly ridiculous with a bulky flak jacket on under his Penney's suit. "Tell the agent what you told me."

The trooper looked icily at Stillwell, resenting the new chain of command. He said to Potter, "I never received that order. I was locked and loaded from the git-go. That's SOP for us, sir."

Stillwell grimaced but he said, "I'll take responsibility, Mr. Potter."

"Oh, brother. . . ." Charlie Budd stepped forward. "Sir," he said formally to Potter, "I have to say—it's my fault. Mine alone."

Potter lifted an inquiring hand toward him.

"I didn't tell the snipers to unchamber. I should've, like you ordered me to. The fact is, I concluded that I wasn't going to have troopers in the field unprotected. It's my fault. Not this man's. Not Dean's."

Potter considered this and said to the sniper, "You'll stand down and assist at the rear staging area. Go report to Agent-in-Charge Henderson."

"But I slipped, sir. It wasn't my fault. It was an accident."

"There're no accidents in my barricades," Potter said coldly.

"But—"

"That's all, Trooper," Dean Stillwell said. "You heard your order. Dismissed." The man snagged his weapon then stormed out of the van.

Budd said, "I'll do the same, sir. I'm sorry. I really am. You should have Dean here assist you. I—"

Potter pulled the captain aside. He said in a whisper, "I need your help, Charlie. But what you did, it was a personal judgment call. That, I *don't* need from you. Understand?"

"Yessir."

"You still want to be on the team?"

Budd nodded slowly.

"Okay, now go on out there and give them the order to unchamber."

"Sir—"

"Arthur."

"I've got to go home and look my wife in the eye and tell her that I disobeyed an FBI agent's direct order."

"How long you been married?"

"Thirteen years."

"Get hitched in junior high?"

Budd smiled grimly.

"What's her name?"

"Meg. Margaret."

"You have children?"

"Two girls." Budd's face remained miserable.

"Go on now. Do what I asked." Potter held his eyes.

The captain sighed. "I will, yessir. It won't happen again."

"Keep your head down." Potter smiled. "And don't delegate this one, Charlie."

"No sir. I'll check everybody."

Stillwell looked on sympathetically as Budd, hangtail, walked out the door.

Tobe was stacking up audiocassettes. All conversations with the takers would be recorded. The tape recorder was a special unit with a two-second delay built in, so that an electronic voice added a minute-by-minute time stamp onto the recording yet didn't block out the conversation. He looked up at Potter. "Who was it who said, 'I've met the enemy and he is us'? Was that Napoleon? Or Eisenhower, or somebody?"

"I think it was Pogo," Potter said.

"Who?"

"Comic strip," Henry LeBow said. "Before your time."

12:33 P.M.

The room was growing dark.

It was only early afternoon but the sky had filled with purple clouds and the windows in the slaughterhouse were small. Need that juice and need it now, Lou Handy thought, peering through the dimness.

Water dripped and chains hung from the gloomy shadows of the ceiling. Hooks everywhere and overhead conveyors. There were rusted machines that looked like parts of cars a giant had been playing with and said fuck it and tossed down on the floor.

Giant, Handy laughed to himself. What the hell'm I talking about?

He wandered through the ground floor. Wild place. What's it like to make money knocking off animals? he wondered. Handy had worked dozens of jobs. Usually sweat labor. Nobody ever let him operate fancy equipment, which would have doubled or tripled his salary. The jobs always ended after a month or two. Arguments with the foreman, complaints, fights, drinking in the locker room. He had no patience to wait it out with people who couldn't understood that he wasn't your average person. He was *special*. Nofuckingbody in the world had ever caught on to this.

The floor was wood, solid as concrete. Beautifully joined oak. Handy was no craftsman, like Rudy'd been, but he could appreciate good work. His brother had laid flooring for a living. Handy was suddenly angry at that asshole Potter. For some reason the agent had brought Rudy to mind. It infuriated Handy, made him want to get even.

He walked to the room where they'd put the hostages. It was semicircular, sided in porcelain tile, windowless. The blood drain. He guessed that if somebody fired a gun in the middle of the room it'd be loud enough to shatter eardrums.

Didn't much matter with this buncha birds, he thought. He looked them over. What was weird was that these girls—most of 'em—were *pretty*. That oldest one especially, the one with the black hair. The one looking back at him with a go-to-fucking-hell expression on her face. She's what, seventeen, eighteen? He smiled at her. She stared back. Handy gazed at the rest of them. Yep, pretty. It blew him away. They're freaks and all and you'd think they'd look a little gross, like retards do— like no matter how pretty, there's still something wrong, the corners don't meet even. But no, they looked normal. But damn, they cry a lot. *That* was irritating . . . that sound their throats make. They're fucking deaf— they shouldn't be making those fucking sounds!

Suddenly, in his mind, Lou Handy saw his brother.

The red dot appearing where Rudy's skull joined his spine. Then more dots, the tiny gun bucking in his fingers. The shudder in his brother's shoulders as the man stiffened, did a spooky little dance, and fell dead.

Handy decided he hated Art Potter even more than he'd thought.

He ambled back to Wilcox and Bonner, pulled the remote control out of the canvas bag, and channel-surfed on the tiny battery-powered TV that rested on an oil drum. All the local stations and one network were reporting about them. One newscaster said this would be Lou Handy's fifteen minutes of fame, whatever the hell that meant. The cops had ordered the reporters so far back from the action that he couldn't see anything helpful on the screen. He remembered the O. J. Simpson case, watching the white Bronco cruise down the highway, park at the man's house. The choppers were close enough to see the faces of the guy who was driving and the cop in his driveway. Everybody white in the prison rec room thinking, Blow your fucking brains out, nigger. Everybody black thinking, Go, O.J.! We're with you, homes!

Handy turned down the sound on the TV. Fucking place, he thought, looking around the slaughterhouse. He smelled rotting carcasses.

A voice startled him, "Let them go. Keep me."

He wandered over to the tiled room. He crouched down and looked at the woman. "Who're you?"

"I'm their teacher."

"You can do that sign language stuff, right?"

"Yes." She gazed at Handy with defiant eyes.

"Uck," Handy said. "Freaky."

"Please, let them go. Keep me."

"Shut up," Handy said, and walked away.

He looked out the window. A tall police van sat on the crest of a hill. He bet that was where Art Potter was sitting. He took his pistol from his pocket and aimed at a yellow square on its side. He compensated for the distance and the wind. He lowered the gun. "Coulda nailed you, they wanted to," he called to Wilcox. "That's what he told me."

Wilcox too was gazing out a window. "There's a lot of 'em," he mused. Then: "Who was he? Th'asshole you were talking to."

"FBI."

Bonner said, "Oh, man. You mean we got a Feebie out there?"

"Was a federal prison we broke outta. Who the fuck you think they'd have after us?"

"Tommy Lee Jones," Bonner said. The big man kept his eyes on the teacher for a moment. Then on the little girl in the flowered dress and white stockings.

Handy saw his eyes. That cocksucker. "Nup, Sonny. Keep it inside them stinky jeans of yours, you hear me? Or you'll lose it."

Bonner grunted. When accused of doing just what he was guilty of Bonner always got pissed. Fast as a hedgehog rolls up. "Fuck you."

"Hope I gave one of 'em a new asshole," Wilcox said, but in his lazy-as-could-be voice, one of the reasons why Handy liked him.

"So what've we got?" Handy asked.

Wilcox answered, "The two shotguns. And close to forty shells. One Smitty only six rounds. No, make that five. But we've got the Glocks and beaucoup de ammo there. Three hundred rounds."

Handy paced around the slaughterhouse floor, dancing over the pools of standing water.

"Damn cryin's getting on my nerves," Handy snapped. "It's fucking with my mind. That fat one, shit. Lookit her. And I don't know what's going on out there. That agent sounded too slick. I don't trust his ass. Sonny, you stay with our girls. Shep 'n' me're gonna poke around."

"What about tear gas?" Bonner looked out the window uncertainly. "We shoulda got some masks."

"They shoot tear gas in," Handy explained, "just piss on the canisters."

"That works? To stop it?"

"Yep."

"How 'bout that."

Handy glanced into the tiled room. The older teacher gazed at him with her muddy eyes. Sort of defiant, sort of something else.

"What's your name?"

"Donna Harstrawn. I—"

"Tell me, Donna, what's her name?" he asked slowly, pointing to the oldest student, the pretty one with the long black hair.

Before the teacher could answer, the girl lifted her middle finger toward him. Handy roared with laughter.

Bonner stepped forward, lifting his arm. "You little shit."

Donna scrambled in front of the girl, who drew back her fists, grinning. The little girls made their fucking spooky bird noises and the scared blond teacher held up a pitiful, pleading hand.

Handy grabbed Bonner's hand and pushed him away. "Don't hit 'em 'less I tell you to." He pointed at the teenager and asked the teacher, "What's her fucking name?"

"Susan. Please, will you—"

"And what's hers?" Pointing at the blond, the younger teacher.

"Melanie."

Mel-a-nee. She was the one that really pissed him off. When he'd found her looking out the window just after the shooting he'd grabbed her arm and she'd gone apeshit, totally freaked. He'd let her wander around 'cause he knew she wouldn't cause any trouble. At first he'd thought it was funny, her being such a little mouse. Then it made him mad—that skittish light in her eyes that made him want to stamp his foot just to see her jump. It *always* pissed him off, seeing no spirit in a woman.

This little bitch was the opposite of Pris. Oh, he'd like to see the two of them tangle. Pris'd pull out that Buck knife she kept down her bra sometimes, hot against her left tit, open it up, and come after her. Little blondie here'd take a dump in her pants. She seemed a hell of a lot younger than that Susan.

Now, *she* interested him, Suze did. Good old Donna had her muddy eyes that told him nothing, and the younger teacher had her scared eyes that hid everything. But Miss Teenager here . . . well, her eyes said a lot and she didn't care if he read it. He figured that she was smarter than the other two put together.

And ballsier.

Like Pris, he thought, with approval. "Susan," Handy said slowly. "I like you. You've got spunk. You don't know what the fuck I'm saying. But I like you." To the older teacher he said, "Tell her that."

After a pause Donna gestured with her hands.

Susan gave him a drop-dead look and responded.

"What'd she say?" Handy barked.

"She said to please let the little girls go."

Handy grabbed the woman's hair and pulled hard. More little bird screeches. Melanie shook her head, tears streaming. "What the fuck did she say?"

"She said, 'Go to hell.' "

He pulled her hair harder; tufts of the dyed strands popped from her skull. She whined in pain. "She said," Donna gasped, "she said, 'You're an asshole.' "

Handy laughed hard and shoved the teacher to the ground.

"Please," she called. "Let them go, the girls. Keep me. What does it matter if you have one hostage or six?"

"Because, you stupid cunt, I can shoot a couple of 'em and still have some left over."

She gasped and turned away quickly, as if she'd just walked into a room and found a naked man leering at her.

Handy walked to Melanie. "You think I'm an asshole too?"

The other teacher started to move her hands but Melanie responded before she'd gotten the question out.

"What'd she say?"

"She said, 'Why do you want to hurt us, Brutus? We didn't hurt you.' "

"Brutus?"

"That's what she calls you."

Brutus. Sounded familiar but he couldn't remember where he'd heard it. He frowned slightly. "Tell her she knows the fucking answer to that question." As he walked out the doorway Handy called, "Hey, Sonny, I'm learning sign language. Lemme show you."

Bonner looked up.

Handy extended his middle finger. The three men laughed and Handy and Wilcox started down the corridor into the back of the slaughterhouse. When they were exploring the maze of hallways and butcher and processing rooms Handy asked Wilcox, "Think he'll behave?"

"Sonny? Fuck, I guess. Any other time he'd be on 'em like a rooster. But there ain't nothing like having a hundred armed cops outside your door to keep a pecker limp. What the fuck d'they do here?" Wilcox was gazing at the machinery, the long tables, gears and governors and belts.

"Whatta you think?"

"I don't know."

"It's a fucking slaughterhouse."

" 'Processing,' that's what it means?"

"Shoot 'em and gut 'em. Yeah. Processing."

Wilcox pointed to an old machine. "What's that?"

Handy walked over and looked at it. He grinned. "Shit. It's a old steam engine. Hell, lookit."

"What'd they use that for here?"

"See," Handy explained, "this is why the world's got itself into deep shit. Back then, see, that was a turbine." He pointed to an old rusted spine covered with rotting fan blades. "That was how things worked. It went around and did things. That was the steam age and it was like the gas age too. Then we got into the electric age and you couldn't see what things did too well. Like you can see steam and fire but you can't see electricity doing anything. That's what got us into World War Two. Now we're in the *electronic* age. It's computers and everything and it's fucking impossible to see how things work. You can look at a computer chip and not see a thing even though it's totally doing what it oughta do. We've lost control."

"It's all pretty fucked up."

"What? Life or what I'm saying?"

"I don't know. It just sounds all fucked up. Life, I guess."

They'd emerged into a large dim cavern. Must have been the warehouse. They tied or chocked shut the back doors.

"They can blow 'em open," Wilcox said. "A couple cutting charges'd do it."

"They could drop an A-bomb on us too. Either way them girls die. If that's what they want that's what they'll get."

"Elevator?"

"Nothing much we can do 'bout that," Handy said, looking at the big service elevator. "They wanta come rappelling in, we can get the first half-dozen of 'em. You know, their necks. Always aim for their necks."

Wilcox glanced at him then drawled, "So, whatcha thinking?"

I do get that look in my eyes, Handy thought. Pris says so all the time. Damn, he missed her. He wanted to smell her hair, listen to the sound of her bracelet as she shifted gears in her car, wanted to feel her underneath him as they fucked on the shag carpet of her apartment.

"Let's send one back to 'em," Handy said.

"One of the girls?"

"Yeah."

"Which one?"

"I don't know. That Susan maybe. She's all right. I like her."

Wilcox said, "I'd vote her most likely to hump. Not a bad idea to get her out of Bonner's sight. He'd be sniffing her lickety-split 'fore sunset. Or that other one, Melanie."

Handy said, "Naw, let's keep her. We oughta hang on to the weak ones."

"Second that."

"Okay, it'll be Susan." He laughed. "Not many girls around can look me in the eye and tell me I'm an asshole, I'll tell you that."

Melanie kept her arm tight around Kielle's shoulders, which were oddly muscular for an eight-year-old, and reached out a little further to rub the arm of one of the twins.

The girls were sandwiched in between her and Susan, and Melanie admitted reluctantly to herself that her gesture was only partially to re-assure the younger ones; she also wanted the comfort for herself, the comfort of being close to her favorite student.

Melanie's hands were still shaking. She'd been unnerved when Brutus had grabbed her earlier as she was looking out the window, sending her message to the policeman in the field. And downright terrified when he'd pointed at her a few minutes ago and demanded to know her name.

She glanced at Susan and saw her looking angrily at Mrs. Harstrawn.

"What's the matter?" Melanie signed.

"My name. Giving it to him. Shouldn't have done that. Don't cooperate."

"We have to," the older teacher signed.

Melanie added, "Can't make them mad at us."

Susan laughed derisively. "What difference does it make if they're mad? Don't give in. They're assholes. They're worst type of Other."

"We can't—" Melanie began.

Bear stamped his foot. Melanie felt the vibrations and jumped. His fat lips were working fast and all she could make out was "Shut up." Melanie looked away. She couldn't stand the sight of his face, the way the black hairs at the edge of his beard curled outward, his fat pores.

His eyes kept returning to Mrs. Harstrawn. And Emily.

When he looked away Melanie slowly brought her hand up and switched from American Sign Language to Signed Exact English and fingerspelling. This was a clumsy way of communicating—she had to spell out words and put them into English word order. But it allowed the use of small hand motions and avoided the broad gestures necessary to communicate in ASL.

"Don't make them mad," she told Susan. "Take it easy."

"They're assholes." Susan refused to switch from ASL.

"Sure. But don't provoke!"

"They won't hurt us. We're no good to them dead."

Exasperated, Melanie said, "They can hurt us without killing us."

Susan just grimaced and looked away.

Well, what does she want us to do? Melanie thought angrily. Grab their guns away and shoot them? Yet at the same time she thought: Oh, why can't I be like her? Look at her eyes! How strong she is! She's eight years younger than me but I feel like the child when I'm around her.

Some of her envy could be attributed to the fact that Susan was the highest in the hierarchy of the world of the Deaf. She was prelingually deaf—born deaf. But more than that, she was Deaf of Deaf: both her parents had been deaf. Politically active in Deaf issues even at seventeen, accepted at Gallaudet in Washington, D.C., on a full scholarship, unyielding about the use of ASL versus SEE, militantly rejecting oralism—the practice of forcing the deaf to try to speak. Susan Phillips was the chic, up-to-the-minute Deaf young woman, beautiful and strong, and Melanie would rather have one Susan by her side at a time like this than a roomful of men.

She felt a small hand tug at her blouse.

"Don't worry," she signed to Anna. The twins hugged each other, their cheeks together, their remarkable eyes wide and tearful. Beverly sat by herself, her hands in her lap, and stared mournfully at the floor, struggling to breathe.

Kielle signed, "We need Jean Grey and Cyclops," referring to two of her favorite X-Men. "They'd tear them apart."

Shannon responded, "No, we need Beast. Remember? He had the blind girlfriend?" Shannon studied Jack Kirby's art religiously and intended to be a superhero-comic artist.

"Gambit too," Kielle signed. Pointing to Shannon's tattoo.

Shannon's own comics—surprisingly good, Melanie thought, for an eight-year-old—featured characters with disabilities, like blindness and deafness, that they could mutate to their advantage as they solved crimes and saved people. The two girls—Shannon, gangly and dark; Kielle, compact and fair—fell into a discussion of whether optic blasts, plasmoids, or psychic blades would be the weapons of choice to save them now.

Emily cried for a moment into the sleeve of her dress, printed with black and purple flowers. Then she bowed her head, praying. Melanie saw her two fists lift and open outward. It was the ASL word for "sacrifice."

"Don't worry," Melanie repeated to those girls who were looking at her. But no one paid attention. If they focused on anyone it was on Susan though the girl was signing nothing, merely gazing steadily at Bear, who stood near the entrance to the killing room. Susan was their rallying point. Her presence alone gave them confidence. Melanie found herself struggling to keep from crying.

And it'll be so dark in here tonight!

Melanie leaned forward and looked out the window. She saw the grass bending in the wind. The Kansas wind, relentless. Melanie remembered her father telling her about the sea captain Edward Smith, who came to Wichita in the 1800s and got the idea of mounting sails on Conestoga wagons—literally prairie schooners. She'd laughed at the idea and at her father's humorous telling of the tale, never knowing whether to believe it or not. Now, she was stung at the memory of the storytelling and wished desperately for anything, mythical or real, to sweep her away from the killing room.

She thought suddenly: And what about that man outside? The policeman?

There had been something so reassuring in the way he'd stood up there on the hill after Brutus had fired his gun out the window and Bear was running around, his fat belly jiggling, ripping open boxes of bullets in a panic. The man stood on the hilltop waving his arms, trying to calm things down, stop the shooting. He was looking directly at her.

What would she call him? No animals came to mind. Nothing sleek and heroic anyway. He was old—twice her age probably. And he dressed frumpy. His glasses seemed thick and he was a few pounds heavy.

Then it occurred to her. De l'Epée.

That's what she'd call him. After Charles Michel de l'Epée, the eighteenth-century abbé who was one of the first people in the world to really care about the Deaf, to treat them as intelligent human beings. The man who created French Sign Language, the predecessor of ASL.

It was a perfect name for the man in the field, thought Melanie, who could read French and knew that the name itself meant a kind of sword. Her de l'Epée was brave. Just the way his namesake had stood up to the Church and the popular sentiment that the Deaf were retarded and freaks, he was standing up to Stoat and Brutus, up there on the hill, bullets flying around him.

Well, she *had* sent him a message—a prayer, in a way. A prayer and a warning. Had he seen her? Could he understand what she'd said even if he had? She closed her eyes for a brief moment, concentrating all her thoughts on de l'Epée. But all she sensed was the temperature, which had grown cooler, her fear, and—to her dismay—the vibration of footsteps as a man, no, *two* men, approached slowly over the resonant oak floor.

As Brutus and Stoat appeared in the doorway Melanie glanced at Susan, whose face hardened once again, looking up at their captors.

I'll make my face hard too.

She tried but it trembled and soon she was crying again.

Susan! Why can't I be like you?

Bear walked up to the other men. He was gesturing to the main room. The light was dim and the phony science of lipreading gave her a distorted message. She believed he said something about the phone.

Brutus responded, "So let the fucker ring."

This was very strange, Melanie reflected, as the urge to cry diminished. Why, she thought again, can I understand *him* so well? Why him and not the others?

"We're going to send one back."

Bear asked a question.

Brutus answered, "Miss Deaf Teen." He nodded at Susan. Mrs. Harstrawn's face blossomed with relief.

My God, thought Melanie in despair, they're going to let her go! We'll be here all alone without her. Without Susan! No! She choked a sob.

"Stand up, honey," Brutus said. "Your . . . day. You're going home."

Susan was shaking her head. She turned to Mrs. Harstrawn and signed a defiant message, with her fast, crisp signing. "She says she isn't going. She wants you to release the twins."

Brutus laughed. "She wants me. . . ."

Stoat said, "Get . . . up." He pulled Susan to her feet.

And then Melanie's heart was pounding, her face burned red, for, to her horror, she realized that the first thought in her mind was: Why couldn't it have been me?

Forgive me, God. De l'Epée, please forgive me! But then she made her shameful wish once again. And again still. It looped through her mind endlessly. I want to go home. I want to sit down by myself with a big bowl of popcorn, I want to watch closed-captioned TV, I want to clap the Koss headsets around my ears and feel the vibrations of Beethoven and Smetana and Gordon Bok. . . .

Susan struggled away from Stoat's grip. She thrust the twins toward him. But he pushed the little girls aside and brutally tied Susan's hands behind her. Brutus stared out through the half-open window. "Hold up here," Brutus said, pushing Susan to the floor beside the door. He glanced back. "Sonny, go keep our lady friends company . . . that scatter-gun with you."

Susan looked back into the killing room.

In the girl's face Melanie saw the message: Don't worry. You'll be all right. I'll see to it.

Melanie held her gaze for only a moment then looked away, afraid that Susan would read her own thoughts and would see in them the shameful question: Why can't it be me, why can't it be me, why can't it be me?

1:01 P.M.

Arthur Potter gazed at the slaughterhouse and the fields surrounding it through the jaundice glass of the van's window. He was watching a trooper run the electrical line up to the front door. Five caged lights hung from the end of the cable. The officer backed away and Wilcox came out once more, pistol in hand, to retrieve the wire. He didn't, as Potter had hoped, run the line through the door, which would then have to remain open, but fed it through a window. He returned inside and the thick metal door swung tightly shut.

"Door is still secure," the negotiator said absently, and LeBow typed.

More faxes arrived. More background on Handy and on the hostages from the school the girls attended. LeBow greedily looked over the sheets and entered relevant data in the "Profiles" computer. The engineering and architect's diagrams had been transmitted. They were helpful only for the negatives they presented—how hard an assault would be. There were no tunnels leading into the slaughterhouse and if the P&Z variance documents from 1938 were accurate there had been significant construction on the roof of the building—with plans to create a fourth story—which would make a helicopter assault very difficult.

Tobe stiffened suddenly. "They've popped the cover on the phone." His eyes stared intently at a row of dials.

"Is it still working?"

"So far."

Looking for bugs.

The young agent relaxed. "It's back together again. Whoever did it knows his equipment."

"Henry, who?"

"No way of knowing yet. I'd have to guess Handy. The military training, you know."

"Downlink," Tobe called.

Potter lifted a curious eyebrow at LeBow and picked up the phone as it rang.

"Hello. That you, Lou?"

"Thanks for the lights. We checked 'em for microphones . . . the phone too. Didn't find a fucking thing. A man of your word."

Honor. It means something to him, Potter noted, trying once again to comprehend the unfathomable.

"Say, what are you, Art, a senior agent? Agent in Charge? That's what they call 'em, right?"

Never let the HT think you're in a position to make important decisions by yourself. You want the option to stall while you pretend to talk to your superiors.

"Nope. Just a run-of-the-mill special agent who happens to like talking."

"So you say."

"I'm a man of my word, remember?" Potter said, glancing at the "Deceptions" board.

Time to defuse things, build up some rapport. "So what about some food, Lou? We could start grilling up some burgers. How do you like 'em?"

Blood red, Potter speculated.

But he was wrong.

"Listen up, Art. I just want you to know what kind of nice fellow I am. I'm letting one of 'em go."

This news depressed Potter immeasurably. Curiously, with this act of spontaneous generosity, Handy had put them on the defensive. It was tactically brilliant. Potter was now indebted to him and he felt again a shift in the balance of power between predator and prey.

"I want you to understand that I ain't all bad."

"Well, Lou, I appreciate that. Is it Beverly? The sick girl?"

"Uh-uh."

Potter and the other cops craned forward to look outside. They could see a slight splinter of light as the door opened. Then a blur of white.

Keep his mind off the hostages, Potter thought. "You done any more thinking about what you folks're interested in? It's time to get down to some serious horse trading, Lou. What do you say—"

The phone clicked into dull static.

The door to the van suddenly swung open. Dean Stillwell's head poked in. The sheriff said, "They're releasing one of them."

"We know."

Stillwell disappeared outside again.

Potter spun about in the swivel chair. He couldn't see clearly. The clouds were very dense now and the fields dim, as if an eclipse had suddenly dipped the earth into shadow.

"Let's try the video, Tobe."

A video screen burst to life, showing in crisp black-and-white the front of the slaughterhouse. The door was open. They had all five lamps burning, it seemed.

Tobe adjusted the sensitivity and the picture settled.

"Who, Henry?"

"It's the older girl, Susan Phillips. Seventeen."

Budd laughed. "Hey, looks like it may be easier than we thought. If he's just gonna give 'em away."

On the screen Susan looked back into the doorway. A hand pushed her forward. Then the door closed.

"This is great," LeBow said enthusiastically, looking out the window, his head close to Potter's. "Seventeen. And she's a top student. She'll tell us a truckload of stuff about the inside."

The girl walked in a straight line away from the building. Through the glasses Potter could see how grim her face was. Her hands were tied behind her but she didn't seem to have suffered from the brief captivity.

"Dean," Potter said into the radio microphone, "send one of your men to meet her."

"Yessir." The sheriff was now speaking in a normal tone into his throat mike; he'd finally gotten the hang of the gear.

A state trooper in body armor and helmet slipped from behind a squad car and cautiously started in a crouch toward the girl, who'd made her way fifty feet from the slaughterhouse.

The gasp came from deep in Arthur Potter's throat.

As if his whole body'd been submerged in ice water he shuddered, understanding perfectly what was happening.

It was intuition probably, a feeling gleaned from the hundreds of barricades he'd negotiated. The fact that no taker had ever spontaneously released a hostage this early. The fact that Handy was a killer without remorse.

He couldn't say for sure what tipped him but the absolute horror of what was about to occur gripped his heart. "No!" The negotiator leapt to his feet, knocking the chair over with a huge crash.

LeBow glanced at him. "Oh, no! Oh, Christ, no."

Charlie Budd's head swiveled back and forth. He whispered, "What's wrong? What's going on?"

"He's going to kill her," LeBow whispered.

Potter tore the door open and ran outside, his heart slugging away in his chest. Snatching a flak jacket from the ground, he slipped between two cars and, gasping, ran straight toward the girl, passing the man Dean Stillwell had sent to meet her. His urgency made the troopers in the field uneasy but some of them smiled at the sight of the pudgy man running, holding the heavy flak jacket in one hand and waving a white Kleenex in the other.

Susan was forty feet from him, walking steadily over the grass. She adjusted her course slightly so they would meet.

"Get down, drop down!" Potter cried. He released the tissue, which floated ahead of him on the fast breeze, and he gestured madly at the ground. "Down! Get down!"

But she couldn't hear, of course, and merely frowned.

Several of the troopers had heard Potter and stepped away from the cars they were using as cover. Reaching tentatively for their guns.

Potter's shouts were joined by others. One woman trooper waved madly. "No, no, honey! Get down, for the love of God!"

Susan never heard a word of it. She'd stopped and was looking carefully at the ground, perhaps thinking that he was warning her about a hidden well or wire she might trip over.

Gasping, his middle-aged heart in agony, Potter narrowed the gap to fifteen feet.

The agent was so close that when the single bullet struck her squarely in the back, and a flower of dark red blossomed over her right breast, he heard the nauseating sound of the impact, followed by an unworldly groan from deep within a throat unaccustomed to speaking.

She stopped abruptly then spiraled to the ground.

No, no, no . . .

Potter ran to the girl and propped the flak jacket around her head. The trooper ran up, crouching, muttering, "My God, my God," over and over. He aimed his pistol toward the window.

"Don't shoot," Potter commanded.

"But—"

"No!" Potter lifted his gaze from Susan's dull eyes to the slaughterhouse. He saw in the window just to the left of the door the lean face of Lou Handy. And through the right, perhaps thirty feet inside the dim interior, the negotiator could make out the stunned face of the young teacher, the blond one, who'd sent him the cryptic message earlier and whose name he could not now recall.

You feel sounds.

Sound is merely a disturbance of air, a vibration, and it laps upon our bodies like waves, it touches our brows like a lover's hand, it stings and it can make us cry.

Within her chest she still felt the sound of the gunshot.

No, Melanie thought. No. This isn't possible.

It *can't* be. . . .

But she knew what she'd seen. She didn't trust voices but her eyes were rarely wrong.

Susan, Deaf of Deaf.

Susan, braver than I could ever be.

Susan, who had the world of the Deaf and the world of the Others at her feet.

The girl had stepped into the horrible Outside and it had killed her. She was gone forever. A tiny hole opening in her back, kicking aside her dark hair. The abrupt halt as she walked the route that Melanie had shamefully prayed that she herself would be walking.

Melanie's breath grew shallow and the edges of her vision crumbled to blackness. The room tilted and sweat appeared in sheets on her face and neck. She turned slowly and looked at Brutus, who was slipping the still-smoking pistol into his waistband. What she saw filled her with hopelessness. For she could see no satisfaction, no lust, no malice. She saw only that he'd done what he planned to—and had already forgotten about the girl's death.

He clicked on the TV again and glanced toward the killing room, in whose doorway the seven girls stood or sat in a ragged line, some staring at Melanie, some staring at Mrs. Harstrawn, who had collapsed on the floor, sobbing, gripping her hair, her face contorted like a hideous red mask. The teacher had apparently seen the gunshot and understood what it meant. The other girls had not. Jocylyn wiped from her face a sheet of her dark hair, unfortunately self-cut. She lifted her hands, signing repeatedly, "What happened? What happened? What happened?"

I have to tell them, Melanie thought.

But I can't.

Beverly, the next oldest after Susan, understood something terrible had occurred but didn't quite know—or admit—what. She took Jocylyn's pudgy hand and gazed at Melanie. She sucked air deep into her damaged lungs and put her other arm around the inseparable twins.

Melanie did not spell the name Susan. She couldn't, for some reason. She used the impersonal "she," accompanied by a gesture toward the field.

"She . . ."

How do I say it? Oh, God, I have absolutely no idea. It took her a moment to remember the word for "killed." The word was constructed by moving the extended index finger of the right hand up under the left hand, held cupped, palm down.

Exactly like a bullet entering the body, she thought.

She couldn't say it. Saw Susan's hair pop up under the impact. Saw her ease to the ground.

"She's dead," Melanie finally signed. "Dead" was a different gesture, turning over the flattened, palm-up right hand so that it was palm down; simultaneously doing the opposite with the left. It was at her right hand that Melanie stared, thinking how the gesture of this hand mimicked scooping earth onto a grave.

The girls' reactions were different but really all the same: the tears, the silent gasps, the eyes filling with horror.

Her hands trembling, Melanie turned back to the window. De l'Epée had picked up Susan's body and was walking back to the police line with it. Melanie watched her friend's dangling arms, the cascade of black hair, the feet—one shoe on, one shoe off.

Beautiful Susan.

Susan, the person I would be if I could be anybody.

As she watched de l'Epée disappear behind a police car, part of Melanie's silent world grew slightly more silent. And that was something she could scarcely afford.

"I'm resigning, sir," Charlie Budd said softly.

Potter stepped into the john of the van to put on the fresh shirt that had somehow appeared in the hands of one of Dean Stillwell's officers. He dropped his own bloodstained shirt into a wastebasket and pulled on the new one; the bullet that had killed Susan had spattered him copiously.

"What's that, Charlie?" Potter asked absently, stepping back to the desk. Tobe and Derek sat silently at their consoles. Even Henry LeBow had stopped typing and stared out the window, which from the angle at which he sat revealed nothing but distant wheat fields, distorted and tinted ocher by the thick grass.

Through the window on the other side of the van the ambulance lights flashed as they took the girl's body away.

"I'm quitting," Budd continued. "This assignment and the force too." His voice was steady. "That was my fault. It was because of that shot a half-hour ago. When I didn't tell the snipers to unchamber. I'll call Topeka and get a replacement in here."

Potter turned back, tucking the crisp shirt in. "Stick around, Charlie. I need you."

"Nosir. I made a mistake and I'll shoulder the consequences."

"You may have plenty of opportunity to take responsibility for your screwups before this night is through," Potter told him evenly. "But that sniper shot wasn't one of them. What Handy just did had nothing to do with you."

"Then why? Why in God's name would he do that?"

"Because he's putting his cards on the table. He's telling us he's serious. We can't buy him out of there cheap."

"By shooting a hostage in cold blood?"

LeBow said, "This's the hardest kind of negotiation there is, Charlie. After a killing up front, usually the only way to save any hostage is a flat-out assault."

"High stakes," Derek Elb muttered.

Extreme stakes, Arthur Potter thought. Then: Jesus, what a day this's going to be.

"Downlink," Tobe said, and a moment later the phone buzzed. The tape recorder began turning automatically.

Potter picked up the receiver. "Lou?" he said evenly.

"There's something you gotta understand 'bout me, Art. I don't *care* about these girls. They're just little birds to me that I used to shoot off my back porch at home. I aim to get outta here and if it means I gotta shoot nine more of 'em dead as posts then that's the way it's gonna be. You hear me?"

Potter said, "I do hear you, Lou. But we've got to get one other thing straight. I'm the only man in this universe can get you out of there alive. There's nobody else. So I'm the one to reckon with. Now do *you* hear *me?*"

"I'll call you back with our demands."

1:25 P.M.

This was tricky, this was dangerous, this was not about re-election.

This was about decency and life.

So Daniel Tremain told himself as he walked into the governor's mansion.

Standing upright as a birch rod, he headed through the surprisingly modest home into a large den.

Decency and life.

"Officer."

"Governor."

The Right Honorable Governor of the state of Kansas, A. R. Stepps, was looking at the faint horizon—fields of grain identical to those that had funded his father's insurance company, which had in turn allowed Stepps to be a public servant. Tremain believed Stepps was the perfect governor: connected, distrustful of Washington, infuriated about crime in Topeka and the felons that Missouri sloughed off into *his* Kansas City but able to live with it all, his eye no further than the low star of a retirement spent teaching in Lawrence and cruising Scandia Lines routes with the wife.

But now there was Crow Ridge.

The governor's eyes lifted from a fax he'd been reading and scanned Tremain.

Look me over if you want. Go right ahead. His blue-and-black operations gear certainly looked incongruous here among the framed prints of shot ducks, the Lemon-Pledged mahogany antiques. Most frequently Stepps's eyes dipped to the large automatic pistol, which the trooper adjusted as he sat in the irritatingly scrolly chair.

"He's killed one?"

Tremain nodded his head, which was covered with a thinning crew cut. He noted that the governor had a tiny hole in the elbow of his baby-blue cardigan and that he was absolutely terrified.

"What happened?"

"Premeditated, looks like. I'm getting a full report but it looks like there was no reason for it. Sent her out like he was giving her up and shot her in the back."

"Oh, dear God. How young was she?"

"The oldest. A teenager. But still . . ."

The governor nodded toward a silver service. "Coffee? Tea? . . . No? You've never been here before, have you?"

"The governor's mansion? No." Though it wasn't a mansion; it was just a nice house, a house that rang with the sounds of family.

"I need some help here, Officer. Some of your expertise."

"I'll do whatever I can, sir."

"An odd situation. These prisoners escaped from a federal penitentiary. . . . What is it, Captain?"

"With all respect, sir, that prison at Callana's like it's got a revolving door in it." Tremain recalled four breakouts in the last five years. His own men had captured a number of the escapees, a record better than that of the U.S. marshals, who in Tremain's opinion were overpaid baby-sitters.

The governor began cautiously, like a man stepping onto November ice. "So they're technically federal escapees but they also're lined up for state sentences. Won't be till the year three thousand maybe but the fact is they're state felons too."

"But the FBI's in charge of the barricade." Tremain had been told specifically by the assistant attorney general that his services would not be required in this matter. The trooper was no expert on the hierarchy of state government but even schoolchildren knew that the AG and his underlings worked for the governor. Executive branch. "We have to defer to them, of course. And maybe it's for the best."

The governor said, "This Potter's a fine man. . . ." His voice seemed not to stop but to deflate until it became a dwelling question mark.

Dan Tremain was a career law enforcer and had learned never to say anything that could be quoted back against him even before he'd learned how to cover two opposing doors when diving through a barricade window. "Pride of the FBI, I'm told," the trooper said, assuming that a tape recorder was running somewhere nearby, though it probably wasn't.

"But?" The governor raised an eyebrow.

"I understand he's taking a hard line."

"Which means what?"

Outside the window, threshers moved back and forth.

"It means that he's going to try to wear Handy down and get him to surrender."

"Will Potter attack eventually? If he has to?"

"He's just a negotiator. A federal hostage rescue team's being assembled. They should be here by early evening."

"And if Handy doesn't surrender they'll go in and . . ."

"Neutralize him."

The round face smiled. The governor looked nostalgically at an ashtray and then back to Tremain. "How soon after they get there will they attack?"

"The rule is that you don't assault except as a last resort. Rand Corporation did a study a few years ago and found that ninety percent of the hostages killed in a barricade are killed when the situation goes hot—when there's an assault. I was going to say something else, sir."

"Please. Speak frankly."

The corner of a sheet of paper peeked out from under the governor's repulsively blue sweater. Tremain recognized it as his own résumé. He was proud of his record with the state police though he wondered if he wasn't here now because the governor had read the brief paragraph referring to a "consulting" career, which had taken Tremain to Africa and Guatemala after his discharge from the Marines.

"The Rand Corporation study is pretty accurate as far as it goes. But there's something else that bears on this situation, sir. That if there's a killing early in the barricade, negotiations rarely work. The HT—the hostage taker—has little to lose. Sometimes there's a psychological thing that happens and the taker feels so powerful that he'll just keep upping his demands so that they *can't* be met, just so he'll have an excuse to kill the hostages."

The governor nodded.

"What's your assessment of Handy?"

"I read the file on the way over here and I came up with a profile."

"Which is?"

"He's not psychotic. But he's certainly amoral."

The governor's thin lips twitched into a momentary smile. Because, Tremain thought, I'm a mercenary thug who used the word *amoral?*

"I think," Tremain continued slowly, "that he's going to kill more of the girls. Maybe all of them ultimately. If he goes mobile and gets away from us I think he'll kill them just for the symmetry of it."

Symmetry. How do you like *that,* sir? Check out the education portion of my résumé. I was cum laude from Lawrence. Top of my class at OCS.

"One other thing we have to consider," the captain continued. "He didn't try very hard to escape from that trooper who found them this afternoon."

"No?"

"There was just that one officer and the three takers, with guns and hostages. It was like Handy's goal wasn't so much to get away but to spend some time . . ."

"Some time what?"

"With the hostages. If you get what I'm saying. They *are* all female."

The governor lifted his bulky weight from the chair. He walked to the window. Outside the combines combed the flat landscape, two of the ungainly machines slowly converging. The man sighed deeply.

Fucking symmetrically amoral life, ain't it, sir?

"He simply isn't your typical hostage taker, Governor. There's a sadistic streak in him."

"And you really think he'd . . . hurt the girls? You know what I mean?"

"I believe he would. If he could keep an eye out the window at the same time. And one of the fellows in there with him, Sonny Bonner, he's doing time for rape. Well, interstate transport. But rape was at the bottom of it."

On the governor's desk were pictures of his blond family, a black Labrador retriever, and Jesus Christ.

"How good is your team, Captain?" Whispering now.

"We're very, very good, sir."

The governor rubbed his sleepy eyes. "Can you get them out?"

"Yes. To know how many casualties, I'd have to do a preliminary plan of the tactical operation and then run a damage assessment."

"How soon could you do that?"

"I've asked Lieutenant Carfallo to obtain terrain maps and architectural drawings of the building."

"Where is he now?"

Tremain glanced at his watch. "He happens to be outside, sir."

The governor's eyes twitched again. "Why don't you ask him in?"

A moment later the lieutenant, a short, stocky young officer, was unfurling maps and old drawings.

"Lieutenant," Tremain barked, "give us your assessment."

A stubby finger touched several places on the architectural drawings. "Breachable here and here. Move in, use stun grenades, set up crossfire zones." The young man said this cheerfully and the governor seemed to grow uneasy again. As well he ought to. Carfallo was a scary little weasel. The lieutenant continued, "I'd estimate six to eight seconds, bang to bullets."

"He means," Tremain explained, "it's six seconds from the time the door blows until we acquire all three targets—um, have guns pointed at all the HTs."

"Is that good?"

"Excellent. It means that hostage casualties would be minimal or nonexistent. But of course I can't guarantee that there'd be none."

"God doesn't give us guarantees."

"No, He doesn't."

"Thank you, Lieutenant," the governor said.

"Dismissed," Tremain snapped, and the young man's face went still as he turned and vanished.

"What about Potter?" the governor asked. "He *is* in charge after all."

Tremain said, "And the related issue—there'd have to be some reason to green-light an assault."

"Some excuse," the governor mused, very carelessly. Then he stiffened and picked at a renegade powder-blue thread on his cuff.

"Say something happened to sever communications between Potter and Handy and the men in the field. And then say someone in my team observed a high-risk activity inside the slaughterhouse, some activity that jeopardized troopers or the hostages. Something Potter wasn't able to respond to. I'd think that—well, even legally—we'd be fully authorized to move in and secure the premises."

"Yes, yes. I'd think you would be." The governor lifted an inquiring eyebrow then thought better of saying whatever he'd been about to say. He slapped the desktop. "All right, Captain. My instructions: You're to move the state Hostage Rescue Unit to Crow Ridge and provide any backup assistance you can to Agent Potter. If for some reason Agent Potter is unable to remain in command of the situation and the convicts present an immediate threat to anyone—hostages or troopers or . . . just plain anyone— you're authorized to do whatever's necessary to neutralize the situation."

Entrust that to tape if you want. Who could argue with the wisdom and prudence of the words?

"Yessir." Tremain rolled up the maps and diagrams. "Is there anything else, sir?"

"I know that time is of the essence," the governor said slowly, applying his last test to the solemn trooper, "but do you think we could spend a moment in prayer?"

"I'd be honored, sir."

And the soldier took the sovereign's hand and they both dropped to their knees. Tremain closed his piercing blue eyes. A stream of words filled the room, rapid and articulate, as if they flowed straight from the heart of an Almighty worried sick about those poor girls about to die in the corridors of the Webber & Stoltz Processing Company, Inc.

So you'll be home then.

Melanie watched the lump of a woman and thought: it's impossible

for someone to cry that much. She tapped Mrs. Harstrawn's arm but all
the teacher did was cry even harder.

They were still in the little hellhole of the killing room. Scummy water
on the floor, ringed like a rainbow from spilled oil. Filthy ceramic tile. No
windows. It smelled of mold and shit. And decayed, dead animals in the
walls. It reminded Melanie of the shower room in *Schindler's List.*

Her eyes kept falling on the center of the room: a large drain from
which radiated spider legs of troughs. All stained brown. Old, old
blood. She pictured a young calf braying then struggling as its throat
was cut, the blood pulsing out, down the drain.

Melanie started to cry and once again heard her father's voice from last
spring, *So you'll be home then. You'll be home then you'll be home then.* . . .

From there her thoughts leapt to her brother, lying in a hospital bed
six hundred miles away. He'd have heard by now, heard about the murder of the couple in the Cadillac, the kidnaping. He'd be worried sick.
I'm sorry, Danny. I wish I were with you!

Blood spraying through the air. . . .

Mrs. Harstrawn huddled and shook. Her face was a remarkable blue
and Melanie's horror at Susan's death was momentarily replaced by the
fear that the teacher was having a stroke.

"Please," she signed. "Girls are scared."

But the woman didn't notice or, if she did, couldn't respond.

So you'll . . .

Melanie wiped her face and lowered her head into her arms.

. . . be home then.

And if she'd been home, like her parents wanted (well, her *father,*
but her father's decision *was* her parents'), she wouldn't be here now.

None of them would.

And Susan would still be alive.

Stop thinking about it!

Bear walked past the killing room and looked in. He squeezed his
crotch, half hidden beneath his belly, and barked something at Shannon. He offered his knee, said something about did she want to kick
him again? She tried to give him a defiant look but stared down at her
arm, rubbing the faded self-drawn tattoo of the superhero.

Brutus called something and Bear looked up. The big man was afraid of him, Melanie understood suddenly, seeing the look in Bear's eyes. He laughed humorlessly, sneering. Glanced once at Mrs. Harstrawn. But his eyes lingered longest on the little girls, especially the twins and Emily, her dress, her white stockings and black patent-leather shoes, the dress bought just for the occasion of Melanie's performance at the Kansas State Theater of the Deaf Summer Recital. How long the gaze coursed over the little girl. He reluctantly walked back into the main room of the slaughterhouse.

Get them out, Melanie told herself. Whatever you have to do, *get them out.*

Then: But I can't. Brutus will kill me. He'll rape me. He's evil, he's the Outside. She thought of Susan and wept again. He was right, her father.

So you'll be home then.

She'd be alive.

There'd have been no secret appointments after the recital in Topeka. No lies, no hard decisions.

"Get back, against the wall," she signed to the girls. She had to get them away from Bear, keep them out of sight. They moved as instructed, tearful all of them except lean, young Shannon, once more angry and defiant, the tomboy. And Kielle too—though she was neither angry nor defiant but eerily subdued. The girl troubled Melanie. What was in her eyes? The shadow of exactly what had been in Susan's? Here was a child with the visage of a woman. My God, there's vindictiveness, chill, raw hatred. Is she the one who's really Susan's heir? Melanie wondered.

"He's Magneto," Kielle signed matter-of-factly, glancing in Brutus's direction and addressing her comment to Shannon. It was her own nickname for Handy. The other girl disagreed. "No. He's Mr. Sinister. Not part of Brotherhood. Worst of the worst."

Kielle considered this. "But I think—"

"Oh, you two, stop!" Beverly burst into their conversation, her hands rising and falling like her struggling chest. "This isn't stupid game."

Melanie nodded. "Don't say anything more." Oh, Mrs. Harstrawn, Melanie raged silently, please ... How you cry! Red face, blue face, quivering. Please don't do this! Her hands rose. "I can't do it alone."

But Mrs. Harstrawn was helpless. She lay on the tile floor of the killing room, her head against a trough where the hot blood of dying calves and lambs flowed and vanished and she said not a word.

Melanie looked up. The girls were staring at her.

I *have* to do something.

But all she remembered was her father's words—phantom words—as he sat on the front porch swing of their farmhouse last spring. A brilliant morning. He said to her, "This is your home and you'll be welcome here. See, it's a question of belonging and what God does to make sure those that oughta stay someplace do. Well, your place is here, working at what you can do, where your, you know, problem doesn't get you into trouble. God's will."

(How perfectly she'd made out the words then, even the impossible sibilants and elusive glottal stops. As clearly as she understood Handy—Brutus—now.)

Her father had finished. "So you'll be home then." And rose to hitch up the ammonia tank without letting her write a single word of response on the pad she carried around the house.

Suddenly Melanie was aware of Beverly's head bobbing up and down. A full-fledged asthma attack. The girl's face darkened and she closed her eyes miserably, struggling ferociously to breathe. Melanie stroked her damp hair.

"Do something," Jocylyn signed with her stubby, inept fingers.

The shadows reaching into the room, shadows of machinery and wires, grew very sharp, then began to sway. Melanie stood and walked into the slaughterhouse. She saw Brutus and Stoat rearranging the lights.

Maybe he'll give us one for our room. Please. . . .

"I hope he dies, I hate him," the blond fireball Kielle signed furiously, her round face contorted with hatred as she gazed at Brutus.

"Quiet."

"I want him to die!"

"Stop!"

Beverly lay down on the floor. She signed, "Please. Help."

In the outer room Brutus and Stoat sat close together under a swaying lamp, the light reflecting off Stoat's pale crew cut. They were watching the small TV, clicking through the channels. Bear stood at the window, counting. Police cars, she guessed.

Melanie walked toward the men. Stopped about ten feet from them. Brutus looked over the dark skirt, the ruddy blouse, the gold necklace—a present from her brother, Danny. He was studying her, that damn curious smile on his face. Not like Bear, not staring at her boobs and legs. Just her face and, especially, her ears. She realized it was the way he'd stared at devastated Mrs. Harstrawn—as if he was adding another specimen to a collection of tragedies.

She mimicked writing something.

"Tell me," he said slowly, and so loudly she felt the useless vibrations pelt her. "Say it."

She pointed to her throat.

"You can't talk neither?"

She wouldn't talk. No. Though there was nothing wrong with her vocal cords. And because she'd become deaf relatively late in life, Melanie knew the fundamentals of word formation. Still, following Susan's model, Melanie avoided oralism because it wasn't chic. The Deaf community resented people who straddled both worlds—the Deaf world and the world of the Others. Melanie hadn't tried to utter a single word in five or six years.

She pointed toward Beverly and breathed in hard. Touched her chest.

"Yeah, the sick one. . . . What about her?"

Melanie mimicked taking medicine.

Brutus shook his head. "I don't give a shit. Go back and sit down."

Melanie pushed her hands together, a prayer, a plea. Brutus and Stoat laughed. Brutus called something to Bear, and Melanie suddenly felt the firm vibrations of his footsteps approach. Then an arm was around her chest and Bear was dragging her across the floor. His fingers squeezed her nipple hard. She yanked his hand away and the tears came again.

In the killing room she pushed away from him and collapsed on the floor. Melanie grabbed one of the lights, which rested on the ground, and clutched it, hot and oily, to her chest. It burned her fingers but she clung to it like a life preserver. Bear looked down, seemed to ask a question.

But just as she'd done that spring day with her father on the farmhouse porch, Melanie gave no response; she simply went away.

That day last May, she'd climbed the creaking stairs and sat in an old rocking chair in her bedroom. Now, she lay on the killing room floor. A child again, younger than the twins. Mercifully she closed her eyes and went away. To anyone watching it seemed that she'd slipped into a faint. But in fact she wasn't here at all; she'd gone someplace else, someplace safe, someplace not another living soul knew about.

When he recruited hostage negotiators Arthur Potter found himself in the peculiar position of interviewing clones of himself. Middle-aged, frumpy, easygoing cops.

For a time it was thought that psychologists ought to be used for negotiating; but even though a barricade resembles a therapy session in many ways, shrinks just didn't work out. They were too analytical, focused too much on diagnostics. The point of talking to a taker isn't to figure out where he fits in the *DSM IV* but to persuade him to come out with his hands up. This requires common sense, concentration, a sharp mind, patience (well, Arthur Potter worked hard at that), a healthy sense of self, the rare gift of speaking well, and the rarer talent of listening.

And most important, a negotiator is a man with controlled emotions.

The very quality that Arthur Potter was wrestling with at the moment. He struggled to forget the image of Susan Phillips's chest exploding before him, feeling the hot tap of blood droplets striking his face. There'd been many deaths in the barricades he'd worked over the years. But he'd never been so close to such a cold-blooded death as this one.

Henderson called. The reporters had heard a gunshot and were champing to get some information. "Tell them I'll make a statement within a half-hour. Don't leak it, Pete, but he just killed one."

"Oh, God, no." But the SAC didn't sound upset at all; he seemed almost pleased—perhaps because Potter had assumed point position on this megatragedy in progress.

"Executed her. Shot her in the back. Listen, this could all go bad in a big way. Get on the horn to Washington and push the HRT assembly, okay?"

"Why'd he do it?"

"No apparent reason," Potter said, and they hung up.

"Henry?" Potter said to LeBow. "I need some help here. What should we stay away from?"

Negotiators try to increase the rapport with their takers by dipping into personal matters. But a question about a sensitive subject can send an agitated taker into a frenzy, even prompting him to kill.

"There's so little data," the intelligence officer said. "I guess I'd avoid his military service. His brother Rudy."

"Parents?"

"Relation unknown. I'd steer clear on general principles until we learn more."

"His girlfriend? What's her name?"

"Priscilla Gunder. No problems there, it looks like. Fancied themselves a regular Bonnie and Clyde."

"Unless," Budd pointed out, "she dumped him when he went to prison."

"Good point," Potter said, deciding to let Handy bring up the girlfriend and just echo or reflect whatever he said.

"Definitely avoid the ex-wife. It seems there was some bad blood there."

"Personal relations in general, then," Potter summarized. It was typical in criminal takings. Usually mentally disturbed takers wanted to talk about the ex-spouse they were still in love with. Potter gazed at the slaughterhouse and announced, "I want to try to get one out. Who should we go for? What do we know about the hostages so far?"

"Just a few isolated facts. We won't have anything substantive till Angie gets here."

"I was thinking . . ." Budd began.

"Yes, go ahead."

"That girl with the asthma. You asked about her before but he's had a spell of her choking up a storm—if I know asthma. Handy's the sort who'd have a short fuse for something like that, seems to me. He's probably ready to boot her out."

"It's a good thought, Charlie," Potter said. "But the psychology of negotiating is that once you've had a refusal you have to go on to a different issue or person. For the time being Beverly's non-negotiable. It'd be weak of us to try to get her and too weak of him to give in when he's already refused. Henry, you have anything at all on the others?"

"Well, this girl Jocylyn Weiderman. I have a note from Angie that she's been in and out of counseling for depression. Cries a lot and has attacks of hysteria. She might try to panic and run. Get herself killed."

"I'll buy that," said Budd.

"Good," Potter announced. "Let's try for her."

As he was reaching for the phone Tobe held up a hand. "Downlink." The phone buzzed; the recorder turned.

"Hello?" Potter asked.

Silence.

"How's everything doing in there, Lou?"

"Not bad."

The thick window of the command van was right next to him but Potter's head was up, gazing at what LeBow had mounted—the CAD diagram of the slaughterhouse. It was a hostage rescue team's nightmare. The spot where Handy seemed to be at the moment was a single large room—a holding pen for the livestock. But in the back of the slaughterhouse were three stories of warrens—small offices, cutting and packing rooms, sausage grinding and stuffing rooms and storage areas, interconnected with narrow corridors.

"You fellows must be pretty tired," Potter offered.

"Listen, Art. I'm gonna tell you what we want. You probably got a tape recorder going but're gonna pretend you don't."

"Sure, we're taking down every word. I'm not going to lie to you. You know the drill."

"You know, I hate the way I sound on tape. One of my trials they played a confession tape of me in court. I didn't like the way I sounded. I don't know why I confessed either. I guess I was just anxious to tell somebody what I done to that girl."

Potter, eager to learn everything about this man, asked, "What *did* you do exactly, Lou?" He speculated: *It was real nasty. I don't think you want to hear about it.*

"Oh, wasn't pleasant, Art. Not pretty at all. I was proud of my work, though."

"Asshole," Tobe muttered.

"Nobody likes how they sound on tape, Lou," Potter continued easily. "I've got to give this training seminar once a year. They tape it. I hate how I sound."

Shut the fuck up, Art. Listen.

"Don't much care, Art. Now, get your pencil ready and listen. We want a chopper. A big one. One that seats eight."

Nine hostages, three HTs, and the pilot. That leaves five left over. What's going to happen to them?

LeBow was writing all this down on his computer. He'd padded the keys with cotton so that they were nearly silent.

"Okay, you want a helicopter. The police and the Bureau only have two-seaters. It'll take some time until we can get—"

"Like I say, Art. Don't much care. Chopper and a pilot. That's number one. Got it?"

"Sure do, Lou. But like I told you before, I'm just a special agent. I don't have the authority to requisition a chopper. I'll have to get on the horn to Washington."

"Art, you ain't listening. That's *your* problem. It's gonna be my theme for the day. Don't. Much. Care. The clock's running, whether you gotta call the airport that's up the road a couple miles or the Pope in his holy city."

"Okay. Keep going."

"We want some food."

"You got it. Anything in particular?"

"McDonald's. Lots of it."

Potter motioned to Budd, who picked up his phone and began whispering orders.

"It's on its way."

Get into him. Get inside his head. He's going to ask for liquor next, Potter guessed.

"And a hundred rounds of twelve-gauge shells, double-ought, body armor, and gas masks."

"Oh, well, Lou, I guess you know I can't do that."

"I don't know that at all."

"I can't give you weapons, Lou."

"Even if I was to give you a girl?"

"Nope, Lou. Weapons and ammunition are deal breakers. Sorry."

"You use my name a lot, Art. Hey, if we *was* to do some horse trading, which one of the girls would you want? Anybody in particular? Say we weren't talking about guns and such."

LeBow raised his eyebrows and nodded. Budd gave Potter a thumbs-up.

Melanie, Potter thought automatically. But he believed their assessment was right and that they had to try for the girl most at risk—Jocylyn, the troubled student.

Potter told him there was one girl in particular they wanted.

"Describe her."

LeBow spun the computer around. Potter read the fine print on the screen then said, "Short dark hair, overweight. Twelve. Her name's Jocylyn."

"Her? That weepy little shit. She whines like a pup with a busted leg. Good riddance. Thanks for picking her, Art. She's the one gets shot in five minutes, you don't agree to the guns 'n' ammo."

Click.

2:00 P.M.

Hell, Potter thought, slamming his fist on the table.

"Oh, brother," muttered Budd. Then: "Oh, Jesus."

Potter picked up the binoculars and saw a young girl appear in the window of the slaughterhouse. She was chubby and her round cheeks glistened with tears. When the muzzle of the gun touched her short-cut hair, she closed her eyes.

"Call it out, Tobe."

"Four minutes thirty."

"That's her?" Potter whispered to LeBow. "Jocylyn?"

"I'm sure."

"You've noted that the scatter guns are twelve-gauge?" Potter asked evenly.

LeBow said he had. "And that they're possibly low on ammo."

Derek glanced at them, shocked at this cold-blooded conversation.

"Jesus God," Budd rasped. "Do something."

"What?" Potter asked.

"Well, call him back and tell him you'll give him the ammo."

"No."

"Four minutes."

"But he's going to shoot her."

"I don't think he will." Will he, won't he? Potter debated. He honestly couldn't tell.

"Look at him," Budd said. "Look out there! That girl's got a gun to her head. I can see her crying from here."

"Which is just what he wants us to see. Calm down, Charlie. You never negotiate weapons or armor."

"But he's going to kill her!"

"Three minutes thirty."

"What if," Potter said, struggling to control his impatience, "he's completely out of ammo? He's sitting in there with two empty pistols and an empty scatter gun?"

"Well, maybe he's got one shell left and he's just about to use it on that girl."

A hostage situation is a homicide in progress.

Potter continued to gaze at the unhappy face of the child. "We have to assume there are nine fatalities right now—the girls inside. A hundred rounds of twelve-gauge shells? That could double the number of casualties."

"Three minutes," Tobe sang out.

Outside Stillwell shifted uncomfortably and ruffled his mop of hair. He looked at the van then back at the slaughterhouse. He hadn't heard the exchange but he, like all the other troopers, could see the poor girl's head in the window.

"Two minutes thirty."

"Send him some blanks. Or some shells that'll jam the guns."

"That's a good idea, Charlie. But we don't have any such thing. He won't waste another hostage this early." Is this true? Potter wondered.

"Waste a hostage?" The voice of another trooper—Derek the technician—cut through the van. Potter believed the man appended in a whisper, "Son of a bitch."

"Two minutes," Tobe said in his unflappable voice.

Potter hunched forward, gazing out the window. He saw the officers behind their Maginot line of cars, some looking back at the van uneasily.

"One minute thirty."

What's Handy doing? What's he thinking? I can't see into him. I need more time. I need to talk to him more. An hour from now I'd *know* whether he'd kill her or not. Right now, all I see is smoke and danger.

"One minute," Tobe called out.

Potter picked up the phone. Pressed the rapid-dial button.

Click.

"Uplink."

"Lou."

"Art, I've decided I want a hundred rounds of Glock ammo too."

"No."

"Make that a hundred and one rounds of Glock. I'm about to lose one in thirty seconds. I'll need something to replace it."

"No ammo, Lou."

Derek leapt forward and grabbed Potter's arm. "Do it. For God's sake!"

"Sergeant!" Budd cried, and pulled the man away, shoved him into the corner.

Handy continued, "Remember that Viet Cong dude got shot? It was on film? In the head? The blood squirting up into the air like a fucking fountain."

"I can't do it, Lou. Don't you follow? We have a bad connection, or something?"

"You're supposed to be negotiating!" Budd whispered. "Talk to him." Now he seemed to regret pulling Derek Elb off.

Potter ignored him.

"Ten seconds, Arthur," Tobe said, fingering his earring hole nervously. He'd turned away from his precious dials and was looking out the window.

The seconds passed, ten minutes or an hour. Absolute silence in the control van, except for the static on the open line, the sound bleeding through the van's speakers. Potter realized he was holding his breath. He resumed breathing.

"Lou, are you there?"

No answer.

"Lou?"

Suddenly the gun lowered and a hand grabbed the girl by the collar. She opened her mouth as she was dragged back into the slaughterhouse.

Potter speculated: *Yo, Art, what's happening, homes?*

"Hey, Art, how's it hanging?" Handy's cheerful voice crackled over the speakers.

"Fair to middlin'. How about you?"

"Doing peachy. Here's the deal. I shoot one an hour till that chopper's here. On the hour, every hour, starting at four."

"Well, Lou, I'll tell you right now we're going to need more time than that to get a big chopper."

Potter guessed: *Fuck that. You'll do what I tell you.*

But with playful menace in his voice Handy said, "How much more time?"

"A couple of hours. Maybe—"

"Fuck no. I'll give you till five."

Potter paused for a judicious moment. "I think we can work with that."

A harsh laugh. Then: "And a whole 'nother thing, Art."

"What's that?"

A pause, tension building. At last, Handy growled, "With those burgers I want some Fritos. Lots of Fritos."

"You got it. But I want that girl."

"Oh, hey," Budd whispered, "maybe you shouldn't push him."

"Which girl?"

"Jocylyn. The one you just had in the window."

"Jocylyn," Handy said with sudden animation, again startling Potter. "Funny 'bout that name."

Potter snapped his fingers, pointed at LeBow's computer. The intelligence officer scrolled through the profile of Handy, and both men tried to find some reference to Jocylyn: mother, sister, probation officer. But there was nothing.

"Why's that funny, Lou?"

" 'Bout ten years ago I fucked a waitress named Jocylyn and enjoyed it very much."

Potter felt the chill run from his legs to his shoulders.

"She was tasty. Before I met Pris of course."

Potter listened to Handy's tone. He closed his eyes. He speculated: *She was a hostage too, that Jocylyn, and I killed her 'cause . . .* He couldn't guess the rest of what Handy might say.

"Haven't thought about her for years. My Jocylyn was a hostage too, just like this one. She didn't do what I told her. I mean, she just *didn't*. So I had to use my knife."

Some of this is part of his act, Potter thought. The cheerful reference to the knife. But there was something revealing in the words too. *Didn't do what I told her.* Potter wrote down the sentence and pushed it to LeBow to type in.

"I want her, Lou," Potter said.

"Oh, don't you worry. I'm faithful to my Pris now."

"When we get the food, let's exchange. How 'bout it, Lou?"

"She's not much good for anything, Art. I think she peed her pants. Or maybe she just don't shower much. Even Bonner wouldn't come close to her. And he's a horny son of a bitch as you probably know."

"We're working on your chopper and you'll have the food there soon. You owe me a girl, Lou. You killed one. You owe me."

Budd and Derek gazed at Potter in disbelief.

"Naw," Handy said. "Don't think so."

"You're only going to have room in the chopper for four or five hostages. Give me that one." Sometimes you have to lie down; sometimes you have to hit. Potter snapped, "Jesus Christ, Lou, I know you're willing to kill them. You made your damn point. So just let her go, all right? I'll send a trooper up with the food; let him come back with the girl."

A pause.

"You really want that one?"

Potter thought: *Actually, I'd like 'em all, Lou.*

Time for a joke? Or too early?

He gambled. "I'd really like them all, Lou."

A harrowing pause.

Then a raucous laugh from the speaker. "You're a pistol, Art. Okay, I'll send her out. Let's synchronize our Timexes, boys. The clock's running. You get the fat one for the food. Fifteen minutes. Or I might change my mind. And a big beautiful chopper at five in the p.m."

Click.

"All right!" Tobe shouted.

Budd was nodding. "Good, Arthur. That was good."

Derek sat sullenly at his control panel for a moment but finally cracked a smile and apologized. Potter, ever willing to forgive youthful enthusiasm, shook the trooper's hand.

Budd was smiling in relief. He said, "Wichita's the aviation capital of the Midwest. Hell, we can get a chopper here in a half-hour."

"We aren't getting him one," Potter said. He gestured to the "Promises/ Deceptions" chart. LeBow wrote, *Helicopter seating eight, due on hourly deadlines. Commencing at 5 p.m.*

"You're not going to give it to him?" Budd whispered.

"Of course not."

"But you lied."

"That's why it's on the 'Deceptions' side of the board."

Typing again, LeBow said, "We can't let him go mobile. Especially in a chopper."

"But he's going to kill another one at five."

"So he says."

"But—"

"That's my *job*, Charlie," Potter said, finding patience somewhere. "It's what I'm doing here, to talk him out of it."

And poured himself a cup of extremely bad coffee from a stainless steel pot.

Potter slipped a cellular phone into his pocket and stepped outside, crouching until he was in the gully, which protected him from the slaughterhouse.

Budd accompanied him part of the way. The young captain had found out that the Hutchinson police were in charge of stopping the river traffic and had ordered them to do so, incurring the wrath of several charterers of container barges bound for Wichita, whose meters were running to the tune of two thousand dollars an hour.

"Can't please everybody," the negotiator observed, distracted.

It was growing even colder—an odd July indeed with temperatures in the mid-fifties—and there was a rich metallic taste to the air, perhaps from the diesel exhaust of the nearby threshers or harvesters or combines, whatever they were. Potter waved at Stillwell, who was walk-

ing back and forth among the troopers, grinning laconically, and ordering troops into position.

Leaving Budd, Potter climbed into a bureau car and drove to the
rear staging area. Already, all the networks and local stations from a
three-state area were here, as were reporters or stringers from the big-
city papers and the wire services.

He had a brief word with Peter Henderson, who—whatever his other
failings and motives—had quickly put together an efficient transport
pool, supply staging area, and press tent.

Potter was known to the press and they descended on him frantically
as he walked from the car. They were as he expected them to be: aggressive, humorless, smart, blindered. They'd never changed in all the
years Potter had been doing this. His first reaction, as always, was how
he would hate to be married to one of them.

He climbed to the podium that Henderson had installed, and looked
into the mass of white video lights. "At about eight-thirty this morning
three escaped felons kidnaped and took hostage two teachers and eight
students from the Laurent Clerc School for the Deaf in Hebron, Kansas.
The felons had earlier in the day escaped from the Callana Federal
Penitentiary.

"They're presently holed up in an abandoned factory along the
Arkansas River about a mile and a half from here, on the border of the
town of Crow Ridge. They are being contained by several hundred
state, local, and federal law enforcers."

More like a hundred, but Potter would rather bend the truth to the
fourth estate than risk nurturing overconfidence on the part of the takers—just in case they happened to catch a news report.

"There has been one fatality among the hostages. . . ."

The reporters gasped and bristled at this and their hands shot up.
They barked questions but Potter said only, "The identity of the victim
and those of the rest of the hostages will not be disclosed until all family members have been notified of the incident. We are in the midst of
negotiations with the felons, who've been identified as Louis Handy,
Shepard Wilcox, and Ray 'Sonny' Bonner. During the course of the negotiations there will be no press access to the barricade site. You'll be

receiving updates as we get new information. That's all I have to say at this time."

"Agent Potter—"

"I'm not answering any questions now."

"Agent Potter—"

"Agent Potter, please—"

"Could you compare this situation to the Koresh situation in Waco?"

"We *need* the press copters released. Our lawyers have already contacted the director—"

"Is this like the Weaver situation a few years—"

Potter walked out of the press tent amid the silent flashes of still cameras and the blaring of videocam lights. He was almost to the car when he heard a voice. "Agent Potter, can I have a minute?"

Potter turned to see a man approaching. He had a limp. He didn't look like a typical newsman. He wasn't a pretty boy and while he seemed aggressive and sullen he was not indignant, which raised him—slightly—in Potter's estimation. Older than his colleagues, he was dark-complected, had a deeply lined face. At least he *looked* like a real journalist. Edward R. Murrow.

The negotiator said, "No individual statements."

"I'm not asking for one. I'm Joe Silbert with KFAL in Kansas City."

"Yessir, if you'll excuse me—"

"You're a prick, Potter," Silbert said with more exhaustion than anger. "Nobody's ever grounded press choppers before."

Extreme stakes, the agent thought. "You'll get the news as soon as anybody."

"Hold up. I know you guys could care less about us. We're a pain in the ass. But we've got our job to do too. This is big news. And you know it. We're going to need fucking more than just press releases and non-briefings like the one we just had. The Admiral's going to be on your ass so fast you'll wish you were back in Waco."

Something about the way he uttered the rank suggested that Silbert knew the FBI director personally.

"There's nothing I can do. Security at the barricade site has to be perfect."

"I have to tell you that if you suppress too much, those youngsters're going to try some pretty desperate things to get inside your perimeter. They're going to be using descrambling scanners to intercept transmissions, they're going to be impersonating officers—"

"All of which is illegal."

"I'm just telling you what some of them have been talking about. There are rumblings out there. And I sure as hell don't want to lose an exclusive to some little asshole law-breaking journalism school graduate."

"I've given orders to arrest any non-law-enforcement personnel within sight of the plant. Reporters included."

Silbert rolled his eyes. "Arnett had it easier in Baghdad. Jesus Christ. You're a negotiator, I thought. Why won't you negotiate?"

"I should be getting back."

"Please! Just listen to my proposal. I want to start a press pool. You allow one or two journalists at a time up near the front. No cameras, radios, recorders. Just typewriters or laptops. Or pen and pencil."

"Joe, we can't risk the takers' getting any information about what we're doing. You know that. They might have a radio inside."

An ominous tone slipped into his voice. "Look, you start suppressing, we'll start speculating."

A barricade in Miami several years ago went hot when the takers heard on their portable radio a newscaster describing an HRT assault on the barricade site. It turned out the reporter was merely speculating as to what *might* happen but the takers thought it was real and began firing at the hostages.

"That's a threat, I assume," Potter said evenly.

"Tornadoes are threats," Silbert responded. "They're also facts of life. Look, Potter, what can I do to convince you?"

"Nothing. Sorry."

Potter turned toward the car. Silbert sighed. "Fuck. How's this? You can read the stories before we file them. You can censor them."

This was a first. Of the hundreds of barricades Potter had negotiated, he'd had good and bad relationships with the press as he tried to balance the First Amendment versus the safety of hostages and cops. But he'd never met a journalist who agreed to let him preview stories.

"That's a prior restraint," said Potter, fourth in his law school class.

"There've already been a half-dozen reporters talking about crossing the barriers. That'll stop if you agree to let a couple of us inside. They'll listen to me."

"And you want to be one of those two."

Silbert grinned. "Of course I fucking want to be one of them. In fact I want to be one of the first two. I've got a deadline in an hour. Come on, what do you think?"

What *did* he think? That half the problem at Waco had been press relations. That he was responsible not only for the lives of the hostages and troopers and fellow agents but for the integrity of the Bureau itself and its image, and that for all his negotiating skills he was an inept player of agency politics. He knew too that most of what Congress, senior Justice officials, and the White House learned about what happened here would be from CNN and the *Washington Post*.

"All right," Potter agreed. "You can set it up. You'll coordinate with Captain Charlie Budd."

He looked at his watch. The food was due. He should be getting back. He drove to the command van, told Budd to set up a small press tent behind it and to meet with Joe Silbert about the pooling arrangement.

"Will do. Where's the food?" Budd asked, gazing anxiously up the road. "Time's getting close."

"Oh," Potter said, "we've got a little flexibility. Once a taker's agreed to release a hostage you're past the biggest hurdle. He's already given Jocylyn up in his mind."

"You think?"

"Go set up that press tent."

He started back to the command van and found himself thinking not of food or helicopters or Louis Handy but rather of Melanie Charrol. And not of how valuable she as a hostage might be to him as a negotiator nor of how much of a benefit or liability she might be in a tactical resolution of the barricade. No, he was mulling over soft information, dicta. Recalling the motion of her mouth as she spoke to him from the dim window of the slaughterhouse.

What could she have been saying?

Speculating mostly about what it would be like to have a conversation with her. Here was a man who'd made his way in the world by listening to other people's words, by talking. And here she was, a deaf-mute.

Lips, teeth, lips.

He mimicked her.

Lips, teeth . . .

Got it, he thought suddenly. And he heard in his mind: "Be forewarned."

He tried it out loud. "Be forewarned."

Yes, that was it. But why such an archaic expression? Of course: So *he* could lip-read it. The movement of the mouth was exaggerated with this phrase. It was obvious. Not "Be careful." Or "Look out." Or "He's dangerous."

Be forewarned.

Henry LeBow should know this.

Potter started toward the van and was only twenty feet from his destination when the limousine appeared silently beside him. It seemed to the agent that as it eased past it turned slightly, as if cutting him off. The door opened and a large, swarthy man climbed out. "Look at all this," he said boisterously. "It looks like D-Day, the troops have landed. You've got everything under control, Ike? Do you? Everything well in *hand?*"

Potter stopped and turned. The man walked up close and his smile, if a smile it had been, fell away. He said, "Agent Potter, we have to talk."

2:20 P.M.

But he didn't talk just at that moment.

He tugged his dark suit closed as a burst of chill wind shot through the gully and he strode to the rise, past Potter, and looked over the slaughterhouse.

The agent noted the state license plate, unhappily speculating as to who the visitor might be, and continued on to the van. "I'd step back," he said. "You're well within rifle range."

The man's large left hand reached out and gripped Potter's arm as they shook. He introduced himself as Roland Marks, the state's assistant attorney general.

Oh, him. Potter recalled the phone conversation earlier. The dusky man gazed at the factory again, still a clear target. "I'd be careful there," Potter repeated impatiently.

"Hell. They have rifles, do they? With laser scopes? Maybe phasers and photon torpedoes. Like *Star Trek*, you know."

I don't have time for this, Potter thought.

The man was tall and large, with a Roman nose, and his presence here was like the blue glow of plutonium in a reactor. Potter said, "One moment please." He stepped inside the command van, lifted an eyebrow.

Tobe nodded toward the slaughterhouse. "As a mouse," he said.

"And the food?"

Budd said it would arrive in a few minutes.

"Marks is outside, Henry. You find anything on him?"

"He's here?" LeBow grimaced. "I made a few calls. He's a hard-line prosecutor. Quick as a whip. Specializes in white-collar crimes. Excellent conviction ratio."

"Take-no-prisoners sort?"

"Exactly. But ambitious. Ran for Congress once. Lost, but still has his eye on Washington, the rumor is. My guess is he's trying to pry some media out of the situation."

Potter had learned long ago that hostage situations are also public relations situations and careers were as much on the line as were human lives. He decided to play Marks carefully.

"Oh, write down that I've translated the message from the hostage. 'Be forewarned.' Assume she's talking about Handy."

LeBow held his eye for a moment. He nodded and turned back to his keys.

Outside again, Potter turned to Marks, the second-most-powerful lawyer in the state. "What can I do for you?"

"So is it true then? What I heard? That he's killed one of them?" Potter nodded slowly. The man closed his eyes and sighed. His mouth tucked into a sorrowful wrinkle. "Why in the name of heaven do a crazy thing like that?"

"His way of telling us he's serious."

"Oh, my good Lord." Marks rubbed his face with large, blunt fingers. "The AG and I've been talking about this at some length, Agent Potter. We've been in a stew about the whole mess and I hightailed it down here to ask if there's anything we can do on the state level. I know about you, Potter. Your reputation. Everybody knows about you, sir."

The agent remained stone-faced. He thought he'd been rude enough on the phone to keep the lawyer out of his life. But it seemed that, to Marks, the earlier conversation had never taken place.

"Play it all close to your chest, do you? But I'd guess you have to. It *is* like playing poker, isn't it. High-stakes poker."

Extreme stakes, Potter thought again, and wished once more that this man would go away. "As I told you I don't really need anything else from the state at the moment. We've got state troopers for containment and I've enlisted Charlie Budd as my second-in-command."

"Budd?"

"You know him?"

"Sure I do. He's a good trooper. And I know all the good troopers." He looked around. "Where are the soldiers?"

"Hostage rescue?"

"I thought for sure they'd be in the thick of things by now."

Potter was still unsure of how the wind from Topeka was blowing. "I'm not using state HRT. The Bureau's team is assembling now and'll be here in the next few hours."

"That's troubling."

"Why's that?" Potter asked innocently, assuming that the man wanted the state rescue team to handle the tactical side.

"You're not thinking of an assault, I hope. Look at the Weaver barricade. Look at Waco. Innocent people killed. I don't want that to happen here."

"No one does. We'll attack only as a last resort."

Marks's boisterous facade fell away and he became deadly serious. "I know you're in charge of the situation, Agent Potter. But I want you to know that the attorney general's position is peaceful resolution at all costs."

Less than four months to the first Tuesday in November, Potter reflected.

"We're hoping things work out peacefully."

"What're his demands?" Marks asked.

Time to tug the leash? Not yet. Potter concluded that an offended Roland Marks could do much harm. "Typical. Chopper, food, ammo. All I'm giving him is food. I'm going to try to get him to surrender or at least get as many girls out as I can before HRT goes in."

He watched Marks's face turn darker than it already was. "I just don't want those little girls hurt."

"Of course not." Potter looked at his watch.

The assistant attorney general continued, "Here's a thought—have him give up the girls and take a chopper. You put one of those clever *Mission: Impossible* things inside and when they land you nail them."

"No."

"Why not?"

"We never let them go mobile if there's any way to avoid it."

"Don't you read Tom Clancy? There're all sorts of bugs and transponders you can use."

"It's still too risky. There's a known quantity of dead right now. The worst he can do is kill the nine remaining hostages, possibly one or two of the HRT." Marks's eyes widened in shock at this. Potter the cold fish continued, "If he gets out he could kill twice that. Three times, or more."

"He's just a bank robber. Hardly a mass murderer."

And how many bodies does it take to qualify somebody as a mass murderer? Potter gazed past the silent combines working their way over hills several miles away. Winter wheat was planted in November, he'd been told by the helicopter pilot, who added that the white man's way of busting sod for wheat planting had mortified the Potawatomi Indians and helped bring on the Depression's dust bowl.

Where was the damn food? Potter thought, now nervous that minutes were slipping past.

"So that's what those girls are then?" Marks asked, none too friendly now. "Acceptable casualties?"

"Let's hope it doesn't come to that."

The door opened and Budd looked out. "That food's almost here, Arthur. Oh, hello, Mr. Marks."

"Charlie Budd. Good luck to you. Tough situation. You'll rise to meet it, though."

"We're doing our best," Budd said cautiously. "Mr. Potter here's really an expert. Agent Potter, I should say."

"I'm going to call in," Marks said. "Brief the governor."

When the limo had vanished, Potter asked Budd, "You know him?"

"Not too well, sir."

"He have an agenda?"

"Suppose he has his eye on Washington in a few years. But he's pretty much a good man."

"Henry thought he might be running for office this fall."

"Don't know 'bout that. But I don't think there's any politics here. His concern'd be the girls. He's a real family man, I heard. A father himself a few times over, all daughters. One of 'em's got some bad health problems so I guess he's feeling this is pretty close to home, those girls being deaf and all."

Potter had noticed Marks's well-worn wedding ring.

"Will he be a problem?"

"I can't imagine how. That way he is, joking and everything, it's kind of a front."

"It's not his sense of humor I'm worried about. How connected is he?"

Budd shrugged. "Oh, well, you know."

"It won't go any further than me, Charlie. I have to know if he can cause us any damage."

"Well, him saying he was going to call the governor? Like they were best buddies?"

"Yes?"

"Doubt the man'll even take his call. See, there're Republicans and then there are *Republicans*."

"Okay, thanks."

"Oh, hey, look, here we go now."

The state police car bounding over the rough road squealed to a stop. But it was not Handy's Big Macs and Fritos. Two women climbed out. Angie Scapello was in a mid-length navy suit, her weapon jutting from the thin blazer and her abundant black hair tumbling to her shoulders. She wore pale sunglasses in turquoise frames. Behind her emerged a young, short-haired brunette in a police uniform.

"Angie." Potter shook her hand. "Meet my right-hand man, Charlie Budd. Kansas State Police. Special Agent Angeline Scapello."

They shook hands and nodded to one another.

Angie introduced the other woman. "Officer Frances Whiting, Hebron PD. She'll be our sign language interpreter." The policewoman shook the men's hands and stole a fast glance at the slaughterhouse, grimaced.

"Please come inside," Potter said, nodding toward the van.

Henry LeBow was pleased by all the data Angie had brought. He rapidly began inputting the information. Potter had been right; the

minute she'd heard about the barricade—before the DomTran Gulfstream was even fueled—she'd spoken with officials at the Laurent
Clerc School and started compiling the profiles of the captives.

"Excellent, Angie," LeBow said, typing madly. "You're a born
biographer."

She opened another folder, offering the contents to Potter. "Tobe,"
he asked, "could you please tape these up?" The young agent took the
photographs of the girls and pinned them to the corkboard, just above
the CAD diagram of the slaughterhouse. Angie had written the names
and ages of the girls in the bottom margin in black marker.

> Anna Morgan, 7
> Suzie Morgan, 7
> Shannon Boyle, 8
> Kielle Stone, 8
> Emily Stoddard, 10
> Jocylyn Weiderman, 12
> Beverly Klemper, 14

The picture of Susan Phillips remained face-up on the table.

"You always do this?" Frances waved at the wall.

Potter, eyes on the pictures, said absently, "You win by having better
knowledge than the enemy." He found himself looking at the adorable
twins, for they were the youngest. Whenever he thought of children he
thought of them as being very young—perhaps because he and Marian
never had any—and the image of the son or daughter that might have
been was thus frozen in time, as if Potter were perpetually a young husband and Marian his bride of, say, twenty-five.

Look at them, he told himself. *Look at them.* And as if he'd spoken
aloud, he realized that everyone except Derek and Tobe, who were
hunched over their dials, had paused and was gazing up at the pictures.

Potter asked Angie for information about the girl who was about to
be released, Jocylyn Weiderman.

Speaking from memory, Angie said, "Apparently she's a troubled girl.
She was postlingually deaf—deaf after she learned to speak. You'd
think that would make things easier and it *does* help with learning de-

velopment. But psychologically what happens is people like that don't take to Deaf culture easily at all. You know what that means? 'Deaf' with a capital *D*?"

Potter, eye on the slaughterhouse, looking again for Melanie, said he didn't.

Angie lifted an eyebrow to Frances, who explained, "The word 'deaf,' small *d*, is the physical condition of not being able to hear. Deaf, upper-case *D*, is used by the Deaf to signify their community, their culture."

Angie continued, "In terms of Deaf status it's best to be born deaf of deaf parents and to shun all oral skills. If you're born hearing of hearing parents and know how to speak and read lips, you don't have the same status. But even that's a notch above someone deaf trying to pass for hearing—which is what Jocylyn's tried to do."

"So the girl has one strike against her to start with."

"She's been rejected by both the hearing and Deaf worlds. Add to that she's overweight. And has pretty undeveloped social skills. Prime candidate for a panic attack. If that happens Handy might think the girl was attacking him. She might even do it."

Potter nodded, thankful as always that Angie Scapello was assisting the threat management team. Her specialty was hostage psychology—helping them to recover and to remember observations that might be useful in future barricades and preparing former hostages to be witnesses at the trials of their takers.

Several years ago it had occurred to Potter to bring her along during ongoing barricades, analyzing the data that hostages reported and evaluating hostages and takers themselves. She often shared the podium with him when he lectured on negotiation strategy.

Potter observed, "Then we've got to try to keep her calm."

Panic during a hostage exchange was infectious. It often led to fatalities.

The negotiator asked Frances, "Could you teach our trooper something to tell her? Something that might help?"

Frances moved her hands and said, "That means 'Stay calm.' But signing's a very difficult skill to learn quickly and to remember. Slight mistakes change the meaning completely. I'd recommend if you have to communicate, use everyday gestures—for 'come here,' 'go there.' "

"And I'd suggest having him smile," Angie said. "Universal language, smiling. That's just what the girl needs. If he has to say something more complex, maybe write it down?"

Frances nodded. "That's a good idea."

"The reading age of prelingually deaf is sometimes below that of their chronological age. But with Jocylyn being postlingual and"—Angie stole back her notes from Henry LeBow, found what she sought—"and having a high IQ, she can read any commands fine."

"Hey, Derek, got any pens and writing pads?"

"Got 'em both right here," Elb replied, producing a stack of pads and a fistful of big black ink markers.

The agent then asked Angie if she happened to have a picture of the teachers. "No, I . . . Wait. I think I have one of Melanie Charrol. The younger of them."

She's twenty-five, Potter reminded himself.

"We're past the food deadline," Tobe announced.

"Ah, here it is," Angie said, handing him a picture.

Be forewarned. . . .

He was surprised. The woman it depicted was more beautiful than he'd thought. Unlike the other photos, this was in color. She had wavy blond hair, very curly bangs, smooth pale skin, radiant eyes. The picture seemed less like a staff photograph than like a model's head shot. There was something childlike about everything except the eyes. He himself pinned it up, next to the picture of the twins.

"Does she have family here?" Potter asked.

Angie looked at her notes. "The dean at Laurent Clerc told me her parents have a farm not far from the school but they're in St. Louis this weekend. Melanie's brother had an accident last year and he's having some kind of fancy surgery tomorrow. She was taking tomorrow off to go visit him."

"Farms," Budd muttered. "Most dangerous places on earth. You should hear some of the calls we get."

A console phone buzzed, a scrambled line, and Tobe pushed the button, spoke into his stalk mike for a moment. "It's the CIA," he announced to the room, then began speaking rapidly into the mike. He tapped several keys, conferred with Derek, and turned on a monitor. "Kwo got a SatSurv image, Arthur. Take a look."

A monitor slowly came to life. The background was dark green, like a glowing radar screen, and you could make out patches of lighter green, yellow, and amber. There was a faint outline of the slaughter-house and a number of red dots surrounding it.

"The green's the ground," Tobe explained. "The yellow and orange, those are trees and natural thermal sources. The red are troopers." The slaughterhouse was a blue-green rectangle. Only toward the front was there any shift in the color, where the windows and doors were located. "There's probably a little heat rising from the lamps. Doesn't tell us much. Other than nobody's actually on the roof."

"Tell them to keep broadcasting."

"You know what it costs, don't you?" Tobe asked.

"Twelve thousand an hour," LeBow said, typing happily, "Now ask him if he cares."

Potter said, "Keep it on-line, Tobe."

"Will do. But I want a cost-of-living this year, we're so rich."

Then the door opened and a trooper entered, brown bags in his arms, and the van filled with the smell of hot greasy burgers and fries. Potter sat down at his chair, gripping the phone in his fingers.

The first exchange was about to begin.

2:45 P.M.

Stevie Oates again.

"Glutton for punishment?" Potter asked.

"Bored just sitting on my butt, sir."

"Nothing to pitch this time, Officer. You'll be going the distance."

Dean Stillwell stood beside the trooper as, Potter instructing, two FBI agents in flak jackets were suiting Oates up with two layers of thin body armor under his regular uniform. They were standing behind the van. Charlie Budd was nearby, directing the placement of the huge halogen spotlights, trained on the slaughterhouse. There was still plenty of summer light left in the day but the overcast had grown thicker and with every passing minute it seemed more like dusk.

"All set, Arthur," Budd announced.

"Hit 'em," Potter ordered, looking up from the trooper for a moment.

The halogens burst to life, shooting their streams of raw white light onto the front and sides of the slaughterhouse. Budd ordered a few adjustments and the lights focused on the door and the windows on either side of it. The wind was gusting sharply and the troopers had to anchor the legs of the lights with sandbags.

Suddenly a curious sound came from the field. "What's that?" Budd wondered aloud.

Stillwell said, "Somebody's laughing. Some of the troopers. Hank, what's going on out there?" the sheriff called over his radio. He listened, then looked at the slaughterhouse through field glasses. "Look in the window."

Potter ducked his head around the van. With the spotlights, nobody in the slaughterhouse would have a prayer of an effective sniper shot. He trained his Leicas on the window.

"Very funny," he muttered.

Lou Handy had put on sunglasses against the glaring lights. With exaggerated gestures he mopped his forehead and mugged for his laughing audience.

"Enough of that," Stillwell radioed sternly, speaking to his troops. "This isn't David Letterman."

Potter turned back to Oates, nodded at the thin armor. "You'll get a nasty bruise if you're shot. But it's important to look unthreatening."

HTs get very nervous, Angie explained, when they see troopers dressed up like alien spacemen plodding toward them. "You've got to dress for success."

"I'm about as unthreatening as can be. 'S'way I feel anyway. Should I leave my sidearm here?"

"No. But keep it out of sight," Potter said. "Your first responsibility is your own safety. Never compromise that. If it's between you and the hostage, save yourself first."

"Well—"

"That's an order, Trooper," Stillwell said solemnly. He'd grown into his role of containment officer like a natural.

Potter continued, "Walk up there slowly, carry the food at your side, in plain view. Don't move fast, whatever happens."

"Okay." Oates seemed to be memorizing these orders.

Tobe Geller stepped out of the doorway of the van, carrying a small box attached to a wire burgeoning into a stubby black rod. He hooked the box to the trooper's back, under the vest. The rod he clipped into Oates's hair with bobby pins.

"Couldn't use this with Arthur here," Tobe said. "Need a full head of hair."

"What is it?"

"Video camera. And earphone."

"That little thing? No foolin'."

Tobe ran the wire down Oates's back and plugged it into the transmitter.

"The resolution isn't very good," Potter said, "but it'll help when you get back."

"How's that?"

"You seem pretty cool, Stevie," LeBow said. "But at best you'll remember about forty percent of what you see up there."

"Oh, he's a fifty percenter," Potter said, "if I'm not mistaken."

"The tape won't tell us too much on its own," the intelligence officer continued, "but it should refresh your memory."

"Gotcha. Say, those burgers sure smell good," Oates joked, while his face said that food was the last thing on his mind.

"Angie?" Potter asked.

The agent walked up to the trooper and tossed the mass of dark, windblown hair from her face. "Here's a picture of the girl who's coming out. Her name's Jocylyn." Quickly, she repeated her assessment on how to best handle her.

"Don't talk to her," Angie concluded. "She won't understand your words and it might make her panic, thinking she's missing something important. And keep smiling."

"Smiling. Sure. Piece of cake." Oates swallowed.

Potter added, "Now, she's overweight and can't run very fast, I'd guess." He unfurled a small map of the grounds of the slaughterhouse. "If she could hustle I'd tell you to duck into that gully there, the one in front of the place, and then just run like hell. You'd be oblique targets. But as it is I think you'll just have to walk straight back."

"Like the girl who got shot?" Budd asked, and nobody was happy he had.

"Now, Stevie," Potter continued, "you should go up to the door. But under no circumstances are you to go inside."

"What if he says he won't release her 'less I do?"

"Then you leave her. Leave the food and walk away. But I think he'll let her go. Get as close as you can to the door. I want you to look inside. Look for what kinds of weapons they have, radios, any signs of blood, any hostages or hostage takers we might not know about."

Budd asked, "How could more've gotten in?"

"They might have been waiting inside for Handy and the others to arrive."

"Oh, sure." Budd looked discouraged. "Didn't think of that."

Potter continued to Oates, "Don't engage him in a dialogue, don't argue, don't say anything, except to answer his questions directly."

"You think he'll ask me stuff?"

Potter looked at Angie, who said, "It's possible. He might want to tease you a little. The sunglasses—he's got a playful streak in him. He might want to test you. Don't rise to the bait."

Oates nodded uncertainly.

Potter continued, "We'll be monitoring your conversations and I can feed you answers through your earphone."

Oates smiled a faint smile. "Those'll be the longest hundred yards of my life."

"There's nothing to worry about," Potter said. "He's a lot more interested in food right now than he is in shooting anybody."

This logic seemed to reassure Oates though the memory loomed in Potter's mind that some years ago he'd said similar words to an officer who a few moments later had been shot in the knee and wrist by a hostage taker who decided impulsively that he didn't want the painkillers and bandages the officer was bringing him.

Potter added an asthma inhaler to the bag of hamburgers. "Don't say anything about that. Just let him find it and decide to give it to Beverly or not."

Budd held up several pads of paper and the markers Derek had provided. "Should we include these?"

Potter considered. The pads and pens would give the hostages a chance to communicate with their captors and improve the Stockholming between them. But sometimes small deviations from what they expected set off HTs. The inhaler was one deviation. How would Handy feel about a second? He asked Angie's opinion.

"He may be a sociopath," she said after a moment. "But he hasn't had any temper tantrums or emotional outbursts, has he?"

"No. He's been pretty cool."

In fact he'd been frighteningly calm.

"Sure," Angie said, "add them."

"Dean, Charlie," Potter said, "come here a minute." The sheriff and the captain huddled. "Who're the best rifle shots you've got?"

"That'd be Sammy Bullock and—what do you think? Chris Felling? That's Christine. I'd say she's better'n Sammy. Dean?"

"If I was a squirrel sitting four hundred yards away from Chrissy and I saw her shoulder her piece, I wouldn't even bother to run. I'd just kiss my be-hind goodbye."

Potter wiped his glasses. "Have her load and lock and get a spotter with glasses to keep a watch on the door and windows. If it looks like Handy or one of the others is about to shoot, she's green-lighted to fire. But she's to aim for the doorjamb or windowsill."

"I thought you said there'd be no warning shots," Budd said.

"That's the rule," Potter said sagely. "And it's absolutely true—unless there's an exception to it."

"Oh."

"Go on and take care of that, Dean."

"Yessir." The sheriff hurried away, crouching.

Potter returned to Oates. "Okay, Trooper. Ready?"

Frances said to the young man, "Can I say 'Good luck'?"

"Please do," Oates said earnestly. Budd patted him on his Kevlared shoulder.

Melanie Charrol knew many Bible-school stories.

The lives of the Deaf used to be tied closely with religion, and many of them still were. The poor lambs of God . . . pat them on the head and force them to learn enough speech to struggle through catechism and Eucharist and confession (always among themselves of course so they didn't embarrass the hearing congregation). Abbé de l'Epée, good-hearted and brilliant though he was, created French Sign Language primarily to make sure his charges' souls could enter heaven.

And of course vows of silence by monks and nuns, adopting the "affliction" of the unfortunate as penance. (Maybe thinking that they could hear God's voice all the better though Melanie could have told them it didn't work worth squat.)

She leaned against the tile walls of the killing room, as horrible a part of the Outside as ever existed. Mrs. Harstrawn lay on her side, ten feet away, staring at the wall. No tears any longer—she was cried out, dry, empty. The woman blinked, she breathed but she might as well have been in a coma. Melanie rose and lifted her leg away from a pool of black water encrusted with green scum and the splintered bodies of a thousand insects.

Religion.

Melanie hugged the twins, feeling their delicate spines through identical powder-blue cowgirl blouses. She sat down beside them, thinking of some story she'd heard in Sunday school. It was about early Christians in ancient Rome, awaiting martyrdom in the Colosseum. They had, of course, refused to deny their faith. Men and women, children, happily praying on their knees while the centurions came for them. The story was ridiculous, the product of a simple-minded textbook writer, and it seemed inexcusable to adult Melanie Charrol that anyone would include it in a children's book. Yet like the cheapest melodrama the story had wrenched her heart then, at age eight or nine. And it wrenched her heart still.

Staring at the distant light, losing herself in the pulsing meditation of the yellow bulb, growing, shrinking, growing, shrinking, seeing the light turn into Susan's face, then into a beautiful young woman's body torn apart by lions' yellow claws.

Eight gray birds, sitting in dark . . .

But no, it's just seven birds now.

Was Jocylyn about to die too? Melanie peeked around the corner, seeing the girl standing at a window. She was sobbing, shaking her head. Stoat had her by the arm. They stood near the partially open door.

Motion nearby. She turned her head—the automatic reaction of a deaf person to the movement of gesturing hands. Kielle had closed her eyes. Melanie watched her hands move in a repetitive pattern, confused about the girl's message until she realized that she was summoning Wolverine, another of her comic-book heros.

"Do something," Shannon signed. "Melanie!" Her tiny hands chopped the air.

Do something. Right.

Melanie thought of de l'Epée. She hoped the thought of him would restart her frozen heart. It didn't. She was as helpless as ever, staring at Jocylyn, who looked back toward the killing room and caught Melanie's eye.

"Going to kill me," Jocylyn signed, sobbing; her cheeks, round and pale as a honeydew, glistened from the tears. "Please, help."

The Outside . . .

"Melanie." Kielle's dark eyes flared. The girl had suddenly appeared beside her. "Do something!"

"What?" Melanie suddenly snapped. "Tell me. Shoot him? Grow wings and fly?"

"Then I will," Kielle said, and turned, bursting toward the men. Without thinking, Melanie leapt after her. The little girl was just past the doorway to the killing room when Bear loomed in front of them. Both Melanie and Kielle stopped abruptly. Melanie put her arm around the girl and looked down, eyes fixed on the black pistol in Bear's waistband.

Grab it. Shoot him. Don't worry what happens. You can do it. His filthy mind is elsewhere. De l'Epée would hear the shot and come running to save them. Grab it. Do it. She actually saw herself pulling the trigger. Her hands began to shake. She stared at the pistol butt, glistening black plastic.

Bear reached forward and touched her hair. The back of his hand, a gentle stroke. A lover's or father's touch.

And whatever strength was within Melanie vanished in that instant. Bear grabbed them by the collars and dragged them back into the killing room, cutting off her view of Jocylyn.

I'm deaf so I can't hear her screams.

I'm deaf so I can't hear her beg me to help her.

I'm deaf, I'm deaf, I'm deaf. . . .

Bear shoved them into the corner and sat down in the doorway. He gazed over the frightened captives.

I'm deaf so I'm dead already. What does it matter; what does anything matter?

Melanie closed her eyes, drew her beautiful hands into her lap, and, untethered, slipped away from the killing room once again.

"Run the HP, Tobe," Potter ordered.

Inside the van Tobe opened an attaché case, revealing the Hewlett-Packard Model 122 VSA, which resembled a cardiac-care monitor.

"These all one-ten, grounded?" He nodded at the outlets. Derek Elb told him yes.

Tobe plugged in and turned on the machine. A small strip of paper, like a cash-register receipt, fed out, and a grid appeared in green on the black screen. He glanced at the others in the room. LeBow pointed at Potter, himself, Angie, and Budd. "In that order."

Frances and Derek looked on curiously.

"Five says you're wrong," Potter offered. "Me, Angie, you, and Charlie."

Budd laughed uneasily. "What're you talking about?"

Tobe said, "Everybody, quiet." He pushed a microphone toward Angie. "The rain in Spain falls—"

"That's enough," Tobe said, holding the microphone out to Potter.

He recited, "The quick brown fox . . ."

Henry LeBow was cut off during a lengthy quotation from *The Tempest*.

Budd nearly went cross-eyed gazing at the encroaching microphone and said, "That thing's making me pretty nervous."

The four FBI agents roared with laughter.

Tobe explained to Frances. "Voice stress analyzer. Gives us some clue about truth telling but mostly it gives us a risk assessment." He pushed a button and the screen divided into four squares. Wavy lines of differing peaks and valleys froze in place.

Tobe tapped the screen and said, "This is Arthur. He never gets rattled. Actually I think he pees his pants regularly but you'll never tell it by the sound of his voice. Then you're number two, Angie. Arthur was right. You get a Cool Cucumber Award. But Henry's not far behind." He laughed, tapping the final grid. "Captain Budd, you are one nervous fellow. Can I suggest yoga and breathing exercises?"

Budd frowned. "If you hadn't been poking that thing into my face

I'da done better. Or told me what it was about in the first place. I get a second chance?"

The negotiator looked outside. "Let's make that phone call. Send him out, Charlie."

"Go ahead, Stevie," Budd said into the radio handset. They saw the trooper move into the gully and make his way toward the slaughterhouse.

Potter pressed the speed dial.

"Uplink."

"Hello, Lou."

"Art. We got the fat one all dressed up like a Thanksgiving turkey. We see your boy coming. He got my chocolate shake?"

"He's the same one who pitched the phone to you. Stevie's his name. Good man."

Potter thought: *Was he one of them was shooting at us before?*

"Maybe," Handy said, "he was the one gave the signal to shoot at our Shep."

"I told you that was an accident, Lou. Say, how's everybody doing in there?"

Who gives a shit?

"Fine. I just checked on 'em."

Curious, the negotiator thought. He hadn't expected this response at all. Is he saying that to reassure me? Is he scared? Does he want to lull me into being careless?

Or did the bad-boy act fall away for a moment and was the real Lou Handy actually giving a legitimate response to a legitimate question?

"I put some of that asthma medicine in the bag."

Fuck her, who cares?

Handy laughed. "Oh, for the one sucking air. It's a pain, Art. How can anybody get any sleep with that little shit gasping for breath?"

"And some paper and pens. In case the girls want to say something to you."

Silence. Potter and LeBow glanced at each other. Was he angry about the paper?

No, he was just talking to someone inside.

Keep his mind busy, off the hostages, off Stevie. "How're those lights working?" Potter asked.

"Good. The ones you've got outside suck, though. Can I shoot 'em out?"

"You know what they cost? It'd come out of my paycheck."

Oates was fifty feet away, walking slowly and steadily. Potter glanced at Tobe, who nodded and pushed buttons on the HP.

"So you're a McDonald's fan, Lou? Big Macs, they're the best."

"How'd *you* know?" Handy asked sarcastically. "You never ate under the golden arches in your life, betcha."

Angie gave him a thumbs-up and Potter nodded, pleased. It's a good sign when the HT refers to the negotiator. The transference process was proceeding.

"Guess again, Lou. You're going to have exactly what I had for dinner twice last week. Well, minus the Fritos. But I did have a milk shake. Vanilla."

"Thought you fancy agents had gourmet meals every night. Steak and lobster. Champagne. Then you fuck the beautiful agent works for you."

"A bacon cheeseburger, not a glass of wine to be had. Oh, and instead of sex I had a second order of fries. I do love my potatoes."

In the faint reflection of the window Potter was aware that Budd was staring at him and he believed the expression was of faint disbelief.

"You fat too, like this little girl I got by her piggy arm?"

"I could lose a few pounds. Maybe more than a few."

Oates was fifty feet from the door.

Potter wanted to probe some more into Handy's likes and dislikes. But he was cautious. He sensed it would rile the man. There's a philosophy in barricade situations that tries to keep the HTs on edge—bombarding them with bad music or playing with the heating and cooling of the barricade site. Potter didn't believe in this approach. Be firm, but establish rapport.

Handy was too quiet. What was distracting him? What was he thinking? *I need more control. That's the problem,* it occurred to Potter. *I can't get control of the situation away from him.*

"I was going to ask you, Lou. . . . This is pretty odd weather for July. Must be cold in there. You want us to rig some heaters or something?"

Potter speculated: *Naw, we got plenty of bodies to keep us warm.*

But Handy responded slowly, "Maybe. How cold's it going to be tonight?"

Again, very logical and matter-of-fact. And behind the words: the implication that he might be planning on a long siege. That might give Potter the chance to push back some of Handy's deadlines. He jotted these impressions on a slip of paper and pushed it toward Henry LeBow to enter into his computer.

"Windy and chilly, I'm told."

"I'll think on it."

And listen to his voice, Potter thought. He sounds so reasonable. What do I make of that? Sometimes he's pure bravado; sometimes he sounds like an insurance salesman. Potter's eyes scanned the diagram of the slaughterhouse. Twelve yellow Post-Its, each representing a taker or a hostage, were stuck on the schematic. Ultimately, Potter hoped, they'd be placed in the exact position where each person was located. At the moment they were clustered off to the side.

"Lou, you there?"

"Sure I'm here. Where the fuck'd I be? Driving down I-70 to Denver?"

"Didn't hear you breathing."

In a low, chilling voice Handy said, "That's 'cause I'm a ghost."

"A ghost?" Potter echoed.

"I slip up quiet as a cat behind you and slit your throat and I'm gone before your blood hits the ground. You think I'm in that building there, that slaughterhouse you're looking at right now. But I'm not."

"Where'd you be?"

"Maybe I'm coming up behind you, that van of yours. See, I know you're in that there truck. Looking out your window. Maybe I'm right outsida that window. Maybe I'm in that stand of buffalo grass your man's walking by right now and I'm going to knife him in the balls when he passes."

"And maybe I'm in the slaughterhouse with you, Lou."

A pause. Potter thought, He'll laugh.

Handy did, a hearty belly laugh. "You get me lotsa Fritos?"

"Lots. Regular and barbecue."

Stevie Oates was at the building.

"Hey, shave and a haircut . . . Somebody's come acalling."

"Got a visual," Tobe whispered. He dimmed the van lights. They turned to the screen broadcasting the picture from the camera above

Stevie Oates's right ear. The image wasn't good. The door of the slaughter-house opened only several feet and the images inside—pipes, machinery, a table—were distorted by light flares. The only person in sight was Jocylyn, in silhouette, hands to her face.

"Here's your boy now. Stevie? I don't think I've ever shot anyone named Stevie. He looks pretty *dayamm* uncomfortable."

What was probably a shotgun barrel protruded slowly and rested against Jocylyn's head. Her hands dropped to her sides, making fists. The sound of her whimpering floated from the speaker. Potter prayed that Stillwell's sniper would exercise restraint.

The video image quivered for a moment.

The shotgun turned toward Oates as a man's silhouette filled the doorway. Through the mike mounted above the trooper's ear came the words: "You got a gun on you?" A voice different from Handy's. Shepard Wilcox's, Potter guessed; Bonner would cast a far bigger shadow.

Potter looked down to make sure he was hitting the right buttons as he cut over to Oates's earphone. "Lie. Be insistent but respectful."

"No, I don't. Here's what you wanted. The food. Now, sir, if you'd let that girl go . . ." The trooper spoke without a quaver in his voice.

"Good, Stevie, you're doing fine. Nod if Jocylyn seems okay."

The picture dipped slightly.

"Keep smiling at her."

Another dip.

Handy asked Oates, "You got a microphone or camera?" Another silhouette had appeared. Handy's. "You recording me?"

"Your call," Potter whispered. "But there'll be no exchange if you say yes."

"No," the trooper said.

"I'll kill you if I find out you're lying to me."

"I don't," Oates said insistently, without hesitation.

Good, good.

"You alone? Anybody sneak up on either side of the door?"

"Can't you see? I'm alone. How's the girl?"

"Can't you see?" Handy mocked, stepping behind Wilcox, in plain view. "Here she is. Look for yourself."

There was no move to release her.

"Let her go," Oates said.

"Maybe you oughta come in and get her."

"No. Let her go."

"You wearing body armor?"

"Under my shirt, yeah."

"Maybe you oughta give me that. We could use it more'n you."

"How do you figure?" Oates said. His voice was no longer so steady.

" 'Cause it won't do you any good. See, we could shoot you in the face and take it offa you and you'd be just as dead as if we shot you in the back when you were walking away. So how 'bout you give it to us now?"

They'd find the video camera and radio transmitter if he gave up the armor. And probably kill him on the spot.

Potter whispers, "Tell him we had a bargain."

"We had a bargain," Oates said firmly. "Here's the food. I want that girl. And I want her now."

A pause that lasted eons.

"Put it on the ground," Handy finally said.

The image on the screen dipped as Oates set the bag down. Still, the trooper kept his head up and pointed directly into the crack of the open door. Unfortunately there was too much contrast in the image; the agents in the van could see virtually nothing inside.

"Here," Handy's voice crackled, "take Miss Piggy. Go wee, wee, wee all the way home." Laughter from several voices. Handy stepped away from the door. They lost sight of him and Wilcox. Was one of them raising the gun to shoot?

"Hiya, honey," Oates said. "Don't you worry, you're gonna be just fine."

"He shouldn't be talking to her," Angie muttered.

"Let's go for a walk, whatta you say? See your mommy and daddy?"

"Lou," Potter called into the throw phone, suddenly concerned that the takers were no longer in sight. No answer. To those in the van he muttered, "I don't trust him. Hell, I don't trust him."

"Lou?"

"Line's still open," Tobe called. "He hasn't hung up."

Potter said to Oates, "Don't say anything to her, Stevie. Might make her panic."

The screen dipped in response.

"Go on. Back on out of there. Go real slow. Then get behind the girl, turn around, and walk straight away. Keep your head up, so your helmet covers as much of your neck as possible. If you're shot, fall on top of the girl. I'll order covering fire and we'll get you out as fast as we can."

A faint disturbed whisper came through the speaker. But there was no other answer.

Suddenly the video screen went mad. There was a burst of light and motion and jiggling images.

"No!" came Oates's voice. Then a deep grunt, followed by a moan.

"He's down," Budd said, looking through the window with binoculars. "Oh, brother."

"Christ!" Derek Elb cried, gazing up at the video monitor.

They'd heard no gunfire but Potter was sure that Wilcox had shot the girl in the head with a silenced pistol and was firing repeatedly at Oates. The screen danced madly with grainy shapes and lens flares.

"Lou!" Potter cried into the phone. "Lou, are you there?"

"Look!" Budd shouted, pointing out the window.

It wasn't what Potter had feared. Jocylyn apparently had panicked and leapt forward. The big girl had knocked Oates flat on his back. She was bounding over the grass and bluestem toward the first row of police cars.

Oates rolled over and was on his feet, going after her.

Potter juggled more buttons. "Lou!" He slapped the console again, activating the radio to Dean Stillwell, who was watching through a night scope with a sniper beside him.

"Dean?" Potter called.

"Yessir."

"Can you see inside?"

"Not much. Door's open only about a foot. There's somebody behind it."

"Windows?"

"No one in 'em yet."

Jocylyn, overweight though she might be, was sprinting like an Olympian directly toward the command van, arms waving, mouth open wide. Oates was gaining on the girl but they were both clear targets.

"Tell the sniper," Potter said, desperately scanning the slaughterhouse windows, "safety off."

Should he order a shot?

"Yessir. Wait. There's Wilcox. Inside about five yards from the window. He's got a shotgun and's drawing a target."

Oh, Lord, Potter thought. If the sniper kills him Handy's sure to murder one of the hostages in retaliation.

Is he going to shoot or not?

Maybe Wilcox's just panicked too, doesn't know what's going on.

"Agent Potter?" Stillwell asked.

"Acquire."

"Yessir. . . . Wilcox's in Chrissy's sights. She's got a shot. Can't miss, she says. Crosshaired on his forehead."

Yes? No?

"Wait," Potter said. "Keep him acquired."

"Yessir."

Jocylyn was thirty yards from the slaughterhouse. Oates close behind her. Perfect targets. A load of twelve-gauge, double-ought buck would cut their legs off.

Sweating, Potter slammed his hand onto two buttons. Into the phone he said, "Lou, you there?"

There was the sound of static, or breathing, or an erratic heartbeat.

"Tell the sniper to stand down," Potter ordered Stillwell suddenly. "Don't shoot. Whatever happens, don't shoot."

"Yessir," Stillwell said.

Potter leaned forward, felt his head tap against the cool glass window.

In two leaps, Stevie Oates grabbed the girl and pulled her down. Her hands and legs flailed and together they tumbled behind the rise, out of sight of the slaughterhouse.

Budd sighed loudly.

"Thank God," muttered Frances.

Angie said nothing but Potter noticed that her hand had strayed to her weapon and now held the grip tightly.

"Lou, you there?" he called. Then again.

There was a crackle, as if the phone were being wrapped in crispy paper. "Can't talk, Art," Handy said through a mouthful of food. "It's suppertime."

"Lou—"

There was a click and then silence.

Potter leaned back in his chair and rubbed his eyes.

Frances applauded, joined by Derek Elb.

"Congratulations," LeBow said quietly. "The first exchange. A success."

Budd was pale. He slowly exhaled a cheekful of air. "Brother."

"All right, everybody, let's not pat ourselves on the back too much," Potter said. "We've only got an hour forty-five minutes till our first helicopter deadline."

Of all the people in the van only young Tobe Geller seemed disturbed.

Arthur Potter, childless father that he was, noticed it immediately. "What is it, Tobe?"

The agent pushed several buttons on the Hewlett-Packard and pointed to the screen. "This was your VSA grid during the exchange, Arthur. Lower anxiety than normal for a mildly stressful event."

"Mildly," Budd muttered, rolling his eyes. "Glad you didn't take mine."

"Here's Handy's average ten-second sequence for the entire exchange." He tapped the screen. It was nearly a flat line. "He was in the doorway with a dozen guns pointed at his heart and that son of a bitch was about as stressed out as most people get ordering a cup of coffee at 7-Eleven."

3:13 P.M.

She felt no thud of gunshots, no quiver of scream resonating in her chest.

Thank you thank you thank you.

The butterball Jocylyn was safe.

Melanie huddled with the twins in the back of the killing room, their long chestnut hair damp from tears, plastered to their faces. She looked up at the bare bulb, which—just barely—kept the crushing waves of the Outside from smashing her to death.

Her finger nervously entwining a strand of hair again. The hand shape for "shine." The word for "brilliance."

The word for "light."

A blur of motion startled her. The huge bearded form of Bear, chewing a hamburger, stormed up to Stoat and snapped a few words. Waited for an answer, got none, and shouted some more. Melanie couldn't read a single word of their conversation. The more emotional people became, the more ragged and fast their words, making them impossible to understand, as if just when it was the most important to say things clearly there could be no clarity.

Brushing his crew cut, Stoat stayed cool and looked back at Bear with a sneer of a smile. A real cowboy, Melanie thought, Stoat is. He's as cruel as the others but he's brave and he has honor and if those are good qualities even in bad people then there's some good in him. Brutus appeared and Bear suddenly stopped talking, grabbed a packet of fries in his fat hand, and wandered off to the front of the slaughterhouse, where he sat down and began shoveling food into his messy beard.

Brutus carried a paper-wrapped hamburger with him. He kept glancing at it in an amused way, as if he'd never had one before. He took a small bite and chewed carefully. He crouched in the doorway of the killing room, looking over the girls and the teachers. Melanie caught his eye once and felt her skin burn with panic. "Hey, miss," he said. She looked down quickly, feeling stomach sick.

She felt a thud and looked up, startled. He'd slapped the floor beside her. From his shirt pocket he took a small blue cardboard box and tossed it to her. It was an asthma inhaler. She opened it slowly and handed it to Beverly, who breathed in the medicine greedily.

Melanie turned to Brutus and was about to mouth "Thank you," but he was looking away, staring once again at Mrs. Harstrawn, who'd fallen into another hysterical crying fit.

"Ain't that something—she . . . keeps going and going."

How can I understand his words if I can't understand *him?* Look at him—he crouches there and watches the poor woman cry. Chewing, chewing, with that damn half-smile on his lips. Nobody can be that cruel.

Or *do* I understand him?

Melanie hears a familiar voice. *So you'll be home then. . . .*

Get up, she raged silently to the other teacher. Stop crying! Get up and do something! Help us. You're supposed to be in charge.

So you'll be—

Suddenly her heart went icy cold and anger vaporized her fear. Anger and . . . what else? A dark fire swirling within her. Her eyes met Brutus's. He'd stopped eating and was looking at her. His lids never flickered but she sensed he was winking at her—as if he knew exactly what she was thinking about Mrs. Harstrawn and that the same thing had occurred to him. For that instant the pathetic woman was the butt of an inexcusable, mutual joke.

In despair she felt the anger vanishing, fear flooding in to fill its place. Stop looking at me! she begged him silently. Please! She lowered her head and began to tremble, crying. And so she did the only thing she could do—what she'd done earlier: closing her eyes, lowering her head, she went away. The place she'd escaped into from the slaughterhouse earlier today. Her secret place, her music room.

It is a room of dark wood, tapestries, pillows, smoky air. Not a window in the place. The Outside cannot get in here.

Here's a harpsichord carved of delicate rosewood, florets and filigree, inlaid with ivory and ebony. Here's a piano whose tone sounds like resonating crystal. A South American berimbau, a set of golden vibes, a crisp, prewar Martin guitar.

Here are walls to reflect Melanie's own voice, which is an amalgam of all the instruments in the orchestra. Mezzo-sopranos and coloratura sopranos and altos.

It was a place that never existed and never would. But it was Melanie's salvation. When the taunts at school had grown too much, when she simply couldn't grasp what someone was saying to her, when she thought of the world she'd never experience, her music room was the only place she could go to be safe, to be comforted.

Forgetting the twins, forgetting gasping Beverly, forgetting the sobs of the paralyzed Mrs. Harstrawn, forgetting the terrible man watching her as he inhaled for sustenance the sorrow of another human being. Forgetting Susan's death, and her own, which was probably all too close.

Melanie, sitting on the comfortable couch in her secret place, decides she doesn't want to be alone. She needs someone with her. Someone to talk with. Someone with whom she can share human words. Whom should I invite?

Melanie thinks of her parents. But she's never invited them here before. Friends from Laurent Clerc, from Hebron, neighbors, students . . . But when she thinks of them she thinks of Susan. And of course she dares not.

Sometimes she invites musicians and composers—people she's read about, even if she's never heard their music: Emmylou Harris, Bonnie Raitt, Gordon Bok, Patrick Ball, Mozart, Sam Barber. Ludwig, of course. Ralph Vaughan Williams. Never Wagner. Mahler came once but didn't stay long.

Her brother used to be a regular visitor to the music room.

In fact, for a time, Danny was her only visitor, for he seemed to be the only person in the family not thrown by her affliction. Her parents struggled to coddle their daughter, keeping her home, never letting her go to town alone, scraping up money for tutors to come to the house, impressing on her the dangers of "her, you know, condition"—all the while avoiding any mention of her being deaf.

Danny wouldn't put up with her timidity. He'd roar into town on his Honda 350 with his sister perched on the back. She wore a black helmet emblazoned with fiery wings. Before her hearing went completely he'd take her to movies and would drive audiences to rage by loudly repeating dialogue for her. To their parents' disgust the boy would walk around the house wearing an airline mechanic's earmuffs, just so he'd know what she was going through. Bless his heart, Danny even learned some basic sign and taught her some phrases (naturally ones that she couldn't repeat in the company of adult Deaf though they would later earn her high esteem in the Laurent Clerc schoolyard).

Ah, but Danny . . .

Ever since the accident last year, she hadn't had the heart to ask him back.

She tries now but can't imagine him here.

And so today, when she opens the door, she finds a middle-aged man with graying hair, wearing an ill-fitting navy-blue jacket and black-framed glasses. The man from the field outside the slaughterhouse.

De l'Epée.

Who else but him?

"Hello," she says in a voice like a glass bell.

"And to you." She pictures him taking her hand and kissing it, rather bashfully, rather firmly.

"You're a policeman, aren't you?" she asks.

"Yes," he says.

She can't see him as clearly as she'd like. The power of desire is unlimited but that of imagination is not.

"I know it's not your name but can I call you de l'Epée?"

Of course he's agreeable to this, gentleman that he is.

"Can we talk for a little while? That's what I miss the most, talking."

Once you've spoken to someone, pelted them with your words and felt theirs in your ears, signing isn't the same at all.

"By all means, let's talk."

"I want to tell you a story. About how I learned I was deaf."

"Please . . ." He seems genuinely curious.

Melanie had planned to be a musician, she tells him. From the time she was four or five. She was no prodigy but did have the gift of perfect pitch. Classical, Celtic, or country-western—she loved it all. She could hear a tune once and pick it out from memory on the family's Yamaha piano.

"And then . . ."

"Tell me about it."

"When I was eight, almost nine, I went to a Judy Collins concert."

She continues, "She was singing a cappella, a song I'd never heard before. It was haunting. . . ."

Conveniently, a Celtic harp begins playing the very tune through the imaginary speakers in the music room.

"My brother had the concert program and I leaned over and asked him what the name of the song was. He told me it was 'A Maiden's Grave.' "

De l'Epée says, "Never heard of it."

Melanie continues, "I wanted to play it on the piano. It was . . . It's hard to describe. Just a feeling, something I *had* to do. I had to learn the song. The day after the concert I asked my brother to stop by a music store and get some sheet music for me. He asked me which song. 'A Maiden's Grave,' I told him.

" 'What song's that?' he asked. He was frowning.

"I laughed. 'At the concert, dummy. The song she finished the concert with. *That* song. You told me the title.'

"Then *he* laughed. 'Who's a dummy? "A Maiden's Grave"? What're you talking about? It was "Amazing Grace." The old gospel. That's what I told you.'

" 'No!' I was sure I heard him say 'A Maiden's Grave.' I was positive! And just then I realized that I'd been leaning forward to hear him and that when either of us turned away I couldn't really hear what he was saying at all. *And* that when I was looking at him I was looking only at his lips, never his eyes or the rest of his face. The same way I'd been looking at everyone else I'd talked to for the last six or eight months.

"I ran straight to the record store downtown—two miles away. I was so desperate, I had to know. I was sure my brother was teasing me and I hated him for it. I swore I'd get even with him. I raced up to the folk section and flipped through the Judy Collins albums. It was true . . . 'Amazing Grace.' Two months later I was diagnosed with a fifty-decibel loss in one ear, seventy in the other. It's about ninety now in both."

"I'm so sorry," de l'Epée says. "What happened to your hearing?"

"An infection. It destroyed the hairs in my ear."

"And there's nothing you can do about it?"

She doesn't answer him. After a moment she says, "I think that you're Deaf."

"Deaf? Me?" He grins awkwardly. "But I can hear."

"Oh, you can be Deaf but hearing."

He looks confused.

"Deaf but hearing," she continues. "See, we call people who can hear the Others. But some of the Others are more like us."

"What sort of people are those?" he asks. Is he proud to be included? She thinks he is.

"People who live according to their own hearts," Melanie answers, "not someone else's."

For a moment she's ashamed, for she's not sure that she always listens to her own.

A Mozart piece begins to play. Or Bach. She isn't sure which. (Why couldn't the infection have come a year later? Think of all the music I could have listened to in twelve months. For God's sake, her father pumped easy-listening KSFT through the farm's loudspeakers. In my bio, they'll find I was reared on "Pearly Shells," Tom Jones, and Barry Manilow.)

"There's more I have to tell you. Something else I've never told anyone."

"I'd like to hear it," he says, agreeable. But then, in an instant, he disappears.

Melanie gasps.

The music room vanishes and she's back in the slaughterhouse.

Her eyes are wide, she looks around, expecting to see Brutus approaching. Or Bear shouting, storming toward her.

But, no, Brutus is gone. And Bear sits by himself outside the killing room, eating, an incongruous smile on his face.

What had dragged her from the music room?

A vibration from a sound? The light?

No, it was a smell. A scent had wakened her out of her daydream. But of what?

Something she detected amid the smell of greasy food, bodies, and oil and gasoline and rusting metal and old blood and rancid lard and a thousand other scents.

Ah, she recognized it clearly. A rich, pungent smell.

"Girls, girls," she signed emphatically to the students. "I want to say something."

Bear's head turned toward them. He noticed the signing. His smile vanished immediately and he climbed to his feet. He seemed to be shouting, "Stop that! Stop!"

"He doesn't like us to sign," Melanie signed quickly. "Pretend we're playing hand-shape game."

One thing Melanie liked about Deaf culture—the love of words. ASL was a language like any other. In fact it was the fifth most widely used language in America. ASL words and phrases could be broken down into smaller structural units (hand shape, motion, and relation of the hand to the body), just like spoken words could be broken down into syllables and phonemes. Those gestures lent themselves to word games, which nearly all Deaf people grew up playing.

Bear stormed up to her. "What the fuck . . . with . . ."

Melanie's hands began to shake violently. She managed to write in the dust on the floor, *Game. We're playing game. See? We make shapes with our hands. Shapes of things.*

"What things?"

This is animal game.

She signed the word "Stupid." With her index and middle fingers extended in a V, the shape vaguely resembled a rabbit.

"What's that . . . be?"

A rabbit, she wrote.

The twins ducked their heads, giggling.

"Rabbit . . . Doesn't . . . fucking rabbit to me," he said.

Please let us play. Can't hurt.

He glanced at Kielle, who signed, "You turd." Smiling, she wrote in the dust, *That was hippo.*

". . . out of your fucking minds." Bear turned back to his fries and soda.

The girls waited until he was out of sight then looked expectantly at Melanie. Kielle, no longer smiling, asked brusquely, "What do you have to say?"

"I'm going to get us out of here," Melanie signed. "That's what."

.

Arthur Potter and Angie Scapello were preparing to debrief Jocylyn Weiderman, who was being examined by medics at that moment, when they heard the first shot.

It was a faint crack and far less alarming than Dean Stillwell's urgent voice breaking over the speaker above their heads. "Arthur, we've got a situation here! Handy's shooting."

Hell.

"There's somebody in the field."

Before he even looked outside Potter pressed the button on the mike and ordered, "Tell everybody, no return fire."

"Yessir."

Potter joined Angie and Charlie Budd in the ocher window of the van.

"That son of a bitch," Budd whispered.

Another shot rang out from the slaughterhouse and the bullet kicked up a cloud of splinters from the rotting stockade post next to the dark-suited man about sixty yards from the command van. A voluminous handkerchief, undoubtedly expensive, billowed around the raised right hand of the intruder.

"Oh, no," Angie whispered in dismay.

Potter's heart sank. "Henry, your profile of the assistant attorney general neglected to mention he's out of his damn mind."

Handy fired again, hitting a rock just behind Roland Marks. The assistant AG stopped, cringing. He waved the handkerchief again. He continued slowly toward the slaughterhouse.

Potter pressed speed dial. As the phone rang and rang he muttered, "Come on, Lou."

No answer.

Dean Stillwell's voice came over the speaker. "Arthur, I don't know what to make of it. Somebody here thinks it's—"

"It's Roland Marks, Dean. Is he saying anything to Handy?"

"Looks like he's shouting. We can't hear."

"Tobe, you have those Big Ears in place still?"

The young agent spoke into his stalk mike and punched buttons. In a few seconds, the mournful yet urgent sound of the wind filled the van. Then Marks's voice.

"Lou Handy! I'm Roland Marks, assistant attorney general of the state of Kansas."

A huge crack of a gunshot, overly amplified, burst into the van. Everyone cringed.

Tobe whispered, "The other Big Ear's trained on the slaughterhouse but we're not getting anything."

Sure. Because Handy's not saying anything. Why talk when you can make your point with bullets?

"This is bad," Angie muttered.

The AG's voice again: "Lou Handy, this isn't a trick. I want you to give up the girls and take me in their place."

"Jesus," Budd whispered. "He's doing that?" He sounded half-impressed and Potter had to restrain himself from scowling at the state police captain.

Another shot, closer. Marks danced sideways.

"For the love of God, Handy," came the desperate voice. "Let those girls go!"

And all the while the phone inside the slaughterhouse rang and rang and rang.

Potter spoke into the radio mike. "Dean, I hate to say it but we've got to stop him. Hail him on the bullhorn and try to get him over to the sidelines. If he doesn't come, send out a couple of men."

"Handy's just playing with him," Budd said. "I don't think he's in any real danger. They could've shot him easy by now, they'd wanted to."

"*He's* not who I'm worried about," Potter snapped.

"What?"

Angie said, "We're trying to get hostages *out,* not in."

"He's making our job harder," Potter said simply, not explaining the terrible mistake Marks was now making.

With a whining ricochet, a bullet split a rock beside the lawyer's leg. Marks remained on his feet. He turned and he was listening to Dean Stillwell, whose voice was being picked up by the Big Ear and relayed into the van. To Potter's relief the sheriff wasn't cowed by the man's authority. "You there, Marks, you're to get under cover immediately or you'll be arrested. Come back this way."

"We've got to save them." Marks's raw voice filled the van. It sounded resolute but terrified and for a moment Potter's heart went out to him.

Another shot.

"No, sir. Do you understand? You're about to be placed under arrest."

Potter called Stillwell and told him he was doing great. "Tell him he's *endangering* the girls doing this."

The sheriff's voice, mixing with the ragged wind, filled the van as he relayed this message.

"No! I'm saving them," the assistant AG shouted and started forward again.

Potter tried the throw phone again. No answer.

"Okay, Dean. Go get him. No covering fire under any circumstances."

Stillwell sighed. "Yessir. I've got some volunteers. I hope it's okay but I green-lighted pepper spray if he resists."

"Give him a blast for me," Potter muttered, and turned back to watch.

Two troopers in body armor and helmets slipped from the line of trees and, crouching, headed through the field.

Handy fired several more times. He hadn't noticed the troopers yet and was aiming only around Marks, the shots always near-misses. But one bullet hit a rock and ricocheted upwards, shattering the windshield of a squad car.

The two troopers kept low to the ground, running perpendicularly to the front of the slaughterhouse. Their hips and sides were easy targets if Handy decided to turn malicious and draw blood. Potter frowned. One of the men looked familiar.

"Who're those troopers?" Potter asked Stillwell. "Is one of them Stevie Oates?"

"Yessir."

Potter exhaled a deep sigh. "He just got *back* from a run, Dean. What's he thinking of?"

"Well, sir, he wanted to go out again. Was really insistent about it."

Potter shook his head.

Marks was now only forty yards from the slaughterhouse, the two troopers closing in slowly, scrambling through the buffalo grass. Marks saw them and shouted for them to get away.

"Sir," the voice through the speaker called—Potter recognized it as Oates's—"our orders're to bring you back."

"Fuck your orders. If you care about those girls just leave me alone."

They heard a whoop of distant laughter the Big Ear was picking up. "Turkey shoot," resounded Handy's voice, riding on the wind. Another deafening gunshot. A rock beside one of the troopers flew into the air. They both dropped to their bellies, began crawling like soldiers toward the assistant AG.

"Marks," Oates called, breathing hard. "We're bringing you back, sir. You're interfering with a federal operation."

Marks whirled around. "What're you going to do to stop me, Trooper? You work for *me*. Don't you forget it."

"Sheriff Stillwell has authorized me to use all necessary force to stop you, sir. And I aim to."

"You're downwind, son. Pepper-spray me and you're the only one who'll get a faceful of it."

Handy fired again. The bullet split an ancient post two feet from Oates's head. The convict, still in a playful mood, laughed hard.

"Jesus," somebody muttered.

"No, sir," Oates said calmly, "my orders're to shoot you in the leg and drag you back."

Potter and LeBow stared at each other. The negotiator's fervent thumb pressed the transmit button. "He *is* bluffing, isn't he, Dean?"

"Yep" was Stillwell's unsteady reply. "But . . . he sounds pretty determined. I mean, don't you think?"

Potter did think.

"Would he do it?" LeBow asked.

Potter shrugged.

Angie said, "He's drawn his weapon."

Oates was aiming steadily at Marks's lower extremities.

Well, this is escalating into a full-blown disaster, Potter thought.

"Sir," Oates called, "I will not miss. I'm an excellent shot and I'm just about to bring you down."

The assistant AG hesitated. The wind ripped the handkerchief from his fingers. It rose a few feet above his head.

A shot.

Handy's bullet struck the white cloth. It jerked and floated away on the breeze.

Again, through the Big Ear, the distant sound of Handy laughing. Marks looked back at the slaughterhouse. Called out, "You son of a bitch, Handy. I hope you rot in hell."

More laughter—or perhaps it was only the wind.

Standing tall, the assistant AG walked off the field. As if strolling through his own backyard. Potter was pleased to see that Stevie Oates and his partner kept low as terriers as they crawled after the man under cover of the sumptuous, windswept grass.

"You could've ruined everything," Arthur Potter snapped. "What the hell were you thinking?"

He had to look up into Marks's eyes—the man was well over six feet tall—but still felt he was talking to a snotty child caught misbehaving.

The assistant attorney general began firmly, "I was thinking—"

"You *never* exchange hostages. The whole point of negotiation is to devalue them. You were as good as saying to him, 'Here I am, I'm worth more than all of those girls combined.' If he'd gotten you it would've made my job impossible."

"I don't see why," Marks answered.

"Because," Angie said, "a hostage like you would have boosted his sense of power and control a hundred times. He'd up his demands and stick to them. We'd never get him to agree to anything reasonable."

"Well, I kept thinking about those girls in there. What they were going through."

"He never would have let them go."

"I was going to talk him into it."

LeBow rolled his eyes and continued to type up the incident.

Potter said, "I'm not going to arrest you." He'd considered it and concluded that the fallout would be too thorny. "But if you interfere in any way with this barricade again I will and I'll have the U.S. Attorney make sure you do time."

To Potter's astonishment, Marks wasn't the least contrite. The witty facade was gone, yes; but he seemed, if anything, irritated that Potter had interfered with *his* plans. "You do things by the book, Potter." A large index finger pointed bluntly at the agent. "But the book doesn't say anything about a psycho who gets his kicks killing children."

The phone buzzed. LeBow took the call and said to Potter, "Jocylyn's gotten a clean bill of health from the medics. She's fine. You want to debrief her now?"

"Yes, thank you, Henry. Tell them to send her in. Stevie Oates too." To Marks he said, "I'll ask you to leave now."

Marks buttoned his suit jacket, brushed away the rock dust that had powdered his jacket from Handy's target practice. He strode to the door and muttered something. Potter believed he heard: "blood on your hands." But as to the other words, he didn't have a clue.

3:40 P.M.

For precious minutes she wept uncontrollably.

Angie Scapello and Arthur Potter sat with Jocylyn and struggled to look calm and reassuring while in their hearts they wanted to grab the girl by the shoulders and shake answers out of her.

Impatience, Arthur Potter's nemesis.

He kept a smile on his face and nodded with reassurance while the chubby twelve-year-old cried and cried, resting her round, red face in her hands.

The door opened and Stevie Oates stepped inside, pulled off his helmet. Despite the cold his hair was damp with sweat. Potter turned his attention from the girl to the trooper.

"You should stand down for a while, Stevie."

"Yessir, I think I will. Those last couple shots were kind of, well . . . close."

"Sobered you up pretty fast, did they?"

"Yessir. Sure did."

"Tell me everything you saw when you went up there with the food."

As Potter expected, even with the aid of the videotape from the camera perched over his ear, Oates couldn't provide much detail about the interior of the slaughterhouse.

"Any thoughts on Handy's state of mind?"

"Seemed calm. Wasn't edgy."

Like he was buying a cup of coffee at 7-Eleven.

"Anybody hurt?"

"Not that I could see."

LeBow dutifully typed in the paltry intelligence. Oates could recall nothing else. Potter pointed out to the discouraged officer that it was good news he *hadn't* seen blood or bodies. Though he knew his own face didn't mask the discouragement he felt; they wouldn't get anything helpful from the twelve-year-old girl, who continued to weep and twine her short dark hair around fingers that ended in chewed nails.

"Thanks, Stevie. That's all for now. Oh, one question. Were you really going to shoot Marks in the leg?"

The young man grew serious for a moment then broke into a cautious grin. "The best way I can put it, sir, is I wasn't going to know until I pulled the trigger. Or didn't pull the trigger. As the case might be."

"Go get some coffee, Trooper," Potter said.

"Yessir."

Potter and Angie turned their attention back to Jocylyn. Her eyes were astonishingly red; she huddled in the blanket one of Stillwell's officers had given her.

Finally the girl was calm enough that Potter could begin to question her through Officer Frances Whiting. The negotiator noted that while Frances's hands moved elegantly and with compact gestures Jocylyn's were broad and awkward, stilted: the difference, he guessed, between someone speaking smoothly and someone inserting "um"s and "you know"s into their speech. He wondered momentarily how Melanie signed. Staccato? Smooth?

"She isn't answering your questions," Frances said.

"What's she saying?" Angie asked, her quick, dark eyes picking up patterns in the signing.

"That she wants her parents."

"Are they at the motel?" he asked Budd.

The captain made a call and told him, "They should be, within the hour."

Frances relayed that information to her. Without acknowledging that she understood, the girl started another jag of crying.

"You're doing fine," Angie said encouragingly.

The negotiator glanced at his watch. A half-hour to the helicopter deadline. "Tell me about the men, Jocylyn. The bad men."

Frances's hands flew and the girl finally responded. "She says there are three of them. Those three there." The girl was gesturing at the wall. "They're sweaty and smell bad. The one there." Pointing at Handy. "Brutus. He's the leader."

"Brutus?" Potter asked, frowning.

Frances asked the question and watched a lengthy response, during which Jocylyn pointed to each of the takers.

"That's what Melanie calls him," she said. "Handy's 'Brutus.' Wilcox is 'Stoat.' And Bonner is 'Bear.' " The officer added, "Signing's very metaphoric. 'Lamb' is sometimes used for 'gentle,' for instance. The Deaf often think in poetic terms."

"Does she have any idea where they are in the slaughterhouse?" He asked this of Frances, and Angie said, "Talk to her directly, Arthur. It'll be more reassuring, make her feel more like an adult. And don't forget to smile."

He repeated the question, smiling, to the girl, and Frances translated her response as she pointed to several locations near the front of the big room then touched Handy's and Wilcox's pictures. Tobe moved the Post-Its emblazoned with their names. LeBow typed.

Jocylyn shook her head. She rose and placed them more exactly. She signed some words to Frances, who said, "Bear—Bonner—is in the room with her friends."

Jocylyn put Bear's Post-It in a large semicircular room about twenty-five feet from the front of the slaughterhouse. Tobe placed all the hostage markers in there.

Jocylyn rearranged them too, being very precise.

"That's where everyone is, she says. Exactly."

Potter's eye strayed to Melanie's tab.

Jocylyn wiped tears, then signed.

"She says Bear watches them all the time. Especially the little girls."

Bonner. The rapist.

Potter asked, "Are there any other doorways or windows that aren't on the diagram?"

Jocylyn studied it carefully. Shook her head.

"Are you sure?"

"Yes."

"Did you see any guns?"

"They all have guns." The girl pointed to Tobe's hip.

He asked, "What kind were they?"

She frowned and pointed to the agent's hip again.

"I mean, were they like this, or did they have cylinders?" He found himself making a circular gesture with his finger. "Revolvers," he said slowly.

Jocylyn shook her head. Her awkward hands spoke again.

"No, she says they were black automatics. Just like that one." Frances smiled. "She asked why don't you believe her."

"You know what an automatic is?"

"She says she watches TV."

Potter laughed and told LeBow to write down that she'd confirmed they were armed with three Glocks or similar weapons.

Jocylyn volunteered that they had two dozen boxes of bullets.

"Boxes?"

"This big," Frances said, as the girl motioned her hands about six inches apart. "Yellow and green."

"Remington," LeBow said.

"And shotguns. Like that. Three of them." Jocylyn pointed to a shotgun on the rack in the van.

"Any rifles?" Potter pointed to an M-16 resting against the wall.

"No."

"They're pretty damn prepared," Budd muttered.

Potter handed off to Angie, who asked, "Is anybody hurt?"

"No."

"Does Handy—Brutus—talk to anybody in particular? Any of the teachers or girls, I mean?"

"No. Mostly he just looks at us." This brought back some memory and, in turn, more tears.

"You're doing great, honey," Angie said, squeezing the girl's shoulder. "Have you been able to tell what the three men are talking about?"

"No. I'm sorry. I can't lip-read good."

"Is Beverly all right?"

"She can't breathe well. But she's had worse attacks. The worst problem is Mrs. Harstrawn."

"Ask her to explain."

Frances watched her hands and said, "It sounds like she's having a breakdown. She was fine until Susan was shot. All she does now is lie on her back and cry."

Potter thought: They're leaderless. The worst situation. They could panic and run. Unless Melanie has taken over.

"How's Melanie?"

"She just sits and stares. Sometimes closes her eyes." Frances added to Potter, "That's not good. The deaf never close their eyes in a tense situation. Their vision is the only warning system they have."

Angie asked, "Do the men fight among themselves?"

Jocylyn didn't know.

"Do they seem nervous? Happy? Scared? Sad?"

"They're not scared. Sometimes they laugh."

LeBow typed this into his computer.

"Okay," Potter said. "You're a very brave girl. You can go to the hotel now. Your parents will be there soon."

The twelve-year-old wiped her nose on her sleeve but didn't leave. She signed awkwardly.

"Is that all you want to ask me?" Frances translated.

"Yes. You can go."

But the girl signed some more. "She asked, 'Don't you want to know about the TV? And the other stuff?'"

Tobe, LeBow, and Budd turned their heads to Potter.

"They have a TV in there?" he whispered, dismayed. Frances translated and Jocylyn nodded.

"Where did they get it?"

"In the bags with the guns. They brought it in with them. It's a little one."

"Do they have a radio?"

"I didn't see one."

"Do they watch the TV a lot?"

She nodded.

"What other stuff do they have?"

"She says they have some tools. New ones. They're in plastic."

"What kind?"

"Silver ones. Wrenches. Pliers. Screwdrivers. A big shiny hammer."

"Offer her a job, Arthur," Henry LeBow said. "She's better than half our agents."

"Anything else you can think of, Jocylyn?"

Her red fingers moved.

"She misses her mommy."

"One more thing," Potter said. He hesitated. He wanted to ask something more about Melanie. He found he couldn't. Instead he asked, "Is it cold inside?"

"Not too bad."

Potter took the girl's round, damp hand and pressed it between his. "Tell her many thanks, Frances. She did a fine job."

After this message was translated Jocylyn wiped her face and smiled for the first time.

Angie asked Frances to tell the girl that she'd take her to the motel in a minute. Jocylyn went outside to wait with a woman state trooper.

LeBow printed out the list of what the men had inside the slaughterhouse with them. He handed it to Tobe, who pinned it up beside the diagram.

Tobe said, "It's like a computer adventure game. 'You're carrying a key, a magic sword, five stones, and a raven in a cage.' "

Potter sat back in his chair slowly, laughing. He looked at the list. "What do you make of it, Henry? Tools, a TV?"

"Knocked over a store on their way out of the prison?"

Potter asked Budd, "Any reports of a commercial burglary between here and Winfield, Charlie?"

"I'm outta that loop. I'll check." He stepped outside.

"I've never had such good intelligence from a hostage who'd been inside so short a time," Potter said. "Her powers of observation are remarkable."

"God compensates," Frances said.

Potter then asked Angie, "What do you think?"

"She's with us, I'd guess."

Because of the Stockholming process hostages have been known to give false information to negotiators and tactical teams. On one of Potter's negotiations—a weeklong terrorist barricade—a released hostage left a handkerchief in front of the window where Potter was hiding so that the barricaded gunman would know where to shoot. A sniper killed the hostage taker before he could fire. Potter testified on the hostage's behalf at her subsequent trial; she got a suspended sentence.

Potter agreed with Angie's assessment. Jocylyn hadn't been inside long enough to skew her feelings about Handy and the others. She was just a scared little girl.

Angie said, "I'm going to take her to the motel. Make sure she's comfortable. Reassure the other parents."

Henry LeBow called, "Arthur, just got some info on Henderson."

Potter said to Angie as she stepped out the door, "While you're down there, check up on him. He makes me nervous."

"Pete Henderson we're talking, the Wichita SAC?"

"Yep."

"Why?"

"Gut feel." Potter told her about the threat. And added that he was more concerned that Henderson hadn't at first volunteered that he'd interviewed Handy after the S&L arson. "It's probably because his boys did a lousy job on the collar, letting the girlfriend get away and ending up with two wounded troopers." The postcollar interrogation too, which Potter now recalled had yielded only unimaginative obscenities on Handy's part. "But he should've told us up front he was involved."

"What do you want me to do?" Angie asked.

Potter shrugged. "Just make sure he's not getting into any trouble."

She offered a gimme-a-break look. Peter Henderson, as Special Agent in Charge of a resident agency, had the rank to get into as much trouble as he liked and it wasn't for underlings like Angie Scapello to do anything about it.

"Try. Please." Potter blew her a kiss.

LeBow handed Potter the printout, explaining with a sneer, "It's only résumé-quality data. But there *are* some details I'll bet he wants to keep under wraps."

Potter was intrigued. He read. Henderson had come up through the ranks, working as an investigator in the Chicago Police Department while he went to DePaul Law School at night. After he got his degree he joined the Bureau, excelled at Quantico, and returned to the Midwest, where he made a name for himself in southern Illinois and St. Louis, primarily investigating RICO crimes. He was a good administrator, fit the Feebie mold, and was clearly destined for a SAC job in Chicago or Miami or even the Southern District of New York. After which the career trajectory would have landed him in D.C.

If not for the lawsuit.

Potter read the press accounts and, supplemented by details from memos Henry LeBow had somehow managed to pry from the Bureau databases, he understood why Henderson had been shunted off to Kansas. Six years ago a dozen black agents had sued the Bureau for discrimination in doling out assignments, promotions, and raises. The St. Louis office was one of the targeted federal districts, and Henderson was quick to offer testimony supporting their claim. Too quick, some said. In the anticipated shakeup following the Title VII suit the then-current Bureau director was expected to resign and be replaced by a young deputy director, who would become the first black head of the FBI and who would—Henderson figured—remember those loyal to the cause.

But Henderson's scheming had blown up in his face. The steam went out of the suit as it bogged down in the federal courts. Some plaintiffs dropped out; others simply couldn't prove discrimination. For reasons stemming from ambition, not ideology, the young black deputy director chose to move to the National Security Council. The existing Bureau director simply retired, amid no scandal, and was replaced by the Admiral.

Turncoat Peter Henderson was administratively drawn and quartered. The man who'd once gotten a tap into syndicate boss Mario Lacosta's Clayton, Missouri, private den was sent packing to the state in which the geographic center of the country could be found and that was indeed known mostly for pilferings at McConnell Air Force Base and internecine battles with Indian Affairs and BATF. The career of the thirty-nine-year-old agent was at a complete standstill.

"Risks?" Potter asked LeBow. "He going to get in our way?"

"He's not in any position to do anything," the intelligence officer said. "Not officially."

"He's desperate."

"I'm sure he is. I said 'not officially.' We still have to keep our eyes on him."

Potter chuckled. "So, we've got an assistant attorney general ready to hand himself over to the takers and a SAC who wants to hand *me* over to them."

We have met the enemy . . .

He turned back to the window, thinking of Melanie, recalling what Jocylyn had said. *She just closes her eyes. Doesn't do anything.* What does that mean? he wondered.

Tobe broke into Potter's musings. "Handy's expecting a chopper in an hour, five minutes."

"Thank you, Tobe," Potter responded.

He looked out over the slaughterhouse and thought: A key, a magic sword, five stones, and a raven in a cage.

"Officer."

Charlie Budd was walking back to the van from his own unmarked car, where he'd just typed in a computer request for 211s in a four-county area. The only robberies today had been a convenience store, a gas station, and a Methodist church. The booty in none of them matched the weapons, TV, and tools that the HTs had brought with them.

"Come over here, Officer," the man's low voice said.

Oh, brother. What now?

Roland Marks leaned against the side of a supply van, smoking a cigarette. Budd thought he'd be ten miles away by now but there was purpose in his eyes and he looked like he was here to stay.

"You witnessed that little travesty," Marks announced. Budd had been in the corner of the van as Potter read the riot act. Budd looked around then wandered through the grass to the dark-featured man and stood upwind of the smoke. He said nothing.

"I love summer afternoons, Captain. Remind me of growing up. I played baseball every day. Did you? You look like could run like the wind."

"Track and field. Four-forty and eight-eighty mostly."

"All right." Marks's voice dropped again, softer than Budd thought it possibly could and still be audible. "We had the luxury, you and I'd dance around a bit like we were on a dinner cruise and you'd get my meaning and then go off and do what you ought to. But there's no time for that."

I was *never* cut out to be an officer, Budd thought, and replayed for the hundredth time the bullet cutting down seventeen-year-old Susan Phillips. He choked suddenly and turned it into an odd-sounding cough. "Say, I'm real busy right now, sir. I have to—"

"Answer me yes or no. Did I see something in your eyes in the van?"

"Don't know what you mean, sir."

"Sure, maybe what I did was out of line. I wasn't thinking too clearly. But you weren't completely sure *Potter* was right either. And— no, hold up there. I think if we took a vote more people in that van'd come down on my side than his."

Budd summoned his courage from somewhere and said, "It's not a popularity contest, sir."

"Oh, no, it's not. That's exactly right. It's a question about whether those girls live, and I think Potter doesn't care if they do or not."

"Noooo. That's not true. Not by a long shot. He cares a lot."

"What'm I seeing in your face, Officer? Just what I saw in the van, right? You're scared shitless for those little things in that slaughterhouse."

Our number-one priority isn't getting those girls out alive. . . .

Marks continued, "Come on now, Officer. Admit it."

"He's a good man," Budd said.

"I know he's a good man. What the fuck does that have to do with anything?"

"He's doing the best—"

"There is no way in hell," Marks said slowly, "I'm letting those girls in there die. Which is something he's willing to do . . . and that's been eating at you all day. Am I right?"

"Well—"

Marks's hand dug into his suit jacket and he pulled out a wallet, flipped
it open. For a crazy moment Budd though he was going to display his AG's
office ID. But what Budd found himself looking at had far more impact on
him. Three photos in glossy sleeves of young girls. One had knitted eyebrows and slightly distorted features. The handicapped daughter.

"You're a father of girls, Budd. Am I right?"

The captain swallowed and tried to look away from the six dark eyes.
He couldn't.

"Just imagine *your* little ones in there. And then imagine someone
like Potter saying, 'Hell, they're expendable.' Imagine that, Captain."

Budd inhaled long. And finally managed to look away. The wallet
snapped closed.

"We have to get him removed."

"What?"

"*He's* signing their death sentences. What did he say about meeting
Handy's demands? Come on, Budd. Answer like an officer."

He looked into Marks's eye and ignored the slap, saying, "He said
Handy wasn't leaving there except in cuffs or a body bag."

And that if those girls had to die, so be it.

"Is that acceptable to you, Officer?"

"It's not my job to say if it is or isn't."

" 'I was only following orders.' "

"That's about the size of it."

Marks spit the cigarette from his mouth. "For God's sake, Captain,
you *can* take a moral position, can't you? Don't you have any higher
values than running errands for a fat FBI agent?"

Budd said stiffly, "He's the senior officer. He's federal, and—"

"You just hold on to those words, Captain," Marks railed like a
pumped-up evangelist. "Tuck 'em under your arm and bring 'em out at
the funerals of those girls. I hope they make you feel better." He
reached into Budd's soul and poked with a fingernail. "There's already
one girl's blood on our hands."

He means your *hands.*

Budd saw Susan Phillips as she fell to her knees. The impact of that
fall made her jaw drop open and distorted her beautiful face for a moment. It became beautiful once more as she died.

"What?" Budd whispered, his eyes on the buggish headlights of the harvesting threshers. "What do you want?" This sounded childish and shamed him but he couldn't stop himself.

"I want Potter out. You or I or somebody state'll take over the negotiations and give those cocksuckers their damn helicopter in exchange for the girls. We'll track 'em down when they land and blow 'em to hell. I've already checked. We can get a chopper here in a half-hour, fitted with a homing device that'll track 'em from a hundred miles away. They'll never know we're following."

"But he says Handy's too dangerous to let out."

"Of course he's dangerous," Marks said. "But once he's out he'll be up against professionals. Men and women who're paid to take risks. Those girls aren't."

Marks had tiny eyes and it seemed to Budd that they were on the verge of tears. He thought of the man's mentally retarded daughter, in and out of hospitals all her short life.

He observed that Marks had said nothing about the effect of Budd's decision on his career. If he had, Budd would have stonewalled. When it came to things like that, cheap shots, the young captain could be a mule. Then it discouraged him immensely to see that Marks had assessed that about him and had pointedly avoided any threats. Budd realized that he was already lying on the mat, shoulders pinned, staring at the ceiling. The count had begun.

Oh, brother.

"But how can we get Potter out?"

He said this to stymie Marks but of course the man was prepared. The small black box appeared in Marks's hand. For an absurd moment Budd actually thought it was a bomb. He stared at the tape recorder. "All I want is for you to get him to say that the hostages are expendable."

"You mean, record him?"

"Exactly."

"And . . . and then what?"

"I've got some friends at a St. Louis radio station. They'll run the tape on the news. Potter'll have to step down."

"That could be the end of his career."

"And it could be the end of *mine*, doing this. But I'm willing to risk it. For chrissake, I was willing to give myself up in exchange for them. You don't see Potter doing that."

"I just don't know."

"Let's save those nine poor girls in there, Captain. What do you say?"

Marks thrust the recorder into Budd's unhappy hands. The officer stared at it then slipped it into his pocket and without a word turned away. His only act of defiance was to offer, "No, you're wrong. There are only eight people inside. He's gotten one out." But Marks was out of earshot when he said it.

4:10 P.M.

Captain Charles R. Budd stood in a gully not far from the command van.

He was delegating, yes, but mostly he was trying to ignore the weight of the tape recorder, a thousand pounds of hot metal, in his hip pocket.

I'll think about that later.

Delegate.

Phil Molto was setting up the press table: a folding fiberboard table, a small portable typewriter, paper and pencils. Budd was no news hog but he supposed this setup would be useless for today's high-tech reporters. Did they even know how to type, those pretty boys and girls? They seemed like spoiled high-school kids.

He guessed, though, that this arrangement had less to do with journalism than with politics. How did Potter know how to handle all these things? Maybe living in the nation's capital helped. Politics one way or another. The earnest young captain felt totally incompetent.

Shame too. The tape recorder melted into fiery plastic and ran down his leg.

Forget about it. Fifty minutes to five—fifty minutes to the deadline. He kept a meaningless smile on his face but he couldn't sweep from his mind the image of the teenage girl falling to ground, dying.

He somehow knew in his heart more blood would be spilled. Marks was right. In the van he *had* sided with the assistant attorney general.

Forty-nine minutes . . .

"Okay," he told his lieutenant. "Guess that'll do. You ride herd on 'em, Phil. Make sure they sit tight. They can wander around a little behind the lines and take notes on whatever they want—"

Was that okay? he wondered. What would Potter say?

"—but suit 'em up in flak jackets and make sure they keep their heads down."

Quiet Phil Molto nodded.

The first car arrived a minute later, containing two men. They climbed out, flashed press credentials, and as they looked around hungrily the older of them said, "I'm Joe Silbert, KFAL. This is Ted Biggins."

Budd got a kick out of their dress—dark suits that didn't fit very well and black running shoes. He pictured them racing down the hall of a TV station, shouting, "Exclusive, exclusive!" while papers spun in their wakes.

Silbert looked at the press table and laughed. Budd introduced himself and Molto and said, "Best we could do."

"It's fine, Officer. Only I hope you don't mind if we use our own stone tablet to write on?"

Biggins hefted a large portable computer onto the table.

"Long as we see what you write before you send it." For so Potter had instructed him.

"File it," Silbert said. "We say 'file it,' not 'send it.' " Budd couldn't tell if he was making a joke.

Biggins poked at the typewriter. "What exactly is this?"

The men laughed. Budd told them the ground rules. Where they could go and where they couldn't. "We've got a couple troopers you can talk to if you want. Phil here'll send 'em over."

"They hostage rescue?"

"No. They're from Troop K, up the road."

"Can we talk to some hostage rescue boys?"

When Budd grinned Silbert smiled too, like a co-conspirator, and the reporter realized he wasn't going to catch the captain in any slip-ups about whether or not HRT was on the scene.

"We're going to want to talk to Potter sometime soon," Silbert groused. "He planning on avoiding us?"

"I'll let him know you're here," Budd said cheerfully, the Switzerland of law enforcers. "Meanwhile Phil here'll bring you up to date. He's got profiles of the escapees and pictures of them. And he'll get you suited up in body armor. Oh, and I was thinking you might want to get the human-interest angle from some troopers. What it's like to be on a barricade. That sort of thing."

The reporters' faces were solemn masks but Budd wondered again if they were laughing at him. Silbert said, "Fact is, we're mostly interested in the hostages. That's where the story is. Anybody here we can talk to about them?"

"I'm just here to set up the press table. Agent Potter'll be by to give you the information he thinks you oughta have." Is that the right way to put it? Budd wondered. "Now I got some things need looking after so I'll leave you be."

"But I won't," said Molto, cracking a rare smile.

"I'm sure you won't, Officer." Their computer whirred to life.

What Melanie had smelled in the air of the killing room, what had forced her from her music room: mud, fish, water, diesel fuel, methane, decaying leaves, wet tree bark.

The river.

The fishy breeze had been strong enough to start the lamp swaying. That told her that somewhere near the back of the slaughterhouse was an open doorway. It occurred to her that maybe de l'Epée had already sent his men around the slaughterhouse looking for places where the girls might get out. Maybe some were even cutting their way in right now to rescue them.

She thought back to their arrival at the slaughterhouse this morning. She remembered seeing groves of trees on either side of the building, a muddy slope down to the river, which glistened gray and cold in the overcast afternoon light, black wood pilings, dotted with tar and creosote, a dock leaning precariously over the water, dangling rotten tires for ship bumpers.

The tires . . . That's what had given her the idea. When she was a girl, every summer in the early evening she and Danny would race down to Seversen Corner on the farm, run over the tractor ruts and through a fog of wheat down to the pond. It was nearly an acre, surrounded by willows and grass and stiff reeds filled with cores like Styrofoam. She ran like the Kansas wind so that she'd be the first one to the hill overlooking the pond, where she'd leap into space, grab the tire swing hanging over the water and sail out above the mirrorlike surface.

Then let go and tumble into the sky and clouds reflected below her.

She and her brother had spent long hours at the pond—even now, that glassy water was often her first thought when she stepped outside into a warm summer evening. Danny had taught her to swim twice. The first time when she was six and he'd taken her hands and eased her into the water of the still but deep pond. The second time was far harder—after she'd lost her hearing and grown afraid of so many things. She was twelve then. But the lanky, blond boy, five years older, refused to let her dodge the swimming hole any longer and, using the sign language he alone in the Charrol family had learned, talked her into letting go her grip on the bald Goodyear. And he calmly trod water, supported her and kept her from panicking while she finally remembered the strokes she'd learned years before.

Swimming. The first thing she'd done that gave her back a splinter of self-confidence after her plunge into deafness.

Thank you, Danny, she thought. For then, and for now. Because it was this memory that she believed was going to save some, if not all, of her students.

The river was wide here. The surface was choppy and the current fast but she remembered a tangle of branches and garbage washed up against a fallen tree that hung into the choppy water maybe a hundred feet downstream. Melanie pictured the girls moving silently through the back corridors of the slaughterhouse, over the dockside, into the water, then drifting with the current to the tree, scrambling out through the branches. Running to safety. . . .

"Never underestimate a body of water," Danny had told her. "Even the calm ones can be dangerous."

Well, there was nothing calm about the Arkansas. Could they manage it? Donna Harstrawn can swim. Kielle and Shannon—superheroes that they are—can swim like otters. (Melanie pictures Kielle's compact body cannonballing off the diving board, while Shannon's willowy frame leisurely completes her laps.) The twins love to play in the water. But they can't swim. Beverly knows how but with her asthma she can't. Melanie doesn't know about pretty Emily; the girl refuses to put her face underwater and always stands demurely in the shallow end of the pool when they go swimming.

She'll have to find something for the ones who can't swim, a paddleboard, a float. But what?

And how do I get them to the back of the slaughterhouse?

She thought of Danny. But Danny wasn't here to help. Panic edged in.

De l'Epée?

She sent her thoughts out to him but all he did was whisper his reassurance that there'll be police to find the girls that escape into the river. (They'll be there, won't they? Yes, she has to believe they will.)

Crap, Melanie thinks. I'm on my own here.

Then, suddenly, the smell changes.

Her eyes open and she finds herself staring into the face of Brutus, a few feet away from her. She no longer smells the river but rather meat and stale breath and sweat. He's so close that she sees, with horror, that the marks on his neck—what she thought were freckles—must be the blood from the woman with the purse, the woman he killed this afternoon. Melanie recoiled in disgust.

"Sit tight, missie," Handy said.

Melanie wondered again, Why can I understand him? *Sit tight.* A phrase almost impossible to lip-read, and yet she knows without a doubt that this is what he said. Brutus took her hands. She tried to resist him but she couldn't. "You were sitting there with your eyes closed . . . hands were twitching like a shot 'coon's paws. Talking to yourself? That what you doing?"

There was movement in the corner. Kielle had sat up and was staring at him. The little girl had an eerily adult look in her face. Her jaw was set. "I'm Jubilee!" Kielle signed. Her favorite X-Man character. "I'm going to kill him!" Melanie dared not sign but her eyes implored the girl to sit down.

Brutus glanced at the little girl, laughed then stepped into the main room of the slaughterhouse, motioning Bear after him. When he returned a moment later he was carrying a large can of gasoline.

Kielle's face went still as she stared at the red can.

"Don't nobody move." Brutus looked into Melanie's eyes as he said this. Then he set a heavy metal canister, a small rendering vat maybe, on top of a shelf above the girls and poured the gasoline into it. Melanie felt the thud as he pitched the gas can into the corner of the room. Then he tied a wire to the edge of the canister and ran it to the other room. Eerie shadows danced on the floor and wall as the light from the other room grew brighter and brighter and Brutus returned suddenly, swinging another of the lights. He unscrewed the cage and tied the unprotected fixture and bulb to a bolt in the floor, directly below the canister of gas.

Bear surveyed the workmanship with approval.

Kielle stepped toward Brutus.

"No," Melanie signed. "Get back!"

Brutus suddenly dropped to his knees and took Kielle by the shoulders. He put his face inches from hers and he spoke slowly.

"Here now, little bird . . . hassles from you . . . or somebody tries to save you, I'll pull that wire and burn you up."

He pushed hard and Kielle fell over one of the blood grooves in the floor.

"What one should I pick?" Brutus asked Bear. The fat man looked them over. His eyes lingered longest on Emily, her flat chest, her white stockings, her black-strapped shoes.

Bear gestured at Shannon. ". . . kicked me. Pick her, man."

Brutus looked down at the girl, tossing her long, dark hair. Like Kielle, she gazed back defiantly. But after a moment she looked down, tears filling her eyes. And Melanie could see the real difference between the girls. Shannon Boyle was one hell of an artist but she wasn't Jubilee or any other kind of hero. She was an eight-year-old tomboy, scared to death.

"You're a kicker, are you?" Brutus asked. "Okay, let's go." They led her out.

What were they going to do with her? Release her, like Jocylyn? Melanie scooted toward the doorway of the killing room—as far as she dared. She looked out and saw Shannon in the greasy window in the front of the slaughterhouse. Brutus took his pistol from his back pocket. Rested the muzzle against the girl's head: No! Oh, no. . . .

Melanie started to rise. Bear's bulbous head swiveled toward her quickly and he raised the shotgun. She sank down to the cold floor and stared hopelessly at her student. Shannon closed her eyes and wrapped her fingers around the pink-and-blue-string friendship bracelet she'd tied on her wrist a month ago. The girl had promised to make a matching bracelet for her, Melanie now recalled, choking back tears, but had never gotten around to it.

Angie Scapello paused on her way back to the van from the rear staging area.

"Hey, Captain."

If he hadn't known it for a fact, Charlie Budd would never have guessed she was a federal agent. "Hi," he said.

She paused and fell into step beside him.

"You worked with Arthur much?" he asked suddenly, flustered. Just trying to make conversation.

"About thirty or forty barricades. Maybe a few more, I guess."

"Hey, you must've started out young."

"I'm older than I look."

He didn't think "older" was a word that applied to her at all.

"This isn't a line—I'm married." Budd awkwardly held up his glistening ring, which happened to match his wife's. "But you ever do any modeling? I only ask 'cause Meg, that's my wife, she gets these magazines. You know, *Vogue* and *Harper's Bazaar*. Like that. I was thinking maybe I saw you in an ad or two?"

"Could've been. I put myself through school doing print ads. Was a few years ago. Undergrad." She laughed. "I was usually cast as a bride for some reason. Don't ask me why."

"Good hair for a veil," Budd suggested, and then went red because the comment sounded like a flirt.

"And I've been in one movie."

"No kiddin'?"

"I was a double for Isabella Rossellini. I stood outside in the snow for long angles."

"I was thinking you looked like her." Though Budd said this uneasily, having no idea who the actress was, and hoped that she wasn't some unknown who'd never appeared in a movie shown in America.

"You're kind of a celebrity in your own right, aren't you?" she asked.

"Me?" Budd laughed.

"They say you came up through the ranks real fast."

"They do?"

"Well, you're a captain and you're a young man."

"I'm older than *I* look," he joked. "And before today's over I'm going to be older still by a long shot." He looked at his watch. "I better be getting inside. Not long till the first deadline. How do you manage to stay calm?"

"I think it's all what you're used to. But what about you? That high-speed chase, the time you went after that sex offender in Hamilton?"

"How on earth d'you hear about that?" Budd laughed. Two years ago. He'd hit speeds of a hundred twenty. On a dirt road. "Didn't think my, you know, exploits made it into *National Law Enforcement Monthly.*"

"You hear things. About certain people anyway."

Her brown eyes bored into Budd's, which were green, exceedingly embarrassed, and growing more and more flummoxed by the second. He rubbed his cheek with his left hand again, just to give her a view of his ring once more, then thought: Hey, get real. You actually think she's coming on to you? No way, he told himself. She's making polite talk to a local rube.

"Better see if there's anything Arthur needs," Budd said.

For some reason he stuck his hand out toward her. Wished he hadn't, but there it was and she reached out, took it in both of hers, and squeezed it hard, stepping close. He smelled perfume. It seemed entirely unnatural for FBI agents to be wearing perfume.

"I'm real glad we're working together, Charlie." She fired a smile at him, the likes of which he hadn't seen in years—since Meg, in fact, had crosshaired him at the junior prom with one of those flirtations that he never would've believed the president of Methodist Girls' Youth Group was capable of.

4:40 P.M.

"Twenty minutes to deadline," Tobe Geller called.

Potter nodded. He punched the speed-dial button. Handy answered by saying, "I've picked the next little bird, Art."

Get off the subject of the hostages; keep him thinking they're valueless. Potter said, "Lou, we're working on that helicopter. It isn't that easy to get one."

"This one's a little trouper, she is, Art. That fat one cried and cried. Man, did that bug me. This one's shedding a tear or two but she's a soldier. Got a fucking tattoo on her arm, you can believe it."

Share some observations. Show him you're concerned, find out a few things about him.

"You sound tired, Lou."

"Not me. I'm right as rain."

"Really? Would've guessed you were up all night planning your big getaway."

"Naw, got my full eight hours. 'Sides, there's nothing like a Mexican standoff to get the old juices flowing." In fact he didn't sound at all tired. He sounded relaxed and at ease. Potter nodded toward LeBow but the officer was already typing.

"So tell me. What's so hard about a chopper, Art?"

Potter trained the glasses out the window at the brown-haired, long-faced girl. He'd already memorized the names and faces. Punching the mute button, he said to Angie, "It's Shannon Boyle. Tell me about her." Then into the phone: "I'll tell you what's so hard, Lou," Potter snapped. "They don't grow on trees and they aren't free."

You're worried about fucking money at a time like this?

"Fuck, you got all the money you need. What with everything you assholes steal from us taxpayers."

"You a taxpayer, Lou?"

"We ain't buying nuclear bombs anymore so spend a little on a chopper and save some lives here."

Angie tapped his shoulder.

"Hold on a second, Lou. Word's coming in about that chopper right now."

"She's eight," Angie whispered, "prelingually deaf. No lip-reading skills to speak of. She's got a personality of her own. Very independent. She's marched in protests to get deaf deans at schools for the deaf in Kansas and Missouri. Signed the petition to increase the deaf faculty at Laurent Clerc and hers was the largest signature on the sheet. She's been in fistfights at school and she usually wins."

Potter nodded. So if they could distract him enough, and if she had an opportunity, the girl might make a run for freedom.

Or use the chance to attack Handy and get herself killed in the process.

He clicked the mute button off. Sounding exasperated: "Look, Lou. We're just talking about a little delay is all. You want a big aircraft. Well, we've got two-seaters galore. But the big ones're hard to find."

"That's your fucking problem, ain't it? I put a bullet into little Fannie Annie here in, lemme see, fifteen minutes by my clock."

Usually, you devalue the hostages.

Sometimes you just have to beg.

"Her name's Shannon, Lou. Come on. She's only eight years old."

"Shannon," Handy mused. "I guess you aren't catching on, Art. You're trying to get me to feel sorry for some poor kid's got a name. Shannon

Shannon Shannon. Those're your rules, right, Art? Written up in your Feebie handbook?"

Page 45, in fact.

"But see, those rules don't take into account somebody like me. The more I know them the more I *want* to kill 'em."

Walk that fine line. Chide, push, trade barbs. He'll back off if you hit the balance just right. Arthur Potter thought this but his hand cramps on the receiver as he said cheerfully, "I think that's bullshit, Lou. I think you're just playing with us."

"Have it your way."

A little edge in the agent's voice: "I'm tired of this crap. We're trying to *work* with you."

"Naw, you want to shoot me down. Why don't you have the balls to admit it? If I had you in my sights I'd drop you like a fucking deer."

"No, I don't want to shoot you, Lou. I don't want anybody to die. We've got a lot of logistic problems. Landing is a real hassle here. The field out front's filled with those old posts from the stockyard pens. And we've got trees everywhere. We can't set a chopper down on the roof because of the weight. We—"

"So you've got diagrams of the building, do you?"

Negotiate from strength—with a reminder to the HT that there's always a tactical solution in the back of your mind (we can kick in the door any time we want and nail you cold, and remember, there're a hell of a lot more of us than of you). Potter laughed and said, "Of course we do. We've got maps and charts and diagrams and graphs and eight-by-ten color glossy photos. You're a damn cover boy in here, Lou. This's no surprise, is it?"

Silence.

Push too far?

No, I don't think so. He'll laugh and sound cool.

It was a chuckle. "You guys're too fucking much."

"And the field to the south," Potter continued, as if Handy hadn't spoken, "look at it. Nothing but gullies and hummocks. To set an eight-person copter down'd be pretty dangerous. And this wind . . . it's a real problem. Our aviation advisor isn't sure what to do about it."

Budd frowned, mouthing, "Aviation advisor?" Potter shrugged, having just made up the job. He pointed to the "Deceptions" board and Budd wrote it down, sighing.

Silver tools, wrapped in plastic, new.

Potter desperately wanted to ask what they were for. But of course he couldn't. It was vitally important that Handy not realize what they knew about the inside of the barricade. Even more vital: if Handy suspected the released hostages were giving Potter quality information he'd think twice about releasing others.

"Art," Handy spat out, "I keep saying, them's your problems." But he was not as flippant now and part of him at least seemed to realize that this had become *his* problem.

"Come on, Lou. This's just a practical thing. I'm not arguing about the chopper. I'm telling you we're having trouble finding one and that I'm not sure where we can set it down. You got any ideas, I'll be happy to take 'em."

Hostage negotiation strategy calls for the negotiator to avoid offering solutions to problems. Shift that burden to the taker. Keep him in a problem-solving mode, uncertain.

A disgusted sigh. "Fuck."

Will he hang up?

Finally Handy said, "How 'bout a pontoon chopper? You can do that, can't you?"

Never agree too quickly.

"Pontoon?" Potter said after a moment. "I don't know. We'd have to look into it. You mean, set her down in the river."

"*Course* that's what I mean. Where'd you think, land in some fucking toilet somewhere?"

"I'll see about it. If there's a sheltered cove it might work out perfectly. But you'll have to give us more time."

You don't have more time.

"You haven't got any more time."

"No, Lou. Pontoons'd be perfect. It's a great idea. I'll get on it right away. But let me buy some time. Tell me something you want."

"A fucking helicopter."

"And you'll have it. It may just take a little longer than we'd hoped. Name something else. Your heart's desire. Isn't there something you can think of you want?"

A pause. Potter thought: guns, X-rated tapes and a VCR, a friend busted out of prison, money, liquor . . .

"Yeah, I want something, Art."

"What?"

"Tell me 'bout yourself."

From out of left field.

Potter looked up into Angie's frown. She shook her head, cautious.

"What?"

"You asked me what I wanted. I want you to tell me about yourself."

You always want the HT to be curious about the negotiator but it usually takes hours, if not days, to establish any serious connection. This was the second time in just a few hours that Handy had expressed an interest in Potter, and the agent had never known an HT to ask the question so directly. Potter knew he was on thin ice here. He could improve the connection between the two or he could drive a wedge between them by not responding the way Handy wished.

Be forewarned. . . .

"What do you want to know?"

"Anything you wanta tell me."

"Well, there's nothing very exciting. I'm just a civil servant." His mind went blank.

"Keep going, Art. Talk to me."

And then, as if a switch had been flicked, Arthur Potter found himself desiring to blurt out every last detail of his life, his loneliness, his sorrow. . . . He wanted Lou Handy to know about him. "Well, I'm a widower. My wife died thirteen years ago, and today's our wedding anniversary."

He remembered that LeBow had told him there'd been bad blood between Handy and his ex; he turned to the intelligence officer, who had already called up a portion of Handy's profile. The convict had been married for two years when he was twenty. His wife had sued for divorce on the grounds of mental cruelty and had gotten a restraining order because he'd beaten her repeatedly. Just after that he'd gone off on a violent robbery spree. Potter was wishing he hadn't brought up the subject of marriage, but when Handy now asked what had happened to Potter's wife he sounded genuinely curious.

"She had cancer. Died about two months after we found out about it."

"Me, I was never married, Art. No woman'll ever tie me down. I'm a freewheelin' spirit, I go where my heart and my dick lead me. You ever get yourself remarried?"

"No, never did."

"What do you do when you want a little pussy?"

"My work keeps me pretty busy, Lou."

"You like your job, do you? How long you been doing it?"

"I've been with the Bureau all my adult life."

"All your adult life?"

My Lord, an amused Potter thought from a remote distance, he's echoing *me*. Coincidence? Or is he playing me the way I should be playing *him*?

"It's the only job I've ever had. Work eighteen hours a day a lot."

"How'd you get into this negotiating shit?"

"Just fell into it. Wanted to be an agent, liked the excitement of it. I was a pretty fair investigator but I think I was a little too easygoing. I could see both sides of everything."

"Oh, yessir," Handy said earnestly, "that'll keep you from moving to the top. Don't you know the sharks swim faster?"

"That's the God's truth, Lou."

"You must meet some real fucking wackos."

"Oh, present company excluded of course."

No laughter from the other end of the line. Only silence. Potter felt stung that the levity had fallen flat and he worried that Handy had heard sarcasm in Potter's voice and was hurt. He felt an urge to apologize.

But Handy just said, "Tell me a war story, Art."

Angie was frowning again. Potter ignored her. "Well, I did a barricade at the West German embassy in Washington about fifteen years ago. Talked for about eighteen hours straight." He laughed. "I had agents racing back and forth to the library bringing me books on political philosophy. Hegel, Kant, Nietzsche . . . Finally I had to send out for Cliff Notes. I was camped out in the backseat of an unmarked car, talking on a hard-wired throw phone to this maniac who thought he was Hitler. Wanted to dictate a new version of *Mein Kampf* to me. I still have no idea what the hell we talked about all that time."

Actually, the man hadn't claimed to be Hitler but Potter felt the urge to exaggerate, to make sure Handy was amused.

"Sounds like a fucking comedy."

"He was funny. His AK-47 was pretty sobering, I have to say."

"You a shrink?"

"Nope. Just a guy who likes to talk."

"You must have a pretty good ego."

"Ego?"

"Sure. You gotta listen to somebody like me say, 'You scurvy piece of dogshit, I'm going to kill you the first chance I get,' and then still ask him if he'd like Diet Coke or iced tea with his burgers."

"You want lemon with that tea, Lou?"

"Haw. This's all you do?"

"Well, I teach too. At the military police school at Fort McClellan. In Alabama. Then I'm head of hostage and barricade training at Quantico in the Bureau's Special Operations and Research Unit."

Now Henry LeBow offered an exasperated expression to Potter. The intelligence officer had never heard his fellow agent give away so much personal information.

Slowly Handy said in a low voice, "Tell me something, Art. You ever done anything bad?"

"Bad?"

"Really bad."

"I suppose I have."

"Did you mean to do it?"

"Mean to do it?"

"Ain't you listening to me?" Testy now. Echoing too frequently can antagonize the hostage taker.

"Well, the things I've done aren't so much intentional, I suppose. One bad thing is that I didn't spend enough time with my wife. Then she died, pretty fast, like I told you, and I realized there was a lot I hadn't said to her."

"Fuck," Handy spat out with a derisive laugh. "That's not bad. You don't know what I'm talking about."

Potter felt deeply hurt by the criticism. He wanted to cry out, "I do! And I *did* feel that I'd done something bad, terribly bad."

Handy continued, "I'm talking about killing somebody, ruining somebody's life, leaving a widow or widower, leaving children to grow up alone. Something *bad.*"

"I've never killed anyone, Lou. Not directly."

Tobe was looking at him. Angie scribbled a note: *You're giving away a lot, Arthur.*

He ignored them, wiped the sweat from his forehead, kept his eyes focused outside on the slaughterhouse. "But people have died because of me. Carelessness. Mistakes. Sometimes intent. You and I, Lou, we both work flip sides of the same business." Feeling the overwhelming urge to make himself understood. "But you know—"

"Don't skip over this shit, Art. Tell me if they bother you, some of the things you've done?"

"I . . . I don't know."

"What about them people dying you was talking about?"

Take his pulse, Potter told himself. What's he thinking?

I can't see a thing. Who the hell knows?

"Yo, Art, keep talkin'. Who were they? Hostages you couldn't save? Troopers you sent in when you shouldn't've?"

"Yes, that's who they were."

And takers too. Though he doesn't say this. Ostrella, he thinks spontaneously, sees her long, beautiful face, serpentine. Dark eyebrows, full lips. *His* Ostrella.

"And that bothers you, huh?"

"Bothers me? Sure it does."

"Fuck," Handy seemed to sneer. Potter again felt the sting. "See, Art, you're proving my point. You've never done anything bad and you and me, we both know it. Take those folks in the Cadillac this afternoon, that couple I killed. *Their* names were Ruth and Hank, by the way. Ruthie and Hank. You know why I killed them?"

"Why, Lou?"

"Same reason I'm putting that little girl—*Shannon*—in the window in a minute or two and shooting her in the back of the head."

Even cool Henry LeBow stirred. Frances Whiting's elegant hands moved to her face.

"Why's that?" Potter asked calmly.

"Because I didn't get what I was owed! Pure and simple. This afternoon, in that field, they fucked up my car, ran right into it. And when I went to take theirs they tried to get away."

Potter had read the report from the Kansas State Police. It looked as if Handy's car had run a stop sign and been hit by the Cadillac, which had the right of way. Potter did not mention this fact.

"That's fair, isn't it? I mean, what could be clearer? They had to die, and it woulda been more painful than it was if I'd had more time. They didn't give me what I shoulda had."

How cold and logical he sounds.

Potter reminded himself: No value judgment. But don't approve of him either. Negotiators are neutral. (And it broke his heart that he didn't in fact feel the disgust that he ought to have been feeling. That a small portion of him believed Handy's words made sense.)

"Man, Art, I don't get it. When I kill somebody for a reason they call me bad. When a cop does it for a reason they give him a paycheck and call him good. Why're some reasons okay and others ain't? You kill when people don't do what they're supposed to. You kill the weak because they'll drag you down. What's wrong with that?"

Henry LeBow typed his notes calmly. Tobe Geller perused his monitors and dials. Charlie Budd sat in the corner, eyes on the floor, Angie beside him, listening carefully. And Officer Frances Whiting stood in the corner, uneasily holding a cup of coffee she'd lost all taste for; police work in Hebron, Kansas, didn't involve the likes of Lou Handy.

A laugh over the speaker. He asked, "Admit it, Art. . . . Haven't you ever wanted to do that? Kill someone for a bad reason?"

"No, I haven't."

"That a fact?" He was skeptical. "I wonder. . . ."

Silence filled the van. A trickle of sweat flowed down Potter's face and he wiped his forehead.

Handy asked, "So, you look like that guy in the old FBI show, Efrem Zimbalist?"

"Not a bit. I'm pretty ordinary. I'm just a humble constable. I eat too many potatoes—"

"Fries," Handy remembered.

"Mashed are my favorite, actually. With pan gravy."

Tobe whispered something to Budd, who wrote down on a slip of paper: *Deadline.*

Potter glanced at the clock. Into the phone he said, "I fancy sports coats. Tweed are my favorite. Or camel's hair. But we have to wear suits in the Bureau."

"Suits, huh? They cover up a lot of fat, don't they? Hold on a second there, Art."

Potter dipped out of his reverie and trained his Leicas on the factory window. A pistol barrel appeared next to Shannon's head, which was covered with her long, brown hair, now mussed.

"That son of a bitch," Budd whispered. "The poor thing's terrified."

Frances leaned forward. "Oh, no. Please . . ."

Potter's fingers tapped buttons. "Dean?"

"Yessir," Stillwell answered.

"Can one of your snipers acquire a target?"

A pause.

"Negative. All they can see is a pistol barrel and slide. He's behind her. There's no shot he can make except into the window frame."

Handy asked, "Hey, Art, you really never shot anyone?"

LeBow looked up, frowning. But Potter answered anyway, "Nope, never have."

His hands stuffed deep into his pockets, Budd began pacing. It was very irritating.

"Ever fired a gun?"

"Of course. On the range at Quantico. I enjoyed it."

"Didja? You know, if you enjoyed shooting you might enjoy shooting some*body*. Killing somebody."

"Sick son of a bitch," Budd muttered.

Potter waved the captain quiet.

"You know something, Art?"

"What's that?"

"You're all right. I mean it."

Potter felt a pleasing burst—from the man's approval.

I *am* good, he thought. He knew that it was the empathy that makes the difference at this job. Not the strategy, not the words, not the calculation or intelligence. It's what I can't teach in the training courses. I was always good, he reflected. But when you died, Marian, I became great. I had nowhere for my heart to go and so I gave it to men like Louis Handy.

And to Ostrella . . .

A terrorist takeover in Washington, D.C. The Estonian woman, blond and brilliant, walking out of the Soviet embassy after twenty hours of negotiating with Potter. Twelve hostages released, four more inside. Finally she'd surrendered, come out with her hands not outstretched but on her head—a violation of the hostage surrender protocol. But Potter knew she was harmless. Knew her as well as he knew Marian. He'd stepped unprotected from the barricade and walked toward her, to greet her, to embrace her, to make sure that when she was arrested the cuffs weren't too tight, that her rights were read to her in her native language. And he'd had to endure the copious spatter of her blood from the sniper who shot her in the head when she pulled the hidden pistol from her collar and shoved it directly toward Potter's face. (And his reaction? To scream to her, "Get down!" And fling his arms around her to protect his new love, as bits of her skull snapped against his skin.)

Have you ever wanted to do something bad?

Be . . .

Yes, Lou, I have. If you must know.

. . . *forewarned.*

Potter was unable to say anything for a moment, afraid to offend Handy, afraid that he'd hang up. Almost as afraid of that as of Handy's killing the girl. "Listen to me, Lou. I tell you in good faith we're working on this chopper and I asked you to tell me something that you'll accept to buy another hour." Potter added, "We're trying to work out a deal. Help me out here."

There was a pause and the confident voice said, "It's thirsty work, here."

Ah, let's play a game. "Diet Pepsi?" the agent asked coyly.

"You know what I'm talking about."

"Lemonade, made out of fresh Sunkist?"

LeBow hit several keys and showed the screen to Potter, who nodded.

"Glass of mother's milk?" Handy sneered.

Reading Wilcox's profile, Potter said, "I don't think liquor's a real good idea, Lou. Shep has a bit of a problem, doesn't he?"

A pause.

"You boys sure seem to know a lot about us."

"That's what they pay me my meager salary for. To know everything in the world."

"Well, that's the deal. One hour for some booze."

"Nothing hard. No way."

"Beer's fine. 'S'more to my liking anyway."

"I'll send in three cans."

"Hold up there. A case."

"No. You get three cans of light beer."

A snicker. "Fuck light beer."

"That's the best I can do."

Frances and Budd were plastered against the window, watching Shannon.

Handy's voice sang, "This little piggy went to market, this little piggy stayed home. . . ." Moving the gun from one of the girl's ears to the other.

Stillwell came on the air to ask what he should tell the snipers.

Potter hesitated. "No fire," he said. "Whatever happens."

"Copy," Stillwell said.

They heard the whimper of the girl as Handy pressed the gun against her forehead.

"I'll give you a six-pack," Potter said, "if you let me have that girl."

Budd whispered, "Don't push it."

A pause. "Give me a reason why I'd want to do that."

LeBow dropped the cursor to a paragraph in the evolving *Biography of Louis Handy*. Potter read, then said, " 'Cause you *love* beer."

Handy had been reprimanded by one of his wardens for whipping up some home brew in prison. Later, his privileges were suspended after he'd smuggled in two cases of Budweiser.

"Come on," Potter chided, "what can it hurt? You'll have plenty of hostages left over." Potter took the chance. "Besides, she's a little pain in the ass, isn't she? That's her reputation at school."

Angie's eyes sprang open. It's a risk to refer to the hostages in any way because it gives them more value to the taker than they already have. You *never* suggest that they have some liability that might irritate or endanger him.

A pause.

Now, set the hook.

The agent said, "What's your favorite brand? Miller? Bud?"

"Mexican."

"You got it, Lou. A six-pack of Corona, you let that girl go and we get another hour for the chopper. Everybody's happy."

"I'd rather shoot her."

Potter and LeBow glanced at each other. Budd was suddenly standing close to Potter, his hands in his pocket, fidgeting.

The negotiator ignored the young captain and said to Handy, "Okay, Lou, then shoot her. I'm tired of this bullshit."

From the corner of his eye he saw Budd shift and for a moment Potter tensed, thinking the captain was going to leap forward, grab the phone, and agree to whatever Handy wanted. But he just kept his hands in his back pockets and turned away. Frances gazed at the negotiator in utter shock.

Potter hit buttons on the phone. "Dean, he may shoot the girl. If he does, make sure nobody returns fire."

A hesitation. "Yessir."

Potter was back on the line with Handy. The man hadn't hung up but he wasn't talking either. Shannon's head swiveled back and forth. The black rectangular pistol was still visible.

Potter jumped inches when Handy's staccato laugh shot into the van. "This's sorta like Monopoly, ain't it? Buying and selling and all?"

Potter struggled to remain silent.

Handy growled, "Two six-packs or I do it right now." Shannon's head bent forward as Handy pressed the gun into it.

"And we get an extra hour for the chopper?" Potter asked. "Makes it about six-fifteen."

"Safety's off," Dean Stillwell sang out.

Potter closed his eyes.

Not a single sound in the van. Complete silence. This is what Melanie lives with day after day after day, Potter thinks.

"Deal, Art," Handy said. "By the way, you *are* one bad motherfucker." *Click.*

Potter slumped into the chair, closed his eyes for a moment. "You get all that, Henry?"

LeBow nodded and typed away. He rose and started to lift Shannon's marker out of the slaughterhouse schematic.

"Wait," said Potter. LeBow paused. "Let's just wait."

"I'll get that beer," Budd said, exhaling a sigh.

Potter smiled. "Getting a little hot for you, Captain?"

"Yeah. Some."

"You'll get used to it," Potter said, just as Budd said, "I'll get used to it." The captain's voice was far less optimistic than Potter's. The agent and the trooper laughed.

Budd started like a rabbit when Angie squeezed his arm. "I'll come with you to see about that beer, Captain. If that's all right with you."

"Uh, well, sure, I guess," he said uncertainly, and they left the van.

"One more hour," LeBow said, nodding.

Potter swiveled around in his chair, staring out the window at the slaughterhouse. "Henry, write down: 'It's the negotiator's conclusion that the stress and anxiety of the initial phase of the barricade have dissipated and subject Handy is calm and thinking rationally.' "

"That makes one of us," said Frances Whiting, whose shaking hands spilled coffee on the floor of the van. Derek Elb, the red-haired trooper, gallantly dropped to hands and knees to clean up the mess.

5:11 P.M.

"What's he doing with Shannon?" Beverly signed, her chest rising and falling as she tried to breathe.

Melanie leaned forward. Shannon's face was emotionless. She was signing and Melanie caught the name Professor X, the founder of the X-Men. Like Emily, the girl was summoning her guardian angels.

Bear and Brutus were talking and she could see their lips. Bear gestured to Shannon and asked Brutus, "Why . . . giving them away?"

"Because," Brutus answered patiently, "if we don't they'll break in the fucking door and . . . shoot us dead."

Melanie scooted back, said, "She's just sitting there. She's all right. They're going to let her go."

Everyone's face lit up.

Everyone except Mrs. Harstrawn's.

And Kielle's. Little Kielle, a blond, freckled bobcat. An eight-year-old with twenty-year-old eyes. The girl glanced impatiently at Melanie and turned away, bent down to the wall beside her, working away at something. What was she doing? Trying to tunnel her way out? Well, let her. It'll keep her out of harm's way.

"I think I'm going to be sick," signed one of the twins, Suzie. Anna signed the same but then she usually echoed everything her very slightly older sister said.

Melanie signed to them that they wouldn't be sick. Everything would be fine. She scooted over beside Emily, who was tearfully examining a rip in her dress. "You and I'll go shopping next week," Melanie signed. "Buy you new one."

And that was when de l'Epée whispered in her useless ear. "The gas can," he said, and vanished immediately.

Melanie felt the chill run down her back. The gas can, yes. She turned her head. It sat beside her, red and yellow, a big two-gallon one. She eased toward it, snapped closed the cover and the pressure hole cap. Then looked around the killing room for the other thing she'd need.

There, yes.

Melanie slid around to the front of the room, examined the back of the slaughterhouse. There were two doors—she could just make them out in the dimness. Which one led to the river? she wondered. She happened to glance down at the floor, where she'd written the messages in the dust about the hand-shape game. Squinting, she looked at the floor in front of each door—there was much less dust in front of the left. That's it—the river breeze blows through that one and has swept away the dust. Enough wind for there to be, just possibly, a window or door open far enough for a little girl to scoot through.

Beverly choked and started a crying fit. She lay on her side, struggling for breath. The inhaler hadn't done her much good. Bear frowned and looked at her, called something.

Shit. Melanie signed to Beverly, "It's hard, honey, but please be quiet."

"Scared, scared."

"I know. But it'll be all—"

Oh, my God. Melanie's eyes went wide and her signing hands stopped in midword as she looked across the room.

Kielle was holding the knife in front of her, an old hook-bladed knife. That's what she'd seen underneath a pile of trash; that's what she'd been digging out.

Melanie shuddered. "No!" she signed. "Put it back."

Kielle had murder in her gray eyes. She slipped the weapon into her pocket. "I'm going to kill Mr. Sinister. You can't stop me!" Her hands slashed the air in front of her as if she were already stabbing him.

"No! Can't do it that way!"

"I'm Jubilee! He can't stop me!"

"That's character in comic book," Melanie's staccato hands shot out. "Not real!"

Kielle ignored her. "Jubilation Lee! I'm going to blow him apart with plasmoids! He's going to die. No one can stop me!" She crawled through the door and disappeared through the shower of water tumbling from the ceiling.

The huge main room of the Webber & Stoltz slaughterhouse, in the front portion of which were clustered the three convicts, had been a series of holding pens and walkways for the beasts that had died here. The space was now used for storing slaughterhouse equipment—butcher blocks, one- and three-bay decapitation guillotines, gutting machines, grinders, huge rendering vats.

It was into this gruesome warehouse that Kielle disappeared, intending, it seemed, to circle around to the front wall, where the men lounged in front of the TV.

No. . . .

Melanie half-rose, looked at Bear—the only one of the three with a clear view of the killing room—and froze. He wasn't looking their way but he had only to turn his greasy head inches to see them. In a panic she looked over the main room. Caught a glimpse of Kielle's blond hair vanishing behind a column.

Melanie eased closer to the doorway, still crouching. Brutus was at the window, beside Shannon, looking out. Bear started to glance toward the room but turned back to Stoat, who was laughing at something. Bear, stroking the shotgun he held, reared back and laughed, closing his eyes.

Now. Do it.

I can't.

Do it, while he can't see you.

A deep breath. Now. Melanie slipped out of the room and crawled under a rotting walkway, indented and bowed from a million hoof-prints. She paused, looking through the cascade of tumbling water. Kielle . . . Where are you? You think you can stab him and just vanish? You and your damn comic books!

She slipped through the water—it was freezing cold and slimy. Shivering in disgust, she made her way into the cavernous room.

What would the girl do? Circle around, she supposed, come up behind him, stab him in the back. Past the machinery, rusting scraps of metal and rotting wood. Piles of chains and meat hooks, stained with blood and barbed with sharp bits of dried flesh. The vats were disgusting. From them emanated a sickening smell and Melanie couldn't rid her mind of the image of animals sinking down into simmering fat and fluid. She felt her gorge rising, started to retch.

No! Be quiet! The least sound'll tell them you're here.

She struggled to control herself, dropping to her knees to breathe the cool moist air from the floor.

Glancing under the legs of a large guillotine, its angular blade rusty and pitted, Melanie saw the little girl's shadow across the room as she scrambled from one column to another.

Melanie started forward quickly. And got only two feet before she felt the numbing thud of her shoulder running into a piece of steel pipe, six feet long, resting against a column. It began a slow fall to the floor.

No!

Melanie flung her arms around the pipe. It must have weighed a hundred pounds.

I can't hold it, can't stop it!

The pipe fell faster, pulling her after it. Just as her grip was about to go she dropped to the floor, rolled under the rusty metal, and took the impact of it on her tensed stomach muscles. She gasped at the pain that surged through her body, praying that the wind and the cascade of water made enough noise to cover the grunting from her throat. She lay stunned for a long moment.

Finally she managed to ease out from underneath the pipe and roll it to the floor—silently, she hoped.

Oh, Kielle, where are you? Don't you understand? You can't kill them all. They'll find us, they'll kill us. Or Bear'll take us into the back of the factory. Haven't you seen his eyes? Don't you know what he wants? No, you probably don't. You don't have a clue—

She risked a look toward the front of the room. The attention of the men was mostly turned toward the TV. Occasionally Bear glanced at the killing room but didn't seem to notice that two of the captives were missing.

Glancing again beneath the legs of the machinery, Melanie caught a glimpse of blond hair. There she was, Kielle, making her way inexorably toward the three men near the window. Crawling, a smile on her face. She probably *did* think she could kill all three.

Struggling to catch her breath from the blow of the pipe, Melanie scrabbled down a corridor, hid behind a rusted column. She turned the corner and saw the blond girl, only twenty or thirty feet from Brutus, whose back was to her as he continued to gaze out the window. His hand casually gripping Shannon's collar. If any one of the three men had stood and walked toward the girl, they'd only have to look down over one of the large vats, which lay on its side, to see her.

Kielle was tensing. About to leap over the vat and charge Brutus.

Melanie thought, Should I just let her do it? What is the worst that would happen? She'd get a few feet toward them, Bear would see her, take the knife away. They'd slap her once or twice, shove her back into the killing room.

Why should I risk my life? Risk Bear's hands on me? Risk Brutus's eyes?

But then Melanie saw Susan. Saw the dot appearing on her back and the puff of black hair, like smoke, rise up.

She saw Bear looking over Emily's boyish body, grinning.

Shit.

Melanie pulled her black shoes off, pushed them under a metal table. She started to sprint. Flat out, down the narrow corridor, dodging overhanging hunks of metal and rods and pipes, leaping over a piece of butcher block.

Just as Kielle stood and reached for the top of the vat Melanie tackled her. One hand around her stomach, the other around her mouth. They went down hard and knocked into the hinged lid of a vat, which slammed closed.

"No!" the little girl signed. "Let me—"

Melanie did something she'd never in her life done: drew back her open palm and aimed directly at the girl's cheek. Kielle's eyes went wide. The teacher lowered her hand and glanced through the crack between two overturned vats. Brutus had turned, looking in their direction. Stoat was shrugging. "Wind," she saw him say. Unsmiling Bear was on his feet, carrying the shotgun, walking toward them.

"Inside," Melanie signed fiercely, gesturing toward a large steel vat nearby, resting on its side. The girl hesitated for a moment and they climbed inside, pulling the lid closed, like a door. The sides were coated with a waxy substance that disgusted Melanie and made her skin crawl. The smell was overpowering and she struggled once again to keep from vomiting.

A shadow fell over the vat and she felt a vibration as Bear stepped into the corridor. He was only two feet from them.

Halfheartedly, he glanced around and then stepped back toward Shannon and the other men.

Kielle turned to her. In the dim light Melanie could just make out the girl's words. "I'm going to kill him! Don't stop me, or I'll kill you too!"

Melanie gasped as the little girl lifted the razor-sharp blade and pointed it at her. "Stop it!" Melanie signed brutally. What should I do? she wondered. Images of Susan were flashing through her mind. Mrs. Harstrawn, her father, her brother.

And de l'Epée.

Susan, help me.

De l'Epée . . .

Then Melanie thought suddenly: There *is* no Susan. She's dead. Dead and already cold.

And Mrs. Harstrawn may as well be.

De l'Epée? He's just a lie. A phony visitor to your phony little room. Another of your sick, imaginary friends, one of the dozens you grew up talking to, going out with, making very solitary love to while you hid from everything real. I get everything wrong! I hear music when there is no music, I hear nothing when people speak to me inches away, I'm afraid when I have to be brave. . . .

A Maiden's Grave.

The little girl reached for the lid of the vat.

"Kielle!" Melanie signed angrily. "Jubilee . . . All right. Listen."

The girl looked at her cautiously, nodded.

"You really want to kill him?"

"Yes!" Kielle's eyes glowed.

"Okay. Then we'll do it together. We'll do it the right way."

A ragged smile blossomed in Kielle's face.

"I'll distract him. You go behind pipe there. See it? Go over there and hide."

"What should I do?"

"Wait until I give you signal to come out. He'll be talking to me, won't look for you."

"And then?"

"Stab him as hard as you can in back. Okay?"

"Yes!" The little girl smiled, her eyes no longer fiery but cold as stone. "I'm Jubilee! No one can stop me!"

Brutus had his back to the interior of the slaughterhouse but he must have seen her reflection in a pane of cracked glass. He turned. "Whatta we got here?"

Melanie had slipped from the vat and circled back toward the killing room. Now she walked toward them, smiled at Shannon.

She looked at Handy and mimicked writing. He handed her a yellow pad and pen. She wrote, *I don't want you to hurt her.* She nodded toward Shannon.

"Hurt her? I'm giving . . . away. Understand?"

Why not both her and the sick girl? she wrote. Mention her name, Melanie thought. Maybe he'll be more sympathetic. *Beverly,* she added.

Brutus grinned and nodded at Bear. "My friend . . . wants to keep the pretty ones . . . for a while."

He's saying this just to be cruel, she thought. Then reflected: He *is* cruel, yes. But what else is he, what else do I feel about him? Something strange; there's some connection. Is it because I can understand his words? Or do I understand him *because* of the connection?

Stoat stepped away from the window and said, ". . . coming . . . two . . .

packs." He winked and continued to chew on a toothpick. But Brutus wasn't looking out the window; he was scanning the slaughterhouse, looking around, squinting.

What can I do to keep him from seeing Kielle?

Try to seduce him? she thought suddenly.

What she knew of love she knew from books, movies, and girl talk. Melanie had had boyfriends but had never slept with any of them. Always, the fear . . . Of what, she didn't know. The dark maybe. Trusting somebody that much. Of course there was the problem that she'd never met anyone interested in making love with her. Oh, there'd been plenty of boys who wanted to fuck her. But that was so different. Look at the two terms: Saying "fuck" pinched the nose and made your features tight and lonely. "Making love" . . . it was soft and opened up your face.

Suddenly Brutus laughed and stepped forward, grabbed her and pulled her close. Maybe he was far smarter than he seemed. Or maybe her eyes could keep nothing secret; in any event he knew exactly what she was thinking. He stroked her hair.

She waited for the hands on her breasts, between her legs. She remembered how she'd recoiled when a boyfriend had slipped his hand up there quickly. She'd leapt off his knee like lightning, smacking her head on the car's hot dome light.

Then Brutus turned his head and said something she didn't catch.

Bear and Stoat were laughing.

Abruptly he shoved her away, leaned his face close, and said, "Why'd I want you? A busted little thing like you? You're like a boy. I want women only." His black eyes bored into hers and she broke into sobs. With satisfaction he looked over the horror and shame in her face. "I got me a real woman. Pris's all I need. She's got herself a woman's body and a woman's eyes. We fuck for hours. You have a boyfriend?"

Melanie couldn't answer. Her arms were weak and hung at her side. In the corner of her eye she saw Kielle slip through the shadows of machinery. She struggled to stop the tears, refused to wipe them away.

"Pris's a real character. A ballbuster . . . Think I'm bad? She's badder. You hate me? You wouldn't like her one bit. Now, *she* might fuck you. She's a bit that way and I'd like to watch. If we get out of this we'll do that, her and me and you."

Melanie stepped away but he took her by the arm. The grip cut off the blood to her hands and she felt them tingle painfully.

Stoat, hand on his crew cut, was calling something. Brutus turned to the window, looked out. Melanie felt a vibration in the air. Brutus looked toward the phone. Smiling, he let go of Melanie's arm and picked up the receiver.

"Hello . . ."

Was he talking to de l'Epée? What were they saying?

Behind the pipes near the door was Kielle's shadow. The girl held the knife in her hand.

". . . almost here," Stoat called, pointing his gun out the window.

Brutus lowered his head and kept talking into the phone, fiddling with the pistol stuffed in his belt. He looked bored; he grimaced and hung up. Picked up a shotgun, pulled back a lever on it, and stepped to the doorway. His back was to Kielle, perhaps ten feet away. The girl leaned her head out. Light from outside, a shaft of brilliant white light, glinted off the blade in her hand. Melanie signed, "Wait."

Stoat grabbed Shannon by the arm and pulled her to the door. Brutus stepped back, pointing the gun outward, and Stoat eased the door open.

A figure appeared in the doorway—a trooper dressed in black. He handed in two six-packs of beer. Stoat shoved the girl out the door.

Now!

Melanie stepped slowly behind Brutus. She smiled at Kielle, who frowned, confused. Then Melanie reached down and simply scooped the little girl off the ground, grabbing the knife from her hand.

Kielle shook her head violently.

But Melanie spun around, moving so fast that Brutus froze in confusion, staring at them, no idea what was going on. Melanie continued to smile as she stepped around him, firmly gripping the astonished girl.

Then flung Kielle out the door into the chest of the trooper.

For an instant no one moved. Melanie, still smiling at Stoat, slowly eased the door closed, shooing her hand lethargically at the astonished cop as if he were a bluetail fly.

"Fuck," Brutus spat out. Stoat started forward, but Melanie slammed the door completely closed and wedged it tight with Kielle's knife. Stoat tugged at the large knob but it wouldn't budge.

Then Melanie dropped to her knees and covered her face, trying to cushion herself from the blow as Stoat's bony fist slammed into her neck and jaw. He pulled her arms away and struck her hard on the forehead and chin.

"You fucking bitch!" Brutus's tendons and jaw quivered.

He hit her once hard and she fell against the floor. Trying to scrabble away, she pulled herself up by the windowsill, glanced outside and saw the trooper carrying both the young X-Men with him, tucked under his arms. Jogging awkwardly through the gully away from the slaughterhouse.

On her neck she heard the vibrations of a man's voice shouting in anger. Brutus was running to the window on the other side of the door. He stepped back from it then aimed the shotgun outside.

Melanie ran at him.

It seemed that her feet didn't even touch the ground. Stoat grabbed for her but caught only a shred of silk collar that tore away. As she collided with Brutus's shoulder she had the satisfaction of seeing his pain and surprise and fear as he fell sideways into a square of butcher block. The gun hit the floor but didn't go off.

Melanie looked out the window once more and saw the two girls and the trooper disappear over a small hill. And then Stoat's gun caught her above the ear that had first gone deaf, years ago, and she dropped to her knees. She fainted not so much from the pain as from the terror that the darkness taking her vision was from a broken nerve and that she would now be blind as well as deaf forever and ever.

5:34 P.M.

"You gave us a bonus, Lou. Thanks much."

"Wasn't me," Handy grumbled.

"No? What happened?"

"Listen here, I'm pissed."

"Why's that?"

"Just shut up and listen, Art. I don't wanta hear your bullshit." His voice was colder than it'd been all day.

"Forty-five minutes for that helicopter. That's all you got and I'll tell you, mister, I'm itching to kill somebody. I almost hope it don't show up. I'm not doing any more bargaining with you."

"How's your beer?"

"I picked the little bitch already. She's ten or eleven. Wearing a pretty dress."

"Emily," Angie said.

"And I'm gonna let Bonner have her first. You know 'bout Bonner, don't you? You got your fucking files on us. You must know all 'bout his little problem."

A negotiator never imposes his own values on the situation—either approval or criticism. Doing so suggests that there are standards of what is and isn't acceptable and is apt to irritate the taker or make his bad behavior seem justified. Even offering reassuring clichés can be dangerous, suggesting that you're not taking the situation seriously.

Reluctantly Potter now said in as blasé a voice as he could muster, "You don't want to do that, Lou. You know you don't."

The cackle of vicious laughter filled the van. "Everybody's telling me what I don't want to do. I *hate* that!"

"We're working on the chopper, Lou. Look outside. We've got twenty-mile-an-hour winds, low overcast, and fog. You wanted pontoons. Well, pontoons don't grow on trees."

"You got twelve-mile-an-hour winds, ceilings of two thousand feet, and no fucking fog that I can see."

The television, Potter remembered, angry with himself for forgetting. Maybe Handy was watching the *Live at Five* weather report at that moment. A long minute of silence. Potter, staring at the speaker above his head, decided they were too focused on the mechanics of the negotiating. It was time for something personal.

"Lou?"

"Yeah."

"You asked me what *I* looked like. Let me ask you about yourself."

"Fuck, you've got pictures in there, I'll bet."

"What do mug shots show?" Potter asked, and laughed.

When Handy spoke, his voice had calmed considerably. "What do I look like?" he mused. "Let me tell you a story, Art. I was in a prison riot one time. All kindsa shit was going down like usual in things like that. What the fuck happens but I find myself in the laundry room with a fellow I'd had it in for for a long time. Now, you know where you hide things when you're inside, don't you? So I crapped this glass knife, unwrapped it, and started to work on him. You know why?"

Echo his questions and comments, Arthur Potter the negotiator thought. But Arthur Potter remained silent.

" 'Cause when I first was in he come up to me, all macho and that shit, and said he didn't like the way I looked."

"So you killed him." A matter-of-fact statement.

"Fuck yes, but that's not my point. While he was dying there, his gut all split open, I leaned down. See, I was curious. I leaned down real close and I asked him what exactly it was he didn't like about the way I looked. And you know what he said? He said, 'You looked like cold death.' Know something, Art? I was sorry I killed him after he told me that. Yessir, cold death."

Don't play his game, Potter thought suddenly. You're falling under his spell. With an edge to his voice he asked, "Lou, give us until seven. You do me that, I think we'll have some good news for you."

"I—"

"That's all. What difference does it make?" Potter kept all supplication from his voice. He made it sound that Handy was being unreasonable. It was a risk but Potter assessed that the man would have no respect at all for whiners.

Still, he was very surprised when Handy said, "All right. Jesus! But have the chopper here, Art. Or the little one in the dress goes."

Click.

Potter calmly instructed Tobe to adjust the deadline clock accordingly.

The door to the van opened and a trooper looked in. "The two girls are here, sir. They're in the medical tent."

"Are they okay?"

"One fell and scraped her elbow. Otherwise they're fine."

"I'll go over there. I could use some fresh air. Frances, could you translate? Henry, get yourself unplugged and come with us. Angie too?"

In a grove of trees not far from the van Potter ushered the girls into folding chairs. Henry LeBow joined them, portable computer in hand. He sat down and smiled at the girls, who stared at the Toshiba.

Potter tried to recall what Frances had taught him and spelled their names in sign language. S-H-A-N-N-O-N and K-I-E-L-L-E, bringing a smile to Shannon's face. They were the same age, Potter knew— eight—but Shannon was taller. Kielle, however, with her grim face and cynical eyes, gave the impression of being far older.

"What's the matter?" Potter asked Kielle.

Frances's face went cold when she received a response. "She said she tried to kill him."

"Who?"

"Handy, I think she means. She calls him Mr. Sinister."

Potter produced the flyer of the fugitives. Kielle's face screwed into a tight mask and she poked a finger at Handy's picture.

"She says he killed Susan and she was going to kill him. Melanie betrayed her. Melanie is a Judas."

"Why?" Angie asked.

More brutal signing.

"She threw her out the door."

"Melanie did that?"

Potter felt the chill down his spine. He knew there'd be a payback of some kind.

Shannon confirmed that the men didn't seem to have any rifles, only shotguns—her father hunted and she knew something about guns. Beverly's asthma was bad, though Handy had given her the medicine. She reiterated that the "big man," Bonner, hovered over the girls and kept looking at Emily because she was "prettier and looked more like a girl."

Angie asked delicately, "Has anyone touched any of you?"

Shannon said that they had. But Kielle waved her hand and signed, "Not the way you mean. But Bear looks a lot."

So, Potter reflected, Bonner's a discrete threat, separate from Handy. And probably more dangerous. Lust-driven criminals always are.

"Who picked you to be released?" Angie asked Shannon.

"Him." She pointed at Handy.

"The one Melanie calls Brutus, right?"

Shannon nodded. "We call him Mr. Sinister. Or Magneto."

"Why did he pick you, do you think? Was there any reason?"

"Because Bear"—Shannon pointed at Bonner's picture—"told him to." Frances looked at Angie and said, "Shannon kicked him and he was mad."

"I didn't mean to kick him. I just didn't think. . . . And then I got really scared. I thought it was my fault he was going to burn us up."

"Burn you up? Why'd you think that?"

Shannon told them about the gas can rigged right above their heads. Frances's face went pale. "He wouldn't."

"Oh, yes he would," Angie said. "Fire. His new toy."

"Damn," Potter muttered. This virtually eliminated the possibility of an HRT rescue. Henry LeBow's concession to the horror was to pause before he typed a description of the device.

Potter walked to the doorway of the van, called Budd out, and then motioned Dean Stillwell over. The negotiator said to them both, "We've got a hot trap inside—"

"Hot?" Budd asked.

"Armed," Potter continued. "We can't give him the least excuse to trip it. There's to be absolutely no action that could be construed as offensive. Double-check—all weapons unchambered."

"Yessir," Stillwell said.

Potter then asked Shannon if there was anything else she could remember about the men and what they did inside.

"They watch TV," Frances translated. "They walk around. Eat. Talk. They're pretty relaxed."

Relaxed. Jocylyn had said the same. Well, this was a first for a barricade.

"You saw the tools they have?"

Shannon nodded.

"Have they used them?"

"No."

"Do you remember what tools they had?"

She shook her head no.

"Can you tell what they talk about?" Potter asked.

"No," Frances explained. "Neither of them can lip-read."

"They watch you all the time?" Angie asked.

"Pretty much. He's scary. Him." Shannon was pointing at Handy. Kielle reached forward viciously and grabbed the picture. She tore it up and signed violently.

"She says she hates Melanie. She could have killed him. And now he's alive to kill more people. She says she wouldn't have minded dying. But Melanie's a coward and she hates her."

As he had done with Jocylyn, Potter warmly shook the girls' hands and thanked them. Shannon smiled; Kielle did not but it was with a strong, self-assured grip that the little girl grasped the agent's hand. Then he sent the two girls off with a trooper, to meet their parents at the motel in Crow Ridge. He conferred with Angie for a few minutes then climbed into the van. She followed him.

The negotiator rubbed his eyes and leaned back and took the cup of the dreadful coffee Derek set beside him. "I don't get it," he said to no one in particular.

"What?" Budd asked.

"A hostage escaped and he's angry. That part I understand. But he doesn't seem angry because he lost a bargaining chip. He's angry for some other reason." He looked across the van. "Angie? Our resident psychologist? Have any ideas?"

She organized her thoughts, then said, "I think Handy's big issue is control. He says he's killed people because they didn't do what he wanted. I've heard that before. A convenience store clerk didn't put the money in the robber's bag as fast as he wanted so *she's* the one guilty of an offense, not him. That gave him, in effect, permission to kill her."

"Is that why he killed Susan?" Budd asked.

Potter rose and paced. "Ah, a very good question, Charlie."

"I agree," Angie said. "A key question."

"Why her?" Potter continued.

"Well, what I actually meant," Budd said, "was why did he *kill* her? Why go to that extreme?"

"Oh, when somebody breaks his rules, however slightly," Angie said, "any punishment's fair. Death, torture, rape. In Handy's world, even misdemeanors are capital offenses. But let's ask *Arthur's* question. Why *her*? Why Susan Phillips? That's the important issue. Henry, tell us about the girl."

LeBow's finger clattered. He read from the screen. "Seventeen. Born of deaf parents. IQ of one hundred and forty-six."

"This is hard to listen to," Budd muttered. Potter nodded for LeBow to go on.

"First in her class at the Laurent Clerc School. And listen to this. She's got a record."

"What?"

"She was a protestor last year at Topeka School for the Deaf, a part of Hammersmith College. They wanted a deaf dean. Fifty students got arrested and Susan slugged a cop. They dropped the charges for assault but gave her a suspended for trespass."

LeBow continued, "Volunteered at the Midwest Bicultural/Bilingual Center. There's an article here—in the material Angie brought." He skimmed it. "Apparently it's an organization that opposes something called 'mainstreaming.'"

Angie said, "The dean of the Clerc School told me about that. It's a movement to force the Deaf into regular schools. It's very controversial. Deaf activists oppose it."

"All right," Potter said. "Let's file that away for a moment. Now, who's Handy given up so far?"

"Jocylyn and Shannon," Angie said.

"Anything in common about them?"

"Doesn't seem to be," Budd said. "In fact, looks like they're opposites. Jocylyn's a timid little thing. Shannon's feisty. She's a little Susan Phillips."

"Angie?" Potter said. "What do you think."

"Control again. Susan was a direct threat to him. She had an in-your-face attitude. She probably challenged his control directly. Now, Shannon, with her kicking Bonner . . . Handy'd sense the same threat but on a smaller scale. He wouldn't feel the need to kill her—to reassert control in the most extreme way possible—but he'd want her out. Jocylyn? She was crying all the time. Sniveling. She got on his nerves. That's a way to eat at his control too."

"What about the adults?" LeBow asked. "I'd think they'd be more of a threat than the children."

"Oh, not necessarily," Angie said. "The older teacher, Donna Harstrawn, is half-comatose, it sounds like. No threat there."

"And Melanie Charrol?"

Angie said, "The dean at the school told me that she's got a reputation for being very timid."

"But look at what she just did," Potter said. "Getting Kielle out."

"A fluke, I'd guess. Probably impulse." She gazed out the window. "He's an odd one, Handy is."

"Unique in my experience," Potter said. "Say, Henry, read to us from your opus. Tell us what we know about him so far."

LeBow sat up slightly and read in a stiff voice. "Louis Jeremiah Handy is thirty-five years old. Mother raised him after his alcoholic father went to jail when the baby was six months. The mother drank too. Child protective services considered placing him and his brothers in foster homes several times but nothing ever came of it. No evidence he was abused or beaten, though when his father returned from prison— Lou was eight—the man was arrested several times for beating up his neighbors. The father finally took off when Handy was thirteen and was killed a year later in a barroom fight. His mother died a year after that."

Officer Frances Whiting shook her head with undirected sympathy.

"Handy killed his first victim at age fifteen. He used a knife though he apparently had a gun on him and could have used the more merciful weapon. It took the victim, a boy his age, a long time to die. Six years in juvenile for that then out long enough to earn a string of GTA arrests, carjackings, assault, D&D. Suspected in ATM stickups and bank robberies. Was almost convicted twice for major jobs but the witnesses were killed before trial. No link to him could be proved.

"His two brothers were in and out of trouble with the law over the years. The eldest was killed five years ago, as I mentioned before. It was thought Handy might have done it. No known whereabouts for the younger brother.

"As Handy's career's progressed," LeBow said to his audience, "he's gotten more violent." It was the severity and randomness of his crimes that seemed to escalate, the intelligence officer explained. Recently he'd taken to killing for no apparent reason and—in the robbery in which he'd most recently been convicted—started committing arson.

Potter interrupted to say, "Tell us specifically what happened at the Wichita robbery. The Farmers & Merchants S&L."

Henry LeBow scrolled through the screen, then continued, "Handy, Wilcox, a two-time felon named Fred Laskey, and Priscilla Gunder— Handy's girlfriend—robbed the Farmers & Merchants S&L in Wichita. Handy ordered a teller to take him into the vault but she moved too slow for him. Handy lost his temper, beat her, and locked her and another woman teller inside the vault, then went outside and got a can of gas. Doused the inside of the bank and lit it. The fire was the reason he was caught. If they'd just run with the twenty thousand they'd have made it but it took him another five minutes or so to torch the place. That gave the cops and Pete Henderson's men time to roll up, silent."

He summarized the rest of the drama: There was a shootout in front of the bank. The girlfriend got away and Handy, Wilcox, and Laskey stole another car but got stopped by a roadblock a mile away. They'd climbed out and walked toward the cops. Handy fired a hidden gun through Laskey's back, killing him and wounding two of the arresting officers before being wounded himself.

"Pointless." Budd shook his head. "That fire. Burning up those women."

"Oh, no, the fire was one way to regain control of the situation," Angie said.

Potter quoted, " 'They didn't do what I wanted. When I wanted it.' "

"Maybe people like Handy'll become your specialty, Arthur," Tobe said.

Two years until retirement; as if I need a specialty, thought Potter. And one that includes the Lou Handys of the world.

Budd sighed.

"You all right, Captain?" Potter asked.

"I don't know if I'm exactly made for this kind of work."

"Ah, you're doing fine."

But of course the young trooper was right. He wasn't made for this line of work; nobody was.

"Listen, Charlie, the troopers're probably getting antsy by now. I want you to make the rounds, you and Dean. Calm 'em down. See about coffee. And for God's sake make sure their heads're down. Keep yours that way too."

"I'll come with you, Charlie," Angie said. "If it's okay with Arthur."

"Catch up with him, Angie. I want to talk to you for a moment."

"I'll meet you outside," she called, and pulled her chair closer to Potter.

"Angie, I need an ally," Potter said. "Someone inside."

She glanced at him. "Melanie?"

"Was that really just a fluke, what she did? Or can I count on some help?"

Angie thought for a minute. "When Melanie was a high-school student there, Laurent Clerc was an oralist school. Signing was forbidden."

"It was?"

"It was a mainstream school. But Melanie realized that was stifling her—which is what all educators are now coming to realize. What she did was to develop her own sign language, one that was very subtle—basically just using the fingers—so the teachers didn't notice it the way you'd see people signing in ASL. Her language spread through the school like wildfire."

"She created a language?"

"Yep. She found that the ten fingers alone weren't enough for a working vocabulary and syntax. So the variable element she introduced was brilliant. It had never been done in sign language before. She used rhythm. She overlaid a temporal structure on the finger shapes. Her inspiration was apparently orchestral conductors."

Arthur Potter, who, after all, made his living with language, was fascinated.

Angie continued, "Right around that time there were protests to shift to a curriculum where ASL was taught and one of the reasons cited by the deaf teachers in favor of doing so was that so many students were using Melanie's language. But Melanie wouldn't have anything to do with the protests. She denied that she'd invented the language—as if she was afraid the administration would punish her for it. All she wanted to do was study and go home. Very talented, very smart. Very scared. She had a chance to go to Gallaudet College in Washington this summer on a fellowship. She turned it down."

"Why?"

"Nobody knew. Her brother's accident maybe."

Potter recalled that the young man was having surgery tomorrow. He wondered if Henderson had gotten in touch with the family. "Maybe," he mused, "there's just a certain timidity that goes along with being deaf."

"Excuse me, Agent Potter." Frances Whiting leaned forward. "Is that like a certain amount of fascism goes along with being a federal agent?"

Potter blinked. "I'm sorry?"

Frances shrugged. "Stereotyping. The Deaf have had to deal with it forever. That they're kings of the beggars. That they're stupid. Deaf and *dumb*. That they're timid. . . . Helen Keller said that blindness cuts you off from *things*, deafness cuts you off from *people*. So the Deaf compensate. There's no other defining physical condition that's given rise to a culture and community the way deafness has. There's a huge diversity among—pick a group: gays, paraplegics, athletes, tall people, short people, the elderly, alcoholics. But the Deaf community is militantly cohesive. And it's anything but timid."

Potter nodded. "I stand chastised." The officer smiled in response.

He looked out over the scruffy field beside them. He said to Angie, "My feeling is that I can get only so far with Handy through negotiations. It could save three or four lives if somebody inside was helping us."

"I'm not sure she's the one who can do it," Angie said.

"Noted," he said. "You better go find Charlie now. He's probably wondering what's become of you."

Angie left the van, Frances too, on her way to the hotel to check on the hostages' families. Potter sat back in the desk chair, picturing the photo of Melanie's face, her wavy blond hair.

How beautiful she is, he mused to himself.

Then he sat up, laughing to himself.

A beautiful face? What was he thinking of?

A negotiator must never Stockholm with hostages. That's the first rule of barricades. He has to be ready to sacrifice them if need be. Still, he couldn't stop thinking about her. This was ironic, for nowadays he rarely thought of women in terms of physical appearance. Since Marian died he'd had only one romantic involvement. A pleasant woman in her late thirties. It was a liaison doomed from the start. Potter now believed you could return successfully to romantic love at age sixty and above. But in your forties and fifties, he suspected, the process was doomed. It's the inflexibility. And the pride. Oh, and always the doubts.

Gazing at the slaughterhouse, he thought: In the past fifteen years, since Marian, the most meaningful conversations I've had have been not with my surrogate cousin Linden or her clansmen or the women who've hung chastely on my arm at functions in the District. No, they've been with men holding oiled guns at the heads of hostages. Women with short black hair and Middle Eastern faces, though very Western code names. Criminals and psychopaths and potential suicides. I've spilled my guts to them and they to me. Oh, they'd lie about tactics and motives (as I did) but everyone told the exquisite truth about themselves: their hopes, their dreams dead and dreams living still, their families, their children, their scorching failures.

They told their stories for the same reasons Arthur Potter told his. To wear the other side down, to establish bonds, to "transfer the emotive response" (as his own highly circulated hostage negotiation guidebook, eighth printing, explained).

And simply because someone seemed to want to listen.

Melanie . . . will we ever have a conversation, the two of us?

He saw Dean Stillwell wave to him and stepped into the fragrant gully to meet the sheriff. He glanced at the shreds of fog wafting around the van. So Handy's weather report wasn't up to date after all. It gave him a fragment of hope—unreasonable perhaps, but hope nonetheless. He looked up at the late-afternoon sky, in which strips of yellow and bruise-colored clouds sped past. In a break between two of the vaporous shapes he saw the moon, a pale crescent sitting over the slaughterhouse, directly above the blood-red brick.

6:03 P.M.

They appeared suddenly, the dozen men.

The slippery wind covered the noise of their approach and by the time the agent was aware of them they'd surrounded him and Dean Stillwell, who was telling Potter about the dock behind the slaughterhouse. Stillwell had looked over the river and the dock and concluded that, even though the current was fast, as Budd had reported, it was too tempting an escape route. He'd put some armored troops in a skiff and anchored them twenty yards offshore.

Potter noticed Dean Stillwell look up and stare at something behind the agent. He turned.

The team was dressed in black and navy-blue combat gear. Potter recognized the outfits—the American Body Armor plated vests, the rubberized ducking uniforms and hoods, the H&K submachine guns with laser sights and flashlights. It was a Hostage Rescue Team, though not his, and Arthur Potter didn't want these men within a hundred miles of the Webber & Stoltz Processing Company.

"Agent Potter?"

A nod. Be gracious. Don't jerk leashes until leashes need to be jerked. He shook the hand of the crew-cut man in his forties.

"I'm Dan Tremain. Commander of the state police Hostage Rescue Unit." His still eyes were confident. And challenging. "I understand you're expecting a Delta team."

"The Bureau's HRT actually. Jurisdiction, you know."

"Course."

Potter introduced him to Stillwell, whom Tremain ignored.

"What's the status?" Tremain asked.

"They're contained. One fatality."

"I heard," Tremain said, rubbing a gold pinky ring on which was a deep etching of a cross.

"We've gotten three girls out unhurt," Potter continued. "There are four other girls inside and two teachers. The HTs've asked for a chopper, which we aren't going to give them. They've threatened to execute another hostage at seven unless we have it here by then."

"You're not going to give him one?"

"No."

"But what'll happen?"

"I'm going to try to talk him through it."

"Well, why don't we deploy just the same? I mean, if it comes down to him killing her, I know you'll want to move in."

"No," Potter said, looking over at the press table, where Joe Silbert and his assistant were diligently typing away on a computer. The reporter looked up glumly. Potter nodded and glanced back at Tremain.

The state police commander said, "You're not saying that you'd let him kill the girl, are you?"

"Let's hope it doesn't come to that."

Acceptable casualties . . .

Tremain held his eye for a moment. "I'm thinking we really ought to move into position. Just in case."

Potter glanced at the men and gestured Tremain aside. They walked into the shadow of the command van. "If it comes down to an assault, and I certainly hope it doesn't, then my team'll be the one doing it— and only my team. Sorry, Captain, that's just the way it is."

Was this going to explode? Shoot straight to the governor and the Admiral in Washington?

Tremain bristled but he shrugged. "You're in charge, sir. But those men are state felons too and our regulations require us to be on the scene. And *that's* just the way it is too."

"I have no objection at all to your presence, Captain. And if they come out, guns ablazing, I'd sure welcome your firepower. But as long as it's understood that you're taking orders from me."

Tremain relented. "Fair enough. Fact is, I told my men that we'll probably be spending three hours drinking coffee and then pack up and go home."

"Let's hope so for all our sakes. If you want to go into position as part of the containment crew, Sheriff Stillwell here's in charge of that."

The two men nodded at each other coolly and every soul within earshot knew there was no way an HRT commander would put his men under the orders of a small-town sheriff. Potter hoped this would guarantee that Tremain would hightail it out of here.

"I think we'll just hang back. Stay out of sight. If you need us we'll be around."

"Whatever you want, Captain," Potter said.

Budd and Angie appeared, striding up the hill, and stopped suddenly. "Hey, Dan," Budd said, recognizing Tremain.

"Charlie." They shook hands. Tremain's eyes took in Angie's hair and face but it was a chaste examination, one of curiosity, and when his eyes dipped downward to her chest it was simply to confirm from her necklace ID that she was in fact an FBI agent.

"You boys heard about our little situation, did you?" Budd said.

Tremain laughed. "How 'bout, anybody watches TV knows about it. Who's working the CP?"

"Derek Elb."

"Derek the Red?" Tremain laughed. "I gotta say hi to him." Now jovial, Tremain said to Potter, "That boy wanted to join HRU but we took one look at that hair on him and thought he'd be just a little too prominent in a sniper's scope."

Potter smiled agreeably, pleased that there'd been no confrontation. Usually state and federal negotiators get along well enough but there's invariably tension between negotiators and tactical units from other branches. As Potter explained in class, "There're talkers and there're shooters. That's night and day and it won't ever change."

Tremain stepped into the van. Potter eyed the dozen men. Somber, artful, and oh-so-pleased to be here. He thought of Robert Duvall in *Apocalypse Now* and supposed these men too loved the smell of napalm in the morning. Potter finished his conversation with Stillwell. When he turned back he was surprised to find that the HRU, to a man, was gone. When he climbed into the van he saw that Tremain too had left.

LeBow entered the information about Stillwell's skiff into his electronic memory.

"Time, Tobe?" Potter was staring at the "Promises/Deceptions" board. The young man glanced at the digital clock.

"Forty-five minutes," Tobe muttered, then said to LeBow, "You tell him."

"Tell me what?"

The intelligence officer said, "We've been playing with the infrared monitor. We caught a glimpse of Handy a minute ago."

"What was he doing?"

"Loading the shotguns."

The Kansas State Police Hostage Rescue Unit, led by Captain Daniel Tremain, slipped silently into a stand of trees a hundred yards from the slaughterhouse.

The trees, Tremain noted at once, were not unoccupied. There were a state police sniper and two or three local deputies in position. Using hand signals Tremain directed his men through the trees and down into a gully that would take them around the side of the slaughterhouse. They passed undetected through the small forest. Tremain looked about and saw—fifty yards toward the river—an abandoned windmill, forty feet high, sitting in the middle of a grassy field. Beside it were two state troopers, standing with their backs to the HRU as they gazed warily at the slaughterhouse. Tremain ordered the two men into a line of trees out of sight of both the north side of the slaughterhouse and the command post.

From the windmill, the HRU team walked into a gully and made their way closer to the slaughterhouse. Tremain held up his hand and they stopped. He tapped his helmet twice and the men responded to the signal by switching on their radios. Lieutenant Carfallo opened the terrain map and the architectural drawings. From his pocket Tremain took the diagram of the inside of the slaughterhouse that Derek the Red, Derek the trooper, Derek the spy, had just slipped him inside the van. It was marked with the location of the hostages and the HTs.

Tremain was encouraged. The girls weren't being held in shield positions by the windows or in front of the HTs. There were no booby traps. Derek reported that the men inside were armed with pistols and shotguns only, no automatic weapons, and they had no flak jackets, helmets, or flashlights. Of course the hostages weren't as far away from the takers as he would have liked, and the room in which they were being kept had no door. But still Handy and the others were twenty or so feet from the girls. It would take a full five seconds for Handy to get to the hostages, and that was assuming he'd already decided that he would kill them the instant he heard the cutting charges. As a rule, in an assault, there were four to ten seconds of confusion and indecision while the takers tried to scope out what was happening before they could take up effective defensive positions.

"Listen up." Hands tapped ears and heads nodded. Tremain pointed at the chart. "There are six hostages inside. Three HTs—located here, here, and here, though they're pretty mobile. One checks on the girls with some frequency." Tremain nodded to one trooper. "Wilson."

"Sir."

"You're to proceed through this gully along the side of the building here and surveil from one of these two windows."

"Sir, can you get them to shift that light?" Trooper Joey Wilson nodded toward the halogens.

"Negative. This is a clandestine operation and you're not to expose yourself to the friendlies."

"Yessir," the young man barked. No questions asked.

"The middle window is hidden by that tree and the school bus. I'd suggest that one."

"Yessir."

"Pfenninger."

"Sir."

"You're to return to the command van and your orders are consistent with what you and I discussed earlier. Is that understood?"

"Yessir."

"The rest of us are moving to this point here. Using those bushes and trees for cover. Harding, you take point. All officers move out now."

And they dispersed into the dusky afternoon, as fluid as the dark river flowing past, more silent than the wind that bent the grass around them.

"Let's have a smoke," Potter said.

"Not me," Budd answered.

"An imaginary one."

"How's that?"

"Let's step outside, Captain."

They wandered away from the van twenty feet into a stand of trees, the agent adjusting his posture automatically to stand more upright; being in the presence of Charlie Budd made you want to do this. Potter paused and spoke with Joe Silbert and the other reporter.

"We've got two more out."

"Two more? Who?" Silbert seemed to be restraining himself.

"No identities," Potter said. "All I'll say is that they're students. Young girls. They've been released unharmed. That leaves a total of four students and two teachers left inside."

"What did you trade for them?"

"We can't release that information."

He'd expected the reporter would be grateful for the scoop but Silbert grumbled, "You're not making this very fucking easy."

Potter glanced at the computer screen. The story was a human-interest piece about an unnamed trooper, waiting for action—the boredom and the edginess of a barricade. Potter thought it was good and told the reporter so.

Silbert snorted. "Oh, it'd sing like poetry if I had some hard news to put in. When can we interview you?"

"Soon."

The agent and the trooper wandered down into a grove of trees out of the line of fire. Potter called in and told Tobe where he was, asked for any calls from Handy to be patched through immediately.

"Say, Charlie, where'd that attorney general get himself to?"

Budd looked around. "I think he went back to the hotel."

Potter shook his head. "Marks wants Handy to get his helicopter. The governor told me he wants Handy dead. The Bureau director'll probably be on the horn in the next half-hour—and there've been times when I've gotten a call from the president himself. Oh, and mark my words, Charlie, somebody's writing the script right at this moment and making *me* out to be the villain."

"You?" Budd asked, with inexplicable glumness. "You'll be the hero."

"Oh, not by a long shot. No, sir. Guns sell advertising, words don't."

"What's this about imaginary cigarettes?"

"When my wife got cancer I quit."

"Lung cancer? My uncle had that."

"No. Pancreas."

Unfortunately the party with whom Potter had been negotiating for his wife's recovery had reneged on the deal. Even so, Potter never took up smoking again.

"So you, what, imagine yourself smoking?"

Potter nodded. "And when I can't sleep I imagine myself taking a sleeping pill."

"When you're, you know, depressed you imagine yourself happy?"

That, Arthur Potter had found, didn't work.

Budd, who'd perhaps asked the question because of the funk he'd been in for the last hour, forgot his dolor momentarily and asked, "What brand aren't you smoking?"

"Camels. Without the filter."

"Hey, why not?" His face slipped and he seemed sad again. "I never smoked. Maybe I'll have me an imaginary Jack Daniel's."

"Have a double while you're at it." Arthur Potter drew hard on his fake cigarette. They stood among flowering catalpa and Osage orange and Potter was looking down at what appeared to be the deep tracks of wagon wheels. He asked Budd about them.

"Those? The real thing. The Santa Fe Trail itself."

"Those're the *original* tracks?" Potter was astonished.

"They call 'em swales. Headed west right through here."

Potter, genealogist that he was, kicked at the deep, rocklike tread mark cut into the dirt, and wondered if Marian's great-great-grandfather Ebb Schneider, who had traveled with his widowed mother from Ohio to Nevada in 1868, had been an infant asleep in the wagon that had made this very track.

Budd nodded toward the slaughterhouse. "The reason that was built was because of the Chisholm Trail. It went south to north right through here too, from San Antonio to Abilene—that's *our* Abilene, in Kansas. They'd drive the longhorns along here, sell off and slaughter some for the Wichita market."

"Got another question," Potter said after a moment.

"I'm not much of a state historian. That's 'bout all I know."

"Mostly, Charlie, I'm wondering why you're looking so damn uneasy."

Budd lost interest in the swales at his feet. "Well, I guess I wonder what exactly you wanted to talk to me about."

"In about forty minutes I've got to go talk Handy out of killing another of the girls. I don't have a lot of ideas. I'd like to get your opinion. What do you think of him?"

"Me?"

"Sure."

"Oh, I don't know."

"We never *know* in this business. Give me an educated guess. You've heard his profile. You've talked to Angie. . . . She's quite a lady, isn't she?"

"Say, 'bout that, Arthur . . . the thing is, I'm a married man. She's been chatting me up an awful lot. I mentioned Meg must've been a dozen times and she doesn't seem to pay any attention to it."

"Consider it flattery, Charlie. You're in control of the situation."

"Sorta in control." He looked back at the van but didn't see the dark-haired agent anywhere.

Potter laughed. "So now, give me some thoughts."

Budd fidgeted with his fingers, maybe thinking he should actually be pretending to hold his glass of whisky. Potter smoked as he had come to do so much else in recent years—not actually doing it, not pantomiming, only imagining. It was for him a type of meditation.

"I guess what I'm thinking," Budd said slowly, "is that Handy's got a plan of some kind."

"Why?"

"Partly it's what Angie was saying. Everything he does has a purpose. He's not a crazed kick killer."

"What sort of plan were you thinking of?"

"Don't know exactly. Something he thinks is gonna outsmart us."

Budd's hands slipped into his rear pockets again. The man's nervous as a fifteen-year-old at his first school dance, Potter reflected.

"Why do you say that?"

"I'm not sure exactly. Just an impression. Maybe because he's got this holier-than-thou attitude. He doesn't respect us. Every time he talks to us what I hear is, you know, contempt. Like he knows it all and we don't know anything."

This was true. Potter had noticed it himself. Not a shred of desperation, no supplication, no nervous banter, no tin defiance; all the things you usually heard from hostage takers were noticeably absent here.

Along with the flattest VSA line Potter had ever seen.

"A breakout," Budd continued. "That's what I'd guess. Maybe setting fire to the place." The captain laughed. "Maybe he's got fireman outfits in there—in those bags he brought in with him. And he'll sneak out in all the confusion."

Potter nodded. "That's happened before."

"Has it?" Budd asked, incredulous that he'd thought of this strategy and, accordingly, very pleased with himself.

"Medical-worker outfits one time. And police uniforms another. But I'd given all the containment officers handouts, like what I distributed earlier, so the HTs were spotted right away. Here, though, I don't know. It doesn't seem to be his style. But you're right on about his attitude. That's the key. It's saying something to us. I just wish I knew what."

Again Budd was fiddling nervously with his pockets.

"Those tools," Potter mused, "might have something to do with it. Maybe they'll set a fire, hide in a piece of machinery or even under the floor. Then climb out when the rescue workers are there. We should make sure that everybody, not just the troopers, has a copy of the profile flyers."

"I'll take care of it." Budd laughed nervously again. "I'll delegate it."

Potter had calmed considerably. He thought of Marian. The infrequent evenings he was home they used to sit together by the radio listening to NPR and share one cigarette and a glass of sherry. Occasionally, once a week, perhaps twice, the cigarette would be stubbed out and they would climb the stairs to their ornate bed and forgo the musical programming for that evening.

"This negotiation stuff," Budd said. "It's pretty confusing to me."

"How so?"

"Well, you don't seem to talk to him about what I'd talk to him about—you know, the stuff he wants and the hostages and everything. Business. Mostly, it seems that you just chat."

"You ever been in therapy, Charlie?"

The young officer seemed to snicker. He shook his head. Maybe analysis was something Kansans didn't go in for.

Potter said, "I was. After my wife died."

"I was going to say, I'm sorry to hear that happened."

"You know what I talked to the therapist about? Genealogy."

"What?"

"It's my hobby. Family trees, you know."

"You were paying good money to a doctor to talk about hobbies?"

"And it was the best money I ever spent. I started to feel what the therapist was feeling and vice versa. We moved closer to each other. What I'm doing here—with Handy—is the same. You don't click a switch and make Handy give up the girls. Just like the doctor doesn't click a switch and make everything better. The point is to create a relationship between him and me. He's got to know me, and I've got to know him."

"Hey, like you're dating?"

"You could say that," Potter said without smiling. "I want to get him into my mind—so he'll realize it's a hopeless situation. So he'll give me the girls and surrender, to make him feel that it's pointless to go on. Not to understand it intellectually, but to *feel* it. You can see it's working a bit. He's given us two and hasn't killed anyone else, even when that other girl snuck out." Potter drew a final breath of his imaginary Camel. Stubbed it out.

He started to imagine climbing stairs, Marian's hand in his. But this image faded quickly.

"And I do it to get into his mind. To understand him."

"So you become his friend?"

"Friend? Not a friend. I'd say that we become linked."

"But, I mean, isn't that a problem? If you have to order HRT to green-light him, you'd be ordering the death of somebody you're close to. Betraying them."

"Oh, yes," the negotiator said softly. "Yes, it's a problem."

Budd blew air out of his cheeks and again studied the harvesting. "You said . . ."

"What?"

"You said before that you're willing to sacrifice those girls to get him. Is that really true?"

Potter looked at him for a moment while Budd's distraught eyes gazed at the steadfast threshers miles away. "Yes, it is. My job is to stop Handy. Those're my orders. And yes, there may have to be sacrifices."

"But they're little girls."

Potter smiled grimly. "How can you make a value judgment? These aren't the days of women and children first. A life is a life. Are those girls more deserving than the family Handy might kidnap and kill next year if he escapes today? Or the two traffic cops he shoots when they stop him for speeding? I have to keep thinking that those hostages are dead already. If I can save some, so much the better. But I can't look at it any other way and still function."

"You're good at what you do, seems."

Potter didn't answer.

"You think there'll be more deaths?"

"Oh, yes, I'm afraid so. Just an educated guess but I do think so."

"The girls?"

Potter didn't answer.

"Our immediate problem, Charlie—what can we use to buy another hour with?"

Budd shrugged. "No guns or ammo, right?"

"That's not negotiable."

"Well, he thinks he's getting his imaginary helicopter, right?"

"Yes."

"As long as we're lying to him 'bout that, why don't we lie to him 'bout something else? Promise him something to go along with it."

"Can't give a kid a toy without giving him batteries, is that what you're saying?"

"I guess I am."

"That's brilliant, Charlie. Let's go kick it around with Henry."

As they climbed into the van Potter clapped the trooper on the shoulder and Budd responded with as hangtail a smile as the agent had ever in his life encountered.

They would divide into three teams, Alpha, Bravo, Charlie.

The HRU officers, under Dan Tremain, were gathered in a cluster on the left side, the northwest side, of the slaughterhouse, hidden in a grove of trees. The men were now wearing black assault coveralls over their body armor. Nomex hoods and gloves. Their goggles rested on the crest of their foreheads.

Alpha and Bravo teams had four men each, two armed with Heckler & Koch MP-5 submachine guns, fitted with B.E.A.M. mounts and halogen flashlights, two armed with H&K Super 90 semiautomatic shotguns. The two HRU troopers in Charlie team had MP-5s as well but were also carrying Accuracy Systems M429 Thunderflash stun grenades and M451 Multistarflash grenades.

Two other troopers had been deployed. Chuck Pfenninger—Outrider One—was in standard uniform beside the command van. Joey Wilson—Outrider Two—in ops armor and camouflage was beneath the middle window to the left of the main door of the slaughterhouse. He was hidden from view of the command post and the troopers in the field by the Laurent Clerc School bus and a ginkgo tree.

Tremain went over the plan one more time in his mind. As soon as Wilson reported that the HTs were as far away from the hostages as they could hope for, Pfenninger would blow the generator in the command van, using an L210 charge, known informally as a mini-Molotov. It was a small gasoline bomb sealed in a special fiberboard container, like single-serving boxes of grape juice or fruit punch. The container would disintegrate under the heat from the blast and would be virtually undetectable by crime-scene technicians. Properly placed, it would cut off all communications and seal the troopers inside the van. The vehicle had been designed to be driven through flames, was well insulated, and had an internal oxygen system. As long as the door remained closed, no one inside would be injured.

Tremain would officially take charge and "declare" that the situation had gone hot.

As soon as this happened HRU's three teams would move into the slaughterhouse. Charlie team would use Model 521 cutting charges to blast a hole in the roof and drop two stun grenades onto the takers. Alpha and Bravo would blow the side and loading-dock doors simultaneously and enter the building while Charlie dropped the second—the flash—grenades, which would explode in a huge burst of blinding light, and then rappel through the opening in the roof. Bravo team would head straight to the hostages, and Alpha and Charlie would advance on the HTs, neutralizing them if there was any resistance.

They were now waiting for three troopers who'd gone to check out the side door, the loading dock, and the roof.

Dan Tremain lay prone beside the steely Lieutenant Carfallo and gazed at the slaughterhouse, which rose above them like a medieval castle, toothy and dark. The captain said to his troops, "You'll be using four-man entry. The first two men will be the key shooters. Machine guns first, followed by shotgun backup. This will be a dynamic shooting entry. You will proceed until all hostile targets have been successfully engaged and neutralized and the premises have been secured. There are six hostages inside, located where I indicated on the map. They're all female, and four are young girls, who may panic and run. You will exercise absolute muzzle control of your weapons at all times you are inside. Do you copy?"

Affirmative answers.

Then came the bad news.

One by one the surveillance troopers called in. The reconnaissance revealed that the side door was far thicker than the diagram indicated: three-inch oak with a sheet steel face. They would have to use four cutting charges. For safety, Alpha team would have to be farther away when it blew than originally planned. That would add as much as six seconds to the time it would take to get to the girls.

It turned out too that there'd been some construction on the roof not reflected in the original architectural drawings—a series of steel plates, covering virtually the entire roof, had been bolted into place years ago. The men on the roof would have to use a large amount of C4 to cut through them. In an old building like this, that much plastic explosive could bring down girders—possibly even major portions of the roof.

Tremain then learned from the third scout that the loading-dock door was jammed open only about eight inches. It was a huge steel sheet, too large to blow.

The captain conferred with Carfallo and they revised their plans. They decided they'd have to forgo the roof and loading-dock assaults and go with a two-team, single-door entry through the north door. Wilson, standing by the front window, would toss in a stun grenade, followed by the flash. This was risky because it would expose him to both the police line and the HTs; he might get shot by either. But Tremain concluded there was no choice.

He needed another hour, he decided, for an effective attack—time to find another unbarred door or window and time to weaken the hinges on the fire door so they could use smaller charges.

But he didn't have an hour. He had twenty minutes until the next deadline.

Until the next girl would die.

Well, then, a single-entrance assault it would be. Tremain said, "Code word 'filly' means green light. Code word 'stallion' means stand down. Acknowledge."

The men responded. Tremain led them into the gully beside the slaughterhouse. There they plastered themselves against the damp earth and fell into absolute stillness and silence, for so they had been instructed, and these were men who lived by their orders before anything else.

6:40 P.M.

Joe Silbert had taught himself to type with two fingers on an Underwood upright that smelled of oil and ink and the bittersweet scent of eraser shavings clogging the carriage.

Technology hadn't changed things for him much and he now pounded away with only his index digits thudding loudly on the large portable Compaq. The orange light of the screen illuminated both him and Ted Biggins, made them look jaundiced and depleted. Silbert supposed that, being almost double Biggins's age, he looked twice as bad.

Philip Molto stood his diligent guard, as instructed by nervous Captain Budd.

"What do you think?" Silbert asked Biggins.

Biggins looked over his colleague's shoulder at the dense single-spaced type on the screen and grunted. "Mind if I take over?" He nodded at the screen.

"Be my guest."

Biggins could touch-type like a demon and his fingers moved quietly and invisibly over the keys. "Hey, I'm a fucking natural at this," he said, his hair perfectly coiffed although he was only an engineer and Silbert was in fact the on-camera reporter.

"Hey, Officer," Silbert called to Molto, "our shift's almost up. We're just going to leave the computer here for the next team. They'll pick up the story where we left it off."

"You guys do that?"

"It's a cooperative thing, you know. You'll keep an eye on the computer?"

"Sure thing, yessir. What's the matter?"

Silbert was frowning, looking out into the stand of trees and juniper bushes behind the police line. "You hear something?"

Biggins was standing up, looking around uneasily. "Yeah."

Molto cocked his head. There were footsteps. A snap of branch, a shuffle.

"There's nobody behind there," the lieutenant said, half to himself. "I mean, nobody's *supposed* to be."

Silbert's face had the cautious look of a man who'd covered combat zones before. Then he broke into a wry grin. "That son of a bitch. Lieutenant, I think we've got a trespasser here."

The trooper, hand on his pistol, stepped into the bushes. When he returned he was escorting two men in black jogging suits. Press credentials bounced on their chests.

"Well, look who it is," Silbert said. "Walter Cronkite and Chet Huntley."

Biggins said to Molto, "If you're going to arrest them, forget trespassing. Charge 'em with being first-degree assholes."

"You boys know each other?"

One of the captives grimaced. "Silbert, you're a son of a bitch. You blow the whistle on us? And don't even let that little shit with you say a word to me."

Silbert said to Molto, "They're with KLTV. Sam Kellog and Tony Bianco. They seem to've forgotten that we're press-pooling."

"Fuck you," Bianco snapped.

Silbert spat out, "I gave up an exclusive just like you did, Kellog. You would've had your turn."

"I'm supposed to arrest you," Molto said to Kellog and Bianco.

"Bullshit, you can't do that."

"I'll think about it on the way back to the press tent. Come on."

"Look, Officer," Kellog said, "as long as we're here . . ."

"How'd you get here anyway, Kellog?" Biggins said. "Crawl on your belly?"

"Fuck you too."

Molto led them away. As soon as the squad car vanished Silbert barked to Biggins, "Now. Do it."

Biggins unhooked the casing of the computer monitor and pulled it open. From it he took a Nippona LL3R video camera—the subminiature model, which cost one hundred and thirty thousand dollars, weighed fourteen ounces, and was equipped with a folding twelve-inch parabolic antenna and transmitter. It produced a broadcast-quality picture in virtual darkness and had a telescopic lens as smooth as a sniper's riflescope. It had an effective range of three miles, which would be more than enough to reach the KFAL mobile transmitting center, where Silbert's colleagues (Tony Bianco and Sam Kellog, as it turned out, not too coincidentally) would soon—if they weren't actually under arrest—be waiting for the transmission. In case they were in fact sacrifices to the First Amendment other technicians were ready to wade into the breach.

Silbert opened his attaché case and took out two black nylon running suits—identical to those that Kellog and Bianco had been wearing, except for one difference: on the back were stenciled the words *U.S. Marshal.* They pulled these on.

"Wait," Silbert said. He bent down to the screen and erased the entire file that Biggins had written—which consisted of the sentence *The quick brown fox jumped over the lazy dog,* written about three hundred times. Shift-F3. He switched screens to the generic cop-on-a-stakeout story, which Silbert had filed about three years ago and had called up tonight as soon as they got the computer booted up. The story that prick Arthur Potter had admired.

The two men slipped into the gully behind the command van and hurried through the night in the direction that Dan Tremain and his silent Hostage Rescue Unit had gone.

The gas can.

This was the first thing in her thoughts as she opened her eyes and looked around the killing room.

Emily, on her knees, playing good Christian nurse, brushed the blood away from Melanie's eye. It was swollen, though not closed. The girl ripped the hem of her precious Laura Ashley dress and wiped more of the blood away.

Melanie lay still, as the terrible pain in her head lessened and her vision improved. One of the twins, Suzie (she *thought* it was Suzie), brushed her hair with her tiny, perfect fingers.

The gas can. There it was.

Finally Melanie sat up and crawled over to Beverly.

"How are you?" she asked the girl.

Sweat had plastered Beverly's blond Dutch-boy hair to her face. She nodded, though her chest continued to rise and fall alarmingly. She used the inhaler again. Melanie had never seen her this sick. The device seemed to be having no effect.

Mrs. Harstrawn still lay on the floor, on her back. She'd been crying again but was now calm. Melanie gently worked the woman's colorful sweater over her shoulders. She muttered some words. Melanie thought she said, "Don't. I'm cold."

"I have to," Melanie signed. Her fingers danced in front of the woman's face but she didn't see the message.

A minute later Mrs. Harstrawn's sweater was off. Melanie looked around and pitched it casually against the wall of the killing room, near the place where the arched opening met the floor toward the rear of the slaughterhouse. Then she scooted forward until she could look into the main room. Bear glanced toward them occasionally but the men were concentrating on the television. Melanie looked at the twins and in faint gestures signed to them, "Go over to gas can."

They looked uneasily at each other, their heads moving identically.

"Do it. Now!" Her signs were urgent—sharp, compact stabs of her fingers.

They rose and crawled slowly toward the red-and-yellow can.

When Suzie looked at her she told the girl to pick up the sweater. Mrs. Harstrawn's mother in Topeka had knitted it. The colors were red and white and blue, very visible—bad news for now; good news once the girls got outside. But Suzie wasn't moving. Melanie repeated the command. There was no time for caution, she explained. "Move! Now!"

Why is she hesitating? She's just staring at me.

No, not at *me*. . . .

Then the shadow fell over her.

She gasped as Brutus took her by the shoulders and spun her around.

"You think . . . a fucking hero, do you? Why, I've shot people for a lot less'n what you did."

She thought for a terrible moment that Brutus could actually read her mind, had an animal's sixth sense, and knew what she was planning with the gas can. But then she understood he was talking about her pitching Kielle out the door. Maybe being pistol-whipped wasn't enough punishment. He pulled his gun and rested it against her head.

Filled with a burst of rage that shocked her, she pushed the gun aside, stood, and walked into the main room of the plant, feeling the vibrations of his shouts on her back. She ignored him and continued to the oil drum that served as a table. Bear rose and stepped toward her but she ignored him too. She picked up the pen and paper and returned to the killing room.

She wrote: *You work real hard to prove you're a bad guy, don't you?* Thrust it in his face.

Brutus laughed. He ripped the pad from her hands, tossed it on the floor. He studied her for a long, long moment, then, eerily calm, he said, ". . . you and me chew the fat. I don't talk much . . . not many people I can talk to. But you I can. Why's that? . . . you can't talk back, I guess. It's good when a woman don't talk back. Pris, she's got a mind of her own. . . . I approve of that. But sometimes she's off someplace else, you know? . . . I just don't get what she's saying. You, I look into your face and I can understand you. You seem like a little mouse, but maybe there's more to you. There is, ain't there?"

Melanie was horrified to find, somewhere in her heart, a splinter of pleasure. This terrible, terrible man was approving of her. He killed Susan, he killed Susan, he killed Susan, she told herself. He'd kill me in an instant if he wanted to. These things she knew but all she sensed at this moment was his approval.

He put the gun away and fiddled with his shoelaces. "You think I'm bad for . . . to your friend. Well, by your thinkin' I am bad. I ain't . . . smart and I don't have no particular talents. But the one thing I am is bad. I'm not saying I don't have a heart or that I haven't cried in my day. I cried for a week when somebody shot my brother. Yes, I did." Brutus paused, his pointy teeth rising from his thin lips, "Now, that sonofabitch out there . . ." He nodded toward the phone.

De l'Epée? Does he mean de l'Epée?

"Him and me, we're in a battle right now. And he's going to lose. . . . Why? Because bad is simple and good is complicated. And the simple always wins. That's what everything comes down to in the end. Simple always wins. That's just nature and you know what kind of trouble people get into ignoring nature. Look at you, all you deaf people. You'll die out before people like me. I need something, I can say, 'Give it to me.' I open my mouth and somebody does what I want. But you, you have to do funny things with your hands. You have to write it down. That's complicated. You're a freak . . . you'll die and I'll live. It's nature.

"Me, I'm taking that girl over there, that flower-dress one, and shooting her in about ten minutes if . . . helicopter don't get here. Which I don't think it will. To me, that's no worse'n scratching an itch or buying a soda pop when you're thirsty."

He looked at Emily, his mouth curling into that faint smile of his.

And in his glance, Melanie suddenly saw much more than a look of a captor toward his victim. She saw all the taunts of her classmates, the grinding frustrations of trying to understand what can be understood only by the miracle of hearing. She saw an empty life without a lover. She saw the cover of a piece of sheet music entitled "Amazing Grace" and inside, merely blank pages.

God's will . . .

Brutus's glance . . .

And so it made sense that she went for his eyes.

Melanie leapt forward, her perfect fingernails clawing at his face.

He gave a gasp of surprise and stumbled backwards, groping for his gun. He pulled it from his belt and she lunged for it. The pistol flew from his grip and slid across the floor. She was out of control, crazed, driven by a consuming anger unlike any she'd ever experienced. An anger that poured from her too quickly, ripping her open, hurting the way the fever had burned her skin when she was eight and took away the simple and made her life so terribly complicated.

Her long fingers, muscular from years of signing, tipped with pearl nails, ripped into his cheek; she slapped his nose, she dug for his eyes. As he fell onto his back she leapt upon his chest, her knee crunching into his solar plexus. He gasped as the breath was forced from his lungs. He struck her once in the chest and she recoiled from him but he had no leverage and his blow was painless.

"Jesus Christ . . . !" His wiry hands reached for her throat but she punched them aside and got a grip on his windpipe, her strong arms fending off his; he couldn't quite reach her. Where was this strength coming from? she wondered, as she banged his head into the concrete and watched his face turn blue.

Perhaps Stoat and Bear were running toward her, perhaps they were aiming their guns at her. Or maybe because Brutus had no air in his lungs he was silent, maybe he was too proud to call for help. She didn't know—or care. Nothing existed for her but this man and his evilness—not the other girls, not Mrs. Harstrawn, not the soul of Susan Phillips, who agnostic Melanie believed floated above them at this moment, a beautiful seraph.

She was going to kill him.

Then suddenly he went limp as a towel. His tongue protruded from his pale lips. And she thought, My God, I've done it! Exultant and terrified, she sat back, looking at the twins, sobbing Emily, gasping Bev.

When his knee rose fast she had no time to deflect it and it caught her between the legs, crashing into her with a raging pain. She inhaled fiercely and cradled her groin as Brutus's fist drove into her chest just below the breastbone. Melanie doubled over, breathless.

He rose easily and she saw that, aside from the scratches on his cheek, he wasn't hurt at all. He'd been playing with her. Roughhousing.

Then he had her by the hair and was dragging her into the front room.

She dug her nails into his hand and he slapped her face hard. Her vision exploded with light and her arms went limp. The next thing she knew she was in the window of the slaughterhouse, staring out at the windy field and the brilliant lights trained on the building.

Her face was against the glass and she thought it might break and slice through her eyes. No, no, not *that* kind of darkness. Permanent darkness. No, please. . . .

Stoat stepped forward but Brutus waved him off. He pulled his pistol out. He spun her around so she could see him speak. "If you could talk like a normal person, maybe you could say something to save yourself. But you can't. No, no. You're a freak of nature and if they don't come through with that chopper you're going to be even more of a freak. Shep, how much time . . . ?"

Stoat seemed to hesitate and said something she didn't understand.

"How much fucking *time?*" Brutus's bloody face was distorted with rage.

He received the answer and lifted the gun to her cheek. Then slowly his hand entwined in her hair and turned her around so that she was facing into the blinding white lights once again.

Melanie. Potter saw her face through his thick field glasses. Melanie was the next victim.

Budd, LeBow, and Frances stared out the window. Stillwell came on the radio and said, "One of my snipers reports that Handy's bleeding. Doesn't seem serious but his face is cut."

"Twelve minutes to deadline," Tobe said. "Downlink coming in."

The phone rang and Potter answered at once. "Lou, what—?"

"I've got a new one, Art," Handy's voice raged. "She's got some spirit. I was gonna forgive her after she gave you that little trouble-maker. But the slut got it into her mind she wanted to have a little fun. Go for a roll in the hay with me."

Stay calm, Potter told himself. He's playing you again. He tamped down his own rage, which mimicked Handy's.

"She's into some sick stuff, Art. One of them S&M pups, looks like. She'll learn, she'll learn. You've got 'bout ten minutes, Art. I don't hear that chopper overhead we're gonna do some nine-millimeter plastic surgery on this here girl. Now I want that fucking helicopter. You got it?"

"We have to bring one in from Topeka. There—"

"There's a goddamn airport three miles west of here. Why the fuck don't you *bring one in* from there?"

"You said you—"

"Ten minutes."

Click.

Potter closed his eyes and sighed.

"Angie?"

"I think we have a problem," the psychologist answered. "He wants to hurt her."

This was a real setback. Potter could probably have gotten an extension of the deadline from a Lou Handy who was in a good frame of mind and in control. Vindictive Lou Handy, embarrassed and angry Lou Handy, wasn't inclined to give them anything and was now in the mood for bloodshed.

Oh, Melanie, why couldn't you have just left well enough alone? (Yet what else did he feel? Pride that she had the guts to resist Hardy when he tried to beat her for saving Kielle? Admiration? And what else?)

Angie's beautiful, exotic face was frowning.

"What is it?" Budd asked her.

"What Handy was saying about plastic surgery. What does he mean?"

"He doesn't want to kill anyone else just yet, I think," Potter said slowly. "He's worried that he's losing too many hostages and we haven't given him anything substantive. So he's going to wound her. Maybe blind her in one eye."

"Lord," Budd whispered.

Tobe called, "Arthur, I'm picking up scrambled signals from nearby."

"What frequency?"

"What megahertz, you mean?"

"I don't care about the numbers. Whose would they be?"

"It's an unassigned frequency."

"Two-way?"

"Yep. And they're retrosignals."

Some operations are so secret that the law enforcers' radios use special coordinated scramblers that change the code every few seconds. Derek confirmed that the state police radios didn't have this feature.

"How nearby?"

"Within a mile radius."

"Press?"

"They don't usually use scramblers but it could be."

Potter couldn't waste time on this now. He made a fist and stared out the window through the Leicas. He saw Melanie's blond hair, the black speck of the pistol. Struggling to keep his voice calm, he said, "Well, Charlie . . . you thought any more about what kind of imaginary batteries he wants for his toy?"

Budd lifted his hands helplessly. "I can't think. I . . . I just don't know." Panic edged into his voice. "Look at the time!"

"Henry?"

LeBow scrolled slowly through the now-lengthy profile of Louis Handy. To nervous Charlie Budd he said, "The more urgent the task, Captain, the more slowly you should perform it. Let's see, there was a lot of grand theft auto when he was a kid. Maybe he's into cars. Should we push that button?"

"No. Charlie's got a point. Let's think about something having to do with his escape."

"What else does he spend his money on?" Angie asked.

"Not much. Never owned property. Never knocked over a jewelry store. . . ."

"Any interests?" Potter wondered.

Angie said suddenly, "His probation reports. You have those in there?"

"I've scanned them in."

"Read them. See if he's ever asked permission to leave a jurisdiction and why."

"Good, Angie," Potter said.

Keys tapped. "Okay. Yes, he has. Twice he left Milwaukee, where he was living following his release, to go fishing in Minnesota. Up near International Falls. And three times up to Canada. Returned all times without incident." LeBow squinted. "Fishing. That reminds me of something. . . ." He typed in a search request. "Here, a prison counselor's report. He likes to fish. Loves it. Worked up merit points for a leave to a trout stream on the grounds at Pennaupsut State Pen."

Potter thought, Minnesota. His home state. Land of a Thousand Lakes. Canada.

Budd—standing tall with his perfect posture—continued to fidget. "Oh, brother." He looked at his watch twice, five seconds apart.

"Please, Charlie."

"We've got seven minutes!"

"I know. You had the brainstorm. What was in your mind?"

"I don't *know* what I meant!"

Potter was staring at Melanie once again. Stop it, he ordered. Forget about her. He sat up suddenly. "Got it. He likes to fish and has a fondness for the north?"

"Right," Budd said. Asking, in effect, So what?

But LeBow understood. He nodded. "You're a poet, Arthur."

"Thank Charlie here. He got me thinking of it."

Budd looked merely perplexed.

"Five minutes," Tobe called.

"We're going to cut a phony escape deal." Potter said quickly, pointing to the "Deceptions" half of the board. LeBow rose to his feet, grabbed the marker. Potter thought for a moment. "Handy's going to want to check what I tell him. He's going to call the FAA regional headquarters. Where is that, Charlie?"

"Topeka."

To Tobe, Potter said, "I want an immediate routing of all calls into the main FAA number sent to that phone right there." He pointed to a console phone. It would be an arduous task, Potter knew, but without a word Tobe set to work pushing buttons and speaking urgently into his headset mike.

"No," Budd protested. "There's no time. Just give him that number. How will *he* know it's not the FAA?"

"Too risky if he checks." Potter picked up the phone and hit redial.

An enthusiastic voice answered, "Yo."

"Lou?"

"Hello, Art. My ears're peeled but I don't hear no chopper. You see my girlfriend here in the window?"

"Say, Lou," Potter said calmly, looking into the window. "I've got a proposition for you."

"Ten, nine, eight . . ."

"Listen—"

"Hey, Art, I just had a thought. Maybe this is your way of doing something bad. Maybe you *are* a son of a bitch."

"The chopper's just about ready."

"And this here girl is just about bleedin'. She's crying a stream, Art. I've had it. I've just fucking had it with you people. You don't take me seriously." He raged, "You don't do what I fucking *want!*"

Angie leaned forward. Charlie Budd's lips moved in a silent prayer.

"All right, Lou," Potter growled. "I know you'll shoot her. But you know I'll let you do it."

Static filled the van.

"Hear me out at least."

"By my clock I'll hear you out for another minute or two."

"Lou, I've been working on this for an hour. I didn't want to say anything until it was in place but I'll tell you anyway. It's almost done."

Let the anticipation build up.

"Well, what? Tell me."

"Give me another hour, don't hurt the girl, and I'll get you a priority FAA-cleared flight plan into Canada."

Silence for a second.

"What the fuck does that mean?"

"You can deal with the FAA directly. We'll never know where you go."

"But the pilot will."

"The pilot'll have handcuffs for himself and the hostages. You set down wherever you want in Canada, disable the chopper and the radio, and you'll be gone hours before we find them."

Silence.

Potter looked at Tobe desperately, eyebrows raised. The young man, sweating heavily, exhaled long and mouthed, "Working on it."

"We'll stock the chopper with food and water. You want backpacks, hiking boots? Hell, Lou, we'll even give you fishing rods. This is a good deal. Don't hurt her. Give us another hour and you'll get the clearance."

"Lemme think."

"I'll get the name of the FAA supervisor and call you right back."

Click.

Unflappable Tobe gazed at his inert dials then hit the console with his fist and said, "Where the fuck is our transfer?"

Potter folded his hands together and stared out the window at the configuration that was Melanie Charrol—tiny glowing shapes of color and light, like pixels on a TV screen.

Captain Dan Tremain leaned forward, pushing aside a branch, silent as snow.

From this angle he could just see the corner of the window in which the young woman was being held. Tremain was one of the best sniper shots in the HRU and often regretted that his command position didn't give him the chance to strap up a Remington and, with the aid of his spotter, acquire and neutralize a target eight hundred, a thousand yards away.

But tonight was a door-entry operation. Snipers would be useless and so he turned his thoughts from the vague target in the window to the job at hand.

Tremain's watch showed seven. "Deadline," he said. "Outrider One. Report."

"Charge loaded in generator."

"Await green-light command."

"Roger."

"Outrider Two, report."

"The subjects are all in the main room, hostages are unattended, except for the woman in the window."

"Roger," Tremain said. "Teams A and B, status?"

"Team A to home base. Loaded and locked."

"Team B, loaded and locked."

Tremain chocked his foot against a rock and eased to one knee. Eyes on Handy. He looked like a sprinter waiting for the gun—which was exactly what he would become in a matter of minutes.

"Done," Tobe called.

He added, "Theoretically, at least."

Potter wiped his palm. He transferred the phone to his other hand, then called Handy back and said the helicopter clearance was arranged. He gave him the number of the FAA office.

"What'sa name?" Handy growled. "Who should I talk to?"

Potter said, "Don Creswell." It was the name of his cousin-in-law Linden's husband. LeBow scrawled it on the nearly filled "Deceptions" board.

"We'll see, Art. I'll call you back. The girl stays right beside me and my big G till I'm satisfied."

Click.

Potter spun around and looked at Tobe's screen. He said, "It'll have to be you, Henry. He knows my voice."

LeBow grimaced. "I could have used time to prepare, Arthur."

"So could we all."

A moment later Tobe said, "Uplink from slaughterhouse.... Not coming here ... digits .... one, nine-one-three, five-five-five, one-two-one-two. Topeka directory assistance."

They heard Handy's voice ask for the number of the FAA regional office. The operator gave it to him. Potter exhaled in relief. Budd said, "You were right. He didn't trust you."

"Uplink terminated," Tobe whispered unnecessarily. "Uplink from slaughterhouse to Topeka, downlink transfer from trunk line to . . ." He pointed to the phone on the desk, and it began to ring. "Curtain up."

LeBow took a deep breath and nodded.

"Wait," Budd said urgently. "He'll be expecting a secretary or receptionist."

"Damn," Potter spat out. "Of course. Angie?"

She was the closest to the phone.

Third ring. Fourth.

She nodded brusquely, snatched up the receiver. "Federal Aviation Administration," she said breezily. "May I help you?"

"I wanta talk to Don Creswell."

"One moment please. Who's calling?"

A laugh. "Lou Handy."

She clapped her hand to the mouthpiece and whispered, "What's hold?"

Tobe took the phone from her and tapped it with a fingernail, then handed it to LeBow. Potter winked at her.

Again LeBow inhaled and said, "Creswell here."

"Hey, Don. You don't know me."

A brief pause. "This is that fellow the FBI called me about? Louis Handy?"

"Yeah, this's that *fellow*. Tell me, is this bullshit he's feeding me? It is, isn't it?"

Pudgy, benign Henry LeBow snapped, "Well, sir, I'll tell you, it's more bullshit for me. 'Cause frankly it's making my life pure hell. I got sixty planes an hour coming into our airspace and this's going to mean rerouting close to three-quarters of them. And that's just the commercial flights. I told the agent no way at first but he's a grade-A pain in the ass, and a FBI pain in the ass to boot. He told me he'd fuck up my life royal if I don't do exactly what you want. So, yeah, it's bullshit but, yeah, I'm going to give him what he asked for."

"What the fuck is that, exactly?"

"Didn't he tell you? An M-4 priority airspace clearance straight into western Ontario."

Good job, Henry, Potter thought, his eyes on Melanie's silhouette.

"A what?"

"It's the highest priority there is. It's reserved for Air Force One and visiting heads of state. We call it 'papal clearance' because it's what the Pope gets. Now listen, you might want to write this down. What you have to do is make sure the helicopter pilot shuts off the transponder. He'll point it out to you and you can shut it off or smash it or whatever, and we won't be able to track you on radar."

"No radar?"

"That's part of the M-4. We do that so radar-seeking missiles can't lock onto a dignitary's jet."

"The transponder. I think I heard about them. How long do we have?"

LeBow looked at Potter, who held up eight fingers.

"We can keep the airspace open for eight hours. After that there's too much commercial traffic and we'd have to rewrite the airspace requirements."

"Okay. Do it."

"It's being done. It'll be effective in, let me see . . ."

Potter held up two fingers.

"About two hours."

"Fuck that. One hour tops, or I kill this pretty little thing next to me."

"Oh, my God. Are you seri—? Well, sure. One hour. But I need a full hour. Only please, mister, don't hurt anybody."

Handy's cold chuckle came through the speaker. "Hey, Don, lemme ask you a question."

"Sure."

"You in Topeka right now?"

Silence in the room.

Potter's head turned away from the window, stared at LeBow.

"Sure am."

Potter snapped his fingers and pointed to LeBow's computer. The intelligence officer's eyes went wide and he nodded. He punched silent buttons. The message came on: "Loading Encyclopedia." The words blinked repeatedly.

"Topeka, huh?" Handy said. "Nice place?"

Loading . . . loading . . .

Come on, Potter thought desperately. Come *on!*

"I like it."

The screen went blank; at last a colorful logo appeared. LeBow typed madly.

"How long you been there?"

How calm Handy sounds, Potter reflected. Holding a gun to a girl's eye and he's still working all the angles, cool as can be.

"About a year," LeBow ad-libbed. "You work for Uncle Sam, they move you around a lot." He typed rapidly. His fingers stopped. An error message appeared. "Invalid Search Request."

The more urgent the task . . .

He started again. Finally a map and text appeared and in the corner of the screen a color photo of a skyline.

"Imagine they do. Like that FBI agent who called you. Andy Palmer. He must move a bunch too."

LeBow took a breath to answer but Potter scrawled on a sheet of paper, "Don't respond to name."

"Hell, I'd guess so."

"That *is* his name, right? Andy?"

"I think so. I don't remember. He just told me the code that let me know it was a real call."

"You got codes? That you use like spies?"

"You know, sir, I really oughta get on this project for you."

"What's that river there?"

"In Topeka, you mean?"

"Yeah."

LeBow leaned forward and read the blurb about the city. "The Kaw, you mean. The Kansas River. The one cuts the town in half?"

"Yeah. That's it. Used to go fishing there. Had a uncle lived in that old neighborhood. It was all la-di-da, fancy old houses. Cobblestoned roads, you know."

Henry LeBow was sitting so far forward he was in danger of tumbling off his chair. He read frantically. "Oh, Potwin Place. He's a lucky man, your uncle. Nice houses. But the streets aren't cobblestoned, they're brick." The agent's bald head glistened with silver beads of sweat.

"What's your favorite restaurant there?"

A pause.

"Denny's. I have six children."

"You son of a bitch," Handy growled.

Click.

"Downlink terminated," Tobe called.

LeBow, hands shaking, stared at the phone.

Four heads jammed into the window.

"Did it work?" Frances muttered.

No one ventured a guess. Only Charlie Budd said anything and the most he dared utter was "Oh, brother."

"Home base to Outrider Two."

"Outrider Two," whispered Lieutenant Joey Wilson, standing just beneath the window of the slaughterhouse, in the shadow of the school bus.

"Positions of subjects?"

The trooper lifted his blackened face quickly, glanced inside, then dropped down again.

"Two takers in the main room by the window, Handy's got a gun on one hostage. A Glock. Right against her head. Can't tell if it's cocked. Wilcox doesn't have a weapon in his hands but's got a Glock in his belt. Bonner's got a Mossberg semiauto twelve-gauge. But he's thirty feet from the hostage room. It's a good scenario. Except for the girl in the window."

"Can you take out Handy?"

"Negative. He's behind pipes. Have no clear shot. Bonner keeps going back and forth. Maybe I can acquire him. I don't know."

"Stand by."

They were well past deadline now. Handy could shoot the poor woman at any moment.

"Outrider One? Report."

"Outrider One. I'm at the generator. Charge is armed."

Lord, let us not fail, Tremain thought, and took a deep breath.

"Outrider One?" Tremain called to Pfenninger, whom he pictured beside the command van's generator, the detonating cord to the L-210 in his hand.

"Outrider One here."

"Code word—"

"Outrider Two to home base!" Wilson's energetic voice cut through the airwaves. "Hostage is safe. Repeat. Outrider Two to home base. Subject Handy is standing down. He's put his weapon away. Subject Bonner's taking the girl back to the room with the rest of the hostages."

Tremain looked. The girl was being pulled out of the window.

"Subject Bonner has left her in the hostage room and has returned to the front of the factory."

"Code word Stallion," Tremain said. "All outriders, all teams, Stallion, Stallion, Stallion. Confirm transmission."

They all did.

Dan Tremain—senior HRU commander and a man who had a reputation for thinking fast—composed and then offered a silent prayer to his just and merciful Lord in Christ, thanking Him for sparing the girl's life. But mostly he gave thanks for providing the extra time in which to prepare for the assault that He had assured Tremain would free the poor lambs from the hands of the barbaric Romans.

"Downlink," Tobe announced. "From him."

Potter let the phone ring twice then answered it. "Art?"

"Lou. Creswell just called."

"He thinks you're a prick. He doesn't even know your fucking name."

"I have my enemies. More of them within the government than without, I'm sorry to say. What about it?"

"Okay, it's a deal," Handy said cheerfully. "You got one more hour."

Potter paused, let the silence build up.

"Art," Handy asked uncertainly, "you still there?"

A subtle sigh issued from the negotiator's mouth.

"What'sa matter? You sound like your fucking dog just died."

"Well . . ."

"Come on, talk to me."

"I don't know how to ask this. You were real good about agreeing to give us the extra time. And . . ."

Test the bonds, Potter was thinking. What exactly *is* Handy thinking about me? How close are we?

"Well, ask me what you gotta, Art. Just fucking do it."

"Creswell said he'll need at least until nine-thirty to do the clearance right. He's got to coordinate with the Canadian authorities. I told him to do it within an hour. But he said they can't do it that fast. I feel like I'm letting you down. . . ."

And part of him did, yes—at the lie he was telling, so blatantly, so coldly.

"Nine-thirty?"

A long hesitation.

"Fuck, I can live with that."

"Really, Lou?" Arthur Potter asked, surprised. "Appreciate it."

"Hey, anything for my good buddy Art."

Take advantage of the good mood. He said, "Lou, let me ask you another question."

"Shoot."

Should I push or not?

Angie was watching him. Their eyes met and she mouthed, "Go for it."

"Lou, how about if you let her go? Melanie."

Okay. Art, I'm in a good mood. I'm going to Canada, so you just bought yourself one.

Handy's voice was like a cold razor blade. "Sometimes you ask for too fucking much, you asshole. I'm the one person in the fucking universe you *don't* want to do that to."

The phone went dead.

Potter raised his eyebrows at the outburst. But the room erupted into applause and laughter. Potter hung up the phone and joined in.

Potter clapped LeBow on the back. "Excellent job." He looked at Angie. "Both of you."

Budd said, "You deserve an Oscar for that. Yessir, I'd vote for you."

"M-4?" Potter said. "What's an M-4 priority?"

"Doris and I went to England last year," LeBow explained. "That was a highway, I seem to recall. Did sound good, didn't it?" He was very pleased with himself.

"That radar missile tracking," Budd said. "That sounded pretty cool."

"All made up."

"Oh, brother. He bought it all."

Then they went somber again as Potter gazed out the window at the place where six hostages still remained, safe for at least a couple of hours—if Handy kept his word. Then simultaneously the entire crowd in the van all laughed once more as Tobe Geller, maven of electronics and coldly rational science, whispered reverently, "Papal clearance," and crossed himself expertly like the good Catholic that he apparently was.

7:15 P.M.

"Well, Charlie, what's the news from the front?"

Budd stood outside the van in a gully. He held his cellular phone pressed hard into his ear—as if that would keep anyone from overhearing. Roland Marks's voice tended to boom.

The assistant attorney general was down at the rear staging area. Budd said, "I'll tell you, it's been a real roller coaster here. Up and down, you know. He's doing some real remarkable things—Agent Potter, I mean."

"Remarkable?" Marks asked sarcastically. "He's brought that girl back to life, has he? A regular Lazarus situation, is it?"

"He's gotten a couple more out safe and he just bought us another couple of hours. He's—"

"Do you have that present for me?" Marks asked evenly.

The door of the van opened and Angie Scapello stepped out.

"Not yet," Budd said, and decided the lie was credible. "Soon. I should go."

"I want that tape within the hour. My friend from the press'll be here then."

"Yessir, that's right," he said. "I'll talk to you later."

He pushed disconnect. And said to Angie, "Bosses. We could do without 'em."

She was carrying two cups of coffee and offered one to him.

"Milk, no sugar. That's how you like it?" she said.

"Agent LeBow has my file too, huh?"

"You live near here, Charlie?"

"My wife and I bought a house about fifteen miles away."

That was good. Work in Meg again.

"I have an apartment in Georgetown. I travel so much it doesn't make sense for me to buy. And just being by myself."

"Never been married?"

"Nope. I'm an old maid."

"Old, there you go again. You must be all of twenty-eight."

She laughed.

"You like life out here in the country?" Angie asked him.

"Sure do. The girls have good schools—I showed you the pictures of my family?"

"You did, yes, Charlie. Twice."

"They have good schools and good teams to be on. They live for soccer. And it's not expensive, really. I'm thirty-two and own my own house on four acres. You couldn't do that on the East Coast, I don't imagine. I went to New York once and what people pay for apartments there—"

"You faithful to your wife, Charlie?" She turned her warm, brown eyes on him.

He gulped down coffee he had absolutely no taste for. "Yes, I am. And as a matter of fact I've been meaning to talk to you. I think you're an interesting person and what you're doing to help us is real valuable. And I'd have to be a blind man not to see how pretty you are—"

"Thank you, Charlie."

"But I'm not even unfaithful in my mind—like that president was, Jimmy Carter? Or somebody, I don't remember." This was all rehearsed and he wished he didn't have to swallow so often. "Meg and I've had our problems, that's for sure. But who hasn't? Problems're part of a relationship and you get through them just like you get through the good times, and you keep going." He stopped abruptly, forgetting completely the end of his speech, which he improvised as "So there. I just wanted to say that."

Angie stepped closer and touched his arm. She leaned up and kissed his cheek. "I'm very glad you told me that, Charlie. I think fidelity is the most important trait in a relationship. Loyalty. And you don't see much of it nowadays."

He hesitated. "No, I guess you don't."

"I'm going down to the motel and visit the girls and their parents. Would you like to come with me?" She smiled. "As a friend and fellow threat management team member?"

"I'd be delighted." And to Budd's unbounded relief she didn't slip her arm through his as they walked to the van to tell Potter where they would be and then proceeded to the squad car for the short drive to the Days Inn.

They sat in the killing room, the entrance to hell, tears on all their faces.

What was happening now—only a few feet in front of them—was worse than they'd ever imagined. Let it be over soon, Melanie thought, her fingers twitching this mute plea. For the love of God.

"Don't look," she finally signed to the girls. But they all did look—no one could turn away from this terrible spectacle.

Bear lay atop poor Mrs. Harstrawn, her blouse open, her skirt up to her waist. Numb, Melanie watched the man's naked ass bob up and down. She watched his hands grip one of Mrs. Harstrawn's breasts, as white as his own bloated skin. She watched him kiss her and stick his wet tongue into her unresponsive mouth.

He paused for a moment and looked back into the main room. There, Brutus and Stoat sat before the TV, drinking beer. Laughing. Like Melanie's father and brother would sit around the TV on Sunday, as if the small black box were something magic that allowed them to talk to one another. Then Bear reared up, hooked his arms beneath Mrs. Harstrawn's knees and lifted her legs into the air. He began his ungainly motion once again.

Melanie grew calm as death.

It's time, she decided. They couldn't wait any longer. Never looking away from Bear's closed eyes, she wrote a note on the pad of paper that Brutus had torn from her hands earlier. She folded it tightly and slipped it into Anna's pocket. The girl looked up. Her twin did too.

"Go into corner," Melanie signed. "By gas can."

They didn't want to. They were terrified of Bear, terrified of the horrible thing he was doing. But so emphatic was Melanie's signing, so cold were her eyes that they moved steadily into the corner of the room. Once again Melanie told them to take Mrs. Harstrawn's sweater.

"Tie it around gas can. Go—"

Suddenly Bear leapt up off the teacher and faced Melanie. His bloody organ was upright and glistened red and purple. The overwhelming scent of musk and sweat and woman's fluid made her gag. He paused, his groin only a foot from her face. He reached down and touched her hair. "Stop that fucking spooky shit. Stop . . . with your hands . . . that bullshit." He mimicked signing.

Melanie understood his reaction. It was common. People have always been frightened by signing. It was why there was such a strong desire to force the deaf to speak and not use sign language—which was a code, a secret language, the hallmark of a mysterious society.

She nodded slowly and lowered her eyes once more to the glistening, erect penis.

Bear strode back to Mrs. Harstrawn, squeezed her breasts, knocked her legs apart, and plunged into her once again. She lifted a hand in a pathetic protest. He slapped it away.

Don't sign. . . .

How could she talk to the girls? Tell the twins what they had to do?

Then she happened to recall her own argot. The language that she had created at age sixteen, when she'd risked getting her knuckles slapped by the teachers—most of them Others—for using ASL or SEE at the Laurent Clerc School. It was a simple language, one that had occurred to her while watching Georg Solti conduct a silent orchestra. In music the meter and rhythm were as much a part of the piece as the melody; she'd kept her hands close to her chin and spoke to her classmates through the shape *and* rhythm of her fingers, combined with facial expressions. She'd shown all her students the basics of the language—when she compared different types of signing—but she didn't know if the twins recalled enough to understand her.

Yet she had no choice. She lifted her hands and moved her fingers in rhythmic patterns.

Anna didn't understand at first and began to respond in ASL.

"No," Melanie instructed, frowning for emphasis. "No signing."

It was vital that she convey her message, for she believed she could save the twins at least, and maybe one more—poor gasping Beverly, or Emily, whose thin white legs Bear had been staring at for long moments before he pulled Donna Harstrawn toward him and spread her legs like a hungry man opening up a package of food.

"Take gas can," Melanie communicated. Somehow. "Tie sweater around it."

After a moment the girls understood. They eased forward. Their tiny hands went to work enwrapping the can with the colorful sweater.

The can was now enwrapped by the sweater.

"Go out back door. One on left."

The doorway swept clean of dust by the breeze from the river.

"Afraid."

Melanie nodded but persisted. "Have to."

A faint, heartbreaking nod. Then another. Emily stirred beside Melanie. The girl was terrified. Melanie took her hand, behind their backs, out of Bear's view. She fingerspelled in English. "Y-o-u w-i-l-l b-e n-e-x-t. D-o n-o-t w-o-r-r-y."

Emily nodded. To the twins Melanie said, "Follow smell of river." She flared her nostrils. "River. Smell."

A nod from both girls.

"Hold on to sweater and jump into water."

Two no shakes. Emphatic.

Melanie's eyes flared. "Yes!"

Then Melanie looked at the teacher and back to the girls, explaining silently what could happen to them. And the twins understood. Anna started to whimper.

Melanie would not allow this. "Stop!" she insisted. "Now. Go."

The twins were behind Bear. He'd have to stand up and turn to see them.

Afraid to use her hands, Anna timidly lowered her face and wiped it on her sleeve. They shook their heads no. In heartbreaking unison.

Melanie's hand rose and she risked fast fingerspellings and hand signs. Bear's eyes were closed; he missed the gestures. "Abbé de l'Epée is out there. Waiting for you."

Their eyes went wide.

De l'Epée?

The savior of the Deaf. A legend. He was Lancelot, he was King Arthur. For heaven's sake, he was *Tom Cruise!* He *couldn't* be outside. Yet Melanie's face was so serious, she was so insistent that they offered faint nods of acquiescence.

"You must find him. Give him note in your pocket."

"Where is he?" Anna signed.

"He's older man, heavy. Gray hair. Glasses and blue sports coat." They nodded enthusiastically (though this was hardly how they pictured the legendary abbé). "Find him and give him note."

Bear looked up and Melanie continued to lift her hand innocently to wipe her red, but dry, eyes as if she'd been crying. He looked down again and continued. Melanie was grateful she couldn't hear the piggish grunts she knew issued from his fat mouth.

"Ready?" she asked the girls.

Indeed they were; they would leap into flames if it meant they could meet their idol. Melanie looked again at Bear, the sweat dripping off his face and falling like rain on poor Mrs. Harstrawn's cheeks and jiggling breasts. His eyes closed. The moment of finishing was near—something Melanie had read about but couldn't quite comprehend.

"Take shoes off. And tell de l'Epée to be careful."

Anna nodded. "I love you," she signed. Suzie did too.

Melanie looked out the doorway and saw Brutus and Stoat, far across the slaughterhouse, staring at the TV. She nodded twice. The girls picked up their gas-can life preserver and vanished around the corner. Melanie watched Bear to see if their passage was silent. Apparently it was.

To distract him she leaned forward, enduring the ugly man's ominous stare, and slowly, cautiously, with her burgundy sleeve wiped the sheen of his sweat from the teacher's face. He was perplexed by the gesture then angered. He shoved her back against the wall. Her head hit the tile with a thud. There she sat until he finished and lay gasping. Finally he rolled off her. Melanie saw a slick pool on the woman's thigh. Blood too. Bear glanced furtively into the other room. He had escaped undetected; Brutus and Stoat hadn't seen. He sat up. He zipped his filthy jeans and pulled down Mrs. Harstrawn's skirt, roughly buttoned her blouse.

Bear leaned forward and put his face inches from Melanie's. She managed to hold his eye—it was terrifying but she would do anything to keep him from looking around the room. He spat out, "You . . . word about . . . you're . . ."

Delay, stall. Buy time for the twins.

She frowned and shook her head.

He tried again, words spitting from his mouth.

Again she shook her head, pointed to her ear. He boiled in frustration.

Finally, she leaned away and pointed to the dusty floor. He wrote, *Say anything and your dead.*

She nodded slowly.

He obliterated the message and buttoned his shirt.

Sometimes all of us, even Others, are mute and deaf and blind as the dead; we perceive only what our desires allow us to see. This is a terrible burden and a danger but can also be, as now, a small miracle. For Bear rose unsteadily, tucked in his shirt, and looked around the killing room with a glazed look of contentment on his flushed face. Then he strode out, never noticing that only four shoes remained in place of the twins and that the girls were gone, floating free of this terrible place.

For a few years I was nothing but Deaf.

I lived Deaf, I ate Deaf, I breathed it.

Melanie is speaking to de l'Epée.

She has gone into her music room because she cannot bear to think about Anna and Suzie, leaping into the waters of the Arkansas River, dark as a coffin. They're better off, she tells herself. She remembers the way Bear looked at the girls. Whatever happens, they're better off.

De l'Epée shifts in his chair and asks what she meant by being nothing but Deaf.

"When I was a junior the Deaf movement came to Laurent Clerc.

Deaf with a capital *D*. Oralism was out and at last the school began teaching Signed Exact English. Which is sort of a half-assed compromise. Eventually, after I graduated, they agreed to switch to ASL. That's American Sign."

"I'm interested in languages. Tell me about it." (Would he say this? It's *my* fantasy; yes, he would.)

"ASL comes from the world's first school for the deaf, founded in France in the 1760s by your namesake. Abbé Charles Michel de l'Epée. He was like Rousseau—he felt that there was a primordial human language. A language that was pure and absolute and unfalteringly clear. It could express every emotion directly and it would be so transparent that you couldn't use it to lie or deceive anyone."

De l'Epée smiles at this.

"With French Sign Language, oh, the Deaf came into their own. A teacher from de l'Epée's school, Laurent Clerc, came to America in the early 1800s with Thomas Gallaudet—he was a minister from Connecticut—and set up a school for the deaf in Hartford. French Sign Language was used there but it got mixed with local signing—especially the dialect used on Martha's Vineyard, where there was a lot of heredity deafness. That's how American Sign Language came about. That, more than anything, allowed the Deaf to live normal lives. See, you have to develop language—some language, either sign or spoken—by age three. Otherwise you basically end up retarded."

De l'Epée looks at her somewhat cynically. "It seems to me that you've rehearsed this."

She can only laugh.

"Once ASL hit the school, as I was saying, I lived for the Deaf movement. I learned the party line. Mostly because of Susan Phillips. It was amazing. I was a student teacher at the time. She saw my eyes flickering up and down as I read somebody's lips. She came up to me and said, 'The word "hearing" means only one thing to me. It's the opposite of who I am.' I felt ashamed. She later said that the term 'hard of hearing' should infuriate us because it defines us in terms of the Other community. 'Oral' is even worse because the Oral deaf want to pass. They haven't come out yet. If somebody's Oral, Susan said, we have to 'rescue' them.

"I knew what she was talking about because for years I'd tried to pass. The rule is 'Plan ahead.' You're always thinking about what's coming, second-guessing what questions you'll be asked, steering people toward streets with noisy traffic or construction, so you'll have an excuse to ask them to shout or repeat what they say.

"But after I met Susan I rejected all that. I was anti-Oral, I was anti-mainstreaming. I taught ASL. I became a poet and gave performances at theaters of the deaf."

"Poet?"

"I did that as a substitute for my music. It seemed the closest I could hope for."

"What are signed poems like?" he asks.

She explains that they "rhymed" not sonically but because the hand shape of the last word of the line was similar to that of the last words in preceding lines. Melanie recited:

"Eight gray birds, sitting in dark.

"Cold wind blows, it isn't kind.

"Sitting on wire, they lift their wings

"And sail off into billowy clouds."

"Dark" and "kind" share a flat, closed hand, the palm facing the body of the signer. "Wings" and "clouds" involve similar movements from the shoulders up into the air above the signer.

De l'Epée listens, fascinated. He watches her sign several other poems. Melanie puts almond-scented cream on them every night and her nails are smooth and translucent as lapidaried stones.

She stopped in mid line. "Oh," she muses, "I did it all. The National Association of the Deaf, the Bicultural Center, the National Athletic Association of the Deaf."

He nods. (She wishes he'd tell her about his life. Is he married? (Please no!) Does he have children? Is he older than I imagine, or younger?)

"I had my career all laid out before me. I was going to be the first deaf woman farm foreman."

"Farm?"

"Ask me about dressing corn. About anhydrous ammonia. You want to know about wheat? Red wheat comes from the Russian steppes. But it's name isn't political—oh, not in Kansas, nosir. It's the color. 'Amber waves of grain . . .' Ask me about the advantages of no-till planting and how to fill out UCC financing statements to collateralize crops that haven't grown yet. 'All the accretions and appurtenances upon said land . . .' "

Her father, she explains, owned six hundred and sixty acres in south-central Kansas. He was a lean man who wore an exhaustion that many people confused with ruggedness. His problem wasn't a lack of willingness but a lack of talent, which he called luck. And he acknowledged—to himself alone—that he needed help from many quarters. He of course put most of his stock in his son but farms are big business now. Harold Charrol planned to invest both son, Danny, and daughter, Melanie, with third-share interests and watch them all prosper as a corporate family.

She had been reluctant about these plans but the prospect of working with her brother had an appeal to it. The unfazable boy had become an easygoing young man, nothing at all like their embittered father. While Harold would mutter darkly about fate when a thresher blade snapped and he stood paralyzed with anger, staring at the splintered wood, Danny might jump down out of the cockpit, vanish for a time, and return with a six-pack and some sandwiches for an impromptu picnic. "We'll fix the son of a bitch tonight. Let's eat."

For a time she believed this could be a pleasant life. She took some ag extension courses and even sent an article to *Silent News* about farm life and Deafness.

But then, last summer, Danny'd had the accident, and lost both the ability, and the will, to work the place. Charrol, with the desperate legitimacy of a man needing heirs, turned to Melanie. She was a woman, yes (this a handicap somewhat worse than her audiologic one), but an educated, hardworking one at least.

Melanie, he planned, would become his full partner. And why not? Since age seven she'd ridden in the air-conditioned cab of the big John Deere, helping him shift up through the infinite number of gears. She'd donned goggles and mask and gloves like a rustic surgeon and filled the ammonia tank, she'd sat in on his meetings with United Produce, and she'd driven with him to the roadside stops, known only to insiders, where the illegal migrant workers hid, waiting for day jobs at harvest.

It's a question of belonging and what God does to make sure those that oughta stay someplace do. Well, your place is here, working at what

*you can do, where your, you know, problem doesn't get you into trouble.
God's will. . . . So you'll be home then.*

Tell him, Melanie thinks.

Yes! If you never tell another soul, tell de l'Epée.

"There's something," she begins, "I want to say."

His placid face gazes at her.

"It's a confession."

"You're too young to have anything to confess."

"After the poetry recital in Topeka I wasn't going back to the school
right away. I was going to see my brother in St. Louis. He's in the hospital. He's having some surgery tomorrow."

De l'Epée nods.

"But before I went to see him there was something I planned to do in
Topeka. I had an appointment to see somebody."

"Tell me."

Should she? Yes, no?

Yes, she decides. She has to. But just as she is about to speak,
something intrudes.

The smell of the river?

The thud of approaching feet.

Brutus?

Alarmed, she opened her eyes. No, there was nothing. The slaughterhouse was peaceful. None of their three captors was nearby. She closed
her eyes and struggled back into the music room. But de l'Epée was gone.

"Where are you?" she cried. But realized that though her lips were
moving she could no longer hear any words.

No! I don't want to leave. Come back, please. . . .

Then Melanie realized that it wasn't the breeze from the river that
booted them out of the room; it was her own self. She had grown timid
once again, ashamed, and could not confess.

Even to the man who seemed more than willing to listen to anything
she wanted to say, however foolish, however dark.

They caught the glint of light about fifty yards away.

Joe Silbert and Ted Biggins walked silently through the field on the left flank of the slaughterhouse. Silbert pointed to the light, a flash off the field glasses or a piece of equipment dangling from the belt of one of the hostage rescue troopers, a reflection from the brilliant halogen lights.

Biggins grumbled that the lights were too bright. There'd be lens flare, he was worried.

"You want me to go fucking shut them off?" Silbert whispered. He wanted a cigarette badly. They continued through the woods until they broke into an open field. Silbert looked through the camera, pushing the zoom button. The troopers, he could see, were clustered on a brush-filled ridge overlooking the slaughterhouse. One of them—hidden behind the school bus—was actually at the slaughterhouse, hovering just below a window.

"Damn, they're good," Silbert whispered. "One of the best teams I've ever seen."

"Fucking lights," muttered Biggins.

"Let's get going."

As they walked through the field Silbert looked for patrolling troops. "I thought we had baby-sitters all over the place."

"Those lights're really a pain."

"This is almost too easy," Silbert muttered.

"Oh, my God." Biggins was looking up in the air.

"Perfecto," Silbert whispered, laughing softly.

The men gazed up at the top of the windmill.

"It'll get us above the lights," Biggins the sticking record said.

Forty feet in the air. They'd have a spectacular view of the field. Silbert grinned and began to climb. At the top they stood on the rickety platform. The mill was long abandoned and the blades were missing. It rocked back and forth in the wind.

"That going to be a problem?"

Biggins pulled a retractable monopod from his pocket and extended it, screwing the joints tight. "So what can I do about it? Like, I've got a Steadicam in my fucking pocket?"

The view was excellent. Silbert could see troopers were clustered on the left side of the slaughterhouse. With grim respect he thought of Agent Arthur Potter, who'd looked him in the eye and said there'd be no assault. It was obvious the troopers were getting ready for an imminent kick-in.

Stillwell took a small sponge-covered microphone from his pocket and held it in his hand. He spoke into his scrambled cellular phone and called the remote transmission van, which was back near the main press tent. "You cocksucker," he said to Kellog when the man answered. "I was hoping they'd bust your ass."

"Naw, I told that trooper they could fuck your wife and they let me go."

"The other guys, they're at the press table?"

"Yep."

Silbert had in fact never told any of the other reporters about the press pool arrangement. He and Biggins, Kellog and Bianco and the two reporters now sitting at the pool site, pretending to type stories on the gutted Compaq, were all employees of KFAL in Kansas City.

Biggins plugged the mike into the camera and unfolded the parabolic antenna. He clipped it to the handrail of the windmill and began speaking into the mike, "Testing, testing, testing . . ."

"Cut the crap, Silbert, you gonna give us some pictures?"

"Ted's sending the level now." Silbert gestured toward the antenna and Biggins adjusted it while he spoke. "I'm switching to radio," the anchorman said, then took the microphone and shoved an earphone in his left ear.

After a moment Kellog said, "There. Five by five. Jesus H. Christ, we got the visual. Where the fuck are you? In a helicopter?"

"The pros know," Silbert said. "Cut into the feed. I'm ready to roll. Let's do it before we get shot down."

There was a staticky click and he heard a Toyota commercial suddenly cut off in mid-disclaimer. "And now from Crow Ridge, Kansas," the baritone announcer said, "We have a live report from Channel 9 anchorman Joe Silbert with exclusive footage from the kidnaping scene, where a number of students from the Laurent Clerc School for the Deaf and two teachers are being held by escaped convicts. Let's go live to you, Joe."

"Ron, we're overlooking the slaughterhouse in which the girls and their teachers are being held. As you can see, there are literally hundreds of troopers surrounding the building. The police have set up a series of those brilliant halogen lights to shine into the slaughterhouse windows, presumably to prevent any sniping from inside.

"The lights and the presence of the troopers, however, didn't prevent the murder of one of the hostages on that spot right about there, in the center of your screen, about six hours ago. A trooper told me that the girl was released by the fugitives and was walking down to join her family and friends when a single shot rang out and she was hit squarely in the back. She was, as you said, Ron, deaf, and the trooper told me he believed she'd used sign language to plead for help and to tell her family that she loved them."

"Joe, do you know the identity of that girl?"

"No, we don't, Ron. The authorities are being very slow in releasing any information."

"How many hostages are involved?"

"At this point it seems there are four students remaining inside and two teachers."

"So some have gotten out?"

"That's right. Three have been released so far, in exchange for demands by the kidnapers. We don't know what concessions the authorities have made."

"Joe, what can you tell us about those policemen off to the side there?"

"Ron, those are members of the elite Kansas State Police Hostage Rescue Unit. We've had no official word about an attempted rescue but I've covered a number of situations like this before and my impression is that they're preparing for an assault."

"What will happen, do you think, Joe? In terms of the assault? How will it proceed?"

"It's hard to say without knowing where the hostages are being kept, what the firepower of the men inside is, and so on."

"Could you speculate for us?"

"Sure, Ron," Silbert said. "I'd be happy to."

And he signaled to Biggins, using the hand gestures they'd developed between them. The sign meant "Zoom in."

They got down to the business at hand, for they didn't know how much time remained until the next deadline.

Captain Dan Tremain spoke on the scrambled radio to Bravo team and learned that they had found a breachable door near the dock in the back of the slaughterhouse but it was in full view of a skiff containing two armed troopers. The boat was anchored about twenty yards offshore.

"They'll see us if we get any closer."

"Any other access to the door?"

"Nosir."

Outrider Two, however, had some good news. Glancing into the plant, Trooper Joey Wilson had scanned the far wall—the southeast side—of the slaughterhouse and saw that, just opposite the fire door that Alpha team was going to breach, was a large piece of sloppily mounted plasterboard. He wondered if it covered a second fire door. The initial exterior surveillance hadn't revealed it. Tremain sent another trooper under the dock to the far side of the building. He made his way to the place Wilson mentioned and reported that it was in fact a door, invisible because it was overgrown with ivy.

Tremain ordered the trooper to drill through the door with a silenced Dremel tool fitted with a long, thin titanium sampling bit. Examining the core samples he found that the door was only an inch thick and had been weakened with wet rot and termite and carpenter ant tunneling. There was a two-inch gap and then he struck plasterboard, which proved to be only three-eighths inch thick. The whole assembly was far weaker than the door on the opposite side. Small cutting charges would rip it open easily.

Tremain was ecstatic. This was even better than going through the loading-dock door, because opposing door entry allowed for immediate dynamic crossfire. The takers wouldn't have a chance to respond. Tremain conferred with Carfallo and divided the men into two new teams. Bravo would make its way under the dock to the southeast side of the slaughterhouse. Alpha would position itself at the north door, further to the back but closer to the hostages.

Upon entry, Alpha would split in two groups, three men going for the hostages, three advancing on the takers, while the four-man Bravo team would enter through the south door and engage the HTs from behind.

Tremain considered the plan: Deep gullies to cover their approach, absolute surprise, stun then flash grenades, crossfire. It was a good scenario.

"Home base to all teams and outriders. On my mark it will be forty-five minutes to green-light order. Are you ready? Counting from my five. . . . Five, four, three, two, one, mark."

The troopers acknowledged the synchronization.

He would—

An urgent, staticky message: "Bravo leader to home base. We have movement here. From the loading dock. Somebody's rabbiting."

"Identify."

"Can't tell. They're slipping out from under the loading-dock door. I can't see clearly. It's just motion."

"An HT?"

"Unknown. The dock's shot to hell and there's crap all over it."

"Mount your suppressors."

"Yessir."

The men had suppressors on their H&Ks—big tubes of silencers. For at least a clip or two of ammunition the sound of the guns would be merely a whispering rattle and with this wind the troopers in the skiff would probably not hear a sound.

"Acquire target. Semiauto fire."

"Acquired."

"What's it look like, Bravo leader?"

"Real hard to make him out but he's wearing a red, white, and blue shirt. I can probably neutralize but can't make a positive ID. Whoever it is, he's staying real low to the ground. Advise."

"If you can make a positive ID on a taker you've got a green light to take him out."

"Yessir."

"Keep him acquired. And wait."

Tremain called Outrider Two, who risked a look through the window. The Trooper responded, "If anybody's bolting, it's Bonner. I can't see him. Only Handy and Wilcox."

Bonner. The rapist. Tremain would love the chance to bring God's revenge down upon him.

"Bravo leader. Status? He's going into the water?"

"Wait, yeah, there he goes. Just slipped in. Lost him. No, got him again. Should I tell the officers in the boat? He'll float right past them."

Tremain debated.

"Home base, do you copy?"

If it was Bonner he might get away. But at least he wouldn't be inside for the assault. One less person to worry about. If—though it seemed impossible—it was a hostage there was a chance she might drown. The current was swift here and the channel deep. But to rescue her he'd have to give away his presence, which would mean calling off the operation and jeopardizing the other hostages. But no, he thought. It couldn't be a hostage. There was no way a little girl could escape from three armed men.

"Negative, Bravo team leader, do not advise the troopers in the boat. Repeat, do not advise of subject's presence."

"I copy, home base. By the way, I don't think we have to worry about him. He's going straight out to mid-river. Doubt we'll ever see him again."

III

ACCEPTABLE CASUALTIES

7:46 P.M.

"What's that?"

Crow Ridge sheriff's deputy Arnold Shaw didn't know and he didn't care.

The lean thirty-year-old, a law enforcer all his young working life, had been in his share of boats. Dropping stinkers for catfish, trolling for bass and muskie. He'd even been water-skiing a couple of times down at Lake of the Ozarks. And he'd never once been as seasick as he was right now.

Oh, man. This is torture.

He and Buzzy Marboro were anchored twenty yards or so into the river, keeping their eyes "glued like epoxy" on the dock of the slaughterhouse, as their boss, Dean Stillwell, had commanded. The wind was bad, even for Kansas, and the shallow skiff bobbed and twisted like a Tilt-A-Whirl carnival ride.

"I'm not doing too well," Shaw muttered.

"There," Marboro said. "Look."

"I don't want to look."

But look he did, where Marboro was pointing. Ten yards downstream, something was floating away from them. The men were armed with battered Remington riot guns and Marboro drew a lazy target at the bobbing mass.

They'd heard a splash coming from the dock not long ago and had looked carefully but found no takers escaping through the water.

"If somebody did jump in—"

"We woulda seen him," Shaw muttered through the wind.

"—he'd be right about there by now. Just where that thing is. *Whatever* it is."

Shaw struggled to rid himself of memories of last night's dinner—his wife's tuna casserole. "I'm not feeling too well here, Buzz. What's your point, exactly?"

"I see a hand!" Marboro was standing up.

"Oh, no, don't do that. We've moving round enough as it is. Sit your heinie down."

Tuna and cream of mushroom soup and peas and those canned fried onions on top.

Oh, man, can't keep it down much longer.

"Looks like a hand and look at that thing—it's red and white—hell, I think it's one of the hostages got away!"

Shaw turned and looked at the debris, just above the surface of the choppy water, rising and falling. Each glimpse lasted no more than a few seconds. He couldn't tell what it was exactly. It looked sort of like a net float, except, as Buzz Marboro had pointed out, it was red and white. Blue too, he now saw.

And moving away from them, straight into midstream, pretty damn fast.

"Don't you see a hand?" Marboro said.

"No. . . . Wait. You know, it *does* look like a hand. Sorta." Reluctantly, and to the great distress of his churning gut; Arnie Shaw rose to his feet. That made him feel, he estimated, about a thousand times worse.

"I can't tell. A branch maybe."

"I don't know. Look how fast it's moving. It'll be in Wichita 'fore too long." Shaw decided he'd rather have a tooth pulled than be seasick. No—two teeth.

"Maybe it's just something the takers threw out to, you know, distract us. We go after it and they get away out the back door."

"Or maybe it's just trash," Shaw said, sitting down. "Hey, what're we thinking of? If they were friendlies they wouldn't've just floated past without calling for help. Hell, we've got our uniforms on. They'd know we're deputies."

"Sure. What'm I thinking of?" Marboro said, sitting down too.

One pair of vigilant eyes returned to the ass end of the slaughterhouse. The other pair closed slowly, as their owner swallowed in a desperate effort to calm his stomach. "I'm dying," Shaw whispered.

Exactly ten seconds later the eyes opened. "Oh, son of a bitch," Shaw spat out slowly. He sat up straight.

"You just remembered too?" Marboro was nodding.

Shaw *had* in fact just remembered—that the hostages were deaf and mute and wouldn't be able to call out for help to save their souls, no matter how close they'd passed by the skiff.

That was one of the reasons for his dismay. The other was that Shaw knew that while he himself had been an intercollegiate state finals swim champion three years running, Buzz Marboro couldn't dog-paddle more than ten yards.

Breathing deeply—not for the impending swim but merely to keep his turbulent stomach at bay—Shaw shed his weapons, body armor, helmet, boots. A final breath. He dove headfirst into the raging, murky water and streaked toward the disappearing flotsam as it headed rapidly southeast in the ornery current.

Arthur Potter gazed at the window where he'd first seen Melanie.

Then at the window where he'd almost seen her shot.

"I think we're moving up against the wall here," he said slowly. "If we're lucky we're going to get maybe one or two more out but that's it. Then we'll either have to get him to surrender or have HRT go in. Somebody tell me the weather." Potter was hoping for a hellsapoppin' storm to justify a longer delay in finding a helicopter.

Derek Elb turned a switch and the Weather Channel snapped on. Potter learned that the rest of the night would be much the same—

windy, with clearing skies. No rain. Winds would be out of the north-west at fifteen to twenty miles an hour.

"We'll have to rely on the wind for an excuse," LeBow said. "And even that's going to be dicey. Fifteen miles an hour? In the service Handy's probably flown in Hueys that've landed in gusts twice that."

Dean Stillwell called in for Henry LeBow, his laconic voice tripping out of the speaker above their heads.

"Yes?" the intelligence officer answered, leaning into his microphone.

"Agent Potter said to relay any information about the takers to you?"

"That's right," LeBow said.

Potter picked up the mike and asked what Stillwell had learned.

"Well, one of the troopers here has a good view inside, sort of an angle. And he said that Handy and Wilcox are walking around inside, looking the place over real carefully."

"Looking it over?"

"Pushing on pipes and machinery. It's like they're looking for something."

"Any idea what?" LeBow asked.

"Nope. I thought maybe they're checking out places to hide."

Potter nodded at Budd, recalling it had been the captain's idea that the takers might don rescue-worker uniforms during the surrender or HRT assault. It also wasn't unheard of for takers to, say, leave a back window open, then hide inside closets or crawl spaces for a day or two until law enforcers concluded they were long gone.

LeBow wrote down the information and thanked Stillwell. Potter said, "I want to make sure everybody's got pictures of the takers. And we'll have to tell Frank and the HRT to go through the place with a fine-tooth comb if it looks like an escape."

He sat in his chair once more, staring out at the factory.

"By the way," Stillwell returned over the radio. "I'm having chow brought in for the troopers and the Heartland's delivering your all's supper any time now."

"Thank you, Dean."

"Heartland? All right," Derek Elb said, looking particularly pleased.

Potter's mind, though, wasn't on food. He was thinking something far graver—whether or not he should meet with Handy. He felt the deadlines compressing, sensed somehow that Handy was growing testy and would start making nonnegotiable ultimatums. Face to face, Potter might be able to wear the convict down more efficiently than through their phone conversations.

Thinking too: It might give me a chance to see Melanie.

It might give me a chance to save her.

Yet a meeting between the taker and the incident commander was the most dangerous form of negotiating. There was the physical risk, of course; hostage takers' feelings, both positive and negative, are their most extreme about the negotiator. They often believe, sometimes subconsciously, that killing the negotiator will give them power they don't otherwise have, that the troopers will fall into chaos or that someone less daunting will take the negotiator's place. Even without violence, however, there's a danger that the negotiator will, in the taker's eyes, shrink in authority and stature and lose his opponent's respect.

Potter leaned against the window. What's inside you, Handy? What's making the wheels go round?

Something's happening in that cold brain of yours.

When you talk I hear silence.

When you don't say a word I hear your voice.

When you smile I see . . . what? What *do* I see? Ah, that's the problem. I just don't know.

The door swung open and the smell of food filled the room. A young deputy from the Crow Ridge Sheriff's Department brought in several boxes, filled with plastic containers of food and cartons of coffee.

Potter's appetite returned suddenly as the trooper set out the containers. He expected tasteless diner fare—hot beef sandwiches and Jell-O. But the trooper pointed to each of the dishes as he laid them out and said, "That's cherry mos, that's zwieback, bratwurst, goat and lamb pie, sauerbraten, dill potatoes."

Derek Elb explained, "Heartland's a famous Mennonite restaurant. People drive there from all over the state."

For ten minutes, they ate, largely in silence. Potter tried to remember the names of the dishes to tell Cousin Linden when he returned to the Windy City. She collected exotic recipes. He was just finishing his second cup of coffee when, from the corner of his eye, he saw Tobe stiffen as a radio transmission came in. "What?" the young agent said in shock into his microphone. "Repeat that, Sheriff."

Potter turned to him.

"One of Dean's men just fished the twins out of the river!"

A collective gasp. Then, spontaneous applause erupted in the van. The intelligence officer plucked the two Post-It tabs representing the girls off the chart and moved them to the margin. He took down their pictures, which joined Jocylyn's, Shannon's, and Kielle's in the "Released" folder of hostage bios.

"They're being checked for hypothermia but they look fine otherwise. Like drowned rats, he said, but we're not supposed to tell the girls that."

"Call the hotel," Potter instructed. "Tell their parents."

Tobe, listening into his headset, laughed. He looked up. "They're on their way over, Arthur. They're insisting on seeing you."

"Me?"

"If you're an older man with glasses and a dark sports coat. Only they think your name is de l'Epée. . . ."

Potter shook his head. "Who?"

Frances laughed briefly. "Abbé de l'Epée. He created the first widely used sign language."

"Why would they call me that?"

Frances shrugged. "I have no idea. He's sort of a patron saint for the Deaf."

The girls arrived five minutes later. Adorable twins, wrapped up in colorful Barney blankets, no less (another of Stillwell's miracles). They no longer resembled wet rodents at all but girls more awestruck than scared as they stared at Potter. In halting sign language they explained through Frances about how Melanie had gotten them out of the slaughterhouse.

"Melanie?" Angie asked, nodding toward Potter. "I was wrong. Seems you do have an ally inside."

Did Handy know what she'd done? Potter wondered. How much more resistance would he tolerate before the payback? And how lethal would it be this time?

His heart froze as he saw Frances Whiting's eyes go wide with horror. She turned to him. "The girls didn't understand exactly what was going on but I think one of them was raping the teacher."

"Melanie?" Potter asked quickly.

"No. Donna Harstrawn."

"Oh, my good Lord, no," Budd muttered. "And they saw it, those girls?"

"Bonner?" Angie asked.

Potter's face showed none of the anguish he felt. He nodded. Of course it would be Bonner. His eyes strayed to the pictures of Beverly and Emily. Both young, both feminine.

And then to the photo of Melanie.

Angie asked the girls if Handy had, in effect, set Bonner on the woman, or if the big man had been acting by himself.

Frances watched the signing, then said, "Bear—that's what they're calling Bonner—looked around a lot while he was doing it. Like he didn't want to get caught. They think Brutus—Handy—would have been mad if he'd seen him."

"Is Brutus friendly with any of you?" Angie asked the twins.

"No. He's terrible. He just looks at us with cold eyes, like somebody in one of Shannon's cartoons. He beat up Melanie."

"Is she all right?"

One girl nodded.

Angie shook her head. "This isn't good." She looked at the diagram of the factory. "They're not that far apart, the hostages and the takers, but there doesn't seem to be *any* Stockholming going on with Handy."

The more I know about them the more I want to kill them.

Potter asked about guns and the tools and the TV. But the little girls could offer nothing new. Then one of them handed him a slip of paper. It was soggy but the lettering, written in the waterproof markers Derek had provided, was clear enough. "It's from Melanie," he said, then read out loud: *"Dear de l'Epée: There is so much to write to you. But no time. Be very careful of Handy. He's evil—more evil than anything. You should know: Handy and Wilcox are friends. Handy hates Bear (the fat one). Bear is greedy."*

LeBow asked for the paper so he could type it into the computer. "It's disintegrating," Potter told him. He read aloud again as the intelligence officer typed.

One of the twins stepped forward and signed timidly. Potter smiled and glanced queryingly at Frances.

"They want your autograph," she said.

"Mine?"

In perfect unison they nodded. Potter took a pen from his shirt pocket, the silver fountain pen that he always carried with him.

"They're expecting," Frances continued, " 'Abbé de l'Epée.' "

"Ah, yes. Of course. And that's what they'll have. One for each."

The girls looked at the two slips of paper and carried them reverently when they left. One girl paused and signed to Frances.

She said, "Melanie said something else. She said to tell you to be careful."

Be forewarned. . . .

"Show me how to say 'Thank you. You're very brave.' "

Frances did, and Potter mimicked the words with halting gestures. The girls broke into identical smiles then took Frances's hands as she escorted them to a trooper outside for the drive to the Days Inn.

Budd sat down next to Potter. "Why," he asked, "would Melanie tell us that?" He pointed to the note. "About Bonner being greedy, about the other two being friends?"

"Because she thinks there's something we can do with it," Angie said.

"What?"

Potter looked down at the soggy slip of paper. It was signed, *"Love, Melanie C."*—which was the reason he hadn't shown the note itself to Henry LeBow. He now folded it up, put the damp paper in his pocket.

"Look up Bonner," Potter instructed.

He read from the screen. Ray "Sonny" Bonner had led a useless life. He'd done time for sex offenses and minor robberies, domestic violence, public disorderliness. Lust-driven, not bright. He was a snitch too; he'd testified against his partner at a robbery trial ten years ago.

Potter and Angie looked up at each other. They smiled.

"Perfect."

The decision had been made. Potter would not meet with Handy face to face. A new strategy had presented itself. Riskier, yes. But perhaps better.

Charlie Budd was suddenly aware that both Angie and Potter were looking at him, studying him.

"What do *you* think, Henry?" Potter asked.

"Say—" Budd began uneasily.

"I think he's perfect," LeBow offered. "Earnest, straightforward. And he's got a great baritone."

Potter said, "You've got quite a performance ahead of you, Charlie."

"Me?" The young captain looked stricken. "How d'you mean that, exactly?"

"You're taking over the negotiation."

"What?"

"And I want you to talk to Handy about surrendering."

"Yessir," Budd answered Potter. Then: "You're kidding."

"You're perfect, Charlie," Angie said.

Potter said, "I've brought up the subject with him. Now it's time to raise surrender as a realistic possibility. Of course he'll say no. But it'll be in his mind as an option. He'll start to weigh the possibilities."

"There'll be a little more to it than that, though," LeBow said, eyes as ever on his screen.

"We're upping the ante," Potter said, and began to jot notes on a yellow pad.

"You know, I'm thinking I wouldn't be very good at this."

"You ever do any acting?" Angie asked.

"I dress up like Santa on Christmas for my kids and my brother's. That's it. Never been on stage, never wanted to be."

"I'll give you a script." Potter thought for a moment, then tore off the top sheets of the yellow pad and began again, writing meticulous notes: two pages' worth of dense writing.

"This is the gist of it. Just ad-lib. Can you read it okay?"

Budd scanned the sheets. "Sure, only I don't think I'm ready. I should practice or something."

"No time for practice," Potter told him. "Just let me give you a few pointers in negotiations."

"You're serious about this, aren't you?"

"Listen, Charlie. Concentrate. You've got to break through his barriers quickly and get him to believe this." He tapped the yellow paper.

Budd's face grew still and he sat forward in front of the desk on which rested the cellular phone.

"Now I want you to echo things he says. He'll say he wants ice cream. You say, 'Ice cream, sure.' He'll say he's angry. You say, 'Angry, are you?' It shows you're interested in what he says without expressing judgment. It wears him down and makes him think. Do it selectively, though. Not every comment or you'll antagonize him."

Budd nodded. He was sweating fiercely.

Angie offered, "Acknowledge his feelings but don't sympathize with him."

"Right," Potter continued. "He's the enemy. We don't sanction violence and therefore he's doing something wrong. But you should explain that you understand why he feels the way he does. Got it? Don't ramble. You have to be aware of how you sound and how fast you're talking. I'll tell you right now you'll be going way too fast. Make a conscious effort to talk slowly and deliberately. To you it'll feel like you're underwater."

Angie said, "If you ask him a question and he doesn't respond just let the silence run up. Don't let pauses rattle you."

"Don't let him manipulate you. He'll do it intentionally and subconsciously—using threats, fast speech, craziness, and silence. Just keep your mind on your goal." Again Potter, rather solemnly this time, tapped the yellow paper. "Most important, don't let him get to you. Let him rant and say terrible things but don't get shook up. Let him laugh at you. Let him insult you. It rolls off you. You're above it all." Potter leaned forward and whispered, "He might tell you he's going to kill all those girls. He may even fire the gun off and let you think he's shot someone. He might tell you he's going to torture them or rape them. Don't let it affect you."

"What do I say?" Budd said desperately. "If he says that, what do I say?"

"It's best not to say anything at all. If you feel compelled to respond you say simply that it wouldn't be in the best interests of a solution to do that."

"Oh, brother."

Potter looked at his watch. "Let's get this show on the road. Ready?" Potter asked.

The young captain nodded.

"Push button one."

"What?"

"It's on speed dial," Tobe explained. "Push number one."

"And then I just talk to him?"

"You understand the script?" Potter asked.

Budd nodded again. Potter pointed to the phone. "Oh, brother." He reached for the phone, dialed.

"Uplink," Tobe whispered.

"Hey. How you doing, Art?" The voice came through the speakers above their heads. Handy seemed to be smirking.

"This is Charlie Budd. Is this Lou Handy?"

"The fuck're you?"

Budd's eyes were on the sheet in front of him. "I'm with the U.S. attorney's office."

"The hell you say."

"I'd like to talk to you for a few minutes."

"Where's Art?"

"He's not here."

"What the fuck's going on?"

Budd swallowed. Come on, Charlie, Potter thought. No time for stage fright. He tapped the pad before Budd. "Going on?" the captain echoed. "What do you mean?"

"I only want to talk to *him*."

"To who?"

"Art Potter. Who the fuck do you think?"

Budd took a deep breath. "Well, why don'tcha talk to me? I'm not such a bad guy."

"U.S. attorney?"

"That's right. I want to talk to you about surrendering."

Slow down, Potter wrote.

"Oh, a shyster with a sense of humor. Well, fuck you."

Budd's face was relaxing. "Hey, don'tcha like lawyers?"

"I love 'em."

Budd said, "You wanta hear a joke, Lou?"

Potter and LeBow looked at each other, eyebrows raised.

"Sure, Charlie."

"A woman goes to her gynecologist and asks can somebody get pregnant by having anal sex. And the doctor says sure you can, where do you think lawyers come from?"

Handy roared with laughter. Budd's face burned crimson.

Potter had never in twenty years of negotiating shared a joke with a taker. Maybe he'd rewrite his instruction book.

Budd continued. "Arthur's seeing about getting you some helicopter or 'nother. Something about pontoons. It should be here soon."

"It fucking well better be here in one hour and twenty fucking minutes."

"Well, all I know is, Lou, he's doing what he can. But look here, even if you get the chopper they're gonna find you sooner or later." Budd stared at the sheet in front of him. "Soon as somebody finds out who you are, the fact you shot a girl in the back, you know what'll happen. They'll collar you and somehow you'll be riding in the back of a meat wagon and some accident'll happen."

"You threatening me?"

"Hell, no. I'm trying to save you. I'm just saying the way it is. The way you *know* it is."

"Ain't nobody gonna find me. So fuck that surrender shit. It ain't gonna happen. You assholes'll have to come in and get me 'fore I'd do that. And you'd find me atop six dead hostages."

Potter pointed to the pictures of the twins. LeBow frowned. Why didn't Handy know they were gone?

Budd continued, "Listen, Lou, we can offer you a deal."

"A deal? What kind of deal?"

"Some immunity. Not complete, but—"

"You know what I done here?"

"What you've done?" Echoing like a pro, Potter thought.

"I killed me a few people today. We're not talking immunity, we're talking . . . what the fuck's that thing priests give you?"

Budd looked up at Potter, who whispered, "Dispensation."

"Dispensation."

"So I don't think so, Charlie the butt-fucked lawyer. I think I need a helicopter or I'm going to turn my good friend Bonner here loose on a girl or two. You know Bonner? He stays hard twenty-four hours a day. Re-fucking-markable. Never seen anybody like him. You should've seen him in prison. Kid comes in for GTA and, bang, there's Bonner next to him 'fore the fingerprints're dry, saying, 'Bend over, pretty boy. Spread 'em.' "

Potter clamped his hand down on Budd's arm, seeing the anguish in his face. He tapped the yellow sheet once more.

"Where's Art?" Handy said suddenly. "I like him better'n you."

"He's out rustling up your helicopter, like I said."

"Fuck if he isn't listening to this right now on the squawk box. How close is he? He could probably stick his dick in your mouth without either of you moving. Hey, you a faggot, Charlie? Sound like one to me."

Budd adjusted his grip on the phone. "Agent Potter's trying to get you what you've been asking for."

They died because they didn't give me what I wanted. Potter nodded approval.

"I want that chopper or Bonner gets a girl."

"You don't need to do that, Lou. Come on. We're all working together here, aren't we?"

"Oh, I wasn't on your team last time I looked, Charlie."

Budd wiped sweat from his forehead. Potter, feeling very much like an orchestra conductor, gestured at Budd and pointed to a portion of the yellow sheet.

"My team?" Budd responded. "Hey now, that's wrong, Lou. I *am* on your team. And I want to offer you a deal. You and Wilcox."

Potter held his finger to his lips, indicating for Budd to pause. The captain swallowed. Angie handed him a cup of water. He drank it down, gave her a rueful smile.

Handy was silent.

Budd started to speak; Potter shook his head.

Finally Handy said, "Me and Shep?"

"That's right."

Cautiously: "What kinda deal?"

Budd looked down at the sheet. "We'll go for life only. No death penalty."

"For us two?"

Potter heard the uncertainty in Handy's voice. Beautiful, he thought. For the first time all night he's not sure what's going on. He gave Budd a thumbs-up.

"Just you and Wilcox," he said firmly.

"What about Bonner?"

Potter held up his wavering hands, indicating uncertainty.

"Well, I'm just talking about you two."

"Why aren't you talking about Bonner?"

Potter frowned angrily. Budd nodded and in a testy voice said, "Because I don't want to talk about Bonner. I'm offering you and Wilcox a deal."

"You're an asshole, Charlie."

"An asshole?"

"You're not telling me everything."

Potter touched his lips.

Silence.

Perfect, thought Potter. He's doing great. Finally he nodded to Budd.

"I *am* telling you everything." Budd gave up on the yellow sheet and stared out the window at the slaughterhouse. "And I'm telling it to you for your benefit as much as anybody's. You oughta surrender, sir. Even if you get out of here in that helicopter you'll be the most wanted man in North America. Your life's gonna be pure hell and if you get caught you'll get death. You know that. No statute of limitations for murder."

"What'm I supposed to say to Bonner?"

Potter made an angry fist.

"I don't much care what you say to him," Budd said gruffly. "He's not included in—"

"Why not?"

Hesitate, Potter wrote.

Handy broke the interminable silence. "What aren't you fucking telling me?"

"Do you want a deal or not? You and Wilcox. It'll save you from lethal injection."

"I want a fucking helicopter and that's what I'm going to get. Tell Art that. Fuck you all."

"No, wait—"

Click.

Budd closed his eyes and rested the phone on the table. His hands shook fiercely.

"Excellent, Charlie." Potter clapped him on the back.

"Good job," Angie said, winking at him.

Budd looked up, perplexed. "Excellent? He's all pissed off. He hung up on me."

"No, he's just where we want him." LeBow typed up the incident in the log and noted the time. On the "Deceptions" side of the board he wrote, *Federal plea bargain by "U.S. Attorney Budd"—Handy and Wilcox. Life sentences in lieu of death.*

Budd stood up. "You think?"

"You planted the seeds. We'll have to see if they take." Potter caught Angie's eye and they exchanged a solemn glance. The negotiator made a point of looking away before Budd noticed.

8:16 P.M.

"Five minutes and counting."

Dan Tremain had called the governor and together they had decided that the HRU rescue would go ahead as planned. Over the scrambled frequency he radioed this to his men.

Outrider One, Chuck Pfenninger, was in position near the command van, and Outrider Two, Joey Wilson, hidden behind the school bus, was prepared to lob the stun grenades through the front window. Alpha and Bravo teams were ready to make the dynamic entry through the northwest and southeast doors as planned.

Tremain was very confident. Although the HTs might be anticipating an attack through the one well-marked fire exit, they'd never expect the assault through the hidden southeast door.

In five minutes it would all be over.

Lou Handy stared down at the phone and felt it for the first time that day: doubt.

Son of a bitch.

"Where is he?" he snarled, looking through the slaughterhouse.

"Bonner? In with the girls," Wilcox answered. "Or eating. I don't know. What's up?"

"Something's funny going on." Handy paced back and forth. "I think maybe he cut a deal." He told Wilcox what the U.S. attorney had said.

"They're offering *us* a deal?"

"Some deal. Life in Leavenworth."

"Beats that little needle. The worst part is you piss. You know that? There's nothing you can do to stop it. I tell you, I'm going out, I don't want to piss my pants in front of everybody."

"Hey, homes." Handy dropped his head, gazed coolly at his partner. "We're getting out. Don't you forget it."

"Right, sure."

"I think that prick's been with 'em all along."

"Why?" Wilcox asked.

"Why the fuck you think? Money. Cut down his hard time."

Wilcox cast his eyes into the dim back of the slaughterhouse. "Sonny's an asshole but he wouldn't do that."

"He did a while back."

"What?"

"Give up somebody. A guy he did a job with."

"You *knew* that?" Wilcox asked, surprised.

"Sure, I knew that," Handy said angrily. "We needed him."

But how had Bonner gotten to the feds? Almost every minute of the big man's time was accounted for from the moment of the breakout.

Though not all of it, Handy now recalled. Bonner was the one who'd gone to pick up the car. After they'd gotten out of the prison Bonner had been gone for a half-hour while he picked up the wheels. Handy remembered thinking that it was taking him a long time and thinking, If he skips on us he's going to die real fucking slow.

Gone a half-hour to get a car eight blocks away. Plenty of time to call the feds.

"But he's a short-timer," Wilcox pointed out. Bonner's interstate transport sentence was four years.

"The kind," Handy countered, "they'd be most likely to cut a deal with. Feds never chop off sentences more'n a couple years."

Besides, Bonner had an incentive: sex offenders were the prisoners who most often woke up with glass shards shoved down their throat, or a tin-can-lid knife in their gut—or who didn't wake up at all.

Uncertainly Wilcox looked into the dim slaughterhouse. "Whatta you think?"

"I think we oughta talk to him."

They walked through the main room, over the rotting ramps the livestock had once ambled along, past the long tables where the animals had been cut apart, the rusting guillotines. The two men stood in the doorway of the killing room. Bonner wasn't there. They heard him standing not far away, pissing a solid stream into a well or sump pump.

Handy stared at the room—the older woman, lying curled into a ball. The gasping girl and the pretty girl. And then there was Melanie, who stared back with eyes that tried to be defiant but were just plain scared. Then he realized something.

"Where," Handy said softly, "are the little ones?"

He gazed at two empty pairs of black patent-leather shoes.

Wilcox spat out, "Son of a bitch." He ran into the hallway, following the tiny footprints in the dust.

Melanie put her arms around the girl with the asthma and cowered against the wall. Just then Bonner came around the corner and stopped. "Hey, buddy." He blinked uneasily, looking at Handy's face.

"Where are they, you fuck?"

"Who?"

"The little girls. The twins?"

"I—" Bonner recoiled. "I was watching 'em. All this time. I swear."

"All this time?"

"I took a piss is all. Look, Lou. They gotta be here someplace. We'll find 'em." The big man swallowed uneasily.

Handy glared at Bonner, who started toward Melanie, shouting, "Where the fuck are they?" He pulled his pistol from his pocket and walked up to her.

"Lou!" Wilcox was calling from the main room. "Jesus Christ."

"What?" Handy screamed, spinning around. "What the fuck is it?"

"We got a worse problem than that. Look here."

Handy hurried back to Wilcox, who was pointing at the TV.

"Holy Christ. Potter, that lying son of a bitch!"

On the screen: A newscast, showing the perfect telephoto image of the front and side of the slaughterhouse. The reporters had snuck through the police line and had set up the camera on something close and tall—maybe that old windmill just to the north. The camera was a little shaky but there was no doubt that they were looking at a fucking SWAT trooper at a front window—only twenty feet away from where Handy and Wilcox now stood.

"Is that more there?" Wilcox cried. He pointed to some bumps in a gully to the north of the slaughterhouse.

"Could be. Shit yes. Must be a dozen of them."

The newscaster said, "It looks like an assault could be imminent. . . ."

Handy looked up at the fire door on the north side of the factory. They'd wedged it shut but he knew that explosive charges could take it down in seconds. He shouted to Bonner, "Get that scatter gun, we got a firefight."

"Shit." Bonner pulled the slide back on the Mossberg, let it snap back.

"The roof?" Wilcox asked.

Those were the only two ways a hostage rescue team could get in quickly—the side door and the roof. The loading dock was too far back. But as he stared at the ceiling he saw a thick network of ducts and vents and conveyors. Even if they blew through the roof itself they'd have to cut through those utility systems.

Handy glanced out over the field in front of the slaughterhouse. Aside from the trooper by the window—hidden from the police lines by the school bus—no other cops seemed to be approaching from that direction.

"They're coming through that side door there."

Handy moved slowly toward the window where the trooper was hiding. He gestured to Wilcox's gun. The lean man grinned and pulled his pistol from his belt, pulled the slide, chambering a round.

"Go behind him," Handy whispered. "Other window. Get his attention."

Wilcox nodded, dropped suddenly to his belly, and crawled off to the far window. Handy too crawled—to the open window outside of which the trooper was hiding. Wilcox put his mouth next to a hole in a shattered pane and gave the warble of a wild turkey. Handy couldn't suppress his smile.

When Wilcox warbled again Handy looked outside quickly. He saw the trooper, only two feet away, turning toward the sound in confusion. Handy reached out the window, grabbed the trooper's helmet, and, jerking hard, lifted him off the ground. The man let go of his machine gun, which dangled from his shoulder by a leather thong, and grasped Handy's wrists, struggling fiercely as the helmet strap choked him. Wilcox leapt to Handy's side and together they muscled the trooper through the window.

As Handy held him in a full nelson Wilcox kicked him in the groin and pulled his machine gun, pistol, and grenades away. He crumpled and fell to the floor.

"You son of a bitch," Handy raged, kicking the man violently. "Lemme look at you!" He ripped off the trooper's helmet, hood, and goggles. He bent his face low. Handy pulled his knife from his pocket and flicked it open, held the blade against the young man's cheek. "Shoot me in the back? That's the kind of balls you have? Come up behind a man like a fucking nigger!"

The trooper struggled. Handy slashed the knife downward, drawing a streak of blood along his jawline. He slammed his fist into the man's face once, then again, a dozen times, stepped away and turned back, kicking him in the belly and groin.

"Hey, Lou, take it—"

"Fuck him! He was going to shoot me in the back! He was going to shoot me in the fucking back! Is that what kind of man you are? That's what you think of honor?"

"Fuck *you*," the trooper gasped, rolling on the floor, helpless. Handy turned him over, slugged him in the lower back, handcuffed him with the boy's own cuffs.

"Where are the rest of 'em?" Handy poked the knife into the trooper's thigh, a shallow cut. "Tell me!" he raged. He pushed further. The man screamed.

Handy leaned his face close, inches away from the trooper's face.

"Straight to hell, Handy. That's where *you* can go."

The knife slipped further in. Another scream. Handy reached out and touched a tiny sphere of the tear. It clung to his finger, which he lifted to his tongue. Pushed the knife into the thigh a little bit more. More screaming.

Let's see when this boy breaks.

"Oh, Jesus," the man moaned.

Have to happen sooner or later. Just work our way north with this little bit o' Buck steel and see when he starts squealing. He begun to saw slowly with the blade, working his way toward the trooper's groin.

"I don't *know* where the rest of 'em are! I'm just fucking reconnaissance."

Handy suddenly got tired of the knife and beat him again with his fist, angrier than ever. "How many? Where're they coming in through?"

The trooper spat on his leg.

And suddenly Handy was back years ago, seeing Rudy sneer at him— well, it was probably a sneer. Seeing him turn away, Handy's two hundred dollars in his brother's wallet—he *thought* it was there, probably was. Seeing Rudy walk away like Handy was a piece of dried shit. The anger cutting through him like a carbon-steel blade in somebody's hot belly.

"Tell me!" he screamed. His fist rose again and again and smashed into the trooper's face. Finally, he stood back. "Fuck him. Fuck 'em all." Handy ran into the killing room and tipped the pot containing the gasoline over. The room filled with the chill liquid, splashing on the women and girls. Melanie the scared mouse-cunt pulled them into a corner but still they were doused.

Handy held the trooper's submachine gun toward the side door. "Shep, they're gonna come through there fast. As soon as they do I'm going to shoot a couple of 'em in the legs. You pitch that"—nodding at the grenade—"into the room, set off the gas. I want to keep some of them cops alive to tell everybody what happened to those girls. What it looked like when they burnt up."

"Yo, homes. You got it." Wilcox pulled the pin out of the smooth black grenade and, holding the delay handle, stepped into the doorway of the killing room. Handy pulled back the bolt of the H&K, aimed it at the door.

"Arthur, we have some movement by the window," Dean Stillwell said over the radio. "The one second to the left from the front door."

Potter acknowledged his transmission and looked out the window with field glasses. His vision of that window was blocked by the school bus and a tree.

"What was it, Dean?"

"One of my men said it looked like somebody going through the window."

"One of the HTs?"

"No, I meant going *in* the window."

"In? Any confirmation?"

"Yessir, another trooper said she saw it too."

"Well—"

"Oh, Jesus," Tobe whispered. "Arthur, look."

"Who are they?" Angie snapped. "Who the hell *are* they?"

Potter turned and glanced at the TV monitor she was gazing at. It took a moment to realize he was looking at a newscast—the monitor that had been tuned to the Weather Channel. To his horror he realized he was watching an assault on the slaughterhouse.

"Wait a minute," Budd said. "What's going on?"

". . . exclusive footage. It appears that one of the troopers outside the slaughterhouse has just been kidnaped himself."

"Where's the camera?" an astounded LeBow said.

"Can't worry about that now," Potter said. The involuntary thought popped into his mind: Is this Henderson's revenge?

"Tremain," LeBow called out. "It's Tremain."

"Fuck," said good Catholic Tobe. "*Those* were the scrambled messages we were picking up. He's put an operation together."

"The trap inside! Tremain doesn't know about it."

"Trap?" Derek asked nervously.

Potter looked up, shocked. He understood instantly the depth of the betrayal. Derek Elb had been feeding the Hostage Rescue Unit information about the barricade. Had to be. "What's Tremain's frequency?" he shouted, leaping over the table and grabbing the young trooper by the collar.

Derek was shaking his head.

"Tell him, goddamnit!" Budd shouted.

"I don't have access. It's field-set. There's no way to break in."

"I can crack it," Tobe said.

"No, it's retrosignaling, it'll take you an hour. I'm sorry, I didn't know. . . . I didn't know anything about a trap." Potter recalled that they had been outside when they'd learned about the bomb—at the field hospital.

Budd raged, "He's got a firebomb rigged up in there, Sergeant."

"Oh, God, no," Derek muttered.

Potter grabbed the phone. He dialed. There was no answer. "Come on, Lou. Come on! . . . Tobe, is SatSurv still on line?"

"Yep." He slammed his finger into a button. A monitor burst to life. It was essentially the same green-and-blue image of the grounds they'd seen before, but now there were ten little red dots clustered on either side of the slaughterhouse.

"They're in those gullies there. Probably going in through the northwest and southeast windows or doors. Give me a high-speed printout."

"You got it. Black-and-white'll be faster."

"Do it!" As the machine buzzed, Potter pressed the phone to his ear, hearing the calm, unanswered ringing on the other end. "Lou, Lou, Lou, come on. . . . Answer!"

He slammed it down. "Henry, what'll they do?"

LeBow leapt up and stared at the printout as it spewed from the machine. "Blow in the door here, on the left. But I don't know what they're doing on the right side. There's no door. You can't use cutting charges to breach a structural wall." He pointed at the mounted diagram of the processing plant. "Look there. That dotted line. That might've been a door at one time. Tremain must have found it. They're going in from both sides."

"Single-file?"

"Two-man entry but tandem, yeah. They'll have to."

"It's—"

The bang was very soft. Suddenly the van went dark. Frances gave a short scream. Only an eerie yellow glow from the thick windows and the twin blue screens of Henry LeBow's computers illuminated the pungent interior.

"Lost power," Tobe said. "We—"

"Arthur!" LeBow was pointing out the window at the flames that were rolling up the side of the van.

"What happened? Jesus, did Handy hit us?"

Potter ran to the door. He pulled it open and cried out, leaping back from the tongue of flames and the searing heat that flowed into the van. Slammed the door.

"We can't power up," Tobe said. "Backup's gone too."

"How long do I have?" he raged at Derek.

"I—"

"Answer me or you'll be in jail in an hour. How long from the time the power goes out till they attack?"

"Four minutes," Derek whispered. "Sir, I was just doing what—"

"No, Arthur," Angie called, "don't open it!"

Potter flung the door open. He flew backwards as his sleeves ignited. Outside all they could see was an ocean of flame. Then the black smoke of burning rubber and oil poured inside, sending them to the floor in search of air.

Disengaging his scrambler, Dan Tremain broadcast, "Agent Potter, Agent Potter! This is Captain Tremain. Come in, please. Are you all right?"

Tremain watched the fire on the hill. It was alarming, the orange flames and the black smoke, swirling in a tornado. He knew all about the van, had used it himself often, and knew that those inside were safe as long as they kept the door closed. Still, it was a terrible conflagration.

No time to think about that now. He called again, "Agent Potter . . . Derek? Is anyone in the command van? Please report."

"This is Sheriff Stillwell, who's calling?"

"Captain Dan Tremain, state police. What's going on?"

"The van's on fire, sir. We don't know. Handy may've made a lucky shot."

Thank you, Sheriff, Tremain thought. The conversations were being recorded at state police headquarters. Stillwell's comment would more than justify Tremain's action.

"Is everyone all right?" the HRU commander asked.

"We can't get close to the van. We don't—"

Tremain cut off the transmission and ordered, on the scrambled frequency, "Alpha team, Bravo team. Code word Filly. Code word Filly. Arm the cutting charges. Sixty seconds to detonation."

"Alpha. Armed."

"Bravo. Armed."

"Fire in the hole," Tremain called, and lowered his head.

Arthur Potter, fifteen pounds overweight and never athletic, rolled to the ground just past the flames that two troopers were trying unsuccessfully to douse with fire extinguishers.

He hit the ground and stared in alarm at his flaming sleeves. One trooper cried out and blasted him with carbon dioxide. The icy spray stung his hands more than the burn had though he saw the wounds on his skin and knew what kind of agony he could anticipate later.

If he lived to later.

No time, no time at all . . .

He rolled to his feet and ignored the embers smoldering on his jacket, the pain searing his skin. He began to jog, clicking on the bullhorn.

Potter struggled across the field, through the line of police cars and directly toward the slaughterhouse. He gasped as he shouted, "Lou Handy, listen to me! Listen. This is Art Potter. Can you hear me?"

Sixty yards, fifty.

No response. Tremain's men would be moving in at any minute.

"Lou, you're about to be attacked. It's an unauthorized operation. I had nothing to do with it. Repeat: It's a mistake. The officers are in two gullies to the north and the south of the slaughterhouse. You can set up a crossfire from the two windows on those sides. Do you hear me, Lou?"

He was gasping for breath and struggling to call out. A pain shot through his chest and he had to slow down.

A perfect target, he stood on the crest of a hill—the very place where Susan Phillips had been shot in the back—and shouted, "They're about to blow the side doors but you can stop them before they get inside. Set up crossfire positions in the southeast and the northwest windows. There's a door on the south side you don't know about. It's covered up but it's there. They're going to blow their way in from there too, Lou. Listen to me. I want you to shoot for their legs. They have body armor. Shoot for their legs! Use shotguns. Shoot for their legs."

No movement inside the slaughterhouse.

Oh, please. . . .

"Lou!"

Silence. Except for the urgent wind.

Then he noticed movement from the gully to the north of the slaughterhouse. A helmet rising from a stand of buffalo grass. A flash as a pair of binoculars turned his way.

Or was it the telescopic sight of an H&K MP-5?

"Lou, do you hear me?" Potter called again. "This is an unauthorized operation. Set up crossfire positions on the north door and the south door. There'll be plasterboard or something covering the doorway on the south."

Nothing . . . silence.

Somebody please . . .

For God's sake, talk to me. Somebody!

Then: movement. Potter looked toward it—just to the north of the slaughterhouse.

On the crest of a hill seventy-five, eighty yards away a man in black stood, his hip cocked, an H&K on a strap at his side, staring at Potter. Then one by one the troopers in the gullies on either side of the slaughterhouse rose and slithered away from the doors. The helmeted heads bobbed up and retreated into the bushes. HRU was standing down.

From the slaughterhouse there was nothing but silence. But Arthur Potter still was heartsick. For he knew that there would have to be a reparation. As amoral and cruel as Handy was, the one thing he'd done consistently was keep his word. Handy's world may have run on a justice of his own making, an evil justice, but justice it was nonetheless. And it was the good guys who'd just broken faith.

Potter, LeBow, and Budd stood back, arms crossed, while Tobe desperately ran wires, cutting and splicing.

Potter watched Derek Elb being escorted away by two of Pete Henderson's agents and asked Tobe, "Sabotage?"

Tobe—nearly as good at ballistics as he was at electronics—couldn't say for certain. "Looks like a simple gasoline fire. We were running a lot of juice out of the generator. But somebody could've slipped in an L210 and we'd be none the wiser. Anyway I can't look for anything now." And he stripped, joined, and taped a dozen wires at once, it seemed.

LeBow said, "You know it is, Arthur."

Potter agreed, of course. Tremain had probably left a remote-controlled incendiary device in the generator of the van.

Incredulous, Budd asked, "He'd do something like that? What are you going to do?"

The negotiator said, "Nothing right now." In his heart he lived too far in the past; in his career, he lived there hardly at all. Potter had no time or taste for revenge. Now he had the hostages to think about. Hurry, Tobe, get the lines running again.

Officer Frances Whiting returned to the van. She'd been inhaling oxygen at the medical tent. Her face was smudged and she breathed with some difficulty, but otherwise she was okay.

"Little more excitement than you're used to in Hebron?" Potter asked her.

"Not counting traffic citations, my last collar was when Bush was in office."

The smell of scorch and burnt rubber and plastic was overwhelming. Potter's arms were streaked with burn. The hair on the backs of his hands was gone and one searing patch on his wrist raged with pain. But he couldn't take the time to see the medics just yet. He had to make contact with Handy first, try to minimize whatever payback was undoubtedly fermenting in Handy's mind.

"Okay," Tobe called. "Got it." The miracle worker had run a line from the remote generator truck and the van was up and running again.

Potter was about to tell Budd to prop the door open to air the place out when he realized there was no door. It had been burned away. He sat down at the desk, grabbed the phone, and dialed.

The electronic sound of a ringing phone filled the van.

No answer.

Behind them Henry LeBow had begun to type again. The sound of the muted keys more than anything else restored Potter's confidence. Back in business, he thought. And turned his attention to the phone.

Answer, Lou. Come on. We've got too much behind us to let it fall apart now. There's too much history, we've gotten too close. . . .

Answer the damn phone!

A loud squeal outside, so close that Potter thought at first it was feedback. Roland Marks's limo bounded to a stop and he leapt from the car, glancing briefly at the scorched van. "I saw the news!" he shouted to no one in particular. "What the fuck happened?"

"Tremain went rogue," Potter said, pressing redial once more and eyeing the lawyer coldly.

"He *what?*"

LeBow explained.

Budd said, "We didn't have a clue, sir."

"I want to talk to that fellow, oh, yes I do," Marks grumbled. "Where—?"

Then there was a rush of motion from the doorway and Potter was knocked sideways. He fell heavily on his back, grunted.

"You son of a bitch!" Tremain cried. "You fucking son of a bitch!"

"Captain!" Marks roared.

Budd and Tobe grabbed the HRU commander's arms, pulled him off. Potter rose slowly. He touched his head where he'd banged it in the fall. No blood. He gestured for the two men to release Tremain. Reluctantly they did.

"He's got one of my men, Potter. Thanks to you, you fucking Judas."

Budd stiffened and stepped forward. Potter waved him down and straightened his tie, glancing at the burns on the backs of his hands. Large blisters had formed and the pain was really quite remarkable.

"Tobe," he said calmly, "run the tape, would you please? The KFAL tape."

There was a hum of a VCR and a monitor burst to life. A red-white-and-blue TV station logo appeared on the bottom of the screen, along with the words *Reporting Live . . . Joe Silbert.*

"Oh, that's brilliant," Marks said sourly, staring at the screen.

"He's got one of your men," Potter said, "because you dismissed the troopers who were preventing reporters from getting near the site."

"What?" Tremain stared at the newscast.

LeBow continued to type. Without looking up he said, "Handy saw you moving in. He's got a TV inside."

Tremain didn't answer. Potter wondered if he was thinking, Name, rank, serial number.

"Expected better of you, Dan," the assistant attorney general said.

"The governor—" he blurted before he thought better of it. "Well, even if he did, we could've saved those girls. They'd be out by now. We still could have gotten them out safe!"

Why aren't I angry? Potter wondered. Why aren't I raging at him, this man who nearly ruined everything? Who nearly killed the girls inside, who nearly killed Melanie? *Why?*

Because it's crueler this way, Potter understood suddenly. To tell him the truth starkly and without emotion.

Ever done anything bad, Art?

"Handy rigged a booby trap, Captain," Potter said, calm as a deferential butler. "A gasoline bomb on a hair trigger. Those girls would've burned to death the instant you blew those doors."

Tremain stared at him. "No," he whispered. "Oh, no. God forgive me. I didn't know." The sinewy man looked like he was going to faint.

"Downlink," Tobe called.

An instant later the phone rang. Potter snatched it up.

"Lou?"

That sucked, Art. I thought you were my friend.

"Well, Art. That was pretty fucking low. Some goddamn friend you are."

"I had nothing to do with it." Potter's eyes were on Tremain. "We had an officer here go rogue."

"These boys have some nice equipment. We've got some grenades and a machine gun now."

Potter pointed to LeBow, who pulled Tremain aside and asked the numb captain what kind of armament the captured trooper had with him.

A figure appeared in the doorway. Angie. Potter waved her in.

"Lou," the negotiator said into the phone, "I'm apologizing for what happened. It won't happen again. You have my word on that. You heard me out there. I gave you good tactical information. You know it wasn't anything I'd planned."

"I suppose you've got those girls by now. The little ones."

"Yes, we do, Lou."

"That U.S. attorney, Budd . . . he set us up, didn't he, Art?"

Again a hesitation. "I have no knowledge to that effect."

He's going to be very reasonable, Potter surmised.

Or go totally nuts.

"Ha. You're a kicker, Art. Well, okay, I believe you about this D-Day shit. You tell me there was some crazy cop doing things he shouldn't oughta've. But you should've been more in charge, Art. It's the way the law works, isn't that right? You're responsible for things people work for you do."

Angie was frowning.

"What?" Budd asked, seeing the hopeless expression on her face. It matched that on Potter's.

"What's the matter?" Frances Whiting whispered.

Potter grabbed the field glasses, wiped the greasy smoke residue off them, and looked out.

Oh, Christ, no . . . Desperately Potter said, "Lou, it was a *mistake*."

"You shoot at Shep it was a mistake. You don't get me my chopper on time it's not your fault. . . . Don't you know me by now, Art?"

Only too well.

Potter set down the glasses. He turned away from the window, glanced up at the pictures above the diagram of the slaughterhouse. Who will it be? he wondered.

Emily?

Donna Harstrawn?

Beverly?

Potter thinks suddenly: Melanie. He's going to pick Melanie.

Frances understood and cried out, "No, please no. Do something!"

"There's nothing *to* do," Angie whispered.

Tremain leaned his miserable face down to the window and looked out.

Handy's voice filled the van. He sounded reasonable, wise. "You're a lot like me, Art. Loyal. That's what I think. You're loyal to them that do what they're supposed to and you don't have time for those that don't." A pause. "You know just what I'm saying, don't you, Art? I'll leave the body outside. You can come get it. Flag of truce."

"Lou, isn't there anything I can do?" Potter heard the desperation in his own voice. Hated it. But it was there just the same.

Who will it be?

Angie had turned away.

Budd shook his head sorrowfully. Even boisterous Roland Marks could find nothing to say.

"Tobe," Potter said softly, "please turn down the volume."

He did. But still everyone jumped at the stark sound of the gunshot, which filled the van as a huge metallic ring.

As he stumbled toward the slaughterhouse, where the body lay pale in the halogen lights, he pulled off his flak jacket and dropped it on the ground. His helmet too he left behind.

Dan Tremain walked on, tears in his eyes, gazing at the still body, the bloody body, lying in the posture of a rag doll.

He crested the rise and saw from the corner of his eye troopers standing from their places of cover. They were staring at him; they knew he was responsible for what had happened, for this unconscionable death. He was walking up Calvary Hill.

And in the window of the processing plant: Lou Handy, a gun pointed directly at Tremain's chest. It made no difference, he was no threat; the captain had dropped the utility belt holding his Glock service pistol some yards back. On he stumbled, nearly falling, then just catching his balance like a drunk with some irrepressible sense of survival. His despair was deepened by Lou Handy's face—the red eyes, set back under bony brows, the narrow jaw, the five o'clock shadow. He was smiling, an innocuous smile of curiosity, as he gazed at the sorrow on the cop's face. Sampling, tasting.

Tremain gazed at the body lying there in front of him. Fifty feet away, forty. Thirty.

I'm mad, Tremain thought. And continued to walk, staring into the black eye of the muzzle of Handy's gun.

Twenty feet. Blood so red, skin so pale.

Handy's mouth was moving but Tremain could hear nothing. Maybe God's judgment is to make me deaf as those poor girls.

Ten feet. Five.

He slowed. The troopers were standing now, all of them, staring at him. Handy could pick any of them off, as they could him, but there would be no shooting. This was the Christmas Eve during World War I when the enemy troops shared carols and food. And helped each other collect and bury the shattered bodies strewn throughout no-man's-land.

"What have I done?" he muttered. He dropped to his knees and touched the cold hand.

He cried for a moment then hefted the body of the trooper in his arms—Joey Wilson, Outrider Two—and lifted it effortlessly, looking into the window. At Handy's face, which was no longer smiling but, oddly, curious. Tremain memorized the foxlike cast of his face, the cold eyes, the way the tip of his tongue lay against his upper lip. They were only feet apart.

Tremain turned and started back to the police line. In his mind he heard a tune, floating aimlessly. He couldn't think of what it might be for a minute then the generic instrument turned into the bagpipe he remembered from years ago and the tune became "Amazing Grace," the traditional song played at the funerals of fallen policemen.

8:45 P.M.

Arthur Potter thought about the nature of silence.

Sitting in the medical tent. Staring at the floor as medics attended to his burnt arms and hands.

Days and weeks of silence. Silence thicker than wood, perpetual silence. Is that what Melanie's day-to-day life was like?

He himself had known quiet. An empty house. Sunday mornings, filled only with the faint tapping of household motors and pumps. Still summer afternoons by himself on a back porch. But Potter was a man who lived in a state of anticipation and for him the silence was, on good days at least, the waiting state before his life might begin again—when he would meet someone like Marian, when he would find someone other than takers and terrorists and psychos with whom he might share his thoughts.

Someone like Melanie? he wondered.

No, of course not.

He felt a chill on the back of his hand and watched the medic apply some kind of ointment, which had the effect of dulling most of the stinging immediately.

Arthur Potter thought of Melanie's photograph, saw it hanging over the diagram of the slaughterhouse. He thought of his reaction when he understood, a few minutes ago, that Handy was going to kill another hostage. She was the first person in his mind.

He stretched. A joint somewhere in his back popped softly and he admonished himself: Don't be a damn fool. . . .

But in another part of his lavish mind Arthur Potter English-lit major thought, If we have to be foolish it ought to be in love. Not in our careers, where lives hang in the balance; not with our gods or in our lust for beauty and learning. Not with our children, so desirous and so unsure. But in love. For love is nothing but the purest folly and we go there for the purpose of *being* impassioned and half-crazy. In matters of the heart the world will always be generous with us, and forgiving.

Then he laughed to himself and shook his head as reality descended once more—like the dull ache that returned along his seared arms. She's twenty-five—less than half your age. She's deaf, both lower- and upper-case. And, for heaven's sake, it's your wedding anniversary today. Twenty-three years. Not a single one missed. Enough nonsense. Get back to the command van. Get to work.

The medic tapped him on the shoulder. Potter looked up, startled.

"You're all set, sir."

"Yes, thank you."

He rose and walked unsteadily back to the van.

A figure appeared in the doorway.

Potter looked up at Peter Henderson. "You all right?" the SAC asked.

He nodded cautiously. Tremain might have been the main perp but Potter would have bet a week's salary that Henderson had played some role in the assault. Ambition? A desire to get back at the Bureau, which betrayed him? Yet this would be even harder to prove than the existence of the suspected gas bomb in the generator. Forensics of the heart are always elusive.

Henderson looked at the burns. "You'll get yourself a medal for this."

"My first wound in the line of duty." Potter smiled.

"Arthur, I just wanted to apologize for losing my temper before. It gets dull down here. I was hoping for some action. You know how it is."

"Sure, Pete."

"I miss the old days."

Potter shook the man's hand. They talked about Joe Silbert and his fellow reporters. They'd refer the matter to the U.S. attorney but concluded there was probably nothing to hold them for. Obstruction of justice is a tricky charge and absent interfering with an ongoing criminal prosecution judges usually come down on the side of the First Amendment. Potter had contented himself by walking ominously up to Silbert, who stood in a circle of troopers, cool as a captured revolutionary leader. The agent had told him that he was going to cooperate in every way with the widow of the dead trooper, who would undoubtedly be bringing a multimillion-dollar wrongful-death action against the TV station and Silbert and Biggins personally.

"I intend to be a plaintiff's witness," Potter explained to the reporter, whose facade cracked momentarily, revealing beneath it a very scared, middle-aged man of questionable talents and paltry liquidity.

The negotiator now sat back in his chair and gazed at the slaughterhouse through the yellow window.

"How many minutes to the next deadline?"

"Forty-five."

Potter sighed. "That's going to be a big one. I'll have to do some thinking about it. Handy's mad now. He lost control in a big way."

Angie said, "And what's worse is that you helped him get it back. Which is a form of losing control in itself."

"So he's resentful in general and resentful at me in particular."

"Though he probably doesn't know it," Angie said.

"It's lose-lose." Potter's eyes were on Budd, gazing mournfully at the slaughterhouse.

The phone buzzed. Tobe picked it up, blew soot off the receiver, and answered. "Yeah," the young man said. "I'll tell him." He hung up. "Charlie, that was Roland Marks. He asked if you could come see him right away. He's got his friend with him. Somebody he wants you to meet. He said it's critical."

The captain kept his eye on the battlefield. "He's . . . Where is he?"

"Down by the rear staging area."

"Uh-huh. Okay. Say, Arthur, can I talk to you for a minute?"

"Sure you can."

"Outside?"

"Taken up imaginary smoking, have you?" Potter asked.

"Arthur started a trend in Special Ops," Tobe said. "Henry's taken up imaginary sex."

"Tobe," barked LeBow, typing away madly.

The young agent added, "I'm not being critical, Henry. *I'm* going to imaginary AA."

Budd smiled wanly and he and Potter stepped outside. The temperature had dropped ten degrees and it seemed to the negotiator that the wind was worse.

"So, what's up, Charlie?"

They stopped walking. The men gazed at the van and the burnt field around it—the devastation that the fire had caused.

"Arthur, there's something I have to tell you." He reached into his pocket and pulled out a tape recorder. He looked down and turned it over and over in his hands.

"Oh," the agent said. "About this?" Potter held up a small cassette.

Budd frowned and flipped open the recorder. There was a cassette inside.

"That one's blank," Potter said. "It's a special cassette. Can't be recorded on."

Budd pushed the play button. The hiss of static brayed from the tiny speaker.

"I knew all about it, Charlie."

"But—"

"Tobe has his magic wands. They pick up magnetic recording equipment. We're always sweeping locations for bugs. He told me somebody had a recorder. He narrowed it down to you."

"You knew?" He stared at the agent, then shook his head in disgust with himself—for having been outsmarted at something he didn't think was very smart to begin with.

"Who was it?" Potter asked. "Marks? Or the governor?"

"Marks. Those girls . . . he's really in a state about them. He wanted to give Handy whatever he wanted in order to get them released. Then he was going to track him down. He had this special homing device he was going to put in the chopper. You could track 'em from a hundred miles away and they'd never know."

Potter nodded at the crestfallen captain. "I figured it was something like that. Any man willing to sacrifice himself is willing to sacrifice somebody else."

"But how'd you swap the cassettes?" Budd asked.

Angie Scapello stepped down through the open doorway of the van and nodded a greeting to the men. She walked past Budd, touching his arm very lightly as she passed.

"Hi, Charlie."

"Hey, Angie," he said, not smiling.

"Say, what time do you have?" she asked him.

He lifted his left wrist. "Hell, it's gone. My watch. Damn. And Meg just gave it to me for my—"

Angie held up the Pulsar.

Budd was nodding, understanding it all. "Got it," he said, and hung his head even lower, if that was possible. "Oh, brother."

"I used to teach the pickpocket recognition course at Baltimore PD," she explained. "I borrowed the recorder when we were strolling around in the gully—having our loyalty talk—and switched cassettes."

Budd smiled miserably. "You're good. I'll give you that. Oh, man. I've been messin' up all night long. I don't know what to say. I've let you down."

"You confessed. No harm done."

"It was Marks?" Angie asked.

"Yep." Budd sighed. "At first I was thinking like him—that we should do anything to save those girls. I gave Arthur an earful about that this morning. But you were right, a life's a life. Doesn't matter if it's a girl or a trooper. We gotta stop him here."

"I appreciate that Marks had noble motives," Potter said. "But we have to do things a certain way. Acceptable losses. Remember?"

Budd closed his eyes. "Man, I almost ruined your career."

The negotiator laughed. "You didn't come close, Captain. Believe me, you were the only one at risk. If you'd given that tape to anyone *your* career in law enforcement would've been over."

Budd looked very flustered then stuck out his hand.

Potter shook it warmly though Budd didn't grip it very hard, either out of shame or out of concern about the fluffy pads of bandages on the agent's skin.

They all fell silent as Potter gazed up at the sky. "When's the deadline?"

Budd looked again at his wrist blankly for a moment then he realized that he was holding his watch in his right hand. "Forty minutes. What's the matter?" The captain's eyes lifted to the same jaundiced cloud that Potter was targeting.

"I'm getting a bad feeling about this one. This deadline."

"Why?"

"I just am."

"Intuition," Angie said. "Listen to him, Charlie. He's usually right."

Budd looked down from the sky and found Potter looking at him. "I'm sorry, Arthur. I'm plumb outta ideas."

Potter's eyes zipped back and forth over the grass, blackened by the fire and by the shadow of the van. "A helicopter," he blurted suddenly.

"What?"

Potter felt a keen sense of urgency seize him. "Get me a helicopter."

"But I thought we weren't going to give him one."

"I just need to show him one. A big one. At least a six-seater— eight- or ten- if you can find one."

"If *I* can find one?" Budd exclaimed. "Where? How?"

A thought slipped into Potter's mind from somewhere.

Airport.

There was an airport nearby. Potter tried to remember. How did he know that? Had somebody told him? He hadn't driven past it. Budd hadn't told him; SAC Henderson hadn't said anything. Where—

It was Lou Handy. The taker had mentioned it as a possible source of a helicopter. He must've driven by it on the way here.

He told this to Budd.

"I know it," the captain said. "They got a couple choppers there but

I don't know if there's anybody's there who can even fly one. I mean, if we found one in Wichita they might make it here in time. But hell, it'll take more'n forty minutes to track down a pilot."

"Well, forty minutes is all we have, Charlie. Get a move on."

"The truth . . ." Melanie is crying.

And de l'Epée is the one person she doesn't want to cry in front of. But cry she does. He rises from his chair and sits on the couch next to her.

"The truth is," she continues, "that I just don't like who I am, what I've become, what I'm a part of."

It's time to confess and nothing can stop her now.

"I told you about how I lived for being Deaf. It became my whole life?"

"Miss Deaf Farmhand of the Year."

"I didn't want any of it. Not. One. Bit." She grows vehement. "I got so damn tired of the self-consciousness of it all. The politics of being part of the Deaf world, the prejudice the Deaf have—oh, it's there. You'd be surprised. Against minorities and other handicapped. I'm tired of it! I'm tired of not having my music. I'm tired of my father . . ."

"Yes, what?" he asks.

"I'm tired of him using it against me. My deafness."

"How does he do that?"

"Because it makes me more scared than I already am! It keeps me at home. That piano I told you about? The one I wanted to play 'A Maiden's Grave' on? They sold it when I was nine. Even though I could still hear enough to play and could for a couple years more. They said—well, *he* said, my father said—they didn't want me to learn to love something that would be taken away from me." She adds, "But the real reason was that he wanted to keep me on the farm."

So you'll be home then.

Melanie looks into de l'Epée's eyes and says what she's never said to anyone. "I can't hate him for wanting me to stay at home. But selling the piano—that hurt so much. Even if I'd had only one day of playing music it would have been better than nothing. I'll never forgive him for that."

"They had no right to do that," he agrees. "But you managed to break away. You've got a job away from home, you're independent. . . ." His voice fades.

And now for the hard part.

"What is it?" de l'Epée asks softly.

"A year ago," she begins, "I bought some new hearing aids. Generally they don't work at all but these seemed to have some effect with certain pitches of music. There was a recital in Topeka I wanted to go to. Kathleen Battle. I'd read in the paper that she was going to sing some spirituals as part of the program and I thought . . ."

"That she'd sing 'Amazing Grace'?"

"I wanted to see if I could hear it. I was desperate to go. But I had no way of getting there. I can't drive and the buses would have taken forever. I begged my brother to take me. He'd been working all day on the farm but he said he'd take me anyway."

"We got there just in time for the concert. Kathleen Battle walked out on stage wearing this beautiful blue dress. She smiled to the audience. . . . And then she began to sing."

"And?"

"It was useless." Melanie breathes deeply, kneads her fingers. "It . . ."

"Why are you so sad?"

"The hearing aids didn't work at all. Everything was muddled. I could hardly hear anything and the notes I could hear were all off key to me. We left at intermission. Danny was doing his best to cheer me up. He . . ."

She falls silent.

"There's more, isn't there? There's something else you want to tell me."

It hurts so much! She only thinks these words but according to the fishy rules of her music room de l'Epée can hear them perfectly. He leans forward. "What hurts? Tell me?"

And there's so much to tell him. She could use a million words to describe that night and never convey the horror of living through it.

"Go ahead," de l'Epée says encouragingly. As her brother used to do, as her father never did. "Go ahead."

"We left the concert hall and got into Danny's car. He asked if I wanted some dinner but I couldn't eat a thing. I asked him just to drive home."

De l'Epée scoots forward. Their knees meet. He touches her arm. "What else?"

"We left town, got onto the highway. We were in Danny's little Toyota. He rebuilt it himself. Everything. He's so good with mechanical things. He's amazing, really. We were going pretty fast."

She pauses for a moment to let the tide of sadness subside. It never does but she takes a deep breath—remembering when she had to take a breath before saying something—and finds herself able to continue. "We were talking in the car."

De l'Epée nods.

"But that means we were signing. And that means we had to look at each other. He kept asking me what I was sad about, that the hearing aids didn't work, was I discouraged, had Dad been hassling me about the farm again? . . . He . . ."

She must breathe deeply again.

"Danny was looking at me, not at the road. Oh, God . . . it was just there, in front of us. I never saw where it came from."

"What?"

"A truck. A big one, carrying a load of metal pipes. I think it changed lanes when Danny wasn't looking and . . . oh, Jesus, there was nothing he could do. All these pipes coming at us at a thousand miles an hour . . ."

The blood. All the blood.

"I know he braked, I know he tried to turn. But it was too late. No . . . Oh, Danny."

Spraying, spraying. Like the blood from the throat of a calf.

"He managed to steer mostly out of the way but one pipe smashed through the windshield. It . . ."

De l'Epée kneads her hand. "Tell me," he whispers.

"It . . ." The words are almost impossible to say. "It took his arm off."

Like the blood running down the gutters into the horrible well in the center of the killing room.

"Right at the shoulder." She sobs at the memory. Of the blood. Of the stunned look on her brother's face as he turned to her and spoke for a long moment, saying words she couldn't figure out then and never had the heart to ask him to repeat.

The blood sprayed to the roof of the car and pooled in his lap, while Melanie struggled to get a tourniquet around the stump and screamed and screamed. She, the vocal one. While Danny, still conscious, nodding madly, sat completely mute.

Melanie says to de l'Epée, "The medics got there just a few minutes later and stopped most of the bleeding. They saved his life. They got him to a hospital and the doctors got his arm reattached within a couple of hours. For the past year he's had all sorts of operations. He's having one tomorrow—that's where my parents are. In St. Louis, visiting him. They think he'll get back maybe fifty percent use of his arm eventually. If he's lucky. But he lost all interest in the farm after that. He's pretty much stayed in bed. He reads, watches TV. That's about all. It's like his life is over with. . . ."

"It wasn't your fault," he says. "You're taking the blame, aren't you?"

"A few days after it happened my father called me out on the porch. There's something about him that's funny—I can lip-read him perfectly."

(Like Brutus, she thinks, and wishes she hadn't.)

"He sat on the porch swing and looked up at me and he said, 'I guess you understand what you've done now. You had no business talking Danny into doing something as foolish as that. And for a selfish reason all your own. What happened was your fault, there's no two ways about it. You might just as well've turned the engine over on a corn picker when Danny was working on a jam inside.

" 'God made you damaged and nobody wants it. It's a shame but it's not a sin—as long as you understand what you have to do. Come home now and make up for what you done. Get that teaching of yours over with, get that last year done. You owe your brother that. And you owe me especially.

" 'This is your home and you'll be welcome here. See, it's a question of belonging and what God does to make sure those that oughta stay someplace do. Well, your place is here, working at what you can do, where your, you know, problem doesn't get you into trouble. God's will.' And then he went to spray ammonia, saying, 'So you'll be home then.' It wasn't a question. It was an order. All decided. No debate. He wanted me to come home this last May. But I held off a few months. I knew I'd give in eventually. I *always* give in. But I just wanted a few more months on my own." She shrugs. "Stalling."

"You don't want the farm?"

"No! I want my music. I want to *hear* it, not just feel vibrations. . . . I

want to hear my lover whisper things to me when I'm in bed with him."
She can't believe she's saying these things to him, intimate things—far
more intimate than she's ever told anyone. "I don't want to be a virgin
anymore."

Now that she's started it's all pouring out. "I hate the poetry, I don't
care about it! I never have. It's stupid. Do you know what I was going to
do in Topeka? After my recital at the Theater of the Deaf? I had that
appointment afterwards." Then his arms are around her and she is
pressing against his body, her head on his shoulder. It's an odd experience, doubly so: being close to a man, and communicating without
looking at him. "There's something called a cochlear implant." She
must pause for a moment before she can continue. "They put a chip in
your inner ear. It's connected by wire to this *thing*, this speech processor that converts the sounds to impulses in the brain . . . I could never
tell Susan. A dozen times I was going to. But she would've hated me.
The idea of trying to cure deafness—she hated that."

"Do they work, these implants?"

"They can. I have a ninety percent hearing loss in both ears but
that's an average. In some registers I can make out sounds and the implants can boost those. But even if they don't work there are other
things to try. There's a lot of new technology that in the next five or six
years'll help people like me—grass-roots deaf and peddlers and just
ordinary people who want to hear."

She thinks: And I *do*. I want to hear . . . I want to hear you whisper
things in my ear while we make love.

"I . . ." He's speaking, his mouth is moving, but the sound dwindles
to nothing.

Fading, fading.

No! Talk to me, keep talking to me. What's wrong?

But now it's Brutus who is standing in the doorway of her music
room. What are you doing here? Leave! Get out! It's *my* room. I don't
want you here!

He smiles, looks at her ears. "Freak of nature," he says.

Then they were back in the killing room and Brutus wasn't talking to
her at all but to Bear, who stood with his arms crossed defensively. The
tension between them was like thick smoke.

"You give us up?" Brutus asked Bear.

Bear shook his head and said something she didn't catch.

"They picked them up outside, those little girls."

The twins! They were safe! Melanie relayed this to Beverly and Emily. The younger girl burst into a smile and her fingers stuttered out a spontaneous prayer of thanks.

"You let them go, didn't you?" Brutus asked Bear. "Your plan all along."

Bear shook his head. Said something she didn't catch.

"I talked to . . ." Brutus snarled.

"Who?" Bear seemed to ask.

"The U.S. attorney you cut a deal with."

Bear's face grew dark. "No way, man. No fucking way."

Wilcox came up behind him and said something. Bear stabbed a finger at Melanie. "She's the one. . . ."

Brutus turned toward her. She gazed back coldly at him then rose and walked slowly over the wet tiles, almost choking on the smell of gasoline. She stopped and stood directly over Donna Harstrawn. With her finger she gestured Brutus forward. Her eyes locked into Bear's, Melanie lifted the woman's skirt a foot or two, revealing bloody thighs. She nodded at Bear.

"You little bitch!" Bear took a step toward her but Brutus caught his arm, pulled Bear's gun from his belt, tossed it to Stoat.

"You stupid asshole!"

"So? I fucked her, so what?"

Brutus lifted an eyebrow and then pulled a gun from his pocket. He pulled the slide and let it snap forward then pushed a button and took out the little metal tube that held the rest of the bullets. He put the pistol in Melanie's hand. It was cold as a rock, it gave her power like raw electrical current and it terrified her.

Bear was muttering something; in the corner of Melanie's eye she saw his lips moving. But she couldn't take her eyes from the gun. Brutus stood behind her and directed the barrel toward Bear's chest. He wrapped her hands in his. She smelled him, a sour scent of unwashed skin.

"Come on!" Bear's face was grim. "Quit fooling . . ."

Brutus was speaking to her; she felt the vibrations on the flesh of her face but she couldn't understand him. She sensed he was excited, almost aroused, and she felt it too—like a fever. Bear raised his hands. He was muttering something. Shaking his head.

The gun burned, radioactive. Bear eased away and Brutus adjusted the pistol to keep the muzzle pointed directly at his chest. Melanie pictured him lying atop Mrs. Harstrawn. She pictured him gazing at the twins' thin legs, their flat chests. Pull the trigger, she thought. Pull it! Her hand started to shake.

She again felt the vibrations of Brutus's words. In her mind, she heard his voice, an oddly soothing voice, the phantom voice. "Go ahead," he said.

Why isn't it firing? I'm ordering my finger to pull.

Nothing.

Bear was crying. Tears down his fat cheeks, running into his beard.

Melanie's hand was shaking badly. Brutus's firm hand curled around hers.

Then the gun silently bucked in her hand. Melanie gasped as the hot wind from the muzzle hit her face. A tiny dot appeared in Bear's chest and he gripped the wound with both hands, looked into the air, and fell backwards.

No, it fired by itself! I didn't do it, I didn't!

I *swear!*

She screamed those words to herself, over and over. And yet . . . yet she wasn't sure. She wasn't sure at all. For an instant—before the horror of what had happened hit home—she was enraged that she might *not* have been the one responsible for his death. That Brutus, not she, had applied the final ounce of pressure.

Brutus stepped away and reloaded the gun, pulled a lever, and the slide snapped forward.

Bear's mouth moved, his eyes darkened. She watched his miserable face, which looked as if all the injustice of the earth were conspiring to cheat a good man out of his life. Melanie didn't even try to figure out what he was saying.

She thought: Every once in a while deafness is a blessing.

Handy stepped past Melanie. He looked down at Bear. Muttered something to him. He fired one shot into the man's leg, which kicked violently in reaction. Bear's face contorted with pain. Then Handy fired again—into his other leg. Finally he aimed leisurely at the huge gut; the gun exploded once more. Bear shuddered once, stiffened, and went still.

Melanie sank to the floor, put her arms around Emily and Beverly.

Brutus bent down and pulled her close. His face was only inches away. "I didn't do that 'cause he fucked that woman. I did it 'cause he didn't do what I'd told him. He let those girls get away and was gonna snitch on us. Now you just sit on back there."

How can I understand his words if I can't understand him?

How? Melanie wonders. I hear him so perfectly, just like I hear my father.

So you'll be home—

How? she wonders.

Handy's eyes looked Melanie up and down as if he clearly knew the answer to her question and was simply waiting for her to catch on. Then he looked at his watch, bent down, grabbed Emily by the arm. He dragged the little girl, hands pressed together in desperate prayer, into the main room.

Handy was singing.

Potter had called and said, "Lou, how're things going in there? Thought we heard a few gunshots."

To the tune of "Streets of Laredo" Handy sang in a half-decent voice, "I see by my Timex you got fifteen minutes. . . ."

"You sound like you're in a bright mood, Lou. You doing okay foodwise?"

His voice didn't reveal his concern. *Were* they gunshots?

"I'm feeling pretty chipper, sure am. But I don't want to talk about my moods. That's fucking boring, isn't it? Tell me about my golden helicopter that's flying through the air right now. You get me one with diamond rotors, Art? Some babe with huge tits in the cockpit?"

What were those shots?

Looking at the monitor, the telescopic camera fixed on the window, he could see ten-year-old Emily Stoddard's waved blond hair, her big eyes, heart-shaped face. The silver glint of Handy's blade rested on her cheek.

"He's going to cut her," Angie whispered. For the first time that day her voice cracked with emotion. Because she, like Potter, knew he'd do it.

"Lou, we *have* your chopper. It's on its way."

Why won't he wear down? Potter wondered. After this much time most criminal takers're climbing the walls. They'll do anything to cut a deal.

"Hold on, Lou. I think that's the pilot now. I'm going to put you on hold. I'll be right back."

"No need. Just get me that chopper in fourteen minutes."

"Just hold on."

Potter hit the mute button and asked, "What do you think, Angie?"

She gazed out the window. Suddenly she announced, "He's serious. He's going to do it. He's tired of the bargaining. And he's still mad about the assault."

"Tobe?"

"It's ringing, there's no answer."

"Damn it. Doesn't he keep the phone in his pocket?"

"You still there, Lou?"

"Time's awasting, Art."

Potter tried to sound distracted as he asked, "Oh, hey, tell me, Lou. What *about* those shots?"

A low chuckle. "You sure are curious about that."

"*Were* they shots?"

"I dunno. Maybe it was all in your head. Maybe you were feeling guilty 'bout that trooper of yours getting accidentally shot after you accidentally tried to attack me. And you heard it, you know, like a delusion."

"Sounded real to us."

"Maybe Sonny accidentally shot himself cleaning his gun."

"That what happened?"

"Be a shame if anybody was counting on him to be a witness and all and what happens but he goes and cleans a Glock without looking to see if there was a round inside."

"There is no deal between him and us, Lou."

"Not now there ain't. I'll guaran-fucking-tee that."

LeBow and Angie looked up at Potter.

"Bonner's dead?" the negotiator asked Handy.

Have you ever done anything bad, Art?

"You got twelve minutes," Handy's cheerful voice said.

Click.

Tobe said, "Got him. Budd."

Potter grabbed the offered phone. "Charlie, you there?"

"I'm at the airport and they've got a helicopter here. But I can't find anybody to fly it."

"There's got to be somebody."

"There's a school here—an aviation school—and some guy lives in the back but he won't answer the door."

"I need a chopper here in ten minutes, Charlie. Just buzz the river and set it down in that big field to the west. The one about a half-mile from here. That's all you've got to do."

"That's *all?* Oh, brother."

Potter said, "Good luck, Charlie." But Charlie was no longer on the line.

Charlie Budd ran underneath the tall Sikorsky helicopter. It was an old model, a big one, the sort that had plucked dripping astronauts from the ocean during the Gemini and Apollo days at NASA. It was orange and red and white, Coast Guard colors, though the insignias had long ago been painted over.

The airport was small. There was no tower, just an air sock beside a grass strip. A half-dozen single-engine Pipers and Cessnas sat idle, tied down securely against Land of Oz twisters.

Budd slammed his fist onto the door of a small shack behind the airport's one hangar. The sign beside the door said, *D. D. Pembroke Helicopter School. Lessons, Rides. Hourly, Daily.*

Despite that claim, however, the place was mostly a residence. A pile of mail sat on the doorstep and through the window in the door Budd could see a yellow light burning, a pile of clothes in a blue plastic hamper, and what appeared to be a man's foot hanging off the end of a cot. A single toe protruded from a hole in his sock.

"Come on!" Budd pounded hard. He shouted, "Police! Open up!"

The toe moved—it twitched, swung in a slow circle—then fell still.

More pounding. "Open up!"

The toe was fast asleep once more.

The window shattered easily under Budd's elbow. He unlocked the door and pushed inside. "Hey, mister!"

A man of about sixty lay on the cot, wearing overalls and a T-shirt. His hair was like straw and spread out from his head in all directions. His snore was as loud as the Sikorsky's engine.

Budd grabbed his arm and shook violently.

D. D. Pembroke, if D. D. Pembroke this was, opened his wet, red eyes momentarily, gazed through Budd, and rolled over. The snoring, at least, stopped.

"Mister, I'm a state trooper. This's an emergency. Wake up! We need that chopper of yours right now."

"Go away," Pembroke mumbled.

Budd sniffed his breath. He found the empty bottle of Dewar's cradled beneath the man's arm like a sleeping kitten.

"Shit. Wake up, mister. We need you to fly."

"I can't fly. How can I fly? Go away." Pembroke didn't move or open his eyes. "How'd you get in here?" he asked without a trace of curiosity.

The captain rolled him over and shook him by the shoulders. The bottle fell to the concrete floor and broke.

"You Pembroke?"

"Yeah. Shit, was that my bottle?"

"Listen, this is a federal emergency." Budd spotted a jar of instant coffee on a filthy, littered tabletop. He ran water in the rusted sink and filled a mug, not waiting for it to turn hot. He dumped four heaping tablespoons into the cold water and thrust the dirty cup into Pembroke's hands. "Drink this, mister. We gotta get going. I need to you fly me to that slaughterhouse up the road."

Pembroke, eyes still closed, sat up and sniffed at the cup. "What slaughterhouse? What's this shit in here?"

"The one by the river."

"Where's my bottle?"

"Drink this down, it'll wake you up." The instant grounds hadn't dissolved; they floated on the top like brown ice. Pembroke sipped it, spit a mouthful onto the bed, and flung the cup away. "Jeeeez!" Only then did he realize that there was a man in a blue suit and body armor standing over him.

"Who the fuck're you? Where's my—"

"I need your helicopter. And I need it now. It's a federal emergency. You gotta fly me to that slaughterhouse by the river."

"There? The old one? It's three fucking miles away. You can drive faster. Fuck, you can walk! God in Hoboken . . . my head. Oooooh."

"I need a chopper. And I need it now. I'm authorized to pay you whatever you want."

Pembroke sagged back onto the bed. His eyes kept closing. Budd figured even if they managed to take off, he'd crash and kill them both.

"Let's go." The trooper pulled him up by his Oshkosh straps.

"When?"

"Now. This instant."

"I can't fly when I'm sleepy like this."

"Sleepy. Right. What do you charge?"

"A hundred twenty an hour."

"I'll pay you five hundred."

"Tomorrow." He started to lie down again, eyes closed, patting the dingy sheets for his bottle. "Get the hell outta here."

"Mister. Open your eyes."

He did.

"Shit," Pembroke muttered as he looked down the barrel of the black automatic pistol.

"Sir," Budd said in a low, respectful voice, "you're going to stand up and walk out to that helicopter and fly it exactly where I tell you. Do you understand me?"

A nod.

"Are you sober?"

"Stone cold," Pembroke said. He kept his eyes open for a whole two seconds before he passed out once more.

Melanie lay against the wall, caressing Beverly's sweaty blond hair, the poor girl gasping with every breath.

The young woman leaned forward and looked out. Emily, crying, stood in the window. Now Brutus turned suddenly and looked at Melanie, gestured her forward.

Don't go, she told herself. Resist.

She hesitated for a moment then walked out of the killing room toward him.

I go because I can't stop myself.

I go because he wants me.

She felt the chill sweeping into her from the floor, from the metal chains and meat hooks, from the cascade of slick water, from the damp walls spattered with mold and old, old blood.

I go because I'm afraid.

I go because he and I just killed a man together.

I go because I can understand him. . . .

Brutus pulled her close. "You think you're better'n me, right? You think you're a good person." She could tell he was whispering. People's faces change when they whisper. They look like they're telling you absolute truths but really they're just making the lie more convincing.

"Why're we selling it? Honey, you know what the doctor said. It's your ears. You can still hear now some, sure, but that'll go, remember what they said. You don't really want to start something you'll have to give up in a few years. We're doing it for you."

"See, I'm going to cut her in about three minutes, that chopper don't show up. I'd kill her I had more hostages. But I can't afford to lose another one. Least not yet."

Emily stood, hands still clasped together, staring out at the window, shaking as she sobbed.

"See"—Brutus closed his fiercely strong fingers around Melanie's arm—"if you were a good person, you were really good, you'd say, 'Take me, not her.' "

Stop it!

He slapped her. "No, keep your eyes open. So if you're not like totally good you must have some bad inside you. Somewhere. To let this little one get cut instead of you. It's not like you'd die. I ain't gonna kill her. Just a little pain. Make sure those assholes out . . . know I mean

business. You won't put up with a little pain for your friend, huh? You
. . . bad. Just like me?"

She shook her head.

His head swiveled. Stoat's too. She guessed the phone was ringing.

"Don't answer it," he said to Stoat. "Too much talking. I'm sick
and tired. . . ." He thumbed the blade. Melanie was frozen. "You?
You for her?" He moved the blade of the knife one way then the
other. Figure eights.

What would Susan have done?

Melanie hesitated though she knew the answer clearly. Finally she
nodded.

"Yeah," he said, eyebrows raised. "You mean it?"

"Two minutes," Stoat called.

Melanie nodded then embraced sobbing Emily, lowered her head to
the girl's cheek, directed her gently away from the window.

Handy leaned close, his head inches from Melanie's, his nose beside
her ear. She couldn't hear his breath, of course, but she had the impression he was inhaling something—the scent of her fear. Her eyes were
fixed on the knife. Which hovered over her skin: her cheek, her nose, then
her lips, her throat. She felt it caress a breast and slide down her belly.

She felt the vibration of his voice, turned to look at his lips. ". . . should
I cut you? Your tit? No loss there—you don't have no boyfriend to feel
you up, do you? Your ear? Hey, that wouldn't matter either. . . . You
see that flick, *Reservoir Dogs*?"

The blade lifted, slipped over her cheek. "How 'bout your eye? Deaf
and blind. You'd be a real freak then."

Finally she could take it no longer and she closed her eyes. She tried to
think of the tune of "Amazing Grace" but it was nowhere in her memory.

A Maiden's Grave . . .

Nothing, nothing, all silence. Music can be vibrations or sound, but
not both.

And for me, neither.

Well, she thought, do whatever the fuck you're going to do and get it
over with.

But then the hands pushed her brutally away and she opened her eyes,
staggering across the floor. Brutus was laughing. She understood that this

little sacrifice scene had been just a game. He'd been playing with her once again. He said, "Naw, naw, I've got other plans for you, little mouse. You're a present for my Pris."

He handed her off to Stoat, who held her firmly. She struggled but he gripped her like a vise. Brutus pulled Emily back into the window. The girl's eyes met Melanie's momentarily, and Emily pushed her hands together, praying, crying.

Brutus caught Emily's head in the crook of his left arm and lifted the tip of the knife to her eyes.

Melanie struggled futilely against Stoat's iron grip.

Brutus looked at his watch. "Time."

Emily sobbed; her joined fingers twitched as they uttered fervent prayers.

Brutus tightened his grip on Emily's head. He drew back a few inches with the knife, aimed right for the center of her closed right eye.

Stoat looked away.

Then suddenly his arms jerked in surprise. He looked straight up at the murky ceiling.

Brutus did too.

And finally Melanie felt it.

A huge thudding overhead, like the roll of a timpani. Then it grew closer and became the continuous sound of a bowed upright bass. An indiscernible pitch that Melanie felt on her face and arms and throat and chest.

Music is sound or vibration. But not both.

Their helicopter was overhead.

Brutus leaned out the window and looked up at the sky. With his bony fingers he dramatically unlocked the blade of his knife and closed it with what Melanie supposed was a loud snap. He laughed and said something to Stoat, words that Melanie was, for some reason, furious to realize she could not understand at all.

9:31 P.M.

"You're looking a little green around the gills there, Charlie."

"That pilot," Budd said to Potter, climbing into the van unsteadily. "Brother, I thought I'd bought the farm. He missed the field altogether, set her down in the middle of Route 346, almost on top of a fire truck. Now, there's an experience for you. Then he puked out the window and fell asleep. I kept shutting stuff off till the engine stopped. This smell in here isn't helping my stomach any." The captain's exemplary posture was shot to hell; he slumped into a chair.

"Well, you did good, Charlie," Potter told him. "Handy's agreed to give us a little more time. HRT'll be here any minute."

"Then what?"

"We shall see what we shall see," Potter mused.

"When I was driving up," Budd said, his eyes firmly on Potter's, "I heard a transmission. There was a shot inside?"

LeBow stopped typing. "Handy shot Bonner," the intelligence officer said. "We think."

"I think Handy and Wilcox," Potter continued, "took our strategy a little more seriously than I'd expected—about Bonner cutting a separate deal. They figured him for a snitch."

"Wasn't anything we could do about it," LeBow said offhandedly. "You can't second-guess stuff like that."

"Couldn't have been foreseen," Tobe recited like a cyborg in one of the science fiction novels he was always reading.

Charlie Budd—the faux U.S. attorney, a naif in the state police—was the only honest one in the group, for he was silent. He continued to look at Potter and their eyes met. The young man's gaze said he understood that Potter had known what would happen when he gave Budd the script; it'd been Potter's intent all along for Budd to plant the seed of distrust that would set Handy against Bonner.

But in Budd's glance was another message. His eyes said, Oh, I get it, Potter. You used me to kill a man. Well, fair's fair; after all, I spied on you. But now our sins have canceled each other out. Mutual betrayals, and what's happened? Well, we're one hostage taker down, all to the good. But listen here: I don't owe you anything anymore.

A phone buzzed—Budd's own cellular phone. He took the call. He listened, punctuating the conversation with several significant "ums," and then clamped a hand over the mouthpiece.

"Well, how 'bout this? It's my division commander, Ted Franklin. He says there's a trooper in McPherson, not too far from here. A woman. She negotiated Handy's surrender five years ago in a convenience store holdup that went bad. He wants to know if he should ask her to come down here and help."

"Handy surrendered to her?"

Budd posed the question and listened for a moment. Then he said, "He did, yes. Seems there were no hostages. They'd all escaped and HRU was about to go in. A lot different from this, sounds like."

Potter and LeBow exchanged glances. "Have her come anyway," the negotiator said. "Whether she can help us directly or not, I can see Henry's licking his chops at the thought of more info on the bad guys."

"Yes indeed."

Budd relayed this to his commander and Potter was momentarily heartened at the thought of having an ally. He sat back in the chair and mused out loud, "Any way we can get another one or two out before HRT gets here?"

Angie asked, "What can we give him that he hasn't asked for? Anything?"

LeBow scrolled through the screen. "He's asked for transportation, food, liquor, guns, vests, electricity. . . ."

Angie said, "All the classic things. What every taker wants."

"But not money," Budd said suddenly.

Frowning, Potter glanced at the "Promises" side of the board, where the things they'd actually given Handy were recorded. "You're right, Charlie."

Angie asked, "He hasn't?" Surprised.

LeBow scrolled through his files and confirmed that Handy had not once mentioned money. He asked the captain, "How'd you think of that?"

"I saw it in a movie," Budd explained.

"It's an opportunistic taking," LeBow offered. "Handy's not out to make a profit. He's an escaping criminal."

"So was this fellow," Budd said. Potter and LeBow glanced at the captain, who, blushing, added, "In the movie, I mean. I think it was Gene Hackman. Or maybe he was the one playing your role, Arthur. He's a good actor, Hackman is."

Angie said, "I agree with Charlie, Henry. It's true that a lot of criminal takers don't want money. But Handy's got a mercenary streak in him. Most of his underlying raps're larceny."

"Let's try to buy a couple of them," Potter said. "What've we got to lose?" He asked Budd, "Can you get your hands on any cash?"

"This time of night?"

"Immediately."

"Geez, I guess so. HQ's got petty cash. Maybe two hundred. How's that?"

"I'm talking about a hundred thousand dollars in small bills, unmarked. Within, say, twenty minutes."

"Oh," Budd said. "In that case, no."

LeBow said, "I'll call the DEA. They've got to have some buy money in Topeka or Wichita. We'll do an interagency transfer." He nodded at Tobe, who flipped through a laminated phone book and pushed in a phone number. LeBow began speaking through his headset in a voice as soft and urgent as his key strokes.

Potter picked up his phone and rang Handy.

"Hey, Art."

"How you doing, Lou? Ready to leave?"

"You bet I am. Go to a nice warm cabin. . . . Or a hotel. Or a desert island."

"Whereabouts, Lou? Maybe I'll come visit."

You got yourself quite a sense of humor, Art.

"I like cops with a sense of humor, you old son of a bitch."

"Where's my chopper?"

"Close as we could get it, Lou. In that field just over the trees. Turned out the river was too choppy after all. Now listen, Lou. You saw that chopper. It's a six-seater. I know you wanted an eight- but that's all we could rustle up." He hoped the man hadn't gotten a very good look at it; you could fit half the Washington Redskins in an old Sikorsky. "So, I've got a proposition. Let me buy a couple of the hostages."

"Buy?"

"Sure. I'm authorized to pay up to fifty thousand each. There just isn't room for the six of you and the pilot. No overhead racks for carry-ons, you know. Let me buy a couple of them."

Shit, Art, I could shoot one of 'em. Then we'd have plenty of space.

But he'll laugh when he says it.

"Hey, I got an idea. 'Stead of giving one of 'em to you, I could shoot her. Then we'd have plenty of room. For us and our matched sets of American Tourister."

The laugh was almost a cackle.

"Ah, but Lou, if you kill her you don't get any money. That'd be a bummer, as my nephew says." Potter said this good-naturedly, for he felt the rapport had been re-established. It was solid, fibrous. The negotiator knew that the man was seriously considering the offer.

"Fifty thousand?"

"Cash. Small, unmarked bills."

A hesitation. "Okay. But only one. I keep the rest."

"Make it two. You'll still have two left. Don't want to be greedy."

Fuck it, Art. Gimme a hundred for one. That's the best I'll do.

"Nope," Handy said. "You get one. Fifty thousand. That's the deal."

Potter glanced at Angie. She shook her head, perplexed. Handy wasn't bargaining. After some feigned horse trading, Potter had been prepared to turn over the full one hundred for a single girl.

"Well, all right, Lou. I accept."

"Only, Art?"

There was a tone in Handy's voice Potter hadn't yet heard and it troubled him. He had no idea what was coming next. Where had he left himself exposed?

"Yes?"

"You have to tell me which one."

"How do you mean, Lou?"

The chuckle again. "Pretty easy question, Art. Which one do you want to buy? You know how it works, good buddy. You go to a car lot and say, I'll take that Chevy or that Ford. You pays your money, you takes your choice. Which one you want?"

His heart. That's where Potter had left himself unprotected. In his heart.

Budd and Angie stared at the agent.

Tobe kept his head down, focusing on his animate dials.

"Well, Lou, now . . ." Potter could think of nothing else to say. For the first time today, indecision crept into Potter's soul. And, worse, he heard it in his voice. This *couldn't* happen. Hesitation was deadly in a negotiation. Takers picked up on it immediately and it gave them power, deadly power. With someone like Handy, a control freak, hearing even a one-second pause in Potter's voice might make him feel invincible.

In the delay Potter sensed he was signing the death warrants for all four hostages. "Well, that's a tough question," Potter tried to joke.

"Must be. Fact, sounds like you're pretty damn flummoxed."

"I just—"

"Lemme help you, Art. Let's take a stroll through the used-hostage lot, why don't we? Well, here's the old one—that teach. Now, she's gotta lot of mileage on her. She's pretty run-down. A clunker, a lemon. That was Bonner's doing. He rode her hard, I tell you. Radiator's still leaking."

"Jesus," Budd muttered.

"That son of a bitch," placid Angie said.

Potter's eyes were firmly fixed on the yellow, homey windows of the slaughterhouse. Thinking: No! Don't do this to me! No!

"Then there's the pretty one. The blond one. Melanie."

Why does he know her name? Potter thought. Unreasonably angry. Did she tell him? Does she talk to him?

Has she fallen for him?

"I myself've taken a shine to her. But she's yours if you want her. Then we have this little shit that can't breathe. Oh, and finally we got the pretty one in the dress just about became Miss One-Eye. Take your pick."

Potter found himself looking at Melanie's picture. No, stop it, Potter commanded himself. Look away. He did. Now think! Who's the most at risk?

Who threatens his control the most?

The older teacher? No, not at all. The little girl, Emily? No, too frail and feminine and young. Beverly? Her illness would, as Budd had suggested, irritate Handy.

And what of Melanie? Handy's comment about taking a shine to her suggested that some Stockholming was going on. Was it enough to make him hesitate to kill her? Probably not. But she's older. How could he ask for an adult before a child?

Melanie, Potter's heart cried helplessly, I want to save you! And the same heart burned with rage for Handy's laying the decision in his lap.

He opened his mouth; he couldn't speak.

Budd frowned. "There isn't much time. He may back down if we don't pick right now."

LeBow touched his arm. He whispered, "It's okay, Arthur. Pick who you want. It doesn't really matter."

But it did. Every decision in a barricade incident mattered. He found himself staring at Melanie's picture again. Blond hair, large eyes.

Be forewarned, de l'Epée.

Potter sat up straight. "Beverly," he said suddenly into the phone. "The girl with the asthma." He closed his eyes.

"Hmmm. Good choice, Art. Her wheezing's gettin' on my nerves. I was getting close to doing her on general principles 'cause of that fucking wheeze-wheeze shit. Okey-dokey, when you get the cash, I'll send her out."

Handy hung up.

No one spoke for a long moment. "I hate that sound," Frances finally muttered. "I never want to hear a phone hang up again."

Potter sat back. LeBow and Tobe were looking at him. Slowly he swung to the window and looked out.

Melanie, forgive me.

"Hello, Arthur. This's a bad one, to hear tell."

Frank D'Angelo was a lanky, mustachioed man, calm as a summer pond. The head of the Bureau's Hostage Rescue Team had been in charge of the hot work in fifty or sixty negotiations Potter had run. The tactical agents—pulled off the Florida and Seattle barricades—had just arrived and were assembled in the gully behind the command van.

"It's been a long day, Frank."

"He's got a booby trap rigged?"

"So it seems. I'm inclined to get him out on a short leash and then apprehend or neutralize. But that's your speciality."

D'Angelo asked, "How many hostages left?"

"Four," Potter answered. "We're getting another one out in about ten minutes."

"You going to make a surrender pitch?"

The ultimate goal of all negotiations is to get the takers to surrender. But if you make your case to them just before they get their helicopter or other means of escape, they might conclude, reasonably, that an offer to surrender is actually a veiled ultimatum and that you're about to nail them. On the other hand, if you just green-light an attack there'll likely be casualties and you'll spend the rest of your life wondering if you might have gotten the takers to give up without any bloodshed.

Then too there was the Judas factor. The betrayal. Potter was promising Handy one thing and delivering something very different. Possibly—likely—the man's death. However evil Handy was, he and the negotiator were partners of sorts, and betraying him was something Potter would also have to live with for a long, long time.

"No," the agent said slowly, "no surrender pitch. He'll hear it as an ultimatum and figure we're planning an assault. Then we'll never get him out."

"What happened here?" D'Angelo pointed at the burned portion of the command van.

"Tell you about it later," Potter responded.

Inside the van D'Angelo, Potter, LeBow, and Budd looked over the architectural plans of the building and the terrain and SatSurv maps. "This is where the hostages are," Potter explained. "That was current as of an hour ago. And as far as we know the gas bomb is still rigged."

LeBow searched for his description of the device and read it aloud.

"And you're confident you'll get one more out?" the tactical agent asked.

"We're buying her for fifty thousand."

"The girl should be able to tell us if the trap's still set," D'Angelo said.

"I don't think it matters," Potter said, looking at Angie, who nodded her agreement. "Bomb or no bomb, he'll nail the hostages. If he's got any time at all, one or two seconds, he'll shoot them or pitch a grenade in."

"Grenade?" D'Angelo frowned. "Have a list of his weaponry?"

LeBow had already printed one out. The HRT commander read through it.

"He's got an MP-5? With scope and suppressor?" He shook his head in dismay.

There was a knocking on the side of the van and a young HRT officer stepped into the doorway. "Sir, we've completed initial reconnaissance."

"Go ahead." D'Angelo nodded at the map.

"This door here is wood with steel facing. Looks like it's rigged already with cutting charges."

D'Angelo looked at Potter.

"Some enthusiastic state troopers. That's how he got the Heckler & Koch."

D'Angelo nodded wryly, brushing his flamboyant mustache.

The trooper continued, "There's another door on the south side, much thinner wood. There's a loading dock in the back, here, by the river. The door's open far enough to get a tunnel rat under if they strip. Couple of the smaller guys. Next to it's a smaller door, reinforced steel, rusted shut. There's a runoff pipe here, a twenty-four-incher, barred with a steel grille. Second-floor windows are all barred with three-eighths-inch rods. These three windows here aren't visible from the HTs' position. The roof is covered with five-sixteenths-inch steel plates and the elevator shaft is sealed. The shaft access door's metal and I estimate bang-to-bullets of twenty to thirty seconds if we go in that way."

"Long time."

"Yessir. If we do four-man entry on the two doors, covering fire from a window, and two men in from the loading dock, I estimate we could engage and secure in eight to twelve seconds."

"Thanks, Tommy," D'Angelo said to his trooper. To Potter he added, "Not bad if it weren't for the trap." He asked Potter, "How Stockholmed is he?"

"Hardly at all," Angie offered. "He claims the more he knows somebody the more inclined he is to kill them."

D'Angelo's mustache received another stroke. "They good shots?"

Potter said. "Let's just say they're cool under fire."

"That's better'n being a good shot."

"And they've killed cops," Budd said.

"Both in firefights and as execution," Potter offered.

"Okay," D'Angelo said slowly. "My feeling is we can't do an entry. Not with the risk of the gas bomb and grenades. And his frame of mind."

"Have him walk to the chopper?" Potter asked. "It's right there." He tapped the map.

D'Angelo gazed at the portion of the map showing the field and nodded. "Think so. We'll pull everybody back out of sight, let the takers and hostages walk through the woods here."

Angie interrupted. "Handy'll pick his own route, don't you think, Arthur?"

"You're right. He'll want to be in charge of that. And it probably won't be the straightest one."

D'Angelo and Potter marked off four likely routes to get from the slaughterhouse to the chopper. LeBow drew them on the map. D'Angelo said, "I'll set up snipers in the trees here and here and here. Put the ground men in deep camouflage along all four routes. When the takers go by, the snipers'll acquire. Then we'll stun the whole group with smokeless. The agents on the ground'll grab the hostages and pull 'em down. The snipers'll take out the HTs if they show any threat. That sound okay to you?"

Potter was staring down at the map.

A moment passed.

"Arthur?"

"Yes, it sounds good, Frank. Very good."

D'Angelo stepped outside to brief his agents.

Potter looked at Melanie's picture and then sat down once more, staring out the window.

"Waiting is the hardest, Charlie. Worse than anything."

"I can see that."

"And this is what you'd call your express barricade," Tobe offered, eyes on his dials and screens. " 'S'only been about eleven hours. That's nothing."

Suddenly someone burst through the open doorway so quickly every law enforcer inside the van except Potter reached for weapons.

Roland Marks stood in the doorway. "Agent Potter," he said coldly. "Do I understand you're going to take him down?"

Potter looked past him at a tree bending in the wind. The breeze had picked up remarkably. It would bolster the lie about the river being too choppy to land a helicopter.

"Yes, we are."

"Well, I was just speaking to your comrade Agent D'Angelo. He shared with me a disturbing fact."

Potter couldn't believe Marks. In the space of a few hours he'd nearly screwed up the negotiations twice and almost lost his life in the process. And here he was on the offensive again. The agent was a few seconds away from arresting him just to get the pushy man out of his life.

Potter lifted an eyebrow.

"That there's a fifty-fifty chance one of the hostages will die."

Potter had assessed it at sixty-forty in the hostages' favor. But Marian had always chided him for being an incurable optimist. The agent rose slowly and stepped through the burnt doorway, motioning the attorney general after him. He took a tape cassette from his pocket, held it up prominently then put it back. Marks's eyes gave a flicker.

"Was there anything else you wanted to say?" Potter asked.

Marks's face suddenly softened but just for a moment, as if he recognized an apology forming in his throat and shot it dead. He said, "I don't want those girls hurt."

"I don't either."

"For God's sake, put him in a chopper, have him release the hostages. When he lands the Canadians can come down upon him like the proverbial Assyrians."

"Oh, but he has no intention of going to Canada," Potter said impatiently.

"I thought . . . But that special clearance you boys put together . . ."

"Handy doesn't believe a word of that. And even if he did he knows we'd put a second transponder in the chopper. His plans are to head straight to Busch Stadium. Or wherever his TV tells him there's a big game tonight."

"What?"

"Or maybe a parking lot at the University of Missouri just as evening classes are letting out. Or McCormick Place. He'll land someplace where there'll be a huge crowd around. There's no way we can take him in a scenario like that. A hundred people could be killed."

Understanding dawned in Marks's eyes. And whether he saw those lives jeopardized, or his career, or perhaps was seeing nothing more than the hopeless plight of his own poor daughter, he nodded. "Of course. Sure, he's the sort who'd do just that. You're right."

Potter chose to read the concession as an apology and decided to let him be.

Tobe pushed his head out of the doorway. "Arthur, I just got a phone call. It's that Kansas State detective Charlie told us about. Sharon Foster. She's on the line."

Potter had doubts that Foster could help them. Introducing a new negotiator in a barricade can have unpredictable results. But one thing Potter had decided might be helpful was her gender. His impression of Handy was that he was threatened by men—the very fact that he'd gone to ground with ten female hostages suggested that he might listen to a woman without his defenses raised.

Inside the van Potter leaned against the wall as he spoke. "Detective Foster? This is Arthur Potter. What's your ETA?"

The woman said that she was proceeding under sirens and lights and should be at the incident site by ten-thirty, ten-forty. The voice was young and matter-of-fact and extremely calm, though she was probably doing a hundred miles an hour.

"Look forward to it," Potter said, a little gruffly, and hung up.

"Good luck," Marks said. He hesitated, as if thinking of something else he might say. He settled for "God save those girls" and left the van.

"DEA's on the way," Tobe announced. "They've got the cash. Coming in by confiscated turbo helicopter. They get the best toys, those pricks."

"Hey," Budd said, "they're bringing a hundred thousand, right?"

Potter nodded.

"Where're we gonna keep the fifty that we don't give him? That's a lot of cash to store."

Potter held his finger to his lips. "We'll split it, Charlie, you and me."

Budd blinked in shock.

At last Potter winked.

The captain laughed hard, as did Angie and Frances.

Tobe and LeBow were more restrained. Those who knew Arthur Potter understood that he rarely made jokes. He tended to do so only when he was at his most nervous.

10:01 P.M.

The killing room had become cold as a freezer.

Beverly and Emily huddled against Melanie as they all watched Mrs. Harstrawn lying ten feet away: eyes open, breathing, but otherwise dead as Bear, who still blocked the entrance to the room and whose body was sending three long fingers of black blood reaching slowly toward them.

Beverly, air rasping into her lungs, as if she'd never breathe again, could not take her eyes off the streams.

Something was going on in the other room. Melanie couldn't see clearly but it seemed that Brutus and Stoat were packing up—guns and bullets and the tiny TV set. They were walking through the large room, looking around. Why? It was as if they felt sentimental about the place.

Maybe they were going to give up. . . .

Then she thought, No way. They're going to get into that helicopter, drag us along with them, and escape. We'll live this same nightmare over and over and over again. Fly to someplace else. There'll be other hostages, other deaths. More dark rooms.

Melanie found her hand once more at her hair, uneasily entwining a finger in the strands, which were now damp and filthy. No "shine" now. No light. No hope. She lowered her hand.

Brutus strode into the room and gazed at Mrs. Harstrawn, looking down at her creased brow. He had that slight smile on his face, the smile Melanie had come to recognize and to hate. He pulled Beverly after him.

"She's going home. Going home." Brutus pushed her out of the door of the killing room. He turned back, pulled a knife from his pocket, opened it, and cut the wire that had run to the canister of gasoline. He tied Melanie's hands behind her back and then her feet. Emily's too.

Brutus laughed. "Tying your hands up—that's like gagging you too. How 'bout that?"

Then he was gone, leaving the three remaining hostages.

All right, she thought. The twins had done it; they would too. They'd get out by following the scent of the river. Melanie turned around, her back toward Emily's, offered her bound hands. The little girl understood and struggled with the knots. But it was useless; Emily admired long fingernails but had none of her own.

Try harder, come on!

Suddenly Melanie shivered as Emily's fingers dug deep into her wrists. She cringed as the little girl's hands tugged once desperately at her fingers then suddenly disappeared. Someone had the girl, was dragging her away!

What's going on?

Frowning, Melanie twisted around.

Bear!

His face bubbling with blood and twisting in rage, he pulled Emily to the wall. He shoved her against the tile. She fell, stunned. Melanie opened her mouth to scream but Bear lunged forward, stuffing a filthy rag into her mouth and clamping his bloody hand on her shoulder.

Melanie fell backward. Bear's huge face dropped down onto her breast and kissed her, wet and bloody. She felt the moisture through her blouse. His blurry eyes looked over her body as she tried to spit the rag from her mouth. He pulled a knife from his pocket. He opened it with a bloody hand and his teeth.

She tried to squirm away but he continued to clutch her breast. He rose up on one elbow and rolled off her. She kicked hard but her bound feet rose only an inch or two. A stream of blood poured from his slacks, where it had been pooling for the past hour, and covered her legs with the cold, thick liquid.

Melanie, sobbing in terror, tried to push away from him, but he gripped the cloth over her breasts with a desperate strength. He threw his leg over her calves, pinning her to the ground as more blood cascaded over her.

Please, help me. Somebody. De l'Epée. . . .

Somebody! Please—

Oh, no. . . . She shivered in horror. Not this. Please, no.

He tugged her skirt above her waist with his knife hand. Yanked down her black tights. The knife started up along her thigh to her pink cotton panties.

No! She tried to struggle away, her ears roaring from the effort. But there was no escape. His huge bulk lay upon her and dripped his heavy blood onto her legs. The blade touched her mound, cut through one seam of the underwear. Through the sparse hair between her legs she felt the cold steel and recoiled.

A hideous grin on his face, he looked at her with icy disks of eyes. The metal sliced the other side of the panties. They fell away.

Her vision grew dim. Don't faint! Don't lose your sight too!

Pinned to the ground by his weight. Afraid to move anyway; the knife hovered an inch above her pink cleft, the faint hair, the pale skin.

With his free hand Bear reached down to his crotch and unzipped. He coughed, spraying more blood upon her, spattering her chest and neck. As he reached in his pants the knife dipped and she groaned, nearly gagging on the rag, as the cold metal slipped in between her legs.

Then the blade rose again as he guided his huge, glistening penis out. She struggled away from him but he let go of himself and once more grabbed her breast, holding her still.

He rubbed against her leg, blood pouring off his twitching organ and running onto her bare thigh. He pressed against her skin once, twice, and then shifted his weight to move further along her body.

And then . . .

Then . . .

Nothing.

She was breathing faster than she believed possible, her chest trembling. Bear was frozen, eyes inches from hers, one hand on her chest, the other holding the blade, point down, poised between her legs, millimeters from her flesh.

She spit the rag from her mouth, smelled his putrid stink, the rich, rusty smell of blood. Sucked in air.

Felt the cold knife twitch against her skin once, twice, and then it went still.

It took a full minute before she realized that he was dead.

Melanie fought down the nausea, sure that she'd be sick. But then slowly the sensation passed. Her legs were numb; his bulk had cut off her circulation. She planted her bound hands firmly on the concrete beneath her and pushed. A huge effort. But the blood was slick, like fresh enamel, and she managed to slide several inches away from him. Try again. Then once more. Soon her legs were almost out from under him.

One more time . . .

Her feet popped out and came to rest exactly where he held the knife. Tensing her stomach muscles, she lifted her feet slightly and began sawing the wire against the steel blade of the knife.

She glanced toward the doorway. No sign of Brutus or Stoat. Her stomach muscles screamed as she sawed against the wire.

Finally . . . snap. It gave way. Melanie climbed to her feet. She kicked Bear's left hand once, then again. The blade fell to the ground. She kicked it to Emily. Gestured for her to pick it up. The little girl sat up, crying silently. She looked at the knife, which was resting in a pool of blood, and shook her head no. Melanie responded with a fierce nod. Emily closed her eyes, turned, and groped in the slick red pool for the weapon. Finally she gripped it, wincing, and held the blade up. Melanie turned and began rubbing the wire binding her wrists against the blade. A few minutes later she felt the strands break. She grabbed the knife and then cut Emily's wire as well.

Melanie stole to the doorway. Brutus and Stoat were at the windows, looking away from the killing room. Beverly was standing by the door and Melanie could see a trooper approaching with an attaché case. So they were exchanging the girl for something. With luck, they'd be busy for some minutes—long enough for Melanie and the others to get to the dock.

Melanie bent over Mrs. Harstrawn, who was now soaked in Bear's blood. The woman stared at the ceiling.

"Come on," Melanie signed. "Get up."

The teacher didn't move.

"Now!" Melanie signed emphatically.

Then the woman signed words Melanie had never seen before in ASL. "Kill me."

"Get up!"

"Can't. You go."

"Come on." Melanie's hands stabbed the air. *"No time!"* She slapped the woman, tried to pull her to her feet; the teacher was dead weight.

Melanie grimaced in disgust. "Come on. Or I'll have to leave you!"

The teacher shook her head and closed her eyes. Melanie put the knife, still open, into the pocket of her skirt and, pulling Emily by the hand, slipped out of the doorway. They stepped into the door leading to the back of the slaughterhouse and vanished through the dim corridors.

Lou Handy looked at the cash, a surprisingly small pile for that much money, and said, "We should've thought of this before. Every little bit helps."

Wilcox looked out the window. "How many snipers you think they got on us?"

"Oh . . . lessee . . . 'bout a hundred. And with us nailing that trooper of theirs, they've probably got one'r two ready to shoot away and pretend they didn't hear the order not to."

"I always thought you'd be a good sniper, Lou."

"Me? Naw, I'm too, you know, impatient. I knew some of 'em in the service. You know what you do mosta the time? You gotta lie on your belly for a couple, three days 'fore you can make one shot. Not move a muscle. What's the fun of that?"

He flashed back to his days in the military. They seemed both easier and harder than life on the run, and very similar to life in prison.

"The shooting'd be fun, though."

"I'll give you that. . . . Oh, fucking hell!"

He'd glanced at the back of the slaughterhouse and saw bloody footprints leading out of the room where the girls had been.

"Shit," Wilcox spat out.

Lou Handy was a man driven by positive forces, he truly believed. He rarely lost his temper and, yes, he was a murderer but when he killed he killed for expediency but hardly ever from rage.

Yet, a few times in his life, a fierce anger bubbled up from his soul and he became the cruelest man on earth. Unstoppably cruel.

"That cunt," he whispered, his voice cracking. "That cocksucking cunt."

They ran to the doorway, where the bloody prints disappeared.

Handy said, "Stay here."

"Lou—"

"Stay the fuck here!" Handy raged. "I'm gonna fix her clock like I shoulda done a long time ago." He plunged into the murky bowels of the slaughterhouse, the knife in his hand, held low, with the blade up, as he'd been taught not in the army but on the streets of Minneapolis.

10:27 P.M.

Sight is a miracle and it's the foremost of our senses. But we are as often informed by the adjunct perception, sound.

The sight of a river tells us what it is but the sound of water also can explain its character: placid or deadly or dying itself. For Melanie Charrol, deprived of this sense, smell had taken over. River rapids were airy and electric. Still water smelled stale. Here the Arkansas River smelled ominous—pungent and deep and decaying, as if it were the grave of many bottom feeders.

Still, it said, Come to me, come to me, I'm your way out.

Melanie followed its call unerringly. Through the maze of the deserted slaughterhouse she led the little girl in the hopeless Laura Ashley dress. The floorboards were rotting through in many places, but the bare bulbs from the main portion of the slaughterhouse were so bright that even back here enough light filtered into these reaches to illuminate their path. Occasionally she paused, lifted her nose, and breathed the air to make certain they were headed in the right direction. Then she'd turn once more toward the river, spinning around and looking behind her when the panic got to be too much.

Smell has not replaced sound as our primitive warning system.

But Brutus and Stoat didn't seem to have noticed the escape yet.

The teacher and student continued through the increasing gloom, pausing often and feeling their way along. The thin shafts of light were Melanie's only salvation, and now she glanced up at them. The upper part of the walls had rotted away and it was from there that the faint heavenly glow filled the murky underworld sky of this part of the slaughterhouse.

Then there it was, in front of them! A narrow door below a sign that said *Dock*. Melanie tightened her grip on Emily's hand and tugged the little girl along behind her. They pushed through the door and found a large loading-dock area. It was mostly empty but there were some oil drums that looked like they might still float. But the large door opening onto the outside was raised only a foot or so—high enough for them to crawl under but not high enough to push out one of the drums.

They walked to it and slipped outside.

Freedom, she thought, breathing the intoxicating air.

She laughed to herself at the irony—here she was rejoicing at being Outside, tearfully thankful for escaping from the horrible Inside. Motion startled her; she saw a boat not far offshore. Two officers in it. Somehow, they'd already spotted the girls and were now rowing toward the dock.

Melanie turned Emily around, signed, "Wait here for them. Stay down, hide behind that post."

Emily shook her head. "But aren't you—"

"I'm going back. I can't leave her."

"Please." The little girl's tears streaked down her face. The wind tossed her hair around her head. "She didn't *want* to come."

"Go."

"Come with me. God wants you to. He told me He does."

Melanie smiled, embraced the little girl, and stepped back. Looked over her tattered, filthy dress. "Next week, we have date. Shopping."

Emily wiped tears and walked to the edge of the dock. The policemen were very close, one smiling at the girl, the other scanning the building with a short black shotgun pointed toward the black windows above their heads.

Melanie glanced at them, waved, then slipped back beneath the loading-dock door. Once inside, she took Bear's knife from the pocket of her bloody skirt and started back into the slaughterhouse, instinctively following the same route she'd taken to arrive here.

Her neck hairs stirred suddenly and she felt a wave of the sixth sense that some deaf people claim they possess. When she looked, yes, yes, there he was—Brutus, about fifty feet away, crouching, making his way from one piece of machinery to another. In his hand he too held a short knife.

She shivered in terror and ducked behind a stack of employee lockers. She thought of climbing into one but remembered that he'd hear any sound she made. Then the sixth sense came back, pelting her neck. Melanie realized, though, that this wasn't anything supernatural at all; it was the vibration of Brutus's voice, calling to Stoat.

What was he saying?

A moment later, she learned. The lights went out and she was plunged into blackness.

She dropped to the ground, paralyzed with terror. Deaf, and now blind. She curled into a ball for a moment, praying she'd faint, the terror was so great. She realized she'd dropped the knife. She patted the ground but soon gave up on it; she knew that Brutus would have heard the sound of the weapon falling and was probably making his way toward her right now. He could be kicking aside everything in his way and she'd never know, while Melanie herself had to crawl carefully over the ground, picking her way silently over bits of metal and wood, machinery and tools.

I have to—

No!

She felt something on her shoulder.

She turned in panic, lashing out with her palm.

But it was just a wire dangling from the ceiling.

Where is he? There? Or there?

Be. Quiet. It's the only thing that'll save you.

Then a reassuring thought: He can hear, yes, but he can't see any better than I can.

Want to hear a joke, Susan? What's worse off than a bird that can't hear?

A fox that can't see.

Eight gray birds, sitting in dark . . .

If I'm absolutely silent he'll never know where I am.

The remarkable internal compass that the otherwise unjust son of a bitch Fate gave Melanie tells her that she's headed in the right direction, back toward the killing room. And by God she *will* carry Donna Harstrawn on her shoulders if she has to.

Slowly. One foot before the other.

Silent. Absolutely silent.

Going to be easier than he'd thought.

Lou Handy was at his worst and he knew it—still fired up with bitterness, aching for a payback, but thinking coolly now. This was when he killed and tortured and enjoyed it the most. He'd followed the bloody footsteps to the loading dock, where, he'd assumed, both of the little shits had gotten out. But then as he was about to start back he'd heard something—a clink of metal, a scrape. And he'd looked down the corridor and seen her, Melanie, the mouse bitch freak of nature, making her way back to the main room of the slaughterhouse.

He'd moved closer and what was that he'd heard?

A *squish, squish* sound.

Her footsteps. Bloody footsteps. Good old Bonner, leaking and gross to the very end, had bled all over her shoes. With every step Melanie took she was broadcasting exactly where she was. So he'd called to Wilcox to shut the lights out.

It was wild how dark the place was. Pitch. Couldn't see your hand. At first he was real careful about making sounds. Then he thought, Why, you fuck, she can't hear you! And he hurried after her, pausing every few minutes to listen for the sound of the wet squish.

There it is.

Beautiful. honey.

Closing in.

Listen. . . .

Squish.

Can't be more than thirty feet away. Look, here we go. There she is.

He saw a ghostly form in front of him, walking back toward the main room of the plant.

Squish, squish.

He walked closer to her. He knocked a table over but her footsteps just kept rollin' along. She didn't hear a fucking thing. Closing the distance now, fifteen feet . . . ten. Five.

Right behind her.

The way he'd been behind Rudy, smelled the man's Vitalis, seen the oak dust on his shirt and the bulge in the back pocket that was a wallet filled with what it shouldn't've been filled with. "You fucker," Handy'd screamed to his brother, not seeing red, like the expression, but seeing black fire, seeing nothing but his rage. Rudy had sneered, kept on walking. And the gun in Handy's fist began firing. A little gun, a .22, loaded with long, not even a long-rifle, slugs. Which left little red dots on the neck and his brother doing the fucking scary little dance before he fell to the floor and died.

Handy raged again at Art Potter for bringing up the thought of Rudy today, like he was planting the memory in Handy's soul the way a pebble got pushed into your palm in a prison yard fight. Raged at Potter and at fat, dead Bonner and at Melanie, the fucking spooked mouse bitch.

Two feet behind her, watching her timid steps.

She didn't have a clue. . . .

This was fucking great, walking in step with her. There were so many possibilities. . . .

Hello, Miss Mouse. . . .

But he picked the simplest. He leaned close and licked the back of her neck.

He thought she'd break her back she leapt away from him so fast, twisting sideways and falling into a stack of rusted sheet metal. His hand closed on her hair and he dragged her after him, twisting and stumbling.

"Yo, Shep, put those lights back on!"

A moment later the room filled with dim light and Handy could make out the doorway to the main part of the slaughterhouse. Melanie struggled to pry his hands from her hair but he had a good grip and she could beat till kingdom come and he'd never let her go.

"You're making strange little peeps. I don't like it. Shut up! Shut the fuck up!" He slapped her in the face. He didn't think she got what he was saying but in any case she shut up. He dragged her through the cascading water, through the aisles of junk.

Straight to a decapitation guillotine.

It was basically a huge piece of butcher block, carved out with an indentation for the pig's or steer's chest. On the top was mounted a frame holding a triangular blade, operated by a long rubber-covered handle. A big fucking paper cutter.

Wilcox watched. He asked, "You really gonna . . . ?"

"What about it?" Handy screamed.

"It's just we're so close to getting out, man."

Handy ignored him, grabbed a piece of wire from the floor, and wrapped it around Melanie's right wrist. Twisted the tourniquet tight. She struggled, hit him in the shoulder with her left fist. "Fucking freak," he muttered, and slugged her hard in the back. She dropped to the floor, where she curled into a ball, moaning, staring in horror at her hand turning blue.

Handy lit his Bic lighter and ran it slowly over the blade of the guillotine. She shook her head violently, eyes huge. "Should've thought about it before you turned on me." He scooped her up from the floor and slammed her against the guillotine.

Sobbing, slapping at him, the mouse bitch tried to struggle away. He figured the pain in her right hand, now deep purple from the wire, was close to unbearable. Handy shoved her groin against the guillotine and pushed her forward, facedown, extending her right arm under the blade. He kicked her legs out from underneath her. She lost all leverage and dangled, helpless, from the machine. Handy easily pinioned her hand in the cutting groove.

He hesitated a moment and looked down at her face, listening to the gasping sound that rose from her throat. "God, I hate that fucking sound you people make. Hold her, Shep."

Wilcox hesitated, stepped forward, and took her arm in both of his hands. "Don't think I want to watch this," he said uneasily, and looked away.

"I do," Handy muttered. Unable to resist the urge, he lowered his head close to her face, inhaled her scent, rubbing his cheek against her tears. Stroked her hair.

Then his hands rose to the lever. He worked it back and forth, loosening it up, dropping the blade to her flesh, lifting it again. It rose to its full height. He took the rubber handle in both hands.

The phone rang.

Handy looked at it.

A pause. Wilcox released Melanie's hand, stepped away from the guillotine.

Shit. Handy debated.

"Answer it."

" 'Lo?" Wilcox asked into the receiver. Then listened. He shrugged and glanced at Handy, who paused. "Yo, homes, it's for you."

"Tell Potter to go to hell."

"It ain't Potter. It's a girl. And I'll tell you, sounds like she's some fox."

10:58 P.M.

Potter sat at the window, looking through his Leica binoculars, while behind him young, fierce Detective Sharon Foster, who'd pulled her cruiser hell-for-leather into the forward staging area ten minutes before, was pacing nervously and swearing like a sailor at Louis Handy.

"The fuck you say, Lou," she snarled. Like many female line officers Foster had that resolute, humorless grit that her pert blond ponytail and pretty face couldn't belie.

"Been a while, you bitch. You a detective now?"

"Yep. I got promoted." She bent down and squinted through the command van's window at the slaughterhouse, her head inches from Potter's. "What the hell've you done with *your* life, Lou? Aside from screwing it up royal?"

"Hey, I'm right proud of my accomplishments." From the speaker came the cold chuckle Potter recognized so well.

"I always knew you were one grade-A fuckup. They could write a book about you."

Potter recognized exactly what Foster was doing. It wasn't his way. He preferred to be more easygoing, Will Rogersish. Tough when he needed to be, but he avoided jousting, which could easily escalate into emotional skirmishes. Arthur Potter hadn't bantered with Marian and he didn't banter with his friends. But sometimes with certain takers—usually brash, overconfident criminals—this young woman's style worked: the barbs, the give-and-take.

Potter continued to stare at the slaughterhouse, trying desperately to get a look at Melanie. The last of the students, Emily, had been picked up by Stillwell's deputies in the skiff behind the building. Through Frances the little girl had explained that Melanie had gotten her out and then gone back for Mrs. Harstrawn. But that had been nearly twenty minutes ago and no one had seen the last two hostages escape. Potter assumed Handy had found her. He was desperate to know if she was all right but would never interrupt a negotiator at work.

"You're an asshole, Lou," Foster continued. "You may get away in that chopper but they're going to catch you. Canada? They'll extradite your ass so fast it'll make your head spin."

"They gotta find me first."

"You think they wear red jackets and Smokey the Bear hats and chase down muggers with whistles? You've killed, Lou—hostages and cops. There isn't a law enforcer in the world gonna stop till they get you."

LeBow and Potter exchanged glances. Potter was growing uneasy. She was pushing him a lot. Potter frowned but she either missed or ignored the expression, above criticism from an older man—and a Feebie at that. He was also feeling the thorns of jealousy. It'd taken him hours to build up a rapport with Handy; Potter was Stockholmed through and through. And here was this new kid on the block, this blond chippy, stealing away his good friend and comrade.

Potter nodded discreetly at the computer. LeBow caught his meaning and went on line to the National Law Enforcement Personnel Database. A moment later he turned the screen for Potter to read. Sharon Foster only looked young and inexperienced; she was in fact thirty-four and had an impressive record as a hostage negotiator. In thirty barricade situations she'd managed clean surrenders in twenty-four. The others had gone hot—HRT assaults had been required—but they'd been EDs. When emotionally disturbed takers are involved, negotiated solutions work only ten percent of the time.

"I like Art better," Handy said. "He don't give me any shit."

"That's my Lou, always looking for the easy way."

"Fuck you," Handy barked.

"Something I've been thinking about, Lou," she added coyly. "I'm wondering if you're really going to Canada."

Now Potter glanced at D'Angelo. The tactical plan required that Handy and Wilcox trek through the woods to the helicopter. If Foster made him think they hadn't believed him, Handy would suspect a trap and stay holed up.

Potter stood up, shaking his head. Foster glanced but ignored him. LeBow and Angie were shocked at the disrespect. Potter sat down again, more embarrassed than hurt.

"Sure, I'm going to Canada. I've got myself a special priority. I've talked to the fucking FAA myself."

As if he hadn't spoken, her southern-accented voice rasped, "You're a cop killer, Lou. You touch down anywhere in these United States, with or without hostages, you're dead meat. Every cop in the country knows your face. Wilcox's too. And believe me, they'll shoot first and read rights to your bleeding body. And I promise you, Lou, any ambulance carrying you to a prison hospital's gonna take its own sweet fucking time gettin' you there."

Potter had heard enough of her hardball tactics. He was sure she'd push Handy right back into his hole. He reached for her shoulder. But he stopped when he heard Handy say, "Nobody can catch me. I'm the worst thing you'll ever come across. I'm cold death."

It wasn't Handy's words that gave Potter pause but the tone of his voice. He sounded like a scared child. Almost pathetic. However unorthodox her style, Foster had touched something in Handy.

She turned to him. "Can I make a surrender offer?"

LeBow, Budd, and D'Angelo all looked at Potter.

What was in Handy's mind? he wondered. A sudden awareness of the hopelessness of the situation? Maybe a reporter had managed to broadcast that federal Hostage Rescue had arrived and surrounded the slaughterhouse, and Handy had heard it on his television.

Or maybe he'd simply gotten tired.

It happened. In an instant the energy dissipates. HTs ready to come out with guns blazing will just sit on the floor when HRT kicks in the door and look at the approaching agents without the energy to lift their hands over their heads.

Yet there was another possibility, one that Potter hated to consider. Which was that this young woman was simply better than he was. That she'd breezed in, assessed Handy, and then pegged him right. Again the jealousy tore at him. *What should I do?*

He thought suddenly of Melanie. What would be most likely to save her?

Potter nodded to the young detective. "Sure. Go ahead."

"Lou, what'll it take to make you come out?"

Potter thought: *Lemme fuck you.*

"Can I fuck you?"

"You'd have to ask my husband and he'd say no."

A pause.

"There's nothing I want but freedom. And I got that."

"Do you?" Foster asked softly.

Another pause. Longer than the first.

Potter speculated. *Fuck, yeah. And nobody's taking it away from me.*

But Handy said, in effect, just the opposite. "I don't . . . I don't want to die."

"Nobody wants to shoot you, Lou."

"Everybody wants to shoot me. And I go back, the judge'll give me the needle."

"We can talk about that." Her voice was gentle, almost motherly.

Potter stared at the yellow square of light. Somewhere in his heart he was beginning to believe that he'd made some very serious mistakes tonight. Mistakes that had cost lives.

Foster turned to the agent. "Who can guarantee the state won't seek the death penalty?"

Potter told her that Roland Marks was nearby, sent Budd to find him. A moment later Marks climbed into the van and Foster explained to him what Handy wanted.

"He'll surrender?" The assistant attorney general's cold eyes were on Potter, who felt all the censure and scorn he'd fired at Marks earlier that day flow right back at himself. For the first time today Potter found he couldn't hold Marks's eye.

"I think I can get him to," Foster said.

"Yes indeed. I'll guarantee whatever he wants. Put a big red seal on it. Ribbons too. I can't get an existing-sentence reduction—"

"No. I'm sure he understands that."

"But I'll guarantee we don't go sticking those little needles in his arm."

"Lou. The state assistant attorney general is here. He's guaranteeing that they won't go after the death penalty if you surrender."

"Yeah?" There was a pause, the sound of a hand over the receiver. Then: "Same for my boy Shep here?"

Foster frowned. LeBow turned his computer to her and she read about Wilcox. She looked at the AG, who nodded.

"Sure, Lou. Both of you. And the other guy with you?"

Potter thought: *Son of a bitch had himself an accident.*

Handy laughed. "Had a accident."

Foster lifted an inquiring eyebrow to Potter, who said, "Believed dead."

"Okay, you and Wilcox," the blond detective said, "you got a deal."

The same deal that Potter, through Charlie Budd, had offered him. Why was Handy accepting it now? A moment later he found out.

"Hold up, you frigid bitch. That's not all."

"I love it when you talk dirty, Lou."

"I also want a guarantee to stay outta Callana. I killed that guard there. I go back and they'll pound me to death for sure. No more federal time."

Foster looked once more at Potter, who nodded to Tobe. "Call Justice," he whispered. "Dick Allen."

The deputy attorney general in Washington.

"Lou," Foster said, "We're checking on it now."

Potter again anticipated: *I'm still horny. Let's fuck.*

Handy's voice brightened and the old devil was back. "Come sit on my cock while we're waiting."

"I would, Lou, but I don't know where it's been."

"In my Jockeys for way too long."

"Just keep it there for a while longer then."

Potter was patched through to Allen, who listened and agreed reluctantly that if Handy was willing to surrender he could serve his state time first. Allen would also waive the federal charges for the escape though not for the murder of the guard. The practical effect of this was that Handy wouldn't have to surrender to any federal jailers until about fifty years after he'd died of old age.

Foster relayed this to Handy. There was a long pause. A moment later Handy's voice said, "Okay, we'll do it."

Foster looked at Potter with a cocked eyebrow. He nodded numbly, dumbfounded.

"But I gotta see it in writing," Handy said.

"Okay, Lou. We can arrange that."

Potter was already writing the terms out longhand. He handed the sheet to Henry LeBow to type and print out.

"So, that's it," LeBow said, eyes on his blue screen. "Score one for the good guys."

Laughter broke out. Potter's face burned as he watched the elation on the faces of Budd and the other federal agents. He smiled too but he understood—as did no one else on the threat management team—that he had both won and lost. And he knew that it was not his strength or courage or intelligence that had failed him but his judgment.

Which is the worst defeat a man can suffer.

"Here we go," LeBow said, offering the printout to Potter. He and Marks signed the document and Stevie Oates made one last run to the slaughterhouse. When he returned he wore a perplexed expression and carried a bottle of Corona beer, which Handy had given him.

"Agent Potter?" Sharon Foster had apparently been calling his name several times. He looked up. "Would you like to coordinate the surrender?"

He stared at her for a moment and nodded. "Yes, of course. Tobe, call Dean Stillwell. Ask him to please come in here."

Tobe made the call. Unfazed, LeBow continued to type in information on the incident log. Detective Sharon Foster glanced at Potter with a look that he took to be one of sympathy; it was patronizing and hurt far more than a snide smile of triumph would have. As he looked at her he felt suddenly very old—as if everything he'd known and done in his life, every way he looked at things, every word he'd said to strangers and to friends was, in an instant, outmoded and invalid.

If not an outright lie.

He was in camouflage gear so no one saw the lean man lying in a stand of starkly white birch not far from the command van.

His hands clasped the night-vision binoculars, sweat dotting his palms copiously.

Dan Tremain had been frozen in this position for an hour, during which time a helicopter had come and gone, the federal HRT had arrived and assembled nearby, and a squad car had streaked up to the van, bearing a young policewoman.

Tremain had taken in the news, which was spreading like fire in a wheat field from trooper to trooper, that Handy had decided to give it up in exchange for an agreement not to seek the death penalty.

But for Dan Tremain this wasn't acceptable.

His trooper, young Joey Wilson, and that poor girl this afternoon had not died so that Lou Handy might live long enough to kill again, certainly to gloat and relive the perverse joy at the carnage he'd caused throughout his pointless life.

Sacrifice was sometimes necessary. And who better than a soldier to give up his life in the name of justice?

"Surrender in ten minutes," a voice called from behind him. Tremain could not possibly have said whether it was the voice of a trooper or that of an angel dipping low from God's own heaven to make this announcement. In any event he nodded and rose to his feet. He stood tall, wiped the tears from his face, adjusted his uniform, brushed his hair with his fingers. Never one to preen, Tremain had decided it was important that he look strong and resolute and proud when he ended his career in the dramatic fashion he had planned.

11:18 P.M.

Surrender is the most critical stage of a barricade.

More lives are lost in surrenders than during any other phase of hostage situations except assaults. And this one would be particularly tricky, Potter knew, because the essence of surrender was Handy's nemesis—giving up control.

Again his natural impatience prodded him to get things over with, to get Handy into custody. But he had to fight this urge. He was running the surrender by the book and had assembled the threat management team before him in the van.

The first thing he did was shake Dean Stillwell's hand. "Dean, I'm putting Frank and the Bureau's HRT in charge of containment and tactical matters now. You've done a fine job. It's just that Frank and I've done this in the past a number of times."

"No problem at all, Arthur. I'm honored you let me help." To Potter's embarrassment Stillwell snapped a salute, which the agent reluctantly returned.

Budd, LeBow, Tobe, and D'Angelo all hunched over the terrain maps and diagram of the slaughterhouse as Potter went through the procedure. Angie, who had no tactical experience and could offer little assistance to D'Angelo and the HRT, was escorting Emily and Beverly to the Days Inn. Intense, young Detective Sharon Foster was outside smoking—very real Camels. Frances was in the van, waiting patiently.

"Everybody's going to be wired up and half-nuts," Potter said. "Our people *and* the takers. We're all tired and there's going to be a lot of carelessness. So we have to choreograph every step." He fell silent and was looking out the window at the square yellow eyes of the building.

"Arthur?" LeBow said.

He meant, Time's awasting.

"Yes, sure."

They bent over the map and he began to give commands. It seemed to him that he'd lost his voice completely and he was surprised to find that the men who stood before him nodded gravely as if listening to words that he himself hardly heard at all.

Twenty minutes later, as Potter lay in a stand of fragrant grass and hit the speed-dial button, it occurred to him that something was very wrong. That Handy was laying a trap.

He thought of Budd's words earlier in the day, about Handy's planning something clever and flamboyant—a breakout maybe, a run for it.

A gut feel. Listen to it. He's usually right.

And now the feeling was undeniable.

The click of an answered phone.

"Lou." Potter began what was probably their last conversation via throw phone.

"Whatsa game plan, Art?"

"Just want to go over a few ground rules." Potter was fifty yards from the slaughterhouse entrance. Frank D'Angelo and Charlie Budd were beside him. LeBow and Tobe remained in the command van. "Is the older woman conscious? The teacher?"

"Zonked out. Told you, Art. She had a bad night. Bonner's—well, *was* a big fella. I'm talking in all ways."

Potter found his voice quavering as he asked, "And the other teacher?"

"The blond one? The little mouse?" There was a pause and Handy offered his famous chuckle. "Why you so interested in her, Art? Seem to recall you asked about her a couple times."

"I want to know how our last hostages are."

"Sure you do." Handy laughed again. "Well, she's probably had better nights herself."

"How do you mean, Lou?" he asked casually. What terrible retribution had he exacted?

"She's too young for an old fart like you, Art."

Damn it, Potter thought, furious. Handy was reading him too clearly. The agent forced himself to put her out of his mind and returned mentally to Chapter 9 of his handbook, entitled "The Surrender Phase." Potter and D'Angelo had decided to send in the tunnel rats—point men—under the loading-dock door to secure the interior and guard the hostages then have the takers come out through the front.

"All right, Lou," Potter continued. "When I tell you to I'd like you to put your weapons down and just step outside, with your arms out to your side. Not on your head."

"Like Christ on the cross."

The wind had grown much worse, bending saplings and stands of sedge and bluestem, Queen Anne's lace, sending up clouds of dust. It would play hell with the snipers' shooting.

"Tell me the truth. Is Bonner dead or wounded?"

Potter had visited Beverly, the poor asthmatic, in one of the hospital tents and learned that the big man indeed had been shot. But the girl explained that she'd done her best to avoid looking at him. She couldn't say for certain if he was still alive.

"Tired of talking, Art. Me and Shep're gonna chat for a few minutes then we'll give it up. Hey, Art?"

"Yes, Lou?"

"I want you out front. Right where I can see you. It's the only way I'm coming out."

I'll do it, Potter thought instinctively. Anything you want.

"I'll be there, Lou."

"Right out front."

"You've got it." A pause. "Now, Lou, I want to tell you exactly—"

"Goodbye, Art. It's been fun."

Click.

Potter found himself gripping the phone long after Handy's voice was replaced by the rush of static. From nowhere the thought formed: The man's bent on suicide. The hopelessness of the situation: the impossibility of escaping, the relentless pursuit, an unbearable prison term awaiting him. He's going out in a flash.

Ostrella, my beloved. . . .

It would be the ultimate control.

D'Angelo broke into the reverie, saying, "We'll assume Bonner's alive and armed until we get a confirmation."

Potter nodded, pressed disconnect, put the phone in his pocket. "Choreograph it carefully, Frank. I think he may go down shooting."

"You think?" Budd whispered, as if Handy had a Big Ear on them.

"A hunch is all. But plan accordingly."

D'Angelo nodded. He got on the horn and doubled the number of snipers in the trees, moved up some explosives experts to the initial takedown team. When they were in place he asked, "Should we move in, Arthur?"

Potter nodded to him. D'Angelo spoke into his microphone and four HRT troopers slipped along the front of the slaughterhouse. Two paused at open windows and the others disappeared into the shadows on either side of the door. The ones by the window had mesh bomb blankets over their shoulders.

Then the HRT commander called the two point men inside the building. He listened for a moment then repeated the report to Potter: "Two hostages, apparently alive, lying on the ground in the room you indicated. Injured but extent unknown. Bonner appears to be dead." The unemotional voice grew troubled. "Man, there's blood everywhere."

Whose? Potter wondered.

"Are Handy and Wilcox armed?"

"No weapons in their hands but they're wearing bulky shirts. Could be hidden."

Injured but extent unknown.

Potter said to D'Angelo, "They had tools. Might've brought tape with them too and taped weapons under their shirts."

The HRT commander nodded.

Blood everywhere . . .

Sharon Foster joined the men on the hillock. She'd put on bulky body armor.

How was this going to end? Potter wondered. He listened to the mournful sound of the wind. He felt a desperate urge to talk to Handy once more. Pressed the speed-dial button on the phone he carried.

A dozen rings, two dozen. No answer.

D'Angelo and LeBow were looking at him. He hung up.

Inside the slaughterhouse, the lights went out. Budd stiffened; Potter motioned him to relax. HTs often doused lights upon leaving, afraid to present a silhouette target even though they were giving up.

The crescent moon had moved fifty degrees through the windy sky. Often there's a sense of familiarity, even a perverse comfort, that a negotiator finds in the setting in which he's spent hours or days. Tonight, though, as he gazed at the black and red brick, all Potter could think of was Handy's phrase "Cold death."

The door opened slowly, stuck halfway, then opened further.

No movement.

What will it be? he wondered. Good or bad? Peaceful or violent?

Ah, my beautiful Ostrella.

During surrenders, he'd seen it all: Terrorists falling to the ground, crying like babies. Unarmed criminals streaking for freedom. Hidden guns. The young Syrian woman who walked slowly from an Israeli consulate, arms properly outstretched, and smiled sweetly at him just before the grenades in her bra blew herself and three HRT agents to pieces.

Be forewarned.

For only the third or fourth time in his career Arthur Potter lifted his weapon from his belt holster, high on his padded hip, and awkwardly pulled the automatic's slide, chambering a round. He replaced the gun, not clicking on the safety.

"Why isn't anything happening?" Budd whispered in irritation.

Potter stifled a sudden, inexplicable urge to laugh hysterically.

"Art?" Handy's voice floated from inside the slaughterhouse, a soft, ragged sound on the wind.

"Yes?" Potter called through the megaphone.

"Where the fuck are you? I don't see you."

Potter looked at Budd. "Here's where I earn my paycheck." He rose unsteadily, polished his glasses on the lapel of his sports coat. Sharon Foster asked if he was sure he wanted to do this. He glanced at her then walked awkwardly down the hill and stepped over an ancient split-rail fence. He paused about thirty yards from the front of the slaughterhouse.

"Here I am, Lou. Come on out."

And there they were.

Handy first. Then Wilcox.

The first thing he noticed was that their arms were at the backs of their heads.

It's all right, Ostrella. Come out however you want. Come home. You'll be okay.

"Lou, stretch your arms out!"

"Hey, take it easy, Art," Handy called. "Don't give yourself a fucking heart attack." Blinking against the powerful glare of the blinding lights. Amused, looking around.

"Lou, you've got a dozen snipers aiming at you—"

"Just a dozen? Shit! Thought I was worth more than that."

"Put your arms out or they'll shoot."

Handy stopped walking. Looked over at Wilcox. They broke into smiles. Potter's hand went to the butt of his pistol.

Slowly the prisoners' arms extended.

"I look like a fucking ballerina, Art."

"You're doing fine, Lou."

"Easy for you to say."

Potter called, "Move in separate directions about ten feet, then lie facedown on the ground."

They walked away from the slaughterhouse, farther than ordered but then dropped to their knees and went prone. The two HRT agents by the door kept their H&Ks trained on the fugitives' backs and stayed clear of the doorway just in case Bonner wasn't in fact dead or there'd been other takers inside that even the hostages hadn't known about.

The two agents hovering by the windows climbed inside, followed by two more, who ran from the shadows and sped through the door. The beams of the powerful flashlights attached to their guns whipped through-out the slaughterhouse.

They'd been briefed about the incendiary device Handy'd rigged and they'd be moving very slowly, looking for tripwires. Potter believed he'd never been so anxious in his life. He expected the interior of the slaughterhouse to blossom into orange flame at any instant.

Outside, two more HRT agents had moved up, covering the two beside the door, who now advanced on Handy and Wilcox.

Did the men have armed grenades on them?

Hidden knives?

It wasn't until they'd been cuffed and patted down that Arthur Potter realized the barricade was over. He'd escaped, alive and unhurt.

And had once again read Handy wrong.

Potter returned to Budd, D'Angelo, and Foster. Told the HRT commander to radio the agents taking the two convicts into custody with orders on how to handle them. Potter remembered that Wilcox was the cowboy in the group, more impulsive than the others. He'd ordered him shackled around the waist as well as cuffed but told them not to do so with Handy. Potter knew Lou would be more willing to cooperate if he retained at least a little control.

Other agents appeared silently and covered the two men. They pulled them to their feet and frisked them again, more carefully, then quickly led them into a gully and hurried them away from the slaughterhouse.

Then the lights went on inside.

A long, long moment of silence, though it was probably just seconds. Where *is* she?

"Go ahead," D'Angelo said into his mike. He listened for a minute then said to Potter, "It's secure. No other takers. No traps. There was something rigged in the room but it's been dismantled."

The others rose to their feet too and watched Handy's progress as he approached up the gully.

"And the hostages?" Potter asked urgently.

D'Angelo listened. He said aloud, "Bonner's dead."

Yes, yes, *yes?*

"And they found two female hostages. One, white, late thirties. Conscious but incoherent."

For chrissake, what about—

"Second one, white, age mid-twenties. Also conscious." D'Angelo winced. "Seriously hurt, he says."

No. Oh, my God.

"What?" Potter cried. "What happened to her?" The negotiator lifted his own radio and cut into the channel. "How is she? The younger woman?"

The HRT agent inside said, "Handy must've really done a number on her, sir."

"How *bad*?" Potter said furiously. Budd and D'Angelo stared at him. Handy was approaching, two agents on either side. Potter found he couldn't look at him.

The agent inside said into the radio, "Well, sir, she doesn't look that badly hurt but the thing is he must've beat the hell out of her. She can't hear a word we're saying."

The surrender had happened so fast he'd forgotten to tell the tactical agents Melanie was deaf.

D'Angelo said something to him and so did Charlie Budd but Potter didn't hear, so loud was his manic, hysterical laughter. Sharon Foster and nearby troopers looked at him uneasily. Potter supposed, without caring, that he sounded like the crazy old man that he was.

"Lou."

"Art, you don't look nothing like what I thought. You *do* have to lose a few pounds."

Handy stood behind the van, hands cuffed behind him. Sharon Foster was nearby, looking over the prisoners. When Handy glanced at her body, grinning, she stared back contemptuously. Potter knew that after a hard negotiation, particularly one in which there'd been a killing, you felt an urge to insult or belittle your enemy. Potter controlled it himself but she was younger and more emotional. She sneered at Handy, walked away. The convict laughed and turned back to Potter.

"Your picture doesn't do you justice," the negotiator said to him.

"Fuckers never do."

As always, after a surrender, the hostage taker appeared minuscule compared with the image in Potter's mind. Handy's features were hard and compact, his face lean and lined and pale. He knew Handy's height and weight but still he was surprised at how diminished he seemed.

Potter scanned the crowd for Melanie. He didn't see her. Troopers, firemen, medics, and Stillwell's now-disbanded containment force were milling about outside the slaughterhouse. The car and the school bus and the processing plant itself were of course crime scenes and since by agreement this was technically now a state operation Budd had formally arrested Handy and Wilcox and was trying to preserve the site for the forensic teams.

Where is she?

There was a brief incident when Potter arrested Handy on federal charges. Handy's eyes went cold. "What the fuck is this?"

"I'm just preserving our rights," Potter said. SAC Henderson explained that it was a mere technicality, and Roland Marks too confirmed that everyone would adhere to the written agreement, though Potter had a bad moment when he thought Marks was going to take a swing at the convict. The assistant AG muttered, "Fucking child killer," and stormed off. Handy laughed at his receding back.

Shep Wilcox, grinning, looked around, disappointed, it seemed, there were no reporters present.

The older teacher, Donna Harstrawn, was brought out on a gurney. Potter went to her and walked alongside the medics. He looked at one of the techs, eyebrow raised. "She'll be okay," the young man whispered. "Physically, I mean."

"Your husband and children are at the Days Inn," he told her.

"It was . . ." she began, and fell silent. Shook her head. "I can't see anyone now. Please. No . . . I don't ever . . ." Her words dissolved, incoherent.

Potter squeezed her arm and stopped walking, watched them carry her up the hill to the waiting ambulance.

He turned back to the slaughterhouse just as Melanie Charrol was being escorted out. Her blond hair in disarray. She too—like Handy— seemed smaller than Potter expected. He started forward but paused. Melanie hadn't seen him; she was walking quickly, her eyes on Donna

Harstrawn. Her clothes were dark—gray skirt, black stockings, burgundy blouse—but it seemed to Potter that they were saturated with blood.

"What's all that blood on her?" he asked one of the HRT agents who'd been inside.

"Not hers," came the response. "Bonner's probably. Man bled out like a gutted twelve-point buck. You want to debrief her?"

He hesitated.

"Later," he said. But in his mind the word was more of a question and the answer was unknown.

Detective Sharon Foster strode up to Potter and shook his hand.

" 'Night, Agent Potter."

"Thanks for everything," he said evenly.

"Piece of cake." She jabbed a blunt finger at him. "Hey, great job with that surrender. Smooth as silk." Then wheeled and returned to her squad car, leaving Potter standing alone. His face burned like that of a rookie dressed down by a tough training sergeant.

Angie Scapello returned momentarily from the Days Inn to collect her bags and say goodbye to Potter and the others. She still had some work ahead of her at the motel, where she would debrief the hostages further and make sure they and their families had the names of therapists who specialized in post-traumatic stress syndrome.

Budd and D'Angelo hitched a ride with Angie to the rear staging area. Potter and two troopers escorted the takers back to the van. Squad cars waited nearby to take them to the state police troop HQ ten miles away.

"Had yourself a fire, looks like," Handy said, looking over the black scorch marks. "You ain't gonna blame that on me, I hope?"

As he gazed at the convict Potter was aware of a man approaching from the shadows of a gully. He paid little mind since there were dozens of troopers milling about. But there was something purposeful about the man's stride, too quick and direct for him to be passing through the crowd casually. He was heading directly for Potter.

"Weapon!" Potter cried as Dan Tremain, twenty feet away, began to lift the gun.

Wilcox and the trooper holding him dove to the ground, as did the second escort trooper, leaving only Handy and Potter standing. Within easy pistol range.

Handy, smiling, turned to face Tremain. Potter drew his own gun, pointed it at the HRU commander, and stepped in front of Handy.

"No, Captain," the agent said firmly.

"Get out of the way, Potter."

"You're already in enough trouble."

The gun in Tremain's hand exploded. Potter felt the bullet snap past his head. He heard Handy laughing.

"Get out of the way!"

"Do it," Handy whispered in Potter's ear. "Pull the trigger. Waste the fucker."

"Shut up!" the agent barked. Around them four or five troopers had pulled their sidearms and were sighting on Tremain. No one knew what to do.

Or wanted to do what they knew they should.

"He's mine," Tremain said.

"It's legal," Handy whispered. "Kill him, Art. You want to anyway. You *know* you do."

"Quiet!" Potter shouted. And yet suddenly he understood that Handy was right. He *did* want to. And what's more, he felt that he had permission—to kill the man who'd nearly burnt his Melanie to death.

"Do it," Handy urged. "You're dying to."

"This'll bring you nothing but grief, Dan," Potter said slowly, ignoring his prisoner. "You don't want to do this."

"There you go, Art. Telling people what they want to do. I'll tell you what *you* want to do. You want to shoot the prick. Man almost got your girlfriend killed. She is your gal, isn't she, Art? Mel-a-nie?"

"Shut your damn mouth!"

"Do it, Art. Shoot him!"

Tremain fired again. Potter cringed as the bullet streaked past his face and dug a chunk out of the slaughterhouse.

The captain steadied the gun, seeking a target.

And Arthur Potter spread his arms, sheltering the man who was his prisoner. And—yes, Charlie, who was his friend.

"Do something bad," Handy whispered in a smooth, reassuring voice. "Just step aside a inch or two. Let him kill me. Or you shoot him."

Potter turned. "Will you—?"

Several FBI agents had drawn guns and were shouting for Tremain to drop his weapon. The state troopers were silently rooting for the HRU commander.

Potter thought: Handy *had* almost killed Melanie.

Just step aside a few inches.

And Tremain had nearly killed her too.

Shoot. Go ahead.

Handy whispered, "He'd had his way, Art, your girlfriend'd have third-degree burns over most of her body now. Her hair and tits all burned up. Even you wouldn't want to fuck somebody like—"

Potter spun, his fist lashing out. It drove into Handy's jaw. The prisoner reeled back and landed on the ground. Tremain, now only ten feet away, aimed once more at the man's chest.

"Drop the gun," Potter commanded, spinning around and stepping forward. "Drop it, Dan. Your life isn't over with yet. But it will be if you pull that trigger. Think about your family." He remembered the ring he'd seen on Tremain's finger. He said softly, "God doesn't want to waste you over somebody as worthless as Handy."

The pistol wavered, dropped to the ground.

Without looking at Potter or Handy again, Tremain walked over to Charlie Budd and held his hands out for the cuffs. Budd looked over his fellow officer, seemed about to say something but chose to remain silent.

As he scrambled to his feet Handy said, "You missed a good bet, Art. Not many people have the chance to waste somebody and—"

Potter had him by the hair, and the pistol's muzzle drove up under Handy's stubbled jaw.

"Not a single word."

Handy reared back, breathing hard. He looked away first, truly scared. But only for a moment. Then he laughed. "You're a real piece of work, Art. Yessir. Let's get it over with. Book me, Dano."

MIDNIGHT

Arthur Potter was alone.

He looked at his hands and saw they were quivering. Until the incident with Tremain they'd been rock solid. He took an imaginary Valium but it had no effect. He realized after a moment that his unease wasn't so much the aftermath of the showdown after all as an overwhelming sense of disappointment. He'd wanted to talk to Handy. Find out more about him, what made him tick.

Why had he really killed Susan? What had he been thinking? What had happened in that room, the killing room?

And what does he think about me?

It was like watching the troopers escort a part of himself away. He gazed at the back of Handy's head, his shaggy hair. The man looked sideways, a hyena grin on his face. Potter caught a glimpse of an acute angle of jawbone.

Be forewarned.

He remembered his pistol. Unchambered the round and replaced it in the clip then holstered the gun. When he looked up again, the two squad cars bearing Wilcox and Handy were gone. At the moment it seemed like the perverse camaraderie between negotiator and taker would never fade. Part of him was heartsick to see the man go.

Potter considered the work left to be done. There'd be an IR-1002 to write up. There'd be a debriefing tonight via phone with the operations director in the District and a live debriefing with the Admiral himself after the man had read the incident report. Potter ought to start preparing the presentation now. The Director liked his briefings to be as short as news bites, and real-life incidents rarely had the courtesy to line up so willingly. Potter had stopped into Peter Henderson's press conference but answered only a few questions before heading out the door, leaving the SAC to take as much credit and apportion as much blame as he wished; Potter didn't care.

He'd also have to figure out how to deal with the aborted assault by the state HRU. Potter knew that Tremain never would have tried what he did without sanction from above—possibly even the governor's. But if that were the case, the chief executive of the state would already have distanced himself from the commander. He might even be planning a subtle offensive maneuver of his own—like the public crucifixion of one Arthur Potter. The agent would have to prepare a defense for that.

And the other question—should he stay here for a few days? Return to Chicago? Return to the District?

He stood not far from the scorched van, abandoned by the crowds of departing officers, waiting to see Melanie. He gazed at the slaughterhouse, wondering what he would say to her. He saw Officer Frances Whiting leaning against her car, looking as exhausted as he felt. He approached her.

"Have time to give me a lesson?" he asked.

"You bet."

Ten minutes later they walked together to the hospital tent.

Inside, Melanie Charrol sat on a low examining table. A medic had bandaged her neck and shoulders. Perhaps to help him she'd twisted her hair into a sloppy French braid.

Potter stepped toward her and—as he'd told himself, had *ordered* himself, not to do—he spoke straight to the medic applying some Betadine to her leg, rather than to Melanie herself. "Is she all right?"

Melanie nodded. She stared at him with an intense smile. The only time her eyes flicked away from his was when he spoke and she glanced at his lips.

"It's not her blood," the medic said.

"It's Bear's?" Potter asked.

Melanie was laughing as she nodded. The smile remained on her face but he noticed that her eyes were hollow. The medic gave her a pill, which she took, then she drank down two glasses of water. The young man said, "I'll leave you alone for a few minutes."

As he left, Frances stepped inside. The two women exchanged fast, abrupt signs. Frances said, "She's asking about the other girls. I'm giving her a rundown."

Melanie turned back to Potter and was staring at him. He met her gaze. The young woman was still unnerved but—despite the bandages and blood—as beautiful as he'd expected. Incredible blue-gray eyes.

He lifted his hands to sign to her what Frances had just taught him and his usually prodigious memory failed him completely. He shook his head at his lapse. Melanie cocked her head.

Potter held up a finger. Wait. He lifted his hands again and froze once more. Then Frances gestured and he remembered. "I'm Arthur Potter," he signed. "It's a pleasure to meet you."

"No, you are Charles Michel de l'Epée," Frances translated Melanie's signing.

"I'm not *that* old." He was speaking now, smiling. "Officer Whiting here said he was born in the eighteenth century. How are you feeling?"

She understood without a translation. Melanie waved at her clothes and gave a mock frown then signed. Frances translated, "My skirt and blouse have had it. Couldn't you have gotten us out just a little earlier?"

"The movie-of-the-week people expect cliffhanger endings."

And as with Handy he felt overwhelmed; there were a thousand things to ask her. None of which found their way from his mind to his voicebox.

He stepped even closer to her. Neither moved for a moment.

Potter thought of another sentence in ASL—words that Frances had taught him earlier in the evening. "You're very brave," he signed.

Melanie looked pleased at this. Frances watched her sign but then the officer frowned and shook her head. Melanie repeated her words. To Potter, Frances said, "I don't understand what she means. What she said was, 'If you hadn't been with me I couldn't have done it.'"

But *he* understood.

He heard a chug of engine and turned to see a harvester. As he watched the ungainly vehicle he believed for a moment it was driving hordes of insects before it. Then he realized he was watching husks and dust thrown skyward by the thresher blades.

"They'll do that all night," Frances translated.

Potter looked at Melanie.

She continued, "Moisture's critical. When conditions're right they run like nobody's business. They have to."

"How do you know that?"

"She says she's a farm girl."

She looked straight into his eyes. He tried to believe that Marian had gazed at him thus so he could root this sensation in sentiment or nostalgia and have done with it. But he couldn't. The look, like the feeling it engendered, like this young woman herself, was an original.

Potter recalled the final phrase that Frances had taught him. He hesitated then impulsively signed the words. As he did it seemed to him that he felt the hand shapes with absolute clarity, as if only his hands could express what he wanted to say.

"I want to see you again," Potter signed. "Maybe tomorrow?"

She paused for an endless moment then nodded yes, smiled.

She reached out suddenly toward him and closed her hands on his arm. He pressed a bandaged hand against her shoulder. They stood in this ambiguous embrace for a moment then he lifted his fingers to her hair and touched the back of her head. She lowered her head and he his lips, nearly touching them to the thick blond plait. But suddenly he smelled the musky scent of her scalp, her sweat, latent perfume, blood. The smells of lovers coupling. And he could not kiss her.

How young she is! And as he thought that, in one instant, his desire to embrace her vanished and his old man's fantasy—never articulated, hardly formed—blew away like the chaff shot from the thresher he'd been staring at.

He knew he had to leave.

Knew he'd never see her again.

He stepped back suddenly and she looked at him, momentarily perplexed.

"I have to go talk to the U.S. attorney," he said abruptly.

Melanie nodded and offered her hand. He mistook it for a signing gesture. He stared down, waiting. Then she extended it further and took his fingers warmly. They both laughed at the misunderstanding. Suddenly she pulled him forward, kissed his cheek.

He walked to the door, stopped, turned. " 'Be forewarned.' That's what you said to me, isn't it?"

Melanie nodded, her eyes hollow once again. Hollow and forlorn. Frances translated her response: "I wanted you to know how dangerous he was. I wanted you to be careful."

Then she smiled and signed some more. Potter laughed when he heard the translation. "You owe me a new skirt and blouse. And I expect to be repaid. You better not forget. I'm Deaf with an attitude. Poor you."

Potter wandered back to the van, thanked Tobe Geller and Henry LeBow, who were taking commercial flights back to their respective homes. A squad car whisked them away. He shook Dean Stillwell's hand once more and felt a ridiculous urge to give him a present of some sort, a ribbon or a medal or a federal agent decoder ring. The sheriff brushed aside his mop of hair and had the presence of mind to order his men—federal and state alike—to walk carefully, reminding them that they were, after all, at a crime scene and evidence still needed to be gathered.

Potter stood beneath one of the halogen lights, looking out at the stark slaughterhouse.

"Night, sir," a voice drawled from behind him.

He turned to Stevie Oates. The negotiator shook his hand. "Couldn't have done it without you, Stevie."

The boy did better dodging bullets than fielding compliments. He looked down at the ground. "Yeah, well, you know."

"A word of advice."

"What's that, sir?"

"Don't volunteer so damn much."

"Yessir." The trooper grinned. "I'll keep that in mind."

Then Potter found Charlie Budd and asked him for a lift to the airport.

"You're not going to hang around for a while?" asked the young captain.

"No, I should go."

They climbed into Budd's unmarked car and sped away. Potter caught a last glimpse of the slaughterhouse; in the stark spotlights the dull red-and-white structure gave the appearance of bloody, exposed bone. He shuddered and turned away.

Halfway to the airport Budd said, "I appreciate the chance you gave me."

"You were good enough to confess something to me, Charlie—"

"After I almost fixed your clock."

"—so I better confess something to you."

The captain rubbed his tawny hair and left it looking like he'd been to the Dean Stillwell hair salon. He meant, Go ahead, I can take it.

"I kept you with me as an assistant 'cause I needed to show everybody that this was a federal operation and state took second place. I was putting you on a leash. You're a smart man and I guess you figured that out."

"Yup. Didn't seem you really needed a high-priced gofer like me. Ordering Fritos and beer and helicopters. It was one of the things made me put that tape recorder in my pocket. But the way you talked to me, treated me, was one of the things that made me take it out."

"Well, you've got a right to be good and mad. But I just wanted to say you did a lot better than I expected. You were really part of the team. Handling that session by yourself—you were a natural. I'd have you negotiate with me any time."

"Oh, brother, not for any money. Tell you what, Arthur—I'll run 'em to ground and you get 'em out of their holes."

Potter laughed. "Fair enough, Charlie."

They drove in silence through the miles and miles of wheat. The windswept grain was alive in the moonlight, like the silken coat of an animal eager to run. "I've got a feeling," Budd said slowly, "you're thinking you made a mistake tonight."

Potter said nothing, watching the bug eyes of the threshers.

"You're thinking that if you'd come up with what that Detective Foster did you could've got 'em out sooner. Maybe even saved that girl's life, and Joey Wilson's."

"It did cross my mind," Potter said after a minute. Oh, how we hate to be pegged and explained. What's so compelling about the idea that our selves are mysteries to everyone but us? I let *you* in on the secrets, Marion. But only you. It's an aspect of love, I think, and reasonable enough there. But how queasy it makes us feel when strangers have the eye to see us so unfurled.

"But you kept 'em alive through three or four deadlines," Budd continued.

"That girl though, Susan . . ."

"But he shot her before you even started negotiating. There was nothing you could've said to save her. Besides, Handy had plenty of chances to ask for what Sharon offered him, and he never did. Not once."

This was true. But if Arthur Potter knew anything about his profession it was that the negotiator was the closest thing to God in a barricade and that every death fell on his shoulders and his only. What he'd learned—and what had saved his heart over the years—was that some of those deaths simply weigh less than others.

They drove another three miles and Potter realized he'd grown hypnotized, staring at the moon-white wheat. Budd was talking to him once again. The subject was domestic, the man's wife and his daughters.

Potter looked away from the streaming grain and listened to what the captain was telling him.

In the tiny jet Arthur Potter slipped two sticks of Wrigley's into his mouth and waved goodbye to Charlie Budd, who was waving back, though the interior of the plane was very dim and Potter doubted that the captain saw him.

Then he sank down into the spongy beige seat of the Grumman Gulfstream. He thought of the flask of Irish whisky in his briefcase but found himself decidedly not in the mood.

How 'bout that, Marian? No nightcap for me and I'm off-duty. What do you say about that?

He saw a phone on a console nearby and thought he should call his cousin Linden and tell her not to wait up for him. Maybe he'd wait until they were airborne. He'd ask to speak to Sean; the boy would be thrilled to know that Uncle Arthur was talking to him from twenty thousand feet in the air. He gazed absently out the window at the constellations of colored lights marking runways and taxiways. Potter took from his pocket the still-damp note Melanie had written him. Read it. Then he crumpled the paper, stuffed it into the pocket of the seat in front of him.

The jets whined powerfully and with a sudden burst of thrust he found the plane not racing down the runway at all but streaking straight into the sky, almost from a dead stop, like a spaceship headed to Mars.

They rose up and up, aiming for the moon, which was an eerie sickle in the hazy sky. The plane pointed itself at the black disk surrounded by the white crescent. Uncharacteristically poetic, Potter thought of this image: the icy thumb and index finger of a witch, reaching for a pinch of nightshade.

The negotiator closed his eyes and sat back in the soft seat.

Just as he did, the Grumman banked fiercely. So sharp was the maneuver that Arthur Potter knew suddenly he was about to die. He considered this fact very calmly. A wing or an engine had fallen off. A bolt holding together the whole airplane had finally fatigued. His eyes sprang open and—yes, yes!—he believed he saw his wife's face clearly in the white glow surrounding the moon as it scythed past. He understood that what had joined the two of them, himself and Marian, for all these years joined them still, just as powerfully, and she was pulling him after her in death.

He closed his eyes again. And felt utterly at peace.

But no, he was not destined to die just yet.

For as the plane completed its acute turn and headed back toward the airport, dropping the landing gear and flaps, sliding down down down to the flat Kansas landscape once more, Potter clutched the telephone to his ear, listening to SAC Peter Henderson tell him in a shaking, grim voice how the real Detective Sharon Foster had been found dead and half-naked not far from her house a half-hour ago and how it was now suspected that the woman who'd impersonated her at the barricade had been Lou Handy's girlfriend.

The four troopers who'd been escorting Handy and Wilcox were dead, as was Wilcox himself—all killed in a violent shootout five miles from the slaughterhouse.

And as for Handy and the woman—they were gone without a trace.

IV

A MAIDEN'S GRAVE

1:01 A.M.

As they drove through the fields beneath the faint moon the couple in the Nissan reflected on the evening at their daughter's home in Enid, which had been exactly as unpleasant as they'd expected.

When they spoke, however, they spoke not about the children's shabby trailer, the unwashed baby grandson, their stringy-haired son-in-law's disappearing act into the trash-filled backyard to sneak Jack Daniel's. No, they talked only about the weather and unusual road signs they happened to pass.

"We'll get rain this fall. Floodin'."

"Might."

"Something 'bout the trout in Minnesota. I read that."

"Trout?"

"Bad rains I'm talking. Stuckey's's only five miles. Look there. You wanta stop?"

Harriet, their daughter, had made a dinner that could be described only as inedible—woefully overdone and oversalted. And the husband had found what he was sure was some cigarette ash in the succotash. Now they were both starving.

"Might do that. For coffee only. Lookit that wind—whooee! Hope you shut the windows at home. Maybe a piece of pie."

"I did."

"You forgot last time," the wife reminded shrilly. "Don't want to lose the lamp again. You know what three-way bulbs cost."

"Well," the husband said. "What's going on here?"

"How's that?"

"I'm being stopped. A police car."

"Pull over!"

"I'm doing it," he said testily. "No point in leaving skid marks. I'm doing it."

"What'd you do?"

"I didn't do *nothing*. I was fifty-seven in a fifty-five zone and that's not a crime in anybody's book."

"Well, pull off the road."

"I'm pulling. Will you just settle? There, happy?"

"Hey, look," the wife offered with astonishment, "there's a lady officer driving!"

"They have 'em now. You know that. You watch *Cops*. Should I get out or are they going to come up here?"

"Maybe," the wife said, "you oughta go to them. Make the effort. That way if they're right on the borderline of giving you a ticket they might not."

"That's a thought. But I still don't know what I done." And, smiling like a Kiwanian on Pancake Day, the husband climbed out of the Nissan and walked back to the squad car, fishing his wallet out of his pocket.

As Lou Handy drove the cruiser deep into the wheat field, cutting a swath in the tall grain, he was lost in the memory of another field—the one that morning, near the intersection where the Cadillac had broadsided them.

He remembered the gray sky overhead. The feel of the bony knife in his hand. The woman's powdery face, black wrinkles in her makeup, dots of her blood spattering her as he drove the knife downward into her soft body. The look in her eyes, hopelessness and sorrow. Her weird scream, choking, grunting. An animal's sounds.

She'd died the same way that the couple in the Nissan just had, the couple now lying in the trunk of the cruiser he was driving. Hell, they had to die, both of the couples. They'd had something *he* needed. Their cars. The Cadillac and the Nissan. This afternoon Hank and Ruth'd smashed the fuck out of his Chevy. And tonight, well, he and Pris *couldn't* keep driving in a stolen squad car. It was impossible. He needed a new car. He *had* to have one.

And when Lou Handy collected what he was owed, when he'd scratched that itch, he was the most contented man on earth.

Tonight he parked the cruiser, which stunk of cordite and blood, in the field, fifty yards from the road. It'd be found by tomorrow morning but that was okay. In a few hours he and Pris'd be out of the state and flying over the Texas-Mexico border, a hundred feet in the air, on their way to San Hidalgo.

Whoa, hold on tight. . . . Damn, the wind was fierce, buffeting the car and sending the stalks of wheat slapping into the windshield with a clatter like birdshot.

Handy climbed out and trotted back to the road, where Pris sat in the driver's seat of the Nissan. She'd ditched the trooper's uniform and was wearing a sweater and jeans and Handy wanted more than anything else at the moment to tug those Levi's down, them and the cheap nylon panties she always wore, and fuck her right on top of the hood of the tinny Jap car. Holding her ponytail in his right hand the way he liked to do.

But he jumped in the passenger's seat and motioned for her to get going. She pitched her cigarette out the window and gunned the engine. The car shot away off the shoulder, hung a tight U, and sped up to sixty.

Heading back in the direction they'd just come from. North.

It seemed crazy, sure. But Handy prided himself on being as off-the-wall nuts as a man could be and still get on in this life. In reality their destination made sense, though—because where they were going was the last place anyone would think to look for them.

Anyway, he thought, fuck it whether it's crazy or not. His mind was made up. He had business back there. Lou Handy was owed.

The Heiligenstadt Testament, written in 1802 by Beethoven to his brothers, chronicles his despair at his progressive deafness, which a decade and a half later became total.

Melanie Charrol knew this, for Beethoven not only was her spiritual mentor and role model but was a frequent visitor to her music room, where he, not surprisingly, could hear as well as she could. They had had many fascinating conversations about music theory and composition. They both lamented the trend away from melody and harmony in modern composition. She called it "medicinal music"—a phrase Ludwig heartily approved of.

She now sat in the living room of her house, breathing deeply, thinking of the great composer and wondering if she was drunk.

At the bar in the motel in Crow Ridge she'd poured down two brandies in the company of Officer Frances Whiting and some of the parents of the hostages. Frances had gotten in touch with Melanie's parents in St. Louis and told them she was fine. They would return immediately after Danny's operation tomorrow and stop by Hebron for a visit—news that for some reason upset Melanie. Did she want them to stop by or not? She had another brandy in lieu of deciding.

Then Melanie had gone to say goodbye to the girls and their parents. The twins had been asleep, Kielle was awake but snubbing her royally—though if Melanie knew anything about children it was that their moods are fickle as the weather; tomorrow or the next day the little girl would drop by Melanie's cubicle at school and sprawl out upon the immaculate desktop to show off her latest X-Men comic or Power Rangers card. Emily was, of course, in an absurdly frilly and feminine nightgown, fast asleep. Shannon, Beverly, and Jocylyn were the centerpiece of the action. At the moment, coddled and the center of loving attention, they were cheerful and defiant and she could see from their gestures that they were recalling aspects of the evening in detail that Melanie herself could not bear. They had even dubbed themselves "the Crow Ridge Ten" and were talking about having T-shirts printed up. Reality would hit home later, when everyone began to feel Susan's absence. But for now, why not? Besides, whatever misgivings she'd shared with de l'Epée about the politics of Deafness, the members of its community were nothing if not resilient.

Melanie said goodnight to everyone, refusing a dozen offers to spend the night. Never before had she signed "No, thank you" as often as she had this evening.

Now, in her home, all the windows were locked, all the doors. She burned some incense, had another brandy—blackberry, her grandmother's cure for cramps—and was sitting in her leather armchair, thinking of de l'Epée . . . well, Arthur Potter. Rubbing the indentation on her right wrist from the wire Brutus had bound it with. She had her Koss headset clamped over her ears and had Beethoven's Fourth Piano Concerto cranked up so loud the volume was redlined. It was a remarkable piece of music. Composed during what music historians call Beethoven's "second period," the one that produced the *Eroica*, when he was aware of, and tormented by, his hearing loss but before he had gone completely deaf.

As she listened to the concerto now she wondered if it had been written by Beethoven in anticipation of future years when the deafness would be worse, if he'd built in certain chords and dynamics so that a deaf old man might still make out at least the soul of the piece—for though there were passages she could not hear at all (as faint and delicate as smoke, she imagined) the passion of the music came from its emphatic low notes, two hands crashing down on the bass keys, the theme spiraling downward like a hawk falling on prey, the orchestra's timpani and low-pitched strings churning out what for her was the hopeful spirit of the concerto. A sensation of galloping.

She could imagine, through vibration and notes and sight-reading the score, most of the concerto. She thought now, as she always did, that she'd give her soul to be able to actually hear the entire piece.

Just once before she died.

It was during the second movement that she glanced outside and saw a car slow suddenly as it passed her house. She thought this was odd because the street in front was little traveled. It was a dead end and she knew everyone who lived on the block and what kind of cars they drove. This one she didn't recognize.

She pulled off the headset and walked to the window. She could see that the car, with two people inside, had parked in front of the Albertsons' house. This was curious too because she was sure the family was away for the week. She squinted at the car. The two people— she couldn't see them clearly, just silhouettes—got out and walked through the Albertsons' gate, disappearing behind the tall hedge that bordered the couple's property, directly across from her house. Then Melanie remembered that the family had several cats. Probably friends were feeding the animals while the couple was away. Returning to her couch, she sat down and pulled on the headset once more.

Yes, yes . . .

The music, what she could hear of it, as limited as the sound was to her, was an incredible comfort. More than the brandy, more than the companionship of the parents of her students, more than thoughts about the inexplicable and inexplicably appealing Arthur Potter; it lifted her away, magically, from the horror of this windy day in July.

Melanie closed her eyes.

1:20 A.M.

Captain Charlie Budd had aged considerably in the last twelve hours.

Potter studied him in the adulterating fluorescent light of the cramped office of the sheriff of Crow Ridge, which was located in a strip mall off the business loop. Budd no longer appeared young and was easily a decade past callow. And like all of them here tonight, his face showed the patina of disgust.

And uncertainty too. For they had no idea if they'd been betrayed and if so by whom. Budd and Potter sat across the desk from Dean Stillwell, who leaned into the phone, nodding gravely. He handed the receiver to Budd.

Tobe and Henry LeBow had just arrived in a mad race from the airport. LeBow's computers were already booted up; they seemed like an extension of his body. Angie's DomTran jet had hung a U-turn somewhere over Nashville and she was due back in Crow Ridge in a half-hour.

"All right," Budd said, hanging up. "Here're the details. They aren't pretty."

The two squad cars carrying Handy and Wilcox had left the slaughterhouse and headed south to the Troop C headquarters in Clements, about ten miles south. Between Crow Ridge and the state facility the lead car, driven by the woman who was presumably Priscilla Gunder, braked so suddenly it left twenty-foot skid marks and sent the second car, behind it, off the road. Apparently the woman pulled her pistol and shot the trooper beside her and the one in the backseat, killing them instantly.

The crime scene investigators speculated that Wilcox, in the second car, had undone his cuffs with the key that Gunder had slipped him and grabbed the gun of the trooper sitting beside him. But because he'd been double-shackled, according to Potter's surrender instructions, it had taken him longer to escape than planned. He'd shot the officer beside him but the driver leapt from the car and fired one shot into Wilcox before Handy, or his girlfriend, shot him in the back.

"Wilcox wasn't killed outright," Budd continued, brushing his hair, as being in Stillwell's presence made you want to do. "He climbed out and crawled to the first squad car. Somebody—they think it was Handy—finished him with a single shot to the forehead."

In his mind Potter heard: *You kill when people don't do what they're supposed to. You kill the weak because they'll drag you down. What's wrong with that?*

"What about Detective Foster?" Potter asked.

"She was found beside a stolen car about a mile from her house. Her husband said she left the place about ten minutes after she got the call about the barricade. They think the Gunder woman flagged her down near the highway, took her uniform, killed her, and stole her cruiser. Prelim forensics show some of the prints were Gunder's."

"What else, Charlie? Tell us." For Potter saw the look on his face.

Budd hesitated. "After the real Sharon Foster had stripped down to her underwear Handy's girlfriend gagged and handcuffed her. Then she used a knife. She didn't have to. But she did. It wasn't too pleasant what she did. It took her a while to die."

"And then she drove to the barricade site," Potter spat out angrily, "and waltzed out with him."

"Where'd they head?" LeBow asked. "Still going south?"

"Nobody's got a clue," Budd said.

"They're in a cruiser," Stillwell said. "Shouldn't be hard to find."

"We've got choppers out looking," Budd offered. "Six of them."

"Oh, he's already switched cars," Potter muttered. "Concentrate on any report of car theft in south-central Kansas. Anything at all."

Tobe said, "The engine block of the cruiser'll retain heat for about three hours. Do the choppers have infrared cameras?"

Budd said, "Three of them do."

LeBow mused, "What route'd put them the furthest away in that time? He must know we'd be on to them pretty soon."

In the otherwise drab, functional office five brilliant, red plants sat on a credenza, the healthiest-looking plant life Potter had ever seen indoors. Stillwell was hovering beside a wall map of the four-county area. "He could cut over to 35—that's the turnpike, take him northeast. Or 81'd take him to I-70."

"How 'bout," Budd asked, "81 all the way into Nebraska, cut over to 29?"

"Yep," Stillwell continued. " 'S'long drive, but it'd take him up to Winnipeg. Eventually."

"Was that Canada thing all smoke screen?" Tobe wondered.

"I don't know," Potter said, feeling that he'd stumbled into a chess game with a man who might be a grand master or who might not even know the movement of the pieces. He stood and stretched, which was tough in the cramped quarters. "The only way we're going to find him, short of luck, is to figure out how the hell he did it. Henry? What was the chronology?"

LeBow punched buttons. He recited, "At nine thirty-three p.m. Captain Budd said he'd received a call from his division commander about a woman detective who'd gotten Handy to surrender several years ago. She was located in McPherson, Kansas. The commander wondered if he should send the woman to the barricade site. Captain Budd conferred with Agent Potter and the decision was made to ask this detective to come to the site.

"At nine forty-nine p.m. a woman representing herself as Detective Sharon Foster called from her cruiser and reported that she would be at the barricade site by ten-thirty or ten-forty.

"At ten forty-five a woman representing herself to be Detective Sharon Foster, wearing a Kansas State Police uniform, arrived at the barricade and commenced negotiations with subject Handy."

"Charlie," Potter asked, "who was the commander?"

"Ted Franklin over at Troop B." He already had the phone in his hand and was dialing the number.

"Commander Franklin please . . . it's an emergency. . . . Ted? It's Charlie Budd. . . . Nope, no news. I'm going to put you on the squawk box." There was a click and static filled the room. "Ted, I've got half the FBI here. Agent Arthur Potter in charge."

"Hey, gentlemen," came Franklin's electronic greeting.

"Evening, Commander," Potter said. "We're trying to track down what happened here. You remember who called you about Sharon Foster this evening?"

"I've been racking my brain, sir, trying to remember. Some trooper or another. I frankly wasn't listening to who he was as much as what he had to say."

"A 'he,' you say?"

"Yessir. Was a man."

"He told you about Detective Foster?"

"That's right."

"Did you know her beforehand?"

"I knew about her. She was an up-and-comer. Good negotiating record."

Potter asked, "Then you called her after this trooper called."

"No, I called Charlie first down in Crow Ridge to see if it'd be all right with you folks. Then I called her."

"So," Stillwell said, "somebody intercepted your call to her and got to Detective Foster's just as she was leaving."

"But how?" Budd asked. "Her husband said she left ten minutes after she got the call. How could Handy's girlfriend've got there in time?"

"Tobe?" Potter asked. "Any way to check for taps?"

"Commander Franklin," Tobe asked, "is your office swept for bugs?"

A chuckle. "Nope. Not the kind you're talking about."

Tobe said to Potter, "We could sweep it, see if there are any. But it'd only tell us yea or nay. There's no way to tell who got the transmission and when."

But no, Potter was thinking. Budd was right. There was simply no time for Priscilla Gunder to get to Foster's house after the phone call from Franklin.

LeBow spoke for all of them. "This just doesn't sound like a tap situation. Besides, who'd know to put the bug in Commander Franklin's office anyway?"

Stillwell said, "Sounds like this was all planned out ahead of time."

Potter agreed. "The trooper who called you, Commander Franklin, wasn't a trooper at all. He was Handy's accomplice. And the girlfriend was probably waiting outside Detective Foster's house all along, while he—whoever *he* is—made the phone call to you."

"That means somebody'd have to know about the real Sharon Foster in the first place," Budd said. "That Handy'd surrendered to her. Who'd know about her?"

There was silence for a moment as the roomful of clever men thought of clever ways to learn about past police negotiations—through the news, computer databases, sources within the department.

LeBow and Budd were tied for first. "Handy!"

Potter had just arrived there himself. He nodded. "Who'd know better than Handy himself? Let's think back. He's trapped in the slaughterhouse. He suspects he isn't going to get his helicopter or that if he does we're going to track him to the ends of the earth—with or without his M-4 clearance—and so he gets word to his accomplice about Foster. The accomplice calls the girlfriend and they plan out the rescue. But Handy couldn't have called on the throw phone. We'd have heard it." Potter closed his eyes and thought back over the evening's events. "Tobe, those scrambled transmissions you were wondering about . . . We thought they were Tremain and the Kansas HRU. Could they have been something else?"

The young man tugged at his pierced earlobe then dug several computer disks from a plastic envelope. He handed them to LeBow, who put one in his laptop. Tobe leaned over and pushed keys. On the screen played a stilted, slow-moving graphic representation of two sine waves, overlapping each other.

"There are two!" he announced, his scientist's eyes glowing at the discovery. "Two different frequencies." He looked up. "Both law-enforcement assigned. And retrosignal scrambled."

"Are they both Tremain's?" Potter wondered aloud.

Ted Franklin asked what the frequencies were.

"Four hundred thirty-seven megahertz and four hundred eighty point four," Tobe responded.

"No," Ted Franklin answered. "The first one is assigned to HRU. The second isn't a state police signal. I don't know whose it is."

"So Handy had another phone in the slaughterhouse?" Potter asked.

"Not a phone," Tobe said. "It'd be a radio. And four eighty is often reserved for federal operations, Arthur."

"Is that right?" Potter considered this, then said, "But a radio wasn't found at the site, was it?"

Budd dug through a black attaché case. He found the sheet that listed the inventory of evidence found at the crime scene and the initial chain of custody. "No radio."

"Could've hidden it, I suppose. There'd be a million nooks and crannies in a place like that." Potter considered something. "Is there any way to trace the transmissions?"

"Not now. You have to triangulate on a real-time signal." Tobe said this as if Potter had asked if it could snow in July.

"Commander Franklin," the agent asked, "you got a phone call, right? From this supposed trooper? It wasn't a radio transmission?"

"A landline, right. And it wasn't patched in from a radio either. You can always tell."

Potter paused and examined one of the flowers. Was it a begonia? A fuchsia? Marian had gardened. "So Handy radioed Mr. X, who then called Commander Franklin. Then X called Handy's girlfriend and gave her the go-ahead to intercept Sharon Foster. Tobe?"

The young agent's eyes flashed with understanding. He snapped his fingers and sat up. "You got it, Arthur," he responded to the request that Potter was about to make. "Pen register of all incoming calls to your office, Commander Franklin. You object to that?"

"Hell, no. I want this boy as much as you do."

"You have a direct line?" Tobe asked.

"I do, yes, but half of my calls come in from the switchboard. And when I pick up I don't know where it's coming in from."

"We'll do them all," Tobe said patiently, undaunted.

Who's Handy's accomplice? Potter wondered.

Tobe asked, "Henry? A warrant request, please."

LeBow printed one out on Stillwell's NEC and handed it to Potter then called up on his screen the *Federal Judiciary Directory*. Potter placed a call to a judge who sat on the district court of Kansas. He explained about the request. At home at this hour, the judge agreed to sign the warrant on the basis of the evidence Potter presented; he'd been watching CNN and knew all about the incident.

As a member of the bars of D.C. and Illinois, Potter signed the warrant request. Tobe faxed it to the judge, who signed and returned it immediately. LeBow then scrolled through Standard & Poor's *Corporation Directory* and found the name of the chief general counsel of Midwestern Bell. They served the warrant via fax to the lawyer at home. One phone conversation and five minutes later the requested files were dumped ingloriously into LeBow's computer.

"Okay, Commander Franklin," LeBow said, scrolling through his screen, "it looks like we have seventy-seven calls coming into your HQ today, thirty-six into your private line."

Potter said, "You're a busy man."

"Heh. The family can attest to that."

Potter asked when the call about Foster came in.

"About nine-thirty."

Potter said, "Make it a twenty-minute window."

Keys tapped.

"We're down to about sixteen total," LeBow said. "That's getting workable."

"If Handy had a radio," Budd said, "what'd the range of that thing be?"

"Good question, Charlie," Tobe said. "That'll narrow things down even more. If it's standard law-enforcement issue I'd guess three miles. Our Mr. X would have to've been pretty close to the barricade."

Potter lowered his head to the screen. "I don't know these towns, other than Crow Ridge, and there's no listing of any calls from there to you, Commander. Charlie, take a look. Tell us what's nearby."

"Hysford's about seventeen miles. Billings, nowhere near."

"That's the missus," volunteered Commander Franklin.

"How 'bout this? A three-minute call from Towsend to your office at nine twenty-six. Was that about how long you talked to the trooper, Commander Franklin?"

"About, yessir."

"Where's Towsend?"

"Borders Crow Ridge," Budd said. "Good-sized town."

"Can you get us an address?" Budd asked Tobe.

The downloaded files from the phone company didn't include addresses but a single call to Midwestern Bell's computer center pinpointed a pay phone.

"Route 236 and Roosevelt Highway."

"It's the main intersection," Stillwell said, discouraged. "Restaurants, hotels, gas stations. And that highway's a feeder for two interstates. Could've been anybody and he could've been on his way to anywhere."

Potter's eyes were on the five red plants. His head rose suddenly and he reached for the telephone. But it was a curious gesture—he stopped suddenly and seemed momentarily flustered, as if he'd committed some grievous social faux pas at a formal dinner party. His hand slipped off the receiver.

"Henry, Tobe, come with me. You too, Charlie. Dean, will you stay here and man the fort?"

"You bet, sir."

"Where are we going?" Charlie asked.

"To talk to somebody who knows Handy better than we do."

2:00 A.M.

He wondered how they'd announce their presence.

There was a button on the jamb of the front door, just like any other. Potter looked at Budd, who shrugged and pushed it.

"I thought I heard something inside. A doorbell. Why's that?"

Potter had heard something too. But he'd also noticed a red light flash inside, through a lace curtain.

There was no response.

Where was she?

Potter found himself about to call, "Melanie?" And when he realized that would be futile, he lifted his fist to knock. He shook his head at that gesture too and lowered his hand. Seeing the lights inside a lifeless house, he felt a stab of uneasiness and he pulled his jacket away from his hip, where the Glock sat. LeBow noticed the gesture but said nothing.

"Wait here," Potter told the three men.

He walked slowly along the dark porch of the Victorian house, looking in the windows of the place. Suddenly he stopped, seeing shoeless feet, legs sprawled on a couch, motionless.

Alarmed now, in a panic, he hurriedly completed his circuit of the porch. But he couldn't get any view of her—only her unmoving legs. He rapped loudly on the glass, shouted her name.

Nothing.

She should be able to feel the vibration, he thought. And there was the red flashing light—the "doorbell"—above the entryway, flashing in her clear view.

"Melanie!"

He drew his pistol. Tried the window. It was locked.

Do it.

His elbow crashed into the glass and sent a shower of shards onto the parquet floor. He reached in, unlocked the window, and started through. He froze when he saw the figure—Melanie herself, sitting up, terrified, staring at the intruder coming through her window. She blinked away the sleep and gasped.

Potter held up his hands to her, as if surrendering, an expression of horror on his own face at the thought of how he must have frightened her. Still, he was more perplexed than anything else: Why on earth, he wondered, would she be wearing stereo headphones?

Melanie Charrol opened the door and motioned her visitors inside.

The first thing that Arthur Potter saw was a large watercolor of a violin, surrounded by surreal quarter- and half-notes in rainbow colors.

"Sorry about the window," he said slowly. "You can deduct it from your taxes."

She smiled.

"Evening, ma'am," Charlie Budd said. And Potter introduced her to Tobe Geller and Henry LeBow. She looked out the door at the car parked two doors down, the two people standing behind a hedge, looking at the house.

He saw her face. He said to her, "They're ours."

Melanie frowned. He explained, "Two troopers. I sent them here earlier tonight to keep an eye on you."

She shook her head, asking, Why?

Potter hesitated. "Let's go inside."

With flashing lights, a Hebron PD squad car pulled up. Angeline Scapello, looking exhausted though no longer soot-smudged, climbed out and hurried up the stairs. She nodded to everyone, and like her fellow threat management team members she wasn't smiling.

Melanie's house had a homey air about it. Thick drapes. In the air, incense. Spicy. Old prints, many of them of classical composers, hung on the walls, which were covered with striped paper, forest green and gold. The largest print was of Beethoven. The room was full of antique tables, beautiful Art Nouveau vases. He thought with some embarrassment of his own Georgetown apartment, a shabby place. He'd stopped decorating it thirteen years ago.

Melanie was wearing blue jeans, a black cashmere sweater. Her hair was no longer in the awkward braid but hung loose. The bruises and cuts on her face and hands were quite prominent, as were the chestnut Betadine stains. Potter turned to her, tried to think of words that required exaggerated lip movements. "Lou Handy's escaped."

She didn't understand at first. When he repeated it her eyes went wide with horror. She started to sign then stopped in frustration and grabbed the stack of paper.

LeBow touched her arm. "Can you type?" He mimicked keyboarding.

She nodded. He opened his two computers, booted them into word-processing programs, hooked up a serial port cable, and set the units side by side. He sat at one, Melanie at the other.

Where did he go? she typed.

We don't know, that's why we came to see you.

Melanie nodded slowly. *Did he kill anyone escaping?* She could touch-type and she kept her eyes on Potter as she asked this.

He nodded. *Wilcox—the one you called Stoat—was killed. Troopers too.*

Again she nodded, frowning, thinking over the implications of this.

Potter typed, *I have to ask you to do something you're not going to want to do.*

She looked at his message, wrote: *I've already been through the worst.* Her hands danced over the keys invisibly, not a single mistake. *God compensates.*

I want you to go back to the slaughterhouse. In your mind.

Her fingers hovered over the keyboard. She wrote nothing but merely nodded.

We don't understand certain things about the barricade. If you can help us to I think we can figure out where he's gone.

"Henry," Potter called, rising and pacing. LeBow and Tobe caught each other's eyes. "Call up his profile and the chronology. What do we know about him?"

LeBow began to read but Potter said, "No, let's just speculate."

"He's a clever boy," Budd offered. "He comes across like a hick but he's got some smarts."

Potter added, *He plays the dummy but that's largely an act, I think.*

Melanie typed, *Amoral.*

Yes.

Dangerous, Budd offered.

Let's go beyond that.

He's evil, she wrote. *Evil personified.*

But what kind of evil?

Silence for a moment. Angie typed, *Cold death.*

Potter nodded and spoke aloud, "Right. Lou Handy's cold evil. Not passionate evil. Let's keep that in mind."

Angie continued, *Not a sadist. Then he'd be passionate. He feels nothing for the pain he causes. If he needs pain or death to get his way, he'll cause pain or death. Like blinding the hostages—simply another tool for him.*

Potter leaned forward and typed, *So, he's calculating.*

"And?" Budd prompted.

Potter shook his head. *Yes, he's calculating, but you're right, Charlie, what does that mean?*

The men stopped speaking while Melanie's fingers danced over the keyboard. Potter walked around her and stood close as she typed. His hand brushed her shoulder and it seemed to him that she leaned into his fingers. She wrote: *Everything he does has a purpose. He's one of those few people who isn't driven by life; he drives it.*

Angie typed, *Control, control, control.*

Potter found his hand was resting on Melanie's shoulder. She lowered her cheek to it. Maybe it just was an accident as her head turned. Maybe not.

"Control and purpose," Potter said. "Yes, that's it. Type this out so she can see it, Henry. Everything he's done today has a purpose. Even if it seemed random. Killing Susan—it was to make clear that he was serious. He demanded a helicopter that seated eight but he had no problem giving away most of the hostages. Why? To keep us busy. To stretch out the time to give his accomplice and girlfriend a chance to set up the real Sharon Foster. He brought with him a TV, a scrambled radio, and guns."

Angie leaned forward to type, *So what is his purpose?*

"Well, escaping," Budd laughed. "What else would it be?" He leaned forward and two-finger typed, *To escape.*

No!! Melanie typed.

"Right!" Potter shouted, and pointed at her, nodding. "Escape wasn't his priority at all. How could it've been? He virtually let himself get trapped. There was only one trooper on his tail after the accident with the Cadillac. The three of them could've ambushed him, taken his car, and escaped. Why would anybody let themselves get trapped?"

"Hell," Budd said, "a spooked rabbit'll run right into a fox's den not even thinking." He dutifully hunted-and-pecked this in.

But he does think, Melanie wrote. *We can't forget that. And he isn't spooked.*

Not spooked at all, Angie offered. *Remember the voice stress analysis.*

Potter nodded to Melanie, smiling and gripping her shoulder once more. *Calm as ordering a cup of coffee at 7-Eleven.*

Melanie typed, *I called him Brutus. But he's really like a ferret.*

Budd continued, *Well, if he's a ferret, then he'd go to ground only if he knew he wasn't trapped at all. If he had an escape route.*

Melanie typed, *When he first walked into the slaughterhouse Bear said that there was no way out. And Brutus said, "It doesn't matter. It doesn't matter at all."*

Potter nodded, mused, "He could've run, but no, he risked taking a detour to the slaughterhouse and getting trapped. But it wasn't that great a risk at all because he knew he could get out. He had guns and he had a radio to call his accomplice and work out some escape plan. Maybe he'd already thought up substituting his girlfriend for Foster." He typed, *Melanie, tell us exactly what happened when they picked you up.*

She typed, *We found the wreck. He was killing those people. In no hurry. He was confident?*

Very. He took his own sweet time, Melanie typed, grim-faced.

Potter unfurled a map. *What route did you drive?*

I don't know roads, Melanie wrote. *Past a radio station, a farm with lots of cows.* She frowned for a moment then traced the route on the map. *Maybe this.*

The prison's south of the slaughterhouse ninety or so miles, Potter typed. *The three of them drove north to here, had the accident with the Cadillac here, took the van and drove all the way around here. . . .* He traced a route that had Handy driving well past the slaughterhouse then doubling back.

Melanie typed, *No. We drove straight to the slaughterhouse. That was one thing I thought funny. He seemed to know where it was.*

But if he went straight there, Potter typed, *when did you pass the airport?*

We didn't, she explained.

So he knew about it ahead of time. When he was asking me for the helicopter he knew there was an airport just two or three miles up the road. How did he know?

Budd typed, *He'd already arranged to fly out of there.*

But, LeBow typed as fast as he could speak the words, *if it was just a few miles up the road, and if there was an airplane or helicopter waiting for him, why go to the slaughterhouse at all?*

"Why?" Potter muttered. "Henry, tell me what we know. Let's start with what he had with him."

You're carrying a key, a magic sword, five stones, and a raven in a cage.

He went into the slaughterhouse with hostages, the guns, a can of gasoline, ammunition, a TV, the radio, a set of tools—

"The tools, yes," Potter said, as LeBow typed. He turned to Melanie. "Did you see him use them?"

No, Melanie answered. *But I was in killing room for most of time. Toward end I remembered them walking around looking at the machinery and fixtures. I thought they were taking a nostalgic look at the place, maybe they were looking for something, though.*

Potter snapped his fingers. "Dean told us something similar."

LeBow scanned through the incident chronology. He read, " 'Seven-fifty-six p.m. Sheriff Stillwell reported that a trooper under his command observed Handy and Wilcox searching the factory, testing doors and fixtures. Reason unknown.' "

"Okay. Good. Let's put the tools on hold for a minute. Those are the things he had with him when he went in. What did we *give* him?"

"Just the food and the beer," Budd said. "Oh, and the money."

"The money!" Potter cried. "Money he didn't ask for in the first place."

Angie typed, *And he never tried to bargain up the fifty thousand. Why not?*

There's only one reason a man doesn't want money, LeBow typed. *He's got more than he needs.*

Potter was nodding excitedly. *There's money hidden in the building. It was part of his plan all along—to stop at the slaughterhouse and pick it up.*

That's why he had the tools—to get the cash out from where it was hidden, Budd managed to type. Potter nodded.

"Where did it come from?" Tobe wondered.

"He's a bank robber," Budd said wryly. "That's one possibility."

"Henry," Potter said, "jump into Lexis/Nexis and let's read about that most recent robbery of his. The arson."

In five minutes LeBow was on-line with Mead Data. He read newspaper accounts and summarized, "Handy was found with twenty thousand stolen from the Farmers & Merchants heist in Wichita."

"Had he ever burned anything before that?"

LeBow scrolled through the news accounts and his own sixteen-page profile of Louis J. Handy. "No prior arson."

Then why the fire? Potter typed.

He always has a purpose, Angie reminded.

Melanie nodded emphatically then shivered and closed her eyes. Potter wondered what terrible memory had intruded into her thoughts. The agent and Budd looked at each other, four eyebrows arched. Then: "Yep, Charlie. That's right." Potter reached down to the keyboard. *He wasn't there to rob that bank at all. He was there to burn it down.*

LeBow was reading the profile. "And he shot his accomplice in the back when they'd been trapped by the troopers. Maybe so no one would find out what he was really doing there."

But why did he do it? Budd typed.

Someone hired him? Potter asked the question. LeBow nodded. "Of course."

"And whoever did," Potter said, "was paying him a ton of money. A lot more than fifty thousand. That's why he didn't think to ask for cash from us. He was already a rich man. Henry, get into the Corporation Trust database and get me the corporate documents on the bank."

The intelligence officer went off-line with Mead and was soon scrolling through the articles of incorporation, bylaws, and securities filings of the bank. "Closely held, so it's limited public information. But we do know that the directors are also the officers. Here we go: Clifton Burbank, Stanley L. Poole, Cynthia G. Grolsch, Herman Gallagher. The ZIP codes are close together. All near Wichita. Burbank and Gallagher live in the city proper. Poole lives in Augusta. Ms. Grolsch is in Derby."

Potter recognized none of the names but any one of them could have some connection to Handy. As could, say, an embezzling teller, a former employee who'd been fired, the spurned lover of one of the directors. But Arthur Potter would much rather have too many possibilities than none at all. "Charlie, what hotels are near that pay phone where Mr. X called Ted Franklin? In Towsend."

"Hell, there's a bunch. Four or five at least. Holiday Inn, a Ramada, I think a Hilton and some local one. Towsend Motor Lodge. Maybe another one or two."

Potter told Tobe to start calling. "Find out if any of those directors were registered in the hotels today or if anybody from any of those towns was registered."

In five minutes they had an answer. Tobe snapped his fingers. Everyone, except Melanie, looked at him. "Somebody registered from Derby, Kansas. Same as Cynthia Grolsch."

"Too much of a coincidence," Potter muttered, taking the phone. He identified himself, spoke to the clerk for a few moments. Finally he shook his head grimly, asked, "And what room?" He jotted down *Holiday Inn. Rm. 611* on a pad. To the clerk he said, "No. And don't mention this call." He hung up, tapped the pad. "May be our Judas. Let's go have a talk with 'em, Charlie."

Melanie glanced at the pad of paper. Her face went still.

Who? Who is it? Her eyes flared. She stood up abruptly, pulled a leather jacket from a hook.

"Let them handle it," Angie said.

Melanie looked back to Potter, her eyes flaring. She typed, *Who is it?*

"Please." Potter took her by the shoulders. "I don't want anything to happen to you."

Slowly she nodded, pulled off the jacket, slung it over her shoulder. She looked like an aviatrix from the thirties.

Potter said, "Henry, Angie, and Tobe stay here. Handy knows about Melanie. He might come back." He said to her, "I'll be back soon." Then he hurried to the door. "Come on, Charlie."

After they'd gone Melanie smiled at the agents who remained. She typed *Tea? Coffee?*

"Not for me," Tobe said.

"No, thank you. Want to play solitaire?" LeBow booted up the game.

She shook her head. *I'm going to take a shower. Long day.*

"Gotcha."

Melanie disappeared and a few minutes later they heard the sound of running water from a bathroom.

Angie began working on her incident report while Tobe called up Doom II on his laptop and started to play. Fifteen minutes later he'd been blown apart by aliens. He stood up and stretched. He looked over Henry LeBow's shoulder, made a suggestion about the red queen, which was not received very generously at all, and then paced in the living room. He glanced at the sideboard, where he'd left the keys to the government pool car. They were gone. He wandered to the front of the house and glanced outside at the empty street. Why, he wondered, would Potter and Budd have taken two separate cars to the Holiday Inn?

But his blood lust was insatiable and he stopped worrying about such a trivial matter as he returned to his computer and prepared to blast his way out of the fortress of Doom.

2:35 A.M.

It had been Hawaiian Night at the Holiday Inn.

Steel guitar still pumped through the PA and limp plastic leis hung around the night clerks' necks.

Agent Arthur Potter and Captain Charles Budd walked between two fake palms and took the elevator up to the sixth floor.

For a change Budd was the law enforcer looking perfectly confident; it was Potter who was ill-at-ease. The last kick-in the agent had been involved in was the arrest of a perp who happened to be wearing a turquoise Edwardian suit and silver floral polyester shirt, which carbon-dated the bust to around 1977.

He remembered that he wasn't supposed to stand in front of the door. What else? He was reassured to glance at Budd, who had a shiny black leather cuffcase on his belt. Potter himself had never cuffed a real suspect—only volunteers at the live-fire hostage rescue drills on the Quantico back lot. "I'll defer to you on this one, Charlie."

Budd raised surprised eyebrows. "Well, sure, Arthur."

"But I'll back you up."

"Oh. Good."

Both men pulled their weapons from the hip holsters. Potter chambered a round again—twice in one night and three years from the last barricade in which a bullet had rested in his gun's receiver and meant business.

At room 611 they stopped, exchanged glances. The negotiator nodded. Budd knocked, a friendly tap. Shave and a haircut.

"Yeah?" the gruff voice called. "Hello? Who's there?"

"It's Charlie Budd. Can you open up for a minute? Just found something interesting."

"Charlie? What's going on?"

The chain fell, a deadbolt clicked, and when Roland Marks opened the door he found himself staring into the muzzles of two identical automatic pistols: one steady, one shaking, and both safeties off.

"Cynthia's a director of the S&L, yes. It's a nominal position. I'm really the one who calls the shots. We kept it in her maiden name. She's not guilty of anything."

The assistant attorney general could protest all he wanted but it would be up to the grand and petit juries to decide his wife's fate.

No raillery. Marks was now playing straight man. His eyes were red and damp and Potter, feeling nothing but contempt, had no trouble holding his gaze.

The AG had been read his rights. It was all over and he knew it. So he decided to cooperate. His statement was being taken down by the very same tape recorder he'd slipped Budd earlier in the evening.

"And what exactly were you doing at the savings and loan?" Potter asked.

"Making bad loans to myself. Well, to fictional people and companies. Writing them off and keeping the money." He shrugged as if to say, Isn't it obvious?

Marks, the prosecutor specializing in white-collar crime, had learned well from his suspects: he'd bled the Wichita institution's stockholders, and the public, for close to five million dollars—much of it spent already, it seemed. "I thought with the turnaround in the real estate market," he continued, "some of the bank's legitimate investments would pay off and we could cover up the shortfall. But when I went over the books I saw we just weren't going to make it."

The Resolution Trust Corporation, the government agency taking over failed banking institutions, was about to come in and seize the place.

"So you hired Lou Handy to burn it down," Budd said. "Destroy all the records."

"How did you know him?" the agent asked.

Budd beat Marks to it. "You prosecuted Handy five years ago, wasn't it? The convenience-store heist—the barricade Sharon Foster talked him out of."

The assistant attorney general nodded. "Oh, yes, I remembered him. Who wouldn't? Smart son of a bitch. He took the stand in his own defense and nearly ran circles around me. Had to do some digging to find him for the S&L job, you can bet. Checked with his parole officer, some of my contacts on the street. Offered him two hundred thousand to torch the place as part of a robbery. Only he got caught. So I had no choice— I had to cut a deal with him. I'd help him escape, otherwise he'd blow the whistle on me. That cost me another three hundred thousand."

"How'd you get him out? Callana's maximum-security."

"Paid two guards their annual salaries in cash to do it."

"Was one of them the guard Handy killed?"

Marks nodded.

"Saved some money there, didn't you?" Charlie Budd asked bitterly.

"You left a car for him with the guns, the scrambled radio, and the TV in it," Potter continued. "And the tools to get the money out of the slaughterhouse where you'd hidden it for him."

"Well, hell, we couldn't exactly leave the money in the car. Too risky. So I sealed it up in this old steam pipe behind the front window."

Potter asked, "What were the escape plans going to be?"

"Originally, I'd arranged for a private plane to fly him and his buddies out of Crow Ridge, from that little airport up the road. But he never made it. He had the accident—with the Cadillac—and lost about a half-hour."

"Why did he take the girls?"

"He needed them. With the delay he knew he didn't have time to get the money *and* make it to the airport—with the cops right on his tail. But he wasn't going to leave without the cash. Lou figured with the hostages inside and me working to get him out, it didn't matter how many cops were at the slaughterhouse. He'd get out sooner or later. He radioed me from inside and I agreed to convince the FBI to give him a helicopter. That didn't work but by then I remembered Sharon Foster's negotiation with Handy a few years ago. I found out where she was stationed now and called Pris Gunder—his girlfriend—and told her to drive over to Foster's house. Then I pretended I was a trooper and called Ted Franklin at state police."

Potter asked, "So your heart-rending offer to give yourself up for the girls . . . that was all an act."

"I *did* want them out. I didn't want anyone to die. Of course not!"

Of course, Potter thought cynically. "Where's Handy now?"

"I have no idea. Once he got out of the barricade that was it. I'd done everything I'd agreed. I told him he was on his own."

Potter shook his head. Budd asked coldly, "Tell me, Marks, how's it feel to've murdered those troopers?"

"No! He promised me he wouldn't kill anyone! His girlfriend was just going to handcuff Foster. He—"

"And the other troopers? The escort?"

Marks stared at the captain for a minute and when no credible lie came to mind whispered, "It wasn't supposed to work out like this. It *wasn't.*"

"Call for some baby-sitters," Potter said. But before Budd could, his phone buzzed.

"Hello?" He listened for a moment. His eyes went wide. "Where? Okay, we're moving."

Potter cocked an eyebrow.

"They found the other squad car, the one Handy and his girlfriend were in. He's going south, looks like. Toward Oklahoma. The cruiser was twenty miles past the booking center. There was a couple in the trunk. Dead. Handy and his girlfriend must've stolen their wheels. No ID on them so we don't have a make or tag yet." Budd stepped close to the assistant AG. The captain growled, "The only good news is that Handy was in a hurry. They died fast."

Marks grunted in pain as Budd spun him around and shoved him hard into the wall. Potter did nothing to interfere. Budd tied the attorney's hands together with plastic wrist restraints then cuffed his right wrist to the bed frame.

"It's too tight," Marks whined.

Budd threw him down on the bed. "Let's go, Arthur. He's got a hell of a lead on us. Brother, he could be nearly to Texas by now."

She was surrounded by the Outside.

And yet it wasn't as hard as she'd thought.

Oh, she supposed the driver had honked furiously at her when she crossed the center line a moment ago. But, all things considered, she was doing fine. Melanie Charrol had never in her life driven a car. Many deaf people did, of course, even if they weren't supposed to, but Melanie had always been too afraid. Her fear wasn't that she'd be in an accident. Rather, she was terrified that she'd do something wrong and be embarrassed. Maybe get in the wrong lane. Stop too far away from a red light or too close. People would gather around the car and laugh at her.

But now she was cruising down Route 677 like a pro. She didn't have musician's ears any longer but she had musician's hands, sensitive and strong. And those fingers learned quickly not to overcompensate on the wheel and she sped straight toward her destination.

Lou Handy had had a purpose; well, so did she.

Bad is simple and good is complicated. And the simple always wins. That's what everything comes down to in the end. Simple always wins . . . that's just nature and you know what kind of trouble people get into ignoring nature.

Through the night, forty miles an hour, fifty, sixty.

She glanced down at the dashboard. Many of the dials and knobs made no sense to her. But she recognized the radio. She turned switches until it lit up: 103.4. Eyes flicking up and down, she figured out which was the volume and pushed the button until the line in the LED indicator was all the way at full. She heard nothing at first but then she turned up the bass level and she heard thumps and occasionally the sliding sound of tones and notes. The low register, Beethoven's register. That portion of her hearing had never deserted her completely.

Maybe his Ninth Symphony was playing, the soaring, inspiring "Ode to Joy." This seemed too coincidental, considering her mission at the moment, and 103.4 was probably rap or heavy metal. But it sent a powerful, irresistible beat through her chest. That was enough for her.

There!

She braked the car to a screeching stop in the deserted parking lot of the hardware supply store. The windows held just the assortment of goods she'd been looking for.

The brick sailed tidily through the glass and if it set off an alarm, which it probably did, she couldn't hear it so she felt no particular pressure to hurry. Melanie leaned forward and selected what seemed to be the sharpest knife in the display, a ten-inch butcher, Chicago Cutlery. She returned leisurely to the driver's seat, dropped the long blade on the seat next to her, then put the car in gear and sped away.

As she forced the engine to speed the car up to seventy through the huge gusts of silent wind, Melanie thought of Susan Phillips. Who would soon be sleeping forever in a grave as silent as her life had been.

A Maiden's Grave . . .

Oh, Susan, Susan . . . I'm not you. I can't be you and I won't even ask you to forgive me for that, though I would have once. After today I know I can't listen to imaginary music for the rest of my life. I know if you were alive now you'd hate me for this. But I want to *hear* words, I want to *hear* streams of snazzy consonants and vowels, I want to *hear* my music.

You were Deaf of Deaf, Susan. That made you strong, even if it killed you. I've been safe because I'm weak. But I can't be weak anymore. I'm an Other and that's just the way it is.

And Melanie realizes now, with a shock, why she could understand that son of a bitch Brutus so well. Because she *is* like him. She feels exactly what he feels.

Oh, I want to hurt, I want to pay them all back: Fate, taking my music away from me. My father, scheming to keep it away. Brutus and the man who hired him, kidnaping us, toying with us, hurting us, every one of us—the students, Mrs. Harstrawn, that poor trooper. And of course Susan.

The car raced through the night, one of her elegant hands on the steering wheel, one caressing the sensuous wooden handle of the knife.

Amazing grace, how sweet the sound . . .

The wind buffeted the car fiercely and, overhead, black strips of clouds raced through the cold sky at a thousand miles an hour.

> *That saved a wretch like me.*
> *I once was lost but now I'm found.*
> *Was blind, but now I see.*

Melanie dropped the knife back onto the seat and gripped the wheel in both hands, listening to the powerful bass beat resonate in her chest. She supposed the wind howled like a mad wolf but of course that was something she couldn't know for sure.

So you'll be home then.

Never.

They were three miles outside of Crow Ridge, speeding south, when Budd sat up straight, making his perfect posture that much better. His head snapped toward Potter.

"Arthur!"

The FBI agent cringed. "Of course. Oh, hell!"

The car skidded to a stop on the highway, ending up perpendicular to the roadway and blocking both lanes.

"Where is it, Charlie? *Where?*"

"A half-mile that way," Budd cried, pointing to the right. "That intersection we just passed. It's a shortcut. It'll take us right there."

Arthur Potter, otherwise the irritatingly prudent driver, took the turn at speed and, on the verge of an irrigation ditch, managed to control his mad, tire-smoking skid.

"Oh, brother," Budd muttered, though it wasn't Potter's insane driving but his own stupidity he was lamenting. "I can't believe I didn't think of it before."

Potter was furious with himself too. He realized exactly where Handy was. Not going south at all but heading directly back to his money. All the other evidence had been removed from the slaughterhouse by the police. But Crime Scene had never gotten the scrambled radio—or the cash. They were still there, hidden. Hundreds of thousands of dollars.

As he drove, hunched over the wheel, Potter asked Budd to call Tobe at Melanie's house. When the connection was completed he took the phone from the captain.

"Where's Frank and HRT?" the agent asked.

"Hold on," Tobe responded. "I'll find out." A moment later he came back on. "They're about to touch down in Virginia."

Potter sighed. "Damn. Okay, call Ted Franklin and Dean Stillwell, have them send some men to the slaughterhouse. Handy's on his way. If he's not there already. But it's vital not to spook him. This might be our only chance to nail him. I want them to roll in without lights and sirens and park at least a half-mile away on side roads. Remember to tell him Handy's armed and extremely dangerous. Tell him we're going to be inside. Charlie and me."

"Where are you now?"

"Hold on." Potter asked Budd, who gave him their whereabouts. Into the phone he said, "Charlie says, Hitchcock Road, just off Route 345. About two minutes away."

A pause.

"Charlie Budd's with you?" Tobe asked uncertainly.

"Well, sure. You saw him leave with me."

"But you took both cars."

"No. We just took mine."

Another pause. "Hold on, Arthur."

Uneasy, Potter said to Budd, "Something's going on there. At Melanie's."

Come on, Tobe. Talk to me.

A moment later the young agent came on. "She's gone, Arthur. Melanie. She left the shower running and took the other car."

A chill ran through him. Potter said, "She's going to the Holiday Inn to kill Marks."

"*What?*" Budd cried.

"She doesn't know his name. But she knows the room number. She saw what I wrote down."

"And I left him trussed up there without a guard. I forgot to call."

Potter remembered the look in her eyes, the cold fire. He asked Tobe, "Did she take a weapon? Was there one in the car?"

Tobe called something to LeBow.

"No, we've both got ours. Nothing in the car."

"Well, get some troopers over to the hotel fast." He had an image of her madly going for Marks despite the troopers. If she had a gun or knife they'd kill her instantly.

"Okay, Arthur," Tobe said. "We're on it."

Just then the sulky landscape took on a familiar tone—déjà vu from a recurring nightmare. A moment later the slaughterhouse loomed ahead of them. The battlefield was littered with coffee cups and tread marks—from squad cars, not the swales of covered wagons. The field was deserted. Potter folded up the phone and handed it back to Budd. He cut the engine and coasted silently the last fifty feet.

"What about Melanie?" Budd whispered.

There was no time to think about her. The agent lifted his finger to his lips and gestured toward the door. The two men stepped outside into the fierce wind.

They were walking through the gully down which Stevie Oates had carried Shannon and Kielle like bags of wheat.

"Through the front door?" Budd whispered.

Potter nodded yes. It was wide open; they could enter without having to risk squeaky hinges. Besides, the windows were five feet off the ground. Budd might make the climb but Potter, already exhausted and breathing heavily, knew that he wouldn't be able to.

They remained motionless for some minutes but there was no sign of Handy. No cars in sight, no headlights approaching, no flashlights. And no sound except that of the extraordinary wind.

Potter nodded toward the front door.

They crouched and hurried between hillocks up to the front of the slaughterhouse, the red-and-white brick, blood and bone. They paused beside the spot where the body of Tremain's trooper had been dumped.

The pipe by the window, Potter remembered. Filled with half a million dollars, the bait drawing Handy back to us.

They paused on either side of the door.

This isn't me, Potter thought suddenly. This isn't what I was meant to do. I'm a man of words, not a soldier. It's not that I'm afraid. But I'm out of my depth.

Not afraid, not afraid . . .

Though he was.

Why? Because, he supposes, for the first time in years, there is some-one else in his life. Somehow, existence has become somewhat more precious to him in the past twelve hours. *Yes, I want to talk to her, to Melanie. I want to tell her things, I want to hear how her day went. And, yes, yes, I want to take her hand and climb the stairs after dinner, feel the heat of her breath on my ear, feel the motion of her body beneath me. I want that! I . . .*

Budd tapped his shoulder. Potter nodded and, guns before them, they stepped inside the slaughterhouse.

Like a cave.

Darkness everywhere. The wind roared through the holes and ill-fitting joints of the old place so loudly that the men could hear virtually nothing else. They stepped instinctively behind a large metal structure, some kind of housing. And waited. Gradually Potter's eyes became accustomed to the inky darkness. He could just make out two slightly lighter squares of the windows on the other side of the door. Beside the closest one was a stubby pipe about two feet in diameter, rising in an L shape from the floor like a vent on a ship. Potter pointed to it and Budd squinted, nodding.

As they made their way forward, like blind men, Potter understood what Melanie had gone through here. The wind stole his hearing, the darkness his vision. And the cold was dulling his sense of touch and smell.

They paused, Potter feeling panic stream down his spine like ice wa-ter. Once he gasped as Budd lifted his hand alarmingly and dropped into a crouch. Potter too had seen the leveraging shadow but it turned out to be merely a piece of sheet metal bending in the breeze.

Then they were five yards from the pipe. Potter stopped, looked around slowly. Heard nothing other than the wind. Turned back.

They started forward but Budd was tapping his shoulder. The cap-tain whispered, "Don't slip. Something's spilled there. Oil, looks like."

Potter too looked underfoot. There were large dots of silvery liquid—more like mercury than water or oil—at the base of the pipe. He bent down, reached forward with a finger.

He touched cold metal.

Not oil.

Steel nuts.

The end plate was off the pipe.

Handy had been here al—

The gunshot came from no more than ten feet away. An ear-shattering bang, ringing painfully off the tile and metal and exposed wet brick.

Potter and Budd spun around.

Nothing, blackness. The faint motion of shadow as clouds obscured the moon.

Then the choked sound of Charlie Budd whispering, "I'm sorry, Arthur."

"What?"

"I'm . . . I'm sorry. I'm hit."

The shot had been fired into his back. He fell to his knees and Potter saw the ragged exit wound low in his belly. Budd keeled over onto the floor.

The agent started forward instinctively. Careful, he reminded himself, turning toward where the gunshot had come from. Guard yourself first.

The piece of pipe caught Potter squarely on the shoulder, knocking the wind out of him. He dropped hard to the ground and felt the sinewy hand yank his pistol from his grip.

"You alone? You two?" Handy's voice was a whisper.

Potter couldn't speak. Handy twisted his arm up behind his back, bent a little finger brutally. The pain surged through Potter's hand into his jaw and head. "Yes, yes. Just the two of us."

Handy grunted as he rolled Potter over and bound his hands before him with thin wire, the strands cutting into his flesh.

"There's no way you're going to—" Potter began.

Then a blurring motion, as Handy was slammed sideways into the pipe where the money'd been hidden. With a hollow ringing sound, the side of his head connected with the metal.

Charlie Budd, face dripping sweat as copious as the blood he shed, drew back his fist once more and slammed it into Handy's kidney. The convict wheezed with pain and pitched forward.

As Potter struggled futilely to get to his feet, Budd groped in the dark for his service automatic. He felt himself starting to black out and lurched sideways. Recovered slightly then staggered into a large cube of stained butcher block.

Handy leapt at him, growling in fury, throwing his arms around Budd's neck, pulling him down to the floor. The convict had been hurt, yes, but he still had his strength; Budd's was draining rapidly from his body.

"Oh, brother," Budd coughed. "I can't—"

Handy took Budd by the hair. "Come on, sport. Only round one."

"Go to hell," the trooper whispered.

"There's a boy." Handy got his arms around Budd and pulled him to his feet. "Ain't heard the bell. Come on. Fans're waiting."

The trooper, bleeding badly, eyes unfocused, pulled away and began flailing at Handy's lean face. One blow struck with surprising force and the convict jerked back in surprise. But after the initial burst of pain dissipated, Handy laughed. "Come on," he taunted. "Sugar Ray, come on. . . ." When Budd connected a final time Handy moved in close and rained a half-dozen blows into his face. Budd dropped to his knees.

"Hey, down for the count."

"Leave him . . . alone," Potter called.

Handy pulled the gun from his belt.

"No!" the agent cried.

"Arthur . . ."

To Potter, Handy said, "He's lucky I'm doing it this way. I had more time, wouldn't be painless. Nosir."

"Listen to me," Potter began desperately.

"Shhh," Handy whispered.

The wind swelled, a mournful wail.

The three gunshots were fast and were soon replaced by the sound of Potter's voice crying. "Oh, Charlie, no, no, no. . . ."

3:00 A.M.

Through the murky chutes, where the condemned longhorns had walked, between rectangular boulders of butcher block, beneath a thousand rusting meat hooks, clanging like bells . . .

And all the while the wind screamed around them, hooting through crevices and broken windows like a steam whistle on a tug.

Potter's wrists stung from the wire. He thought of Melanie's hands. Of her perfect nails. He thought of her hair, spun honey. He wished fervently that he'd kissed her earlier in the evening. With his tongue he pushed a tooth, loosened in his fall, from its precarious perch and spit it out. His mouth filled and he spit again; blood spurted to the floor.

"You poor fuck," Handy said with great satisfaction in his voice. "You just didn't get it, did you, Art? You just didn't fucking get it."

Ahead of them, some illumination. It wasn't light so much as a vague lessening of the darkness. From outside, faint starlight and the sliver of moon.

"You didn't have to kill him," the agent found himself saying.

"This way. Go there." Handy pushed him into a moldy corridor. "You been in this line of work how long, Art?"

Potter didn't answer.

"Probably twenty, twenty-five years, I'd guess. An' I'll bet mosta

that's been doing what you did today—talking to assholes like me."
Handy was a small man but his grip was ferocious. Potter's fingers tin-
gled as he felt the circulation cut off.

They passed through a dozen rooms, black and stinking—the bloody
dream of Messrs. Stoltz and Webber.

Handy pushed Potter through a back doorway. Then they were outside, rocking against the blast of wind.

"Whoa, bumpy ride tonight." Handy tugged Potter toward a grove of
trees. He saw the outline of a car. Engine blocks take three hours to
cool. If he'd had an infrared viewer they'd have seen it.

And Charlie Budd would still be alive. . . .

"Twenty-five years," Handy shouted over the wind. "You always
been on the other side of the police line. The safe side. You ever think
what it'd be like being a hostage yourself? Wouldn't that be a fuckin'
experience? Come on, Art, hustle. I want you to meet Pris. She's a ball
buster, she is.

"Yessir, that's what you're gonna be—a hostage. You know, people
don't experience stuff. Most people've never shot anybody. Most people've never walked into a bank and pulled a gun. Most people've
never looked at a girl and not said a fucking word but just stared and
stared while she cried like a swatted pup and then started taking off
her clothes. 'Cause she figured that's what you want her to do.

"And most people've never been up close when somebody dies. I
mean, touching 'em when it happens. When the last cell of somebody's
body stops swimming around. I done all that. You don't even come
close to feeling stuff like that. Like I've felt. *That's* experience, Art.

"You tried to stop me. You shouldn't've done that. I'm going to kill
you, you probably know that. But not for a while. I'm taking you with
us. And there ain't nothing you can say to stop me. You can't offer me a
six-pack, you can't offer me a M-the-fuck-4 priority to Canada. When
we're safe and away then the only thing I want is you dead. And if we
don't get safe and away, then I want you dead too."

Handy suddenly quivered with fury, grabbed Potter by the lapels.
"You shouldn'ta tried to stop me!"

There was a crinkling sound in Potter's jacket pocket. Handy smiled.
"What've we got here?"

No! Potter thought, twisting away. But Handy reached inside the sports coat and lifted the photo from the pocket.

"What's'is?"

The picture of Melanie Charrol. The one that had been pinned up on the bulletin board in the van.

"Your girlfriend, huh, Art?"

"There's nowhere in the world," Potter said, "you'll be safe."

Handy ignored him. "We'll be away for a while, Pris and me. But I'm gonna hold on to this snapshot here. We'll come back and visit her. Melanie, she's a pistol. She got me down on my back, knocked the wind clean outta me. Did this—see these scratches? And she pitched that little girl out the door 'fore I could say boo. And got that other one, the pretty little one Sonny had his eye on, got her out too. Oh, Melanie'll get her payback." As if revealing trade secrets Handy added, "A man can't let anybody walk on him. Especially a woman. May be a month, may be two months. She'll find Pris and me in her bed waiting for her. And she can't even scream for help."

"You'd be nuts to come back here. Every cop in the state knows your face."

Handy was angry again. "I'm owed! I am fucking owed!" He shoved the photo into his pocket and dragged Potter after him.

They were headed for the airport—"Bumpy ride tonight." They'd kill him as soon as they were safe. Maybe drop him from the airplane, three thousand feet over a wheat field.

"There she is now, Pris." Handy nodded at the Nissan, parked in a grove of trees. "She's quite a gal, Art. I was shot one time, got hit in the side, and the same shit trooper got me'd drawn down on Pris. She had her piece in her hand but he could've nailed her 'fore she could lift it even. What happens but, cool as ice, she unbuttons her blouse, smiling all the time? Yessir, yessir. He wanted to shoot her, that man did! But he couldn't bring himself to. Soon as he glanced down at her titties she lifted her Glock and took him out, pow, pow, pow. Three in the chest. Then walked over and put one in the head in case he was in armor. You think your girlfriend'd be that cool? Oh, I'll betcha not, Art."

Handy stopped, pulled Potter to a halt and then looked around, head up, sniffing the air, frowning. Melanie had called him Brutus and given the other two the names of creatures but the agent knew Handy was more animal-like than either Wilcox or Bonner.

Handy's eyes turned toward the car.

Potter could see the open driver's door and the woman inside, who'd impersonated Sharon Foster, gazing out the windshield. Her blond hair was pulled back in the same ponytail as before. But she'd changed clothes. No longer in uniform, she was now wearing pants and a dark turtleneck.

"Pris?" Handy whispered.

She didn't respond.

"Pris?" Louder. "Prissy?" Rising on the wind.

Handy shoved Potter to the ground. The agent fell and rolled helplessly on the grass then watched as Handy ran to the driver's seat and cradled his girlfriend.

The convict howled in horror and rage.

Potter squinted. No, not a turtleneck, not a garment at all. The slit in the woman's throat extended from one jugular vein to another and the dark sweater was half the blood in her body streaming down over her shoulders and arms and breasts. Her sole plea for help had been to lift a bloody hand to the windshield and gesture madly, leaving a finger-painting of her terror on the dirty glass.

"No, no, no!" Handy cradled her, rocking frantically back and forth.

Potter rolled to his side and tried to scrabble away. He got only three feet then heard the snap of brush and rush of feet. A boot slammed into his ribs. Potter dropped to the ground, lifting his bound hands to his face. "You did this! You snuck up on her! You did this, you fuck!"

Potter curled up, tried to ward off the vicious kicks.

Handy backed up and lifted the pistol.

Potter closed his eyes and lowered his hands.

He tried to picture Marian but she wouldn't come to mind. No, only Melanie was in his thoughts as, for the second time tonight, he prepared to die.

Arthur Potter was suddenly aware of the wind around him. Howling, hissing, it rose and formed words. But they were words not of this earth: eerie syllables rising deep from within some banshee mimicking the language of pitiful humans. He couldn't make out the content at first, a phrase repeated manically, spoken in pure loathing and fury. Then the scream coalesced, and as Handy whirled around Potter heard the malformed words over and over, "I hate you I hate you I hate you. . . ."

The knife plunged deep into Handy's shoulder and he cried in agony as Melanie Charrol's strong hands pulled the long blade from his flesh and drove it again into him—into his right arm. The gun dropped to the ground. Potter rolled forward and scooped it up.

Handy swung a fist at her face but she leapt back easily, still holding the knife in front of her. Handy dropped to his knees, eyes closed, gripping his arm, from which blood poured and poured, spiraling down his right finger, extended like God's in the Sistine Chapel.

Potter struggled to his feet and walked around Handy, stopped beside Melanie. She looked at his hands and untied the wire binding them. The young woman was quivering fiercely. So she too had made the same deduction about Handy that he and Budd had—that he'd be returning here for his money. She hadn't gone after Marks at all.

"Go ahead, do it," Handy snarled to Potter, as if he were the long-suffering victim of tonight's events.

Feeling the weight of the Glock in his fingers, Potter glanced down at Handy's creased, hating face. The agent said nothing, did nothing.

Have you ever done anything bad?

Then suddenly Arthur Potter understood how different he truly was from Handy and had always been. During the barricades the agent was like an actor—he became someone else for a short while, became someone he distrusted, feared, even loathed. But this talent was mercifully balanced by his uncanny ability to relinquish the role, to return.

And so it was Melanie Charrol who stepped forward and drove the long knife deep between Handy's ribs, all the way to the bloody handle.

The thin man choked, coughed blood, and fell backwards, shivering. Slowly she drew the knife out.

Potter took the weapon from her, wiped the handle on his sports coat, dropped it on the ground. He stood back, watching Melanie crouch beside Handy, who was trembling as the last of life fled his wiry body. She crouched over him, her head down, her eyes on him. In the dimness of the night Potter couldn't see her expression clearly though he detected what he believed was a faint smile on her face, one of curiosity.

And he sensed something else. In her posture, in the tilt of her head near his, it seemed as if she were inhaling the man's pain like spiced incense wafting through her house.

Lou Handy's mouth moved. A wet sound rose, a rattle, but so soft that Arthur Potter was nearly as deaf to it as Melanie would be. When the man quivered violently once, then again, and was finally still, Potter helped her to her feet.

His arm around her shoulders, they walked through the night while around them saplings and sedge and buffalo grass whipped from side to side in the sinewy wind. Fifty yards up the road they came to the government car Melanie had commandeered for the drive here from Hebron.

She turned to him, zipping up her battered brown leather jacket.

He gripped her shoulders, felt the wind slap her hair against his hand. A dozen things he might have said to her came to mind. He wanted to ask if she was all right, ask what she was feeling, tell her what he intended to explain to the troopers, tell her how many times he thought about her during the barricade.

But he said nothing. The moon had slipped behind a lesion of black cloud and the field was very dark; she couldn't, he told himself, see his lips anyway. Potter suddenly pulled her to him and kissed her on the mouth, quickly, ready to step away at the least hesitation. But he felt none and held her tightly to him, dropping his face to the cool, fragrant skin of her neck. They remained in this embrace for a long moment. When he stepped back the moon was out once again and there was pale white light on both their faces. But still he remained silent and merely guided her into the driver's seat of the car.

Melanie started the engine and, glancing back, she lifted her hands off the wheel and gestured to him in sign language.

Why would she do that? he wondered. What could she be saying?

Before he could tell her to wait, to write out the words, she put the car in gear and drove to the dirt road, rocking slowly over the uneven field. The car made an abrupt turn and disappeared behind a row of trees. The brake lights flashed once and then she was gone.

He trudged back to the bloody Nissan. Here, he smudged all the fingerprints but his own and then rearranged the bloody knife, the guns, and the two bodies until the crime scene told a credible, if dishonest, story.

"But what exactly is a lie, Charlie? The truth's a pretty slippery thing. Are any words ever one hundred percent honest?"

He was surveying his handiwork when, suddenly, it occurred to him what Melanie had said a few moments before. The words were among the few in his own paltry vocabulary of sign language, words he in fact had signed to her earlier in the evening. "I want to see you again." Was this right? He lifted his hands and repeated the sentence to himself. Awkwardly at first, then smooth as a pro. Yes, he believed that was it.

Arthur Potter saw a car approaching in the distance. Turning his collar against the relentless stream of wind, he sat down on the rocky ground to wait.

JEFFERY DEAVER

THE EMPTY CHAIR

The New Lincoln Rhyme Thriller

When criminalist Lincoln Rhyme travels to a world-famous spinal cord injuries centre in North Carolina for some experimental surgery, he hopes that the operation will give him slightly more movement. He knows that it may kill him.

But before he has a chance to undergo surgery, Rhyme and his assistant Amelia are drafted in by the local police department to use their forensic skills to help find two women kidnapped by a psychotic young man known locally as the Insect Boy. A cat and mouse game through the abandoned swamps of North Carolina is to have more devastating consequences than either Lincoln or Amelia can anticipate.

HODDER AND STOUGHTON PAPERBACKS

JEFFERY DEAVER

THE DEVIL'S TEARDROP

It's Washington, D.C.; it's the last night of the year, and people are dying . . .

At 9 am on New Year's Eve a man gets onto the packed escalator of a metro station and fires a silenced machine gun into the crowd. He escapes without being spotted in the confusion caused by the horror of this vicious attack, which leaves dozens of people killed and injured.

One hour later, a note is delivered to the mayor: twenty million dollars, or the writer will instruct the killer to strike again; at 4 pm, at 9 pm, at midnight . . . hundreds more will die.

The money has to be found, the ransom will have to be paid. But then a hit-and-run victim is identified as the mastermind behind the operation, and suddenly there's no way of stopping the psychotic gunman killing again, and again, and again . . .

The only thing the FBI have to go on is the note. Parker Kincaid, forensic document expert, and agent-in-charge, Margaret Lukas, could be the only people who can stop the killer.

HODDER AND STOUGHTON PAPERBACKS

JEFFERY DEAVER

THE BONE COLLECTOR

Lincoln Rhyme is one of the world's foremost forensic criminalists. He is also a quadriplegic, paralysed from the neck down. He is strapped in his bed and actually planning his suicide when he gets a call he can't ignore from his old partner on the force.

A single human hand has been found, buried on a deserted railway track on New York's West Side – the hand belonging to a man who got into a cab at the airport and never got out. And the driver was the Bone Collector.

The Bone Collector, a killer and kidnapper obsessed with old New York, leaves clues that only Lincoln Rhyme can decipher. As the minutes count down toward each successive death of an innocent, Rhyme and Amelia Sachs, the female police officer acting as his arms and legs, race to locate the victims by unravelling the Bone Collector's clues.

Slowly the criminalist begins to narrow the noose around the kidnapper. But it appears the Bone Collector has his own plans, and is narrowing his own noose – around Lincoln Rhyme.

'Sophisticated chiller . . . compulsive reading' *Guardian*

'Engrossing, entertaining and fizzing with energy, this is a suspense thriller to keep narcolepts awake'
Val McDermid, *Manchester Evening News*

HODDER AND STOUGHTON PAPERBACKS

JEFFERY DEAVER

SPEAKING IN TONGUES

Two men of words . . . One seeking only peace. The other, violence.

Tate Collier, once one of the finest trial lawyers in the country, is now a divorced, gentleman farmer in rural Virginia, trying to forget the past.

Aaron Mathews, a brilliant psychologist, has turned his talents to far deadlier goals than curing patients; he's targeted Tate, his ex-wife and his estranged daughter for unspeakable revenge.

As Mathews's terrifying plan unfolds, destroying the lives of this troubled family and anyone who tries to stop him, Tate and ex-wife must reunite to stop this psychopath whose gift of a glib tongue and talent for coercion and deceit are as dangerous as knives and guns . . .

Filled with the brilliant twists and turns that are Jeffery Deaver's hallmark, this is the long awaited, completely revised paperback debut of his classic thriller.

HODDER AND STOUGHTON PAPERBACKS

JEFFERY DEAVER

THE COFFIN DANCER

The most dangerous and elusive hitman in the world is visiting New York City . . . on business.

Percey Clay, one of America's foremost pilots and the uncompromising owner of a struggling charter flight service, was in the wrong place at the wrong time. Now she's the target of the Coffin Dancer.

Brilliant quadriplegic criminalist Lincoln Rhyme knows the killer only too well. He's a man who's raised murder to a form of high art; whose deadliest weapons aren't guns or knives but his uncanny knowledge of human nature.

Using his astonishing forensic knowledge and his unique insight into the criminal mind, Rhyme must combat both the hitman's amoral genius and Percey's headstrong determination if he is to save her – and keep himself alive.

HODDER AND STOUGHTON PAPERBACKS

JEFFERY DEAVER

THE LESSON OF HER DEATH

Detective Bill Corde looks down at the beautiful face of the murdered girl in the mud, and cannot know that his own life is about to turn into a terrifyingly real nightmare.

For the girl's killer is now on the trail of Corde and his unsuspecting family. His wife. His teenage son. His imaginative but vulnerable daughter, Sarah.

Sarah – who alone knows the identity of the man who took the life of the girl . . . the man who may be responsible for further deaths.

And the lesson Bill Corde is about to learn – the lesson of her death – is an education that no one will ever forget.

HODDER AND STOUGHTON PAPERBACKS